VAMPIRES OF FATE

THE COMPLETE SERIES

BOOK 1-3

JULIE HUTCHINGS

inked entertainment

Vampires of Fate

Running Home (Book 1)

Running Away (Book 2)

Crawling Back (Book 3)

The Harpy Series

The Harpy (Book 1)

The Harpy 2: Evolution (Book 2)

The Harpy 3: Damnation (Book 3)

Betty Bedlam Series

with Connor Ashley

Damned (Book 1, coming soon)

PART I
RUNNING HOME

CHAPTER 1

"So guess what?" Kat flopped girlishly into the thrift store armchair opposite my own. Twirling a tablespoon of pink ice cream into her mouth and topping it with a sugarplum smile that meant trouble, she didn't wait for me to guess. I hid my smile as I looked up from the Christmas scheduling I'd brought home to work on. The more I looked at it the more it seemed to say "unpaid overtime."

"Partypartyparty!" she squeaked in a single breath.

My eyes widened. "Oh, hell no. No more Kat parties! You try to dress me like a human cupcake and you know I—"

"Hear me out!" she yelped, leaning over and shoveling a lot of ice cream into my mouth.

"No, I will not," I mumbled, ice cream making a cold trail down my chin. I'd already lost this argument. She'd gagged me with the atrocity of strawberry artificial flavoring on purpose.

Kat popped in a horror movie, which she hated and I loved; a clear bribe. "Ellie, there's a new attorney at the firm. They never hire new attorneys."

This was Ossipee, New Hampshire. "Law firm" was a loose phrase when applied to a town where every business had a bear or moose in its logo. This may bother some people, but I wasn't one of them. Ossipee was familiar, and fresh, and as close to the earth as I liked without being anywhere near a hippie. I liked being surrounded by wilderness and all things that reminded me of the solitude I loved.

Kat loved people. She had a romanticized view of city life that had not quite panned out in New York, and she brought her small-town-girl-in-the-big-city romance back to the small town. Leave it to Kat, as soon as she returned, she found the one "law firm" with no wildlife on the sign. A few old guys who went to law school twenty years ago were unable to say no to Kat's can-do attitude and need to be employed somewhere that could almost be mistaken for a city job, even if it was as a receptionist.

We were so different, my odd attachment to Kat alarmed me at times. I didn't want to think I clung to her because she was the only person left. A lurking sense of death was my only family, a dirty spirit that darkened any light in my life, making it so grim I never wanted it illuminated again. But Kat made it better.

Relief surged through me when she'd come back to town, and we found an old bed and breakfast that had been repurposed into apartments. It echoed us well. Charming like Kat; left over by the world, half-molded and half-destroyed like me.

Her wild enthusiasm jolted me. "Ellie, this is *such* a big deal! They said they had to have him, even though they hadn't been looking for new blood, but then they realized they needed it if they wanted to handle the whole state, and he's gorgeous—"

"So who is this new attorney?" I interrupted as I pulled my afghan closer to my neck. *Dawn of the Dead* woke up in the background.

"Chris Lynch," she sputtered, clunking the ice cream bowl

on our crappy end table. She was actually pacing the room over this guy, intermittently blocking the movie. "Wait until you meet him, he's *unbelievable!*" All her words came out as tiny screech.

"The firm is having an office party now?"

"NO! No. Chris is having a cocktail party at his home, which he had built in honor of his new position," she bragged, like this was the most impressive thing I would ever hear. "I drove by it the other day on a long car ride. It's HUGE! And he got it built in less than a month!"

"He invited you *and* me?" I threw my schedules on the floor in surrender. Clearly this was not a work-conducive environment.

"Well, sure, me and a guest," she peeped, breaking her pace to touch the tip of my nose. "And of course, there will be plenty of people to meet."

"Not really winning me over here, Kat."

"Lots of eligible men, friends of his. Normal guys."

"Kat!" I interrupted again with more force, not liking the inevitable direction this had taken. She looked at me like a child in time-out. "Kat," I said more softly. "We're in New Hampshire, and he just moved here. How many eligible guys can he know around here, for starters?"

"He only moved here from Boston," she said, like it was down the street. "And we were chatting at my desk and he said—"

"Kat, I have no need to mingle with the rich and self-important, and I definitely don't need you to introduce me to any more men. Remember Jason?"

"That one was not my fault, Ellie. How was I supposed to know he was a cokehead?"

"Oh, I don't know, Kat. The constant bloody noses, the five-inch pinky nail, the bag of coke he always carried. The point is, you get me into these things with people *you* barely know, and I just don't want to do it again. You trust too easily, Kat." She sighed. "I know you want me to be happy, and I swear to God, I am."

"How can you be happy spending *all* your time with me? I'm fun to be with, but you're the one who says only in small doses." We both laughed at that. "You never go out with the guys who ask you out at the shop. You never get near anybody but me."

"I'm not suicidal, I'm just not actively looking for a man. I *am* actively trying to watch zombies, though."

The thought of getting close to anyone sickened me. I couldn't expect her to understand that after stripping me over and over again of anyone that mattered, death had become the only thing I'd never lose. Trying to hold on to a person, any person, it didn't make sense when the crows were circling overhead, when death was right there, eager to slip in. Death chased everyone, but with me, he ran a little faster, grabbed anyone I cared about. Death singled me out. I hadn't been kicked out of the world, I was never meant to be here to begin with.

And even I didn't know what that meant.

Kat sat on the arm of my chair and leaned against my shoulder. "To tell you the truth," she said, hyperactivity dissipating, "I'm actually a little intimidated by him. He's perfect. Besides, you've *got* to see this house with me or I'll have nobody to talk under my breath to."

Here it comes.

"Please?" She had a way of saying the word with such sincerity that it was impossible for me to say no to her most ridiculous requests, of which there were many.

I thunked my head against the back of the chair and closed my eyes, groaning in tune with my zombie movie.

"Yay!" I heard her squeak.

"Call for pizza," was my only reply.

CHAPTER 2

I took my sentence with dignity, and didn't complain about the impending cocktail party that evening. It sprang up on me, sucking the comfort out of my Saturday after a difficult work week filled with tourists and way-too-early holiday shoppers. Even in my exhaustion, it was hard not to be excited with Kat, as giddy as she was.

Kat had been talking to this new attorney, Chris Lynch, all week. She poured our daily bowls of Golden Grahams, telling me that Mr. Lynch was twenty-nine years old, had never been married or even engaged, and hadn't dated since moving to New Hampshire. Upon asking him why he thought he'd never found the right girl, Chris told Kat he believed it was a combination of being difficult to understand and having unreasonable standards. Kat also managed to nonchalantly ask why he'd want to live in so large a home alone. I pointed out that she'd exposed herself as a drive-by stalker, and she ignored me to babble that he'd told her a successful man should be the king of his castle, even if there were no subjects. Then he gave her a wink and a smile. This confirmed to Kat that she was meant to be his queen.

"He came here to meet a woman, Ellie, one that's not as self-involved as a Boston socialite, but that has a flair that makes her a bit too big for Ossipee. I mean, he didn't actually say that, but you know."

"Let me guess; that's you, right?" I jeered from behind my coffee mug. It had a moose on it.

"I really think there could be something between us, Ellie," she said, pulling her knees up to her chest in the kitchen chair. "I think he's different."

I thought it sounded like he knew just the right things to say. In any case, I wanted to meet him and make my own assessment. I wasn't about to see her taken advantage of.

I also really wanted to see this mansion. I mean, really, in our hick town? In a month? How pompous was this guy?

After breakfast, we braved the Ossipee wind and snow to do our poorly organized food shopping like we did every Saturday morning, followed by a cup of coffee at Black Bear Café. This time we took it to go.

"Let me get you a manicure," Kat said, wiggling her eyebrows over her cup.

"Booo, hiss. No, thank you. My nails are fine. I'll be at—"

She rolled her eyes. "Birch Tree. I know." Widening her smile more, she fluttered away in a swish of lilac wool, sunset hair, and peony perfume. She knew it wasn't in season, but would never wear a different scent. I called such things "commitment" when it applied to her. She called it "stubborn" when it applied to me.

My boots pelted the floor with snow as I entered Birch Tree Books. This place was the cable-knit sweater that melted the winter off me. I loved the battered wood floor that had never seen a coat of polish, and creaked underfoot like it remembered every time I'd visited. It had the same character that the mess of shelves had, and the dusty books that lived on them. Some of these books had been in piles on the yard sale shelves for so long, they'd become landmarks to navigate the shop by.

Birch Tree wasn't just my favorite place. It was the only place where I didn't feel like an intruder.

I tried not to knock a lady in Romance over with my super-bulky coat. I let out a breath as I took in the first shelf of Sci-fi and horror paperbacks, and pulled a creased binding down, eradicating thoughts of awkward parties.

Out of nowhere, the scent of warm brownies and peppermint washed over me, leaving me in a fog, reminding me of the warmth of coming home after sledding as a kid. Nobody made brownies at a book store; the scent just *was* the air somehow. I inhaled deeply and stole a glance at Romance Novel Lady. She clearly hadn't noticed anything strange except me, looking at her, sniffing. I put my nose back into the book before I drew any more attention.

"You don't belong here."

I gasped, a voice like thunder in my head. And it was *in* my head. The scent soothed me while the words frightened me, said in a voice I wanted to hear again and again.

"You don't belong here."

I dropped the book, my head snapping up, hair slipping into my mouth. I spun wildly around, searching for the source of this impossibility that was trying to unsettle me here, in this one place that was mine, the one place I didn't want to run screaming from. A clean-shaven man eyed me with concern from the end of the aisle.

"Do you smell that?" I asked him a little too loudly. He frowned, and I looked away.

I left the aisle, stumbling over a footstool, making more of a ruckus with every step, and peered into the next row. Books, on shelves and in stacks, looked back at me, their mustiness briefly cutting through the peppermint brownie haze.

"Who are you?!" the same silky voice demanded.

I stopped, dead still, breathing hard and heavy in my fear, but propelled by that aroma, like it was trying to bring me somewhere that I wasn't sure I wanted to go.

Heady with the delicious scent, panic rising in my throat, I went to the next aisle. I didn't panic easily, and I added 'irritated' to my overwhelming feelings. Birch Tree was *my* place.

"You don't belong here." Stronger this time, no uncertainty. Not threatening me, just stating something I needed to know.

I did know, but I never expected to feel it here.

"Miss? Are you okay?" A blonde woman with a child staring at me, clinging to her leg. I couldn't answer. I clasped my hands to stop them from shaking.

I raced to the door, heart pounding, the bells on the handle clanging like the Liberty Bell, but not loud enough to drown out the words that followed me into the cold.

"You don't belong here."

CHAPTER 3

Before I knew it, we were two hours from the event itself. The Grand Party at New Lawyer's Mansion. The realization added to my jittery shaking from the book store. Those words wouldn't leave me.

"Ellie," Kat said, interrupting my inner meeting-people-panic and book-store-freakout. "What are you going to wear?" she asked in the way a family member asks, "What are you going to do about that mole?" when it can't wait a second longer.

I stared back at her, but had little else to offer. "I have that blue thing," I said meekly, giving away that I knew it sucked.

"Please wear something of mine. And breathe," Kat said sweetly. "You'll be wonderful. You always are." She ran a finger over my hair. Kat misinterpreted the reason for my anxiety, and I didn't set her straight. I couldn't talk about what happened at Birch Tree. Not yet. It hit too close to home, and even Kat wouldn't understand. I pushed it down where feelings belong, and concentrated on the party. Hooray.

"I'm ready to be dressed now, Katherine."

"Gross, stop that."

Despite her ability to down half a pizza, Kat was this petite pinup. I was a little *too* everything. My hips were a little too round, my waist a little too soft, my breasts a little too full, so I was constantly tucking them into my bra. My face was too childish, with invisible cheekbones and wide green eyes that made me look perpetually surprised. There were tiny freckles on my nose. What adult has freckles on her nose?

We both knew Kat's ill-fitting dress would look better than my own dress. I didn't even remember where or when I got The Blue Beast. With a determined head nod, I led the way to her bedroom to begin the fashion show.

Darkness had already settled as we left for Chris Lynch's cocktail party. Kat eased into the driver's side of her only slightly used Jetta. I had to suck my stomach in underneath the body-slimming thing in order to sit down. Kat was looking at me as the engine roared awake in the cold.

"You look so pretty," she said with all the pride of a mom before her ugly daughter's prom.

I let my breath out. "Thanks. The dress is really nice, Kat." And it was. White satin ribbons wrapped over black lace, making me feel French. Thank God I owned a pair of black heels of my very own. I could even walk in them.

"Radio, please." Kat flicked on the CD button, and "Poker Face" blared all around me.

I can't even deny how much I love that song.

It pounded repeatedly throughout the car as Kat and I flitted through spurts of conversation over the beat, and watched miles of dark trees pass by.

Lights illuminated the world in front of us, piercing the

black woods. And in the center of the oversized spotlight was the most massive house I'd ever seen.

One person's house? Ridiculous.

Blazing white, with columns around the door that rivaled the height of the trees; elegant and pretentious. Unnecessary and excessive. Stealing a glance at Kat, I saw the same open-mouthed blankness on her face that I felt, despite that she'd already seen the house once.

"We gotta see this," I said, still staring.

We passed through dozens of non-Ossipee cars on our walk to the giant front door. It opened as we approached. A couple of crows made me shriek as they flapped away from a car hood.

They always turned up around me. This night wouldn't be different.

"Welcome, ladies," a tuxedoed butler guy greeted us.

Kat came to a dead stop in the doorway, causing me to careen into her back, propelling us both forward. There were too many people in the room for anyone to hear the skittering of our heels on the marble floor.

"Kat, what the—?!"

"Shhhh! Look at this place!" she whispered.

I was faced with a monstrous, open room that would have made *Architectural Digest* proud. The ceiling was so high, you barely noticed the crown moulding at the top, attempting to give the illusion of being in Ancient Rome. The room was sparse, with more shades of white than I was aware existed, speckled with marble and glass and granite. Even the body heat of all the mingling guests didn't help warm this ballroom against the New Hampshire winter that followed us inside.

The person who would make this his home must be cold and hard, too.

Stomach sucked in hard, I ambled forward a few steps, willing myself not to slip on the glistening marble, visions of my boobs falling out of the dress making me stifle a groan. I spotted an empty chair in a cluster of three in the corner, with a table between them. I was most certainly headed there to try to ride out the next couple of hours. Gliding along beside me was Kat, wide eyes and sweet smile, Cinderella at the ball. A spray-tanned, silver-haired man swept out of her way with a condescending smirk, like he was the only adult in a roomful of children he didn't like, and Kat was the most annoying of all. Kat noticed nothing. I grimaced at him as we passed.

"For you, miss?" The man offering me wine from a silver tray had such a genuine smile, it was refreshing to smile back.

"Thank you." I took the glass and drank it too fast, while his eyebrows raised. "I sorta wish it was beer," I said to him quietly, and he smiled wider.

Kat had stopped three feet behind me before I realized it, to talk to a woman in a red wrap dress that towered over all of the people near her.

I was on my own.

Maybe fifteen feet from the trio of chairs, I prepared myself to make polite conversation with the two men also seated there. *"You must be—"* and *"I'm—."* *"Great sweater! Very 1980s coke den."* What the hell was I doing here? I'd rather be with the serving staff than any of the guests.

Click click click click. Kat caught up to me, done with her red-dressed friend. "Where are you going?" she asked.

"That way," I answered, still en route.

"No way," she whined, spinning me around.

"Shit!" I cried out as I tried not to fall.

"Sshhh!" Kat fluffed my hair to Texas-sized with magic speed, making it fly in my face and stick in my eyelashes.

"Kat, people are looking."

"Don't talk like that. Talk the other way you talk, that doesn't sound annoying."

"What? I don't talk another—"

"Yes, you do. That's better," she said, her eyes not touching mine, but glued to my hair, her face close enough that I could tell she'd whitened her teeth. "Come meet some people."

"There are people over there," I replied, motioning towards the two guys at the little table.

"Please. Look at that sweater."

"Katherine!" Kat's eyes went deer-in-headlights as she looked over my shoulder. When he stopped next to me, I saw why.

"Katherine, you look breathtaking," he said, with eyes only for her. His voice was silk-smooth with just a hint of a growl in it. Hot.

"Chris!" Her monster crush didn't reveal itself in her voice. Same old bubbly Kat, happy to see him, like she was everyone.

He bent at the waist to kiss her hand, and the sideways glance she gave me said she needed me there to help her hold it together.

Chris Lynch was a weapon of a man. His jet black hair was impeccably styled. Glittering black-brown eyes barely wrinkled up when he flashed a smile that even made *my* knees weak. I'd never seen anything like it. With a smile like that, he could win any court case. It would be impossible for Kat not to fall for him. He was exactly like all the Prince Charming scenarios she'd fantasized about the entire time I'd known her. Amazing. But I sensed something else.

Danger. The word "feral" came to mind.

He turned the smile to me, extending his hand. "Well, I am certainly glad you came, beautiful stranger," he said, eyes growing dark.

Refusing to get flushed, I met his eyes, and firmly shook his hand. I was surprised to find it warm, but I guess he'd had a lot of hands to shake.

"I'm Eliza Morgan. A friend of Kat's." I shot her a look out of the corner of my eye, hoping he'd get the hint.

"I'm glad you came." He lingered on the last word, making me blush.

"Thank you. And thank you for inviting me. Us. You know." Wow. Stupid.

He licked his bottom lip slowly. My cheeks burned, but Kat didn't bat an eyelash. She also couldn't wipe the grin off her face.

"I want more of you around here."

I winced.

Kat realized Chris was about to move on to other guests, and livened up. "Chris, your new home is truly amazing," she said sincerely. "Did you decorate yourself?"

Chris refocused his attention to her, and I let out a breath. Their party chatting soon became infused with brief hand touching, and murmured words that could still pass for casual conversation, but was probably more. They quickly glued together, making me wonder again how deep into him Kat was. Feeling decidedly third wheel, I looked around. Some guests were getting comfortable; well-dressed men laughed loudly in larger groups now, commanding small audiences. A bunch of Boston attorneys and Gift Shop Ellie. Perfect.

The scent hit me before the sight did. Baked bread and cinnamon; it was different, but the same, familiar. My eyes didn't have a second to search for its origin before it was intrusively close, between the three of us.

But it was me he was facing.

I tilted my head back to see his face. An arrogant smirk and tousled dark waves said he didn't really care about this party. I couldn't quite process what I saw in his eyes. The warmest shade of brown, like melted dark chocolate, swirls of caramel throughout, continuously swimming in a way I'd never seen before. They looked so intently into my own, I felt bare. Until I heard that voice, that rich, husky, velvet voice, speaking to me, thank God, to me.

Wait, *to me?*

"I—I'm sorry?" I stammered. His lips curved into a smile that made me forget my name. The rest of the room was a hazy illusion full of white noise.

"That was intrusive of me," the man said, though he didn't make any effort to back away. "I'm Nicholas." And with his words, a complete sense of liquid warmth seeped through my social discomfort, a deep sigh of relief, even as I made the connection.

The book store.

My heart beat so fast, I was sure he could see it through my dress. Did I imagine his eyes dart to my chest where my heart slammed painfully inside me?

"Would you like to step outside with me?" he asked, ignoring Chris and Kat still, who were only inches away.

I didn't have the strength to rip my eyes from his face, as it warmed and taunted me all at once. I gave him my hand, trancelike. His was warm and strong, enveloping mine protectively, unease washing away. I couldn't tell if all eyes were on us or if we were gliding like ghosts in this pure white nothing room.

We went out into the sparkling cold to a huge patio lit with white lights, ten times more charming than the alien planet inside, totally at odds with the New Hampshire woods surrounding it. The further we got from Chris Lynch, the more alive the world became.

I pulled my hand slowly from the man's, and focused again on his breathtaking face, but composed myself. "Why did you… Do I know you?" I asked.

"Didn't you need to get out of there? That isn't you in there. It sure as hell isn't me."

"I just got here, but yeah, okay, I'd rather not be in the Great White Home, sure. Who are you?"

"I told you, Nicholas. And someone who feels a little too close to you. You feel the same, Eliza, don't you?"

"I don't remember telling you my name." Isn't that what the dumb girl always says before she gets killed? He'd drifted very close to me, like we were dancing, and gazed at me, through me, as though looking for some answer to an unasked question. That scent about him wasn't cologne; it emitted from him, like confidence. It was home, like you always wished home was, like cookies were always baking. Familiar, but ever-changing.

"The book store. I know you."

"Don't presume to know me, Eliza. I'm more than you see."

"But you *were* at the book store."

"It's mine, actually."

"Wait. You *own* Birch Tree Books? Why haven't I seen you there before?"

"I only bought it a month ago. I don't hang around, I'm just in the way around there."

"But you were there today," I said, more to myself than him. "How do you associate with these self-proclaimed sophisticates?"

"How do you?"

"What?!" I was offended for no reason.

We were silent again.

"I suppose I should…" I backed toward the door, and a new realm of awkward party talk.

"Then the answer is no?"

Frowning, I removed my hand from the door handle. "No to what? You've asked me too many and also no questions. What *is* this?" Panicked anger rose in my throat. The dress constricted.

He looked up at me with those eyes, sitting more still than I thought possible in a freezing cold wrought iron chaise with no pad on it. "Do you feel close to me?" There was a sadness in his voice that I didn't understand.

But it pained me.

"I'm not sure how I feel right now." My voice was a hoarse whisper.

He was standing, though I hadn't seen him stand, gripping the railing as if to prevent himself from shaking. Leaning back, he studied me. "There's something between you and I. I don't know what it is yet, but it's a solid thing."

The way he spoke to me stole my breath, frightened me. I was so conflicted, I wanted to cry. "That's a lousy pickup line."

He chuckled. "If I were trying to pick you up, I'd use better than that." Now I was really confused. His expression went from flirtatious to grim so quickly it was chilling. I cleared my throat.

"Eliza. Your gut says this world wasn't meant for you, doesn't it? You're right. I can see it all over you." Tears spilled from my eyes, and I couldn't let loose the knot in my gut. How did he know to say something like that? How did he know my deepest fears that I could never speak aloud?

"You're scaring me," I choked out.

Kat burst onto the porch in an explosion of laughter, bringing me back to the world that didn't want me.

"Ellie! I found you!" Her eyes lingered on Nicholas as she added, "I see you're occupied."

"No!" I blurted, eager to distance myself from this whole conversation. It was making my head swim and my stomach twist.

"Later then," Nicholas whispered in my ear, impossibly close to me again. A gasp froze in my heart before entering my throat as he brushed past me.

I couldn't believe how much I wanted "later" to come.

CHAPTER 4

I never read so fast in my life. I laughed off Kat's comments on how I was burning through books. I rationalized that if I was actually reading these books, I wasn't going to Birch Tree to see Nicholas; it was necessary.

It had become necessary twice that week.

My eyes went straight to him at the checkout counter as I walked in, and I realized he'd already been watching the door. Impossible that he had been waiting for me, of course. His eyes held a hint of laughter when I approached the counter.

A great *thud* made me jump. Nicholas drummed his fingers on the book he'd slammed down.

"Maybe *War and Peace* will tide you over for a week or two."

"One of my many skills is uber-fast reading."

"Probably trying to make it to the end of the crap you're buying. Can I suggest something more…appealing?" He smoldered on this last word, heat in his eyes as he leaned over the counter, getting too close once again. Yet, not close enough.

Damnit, it worked. "Like what?"

"Maybe Poe." He pulled away, and my breath flooded out.

"Have you read him since college? It's not the same when you care." He bustled around behind the register, ringing an older, tweeded man up for a book. Nicholas smiled at the man as he gave him his change, but the man didn't smile back.

"You shouldn't talk to me when waiting on someone else. It's rude," I said. *Wow, way to be annoying as all get-out, El.* The older man bustled past me in aggravation.

Nicholas's brow wrinkled, his swirling eyes twinkling with mischief, as they always seemed to be. "You're right," he said in his quick, carefree way. He swaggered out from behind the counter to the door and flipped the sign to "Closed."

"Let me take you to dinner."

"It's two o'clock."

"Okay, a walk."

"It's thirty-five degrees outside."

"To my place, then," he said, grabbing his coat from the old brass rack by the door. The rich scent of him hushed over me as he slid into it. I had to yank myself back to normalcy, right and wrong, smart and stupid, not the idiocy I was considering. My heart pounded. This was reckless. Not my M.O. And yet, who was I fooling, racing through work to get out early, making excuses to go to the book store whenever I could to make friendly with him?

I'd been waiting for this, even if I didn't admit it to myself before.

Our strange conversation at the party was the elephant in the room, and I'd put myself under its feet for answers. I'd do anything to understand the things he'd said, the things he knew, but couldn't know.

My voice was meek. "I'm not in the habit of going home with strange men."

"What did you call me?"

"You know what I mean."

He was upon me, the heat of his cookie scent, a smirk

playing on his lips, his cocoa eyes paralyzing me. The voice broke my gaze again, so velvety and deep, I could almost see the words form.

"So let's be friends, then."

My knees shook.

~

The sky over us was gray, and promised more snow. A dreary mist dampened the world, but I was dazzled by the muted, ocean colors.

"We can take mine," Nicholas said, motioning towards a beat-up Jeep Wagon.

"I'd prefer not to be stranded at a strange man's house, thanks."

"You keep saying that, but you don't seem to really think I'm strange. Fine. Follow me, then."

Deeply entrenched in the woods, but still close to the book store, was Nicholas's log cabin. I wasn't nervous at all entering the "strange man's" home. No, I should have been there my whole adult life.

It was my Cinderella's castle.

The warmth of the living room enveloped me before I even had time to look around. The house wanted me to come in and stay, bringing tears to my eyes. A picturesque log cabin inside and out, of rustic, dark wood on all sides. A huge stone fireplace headed the room with two well-worn but stately armchairs cozied up to it on top of a round braided rug. A picture window with a seat overlooked the little front yard. A big, red plaid sofa sat asked to be sat on, with an afghan that reminded me of my own tossed across it. A coffee mug balanced on the arm, even though an old trunk was within inches, clearly to be used as a coffee table. Behind the sofa was a red barn-looking door that must lead to the kitchen. But above the kitchen door, a rickety ladder leading up to it, a cubby of a loft hid among the rafters. I could see books of all shapes and sizes balancing precariously upon each other, barely leaving space between them for a stack of pillows. I wanted to crawl up there for days, but not just yet.

"You like it?" Nicholas asked over my shoulder, close to my ear in a husky voice. I shivered, but tried to mask it as he took my coat off with the swishing noise of cheap nylon.

"It's perfect," I replied.

"It's home," he said, putting both our coats on a brass rack by the door, just like the one at Birch Tree. It made me smile.

"Hard to believe you've only been here a month."

"I built almost all the furniture, and some of the walls, among other things. I settle in quickly."

He swaggered across the room toward the kitchen door, trailing snow and wetness behind him, but didn't seem to notice or care. I did the same, watching his every move.

The kitchen was just as inviting, with a black and white tile floor that showed its owner did not, in fact, much care about walking around with dirty boots. It looked lived in, and loved, like a kitchen should. An old wood stove on a brick platform kept the room a bit too warm. The cabinets were old, with crackling white paint and mismatched handles. A different kind of light permeated through the windows over the sink; frosty today, but I could imagine the yellow glow a little sunlight would bring. Copper pans hung from a fixture on the ceiling and threatened to hit Nicholas on the head several times as he put on the kettle and retrieved mugs. I pulled out a green wooden chair that matched nothing else, and yet belonged, and sat on the plaid cushion. A black cat meowed and jumped down to settle at the woodstove.

"A stray that's visiting," Nicholas explained. He put a cow-shaped creamer on the table and sat next to me, not across from me, his eyes trained on my face while we waited for the water to boil. I wasn't bothered by it.

It was so serene, rain, not snow, beating on the windows, the creaking of the house settling around us, that we just looked at each other comfortably. My lips upturned, my brow relaxed in response to his mischievous eyes and cockiness, evident even in the way he sat. A sense of ownership coursed through me, but for what I couldn't tell.

"I never went to college, you know," I told him.

"That's okay. I won't hold it against you."

"No, I mean you said if I read Poe now it would be different than reading it in college. I never went, though." *What was I saying?!*

"Coincidentally, have you never read Poe?"

"Just a few poems."

"That's no fun." His eyes bore into mine, and I got the sense of something coming, the same sense I'd felt every time I found my way into his presence. The kettle screamed, and he sprung up. His body moved so artfully; it was thoughtless to just *stare*, but I didn't get the sense Nicholas would be bothered by that. Or that he got bothered by anything, really. The silence with which he moved, every inch seemingly planned, the strength in his body apparent while doing this mundane thing....

Before I blinked, Nicholas was back at the table. He placed a delicate china teacup in my hand, white, decorated with little blue scenes of an Asian village, traces of cracks blistering its sides. He sensed my admiration. "It's very old china," he said nicely.

"Mmm, my favorite tea," I said, breathing in the peppermint steam.

"Mine, too."

We both sat, our hands wrapped around the cups, each looking quizzically at the other.

"You call me Eliza." Sometimes, I wonder why I open my mouth at all.

"Yes. Yes, I do."

"Everyone calls me Ellie."

"Do you want me to join them?"

"No. My mom used to read me a book when I was a kid about a circus elephant named Ellie. Ellie the Elephant."

"Was that Ellie perfectly content being a circus elephant?"

"I think she was."

"You're different, then."

He seemed to know without question that I was…off. That something was never quite right about me. Nicholas knew what I always knew. It wasn't that I didn't fit in; I didn't want to. I had *more*.

"What's happening in that heart of yours, Eliza Morgan?" Nicholas asked, making my hands tremble, no matter how warm the cup. I managed to smile like I wasn't schoolgirl-nervous.

Again came a distinct pull, like at Birch Tree, the comforting scent of brownies masking some other thing luring me in. I let it.

"It's telling me I've always been meant to know you. Even saying that makes me edgy. Like that's the kind of thing I would keep to myself, but I'm not self-conscious with you." Immediately, I was self-conscious. "And I'm confused about the conversation we had at the party."

"But the answer is yes?"

I knew the question he was referring to. *"Do you feel close to me?"*

"Yes," I whispered. "I do. It scares the hell out of me."

Looking down at his teacup, he murmured, "I don't want you to be afraid of me, Eliza." The contrast to the sarcastic, confident man I was beginning to know made him even more alluring. My heart pounded at the thought that *I* made him feel vulnerable.

"I want to know how you're suddenly central in my life. And how you know things about me, my name, what I do and don't like…" I became aware that what I'd say next would sound as crazy as this entire picture was. "How I *heard* you, in the book store. Why did you say that?" My breath quickened as I heard the words come out of my mouth.

He looked up at me, away from his own hands on the cup. His eyes were soft and warm, the rich colors churning. "Intuition. I read people pretty well. I'd be willing to say you do too, or you wouldn't be here with a near stranger, engaging in a clearly uncomfortable subject. As a matter of fact, you wouldn't be with any people at all if you had the choice." I was about to tell him I did have a choice, but I was chilled to realize I didn't really believe that. The wood stove crackled, and he took his first sip of tea. "This bores me. Tell me something about yourself. Now that's worth cornering you in my house for."

"I don't want to." I wasn't even sure that was true. Nothing was clear. Nicholas gave me a look of mock offense.

"Don't be embarrassed. You already fascinate me." That helped me let my shoulders down, and unfurl the knot in my gut.

"Uh, well, I'm twenty-six. I've lived in New Hampshire my whole life."

"Boooooring," he dragged out, rolling his eyes. "Tell me why you work at that…. What do you *do* there?"

Shocked he even remembered the slight mention of my job, I said, "I work at On A Clear Day. It's a gift shop." That's about all I really cared to say about it. I'd been there a long time, and day one was pretty much the same as day 246. His brows knitted together, his eyes darkened and stilled.

"You were meant for more."

I blinked. "Really. How so?"

"You sound skeptical. Why?" He leaned back in his chair, legs splayed under the table, his foot resting against my own. He didn't move it, and my knee twitched with his proximity. The sexiest smile played at his lips. He asked, "Are you surprised to hear that being middle management isn't your big picture?"

I shook my head, not in response, but at the certainty with which he said these things. "What do you know that I don't know?"

His laugh was hearty and full of joy, none of the sarcasm that I was getting used to from him. It made my heart leap to hear and I laughed with him. He jumped up, taking the empty teacup from me, and brought it to the counter, instinctively pouring me more. When he turned back to the table, cup in hand, eyes with a new kind of excitement in them, I got another sweep of his enticing scent. Spicy apples, like Christmas. Always a little different, but always tasty and comforting, like a big bowl of soup after a day in the cold.

He was becoming the bowl of soup in my cold life.

But my extreme confusion at his words fought with my contentment. I had to remind myself we'd been talking, and not get caught up in my own mind.

"Please get to the point. Are you trying to loop me into some pyramid scheme?"

He paused, eyeing me with a burning intensity. "Eliza. When I look at you, I *see you*. You think about things no one else does, you keep to yourself by choice—you *can* fit in—you don't want to. People repel you." This made him smile. "The daily workings of your life—your job, worrying about bills, parties, even your friendships have a tendency to bore you to tears. Don't they?"

He could see the answer in my clenched jaw.

"You engulf yourself in books, movies, your own imagination, because it's where you're yourself. And where you have nothing to lose. Where nothing else can be taken from you. Where the world doesn't reject you and you don't reject the world." He leaned forward, gaze searing. "What *I* know is that *you* think you're different. You think you're better."

He waited for a response. I had none. So, he continued.

"You're in waiting to do something *real.* Aren't you so alone in this world you're embedded in?"

So this was about religion then?

He dipped his head to look into my downturned eyes. In a moment that raised goosebumps across my arms, he lifted my chin with a touch of his rough finger. In a sultry, pleading voice, he asked, "Would you stop doubting me for just a second and try to understand what I'm telling you, Eliza?"

The finger on my jaw gluing me in place inches from him, we sat together for years, I think, as I memorized every inch of his impeccable face. The pout of his lips, the laugh lines that framed them, the flawless angle of his nose, the strong contour of his cheek and jaw. Nothing, however, matched his eyes, which moved with a life of their own.

"I trust you," I whispered, fearing the words as I spoke them, so foreign were they to me. In the midst of my trance, I'd nearly forgotten the sincerity of his own words.

His lips curved into the gentlest smile I'd seen from him yet. He blinked, and released my gaze. "Thank you," he humbly answered. Shadows flickered across the floor, and we both glanced at the window to see dusk taking over the rainy sky. For a silent moment, we enjoyed the warmth of the wood stove on a day like this, the steaming cups in front of us, and the strange comfort we took in the other's company. I closed my eyes and sighed.

"Tell me about you," I asked, genuinely wanting to know. I leaned forward, eager to hear where he'd begin. He looked at me, unblinking, and grimaced, like he was rearing up for a challenge.

"No. Another time."

So there would be another time.

"Wait! Why?"

"In all fairness, I don't believe you've answered my own questions. As long as you stall, so will I." We both snickered, and stalled some more.

CHAPTER 5

After our mutual decision to drag our time out together, the conversation lightened up to things normal people talk about; books, movies, likes, and our apparently many dislikes. I shocked myself by telling him about the deaths of my parents when I was fifteen. I went to live with my grandmother, but she was seventy-six, and gone two years later. I couldn't bear the thought of living with any one of a number of crazy relatives, so I moved out on my own. Besides, death seemed to have stuck to me, and I didn't want to inflict it on anyone else. It was waiting to take some more.

The only good thing that came out of my late teenage years was that it had, through odd twists of fate, connected me to Kat. And she insisted on sticking around, despite the luck I brought with me. Aside from her, life then was lonely, and hard, and a subject I typically avoided at all costs. Nicholas raised his eyebrows, as if to ask if I was all right.

I was. I was all right speaking to him about the hard things.

He stared at me in that way I was becoming accustomed to, drumming his fingers on the table. "You've lost much in life."

I shrugged.

"It's funny that you're a horror movie buff, when they're all about death and killing and dying, considering your past. Ever think of that?"

My stomach dropped as I said out loud something that I didn't ever admit, even to myself. "Not that funny. Fear is something I recognize. Fear is familiar to me. Death is something I know. What I can't stand is movies about people falling madly in love, running halfway across the world to each other, screwing each other over only to fall into a pit of despair that's totally dependent on another person who's going to probably leave them, and definitely will die. Why do that to yourself? I don't mind being afraid of death, it's a perfectly valid fear. Inevitable. When you love a person, you never know what's coming next. That right there, is a fear I'd rather avoid."

"Fair enough." The way he'd been looking at me changed ever so slightly.

The sky darkened to a purple shade that only happens deep in the woods. The rain slowed again to a rhythmic drizzle. Nicholas and I had long since found ourselves in the two armchairs in his living room, enjoying the fire.

"Your friend is probably worried about you," he said.

"Is that your way of throwing me out?" I asked through a smile.

He rose from his chair and took my hand, pulling me to my feet. That same purely sexual smile danced on his lips and in his eyes. "Far be it from me to throw a beautiful woman from my home, but truthfully, it is late, and you *are* at a strange man's house in the woods."

"We're friends now, aren't we?" My ability to reply astounded me, as he hadn't let go of my hand, and was so close I could barely think.

Letting my hand fall, and his smile with it, he grimly said, "I don't need to tell you, of all people, to choose your friends carefully." He turned on me, and crossed the room to get my coat, trailing his scent behind him. It made me want to curl up in front of that fire forever. But it did give me a second to absorb his odd sentiment.

"I'm not one to make foolish choices," I said, now putting on my puffy winter coat.

He gave me a knowing smile, with a nod, and patted lint off my shoulder.

"It's one of the many things I see about you."

CHAPTER 6

Sleeping that night was a project. My dreams were littered with images of Nicholas's irresistible face and Lynch's snide, arrogant one. I peeled my puffy eyes open for work, early so I could restock our emptying shelves. With a pang of misery, I accepted the end of my night's visions, and turned giddy instead that Nicholas was my last thought before sleep, and the first thing my mind raced to when I woke. I couldn't even put a name to any man I'd met that sparked interest in me, and never had a crush eclipsed the rest of my world, become the blazing center of my earth. It was all-consuming, both exciting and painful.

The pain came with knowing that there was more I didn't know. This man was pursuing me, and hiding from me all at once. In some romance novel like Kat was always reading, this may have added to his mystery and allure, but for me it was just pure terror that the discovery of whatever secret he was harboring would end how I felt.

Getting dressed in a beyond average white collared shirt and old gray skirt I'd probably had since I was fifteen, I wondered if Nicholas would be disappointed in this outfit.

(He most certainly would be.) Feeling utterly ridiculous, I made my own heart race imagining Nicholas pushing me into one of the rooms of the shop and unbuttoning my shirt. Eating my Golden Grahams, I wondered if he was also up at the tender hour of six a.m., and what his breakfast was like. Was he shirtless, with pajama bottoms, hair more disheveled than usual, body smelling slightly salty after a good night's sleep? Was he sprawled in a fuzzy bathrobe on his armchair in front of the fire, with a strong cup of coffee?

Was there a chance he was thinking of me at that very moment, maybe wishing I was right there beside him, listening to the unparalleled silence of early morning?

I wrote a note in Sharpie on the back of the cereal box to Kat;

Have fun at work—tell Lynch I said "hi."

Love,

me

She'd get a kick out of it. Seriously, I would probably never like Lynch enough to relay a message to him at all.

The cold of the morning dark bit at me like an animal as I took tiny, fast steps to my car. In my laziness, I preferred to tough it out in the freezing car, waiting for it to defrost, than get out and scrape the ice. The local morning show mumbled on the radio, all but unheard over the powerful blast of the heater.

This was usually a lonely part of the day for me, but it was tolerable now. Because he even had a presence in this.

Work was a series of people picking out trinkets with the care of choosing a casket, and refilling those same shelves with all new trinkets of little value but great glitter. It wasn't unpleasant, just ordinary, but for the imaginary presence of the world's most interesting man.

I was very aware that these thoughts were bordering

obsessive, but they just came. I guess any old stalker would say the same. And the thoughts felt unreasonably *good*.

Quitting time didn't come quickly. I guess my obsessive thoughts couldn't speed up time. My work day was long, and it was cold—still—again—when I left the shop. There was a message on my phone from Kat, as always, saying she was bringing home pizza. It was 5:30, and Kat left the "law firm" at six. That pizza, and Kat, wouldn't be home until seven. A long, hot bath would pass the time, followed by a George Romero documentary I'd been dying to see.

The apartment door shut with a satisfying *clunk*, closing my work persona out. I peeled off cold layers and mentally prepared for a relaxing night. It was nice and quiet, and warm, and inadvertently reminded me of Nicholas's fireplace, and his warm tea, and his warm lips on mine...

Nope. Not spending any more time fantasizing about anybody today. I poured a beer, and ran the hot water for my bath. The vanilla bath salts brought me back to Nicholas's scent, like Christmas morning.

I sank into the tub, and opened up the copy of Poe he'd given to me. God help me, I actually smelled it, but it just smelled like a loved, musty old book. No trace of the man who gave it to me. He loved this book, but let me take it.

I was reading *The Masque of the Red Death*, Nicholas's recommended reading. I immediately loved the boldness of the story, the drama of the color, and the masquerade ball. It unnerved me that in all the noise, company and wildness Prospero had surrounded himself with, the silence of death still found him. His fate was undeniable.

Kat said once that she understood my fear of death, considering how it had stolen so much from me. I appreciated her for saying it, but there was nothing to understand. Death is the ultimate fear, for anyone, whether they know it or not. I happened to know it.

Falling into thought, I was jolted by the ringing of the phone. I'd forgotten I was in the bathtub, if that's possible, and splashed water into my own face as a result. Ignoring the phone, I sunk deeper into the water, and pulled a facecloth over my eyes.

I heard the answering machine, (yes, we still had one), kick on, undoubtedly for Kat, but the saturated voice on the other end said my name.

"…was hoping you'd like to join me for a late cup of coffee, but it seems you aren't available." A sigh. I flip-flopped to get out of the tub, slipping and smashing my knee on the faucet, and nearly crashing head-first into the toilet. "…continue our talk in private. Hope to see you soon. Bye."

I hopped to the phone, rubbing my knee, just as I heard the click on the other end. Okay, just call him back, Eliza. I looked at the off-color answering machine. Blocked number?! How had I managed to not get his phone number all this time? Don't panic, someone has his number, obviously. But who? Lynch? My own unwarranted revulsion at asking the man for anything surprised me some.

I brimmed with hatred at the thought of him, I realized.

I struggled to put jeans on my damp body, hair dripping. I didn't even own a blowdryer. "What am I *doing?*" I asked myself, but I knew the answer.

I was going to his house. I would have gone to Antarctica if he'd asked.

I pulled on a red sweater, and was kicking on ballet flats when Kat walked in bearing pizza. Her face fell as I swung open my bedroom door, fully clothed, but still wet.

"Where are you going?" she whined. Two movies were stacked on top of the pizza box. One would be *Texas Chainsaw Massacre*, the other a romantic comedy.

"Nowhere." What? Obviously not true. Kat set the boxes

down on the coffee table, her eyes never leaving mine, red lips curling into a smile.

"Do you have a date, Ellie?"

"No, I don't." And I didn't.

"I've never seen you so ready to get out after work!"

I grinned, despite myself. "I'm…gonna go," I said, pulling a piece of pepperoni pizza out of the box. "Tomorrow I promise we'll reheat this." Pizza sauce smeared the sleeve of my coat as I pulled it on.

"Are you in love with Nicholas?"

My eyes widened like I'd been caught killing a kitten or something. "Wow. We just talked a few times, and I smelled him in a book store." That sounded bad, didn't it?

Kat was gaping at me, slack-jawed, and gave me the slow nod. "Right. What do you two talk about, anyway?" She grabbed a piece of pizza, and lounged across the couch. "You've been keeping this whole thing very quiet, Eliza Morgan."

I pursed my lips, stopping myself from bursting out the door. I was being foolish, just going to his house. And Kat deserved to hear more. Sighing, I pulled off my coat, getting more sauce on the sleeve, and plopped into my chair, pulling my afghan around me. I relived the odd scene at Lynch's cocktail party for her, and the just as strange conversation we'd had at his house. I left out my impromptu visits to Birch Tree Books, not really knowing why. "We have a connection," I said timidly. "An indescribable connection." My confusion returned, followed by the butterflies, and the warm flood in my limbs and cheeks. I stood up and paced the room.

"Kat, I don't know what's happening." I was getting flustered, and I was angry about it. "He knows things about who I am, things he can't possibly know. It makes me—nervous— and yet the thought of him—"

She was smiling.

Shaking my head, I continued. She wasn't getting it. "It's not just… I'm also scared. And I don't know at all how he feels."

Kat pulled me by the arm onto the couch beside her, and handed me another slice of pizza. "You stay here with me tonight. Enjoy falling in love. Tell me all about it. It *is* scary, but this could be *fate*!"

Fate? The idea had crossed my mind, but seemed so fairy-tale-ish and just plain dumb. But Nicholas was too incredibly exactly what I wanted, what I needed in every aspect, no matter how out of sorts it made me.

There was no denying that he did scare me a little, and I hated that. It didn't make any sense. And I didn't know what the hell he was talking about half the time. His voice roiled through me as I replayed his phone message in my head: "…*continue our talk in private.*" I did desperately want to hear more about the things he knew of me, but I feared his questions almost as much as his answers.

My desire to just be near him overtook any fears I may have had.

Kat read my mind again. "Not tonight, Ellie." She gave me a little pixie smile that spoke volumes of how much she knew the business of dating. She nudged my shoulder with her own. "Let him wait. Let him miss you, too."

～

For days my not-quite-date with Nicholas overwhelmed my thoughts, struggling with his so-called intuitiveness and the possibility he was like a roadside fortune teller, using tricks to make me believe.

My mind kept wandering while I was at work. The owner, Vivienne, wore a shirt was the same color as Nicholas's hair. Customers made me think of his disapproval of my job. The tourist chatter was as droning as the rain on his windows that night.

But nothing could compare to his scent, or his voice. It was like finding a home I'd never known could exist again. I needed nothing at all to make me remember that.

"Ellie?"

I snapped back yet again from staring at the counter. "I finished the schedule an hour ago, Viv."

She smiled at that. "Even when you aren't there, you get your shit done, Ellie," she said into my ear with a smile, and squeezed my shoulder. The one that Nicholas had brushed lint off of.

I glanced at the clock. 4:15. In forty five minutes the store would close up. Kat and I had a wild night of food shopping ahead of us, for all the stuff we missed on Saturday. This was Wednesday. Friday was the last time I saw him. My eye twitched.

I dusted four glass shelves. I rang out a handful of customers, some regulars. I drank two paper cups of water from the bubbler. 4:45.

"Is it all right if I take off a little early, Viv?" I asked, already putting on the obnoxious bulky coat.

"Sure, Ells. See you tomorrow. Hey, get some rest, would you? You seem—off, Ellie. Have an early night."

So it was that noticeable, then.

I smiled. "Sure. You're right. Tomorrow, I will be on. All day long."

"Christmas is coming!" she sang. "It will be busier every day!"

"Yes!" I failed to make it sound enthusiastic.

My phone buzzed with a text from Kat as I was going through the door. *"Ready for food shopping! Must have red velvet cake!"*

Yes. My fave. I texted back, *"How did you know? You're the best.*"

My inattention made me bump into Richard in the doorway, a regular customer who was only regular so he could ask me out. I knew for a fact he ate raw hot dogs every day for lunch. He told me.

"Hey, Richard," I said, trying to bustle past.

"Ellie, will you ever give me the time of day?"

I stopped on the sidewalk and turned around. "Richard. Sorry, but no."

"Well, I'm sorry, too," he huffed, and pushed his way through the door. I sighed.

It was a short drive in Ossipee time. I parked next to Kat. She was still in her car, on the phone, laughter rustling her coppery red hair. I opened her door for her.

"I'll see what I can do. Okay." Another laugh. "Okay. I'll call you. Bye," she said softly.

"Who was that?" I asked, knowing.

Smiling, she said, "That was Chris. He finally asked me out!"

"I got asked out, too! By Richard! He's taking me to a very exclusive restaurant, says I *need* to try their signature hot dogs wrapped in hot dogs with hot dog sauce. Then we're getting married—quick, I know—by Oscar Meyer, and we'll grow old together, until I get scurvy from eating nothing but hot dogs."

Kat just blinked at me until she gave way to laughter.

At the grocery store, I pushed the shopping cart to the deli and pulled a ticket, trying not to think of Richard as I looked at the meat in the case. I thought instead about the playboy who owned that foolishly large house and was putting the moves on Kat.

"So he's not seeing anyone else, is he?" I asked.-

"Nobody serious. Do we need pickles?"

"Always," I said. "Where is he taking you?"

"Some fancy French restaurant!" She beamed. Where was

there anything fancy around here? I took the cheese from the kid at the counter while an old lady jostled me aside. This place was itty bitty and claustrophobic like the world's smallest elevator.

"That sounds lovely. Just be careful, Kat, okay?"

"Well, it'll be easy to be good while you're there." We both stopped moving. Her, with a wicked grin, me with mouth agape.

"Oh no you don't! No double dates, Katherine! Are you kidding me? What am I going to wear to a fancy anything, the same dress you let me borrow before? What am I going to talk about with some stranger?"

She put a box of Wheat Thins in the carriage. "We'll go shopping. My treat."

"Oh, clothes shopping, my favorite!"

Head tilted, she pleaded like a child. "Pleeeease, Ellie? I really want to go! One night?"

"Kat, have you already planned my date for me? You have." I spun on my heel to leave the aisle and slammed right into someone carrying a cake that smelled fantastic as it hurtled toward the floor.

"Oh, sorry, sorry!" I blubbered, stumbling. A large hand reached down with flickering speed and caught the box before it hit the floor.

"No date? Maybe I could arrange something?" That rich voice. That scent. It hadn't come from the box.

It was like I'd been holding my breath since Friday. I actually closed my eyes and exhaled, letting my shoulders droop. We both rose from our cake-catching crouches, our eyes not faltering from each other.

Nicholas.

Another man cleared his throat, causing Nicholas to gently pull the cake towards himself with a smile, and put it in his cart. Nicholas nodded to the man pushing it.

"Eliza, Kat, this is my brother, Roman. Hobbies include irresistible brooding and…" he pretended to think. "No, that's it." Roman glared tiredly at Nicholas in a way I recognized from Kat. "What? It's a perfectly respectable hobby."

As stunning as his brother, if not his opposite in every way, I estimated Roman to be around our own age, twenty-seven, thirty maybe, while Nicholas was probably ten years older. Shimmering blond hair brushed his thoughtful, blue eyes. For every bit as self-assured and egotistical as Nicholas was, Roman was visibly shy and reserved. Both brothers had the same inherent strength of character, evident upon meeting them, not to mention similar lithe, muscular bodies, reminiscent of Spartan warriors.

I watched Nicholas's eyes roam to Kat, a smirk on his lips. Without looking myself, I knew Roman had…made an impression.

"Nice to meet you, Roman," I managed, which was more than Kat could do. She just showed a lot of teeth.

Nicholas was looking at me again, but speaking to his brother. "Roman, I believe I've mentioned my friend, Eliza."

"Yes, you most certainly have," he said. "It's a pleasure." He smiled genuinely.

I would have killed a man to know what Nicholas had told his brother.

The pastry aisle was crowded with the four of us, Kat's eyes glued to Roman's face, myself to Nicholas's. Other customers mumbled, trying to get by. Nicholas snapped us all out of it, but made no attempt to accommodate the huffing shoppers.

"Eliza, I was thinking of having a few people over to help decorate our Christmas tree. Would you ladies please grace us with your presence?" Just like at the cocktail party, it felt too intimate to be speaking to him with anyone nearby.

"I'd love to!" Kat blurted out from a distance behind me.

Roman laughed; it was an attractive laugh that wrinkled his eyes and showed gleaming teeth. I could see why Kat was dazzled by him. I would have been, too.

Had it not been for the man before me that clutched my very soul.

"Eliza?" Nicholas asked through a laugh of his own.

"I would also love to."

"Good. Now when is this other, less important event, that you need a date for?" he asked. I flushed with embarrassment at the notion of an actual double date.

Kat found her voice. Wrong time. "Well, actually, Ellie, Chris has a friend he was thinking—"

"Don't be shy, Eliza!" Nicholas interrupted with a grin. "I'd like to accompany you…" His voice lowered, just for me. "…if you'll have me." Most definitely.

"Oh, I'll just tell Chris you have a date already, then," Kat yelped, excited to see her plan coming to fruition. "Now this won't be awkward at all, because you know Chris," Kat said, motioning to Nicholas.

Nicholas had been watching her as she rambled in a patronizing manner. He looked back to me. "Ah, our mutual friend, Chris." I got the impression Nicholas was not actually friendly with Lynch at all. "Is he trying to bring you to that French restaurant he knows? It's terrible. Instead, invite him to our place this Sunday for our little party. Roman will cook," he added. Roman made a face. I was hard put to find a better resolution to all of these date scenarios, and he saw it. "It's settled, then!"

In the background, Roman rolled his eyes. He must always have lived in his brother's shadow, as dynamic as Nicholas was, I thought.

"It's a date," I whispered.

"Come by around seven. Or earlier if you like."

"Sounds great." Would sound better if we were alone. For a moment, he closely studied my face, and we were.

In a whisper, he replied, "Four days, then."

Eyes closed, I mouthed back, "Four days."

CHAPTER 7

For the rest of that night, Kat babbled in her sweet, girlish way about Roman—his eyes, how gentle he seemed to be, wouldn't it be nice to date a smart, nice guy for once? She seemed to forget that she actually had a date for this little party at the brothers' house. She was displeased when I brought it up.

Slapping her forehead, she cried, "Oh, Christ! You're right! What are the chances I can find my date a date?" We both laughed, but both knew Lynch was a little more important to her than that. I fell into my armchair. Kat crossed her legs under her and threw down her magazine, ready to talk.

"Seriously, though, how do I tell Chris I've totally changed our date, now with a new and improved fifth wheel? Especially when I'm not totally sure who I want the fifth wheel to be."

My brow wrinkled. "Well, first tell him I am deathly allergic to croissants, or crème brule, and cannot ever eat at a French restaurant, no matter how fancy. And don't be so quick to say he's not your date, Kat. You've been so gung-ho about him, I think that would be a mistake."

"I'll just tell him we thought we'd kill two birds with one stone. Dinner and Christmas decorating party."

"Good," I answered, totally unable to picture Lynch decorating a Christmas tree. "We were overthinking it." I flipped through television channels while she dialed Lynch. She gave me a hilarious puking face when he answered. They chatted for a minute, and then Kat worked in her news.

"So, Ellie's asked Nicholas on our date—"

"She did what?" I could hear from the other end. I flinched.

"Um, yes," Kat replied, her surprise obvious. "And anyway, Nicholas thought instead of going out, we could all go to his house for dinner and a little Christmas party." She tried to sound more excited than hesitant during the long pause. "Did I mention Ellie's allergic to French restaurants?"

"Kat!" I whispered, shaking my head.

A look of distaste wrinkled her face, at the voice on the other end of the phone, not at me. "Well, yes, she's been talking to Nicholas lately. Look if you want to cancel, that's fine—"

"No!" I heard Lynch say, loud and clear, followed by some mumbling. When they hung up, it was with a grumpy undercurrent.

"He's coming," she told me, without enthusiasm. Score one against Chris Lynch, if there was anything to Kat's crush at first sight on Roman. "He said he'll be here at 6:30. He knows where they live."

Why did Lynch seem so resentful? Did it really matter what we did on the date?

As if she could read my thoughts, Kat said, "He seemed like…he was *definitely* mad that Nicholas is your date." She looked as confused as I was.

"Did he have someone else in mind for me or something?"

She fidgeted with her hair, and shook her head. "No, it's not that."

"So it's Nicholas in particular. But—"

"—they're friends," she finished for me.

I turned off the TV, unable to think straight. Bits of my conversation with Nicholas the night of Lynch's party flickered forth from my memory. "You know, I asked Nicholas how he knew Lynch, that night, at the party, when we were talking outside. He didn't seem to be in the right company that night." I remembered every part of our talk, even this insignificant thing. "I mean Lynch…Chris…with that house, and all the cars, and rich friends; that just isn't how Nicholas is. Come to think of it, he only moved here a month ago, too."

"Just like Chris."

"Right," I answered, both of us puzzled. "I asked him how he was a part of that crowd, but he didn't really answer me." A smirk twinged my lips, and I heated up. "He just knew I didn't belong there, either."

Kat looked concerned. "How did he know…how did you know that wasn't his scene? You'd just met. He seemed to fit in well enough to me." She peered at me suspiciously, like I was holding out on her. I wasn't. I still didn't truly have an answer to that myself.

"He fits in everywhere, I think. I dunno. We just picked up on that in each other." I paused. "He sorta seemed to know things about me," I added, unsure that I wanted to pursue this angle.

"What things?" Kat did not look happy.

I snapped back, realizing how odd my conversation with Nicholas would have seemed, even to Kat. "Oh, just, I think he was just really good with pickup lines."

I know she didn't buy that, but Kat was never the type to drag something out if I didn't want it to be dragged out. Temporarily refocused on her own situation, she said, "Well, Chris and Nicholas have that in common, then. I don't know if any woman has ever turned Chris down. It seems like he knows a lot of women, but that they never stick around for long, the way he talks. He'll mention some woman's name absentmindedly, and then drop it, but he doesn't seem very upset or anything."

My disapproval of him couldn't be hidden anymore. "Kat, why would you want a man like that?"

She looked at me like I was out of my mind. "Probably because he's gorgeous, and rich, Ellie. It's a good starting point."

"But he seems like—"

"And he is, I guess." She got up and started towards her bedroom, upset by my mouth. "But he has a certain appeal. I'm somebody with him."

"Oh Kat, no," I moaned, her words twisting my heart. I tried to see it from Kat's perspective, but I hated that she thought of herself that way.

But what I couldn't see was the reason for Lynch's anger towards Nicholas, or why Nicholas didn't like him either, and yet still associated with him. And they all came to town at the same time? More was being hidden from me than I thought.

These next few days were going to be nail biters, waiting to see what would unfold between the old "friends" this weekend.

~

Christmas was getting close. I'd scarcely noticed until Nicholas invited us for Christmas tree decorating. I'd been so wrapped up in what Nicholas was doing next that a lot of the world was just a necessary, albeit unwelcome, distraction. Now that the holidays included him, the red bows were more festive, the lights were brighter, wreaths smelled fresher. The snow created a mystical, sparkling scene where before there was just sludgy blacktop and unshoveled walkways.

I liked Christmas, but it could be difficult for me. Kat went to her grandparents' home in Connecticut every year. I'd gone with her many times. It was lovely to be there, like being in a Lifetime movie. The whole house took on a golden glow with candles and twinkling white lights wound around doorways and banisters. Evergreen garlands on mantelpieces and table-tops filled the air with the scent of fresh woods. It seemed Burl Ives was playing in the background from the minute we woke up to stumble downstairs and join each other around the Christmas tree. The tree was massive. Rockefeller Center's was smaller. Family was everywhere, sipping mimosas as breakfast dishes were brought carefully away from the grand dining table, "just this once," so as not to prolong gift unwrap-ping. Endless cousins and aunts smiled and hugged, and laughed, and warmth emanated from every one of them unsparingly.

I'd never felt so alone.

Without family since seventeen, left to my own devices, I managed to turn out okay; mostly emotionally sound. But the holidays weren't easy when surrounded by the constant Christmas village that was New Hampshire for all of about two months a year, and the memories of celebrating with my family were everywhere. And it would never be just like that again.

But now, I trudged through the snowy sidewalks with pleasure, the store windows, with their over-the-top displays of trains and Santas and party dresses and toppling red-wrapped boxes all reeling me in. The big bows on the street-lamps in Conway… Had they been there every year? And the music! The angelic voices caused my eyes to well up, like a damn fool.

And soon I'd be with Nicholas to enjoy it all. My heart

swelled, and I didn't even sigh with protest as I crossed the street to work. On A Clear Day had taken on a life of its own in these last shopping days, and I'd been swept up in the magic of Vivienne's stunning toy-shopesque décor like the customers.

Tired after work, but smiling, I took a detour to Singing Pines Park across from the shop. It was dark, offsetting the Christmas colors from the nearby street as if they were on stage. Lightly snowing now, I wanted to see it all dance on the icy pond.

But as I opened the wrought iron park gate, a strange unease quivered through me. Undaunted, I closed the gate behind me, and went to the bench facing the pond, insistent on enjoying the crisp air in this vacated public spot after so many people around me all day.

Because no amount of Christmas spirit could entirely erase the gap between me and everyone else. A crow landed on the back of the bench and cawed at me in agreement. I brushed the gathering snow from the bench and sat with a long, deep sigh. I looked across the pond, and my breath caught painfully in my chest. *What the…*

A dark-haired man was bent over a woman with cascades of blonde curls. She was crying I think, but the air around them shimmered and fizzled, like popping soap bubbles. Nothing was clear. He held her tightly, and she was struggling, I was sure of it. I jumped to my feet, unsure what to do, but I *would* do something, and then—

Nothing. Nothing there. Not even a hint in the snow that someone had stood there. The air was pure and clear through the dwindling flurries.

"I didn't imagine that," I said out loud. I swept my foot across the snow, as if I could uncover footprints below. The snow hadn't been falling fast enough, my own footprints still left a trail behind me.

The vision was a freeze-frame in my head; unsettling, grotesque even, so displaced in this beautiful, silent scene. They may have been lovers, enjoying the solitude themselves, and I'd ruined it, misinterpreted. They fled so quickly.

If they'd been there at all.

Before I knew it, I was home, unable to stay at the park for a second longer. Kat was already home. The mere sight of her car helped me breathe out as I rushed inside.

I'd replayed the scene a hundred times in my head on the way home, and it became more and more unclear why it had terrified me. At first, it was only disturbing, and the more I reflected on it, the more afraid I was. The stark snow was a stage for the struggling woman, golden hair shimmering as it shook, hot pink mouth flashing in and out of my vision. I had seen her eyes…hadn't I? Blue? But not his, covered by her body, as he bent over her, clutched her. Only his dark hair, and lithe build, his black coat… Bits and pieces came to me, things I didn't remember seeing, but were in my mind somehow. How long had I watched?

A drop of burgundy blood fell to the snow.

I ran to the bathroom, not stopping to remove my coat, and threw handfuls of warm water on my face. Realizing my gloves were still on, I whipped them off onto the floor, and looked at myself in the mirror. I was blotchy with anxiety and pale as all hell.

I jumped when Kat knocked on the door. "Ellie? Ellie, are you sick?" She came in before I could answer. "Oh! You look awful!" She spotted my wet gloves on the floor, and her eyes darted back to me, taking in the mess I knew I was. Unable to speak, I only shook my head. How to describe what I thought I'd seen, but wasn't there? Was there *blood* and I'd done nothing?

"I…I…thought I saw something terrible, but it was my

imagination." My voice was hoarse. I didn't realize I'd been crying.

Kat patted my hair, and took my coat off for me. "Let's get these wet clothes off of you. Were you in the snow? I'll get you some tea." She walked me to my room and helped me get my clothes off, the whole time muttering that I was shaking because I was so cold. How long *had* I been out there?

It wasn't long before I was wrapped in my favorite afghan, in flannel pajamas, with a mug of tea that smelled like honey and flowers. Kat was right beside me, looking very worried, but I didn't know what to say. We sat like that, watching some cooking show until it was over, and I'd finished my tea. I blinked long and hard, shook my head to clear my mind, and smiled at my best friend to ease her mind, too.

"This was just what I needed, Kitty Kat, thank you."

"Ellie. What happened?"

I told her what I saw, knowing she wouldn't think me nuts, even if she didn't believe me. I wasn't sure I believed myself.

"What do you think it was?" she asked me sincerely.

I wound my hands tightly into my afghan, and pulled my knees to my chin, blanket pooling around my feet.

"I think she's dead."

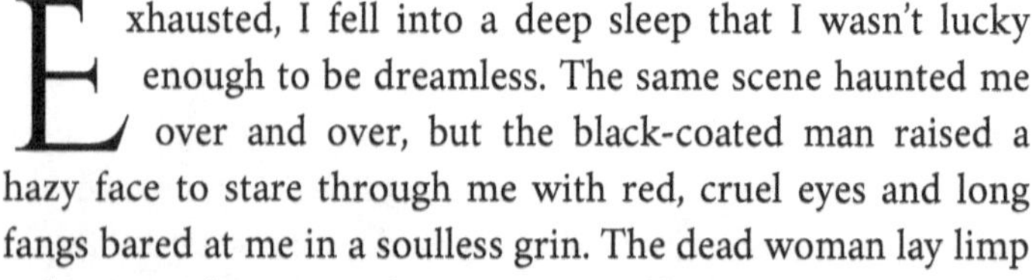

Exhausted, I fell into a deep sleep that I wasn't lucky enough to be dreamless. The same scene haunted me over and over, but the black-coated man raised a hazy face to stare through me with red, cruel eyes and long fangs bared at me in a soulless grin. The dead woman lay limp in his arms, face twisted in a grimace of horror.

Then, a change. The one drop of blood I remembered, or imagined, fell to the snow, and grew and grew, blanketing the white with red, covering the icy pond and melting it, turning it into a wound itself. The blood welled over my feet, my ankles. I couldn't move, the blood was a lake of quicksand, and I screamed, even as she screamed.

Then he was there. My Nicholas appeared in front of me, but with those bestial fangs, and blood on his hands. He smiled, like he was comforting me, like there could be any comfort ever again, and simply said, "ssshhh," a sound more terrible than the screaming or the blood gurgling around us.

I awoke abruptly, the scream a being all its own. Kat was at my door, awoken by my fit. She ran to my side, as I tried to compose myself. I cleared my aching throat. "Just nightmares. Of course."

Quiet for a minute. "Ellie, I watched the eleven o'clock news…" I looked at her sharply, not knowing what I wanted to hear. Either I was crazy, or a woman was dead. And if she was…who was that man?

Christ, was he there, was Nicholas *there?*

"Ellie! You're shaking again, Ellie. Please listen to me. Nothing on the news about it. I called the police, too. I told them I thought I saw something at the pond. They checked it out, and called back to thank me, but nothing was there. No trace of anyone on that side of the pond, or anything." I smiled with pursed lips. We both knew, of course, that this was fantastic, but what did it mean—for me?

"Get some more sleep, Ellie."

The idea seemed insane. "I don't need sleep." I threw off the covers angrily. "Sleep won't help. What…did…I…*see?*" I bit back the panic with gritted teeth as it rose in my heart, my chest, my throat, like the blood in my nightmare. Kat rested her hand on mine. I wanted to snap at her for patronizing me, but her sympathy was real. Nearly made me hate it more.

"Ellie, you saw nothing. It's fine. A trick of the lights, the dark… And we don't need to worry about it unless it happens again. Which it won't." I cocked my head, and she smiled, the least sane thing she could do, and it was the perfect reaction. I smiled, too.

"Ugh. Three in the morning? Way too early for breakfast." I pulled the covers back up, Kat kissed me on the cheek, and we both went back to bed for as long as we could.

CHAPTER 8

A bowl of Golden Grahams and a strong pot of coffee much later, Kat and I had both made a conscious effort to put the apparently non-existent events of the night before behind us, and enjoy our highly anticipated weekend. Despite my last vision of Nicholas being a nightmare beyond words, only stomach butterflies and inner hysteria accompanied the thoughts of our Sunday night date, even if we wouldn't be alone. Kat, ignoring the potential problem on the horizon, was equally jittery about seeing Roman again. Lynch was all but forgotten.

"What should I wear?" she debated with herself as she sipped her orange juice. I never put much thought into clothes, so I suppose it was really good that she did.

"It's only a little thingy at his house, and he's pretty laid back, so don't go prom gown on me." She made a face at me. I responded with, "We could still just go out to dinner. You know, the *four* of us." She was pouting, clearly looking for a reason to get dressed up. "Wear whatever you want, Kat, but I'm not getting out of control, wardrobe-wise." As weird as it was, I sorta did want to look better than usual. Maybe I'd let Kat dress me again.

We spent the morning making sugar cookies to bring with us which was about the extent of our baking skills, individual or as a team. The kitchen was bursting with the sweet scent that reminded me so much of the first time I sensed Nicholas at the book store. It made me shaky with excitement to see him. I spent no time muddling through my confusion over why I was so entranced by him, or why it scared me to answer his weird questions. I didn't wonder how he was hardwired to a part of my being that even I was unfamiliar with. And I definitely didn't imagine he was connected with the non-incident at the park, or my subsequent nightmare.

No, this weekend was about being happy for the holidays, and about the new possibilities that getting to know Nicholas might open in my heart. Today I would enjoy that I was falling in love with a man that I hardly knew.

I danced with Kat to an eighties mixed cd, as we made a mess in the kitchen that we wouldn't clean up for hours. We laughed about all the Christmases we'd spent together, from our numerous poor gift choices, to the time our tree fell off the roof of my car, to the time we gave our last pooled hundred bucks to a mom at Walmart. Kat's usual childlike enthusiasm infected me, where sometimes it just plain puzzled me.

"You realize that we never put up Christmas decorations of our own this year, right?" I said, sometime around our third batch of partially burnt cookies.

She looked at me in wonder. "Oh my God! I've been so— you know, and how did Christmas get so close? Well, let's go get a tree!"

"Tree time. Let's go."

~

I n glorified pajamas, we wandered through the lot by the same grocery store, run by the same family, our breath making little puffs around our faces as we examined tree after tree. We'd been smart enough to get hot chocolate to keep our hands warm in the twenty degree weather, and I took a deep sip, closing my eyes. When I lowered the cup, the delicious scent lingered, mixed with the aroma of pine. Kat was giggling about sap stuck to her boots. This was a good day.

When I opened my eyes, it got better.

"I wish I had hot chocolate. Roman, take note, hot chocolate." He stood in front of me in rugged glory, disheveled dark waves, stubbly cheeks, eyes searching me. His bake sale scent overpowered everything. I gathered my senses the best I could.

"Hi, Nicholas," I breathed. I peeled my eyes from his, as he unashamedly stared at me. Peering over his shoulder, I smiled. "Roman."

"Fancy meeting you here," he said, grinning, looking like a male model, but one that you like.

While I looked at Roman, my body was intensely aware of Nicholas's presence, once again a little too close for casual meeting. I tried to ignore the black wool coat of my nightmare.

"I was sorry not to hear from you…" he started, obviously expecting an answer. I fought with myself, wanting to apologize while hating his entitlement to an explanation.

I hated most of all how I loathed the idea of disappointing him.

Kat saved me. "She was trying to get out, but I kept her home. All my fault."

Roman sidled up next to Nicholas, almost a chastising look about him. "It's okay, Ellie."

"Eliza," Nicholas grumbled, his eyes still attached to mine.

Roman continued, probably used to Nicholas talking to him that way. "It's okay, Eliza. He has no right demanding more of your time." Well, that was a funny way of looking at it.

Nicholas turned his head with such a bemused, arrogant twist to look at Roman, that *I* was intimidated. Roman not only didn't flinch, but punched him in the arm. Nicholas just grinned.

"Ladies, it will be our pleasure to spend tomorrow night with you…and Chris," Nicholas said. I guess we all found the odd-man-out circumstances funny.

We picked out two robust, fragrant Christmas trees together. Roman tied ours to the roof of my car in a stunning display of musculature. I was certain this one wouldn't fall off.

Kat stood by quietly while I harnessed the opportunity to be with the man that stole all the air from my lungs. Nicholas and I spoke softly in a cluster of trees.

"Why did you want to speak to me the other night?" I questioned, hoping beyond hope that the answer was that he just needed to hear my voice.

"I'm greatly interested in finishing our talk. Where were you?" was all he said, but I was helpless to keep from him the wild events of the night before, what I was sure deep down had to have been the killing of that blonde woman in the park. The story poured out of me in a tearless sob.

He looked almost *angry*; not what I would have expected, but I should've learned to expect the unexpected with Nicholas. He grabbed both my arms and pulled me to him with a touch of roughness.

"Eliza, I swear to you, soon enough, things, though they may not make sense, will at least be more clear to you. Do you understand?" His words weren't comforting, but his stomach, black wool coat open, was pressed against me. My body read his tension, sensed his muscles tightening as he breathed out his cryptic words. His lips were close, so close, but he was anxious as he spoke, more anxious than I thought he knew how to be. He wasn't longing to kiss me. I shuddered and could only nod. "And I want to know the answers to every question I have about you, too," he finished.

I was still reeling from having told him about the park, and from his nearness, and all the things I'd certainly never understand. It was moments like this with him, the confusion that brought on a resentful anger in me.

"This isn't the time," he said. "Let's just enjoy the holiday together, quietly."

I don't know how I didn't scream at the broken conversation, except that his eyes kept me focused, his voice stilled me, though his words confounded me. The world was closing in.

"This promises me another date, then?" I asked, my eyes fluttering closed. His voice lulled me like gently lapping waves.

His breath tickled my face as he sighed. "You may see more of me than you care to, young lady."

His scent enveloped me like a sugary fog, then was penetrated by a cooler, more watery aroma. Roman was there, I knew, before I opened my eyes.

"Is he boring you to unconsciousness, Ellie?" It was a joke, of course, but with a bite meant for Nicholas.

"Uh, no, of course not, no." That sounded smart.

Roman flashed a look at Nicholas, and then smiled warmly at me. "Your Christmas tree is all ready to go. No thanks to the cranky tree lot guy."

"Thank you! So, I won't tip the guy on the way out, then?" Nicholas mouthed, *He's right behind you,* to me. My eyes widened as Nicholas and Roman had a good laugh at my expense.

"Jerks," I said, laughing.

"Let's go, Ellie!" Kat called from the car.

Nicholas bent his knees to come to my eye level. "Until tomorrow night, then." He kissed my cold fingertips, exposed in the fingerless gloves. I stopped thinking.

With a note of harshness, Roman said, "Time for us to go, too, brother." I knew I hadn't imagined his tense attitude this time. It came and went, seemingly whenever Nicholas got close to me. I tried to ignore it for now. I wrapped my red scarf tighter, and joined Kat in the car. *Holly, Jolly Christmas* greeted me as I sat on the cold, cracked seat. I closed my eyes for a second, and just listened, waiting for the warmth to flood back into my toes under the heater, and took a deep breath. Kat's eyes bore into me.

"What?"

"Oh, nothing. It's just nice to not be the one in puppy love."

I snickered. "Said the girl with two dates."

"I do not have two dates. Roman is just a lucky coincidence. Besides, he hasn't even spoken to me, really." She wrinkled her nose with a smile. "I wish he was my date," she confided. I laughed a little too loud, still giddy from being so close to Nicholas.

"It feels good," I said, without even really knowing why I said it.

"I know," Kat said through a smile.

We pulled onto the poorly plowed street, and I kept talking, surprising myself. "It feels good to *want* to get close to him. I want him to trust me. I can't even remember the last time I cared." A stab of memory of my mother carrying a birthday cake from the kitchen.

"I know." Kat always knew. It made me sad for myself. I made these choices to be alone, and I regretted nothing.

Quietly, I said, "He's something I needed."

∼

It took an hour just to get the tree into our apartment. Every year we wonder why we do it. Then we'd remember when those lights cast a rainbow glow in the room perfect for reading by, and when we pulled out the boxes of ornaments we'd accumulated through the years, each with a story.

"I wish I could still get away with giving a photo of myself glued to an ashtray as a gift," I said as I hung my third grade ornament right in front.

"I would take it," Kat said. I knew she would, too. Suddenly, her eyes lit up as she nearly dropped a flat dog decoration that was missing an eye. "Oh my god, let's make them for Nicholas and Roman's tree! And one for Chris," she said as an afterthought.

"You're right. We have to do this," I answered, like I was agreeing to a secret spy mission. "We'll put them on their tree and see if they even notice!"

We were resolved. Kat found a recent picture of us in front of the gorilla exhibit at Roger Williams Park Zoo in Rhode Island. We glued it to a cardboard coaster we'd taken home from a bar, and put one of Kat's hair ribbons through it as a hanger. It was just ridiculous enough for Nicholas to find hilarious. Come to think of it, we never did bother to make one for Lynch, like he'd even bring it into the gaudiest home in New Hampshire.

That day was everything the holidays should be, full of love. Kat and I spent the whole day together decorating, and eventually cleaning up all the messes we'd made in the process. We changed from sweatpants into just as comfortable jammies, and watched Christmas specials until after midnight over hot chocolate and way too many cookies.

"I should never have eaten that many cookies if I plan on

fitting into anything of value tomorrow night," Kat groaned, leaning back into the couch.

"I never even bothered to think of that," I said. "What's wrong with me? I still don't care. I could wear sweatpants tomorrow and feel underdressed for like, one second." Meaning I breathed confidence, or I was just that fashion-foolish.

"You've got it for Nicholas bad. If you two don't even notice what the other's wearing, that's all it could mean."

My nose wrinkled up in distaste. "I don't know if he notices or not. I'm so…"

"Entranced?" Kat offered up.

I glanced at her. "I guess so. I guess I am. But I think he likes me, too. I think." He felt like so much more than emotions and guesswork.

It felt like my family consisting of just me and Kat was growing, and it felt unimaginably wonderful.

CHAPTER 9

S unday. I'd been waiting for this day for about twelve
years, it seemed.

"We should have mimosas with this," Kat said as she put
my bowl of Golden Grahams on the table, and sat down with
me, fuzzy bathrobe swirling around her.

"You're right. The best thing to do before going to an over-
crowded grocery store in the morning is to drink. Especially
when you're going to drink even more later."

Through a laugh, she whined, "Do we really have to go
food shopping? Today should be pure fun. All fun."

I dropped my spoon loudly in the bowl, making us both
wince. "That's what fun does to me, I guess. No, seriously, we
have milk and mustard. Unless you want me to make milk-
mustard casserole again, don't fight me."

"We just went food shopping, though."

"And we never get the right stuff. We'll have fun. Before
you know it, you'll be dressing me in something I don't want
to wear, its seams will scream your name when I cram myself
into it, and we'll be on our way to Saint Nicholas's house." My
heart pounded.

"Okay, okay, we'll go." Her eyes glinted at me over her spoonful. "You'll help me not make a mess tonight, right? Chris is, well, he's amazing, but to have him and Roman in the same room? Wow. I don't want to ruin anything."

I smiled. "Kat, what are you talking about? It's not like you haven't been in the same room with two attractive guys before. Just don't flirt with Roman. Just don't, that's all." I couldn't believe I was giving her advice on how to strengthen her relationship with frigging Lynch, but hey. "If you really care about Lynch, you won't care how good looking Roman is for long."

"Right. Of course you're right." Her smile lit up as her worry drained away, and joy over her favorite thing, parties, ensued. "So, what *are* you going to wear?"

Rolling my eyes, "I don't know. And for the record, I cannot wait until the holidays are over for the mere fact that I won't have to worry about holiday parties anymore. I mean, really, how much dressing up can I be expected to do?"

"Well, now, you have Valentine's day to think of!"

"Over my dead body."

~

Kat limped toward the door. "These shoes are hurting my feet."

"This shirt is hurting my feelings. Seriously, why did I attempt a button down?" I said, trying to pull the little hole that revealed my bra closed. "36D, and you talk me into a button—"

"Shut up," she said without malice as she opened the door.

Though he tried to smile through it as he kissed Kat on the cheek, Lynch was visibly annoyed. His quiet dinner plan had become a party that he no longer had any control over. He seemed to be a man who liked his control. The best he could get was insisting on driving, and not letting Nicholas come by the apartment to get us.

"You look very nice," Lynch said to me, his eye going directly to the gap between the buttons I'd tried without success to close.

"Thank you, Lynch."

"You can call me Chris," he said, more implying that I should than that I could.

My eyes darted to his. "I know." I gave him a tight-lipped smile as Kat finished putting on her coat, and grabbed both of our purses. I would have forgotten mine.

Kat sat in the passenger seat of his white Porsche. She looked really pretty for her date. Her red hair was knotted loosely into a "chignon," in a way I would never have been able to do. She wore an emerald green cocktail dress like she was born in it. Lynch seemed so enamored of her, always glancing her way as he drove, talking too low for me to hear in the baby-beanie-sized back seat.

Despite being crammed into the Chihuahua bed that was the sportscar's back seat, I was happy to sink into my constant thoughts of Nicholas and not have to play it cool. Somehow, having this night not alone made our connection stronger, like we were real if other people saw us together. I was nervous like I was going on stage. *This outfit was meant for the stage*, I thought, rolling my eyes at it. I pulled the silver satin blouse pointlessly, and tugged the blue pencil skirt down as best I could. Even the heels were too much. Kat insisted that I look sophisticated. I had believed her.

When we started to get close to the deep woods where Nicholas and Roman lived, a calm came over me, and I attempted to accept my forced clothing choice. This was about the holidays, and being together. And Nicholas.

I could see through the bay window as the car crunched over the snow that multicolored lights were already on the tree. I breathed a sigh of relief. There are two types of people in this world—colored lights people, and white lights people.

Nicholas was like me.

Lynch opened both Kat's door and my own, and the three of us made our way to the cabin. Roman opened it with a stunning smile before we knocked.

"Welcome! Merry Christmas!" he said as he took our coats and purses. "Good to see you again. Even you, Chris," he joked, shaking his hand.

Charming is the only way the little house could be described, but now it exuded Christmas spirit. I hoped no one saw the inexplicable tears I choked back. How asinine it would have seemed. Christmas was never the way it should have been.

This is how it should have been.

Nat King Cole bellowed out *O Holy Night*, resounding through the living room alongside the crackling fire and Nicholas's voice from the kitchen; a flurry of curses at the oven. Beaten-up cardboard boxes were stacked near the chubby little Christmas tree, presumably full of ornaments. The black "stray" cat, that definitely lived there, was curled in a ball on an armchair by the oversized stone fireplace. I went to him and ruffled his fur, enjoying it as much as he did on my chilled fingers. My friends chatted and laughed behind me, and I closed my eyes to relish the sounds. The air smelled of comfort food. My world was comfort food at that moment.

My eyes fluttered open to the boughs of greenery on the mantle, wound amidst a few Christmas cards and picture frames. I smiled at a great photo of Roman and Nicholas fishing, and wondered briefly who had taken it. Next was the bright smile of a young, pretty woman with curly dark hair, climbing aboard a ship. She had a feminine body, curvy, like my own, but she was strong in stature, powerful. In a second photo, she wore a body-hugging gown in front of a theatre; this shot was black and white, and yellowing. Her hair was different, in pin curls, dark lipstick drawing attention to her bow-shaped mouth. I tried not to frown. Who was she?

The other framed pictures of friends, or relatives covered a wide expanse of times. How lucky they were to have such an in-depth family history. The resemblances to the brothers across the years were amazing.

My attention was wrested away as I heard his footsteps across the kitchen floor. Butterflies flitted in the pit of my stomach, and I tried to smooth the stupid shirt one last time. I tucked my hair behind my ear, then untucked it.

He pushed through the swinging barn door, just catching one of the overflowing plates as it slipped from his grasp. Smiling at his mumbled swears, I rushed to hold the door open, but he had it under control, leaving me standing too close to him without an apparent reason. My breath caught, again and as usual, when his swirling cocoa cream eyes penetrated mine, followed by a visual sweep of the rest of me. My cheeks heated.

"You look beautiful." The raspiness of his voice was so blatantly sexual that it immediately brought me to another uninhibited place. A crooked grin shifted the corner of his mouth. "Not like you. But beautiful all the same." His hand breezed by my hot cheek to brush a strand of hair. "I like that you didn't change your hair. This is yours."

It was difficult to meet his eyes, and impossible to tear myself away from them. "Thank you," I mumbled.

The delicious smell of the plates he held was still not as enticing as the scent of the man himself. "Mmmm," he groaned, closing his eyes, as though he'd tasted some wonderful thing. "You smell fantastic today."

"I was thinking the same thing," I breathed. His lips curved.

"Roman!" he yelled out of nowhere, making my ear pop,

breaking the spell like a twig underfoot. "Come get one or three of these plates, for crying out loud!"

Roman took my place in the doorway, arguing with Nicholas over who was doing more host work. I stole a glance at Kat, who looked eagerly back at me, grinning like a kid with the last cookie. Her hand was entwined with Lynch's. I gave her a thumbs-up when I thought no one could see, but Lynch turned at just that exact time, and gave me a thumbs-up back, with a flash of his impossibly brilliant smile. I mumbled a "blech" accidentally.

Despite his vast expanse of glittering white teeth, I only distrusted Lynch. His charm relied on always having the right thing to say, driven home with that shark grin. He didn't so much listen when spoken to, as measure people up, analyzing them. It unnerved me. He let out a long laugh at something he, himself, had said. I looked away.

Nicholas popped his head up from his spot next to Roman on the sofa, and gave me wide, bored eyes. I took the signal, and went to sit on the other side of him. We faced Kat and Lynch over the old chest that served as a coffee table, full of snacks. Nicholas handed me a mug full of a hot, frothy drink bubbling with whipped cream, and frightening amounts of alcohol. He couldn't even pretend to care what Lynch was yapping about.

"So you won't be with your family on Christmas?" Kat asked, sadness filling her voice, as she intently listened to Lynch.

"No, I have a lot of work to do. I have no family left, actually," he answered casually. It didn't appear to bother him.

"Oh, don't be silly. We're your family!" Nicholas spoke up, sarcasm dripping. He drew in a sharp breath when Roman elbowed him in the ribs.

Lynch either didn't catch on, or ignored him. "Thanks,

Nick," was all he said. Nicholas grumbled about being called Nick.

Clearing his throat, Roman said, "Yes, well, we always do invite Chris for the holidays."

"I'm less sentimental than most," Lynch simply stated.

Finishing the last bite of a stuffed mushroom, Kat asked how it was that Chris knew the brothers. Nicholas replied that Chris was an old friend of Roman's, before Lynch even opened his mouth.

Turning to Roman, Kat asked, "Did you go to school together? You're about the same age, right?"

Roman said "yes," while Lynch said "no." Nicholas steered the conversation again by saying that the two had taken martial arts from the same teacher.

"I had no idea!" Kat exclaimed, spinning her head from one man to the other, biting a sugar cookie. "That's interesting," she said, focused more on Roman than on Chris. Roman shied away.

"Nicholas is better than both of us," Roman said.

Now my head snapped up from probably my twentieth appetizer. Mouth full, I looked at the man next to me, always giving me some unexpected thing to ponder.

"Wow, really?" I said in a food-filled whisper. I wasn't sure why it impressed me so, but it did.

"He exaggerates," Nicholas said coolly, smirking at me, purposely and falteringly humble.

"I'm not so sure he is better," Lynch said to no one in particular, as a grape dropped into his mouth from his hand overhead. Smug as always.

"Really?" Nicholas bit at the bait. In a war of words here, Lynch didn't stand a chance, despite his quick lawyer-speak. "What do you base your assumption on?" Nicholas asked.

"You're too bulky, Nick. You've got to be lithe, and swift." Chris cocked his head. "I think I could take you."

There was no movement, but Nicholas was over the table, or around it, his hands encircling Lynch's throat. Lynch's eyes bulged as he bucked off the couch. More alarming was that Kat just reached for her drink, completely okay with this somehow? I was stunned, gulping in shocked breaths.

This got ugly fast. "Guys, it's Christmas. Let's just not, okay?" I pleaded. Nicholas's shoulders relaxed, the muscles of his back loosening visibly under his thermal shirt. He casually rounded the trunk and sat next to me. I gaped at him.

"The jungle cat pairs speed and agility with mass and strength."

"Oh, very philosophical," Lynch muttered, rubbing his neck gingerly.

Nicholas was still getting heated at the attorney's boldness. "And a jungle cat could rip your eyes from their sockets. You know, if so inclined," he added for fun.

I looked at Kat in silent disbelief. She shook her head, and I shrugged. I made another dive for the amazing array of treats on the table; all kinds of cookies, macaroni and cheese bites, chocolate dipped strawberries, too much to take in. I could feel Nicholas's eyes on me as I sat back, stupid satin shirt bunching up where it shouldn't.

"What?" I said, eyes wide, wondering what I had on my face.

"I'm just glad you're enjoying yourself, that's all," he said quietly. Kat and Lynch were talking amongst themselves again, and Roman had momentarily disappeared.

"Is that a crack about how I'll eat anything? Also, I'd be able to enjoy myself a lot more if you and Lynch were about to have a cage match."

He blinked. A surprised blink, but he recovered predictably fast. "Oh, don't worry about us. We'll be doing this until the end of time."

"You're so different from him," I whispered. "Why do you guys spend time with him at all?"

Nicholas's eyes darted to Lynch, who was refilling Kat's wine glass. Lynch met his gaze, and smiled…differently than usual. Not his bright, practiced grin for the masses, but an ominous thing. Then he sauntered to the kitchen, leaving us looking behind him.

"So!" Kat piped up, folding her hands in her lap. She looked like such a little girl to me then. "When do we decorate?"

"Let's not rush," Nicholas answered. "Enjoy yourself!" Nicholas got up, and a black hole seemed to open up beside me. "I want to see what Roman set off to do." With a sideways glance to me, he was in the kitchen, and Kat and I were alone. She hopped over to sit next to me.

"What was that all about?" she said, a conspiratorial grin spreading across her face.

Shaking my head, I said, "I don't know, but I intend to find out."

"Oooh, you're getting crafty, I can just smell it."

"All in good time, Kat, all in good time."

CHAPTER 10

The remainder of the evening was all pleasant, if not a little forced on Lynch's behalf whenever the conversation veered away from him. Kat had convinced me to take a personal day on Monday so she wouldn't have to worry about me spoiling her night early. Thank goodness, because Nicholas's warm alcohol concoctions went down quick, and before I knew to stop I was getting smart alecky. Nicholas loved it, and that made me lose my inhibitions even more. Roman and Kat unexpectedly found lots of things to talk about, and I was pleased to see Kat taking a friendly interest in him, that Roman returned. He'd seen through Kat's playfulness that some took as bimbo-ness. Pompous Lynch didn't seem threatened at all.

We decorated the adorable tree, and laughed, and ate until I couldn't move anymore. Kat found the perfect opportunity in our impending food comas to pull our handmade decoration from her purse.

"This thing is unbelievable," I said as we found a spot for it on the tree. "I hope nobody finds it before we leave. I want it to have the proper *what the hell* impact." Christmas was in the air.

As the night wiled away, Kat and Lynch became inseparable, and eventually Kat hinted to me that she hoped Nicholas would drive me home, so the two of them could be alone. I didn't love the idea of their relationship going in the direction I knew it was going to go, but she was a big girl, and I did love the idea of having time alone with Nicholas.

Soon enough, the wind outside began to howl and moan, blowing a chunk of tree into the side of the cabin. Roman insisted I stay the night, and my heart stopped dead in my chest. He sat now in one of the Victorian armchairs in front of the fire, a thick book resting in his lap as he took a sip of wine. The black cat slept in a ball at his feet, dangerously close to the fire. I was glad he wasn't outside in the frigid winter, that he was cared for.

I stood at the window, watching the snow swirl in puffs and bursts, covering the pebbly driveway and the thick rows of trees that framed it. The golden glow from the single lamppost highlighted shivers of snow like they were on stage. Little drifts gathered in the wooden slats of the window panes, and a gust shook the glass. I pulled my hands further into the sleeves of the tattered sage green sweater that Nicholas had let me borrow. It was soft with wear and smelled like cloves.

He would never get this back.

I listened to the comforting clanking of cups, cabinet doors closing, the kettle whistling in the kitchen. Suddenly, Nicholas was behind me with a steaming mug of hot chocolate and marshmallows, just like I'd had as a kid after sledding and before a nap. I smiled over my shoulder as I took the cup. I wished with all my heart that he would slip an arm around my waist from behind, and tried to catch my breath before it got ahead of me. The house creaked with another gust.

"It's so peaceful here, even in the storm," I said.

"I'm glad you like it here," Nicholas answered.

I could scarcely believe how in days, literally days, this place I hadn't even seen all the rooms of, felt like home. The comfort that wrapped around me and pulled me in was completely at odds with my normal hesitation to, well, not get too comfortable.

"No, it's not just that I like it." I heard Roman stir in his chair, but he couldn't possibly hear us. "I don't get comfortable easily."

He moved to my side, and my comfort increased even more. "You think I don't know that?"

We turned to face each other, he with a smug smile, but a depth in his eyes that betrayed something else. "How? How do you know that when I've barely realized it myself?" I fired the question at him, but he was unperturbed. "Nicholas, I'm confused. You know things you shouldn't, and I'm, I don't know, in the middle of something."

Roman slammed his book shut, making me jump. Once again, Nicholas looked almost like he expected it. With a tight smile for me, Roman said, "It's late. I'm heading to bed. Good night Eliza, and thank you for making this such a nice Christmas already." He shot a heavy glance at Nicholas, and abruptly left down the hall, the cat at his heels.

"Good night," I managed, thrown again by the sudden tension. I almost relieved to see Nicholas was clearly struggling for words. It meant that the ever-present mood swings weren't my imagination.

Frankly, after the park incident, I was a little afraid of my imagination. And I was tired of being afraid.

My need to know all of the corners of this maze that had become my quick relationship with Nicholas overwhelmed me, took over my soul, and I drowned in it.

"As right as everything seems now that I've met you, everything has gone weird, too. Just say what you need to say, Nicholas. Please," I whispered to him.

"Do you think if it were so simple—"

"Make it that simple, Nicholas!" I slammed the mug down on the windowsill, sloshing it over. It was all I could do not to throw it into the wall. "What *is* this? The riddles, the way I feel?" My throat turned into quicksand at the words. "There's more than what you're telling me, and it's *about* me. It's not fair to leave me in the dark!"

"Not fair? What is this, elementary school?" He turned his head, and looked so suddenly sad, that a pang of guilt stabbed me. Not just guilt—*pain.* It actually hurt me to see him in pain. And yet, *that* didn't confuse me.

I knew what that meant.

Nicholas was talking more to himself than me when he said, "It's not fair. Roman said the same thing." Roman? What? "And you're both right. I have to do this now." A strange excitement crossed his face.

Then, he walked away. I followed him.

CHAPTER 11

O nce again, we were in the kitchen, but its comforts were lost on me this time.

"Sit down please, Eliza." Nicholas's back was to me, rinsing our mugs in the porcelain sink. Even now, he awed me in his ordinary tasks and movements. As he poured hot water from the kettle, his biceps tensed under his thermal shirt. The slight movement of his legs toward the counter rippled his pants over the muscular curves of his body. His beautiful face was calm and thoughtful when he sat at the table, stirring the steaming contents of the mugs. So extraordinarily perfect.

He'd seated himself across the table from me; I hadn't even seen him cross the room in my stupor.

He spoke to me like he was reading an IKEA manual. "What I need to tell you will change everything. It will change how you see the world. It will certainly change how you see me." Some emotion was betrayed, but he was so hard to read then, like a hazy screen was up between us. "Forgive me. I've never told anyone *this* before." He rubbed his forehead hard, chuckling nervously, but all nerve and humor evaporated when his eyes met mine. "This is going to scare you. I can say try not to be afraid but you will be."

"Just say it. No more hiding." I gripped the arms of my chair with shaking hands.

"Tell you or show you?"

I pursed my lips impatiently.

He stiffened. "Fine. Enjoy." Just then, the woodstove-warmed room chilled as though the back door had been opened to the raging storm outside. I quickly turned in my seat to check, but the door was closed, woodstove burning. As I swiveled back to face Nicholas, I saw my breath cloud in front of my face.

"What—" I began. And stopped.

Nicholas's face, the warm chocolate eyes, had turned to an unbelievable cold shade of red, predatory gleam lighting them. Sharp, slightly elongated *fangs* dimpled into his bottom lip. The chill of old death overpowered the room.

I leaped backward out of my chair, my cup crashing deafeningly to the floor, a scream escaping my lips to match the howling wind outside. In a flash, he was right there beside me, and grabbed my hands. His were icy. Clammy.

Like a dead man's.

"Eliza. Stop. You know I won't hurt you."

His sugary voice was the same one I dreamed of. It settled me even as I reconciled the corpse-like grip and the brutal stare that I didn't recognize. Nicholas released my hands, my labored breathing the only sound cutting through the frozen silence in the inches between us. I swallowed hard, and relaxed my shoulders with effort.

"Can you please make it warm again?" I whispered, averting my eyes to the floor.

He let out a breath, the sweetness at once warming my nose and cold lips. When I found the courage to look at him again, the fangs were gone, and his eyes were a swirling tempest of death red and cocoa brown.

Finally, his eyes settled into their usual richness, and he was himself again. Coincidentally, the kitchen regained its cozy warmth. It was as if the insanity of these last moments had never existed.

"Well, I guess I asked for it," I said. I circled around him, and sat in my chair. He quickly joined me. "How did you do that?"

"Make the room cold?" I nodded, and he continued with a deep breath. "When I change, it happens. I lose all my human warmth, and it sucks it from the air around me as well." It had felt like I'd walked into a living tomb, like the decay that filled the air was sentient.

I folded my quivering hands in front of me on the table, a chill shaking my spine. Like a camera flash, he was gone from the room, and returned with a fleecy white blanket, which he wrapped around me. His rough fingers grazed my neck, and they were warm again.

Before I had let out a breath, he was seated. What was I supposed to say? I'd be impressed with myself if I could speak at all. He saw my frustration, and took hold.

"I am sorry I didn't tell you sooner. I probably shouldn't have told you this way, but I'm not a spectacular planner. Did I mention that I've never told a person before that I'm a vampire?" I drew a deep breath and held it, as his slight smirk resigned to a thin, hard line. "I am a vampire, Eliza."

"So are you going to kill me?" I knew the answer to the question, and regretted asking it.

"NO!" A blaze of hot anger and disgust. "What kind of *thing* do you think I am, that I'd befriend you, only to destroy you?"

I couldn't have contained my laughter, even if I'd wanted to. "You're a goddamn vampire, Nicholas! How in hell do I know your hunting tactics?!"

He shook his head, a wan smile appearing. "Of course you're right." He paused. "Eliza, you do realize what you just said, right?"

"You're a vampire. Christ."

He slapped the table and gave me a boisterous laugh. "Christ is right! Why haven't you passed out yet?"

"I don't know. I always knew you were too good to be true. And I knew something was different about you. Good lord, I heard your voice—" I almost said that I heard his voice in my head, and I stopped for a second to gauge his reaction. He was spot on, I should be terrified, and I shouldn't believe any of this.

But I did. I believed him, and I was barely put off by it. Even still…

"No way. No way you're a vampire. Not even real. I want a new explanation."

"Nope. Only explanation."

"Why is it so easy for me to accept? You know, don't you?"

"Not exactly."

"But you think you know."

I wondered who had the harder job at that time. He shook his head. "I don't know what exactly I'm dealing with here," he waved his arm up and down, indicating me, "but you're almost as scary as I am."

"Maybe I am in shock." We both knew I wasn't. "So, tell me about it."

He let out a long, deep breath. "We aren't just killers. We're more than that." The wind whipped some object at the kitchen window, but I didn't even flinch.

His voice deepened, he cleared his throat. I reached for his hand across the table, and was surprised to find it warm again. His hand grasped mine. He watched our fingers nervously twist in and around each other.

"We are called *Shinigami,* gods of death."

Gods of death? Scarier than the word 'vampire.' "Japanese?"

He smiled a little, nodding. "Japan is where our Master is, the creator of our race."

"So you're not *just* killers. But you do kill."

"What if I told you that we are not the murderers you think we are?" He cocked his head. "Well, not all of us."

"I'd probably say that everyone in prison claims to be innocent, too. But now. Now, I've met you, haven't I?" I swallowed, trying to comprehend what was happening without letting my heartstrings decide for me.

"Our prey is chosen by a greater force than our hunger, as if our hunger isn't enough." He smirked, and his eyes smoldered with sensuality at the thought, swimming with coffee and death. "Fate chooses our victims, and we listen." I shook my head at his pause, not understanding. Through his almost sexual excitement that had me fidgeting in my seat, I sensed his feeling at the horrifying words, *prey* and *victim.*

Disgust.

They did not disgust me. This was more than shock. I accepted it. And him.

"Why are those victims chosen? I don't understand."

He leaned in, pulling his hands from mine, a restlessness brewing in him. "They are *unmei nashi.*" His voice lowered. "No fate."

He stopped as my heart started pounding, his glinting eyes darting to my chest, until I motioned for him to go on. Equal parts reeling and fascinated, I could barely breathe while I waited for him to explain what he was—a killer.

"There are worse ways to die, than having the life drained from you by one of us. The *unmei nashi* are chosen for us because they're destined for darker than the death a vampire delivers."

Rippling confusion urged me on. "How does it work? How do you find them?"

Frowning grimly, he stood, and paced. "We are called to our victims, compelled to go to them, and we cannot refuse, not that we'd want to. And, in the end, it's the more peaceful way to go."

"How can you know that?"

"We know. We may not know what that other death is that awaits them, but there are numerous legends among our kind about vampires that didn't take their victims, the other fates that awaited them. A Japanese woman, murdered in her home in front of her children, their grief-stricken father then killing himself. A should-have-been victim who turned out to be Jack the Ripper. Cult followers and leaders, politicians, they go on and on." He put his hand up between us. "Before you ask, we don't know why some humans are allowed to succumb to awful deaths, or awful lives for that matter, but *Shinigami* legend tells us that allowing *unmei nashi* to live will have a negative impact on humanity as a whole. It's all we have."

My head swam. The heat in the kitchen, the violent storm outside, Nicholas's scent, his eyes, all of it made me weak. This wasn't in any movie, and it certainly couldn't be real, but I had seen his *fangs*, and it was impossible.

"Eliza," Nicholas said, placing his hands in front of mine on the table, but being careful not to touch me. His eyes were luminous with passion. How long had he waited to tell someone all of this? "We, Eliza, are the instruments of fate. The original angels of death. We are—heroes to humanity."

Heroes? Killers. No matter how you see it, a killer. Nicholas, my Nicholas, a murderer.

Sensing my fear settling in, he continued, more defensive, and with more conviction. "We do what must be done. Not what is right, but what is best. It's not a matter of best being fair. We're a race that was created for a purpose, and we do what we must to go on." He burned with ferocious emotion.

I was ashamed that I may have caused it.

"I'm sorry," I whispered.

He snorted with bitterness. "You're sorry you called me out as being a murderer?"

I shyly smiled, inappropriately I'm sure. "You're more than that. Aren't you?" My gut knew he was more than that. I knew he was good, just *good*, no matter what he said, or what he did. The goodness radiate from him like an electric current.

Nicholas eyed me as I mulled it over. He was so still. He smiled, and sipped from his mug.

I'd seen every vampire movie that existed, knew of ones that hadn't been made yet. None of them were like this.

"I swear, in time, I'll answer all the questions you must be conjuring up. I respond better than Bela Lugosi."

I gasped. "Did you just read my mind?!" His laugh echoed off the walls. He rocked on the back legs of his chair, like a high school delinquent.

"We're more intuitive than humans but we can't read minds," he said, bugging his eyes out and wiggling his fingers at me with mock spookiness. "Obviously you have questions, who wouldn't? It hardly takes a mind reader."

More than a little embarrassed, I squirmed in my chair, afraid of how nuts I'd look if I just asked what I needed to know, and then decided I didn't care. "But that day, at Birch Tree Books, I *heard* you in my head. It was you. You told me I didn't belong."

"Well, as all-knowing as I come across, I'm still trying to figure the hell out of that one."

I loosened up as the dense morbidity that hung over us was replaced with a little of the sarcastic language we usually spoke in.

"Okay, so you said that one of those...missed victims...of legend, she was just a woman, with kids and a husband, right? A good person?" He nodded. "But one was Jack the Ripper?" Another nod. "So you have to kill both good and bad people?"

"That's right." Another sip.

I wasn't sure my lungs could handle another deep breath. "You're not okay with that. Are you?"

Rocking back on his chair legs, "I kinda like it. Keeps me guessing."

"I know the sarcasm hides how sad you really are." We both grinned. We were both guilty of that. Quick tears glassed my eyes, and I hung my head to mask them. "I wish you could be at peace as much as you pretend you are."

"Well." His grin faded. "Looks like you don't have to be *Shinagami* to be intuitive."

My heart softened more as I realized how impossible it must be to be Nicholas French. The sincere happiness, if not tinged with irony. The knowledge of what he's done, and what he will do, no matter for good cause or not, just to survive. The weight that must have buried the purity of his soul until he could barely feel it anymore. Sorrow for him filled me to sickness. My eyes spilled over.

"No, no," he pleaded, coming to kneel by me, putting his hands over mine as they worried at each other in my lap. His expression had an edge, but his heart poured his words. "You cannot cry for me, Eliza. I do this, I *am* this because it is my part in fate's plans. My duty is an icy shadow, and it follows me forever, but I can make the hard choices, and live with the worse consequences. *I do what is right*—even if there's nobody to thank me for it. We all have a destiny to answer to. I'm nothing to cry over."

I smiled through my tears. "You're worth the trouble."

That was worth a sad, tired smile back that still gleamed and sparkled, and that I would later take with me through a deep sleep.

He stood, still holding my hands, and lost his grimness as he pulled me to my feet and tightened the blanket around my shoulders. "It's not all guts and murder, you know," he said.

How could it be, and leave such beauty in its wake?

"Would you like to take a walk?"

I laughed too loud, glancing at the snow outside the window, blinding us to the trees beyond. "Sure," I chuckled.

And he was gone, with a white streak of brownie-scented air replacing him. Before I finished breathing it in, he was back, slipping the blanket off of my shoulders, and my big puffy coat on. He put my fingerless gloves on for me, like my mom used to do.

"You're not serious, Nicholas?"

"What I'm serious about is that it's stupid to have fingerless gloves in Snow Country." He closed my gaping mouth with one finger. For this second, all was as it should be. He bent his knees so he could look straight into my eyes, and I thought I'd pass out from the privacy of the moment. My heart stopped and started again, like a coin had been thrown in the gears. Now I knew why he sometimes glanced at my chest.

He could feel my heart, too.

Narrowing his eyes, he bit his lip; my heart quickened more. "Do you trust me?" he asked.

I nodded. "I do."

"Still?"

"Yes. Still."

"Good. Let's go."

In one movement, we were across the kitchen, through the door, and in the storm outside.

But I was warm, and dry.

A little halo of clear air surrounded us, a shimmering bubble that Nicholas had created somehow, like he'd breathed life into the sky itself. I was able to take in the beauty of nature's ferocity in the thick of it. The trees were so dense and towering, miles high, it was incomprehensible that there was civilization anywhere near here. The branches, leaden with snow, swayed dangerously. Darkness enveloped the senses, but for a piercing howl of a coyote that matched the winds.

It was dreamlike, beautiful, the startling tranquility and wildness of the night. Chaotic and yet, silent. I could hear my heart slowly beating, my breathing steady. I'd never been so aware of anything in all my life as I was of every living thing that night. I saw Nicholas out of the corner of my eye, watching me with the most gentle appreciation.

"This is…there are no words."

He smiled warmly. "I knew you'd get it. Let's walk."

There was no end to the surprises with him.

He wound his fingers between mine, causing my heart to jump to my throat, but it didn't disturb my peace here. We took our first steps across his vast yard. The sphere around us walked with. I could hear owls in the woods over the hush of our boots on the thick snow. A deer came to the edge of the trees to watch the intruders pass by. Nicholas, however, wasn't out of place here; he belonged to this wilderness and depth of night. I was lucky to be a part of it.

We walked up the sloping path at the back of the yard, so high only the treetops were visible on the other side. Beyond a toolshed in disrepair was another slope downward in this neverending landscape. As we rounded the shed, I was able to look down the hill.

"Oh, Nicholas. It's just stunning." Immediately, I began the descent, pulling him behind me.

I knew instantly that he'd created the hidden heaven here, and it spoke to me like it had been waiting for me to find it.

Snow-coated hedges formed a shallow cave in which an ornate little iron table stood with two matching chairs, their black filigree nearly glowing in the carpet of white. Steps away was a fish pond covered in a thin layer of ice, surrounded by purple and red lanterns. The dim light cast a puppet show of shadows on the snow as a rabbit skipped by, unafraid. Having zero knowledge of gardening, I was amazed by the violet and pink flowers that filled the air with delicious sweetness in this winter wonderland. The scents, mingling with the indulgent aroma that was Nicholas, made me heady, but clear-minded. Like magic. A hammock hung between two sturdy trees close by, and I could imagine Nicholas dozing there when summer heated up, and probably even in the winter as icicles hung from the ropes.

I realized the storm had picked up again, but this place was subject only to the most perfect flurries. Amazed, I looked up to see cruel gusts beating against the trees. Whirling clouds of snow pounded Nicholas's snowglobe that encased this haven in its simple perfection, and the two of us with it.

"Yes, that's me," Nicholas said, motioning toward the clear case that shielded us from the storm. He walked a few paces from me and bent to the water, gently breaking the ice with a finger. The rabbit hopped right up next to him as though they were old friends.

I joined him at the water's edge, watching his face bathed in the lantern light, creating a blush where before there was the sheen of a pearl. I caught him gazing at my chest; my heart had betrayed me again. He turned nonchalantly to face the pond. Fish were visible right beneath the surface. *How quiet it must be under there*, I thought, and then thought how perfectly quiet it was in this dome, with Nicholas by my side. So serene, so apart from what I knew I shared this space with, underneath it all.

He closed his eyes lightly, and stray flakes clung to his lashes.

"I love standing in the snow," he murmured with love in his voice. I'm certain I groaned. "Close your eyes."

"I don't want to."

He snuck a glance at me, and nodded, as if to say it was okay, that this would all still be here when I reopened them. I couldn't take my eyes off of him, standing blissfully in the evening snow, peace at its most wonderful. Tears sprang to my eyes, too cold to drop.

"For me, I can *hear* the snow, I can smell it. Like you can," he added, fluttering his eyes over to me, "but for me it's *alive*." He inhaled deeply, then opened his eyes. "*And* I never get cold," he said smugly. He sidled over to me, an impish grin alight on his face. His pearl and roses face.

It was easier to believe he was an angel.

"But you, my dear, must be getting cold." He gestured to our private snowglobe. "This can only keep the cold out for so long."

"Can we stay a little longer?" I asked, like a child. He pulled my coat closer at the neck. "I could stay here all night."

"Let's go in there, where it's warmer." His husky voice, not the cold air, sent shivers down my spine. The sheltered seating area for two was like *The Secret Garden* pages came to life. The wrought iron filigree chairs were made more inviting with blue velvet cushions. Once inside, I could see the veil of white lights clinging to the interior of the hedge cover, trailing down the sides. What chill and wind there was in our snowglobe disappeared in here.

I sat cross-legged in one chair, and he in the other. I drank him in for a moment, and he let me, knowing that I needed to make sense of all that I'd seen and learned.

Did he know that I couldn't make sense of what I felt for him?

"In the summer I'll be able to sit here and see the sun without it burning me," he said, leaning back.

"That's right, you just made all of this," I said in wonder.

"I can work around the clock for free, and I have good friends who do what I tell them."

"That shed back there, though, it's old. A mess, actually."

"Yeah, I brought it with me. It almost fell apart a hundred

times, but I couldn't leave the old thing to die on its own. It's lived a good, simple life so far."

I smiled. "But wait, I've seen you in the sunlight." I was again, confused, unable to keep a clear train of thought. The confusion when I was near him was like a spell he put on me. It was impossible to see reason through the haze that was Nicholas.

His eyes darted nervously at my questioning remark. "Yes, I can go out in the daytime, we all can." *All? How many?* He rubbed his thighs as though to warm them. "How do I explain? When a vampire drinks, the human blood leaves a…residue. And for a while, the vampire can do human things, like go in the sun." He shrugged. "It always burns a little, though."

"So, when I've seen you out in the daylight, you've recently —fed?"

"Yes."

Startled as I was, I wanted to know more. "What else about feeding? What else happens to you?"

"Oh, all the hard ones tonight, huh?" He let out a long breath, gearing up. "One of the most difficult things about our *affliction* is that human imprint we steal. If we feed on an essentially bad person, and there's as many of those out there as you think, we take on more—evil—traits. Temporarily. More aggressive, more will to feed unnecessarily, isolating ourselves, not able to bear the sunlight. That's where the vampire stereotype really gets exciting.

"When we feed on genuinely good, kind people, something different happens. The *Shinagami* becomes, in essence, good, and will take on some of that victim's personality for a time. There will be a need to spend time with people, positive outlook that draws people in, the ability to love, and to withstand annoying people, and/or public television." He squinted, like he was trying to swallow something disgusting. "It, uh— hurts—in a lot of ways, too." My heart clenched. "It hurts me."

A pitiful whimper lodged in my chest. To see this strong, wonderful man express such a thing was horrible for me. I reached for his hand across the table and he took it quickly.

His words became fast, falling out like the seeds of rotting fruit, but he slumped in the small chair, all of his energy sapped by what he was saying. "The Master, and all the teachings we receive in Japan tell us how to adjust to killing, that this is a part of life, but I just *feel* murderous, no matter what the big picture. It's *savage* to take a good man's life. To feel the soul of a good man as you suck him dry, you see what you've stolen from the world, and part of it becomes you. You've taken the best of him for yourself, and left nothing behind. There's no way to comfort yourself for it, no pat on the back that can help. And there's no end! There can never be an end." He laughed bitterly. "Sometimes I wonder if there's any goodwill left in me at all, or if I just body-snatched all of my humanity from the people I kill."

Speechless doesn't begin to explain how I felt at the depth of his agony. I could read it in his eyes like words on a page.

He shook his head to clear it and actually said, "I must be boring you."

"You can't be serious, Nicholas." How much was I willing to say here? "Nicholas, you are a good man."

"Interesting use of the word *man*."

"Stop." I grabbed his hand from the table, pulling him as close to me as I could. "You're a good man to do what you do, when it costs you this way. I never—I can't imagine how it hurts."

That white flash again, and his furious face was inches from mine, bringing with it a deathly chill. "How can you be so foolish?! Whether I want to do it or not, *I will do it* because otherwise I'll wither and eventually die! The guilt doesn't matter; I'm too self-important to make it stop!"

His bellowing voice echoed, and I saw him realize how

frightening he'd become. The transformation was unintentional, and now he struggled to right himself. The fangs were menacing, but not as much as the anguish in his red eyes that left behind the mocha swirls so quickly. My eyelashes froze from the cold he emanated. He backed away from me, his face still shaking with the sudden ferocity. I sat completely still, not breathing, not moving, and so cold.

"Being a *hero*," he spat, "is a convenient side effect of the thirst." The anger still bubbled below the surface, his fangs still prominent.

"Stop being a hypocrite," I let out in a fast breath.

He gasped. I had surprised *him*, finally. "What?"

"You know, in the kitchen you make yourself out to be a champion for humanity," I said, flailing my arms, raising my eyebrows, unable not to mock him. "Now you say that you only do it because, because you're *hungry*?" Now I was angry. "You're a martyr. Every good hero is! If it were easy, anyone could do it. But it's not anyone, it's you! You were chosen too, for a reason. You said yourself fate has a plan, and you're part of it. Well, you have needs, and guilt, and anger, a life beyond your purpose, Nicholas!" I suppressed tears. "Don't let the terrible side effects swallow your purpose. How can you doubt that you're a good man when you shoulder this, this *punishing* life, when you could just *not care*?"

He stared at me, unreadable. "Once, I could actually remember this man's memories. Never happened before or since, thank God. I remembered the good life he led, just ordinary, and humble. Good guy. He worked hard. I ended it all. He'll never hold the door for his wife again. And I know the look on her face when he'd do it, how it warmed his heart to see that. I wanted his favorite dinner—chicken and rice. So plain. I stole it all from him. From his entire family. What right do I have to consider myself a hero?" He looked so defeated. The goodness in him was a lighthouse beacon he couldn't see.

I went to him, and took his face in my hands. "Because you have to. This burden is your destiny." Those words rooted inside me, and my heart welcomed them. I was ready to burst, and understood not a thing of it.

Unshed tears in his eyes were a reflection of my own. He put his hands over mine on his stubbly cheeks. "Thank you." Such simple words, but a depth of gratitude for my understanding drenched them like syrup.

I smiled. "Don't mention it. Now, I am cold. And it's late. Let's go back to the house." It was my turn to pull him to his feet.

We walked back to the house hand in hand, in silence. The storm had abruptly conceded, and the protection Nicholas had created was no longer necessary. He was so clearly exhausted, I don't think he could have done it anyway.

He held the kitchen door open for me. I winced, his story still vivid in my mind. And the distinct sense that there was more happening, inside of me, wouldn't go away.

The house welcomed us with warmth I could've kissed after being so cold. My shoulders and spine clenched and I let out the frozen breath I'd been holding. That blanket from earlier was magically around me again. How did he keep *doing* that?

"Do you need a hot drink to bring back sensation?"

I did, but I was so spent, I couldn't even think about holding the cup. Nicholas could see it through his own emotional drainage.

"Never mind. A hot water bottle to bring to bed with you?"

"You mean like old people use?"

"Yes."

I smiled sleepily. "That sounds nice."

We waited for the water to boil, sitting quietly, the wood

stove's comforting crackles and hisses filling the silence. The whistle blew, and Nicholas pulled the bottle from the cabinet. I wondered, as I watched him, how I'd ever thought he was just a regular person. Once filled, he handed the water bottle to me, and I held it tight to my chest. I was still in his old green sweater. I was so ready to sleep.

"Follow me." *Anywhere.*

I trailed him out of the kitchen, back through the now-dark living room, the sloshing bottle at my side. He pointed to a hallway off the main room. "There's a spare room down that hall. It's ready for you. My room," he smirked, "is right at the end of the hallway, if you need anything. And, yes, I *sleep* there. I do get tired occasionally."

I hesitated to ask, but I needed to. "And Roman?"

"His room is down there, too, on the left."

"Not what I meant."

"I know. Yeah, he's also a vampire. You probably assumed. We stick together." Such a lot of information unearthed, and more to be found.

I nodded. "Okay, yeah, I could have figured that out on my own." We both laughed a little.

"You're beat. Me too. Have a good night's sleep, Eliza."

"You too. And thank you. For trusting me with this."

"Thank you for getting it."

"I think part of me was waiting to hear it. It doesn't make sense, but there it is. You know what I mean, don't you? Because I think you've been waiting a very long time to tell me."

In one last effort to make me faint, he quickly kissed my hand, his lips warm and buttery. My stomach twitched. I knew where that all too human warmth may have come from. "Some things are worth waiting for."

With that, he swaggered down the hall, and I watched as its darkness took him from me.

I stumbled to the spare room and had just shut the door when I heard the strangest words between Nicholas—who'd been apparently lurking like a creep in the hall—and Roman.

"You didn't tell her, did you?" Roman said as his door creaked open a little.

Nicholas sighed. "No. I did what I could today. I need rest." And two doors shut with soft clicks.

I was asleep before I hit the bed.

CHAPTER 12

M orning sunlight played on the bedspread and walls, waking me gently. I sat up, breathing in the scent of Nicholas still on the sweater I'd worn to bed—or collapsed in. Outside the window of the cozy little spare room the snow gleamed in hills as far as the eye could see. My heart pounded as I looked out across the backyard, and the night before rushed back into memory. I slept cloaked in the feeling of him all around me. And a faint, broken sequence of him speaking to his brother, right outside this very door, that didn't fit or make sense.

Just like my dreams, none of the horror or anger followed my memories; only him. The brilliance of him in the snow. The beautiful sanctuary he'd created. His closeness. His lips on my hand. And what he had endured.

I shook off the thoughts of his misery. It pained me too much, and it was too early.

I threw my legs over the bed, and curled my toes into the throw rug on the wood floor. Nothing like a solid stretch after such a pleasant sleep. I found a mirror on the back of the door, and tried to look decent. Well, as decent as possible. I looked down at the green sweater and black sweatpants Nicholas had dug up for me. After all, I'd worn this after the party. Then out in a snowstorm. Then to bed. I sighed, smoothed my hair, and popped in a breath mint out of my purse on the floor, the first time I touched the purse that Kat had been good enough to pack for me.

The house was so quiet that the click of the door opening seemed to explode down the hallway. Glancing at Nicholas's bedroom door, I padded out to the living room. It was bathed in sunlight, miniscule fairies of dust flitting through the rays.

Maybe they really were fairies. I believed in vampires now. Why not?

The thought made me smile wider. I realized I'd been smiling since I woke up. Even while I noted my dreadful appearance, I was happy, really happy. And yet, my entire world had been changed, and monsters were real. And monsters were in this house.

Nicholas must still be asleep. What time was it? I wandered into the kitchen, and jumped when I discovered Roman at the table reading the paper.

"Oh! I didn't think anyone was up," I said. Truthfully, I had sorta forgotten Roman was here, so wrapped in Nicholas as I was.

Folding his paper, he said, "I went to bed much earlier than you." He smiled a sincere, almost apologetic smile. I wondered how much he knew about last night.

I took out a carton of orange juice from the fridge, then reached for a glass in the cabinet. I was both completely comfortable treating the kitchen as my own, and slightly embarrassed. I couldn't look at Roman. I drank the juice standing at the counter, my back to him. Didn't make it easier, though.

"So you know about us then?"

I coughed a painful mouthful of orange juice. I turned and

faced him, willing my eyes to make contact and not look weak.

"Yes. Nicholas told me you're both vampires." Despite my unfaltering gaze, I blurted it out like I'd done something wrong.

Roman smiled at me warmly, making my discomfort funny. I smiled shyly in return, and looked at the black and white floor.

"I'm sorry. I guess I'm just nervous."

I think I was making him nervous, too. But when his eyes focused on mine again, they were filled with determination.

"Do you know *why* he told you?" Silently, without even a breeze, he was in front of me, watching the same patch of floor. This was my chance. To find out why Roman always seemed so agitated with Nicholas when I was around. Why I'd been picked to hear their story. To understand what was said in the hall between the two of them the night before, to hear what it had to do with me. But I couldn't open my mouth.

At that moment, Nicholas burst through the kitchen door in full strut, like he'd won an award, in a black hoodie and sweats.

"Morning, ladies!"

We both looked at him, me awed, Roman bored.

"Hi," I bleated. He stopped his stroll to the fridge to look at me with mock suspicion.

"What are you two doing?" He wiggled his eyebrows, and I shook my head at him in disbelief.

"Making out," Roman snapped.

"Cut it out. You're too self-depriving." Nicholas steered me to the table like a small child, and with a white flash put a plate of toast and jam in front of me that I was sure Roman had intended for himself. The whole time he bustled around the kitchen he worked at getting under Roman's skin with sense- less, silly comments. I smiled to myself. The aroma of fresh coffee filled the kitchen. I munched on my toast and watched two sparrows on the bird feeder, twittering in the sun and snow. Roman and Nicholas alternately laughed and needled each other over their breakfasts. I felt so warm, so at home. I didn't have to remind myself to let my shoulders drop—they weren't tensed up. I did have to remind myself that I was in the company of mythical killers.

And for the first time in a long, long time, I wasn't alone.

I snapped back as toast crust flew past me at Nicholas with a sinister laugh.

"Have you two been like this since you were kids?"

They glanced at each other, Nicholas with a wicked grin, Roman with a look of distaste. My eyes widened with sudden understanding.

"You aren't brothers," I said, squeezing my eyes shut at my stupidity.

"No." Roman was a man of few words.

"Why would you lie about something so silly?" I smiled despite myself as I asked. Nicholas answered simply and unbelievably.

"Well, otherwise, hot chicks would think we were gay."

My heart pumped happily to laugh that hard. "You care what hot chicks think?"

"Uh, yeah." *Sarcastic little...* "It doesn't matter that we're vampires. It doesn't stop in afterlife that straight men want hot chicks to know they're straight." He pointed a wagging finger at Roman. "Even you can't deny it, whether or not you allow yourself to do anything fun with any of them." Roman rolled his eyes in response.

Roman's brilliant smile made an appearance. "We may as well be brothers. I'm embarrassed to be seen with him."

"Awww, that's cute," Nicholas said with a pouty bottom lip that I wanted to bite. "We've known each other a very, very long time and sticking together just comes naturally to *Shinagami*. We're not gay, though."

I laughed again. "Well, thanks for considering me a hot chick," I joked, but jealousy at the thought of any other woman in his mind bubbled under the surface.

In light of the open conversation, I asked if all vampires could make the dome, the magical snowglobe that Nicholas created. Thoughts of it made my stomach flutter.

Roman answered quickly, "Oh, I don't know any *Shinagami* with enough control to do it like Nicholas can, but we can all do it." He sipped his coffee.

"I'm better at everything," Nicholas said. Arrogant thing.

Roman kicked him under the table. "I'm sure she already noticed there are few things you don't excel at." Looking at me more seriously, he went on. "But Nicholas can channel his energy better than any vampire I've ever known. They always fizzle out, even with extreme concentration, and some can't hold a shield at all. The Master says Nicholas has powers unlike any other *Shinigami*." Roman was proud of him. It was wonderful to see.

"Yeah, I'm kind of a rock star in Japan."

Roman and I both rolled our eyes.

We all laughed plenty at breakfast that day. It was incomprehensible that I was so at home with two vampires, and that they were so comfortable with me. The latter was stranger. Why would two vampires be okay with letting go of the information I'd been made privy to? I was thankful for the ease of our friendships—but I sure as hell didn't understand them.

"So, what's on the agenda today?" I piped up. I assumed it was okay for me to include myself in any and all of their plans. What was wrong with me? It didn't seem to faze either of them, though.

Roman answered first. "I need to spend some time with *Chris* today." I noticed a meaningful glance at the folded newspaper on the table. Nicholas actually looked a little ruffled by that. More questions reared in my mind. How deep did this well of secrets go? "Do you have any *intentions* today, Nicholas?" Roman asked coolly.

"I have every intention of doing what I intend to do today. Thank you for asking."

Roman flashed out of the room the way they do, with a quick, polite goodbye to me. Nicholas had invisibly moved into Roman's chair, and was watching me for some reaction.

"What you said, about what you intend to do…" I was given a cat-that-ate-the-canary face. "Well, what is it?"

I expected something snide and diverting. It didn't take long to learn that most of his answers should come with CliffsNotes, subtitles maybe. But, what I got was actually what I needed this time.

He moved his chair closer to me, the determined urgency in his voice taking me by surprise. "I intend on answering some of your questions today. I owe you that." His brow wrinkled, and he averted his eyes. "This—secrecy—it's just because I don't know how to tell such a sordid, completely ridiculous story. I have to build it from the ground up, from a place that doesn't exist for you." He stopped, clearly already overwhelmed by the enormity of his task.

So unreal to be convincing this man, a man who'd undertaken a path that defied goodness, who'd built a house in a month, that talking to me wouldn't be as difficult as he thought. But that was what I did.

I took his hand in both of mine. He flinched, and I tried not to ache over it. I told him, "You have eternity to tell your story. You don't owe me any answers." It tasted bitter in my mouth to say, I so desperately yearned to hear more. "But I promise to hang on your every word."

A momentary shyness crossed his perfect features,

endearing him to me even more. I hadn't known that was possible.

He was at the kitchen doorway now, asking me over his shoulder to join him. "I do have a last minute Christmas gift to pick up. Keep me company." A pounding in my chest threatened to make me throw up.

I sprang from my chair and caught up to him as quickly as I could. "I know my first question," I half-yelled to him. He was at the window in the living room, before I'd gotten close enough to run my hands down his back. My need to touch him had to be put on the backburner so that I could learn… well, anything about our situation. I joined him at the window.

I may have been in puppy love, I may have been charmed by some mystical vampire force, and I may have been living briefly in a fantasy world, but I knew one thing.

This was definitely *our* situation.

I was *involved* in his life now, both of their lives actually, and it was this way for a reason. Nicholas had decided to tell me he was a vampire, but why? What part could I possibly play?

He turned to face me. "Okay, shoot."

"How do you move like that? So fast? Here one second, there the next?"

"Really? Okay, an easy one. It's cool. We don't actually take the steps to go here to there all the time. Like, just now." He nodded toward the kitchen. "If we want to speed it up, all we have to do is picture ourselves there, and it happens."

Already I was amazed. "What, you teleport?"

"No, that's Star Trek, not vampires. You know how you only use one third of your brain's capacity? Well, vampires know how to use the rest. A lot becomes blindingly obvious in death." I couldn't tell if he was being condescending or not.

"That makes sense. Okay, but how is it that nobody sees it happen?"

He leaned in close, slowly, taking my breath away with the intimacy in his eyes, his conspiring smile with the reassuring scent to match.

"Because no one is looking."

I was stunned to silence. Impossible that an entire supernatural world existed right under our noses, and humanity just never noticed. "That's ridiculous."

"Is it?" A satisfied grin spread across his face. "People don't like change. The human race as a whole likes a solid world with clear borders. Not to mention that people rarely ever break attention from their own little bubbles. I could probably walk around naked all day and nobody would notice." He looked a little sad. "People so seldom stop to think about possibility, about anyone but themselves. It's very easy to go unnoticed in this world if you have the advantages we do."

The simplicity of this humbled me. I thought quickly of how I had no idea what half the people looked like that I talked to in a day. "What else can you do that we don't see?" I asked in a whisper.

With the cocky smirk that defines him, he suddenly appeared across the room next to the sofa, and lifted it in the air at head height from the bottom, the other hand running through his messy hair. After making his point, he set it lightly down and slapped his hands together to brush off the dust.

"Very impressive."

He plopped down onto the sofa. "Yeah, stuff like that." He patted the cushion next to him and I nearly tripped over my own feet to get to it. My arm brushed his as we both leaned them on the back of the sofa to face each other. Was that the sugary smell of the caramels I'd loved as a little girl?

His tongue slowly wet his lips as he crossed his ankle over his leg and settled into the sofa. Every part of me burned for him with that simple gesture. His eyes didn't falter from mine, and I was sure I was red as a chunky strawberry.

Clearing his throat, he ripped through the heavy silence. He began again, in a sultry, soft voice that had me leaning in, not to hear, but to get closer to its owner. I was mesmerized.

"The shield I created last night," brief flash of him standing in a gentle flurry as the storm destroyed the calm above and around us, "can be used in all sorts of situations. For protection, as if we need it." He paused. "We can use it when we take a victim," he said slowly, watching my eyes for a show of disgust. He didn't get one. "No one will see us, the elements won't touch us. Do you remember much of our party last night?"

"Yes, I'm not slow."

"Shut up. Lynch and I had a loud argument. Not our worst. But the shield prevented you and Kat from hearing and seeing."

I was lost.

"I know what happened," I said.

Now it was his turn to be lost. "What do you mean?"

"I saw it all, and heard it. I didn't entirely get it, but some of it…" He was clearly surprised, even as I began to piece it together. "Lynch is a vampire, too, then?" I asked wide-eyed.

"You heard? You saw me with my hands on his throat? All of it?"

"Yes, yes. Lynch, though. I'm not comfortable with him around. Not like you and Roman."

He searched my face with a hint of suspicion. "Well, yeah. You are definitely special," he said under his breath. "Intuitive —about stuff that matters." Now he smiled, pleased. "You aren't like everyone else. You *want* to see the world around you for what it is."

The quick array of compliments made me blush and drop

my chin to my chest. *I have to change these clothes.* He quietly waited for me to recover myself.

"What is it about Lynch, Nicholas? He's not like you."

Frustration creased his brow. "He's not. But who is? We'll get to that. For now, I need to get ready for the day." He eyed my mess of attire and disheveled hair. "As cute as you are, you could use a shower. You'll find everything you need in my bathroom."

I grimaced at the thought of redressing in that abysmal satin shirt and tight skirt, especially after eating as much as I had, and I certainly didn't want to put them on a freshly cleaned me. Then I realized in a heartbeat that I was to use his personal bathroom. I blushed like an idiot. "Thanks," I said. "That sounds good." The worn sofa creaked as I got up, but Nicholas had flashed to standing silently. "Quit showing off," I joked as I brushed past him towards the hall.

"That would defy my nature," I heard him say behind me.

CHAPTER 13

When I pulled back the shower door, I just stared at the linen chest near the sink. My purse, and a clear plastic bag of toiletries sat nicely upon it. Under that was a fresh pair of cargo pants, a blue long-sleeved tee, socks, and… a bra and panty set. My bra. And my panty. From home. All of this stuff was from my apartment.

Then, the cell phone in my purse blared "Shout" by Tears for Fears, and shout is exactly what I did as I nearly fell out of the tub to get to it.

"Oh my God, Ellie, tell me all about it!" I listened to Kat presume why Nicholas hadn't brought me home the night before. I half-ignored her as I dangled the pink 36D in front of me, imagining it in his hands, the lacy panty nobody would have pegged me for wearing staring at me from atop the pile of clothes.

"No, Kat, nothing like that," I managed to answer. "We just talked. I slept in the spare room." I walked around the bathroom in my borrowed towel as I diffused Kat's imagination into disappointment. Basics. Toothbrush. Toothpaste. No cologne. Of course not.

"Oh, Ellie, when are you going to make something happen with him? Has he even kissed you?"

Not really. And yet, it felt like—I was *his*. It felt like we were together, at least for me. Was it only me? I didn't think so, but I couldn't be sure how clearly I was thinking.

"Kat, I'll talk to you later, okay? I need to get dressed, and find Nicholas. I'll be home for dinner."

"Dinner? But, it's only nine in the morning. What are you doing today? You're not working."

"I'm not sure, but I know I need to spend it with him. I hope you didn't—"

"No, no, I've monopolized your time for far too long. Go, have fun. And have a story when you get back or else."

I grinned, dropping the towel. "It's too early to use words like 'monopolized.' I can assure you I'll have a story." Possibly not the one she was expecting, but hey.

I think I blushed the entire time I was getting dressed, knowing Nicholas had been looking through my things. It dawned on me that I probably should be angry. I knew he only did it to make me comfortable, and maybe a little to show off that he could somehow get in and out of my apartment without disturbing Kat.

My breath caught. Just how many vampires could do that? I shriveled, thinking of Lynch near Kat without her knowing it. I also realized that I never bothered to ask Kat exactly what the two of them had done last night after leaving our company.

I was beginning to think that my aversion to Lynch was probably the normal reaction to a vampire, and how easy I was about Nicholas and even Roman, was not. Lynch's personality definitely didn't disturb Kat, or a lot of other women apparently. Of course, Kat always was too trusting and romantic, making falling for a suave, mysterious rich guy pretty predictable.

I finished dressing, and putting on my mascara/lip gloss makeup non-routine, and left the steamy bathroom to find Nicholas.

I opened the wrong door.

I smelled mint and a touch of lime, and fresh cut grass. The need to inhale its purity stopped me in my tracks. It was as though spring had come alive in here, defeating the months of cold, gray skies. My eyes shut, my back straightened, my head tilted back in an effort to take as much of it in as I could. A fluid, tangible peace flooded my being.

When I opened my eyes, the tranquility of the room overtook me.

I was in his bedroom, facing glass doors to a small patio, surrounded by the snowy treetops of his land. The rest of the walls were covered in rice paper framed with bamboo, like in a Japanese tea room, I thought. The room was very tidy, with little furniture or visible belongings, but it still rang of him to me. A flush of heat rushed to my face as I looked at his bed, very low to the ground, with a short headboard of light wood. Soft, mossy green blankets and pillows beckoned to me. White vases of bamboo sat on a shelf, reaching for the ceiling.

And there he was. Cross-legged on a straw mat by the glass door, his bare back to me, ferociously muscular and lean, glistening with beads of sweat. His body was perfection, strong, but comfortably so, like a warrior, with inherent, jungle-cat sensuality.

I couldn't breathe until I realized that I shouldn't be in there, and foolishly tried to turn and sneak out the way I'd come in. I stifled a scream as he flashed in front of me, blocking my way. His magnificent arms stretched over his head, fingers curled around the top of the doorframe. My eyes were directly level with the curves of his chest. I tried to avert them, but they fell on the carved stomach that flexed with each breath. I whimpered, defeated.

"Going somewhere?"

Obviously frazzled, I said, "Uh, the wrong way? I don't know, I just finished showering, and I didn't mean to disturb your workout or whatever, I mean clearly you were working out—" I gestured stupidly at the gleaming musculature that loomed over me. I cleared my throat. "You weren't expecting me."

The bastard knew how he looked. That sexy, confident grin and smoldering eyes that knew no embarrassment.

"Are you sure I wasn't? It looks like you were the one taken by surprise." He bit his lip, and my knees knocked together.

He breezed by me with deliberate slowness, smelling sweetly of iced tea despite the perspiration. He sat on the bed, his knees nearly shoulder level, it was so close to the floor. "Come sit," he said. It sounded so loud to my ears that he'd just told me to sit on his bed with him, like a gong had been banged in my head, reverberating. And he had no shirt on.

Nervously, I brushed a wet hair from my cheek and mumbled, "It's so low. Your bed."

He gave me a mocking smile, amused by my discomfort. "It's a Japanese design. I've spent much time there."

Some of my nerves turned to curiosity. "You must have traveled a lot in your…life."

"I've seen too much of the world; I prefer the comforts of home. No matter how old I get, foreign lands are always foreign." He looked around the room, then back to me, as I still stood in the doorway. "Japan was home to me for a long time."

Japanese culture was so notoriously different from our own, with our constant need of things and noise and our gluttony of life.

But Nicholas isn't like that, I thought warmly.

"So that's where vampires grow up?" I asked, edging toward the bed.

He leaned back on his elbows, his stomach muscles tensing, the beautiful length of his body stretched out within arms' reach. "I was made *Shinigami* when I was thirty-four. I taught literature—a rewarding job, but I still had no direction. I had something better than that and I knew it. And I knew I was nowhere near discovering what it was." He was thoughtful for a moment, and I was entranced. I'd gravitated to the empty spot beside him on the bed. He scanned my body, and continued. "I'd known since I was a teenager, actually. A viciously rebellious teenager, of course, who answered to no one." He smiled, egotistical pride flourishing. "I guess, looking back, that becoming an authority figure after hating them all probably played a part in my—hopelessness—as an adult. Because that's what I was. Hopeless. Exhausted by shallow relationships, by trying to be something I couldn't be, by trying too hard in general. I had grown empty."

I'd swallowed a lead weight. I briefly wondered if he had ever told this story, so fresh it still seemed, so heavy in the air.

"When my time came, I never looked back. *Unmei shinsu;* it means 'chosen for new life.' Leaving that horrifically average life was all I'd ever wanted since I started living it," he grimaced.

"Being ordinary to you, it's a fate worse than death?" I smiled a little, but he was completely serious when he furrowed his brows and gave a single, assured nod.

"The Master brought me to Japan. You'll hear more of him, but this isn't his story, it's mine. He was volatile, cruel to me at first, but I was such a willing student, that we warmed to one another quickly. I just wanted to learn. I wanted to change, and I had talent that was amplified by my need to be something new. All that stood in my way was my own self-defeat. As much as I wanted to grow into what I was sure was my place in the world, I couldn't believe I'd succeed. Superiority complex or not, it was hard to believe I was good enough to fill such an epic role in life. My talent and unparalleled intelligence couldn't supersede that rawness.

"I discouraged the hell out of the Master. He told me that he'd never had such an absurd challenge, a self-defeating overachiever. He believed in me so thoroughly, the way no one else ever had…" He trailed off dreamily. "I'd never had that before." We shared a soft silence. I was choked up at this side he had revealed to me.

"That sounded a little pathetic," he said. That was the Nicholas I knew and loved. "I was loved in life, my family and friends were wonderful to me. But it was different when this near-stranger saw a glimmer of something great in me, it renewed me. To have something new and great to achieve, and live for. When someone does that for you… I would do anything not to disappoint him."

The excitement in his eyes was inspiring, even if I didn't entirely understand it. He was so passionate about this transformation going to the Master had brought on. I couldn't imagine having someone that showed up out of the blue to believe in me so strongly.

"He sounds very important to you," I said.

"I owe him my life. It's because of him that I want it at all."

He'd sat up, twisting to face me, that excitement still transforming, heating him.

"I see the same greatness in you, Eliza. I see myself in you. The averageness of your life, Eliza, it isn't you! It isn't what you were meant for."

I was shocked, and hurt some. Again, with the telling me how dull I am, and when he was so exciting to me. It hit hard.

I leapt to my feet in a rush of anger. The serenity of this room and his calming presence couldn't settle me. The compliment he paid me was so overshadowed by the insult.

"You spend a lot of time telling me how boring I am. Why bother if I bore you so much?"

He looked unsurprised by my outburst. "You don't bore me. This shadow of a life you lead does."

His sincerity took the edge off, although I was sure I should still be insulted. I let out a breath and sat back down. "Your formerly touching story of self-awareness seems a little self-righteous now."

Chills shot down my spine as he ran his hand down my arm. "It's not untrue. I meant it all then, and I still mean it now. You and I, we're alike. You can't tell me you don't want more."

"What are you saying?" I whispered.

In that way he moves, he was inches from my face, his sweet breath mingling with my own, his scent sending me back to the bakery I visited on Sundays with my dad. His eyes fixed on mine, silencing me.

"It really doesn't speak to you inside this heart?" His hot palm rested on my chest, my heart jumping to reach it. My soul felt full to bursting with all that he was implying, my head swam with an elevated mix of every emotion I could ever remember having. The haze of Nicholas overtook my senses again. Was I really here, on this incredible man's bed, was he saying that he knew what I was trying to tell him, that my heart was right? Was I right about him, or right about me? That I was *wrong* somehow? A pair of crows flapped to the ground at the glass door, staring inside, waking me from my thoughts.

The richness of his eyes centered me, the shade of fresh soil that I loved to sink my toes into, lulling my confusion. They bore into my own, yearning for my understanding, my companionship, as real as my short breaths. Like strong arms, his ever-changing aroma wrapped around me, spring rain and grapefruit. I was defenseless, my lips tingling as I anticipated meeting his.

I flinched.

An inappropriate time for my memory to dredge up the other things he inspired in me.

You don't belong here.

"You told me that I don't belong here. In one breath you tell me we're alike, and you make me feel like I finally belong, but that wasn't your first reaction. You rejected me, you chased me away, I *repelled* you. Ready to answer questions? Answer me this, Nicholas. What would make you say I don't belong here?"

"I didn't say it, I thought it. And I was right. Still am. You don't belong walking around with regular people, you're not a regular person." He twisted a curl of my hair between his fingers. "You stand out like a peacock among parakeets."

Scarcely could I choke out the words I so desperately needed to. "And what do you know about how I feel? Do you feel it, too?"

"I told you that I do. I know you feel misplaced."

"That's not what I meant," I said quietly, eyes downcast. "Do you care at all about me? Really?"

He rolled his eyes, much to my dismay. "Why do we have to analyze our need to be together? It's one of those human things I didn't even get when I *was* human. Isn't it enough that we're with one another now?"

"I want more."

A knowing smile lit up his face. "That's what I mean. Your want for more—I'm overcome by it, and I'm not overcome by much of anything. Even if you don't see it." My jaw went tense, because I knew this conversation already, in all its many forms. It began with telling me that I'm better than the life I lead, followed by a series of compliments that I didn't understand, and me being confused and a little bit pissed.

I imagined myself saying if he so believed my existence was pathetic, make it better for me. If he really thought I was special, show me with all your tricks and crazy abilities and "unparalleled intelligence."

"I'd better go," I said instead, and rose to my feet. I needed time to think, and sort myself out before my heart got ahead of me. Not to mention, my grudge-holding side wanted to leave him there, wondering what he'd done wrong.

He blocked my way to the door. "Please don't go." Not pleading, a statement. A certainty that I'd oblige.

I sighed, melting at his inexplicable desire to keep me with him, but I grimaced at his self-assured power over me.

I laid my hand on the side of his cheek. His eyes closed, giving me a second to relish the stubble on his warm skin under my fingertips.

"Nicholas, whatever it is you're trying to say to me, you're not ready to say it. I'd like to tell you I understand, but I don't. I don't know if I'm reading you right, or if I'm blowing it out of proportion. And I don't know why it's so hard for you to make it clear to me."

"Eliza..."

I moved my finger to his soft, inviting lips. "It's okay. But I need to sort out how it is that you have this *attachment* to me, and yet you can't open up to me about this important thing between us. It's real." Saying it made my throat tighten. "I know what I want it to mean, but I know there's more you need to tell me, and I won't wound myself waiting."

He looked impossibly sad, grief-stricken. I'd done this. The constriction in my throat forced tears to my eyes.

"Please, Nicholas. I'm not saying goodbye, not like you think. I couldn't." I swallowed hard. "I can't."

"I know," he whispered.

～

Nicholas persuaded Roman to get my car early before I even knew it, claiming he'd do it himself but didn't want to. I'd gathered the few things I had with me, most of which Nicholas's scent still clung to—tea with lemon this time. A familiar smell that usually meant I was comforted, safe, but stressed out. His aroma was never the same, and always exactly what I needed; warm and cozy when I felt alone, fresh and natural when I needed peace. It was the perfect remedy to whatever I was missing, preying upon my vulnerability to give me the illusion that everything was as it should be.

And it meant he was there. The same illusion came with him. My world was whole when he was near me, and yet the needling idea that it was all some magic trick was too strong to ignore.

As I entered the living room, I could hear Nicholas and Roman arguing in the kitchen.

"—dragging it out. She needs to know."

"I've just told her I'm a vampire, Roman. Give her time to absorb—"

"More time with you will only make her want you more! You know all this! *I* know because of *you*! It's not a secret to you why you're kindred spirits, but she can only know it as one thing—love."

"She is *not* in love with me."

"I disagree."

Quiet for a moment, except for my pounding heart and the blood rushing to my ears.

"She may be able to hear us," Nicholas said in a guarded voice.

With more control in his, Roman replied, "Nicholas, I know you don't mean harm, but you may be causing it. You know what the *Shinigami* allure does, why we have it." Roman paused, and my heart stopped, thinking they'd caught on I was listening until he spoke again, more comfortingly. "It's natural for you to want her. I know you need her with you, what it does to be apart from her right now, I've been there. But if you tell her why, neither of you will be confused anymore."

"We don't know that she's my—"

"I do, Nicholas. I've had one of my own."

"I know what I need to do." The steely snideness returned to Nicholas's formerly weakened voice. "You're not the authority on the matter. We all see how Lynch turned out."

A numbing cold came over me, and I realized with a shock that a frost was crawling across the floor, rooting from under the kitchen door, along with a throaty growl.

I bolted into the kitchen.

"NO!" I screamed, and they both whipped their heads toward me, animals caught stalking prey. Roman's body shook with volcanic anger that I couldn't believe he was capable of. The frost touched everything I saw. "No," I said again.

Roman seemed to emerge from a trance, as though unaware of what had come over him. Nicholas loosened up slightly, and magically the room lost some of its frigidity.

We all stood immersed in the silence. What to say first?

Nicholas shrugged, eyebrow cocked. "I knew you were out there the whole time, don't get cocky about it." Roman's eyes rolled and the tension eased, but didn't disappear.

"I'm going to Chris now," Roman said, head hung, grazing me as he left the room. Goosebumps covered every inch of my skin with his touch.

Nicholas slumped against the counter, looking defeated and tired despite his wit. I went to him, needing to reassure him as much as he needed to be reassured.

"I shouldn't have said anything about Lynch to him," he mumbled as I rubbed his shoulder. Frost wet my fingers.

"You didn't mean to hurt him."

"It doesn't matter if I meant to. It was wrong." His voice became heavy with emotion. "I was a jerk to say it. He's so strong to take on this burden, it isn't his fault that Lynch is what he is," he rambled. "But that guilt will haunt him forever, and I've made it worse. Me, of all people." He never lifted his eyes from the floor, lost in regret.

"I have no idea what you mean," I said as gently as I could. "What were you two talking about?"

He met my eyes finally, and with that, warmth seemed to fully return to the room. But the cast on his face was anything but warm.

"You shouldn't have been listening. You shouldn't have been *able* to. Don't try to use this to your advantage."

My hand dragged down his arm as it fell, recognizing the ripples there, even as my anger grew.

"I was only trying to help. A 'thank you for not letting my friend attack me' might even be in order."

"It's partly because of you—!" He stopped himself. He didn't want to say anything else hurtful.

"I'm taking my big mouth and going home. But I'll be waiting for you to see more clearly."

As I forced myself to leave, I caught a glimpse of the headline on the paper Roman had left on the kitchen table.

Body of Missing Woman Found in Pines Pond

CHAPTER 14

With the subtle click of his front door, a savage cold took me. Colder than his kitchen when he'd changed, colder than the blustering storm we spent our evening in. It was a bitterness that began in my soul and froze the world around me more with every inch between us.

It didn't feel like an ending, and it wasn't what I'd heard that caused this coldness bordering on torture. It reminded me of that phrase "phantom pain." It was a burning like I'd left behind so much of myself that the rest couldn't function on its own.

It took all my energy to plod my left foot onto the clear walkway. The understanding that he'd moved the massive tree branches and rubble from the storm with that inconceivable power and speed consumed my second step.

My stomach lurched with each agonizing movement toward my car, further from him. Part of my pain was guilt—I knew Nicholas was hurting, too. My guilt stemmed from both causing it, and relief that he felt our connection as much as I did.

Bile rose to my throat as I pulled down the driveway, also

free of debris. He'd cleared this, too. He'd even heated up my car for me, though we'd argued. Of course, I'd never seen him do it. Pins and needles flitted across my chest and back.

The road stretched ahead, and a venomous sting in my soul nearly caused me to double over. The absurdity of such dramatic reaction, when I was just going home, was not lost on me. I'd never wanted to be attached to someone less.

Nicholas had told me what *Shinigami* do to lure—to trap— their victims. Their scent was always just the right mix. Their intuitiveness that makes the victim trust them, as if they'd always been friends. Their *allure*.

Was all this pain just part of the trap? That I needed to be with him, just to breathe?

But, I wasn't his victim.

What was I to him? Why had Roman said it was natural for him to want me?

The increasing pain propelled me home. Driving took the focus off of its intensity, and I didn't want to get out of the car. Kat was home, which made this infinitely more difficult. She was expecting a play by play, and I could tell her nothing. She wasn't expecting me home either; she'd know something had gone wrong.

The dull throb in the back of my head got thicker when I entered our apartment. I went in quietly and straight to my room, where I lay in the dark, trying not to hear anything, to just sleep. The throbbing lulled at times, but if I moved, it grew. And if I pictured him, it grew more still. I stayed like that for a couple of hours, sneaking once to the bathroom for painkillers. They helped not at all. It wasn't a pain that any amount of aspirin could cure.

Kat had been back and forth by my room doing laundry. The hum of the machine was like a chainsaw to me. I must have groaned too loudly at one pass because she nudged the door open to see me face-down on the bed through the darkness.

"You're home?" she asked in surprise. I groaned in response. She continued with a strain of questions: *are you okay, what happened, did he hurt you.* How could I keep this brief? I rolled over to look at her.

"I'm like, pukey, and I had a fight with Nicholas. I guess I could use some more sleep."

Just speaking made tears spring to my eyes. An assault of images—Nicholas standing in the snow, his eyes staring deeply into mine, so many times his finger lifting my chin, the word "vampire" from his lips. Hysterical rambling escaped me, pieces of which even I couldn't understand. Kat's hands were on my shoulders, but it did nothing to help me. My head lolled around the pillow, my stomach rolled.

Kat somehow weeded through my frenzy and interpreted this all so simply. As she spoke, I wrung the aches from my hands. She squeezed my shoulders, softly reassuring me. "Ugh. Men suck. He's gotten you wrapped around his finger, he's leading you on."

I tried to get a hold of myself, aware that I'd nearly told her Nicholas's and Roman's secret.

And Lynch's.

My problem became more multi-faceted. I regained control, telling myself that this was about more than me, and my discomfort. Kat was involved, and she didn't have a clue. I had her to think of, as well as Roman and Nicholas. They'd welcomed me into their world, and given me a home I hadn't had in a long time, and told me something that maybe no other human knew. And no matter my confusion, my heart was sheltered with Nicholas in a way that it never had been before.

No matter how or why, we were meant to be together.

Nicholas knew it, too. This burning pain that engulfed my very being was the same for him, I sensed it.

I needed to return to him *now*.

"Kat, I'm all right," I said, wiping my eyes, and sitting up with effort.

"Yeah, you seem just fine," she said.

"I know what I need to do," I resolved. "I'm going to give him an ultimatum."

CHAPTER 15

A sense of calm came over me as I readied myself to go back to Nicholas's house. With the slow precision of a man walking to his execution, I washed the distress from my face, and reapplied lotion and mascara. I pulled my uncontrollable away hair back into a ponytail at the nape of my neck. I raised a bottle of vanilla perfume to my throat, and just as slowly lowered it, recalling that Nicholas's perfect fragrance would circle me like the arms of a romance novel hero. Or a shark in a feeding frenzy. I sniffed at the thought.

Bitterness at my own feelings, at Nicholas's cruelty, at this world I'd walked so willingly into, flooded me. My own pain angered me. People didn't feel physical pain at separation from one another.

This was part of his thrall, or whatever you want to call it. I *was* his victim. And I'd signed on for it.

I piled myself into my car in the late afternoon. The sun was still strong. I curled my lip at that, too. Was today a day that Nicholas could go outside?

I began driving to the place I had come to see as my second

home. I'd rooted in there so fast, I had to assume that was part of the bait, too.

My pain diminished more and more as I got closer to Nicholas. I was able to think again, going over the events of the morning in particular. Rationalizing my growing attachment to Nicholas with the bitterness over my lack of control was exhausting. The regret of our argument in the back of my mind, I was now trying to fit in the new fragments about Lynch's role in their lives. He was disliked at best by Nicholas, and resented by Roman. Roman appeared to have an obligation to him. I recalled the knowing look that Nicholas and Roman had exchanged at the headline in the paper. Roman had changed his plans to go to Lynch's house. *"We all see how Lynch turned out,"* Nicholas had said. Why did Roman take such offense to that?

I knew one thing. I never trusted Chris Lynch, and I didn't want him anywhere near Kat.

I shook my head painfully to clear it, anxiety welling in me. A flurry of light snow had begun to fall, adding to the vast expanse of crystal white that framed the road. Cracking the window, I attempted to enjoy the sparkling scenery in effort to erase some of my tension. The cold, pure scent instantly brought me back to the nighttime walk with Nicholas. It seemed like months ago—the tranquility of the forces of nature that surrounded his home, and Nicholas in the center of it, taking me with him, slipping unseen into its welcoming heart. In the fury of that storm, its purity and perfection, was the most peace I could ever remember experiencing. With him at my side, it all felt elemental. Like the storm was inside me.

Tears for Fears yelled at me from the passenger seat. I grabbed the phone.

Nicholas.

I swallowed hard and answered.

"Eliza," the sad, husky voice moaned.

Starting at the top of my head and pouring over my body inch by slow inch, warmth replaced the pain, until my very fingertips tingled with pleasure.

"Nicholas," I breathed out.

"Eliza, I need you to come back." He tried to mask it, but I could feel as much as hear the pain in his voice.

"I'm almost there already."

He let out a long sigh, his relief flooding over into me.

"Oh, Eliza. I could never do enough to deserve you."

"You don't have to do anything, Nicholas," I replied, irony making my words as cold as the snow. "There's no other choice for us. I'll see you soon."

I hung up the phone.

CHAPTER 16

An eternity of minutes later, I pulled up to the vampire house. Nicholas stood statue-still at the front door, then with a *crack* that sounded like lightning, he appeared at my car door to open it. His porcelain face was devoid of emotion, the devilish glint in his eye dormant.

Our eyes never left one another's as I got out and stood to face him. I couldn't begin to vocalize my thoughts in that silent moment. I'm not sure I *could* think, but I knew that we'd crossed a boundary here.

We needed each other. And now we'd both admitted it.

"Come inside." His sultry voice was mournful. He took my hand, and in a blink we were in the house, the door clicking behind us

In the same motion, his arms enveloped me so totally, I could do nothing but breathe in his essence. If you've never smelled sunlight, it's like daffodils, honey and Heaven. A single sob broke loose in his hold. I barely noticed the cat winding his way between my ankles in greeting.

I'd expected the wrenching pain to disappear when I was

in Nicholas's presence, but the effect was more than that; rejuvenation, dipped in the fountain of youth. Curious, I forced myself to pull out of his impossibly perfect embrace. The creases in his face had been erased, the tightness in his mouth relaxed. The vanilla and caramel in his forest-deep eyes danced and played again.

"You hurt the way I did," I said.

He swallowed. "I have never experienced pain like that in my countless years."

No amount of physical pain could equal the glimmer of hurt in his eyes, and the agony of knowing that I'd had a part in it.

And yet, I pursued. Because I'd come here for more than one reason. I needed answers as much as I needed him.

So quietly that he wouldn't have heard me if he weren't a vampire, I asked him one question, with more determination than I felt. "Did you know that you'd feel the pain too, when you did this to me, Nicholas?"

He recoiled from me as though I'd bitten him with my words. A hiss rumbled deep in his throat, and I became very cold.

In a booming voice he bellowed, "You think *I* did this?! You think that I would hurt you on purpose?!" Determined not to be terrified, I raised my chin, staring him down, but all I felt was guilt. Giving up, I plopped into one of the worn armchairs by the fireplace, and was glad it was when I lost my strength. Nicholas stood, shaking, forever-moving eyes wide with fury.

I kept my plan on course, but already this was harder than I thought it would be. "Then how did it happen? You know the answer. You know why our connection is stronger and stronger every minute. You know and you won't tell me!" Now *my* anger had taken center stage. My fingernails dug into the arms of the chair.

I watched the man I loved go through his own flurry of

emotion. I didn't want him to be confused. I didn't want him to be afraid of his own heart.

I didn't want him to hurt like I did.

"Nicholas, we hurt each other. Now, I can't deny that I have a…need… for you. And I know you have a need for me. I need real answers. Now. If you don't give them to me, I *will* walk out that door. And I *will* find a way not to come back." It took all my vitality to say these things and truly mean it, to prepare myself to follow through. To endure agony from Hell indefinitely and erase Nicholas from my past, present, and future.

No amount of preparation could have ever made me ready for the hearty laugh that was his horribly inappropriate and ill-timed reaction.

"What?" I spat through gritted teeth.

All of his fury had vanished. The mournfulness returned to his downcast eyes, the black lashes so thick that I could see them across the room. I tried not to let it skew my will.

"Never did I think *this* would be how I'd finally get snuffed."

Frowning and shaking my head, I blurted out, "What in Hell are you talking about?"

He raised an eyebrow, chin raised, sizing me up. "Your threshold for pain must far exceed mine."

"The pain was excruciating. But not knowing your intentions, your purpose for pulling me in, is debilitating."

"You've gone through the motions for your entire life without knowing your purpose!" he snorted at me. "Why should this be any different?"

My upper lip curled back in a snarl. "You. Can't. Say things like that to me anymore. I know you mean them. I don't care if you smile afterwards, it's cruel." I stood up. "And I've dealt with enough cruelty at your hands."

"I figured it out," he said joyously as I made my way across the room, blurry with tears. I stopped, but couldn't look at him. Not yet. This may not be enough.

"Enlighten me."

"I figured out why there was pain this time, not the other times we were apart." He paused, to gather strength I guessed. "Because I didn't know if you were coming back. I didn't *know* if you really would return to me, even though you said you would. And you, you weren't sure this would still be your home. Were you?"

Correct. I knew it. This feeling of home, and of something else unique, special. I only knew it at Birch Tree Books. Welcomed, *owned.* Like the sensation of lurking death that was the only thing I knew all the way to my core, could be put to rest here. I feared losing that hopefulness as much as I feared losing Nicholas.

"Then you know how difficult it is for me to give you this ultimatum. You see what I stand to lose."

"Yes. I know your threat—"

"—ultimatum—"

"—is a sacrificial one. You think the only thing you can take from me is yourself. I think you may be right." Then he was at my side, pleading. "All I can ask is that you please trust me, that I'm trying to do right by you, Eliza."

I gasped for air, unsure how long it had been since I breathed. "You have a choice. You can tell me the whole goddamn story, Nicholas. Let me be in control for once."

"This isn't about control, Eliza."

"Said the man in control."

Nicholas sighed. He gave in, to a degree. Now he was the one to sink into the closest armchair. I looked down at him, slightly uncomfortable with his vulnerability.

"Please, then. Please let me do this in my time, as a favor to me. Because I need it, Eliza. Time is all I have on my side, the only tool I can use so I don't feel completely at the mercy of what I am." He looked up with those soap opera eyes. "Please don't leave me. Not now. Please don't ever leave me."

I sat in the other armchair.

CHAPTER 17

In the end, it didn't matter that I was curious or proud. That's really all it was that caused me to nearly give it all up.

What mattered in the end was that Nicholas and I belonged together. The force that gave us the horrible pain I remembered too clearly was telling me so, even if Nicholas wouldn't. In the end, it didn't matter that he hadn't told me everything yet. It mattered that he was trying to do things the right way, as he saw it. How could I not support that?

It was this that mattered. He and I, in front of the crackling fire in those same armchairs, drinking tea from well-worn cups, the stray purring the loudest sound in the room. This was the only place aside from Birch Tree that didn't want to throw me out.

Relieved to the point of tears just to be together, and not hurting, we talked about anything besides my draw to him. He told me how he and Roman met, and more about the creature they called the Master. We had a heated debate on what was scarier, David Lynch or George Romero. (Nicholas, a die-hard *Nightmare on Elm Street* fan, was unable to make an informed decision.) We sat like that for hours. It was shocking to me how I'd spent more time sitting in front of a fire than I ever had in the short time I'd known Nicholas, and how it had been the most transformative and tiring time of my life.

Darkness descended again. The Christmas tree cast multicolored prisms on the floor. Another day, come and gone. This one nearly had ended with the greatest loss since my parents died. Exhausted by the emotional rending from my long weekend, I groaned to think of dealing with Christmas shoppers the following morning. Nicholas took the opportunity quickly.

"Stay tonight. It's late. And the chance of reliving that..." He shook with a chill at the thought of our mutual pain. "Well, just stay. Don't go away tonight. I took the liberty of—"

"Let me guess," I jeered. "Robbing my apartment of pajamas and fresh underwear."

"No, not this time," he said, not worried at all by my embarrassment. "This time I went out and picked up a few things to keep here, just in case. Like pajamas and underwear." He grinned and wiggled his eyebrows.

Joking with him about such intimate things made me glow. He was easy to trust, whether it be the vampire in him, or just him. It was fruitless to separate them anymore.

"I don't know, Nicholas. There's just something about sleeping in your own bed, especially before work, you know?"

"So, I'll bring your bed here," he said with a shrug.

I laughed, sipping my tea, and realized he was just looking at me, blinking.

"Oh my God, you're serious. You want to dash to my place tonight and—"

"—carry your bed here. Like a more gas-efficient U-Haul. And better looking. Smarter." He cocked his head to one side in thoughtfulness.

I played along. "And you bring it back tomorrow? What if someone sees you?"

"Vampire shield."

"You have an answer for everything."

"Not according to your ultimatum. I have one more answer. How about I don't bring it back?"

"Bring what back?"

"The bed."

"If my bed was here, where would I sleep at home?" My breath caught as I figured out how dumb I was. "You want me to move in?" What was happening?!

"Why not? You like it here. We're happier together. I don't like torturous pain. Why make things hard on ourselves? Unless you have an attachment to that dismal apartment?" He crossed and uncrossed his legs.

Waking up to Nicholas. Going to sleep to Nicholas's voice. (Certain) mealtimes with Nicholas. It sounded like a dream. In theory. But I knew it wouldn't be the way I had dreamed it. I could make some compromises to foster this odd relationship, but I couldn't give in this time. Moving in here would do nothing but confuse me more, and give me false hope that we had a relationship more than just vampire and...essential friend, I guess.

"Not now, Nicholas. I'm not ready to change my entire life over to the unknown just yet." He smiled, rather than look disappointed, but it didn't bother me. There was a satisfaction behind that smile, like he'd confirmed something. "You're not upset?" I asked him.

"I was serious. I'd love to have you here, but I agree. I don't think you're ready yet."

~

Nicholas and I were up late. He didn't remember what it was like to be tired from a hard day because he got tired so rarely, but before long I'd nodded off mid-sentence in that wonderful armchair, the fire warming my face. I briefly woke to Nicholas sliding me into the guest bed, making this an extended stay. I remembered my shoes hitting the floor, and I finished getting undressed myself. He'd taken a luxurious pair of blue silk pajamas out of the dresser and left the room quietly.

I awoke Tuesday morning to a symphony of birds outside. I should have jumped from bed, as I still thought I had enough time to get to On A Clear Day; instead I lay for a minute, stretching and breathing in long, slow breaths, utterly relaxed. The day before, I awoke with a smile. My new silk pajamas, which I'd never have bought for myself, slipped under the covers with ease as I pulled them up to my chin again.

When I gathered up the will to move in the sunlight-warmed bed, I rolled over and picked up my phone on the nightstand, and dialed the number before I lost my nerve.

"Hey, Viv, it's Ellie." I hated calling myself Ellie, but I don't know if she actually knew my real name. "I'm really sorry but I'm sick, puking today, and need to take the day off. I'll see you in the morning." Thank God for voicemail. I smiled again, and before I knew it, my face was in the pillow so I could conceal my laughter. Blowing off work following a personal day was some kind of record. I'd broken free! How friggin' ridiculous.

I threw my feet over the edge of the bed finally, where they were greeted by my own fuzzy slippers. A vision of Nicholas carrying my dirty slippers with lightning speed made me laugh again.

It was early, so I figured I'd get a jump on the day. I checked my phone first, having forgotten that I turned the ringer off so my ultimatum speech to Nicholas wouldn't be interrupted. Kat had texted me of course, the night before: *"On my way to Chris's for dinner, maybe more..."*

With a grimace I tossed the phone onto the bed and took a hot shower. It helped to take my mind off of Kat, and hoping she was home safe in bed, away from Lynch.

It still wasn't' even seven in the morning when I finished dressing, but I couldn't wait to get in touch with her anymore. I texted her: *"Just checking in. Hope dinner went well. Home now?* My brain screamed when I didn't get an immediate answer.

Like the day before, quiet was all around me in the living room. No one was in the kitchen either. Coffee was made, so someone was awake. Someone was always awake in this house. I proceeded to start on breakfast while I waited for one of them to turn up. As I stood over my eggs on the stove, I caught a glimpse of movement out the window.

My body breathed a sigh as I watched Nicholas perform a series of exotic, fluid movements diligently in the snow. Powerful punches, effortless kicks, leaps and mimed blocks. He was extraordinary, oblivious to the ice and snow, with veil of perspiration shimmering on his torso. His concentration was magnificent. I'd never tried to do something with such heart in all my life.

I stood at the window with my coffee, in quiet contemplation of Nicholas's talent. I was sure that even without the added vampiric strength and agility, he would still have been magical to watch. I imagined him practicing like that in life, as a human.

I wondered if I could do it, too.

I finished my eggs, still standing, and was relishing my next cup of coffee in my short time alone. Yesterday's newspaper was still folded on the table. I flipped it open, and made an ugly sound at the quarter-page high school photo. The sweet-looking girl with curly blonde hair smiled back brilliantly at me. Fresh-faced, plump, and joyful to see.

She looked different than when I'd seen her in the park.

I read the story with roving eyes.

Nearly 2 weeks after 24 year old Christine Simmons was reported missing, the young woman's body was discovered at the bottom of Pines Pond in Singing Pines Park. Though foul play is suspected, the exact cause of death is yet to be released.

"Christine was the light of all our lives," said the victim's grandmother, Anabelle Collins.

The story went on to tell of the police's frantic search for Christine after her parents, who live in Florida, hadn't heard from her in over a week. After a preliminary investigation, it was discovered she hadn't been to her scheduled shifts at the local drug store, and had been thought of as abandoning her job when she made no contact with her boss.

I stopped reading when the article delved into Christine's active participation at the local shelter's food drives, and what a popular and well-loved girl she'd been with all those who knew her.

I thought I might throw up.

Nicholas had been reading over my shoulder. Eventually I smelled the berry-scented perspiration up close. I didn't turn around.

"Lynch fed on her, didn't he?"

Nicholas poured me more coffee, and simply stated, "yes." He moved me into a chair, sat down across from me with his own mug, and watched.

"I saw him, you know," I said thickly. "I watched him do it. I thought I was insane. Kat thought so, too." Oh God, Kat. Unsuspecting in the company of…

…exactly what I was in the company of. But it was different.

"Nicholas, why is it so awful, I *feel* that it's even more awful, that *she* was killed? I mean, you have to kill all the time." More nausea swept over me with a surge of heat.

He wrapped his hands around the hot mug for comfort. "Lynch doesn't kill because he's a vampire; Lynch kills because he's a killer. Christine is one of many that didn't need to die. Not yet."

How do you reconcile the difference between someone who kills for a reason and someone who kills for fun? I didn't need to. The difference was in Nicholas's compassion and humility masked with egotism and self-loathing. But the Cheshire cat smile, the very real superiority complex, the way he makes you think he has something on you—Lynch was brutal. The vampire from old movies, but much closer to home.

"Why are you so close to him? Why is Roman protecting him?"

"Oh, I'm not close to him by choice, and you can't be either."

Nicholas leaned back in his chair. I could see the protectiveness for me around him like a cloud. "Eliza, Roman is Lynch's creator. Roman was the one who made Lynch *Shinigami* not so long ago."

How had I not seen that coming? It was obvious. "He feels obligated to him," I said aloud to myself. "He must feel like a father gone wrong." My heart ached for the hurt this must cause Roman, such a gentle soul, paired with such a vile one for all eternity.

"He does think he's a failure. I remind him that he didn't make Lynch's chemistry and brain function, only his dental impression. He sees no humor in it. Well, it's Roman."

"So, was Lynch a murderer in life? How did Roman pick him? Why?"

I could tell I was asking troublesome things, but I didn't tell Nicholas that he didn't have to answer if he didn't want to.

"Yes, he killed several women as a human. He was never caught. He was far too quick, even then, his mind too intricate. Roman was absolutely disgusted by the idea of immortalizing someone so vicious. It was months before he could bring himself to make the change, but he was powerless against the urge. I was with him through it all." His eyes became faraway. "It tortured him. He became a shell of himself, refusing to feed when the call came, which only caused more heartache when he saw the alternate ending for his destined victims." He shook his head. "He was meant to drink from a father of three, and he couldn't. Roman tried to deny all things vampire-related. But this guy was in the line of fire, he was a cop, and his partner jumped in front of him, a woman. She was killed. Turned out she was pregnant, after having tried for years with her husband. Well, the husband went mental, and killed her partner, Roman's would-be victim anyway, convinced it was all his fault."

I'd stopped breathing and never wanted to breathe again. What an atrocity for anyone involved, and Roman, so good. I wished he was there for me to hug.

Nicholas's angry voice brought me to attention. "The same rule applies for victims who aren't chosen. If they aren't *unmei nashi*, but murdered anyway? Who knows what Christine's future could have held for her? For all of us? She may have just been anyone, but we'll never know the impact she may have had on the world. Now, she can't possibly be at peace. The Japanese have very strong beliefs about what happens in death; it's a way of life for the *Shinigami* to honor their victims, their dead. But there can be no honor in this.

"Lynch was destined for vampirism. All *Shinigami* are. That incident made Roman understand that he has no idea what's best in the long run. Chris Lynch is needed for a reason. Roman made the change happen. Now he's tied to him forever, and tied to all he does." Nicholas sighed, and smiled sadly. "Until Lynch's higher purpose is realized, all we can do is try to control his urges, keep him in check. God, I hate him." He rolled his eyes. I smiled a little, but panic overtook.

"Kat's really falling for him. I have to stop it. I wish he were ugly and poor."

I think a wave of jealousy stirred in Nicholas. Good.

"She can never be safe with him, but Roman is vigilant. He's done this for sixty years with that ass, when any other vampire would have severed ties with the monster and cut losses. And Roman really likes Kat, and he knows what she means to you. Otherwise I'd be even more freaked out that Lynch has sunk his claws into her."

"So, Roman didn't want to make Lynch a vampire, but you said the urge was too much?"

"Yes." He got up and pulled me to my feet, his touch making me tremble. "I'll explain. But we have things to do." He grinned. "You called in sick to work, didn't you?"

I grinned back. "You're a bad influence."

The slightly evil, entirely mischievous glimmer in his eye held me. "If that's the worst bad habit you pick up from hanging with vampires, I think you'll be okay."

CHAPTER 18

Christmas was two days away. I usually only had Kat to find a gift for, and I'd gotten my boss the same bottle of tasteless wine as always. Getting gifts for Nicholas and Roman made me squeaky, like when I was little and gave Dad a tie for Father's Day. I had zero ideas. What in the hell would I get for the man who had eternity to find everything?

So I was relieved when Nicholas reminded me he still had a last minute gift to get. It was a welcome, ordinary thing to do, and I hadn't done anything ordinary as of late.

The brightness of the morning sun did little to warm the air. It was just right for Christmas week. We'd started driving early in his black SUV, right after our breakfast talk about Lynch. It was always going to be strange to see Nicholas could go out in the sunlight. I wondered how long it would be before he couldn't—between... meals.

"You have a message," Nicholas said.

"Huh?"

"You have a message." He never took his eyes off the road.

"My ringer is off."

"I know."

Shaking my head, I went through the underused purse for my phone. The text from Kat read: *"At work now. Spent the night at Lynch's. I know what you're thinking.... you're right!"*

I groaned.

"What's wrong?" Nicholas asked.

"Uh, Kat slept with your buddy, Lynch."

"He's not my buddy."

"I know, but I'm mad, and it's easier to make it your fault." Nicholas's lips puckered. His attempt to hold back a smile settled me.

"You know, I think he cares more strongly for Kat than the other women he's taken advantage of."

"Somehow I'm not comforted."

"You shouldn't be, really. It doesn't make her safe."

Clearing my throat, I said, "I have to tell her. About what you all are."

The complete shock on his face as he spun his head around, mouth agape, was a complete shock to *me*.

"You can't possibly be serious, Eliza."

"No, *you* can't be serious."

"I know you are, but what am I," he muttered.

"My best friend is dating a serial killer vampire, and I know it. How can I not tell her? You can't expect me to keep something like that from her."

He sighed heavily, irritated with me, but I didn't care. "El, our rules don't work like human rules. You're a smart girl, you must understand that. Yes, Lynch kills when he shouldn't—" I had to stifle a laugh to prevent irritating him more. He glared at me as he continued. "But he's still a part of the big picture. His purpose is yet to be served."

My turn to shake my head. "How can that matter?"

Quiet in the car, not the comfortable kind. But neither of us wanted to fight again.

"How is it I was able to see him kill that girl?" I asked,

working not so hard to change the subject. I shouldn't have seen through Lynch's shield.

"The clown gets careless. Lust overcomes him. He gets lost in the blood." I was surprised to hear him sound so sympathetic about it, and my eyebrows wrinkled. "It can be hard not to, but he doesn't even try to control himself. He's told Roman that he doesn't bother to put the shield up much of the time." He glanced at me, narrowing his eyes. "But maybe you could see through it. You're different. And you were in the wrong place at the wrong time."

"Nicholas," I said, voice softening, "don't pity me."

"Shouldn't I?"

"No. I'm glad to know about it all. My life isn't worse for having you in it."

He pursed his lips in a show of shyness. "I don't think you should make that call yet."

Turning to him in my seat, I tried to meet his eyes when they looked away from the road. We drove together for a long time. I had no idea where we were going, but nothing could touch me there, with him beside me. I found it impossible to agonize over Kat's imminent danger. Things were far from perfect, but they were *whole,* and I'd be lying if I said I didn't like it.

"You're smiling," he said, pausing his Christmas singalong with the radio. I gave in to my inappropriate happiness and shared the smile with him. After all, he was the cause of it. And the distinct memory of his absence was enough to make me relish the simplicity of the car ride.

"Yeah, I am smiling. Because despite it all, I think I'm really happy. Aren't you?" Trepidation hovered with the question.

The crease in his forehead deepened. "I'll admit there's an irrational joy that fills me when you're around," he said, and smiled again.

Heat rushed to my cheeks. "Do you mean these things you

say to me?" I asked quietly. I wished I didn't have to question every little damn thing sometimes.

Glancing my way, meeting my eyes, a stray curl grazed his eyebrow. My mind took mental snapshots of every one of those moments.

"I never say anything I don't mean."

I couldn't respond. Nagging confusion corrupted my exhilaration. He may have meant it, but the suspicion always lingered. His words and actions could be so contradictory.

One day, I vowed, *I'll just kiss him out of nowhere to get a reaction. He'd be able to stop me if he wanted.*

Trees thickened, something I didn't know was possible in New Hampshire, and I still had no idea where we were driving to. *Maybe it's all a sick joke and he's bringing me somewhere to kill me after all.*

He finally parked in front of a small, once-white house with a tattered fence, forever away from anywhere else. "Dolman Antiques" was written freehand on the mailbox, echoed by a small wooden sign that hung off a nearby lamp post. It looked as if nobody had been here for weeks, or longer. The snow was a fortress around the house, and there were no footprints to be seen anywhere.

"Here we are," Nicholas said cheerily as he shut off the engine. "Nice, isn't it?" My look showed him that I disagreed, and he liked that.

Crossing the lawn to the front door was a challenge, but after a fair amount of stumbling and swearing from us both, we made it. Turned out there wasn't a vampire intuitiveness about the depth of snow. Nicholas knocked loudly on the door and tried to peer in the window, but nobody came.

"I know he's open," he grumbled. "I told him we'd be here." He went to the next window.

The door flew open with a rusty screech, hurling aside a

welcome mat we'd uncovered ourselves. A thin, unkempt elderly man glared at us from the doorway.

"Yeah?"

Nicholas pushed through the snow back to the door. "I'm Nicholas French. We spoke," Nicholas said with that cryptic tone of his.

The old man looked a little surprised, and nodded. Then he opened the door more for Nicholas and I.

Inside was an appalling mess. I couldn't imagine the place was ever open to the public. It wasn't a store, at least not anymore. It was just an old man's cluttered house. It had barely enough light to see the cobwebs. The old man, who'd introduced himself as Walter, ambled ahead, mumbling about not getting many visitors. Nicholas was wandering, picking up this and that, turning things over and putting them back down, while his eyes moved to the next object. Walter was still talking with growing enthusiasm from another room, to himself mostly.

I sped up to Nicholas, trying to take in the overwhelming space. Three canoes hung from beams overhead. Paintings were propped up against rolled up, dusty carpets. Piles of books, cardboard boxes, curio cabinets.... The room was so overstuffed that it would be impossible to find a particular item, though everything had an aura like it had been carefully selected. An entire life of treasures that I wanted to dig through myself.

"Nicholas, what are we doing here?" I whispered.

He didn't look at me, but continued the frenzied hunt. Under his breath he said, "I know it's here, it has to be."

"Pretty sure we basically broke into this guy's house, Nicholas. Nobody's visited here for years."

"Just, just...." He waved his hand at me, swatting me away. "Go sit down or something. Keep ol' Walt company."

I glanced toward the doorway where Walter had gone. "Well, can't I look with you? What are you looking for?"

He slowed down for a millisecond, as if he'd just realized how weird the whole thing was. "I'll know it when I see it. It's a gift for Roman."

Walter had returned, two glasses of water in his hands. I was weary of drinking from a glass that might not have been washed for ten years, but took it when offered. Nicholas refused, so Walter took a sip as he motioned for me to sit down. The chair was rickety at best. I couldn't even see another one until Walter moved a few things.

"Interesting shop here, Walter," was all I managed to say as I tried to ignore the crash behind me, followed by Nicholas's angry swearing.

"You remind me of her, in the way you sit, maybe. I can't put my finger on it..." Walter trailed off, staring at me. "Emily," he said, expecting the name to clear up what he was talking about.

Nicholas was at my side without a flicker of motion.

"I haven't told her the story, Walter."

"Oh!" Walter clapped his hands, a wide smile lighting up his face. He set his glass on an old packing crate. "Allow me."

I found Walter to be sharper than I'd assumed, and was eager to hear whatever tale he had to tell. I smiled in encouragement.

"She's long since passed away, but I had a twin sister, Emily. I loved her dearly, we were very close. We spent most of our time together, some out of necessity, but mostly by choice. She was the kindest, most gentle person I've ever known." He chuckled. "She would say the same of me." Nicholas chuckled too, and I relaxed more, drinking my water.

"We were very protective of each other, my sister and I. I

never liked her many suitors," he said with a wag of his finger and a smile. "Until I met her Roman."

I gasped. Nicholas's hand enclosed mine, and I knew to keep my poker face.

A wistful stare took over Walter's sharp eyes. "I'd never seen my sister so overjoyed with our more than humble lives. Our whole family took in Roman as one of our own. He was a hard-working man, like we were, and always helped us out around the farm. He fenced in all of our land so my father wouldn't have to. He bought Emily fabric for new skirts when hers became worn. He was so giving, so pleased just to share, taking care of his own parents as well as ours. Our families dined together often, all of us tied by our regard for him."

Tears sprang to my eyes.

"Roman's second summer in our company was when he asked my father permission to propose to Emily, which of course he was granted." Walter stopped, and I smiled. But the tension grew around us. "Mere months after the wedding, Roman was murdered in town after work. No one had seen these strangers before that night. The local barkeep saw a struggle in the alley, and alerted the police, but when they arrived, there was only....blood." His voice shrank to a whisper. "Just blood."

I tore myself from Walter long enough to look at Nicholas's reaction. He was concentrated completely on Walter's face, as if he could see the story there.

"Worse than Roman's untimely death... and there was not much worse for all of us... was that we soon learned Emily was with child."

My jaw dropped. *Poor Roman, and all that he'd lost.*

"It was a terrible pregnancy for Emily. Her illness was unusual. I'm sure more because of losing her beloved than because of the morning sickness." He wiped a tear with a handkerchief from his shirt pocket.

Nicholas's silky voice put a stopper in the terrible story. "Walter you don't have to continue."

Walter fixated on him with intent, but kind eyes. "Dear boy, the pain of telling the tale is dwarfed by living it." Nicholas hung his head to concede.

"Emily and Roman's little boy was never well. He graced us with his beauty for just over two years, and God took him home. Then our Emily took herself."

My stomach turned, but I held it together with a sob. I'd known Roman for such a short time. I couldn't imagine what hearing this did to Nicholas, who loved him so much.

"So, young man, I believe you were looking for this." Forced cheerfulness helped Walter produce a small silver box, tarnished with antiquity, from his pocket. "Roman gave this little trinket to my sister." I saw the detail of it as Walter passed it to Nicholas. A mushroom-shaped box, no larger than a quarter, with a tiny mouse perched on top. It was perfection.

Nicholas couldn't mask the heaviness of his heart as he took it from Walter.

"It's lovely," I breathed.

"Open it," Walter answered with a smile.

Nicholas did so, and read the engraving on the bottom of the little lid. *Love the small things.* He smiled at it for a second, choking back emotion, and reached gingerly inside.

A tiny blond curl held in place with a baby blue silk bow.

"William," Walter whispered. It was all he had to say. I couldn't stop the tears that fled my eyes. Nicholas put a hand on the back of my neck. "Bring it to your friend, Nicholas, the great grandson and namesake of my brother-in-law. I trust that he is loved, as well."

Nicholas stood slowly, even for a human, and helping Walter to his feet, pulled him into his arms. "This will mean more than words can say to Roman. You're a good man to share it with us," Nicholas said quietly into the old man's ear.

"We are a family that's lucky to have a friend in you, Mr. French. Thank you for not letting our history die with me." Nicholas pulled away and put a hand on Walter's shoulder, beckoning to me with the other.

"Time to go, Eliza."

With an embrace for Walter, I followed Nicholas through the maze of artifacts and out into the cold. Once in the car again, I looked back to the house, but Walter had closed the door, and like that, the chunk of history ended. I knew I would never see the sweet old man again.

"Are you okay?" Nicholas asked me gently.

"I'm okay. Are you? I mean, it was about Roman, such a terrible thing about Roman's life."

"No, no. *Part* of it was terrible, absolutely terrible. But he loved Emily so much, still does. He was whole for that time."

"But to be taken away—that was when he was made *Shinigami*, right? To lose your wife, your family… Did he ever see his baby, William?" My throat tightened.

In a whisper, "Once." Louder, "Just once, he snuck back to his old home. By that time, he'd been shown the necessity of leaving loved ones behind."

It couldn't be that simple. "Why? It's not like you're all evil!" I was heated by the idea of so much mourning, when all that had to be done was tell the truth. "His family would have understood, he's still the same man!"

"Eliza, this was 1915. Think of what people would have thought of such a creature as we are when they were such church-going folk, no matter how much they loved him. We were a crime against God, demons, straight from Hell. People react differently to the idea of a vampire these days. Besides," he cleared his throat, "*anyone* might be a chosen victim. You need to think like you're playing chess. I can tell you, Roman would never endanger his family like that. The risk of exposure, well, it could be the reason for the deaths of all those who meant anything to him."

I feared asking, but I did it. "Did you leave anyone behind?"

His reply was easy and honest. "No," he said, unblinking.

"I understand the danger," I said. "What I don't understand is why you would put me in it."

Nicholas quickly turned my way, then averted his eyes. "You aren't in any danger, Eliza."

"But how can you be sure?"

"I just am. You'll see, in time."

"How. Much. Time?" I asked, no longer caring to hide my impatience. Maddeningly, he grinned.

"You've forgotten the 'trust me' conversation already, eh?"

"No," I grumbled like a nine-year-old being sent to her room. I got over myself and changed the subject.

"You know, Roman is lucky to have such an incredible friend. That was amazing, what you did today." Tears pricked my eyes again.

I think Nicholas actually blushed. "He's the purest person I've ever met, and the way he was turned was so gruesome. I can never do enough."

"So he really was murdered?"

"In a sense. His creator was brutal, ruthless, treated him like an animal, all but leaving him for dead. But we've learned that all things happen for a reason, no matter how difficult."

"I don't buy that you believe that," I said. But he didn't answer. Silence overcame us for the rest of the ride. There was such a horrific sting to it all. A good man, killed at the prime of his life to become what was considered a demon by his community, then to create another vampire of an atrocious person, who's allowed to live a life he never deserved. All the while, these vampires are slaves to a fate that gives them few answers, forcing them to a life of solitude.

I was crying *again*.

Nicholas turned off the engine. We'd arrived home—his home.

The warmth of his hand on my arm sent a trickle-down effect through me, destroying all my defenses in a row, and I couldn't hold back my sorrow and fear any longer. He whispered that we should get inside. I threw myself into his arms, burying my face in the crook of his neck, needing that hot chocolate scent and the memories it fueled so avidly. Quickly, I thought, *how much more harsh is the need for blood, when he's in this very same position?* I cried harder, turning my mouth from his neck to his shoulder.

When my trembling hysteria ended a few minutes later, Nicholas drew away from me with the oddest look on his face. "I guess my reaction to the whole vampire world was a little delayed," I said, wiping my nose.

"Yeah. This is more like it," he said.

~

Roman still hadn't returned home when I left the house in the early evening. Nicholas had made tea to settle me down, and we talked about the many Christmases he'd seen. The fire's shadows mingled with the Christmas lights, and it was quiet. I felt much better, but was anxious to get to my apartment and see for myself that Kat was okay.

Parting with Nicholas was never easy, but this time there was no sadness, no pain, physical or mental. He waved to me from the snow-framed doorway, the Christmas tree only slightly visible behind him. Not that it could outshine his smile, or my own. I sang with the Christmas music all the way home.

~

"Y*ou* ditched work? I guess I'm not the only irresponsible person that lives here!" Kat exclaimed, laughter tickling her voice.

"No kidding. A first for me, though I have a hunch your night was sexier." Flashes of Nicholas's mischievous smile, his arms around me, the sound of him asking me to move in... No, I had the sexier night. He bought me pajamas and panties, for crying out loud.

"It was really nice, Ellie," she began, starry-eyed. "He cooked me dinner, his Gramma Annabelle's specialty." My skin froze, my hands curled into claws around the pillow in my lap.

Anabelle. Christine Simmons's grandmother. Nicholas's words echoed in my head: "*...the human leaves a residue.*"

"...and he's a great dancer, like a professional or something. Nobody dances like that in real life." She giggled. Had I not known the monster she spoke of, I would have been overjoyed for her in this state. It was sweet and fresh. For her.

For him, it was the appetizer.

Unfortunately, I'd cried wolf too many times about the men in her life, and Kat wouldn't take me seriously now about her boyfriend choice. She was still giving me her fairy tale rendition, but I'd phased her out, wrapped in my own very real concerns, and just glad, for the time being, that she still breathed.

Cynicism and morbidity created a vision in my head of Lynch stealing my best friend's habits, like the way she bit her pinky nail when she was tired. I gulped back a dry heave.

"Kat, I know I say it all the time, but I have a really bad feeling about Lynch." I should have kept my mouth shut.

Eyes narrowed, she asked, "You didn't send Roman to Chris's house to distract me, did you?"

"No! He went on his own!"

She puffed with irritation, blowing a piece of fiery hair

from her forehead. "If you'd told me a week ago that a man who looks and sounds and smells like Roman does could be so annoying…"

She made me smile. "Put a damper on your plans, did he?"

"Not for long," she said with triumph. "But Roman definitely showed up at just the wrong time, dragged Chris off into the next room, and when he came back, the mood was different." She grimaced. I imagined a screaming argument mere feet away from her as Roman cornered Lynch in his vigilance to keep Kat safe.

"After, Roman actually sat down and flipped on the TV! Like he'd been invited! We all watched a re-run of *The Golden Girls*, and then he finally left. It was so weird! And annoying." She sighed, her aggravation dwindling. "Then it was just the two of us, and it was so romantic. Like he knows me so well, he just says and does all the right things, it's amazing. I mean, it wasn't as passionate as it had been before Roman busted in, but it was wonderful."

Not as passionate. I bet. Son of a bitch. I shook my head of the thought and realized Roman hadn't stayed very long at Lynch's, by Kat's account. Where had he been all night?

Feeding time at the zoo. I shivered, but was markedly less distressed about the notion of Roman feeding than Lynch.

"Well, let's not pick out a wedding dress just yet, Kat."

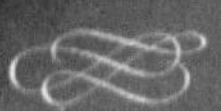

CHAPTER 19

When I was a child, Christmas Eve was full of love and excitement. It had been a long time since I didn't feel any sense of alienation, or pressure to enjoy myself as Kat's family doted on me. I'm sure they thought I was a little strange. I bet they asked Kat what my story was, and I don't even know want to know what her answer might have been. This year, Kat was heading to Connecticut alone to celebrate with her family. I was invited, but this year, I had another invitation. One I intended to take.

So, Christmas came a little early to our apartment. Christmas Eve morning was quiet and comfortable. Kat and I had our morning coffee over the stockings we insisted on filling for each other to bursting every year with lots of silly little things and chocolate. We exchanged gifts early so she could start her long drive by noon. She gave me the sweetest pearl bracelet that she insisted hadn't cost much. I gave her tickets to Blue Man Group in Boston. As expected, she was more excited to stay at the Hotel Marlowe and shop in Boston.

Parting for Christmas was unusual for us, so it was a little more emotional than I liked. I was sad to be apart from her, but I needed to *be* this with Nicholas, and Kat nearly slapped me when I told her I felt guilty. This arrangement seemed right to both of us. Kat realized the bond between Nicholas and I was growing, even if she, like I, didn't fully understand it. She joked that maybe a holiday was what he needed to finally kiss me. The joke made me see even more clearly how odd our relationship truly was. I laughed, but I secretly wondered if he *would* make a move, like a regular man would with a regular woman. Was he capable of a real relationship? I didn't think it with discontent, only curiosity.

Vivienne always gave me Christmas Eve off. Claimed the store was too crowded already. Every year, I stopped by anyway to give her the usual gift, which she was predictably happy with. I admitted to myself that she knew I didn't have the emotional capacity to pick out anything more thoughtful for her, thus admitting that I actually cared about her. This year, I was sorry for it. Having Nicholas made me even more detached from the solid, functional world.

When I came back to my empty apartment, I wanted to be alone, just watching Christmas movies, reading, and wrapping Nicholas's gift while drinking lots and lots of tea. It was blasphemous to leave our Christmas tree all alone for its last hurrah, and I really wanted time to just be *me*. Me without Kat, without Nicholas, without anything but me. Me without trying to be anything else.

I was up early Christmas morning. I lingered over a cup of coffee in silence, my knees up to my chin, covered in my afghan. I wondered how Kat's Christmas was, and knew as soon as I wondered that it was good. It always was. She had a way of making everything and everyone around her good.

After a long, hot shower, I was quickly ready to go, to have him next to me.

As promised, when I arrived at their house, Nicholas and Roman were in pajamas and their own old bathrobes.

Nicholas was serious that Christmas was a holiday best spent in pajamas, and if I wanted to enjoy it with them, I was not allowed to wear clothes that would be seen as acceptable in modern society. Roman confirmed it was a tradition.

I didn't hold back. I drove over in my favorite red striped pajama pants, now wet at the ankles with snow, and a white long-sleeved tee with a silkscreened picture of Santa on it. It showed the spots where my bra didn't quite cut it, but there was little to be done. Kat got us the matching shirts as a joke a few years before, and now we wore them every Christmas morning. No bra would stand in the way of it.

I looked like a fool as I stood at the door of the cabin, and I couldn't have cared less. The world's most amazing creature answered the door, and my smile was so wide it almost hurt.

"Your pajamas are wet," he said, looking at my striped ankles. "Get in here. Give me your coat so we can get you in front of the fire."

The fire drew me like a magnet. The "stray" was meowing, ready to curl up in my lap.

Nicholas took one look at my shirt, and said, "nice" in a way that told me he perfectly well understood why I loved it. "Good choice." His smile sent a burning through my chest.

Plunking down in the armchair that I always claimed, Roman presented me with a reindeer-adorned mug of hot chocolate with marshmallows and a thick blanket. I smiled up at him, and he smiled back. "No Kat today?" he asked in disappointment. He'd grown quite fond of her in a brotherly way that I found sweet. It was good for Kat, too. Men fell for her so quickly that she rarely had a good friend like that in a man.

"Kat went to see her family. They do a big thing," I said, sipping my cocoa and patting the cat in my lap.

"Well, thank you for being here for our little thing."

"No problem," I replied, mimicking his lighthearted grin. He left for the kitchen, and I took a moment to close my eyes and enjoy. The fire toasted my frozen toes and warmed my wet cuffs. The smell of evergreen and peppermint permeated the air. I chuckled when I heard "you'll shoot your eye out!" from *A Christmas Story* on TV. *This* was Christmas. I hadn't felt it for years.

I blinked back a tear when the new, yet familiar scent of gingerbread re-entered the room. The piece de resistance. The smell wafted over as he sat in his armchair.

Opening my eyes, I drank in the man who had recharged the tired holiday for me. He slouched in the chair, flannel-clad legs splayed in front of him, the fuzzy collar of his navy robe brushing his cheek. A sheepish smile of contentment on the full, fresh blooms of lips. The warmth of his chocolate eyes deepened as he looked at me.

He'd been missing something, too.

"Thank you for having me," I whispered, curling the blanket higher around my neck.

"I haven't had you yet."

A surprised too-loud laugh escaped me. "Classy, Nicholas."

He giggled and looked back to the fire. "It's nice to have a real person to spend the holiday with. You don't have to put as much effort into enjoying it."

"I've probably had to put in my fair share of effort, too."

"Well," he said, "it looks like we're a perfect fit."

We both sighed and watched the fire beat in and out of orange and red. A clanking glass in the kitchen broke my gaze. Nicholas shot me a look and rolled his eyes.

"What is it?"

"Roman."

At that moment, Roman stumbled through the kitchen door, which was alarming in itself. Vampirism had given Roman an especially ghost-like grace. More startling was the glass of what looked very much like brandy in his hand. I had seen in Nicholas, and even Lynch, that vampires sometimes ate or drank as a comforting habit, but I rarely saw Roman indulge. Today, he'd clearly been indulging in brandy, though I hadn't noticed at first. He giggled as he bumped into Nicholas's chair, but Nicholas didn't look annoyed.

"It's early yet, brother, maybe you should slow down," Nicholas said in a voice of reason that I didn't expect from him.

"Oh, cut it out, Nicholas, it's Christmas. And we're *Shinigami*. We can do what we want." He flicked a silver ornament on the tree with his finger and swayed, his untied red robe swirling around him.

I laughed as I said, "This happened quickly," out of the corner of my mouth to Nicholas. "I've never seen him drink before."

Without meeting my eyes, Nicholas replied, "He doesn't ever. Until this last feeding."

Where Roman had gone the other night when he left Lynch's! Of course! For a moment I was troubled by the idea of some human's drinking problem infiltrating my friend's body. Then I remembered…that human was now dead. And Roman had killed him.

Knowing that Roman and Nicholas had to kill people was one thing, but this was the first time I'd been in the picture when it happened. I was disturbed, but there was never a question of having to forgive him for it.

"Are you two talking about me? *Oh, Roman ate an alcoholic!*" His crazy hand gestures and googly eyes were too funny not to laugh.

"Welcome to the dark side, Eliza," Nicholas said.

We spent much of the late morning laughing together and doing our best to help Roman sober up. Once he had, he was beyond embarrassed, but without need. I understood.

Nicholas seemed to be watching for me to be repulsed by

Roman's alcoholic bout and his inappropriate jokes, but I left him dissatisfied.

At one point, Roman and I were alone while Nicholas made a phone call to wish his few employees from Birch Tree Books a merry Christmas. "Does it bother you?" I asked him.

Roman smirked cynically, another mannerism not his own, but he told me something he never would have if it was only him occupying that soul. "I hate losing any part of me to someone else. And killing is…you want to do it so badly, and it's mind-numbingly awful, but the taste of that blood is all worth it."

I couldn't mask my shock at the sentiment, and he noticed. I'm sure his vampire sensibility knew my spine tingled. He looked at me with an emotion near pity, but a wicked twinkle in his eyes.

"Alas, my dear, we are still vampires."

And that statement was all his own.

CHAPTER 20

The time came to exchange gifts. Nicholas's glee at having found Roman the perfect gift was bittersweet due to what that gift was. I held my breath as Roman opened the tiny box that Nicholas had gone to great pains in wrapping.

"Every year it gets harder to buy presents," Roman said, still a little tipsy, his fingers carefully tearing the paper. "A flask of hot blood only goes—" He stopped as his finger touched the tiny mouse perched on the intricate box. The rainbow of lights from the Christmas tree sparkled and danced on the little silver mouse, and he became something from another land.

For Roman, it was.

I couldn't breathe as Roman took off the acorn-cap sized lid. When he saw what rested inside, a sob resounded in the silent room. It was the most difficult thing I'd ever watched for the gentle, tragic man to lift that single curl to his cheek and lightly brush it past. A clear red teardrop stained his cheek and was left there, not to be wiped away. With a surgeon's movements, he placed the lock back inside the box, and lifted his head to Nicholas with a face full of wonder.

"There is nothing you need to say," Nicholas murmured in a quavering voice. Still, Roman tried, but Nicholas stopped him. "Someday, if you want to hear how I found it, I'll tell you, but now—"

"Thank you, Nicholas," he said heavily, love and pain and alcohol mingled.

"Yes, well, you're welcome."

Roman excused himself to his room, cradling the tiny box with such fragile love, I thought my heart would shatter.

"He would have been an amazing father," I whispered, after his bedroom door clicked shut. Nicholas stared at the tree, centuries of emotion bubbling behind his eyes.

"When people say life is cruel, they don't know that eternity can be worse." My chest heaved at the prospect of either of them suffering forever with the losses they must have endured, and created. Nicholas glanced at my chest as the rhythm of my heart quickened.

"This is Christmas!" he exclaimed. "And it's present time!" His jovial mood returned to mask his other depths, and mine followed, drawn in by his enthusiasm. "Now give me what's mine," he added, playfully.

Breath held, I handed him the box I'd wrapped in cinnamon red with plaid ribbon.

He shook the box and smelled it deeply. "Cashmere?"

"Wow. Way to ruin everything," I said with fake glumness. "You can seriously *smell* that?"

He grinned. "Cool, right?"

As he pulled apart the paper, I got the usual shyness I get whenever I give a gift. This time it seemed so utterly insane that I would give a vampire a goddamn sweater. Really? Sweat beaded on my back.

But as he lifted the lid, a dazzling smile grew across his face. "I love it," he said simply.

"It's stupid," I replied.

He pulled off his robe, then his shirt. His sudden half-nudity took me by pleasant surprise, but he pulled the sweater on all too quickly. "See? Perfect," he said, holding his arms out, the fabric clinging to his chiseled curves. His tousled dark hair stood up spiky in spots from the static.

I struggled to put order back into my thoughts. "Um, yeah, I thought it could replace—"

"—the one you stole?" he laughed, and ran his finger over its neckline. "No, this one is much better. So why does it seem like you're unhappy that I like it?"

I mumbled, "It's not good enough."

"Eliza," he said, making my breath flutter. "When you have hundreds of Christmases with the same company, year after year, gifts are morbid. Reminders of our stagnant existence. Case in point, my terrible, wonderful gift to Roman. This," he went on, clutching the folds of the sweater on his body, "is simply thoughtful, and sweet. Human. And it's from you."

I blushed. He had a unique way of making me do that. And a way of making me feel like I meant something to someone who couldn't possibly be all that impressed by me. He once told me I was dull.

In that blinding flash of nothing, he was next to me, his hand covering my own. My breath stopped. His own cool breath kissed my face when he spoke.

"Thank you. You've brought back to me some of the easiness of life." His hand rose to stroke my hair. I thought I would pass out. "And I've missed it so much."

Sometimes his sincerity could bring me to my knees.

Out of the blue, he said cheerily, "Now mine!"

Nicholas dropped a gift wrapped in blue in front of me. I

couldn't think of anything he could give me to equal just being with him.

I opened the gift.

"What is this?" I asked. It was full of things I kept at On A Clear Day; my Black Bear Café coffee mug, a black hoodie, even a half-eaten box of Raisinets. "You gave me crap I already own," I said, my fingers roaming through the box.

"I've given you some freedom," he said obscurely.

"I don't get it."

Nicholas sighed, as though annoyed that I couldn't catch on. "I convinced Vivienne to lay you off. Well, fire you."

A gurgle erupted as I gulped in air, trying not to throw up. "What the hell are you talking about?"

My panic didn't unsettle Nicholas. He sat calmly as I paced the floor in my stupid pajamas, talking myself through the funds I owned that I could live on. My thoughts went to Kat, and how she wouldn't be able to support us both; we'd lose our apartment. Sweat broke out on my forehead. "Oh my God, oh my God."

"Are you okay to listen to me now?' the buttery voice asked. I sat down slowly, unsure and curious about the spin he could possibly put on the mess he'd created. "Eliza, you're wasting your life in that menial job. You're meant for greater things."

"Wait, wait, wait. Is this another speech about how dull I am?"

"No. Now you can do real things, meaningful work. Enjoy life while you have it."

"So this is about you! About your life and how you wish you spent it." Then it dawned on me. "Is this so I can spend more time with you?"

His possessiveness should have unnerved me at best, but instead it was a little thrilling.

"Would that be so terrible?" he questioned with a shyness lurking behind that overconfident prying he did with his eyes.

"You got me fired for Christmas? The gift of financial instability. Your answer to our need to be together is making me poor and giving me nothing else to do?"

He sensed at once the involuntary lightening of my tone and jumped on. "I'll take care of you," he said with such urgency, I could tell he'd been planning this part. "I can help you with your finances. I have plenty for all of us." I'm not sure why I was surprised but he saw it. With a smile he said, "You can amass quite a savings over a couple of hundred years. You don't have to live *here,* but I've set up a bank account for you to use as you will."

Speechless. Unemployed.

Free.

Was that all it took then? He was right. As much as I disliked hearing it, my life was routine and boring. Even the word 'boring' made me feel ordinary, and I didn't want to be ordinary. And being at the store turned me into no one in a sea of people, isolated me even more. Nicholas's searching gaze as I ran my new life through my head made my cheeks warm, and I was already sweating with nerves and too much *comfort* all around me. I wasn't a woman meant to be comfortable. I tried, I wanted it, but comfort wasn't something I was supposed to have. Not since death showed up.

I needed to say something.

"Thank you," I choked out. A slow smile spread across his face, the one that said he knew he was right all along. My heart pounded unsteadily in response.

"Merry Christmas," he said, and leaned over the coffee table to kiss my forehead. A tiny fever grew there. A distant hiccup cured it. And the Whos sang in Whoville on TV.

CHAPTER 21

"You want cocoa?" I asked, pushing the plaid throw off. Roman had soundlessly left his room and I met him in the warm little kitchen unexpectedly. He leaned over the counter. A half empty bottle of rum glared back at him.

"Roman?" I whispered from the doorway.

He only hung his head and swooned. "Yes?" he answered, annoyed.

"New plan, making coffee. Maybe you should have some."

He turned with excruciating slowness, his sharp blue eyes blurred and bloodshot. I should never have laughed at his drunken antics earlier. Now his sweet face was drawn with guilt and tortured memories.

"I don't think coffee will help me."

"Roman—"

He was very close now. He'd killed, recently. This time, a man with his own painful past, which now seeped into Roman's mixed memories of a life he should have led. The memories of an alcoholic mingled with hopeful ones of an adored wife, and a baby that *we'd* reminded him of. But Nicholas and I were all he had.

"Roman," I blurted, catching his hand in my own. "I'm so sorry."

"Please," he begged me. "Please just let me enjoy Christmas. I swear, it's not as bad for me as you think."

"How could you possibly be enjoying this?" I asked, exasperated.

He looked at me like I was a little girl who had just done the silliest thing. "It's not bad to feel *all* of your feelings," he said quietly. "Or part of someone else's, I guess." We both laughed a little. "But thank you."

His simple words eased my mind. It was easy to admire the wisdom he'd accrued in his many years, the Zen-like quality he took to it.

"Let's have cocoa," I said, putting on the kettle.

"That sounds great."

~

Roman was right about feeling all of my feelings. That Christmas, I was overcome by every emotion I didn't want—but also longed for—in one full-to-bursting memory. It was toasty, soft, sweet, twinkling, sugary, everything I missed and some of what I never had. I loved Nicholas and Roman a little bit more that day. Nicholas's way of making me feel like I was in on some private joke, sinfully sarcastic, but unbelievably sincere and thoughtful. And Roman was endlessly comforting, kind, inspiring. He was full of love, even in his detachment.

All the jewels and decorations of Kat's big family holiday couldn't compare to that little firelit cabin shrouded by snowy woods, gleaming with warm hues. All of my favorite Christmas songs and movies were there, and the enticing scents of cookies and cocoa, peppermint and gingerbread, combined with pine and firewood. It all smelled like Nicholas.

It was the first time I ever wished a day wouldn't end, rather than fearing the moment it would.

The exhaustion took over eventually, well after midnight. I let my experience turn into memory, and drifted off into a sweet sleep, still smiling.

Nothing could have prepared me for the emotional onslaught the night would bring.

Hours later, but still with starlit darkness seeping in the window of the guest room, I awoke. I'd been dreaming of Nicholas, but it was an awareness of Roman that jolted me. Quietly, I tiptoed barefoot out of my room to Roman's door. I squeezed my arms around myself when I heard a groan, accompanied by the clank of bottles from the other side.

I should not have done what I did next.

"Roman?" I called through the door. "Roman, can I come in?"

In an awful moment, the door flew open. Roman pulled me inside and slammed it shut in one movement. He reappeared on his bed, amongst several empty bottles of hard alcohol.

"Please, amuse me with your thoughts on how much better I am than all of this," he said, sweeping his arm across the disheveled room.

Suddenly I wasn't sure why I had come, and wished to God I hadn't. Roman had to have been hiding the whole day his real anguish, his memories, his victim's memories. Now he could unleash them the way the blood begged him to, a last alcoholic farewell to a dead man and a child who'd barely lived.

"Just wanted to check on you, let you know I was thinking of you."

And in the snap of a finger he was too close to me, the stinging odor of booze coming in waves from his body. He pinned my arms to my sides, and I struggled to turn my head away from his rancorous breath.

"Thinking of me, were you? Now, what could you have been thinking about me, late at night, alone?" His tongue swirled hard and fast inside my mouth, stifling my cry. His fangs penetrated my bottom lip, hot metallic blood filled my mouth and dripped down my chin. I managed to break free of the forced kiss to whimper, "Roman, stop this," but his attention was directed to the blood on my mouth.

"Oh," he moaned. It was like my blood froze and put the rest of my body under Roman's icy spell. His fingers were bruising my arms, then the back of my neck as he tried to twist my head sideways. "Just a taste, then…"

A violent, freezing wind invaded the room, making a hurricane of the mess around it, and slamming Roman into the opposite wall, high near the ceiling.

I cried out in shock when Nicholas's figure formed from thin air. He came together where before there was nothing. Thousands of tiny crystals migrated from the cold in the room to one spot, where they joined together to somehow form his sinewy body. The cold had become him with such force that his lips were blue, his face and hands ashen gray, like he'd been in a frozen grave.

"Nicholas," I breathed.

Roman had slid down the wall, falling into a pile of clothes and bottles in a slump. I hadn't realized how much a vampire can apparently drink.

Fully formed, Nicholas stood, chest heaving, staring at Roman as he lie in a heap on the floor. "What the hell were you doing?!" he demanded in a growl. His bellowing voice shook the room, dripping icicles fell the floor.

Struggling to his feet, Roman spluttered and slipped, the blood from my lip still on the tips of his exposed fangs. His gentle face wasn't meant to wear a snarl like this. I was afraid of him, and for him; Nicholas was so terribly angry, he showed no sign of compassion for his friend.

"Oh, she wanted it, just not from me," Roman was stupid enough to voice.

A loud *crack* resounded in the room as Nicholas broke some barrier of light, sound, and speed with his movement, and another *crack* with the terrible uppercut he delivered to Roman's chin. Roman went reeling again, destroying a shelf and smashing a hole in the wall.

Roman actually chuckled sadistically as he snapped his slackened jaw back into place.

"Shut up!" Nicholas spat, eyes burning. "You don't ever speak of her, or what she wants!"

"Oh, *you* shut up, you pompous ass! You're always telling me to live my life instead of just enduring it, and what do you think I'm trying to do?" I was astonished at this side of Roman, and was equally certain this was him at all.

Nicholas growled, "Not. With. Her. Never with Eliza. You keep your distance from her until I goddamn say you're okay." He crossed the room with another *crack* and a flash until he was breathing the same air as Roman. Low and cruel, he spat, "She is mine."

My heart stopped for a moment. I was. I was his. I was not ashamed to let him have my entirety.

"Get out of here," Roman mumbled, eyes downcast. Nicholas backed off some, and told me to leave the room, his eyes still trained on Roman's face.

I left without a word, and before I knew it, Nicholas was next to me, closing the door behind him. He traced the vein in my neck with his finger, and despite my recent terror, my body responded with heat.

"Are you all right? Did he hurt you?"

I swallowed and faced him. "I'm okay. Just shocked."

His molten eyes bore into mine, all that rage gone as though it never existed. His hand cupped the back of my neck, but the coolness of it did nothing to cool me.

"No one can hurt you. I will always save you."

I doubted anyone could save me, but at that moment, I couldn't survive without him. "Promise me. Promise me you'll always be with me."

His eyes searched my face, my hair, my throat, his fingers still and reassuring on my neck.

"By my very blood I am bonded to you."

When his voice smoldered in that way, I fell, helpless under his spell, every time. His words may be confusing, but I found it hard to care.

The tip of his thumb still caressed my jugular. I drowsily opened my eyes to find him staring at the cold line his fingers drew.

"You caught me," he said in that same irresistible tone. "Sorry. Your lip is still bleeding. It's tough not to…"

My fingers went to my lip and came back stained red. He licked his lips. "Let me go handle that," I said shyly, stepping away. He pulled me back.

"No. Let me." Slowly, more slowly than I thought he could move, he leaned his head to me. One silky brown curl fell to his forehead and fanned to me the aroma of chocolate and campfire that only Nicholas could carry. I saw the tips of his fangs between the plump lips, so near to me, but it was his tongue that delicately licked my bottom lip. I couldn't breathe.

When I didn't dare to think it could get better, his fingers wove through the hair at the nape of my neck, now damp. His sweet breath mingled with my own as his lips suddenly smothered mine, finally, better than I'd imagined it for so long.

I came back to this world when I felt those hands, so powerful, wrap around my arms and tug me gently away from his sensuous lips that tasted like oranges and butter cookies. I finally allowed my eyes to open, unable to bear the idea of ever feeling any different than I did then.

Nicholas's eyes, filled with savage intensity, were waiting for me when I opened my own. He took one of his iron-grip hands from my arm to run it through his messy curls.

"Nicholas," was all I could say, all I could think, all that mattered, all I could hope for.

"Eliza." I swayed and there he was, an angel of iron and frost, his ever-changing pumpkin butter scent engulfing me so that I just wished for sleep, to dream of this for eternity.

"Eliza, I'm sorry about what happened in there, and about…"

"No, don't apologize for him. I should have known better. And don't you dare apologize for this."

I winced when I saw that he looked ashamed. "It isn't fair to you, any of this. I can only promise it will make sense soon."

I wasn't willing to let go of this moment in exchange for more promises and secrets. Without anger or disappointment I began to walk to my room to relive this event for as long as I could.

But first I turned around. "Roman was right, you know." He shook his head a little. "About me…wanting it. But not from him. I want all of it." And I walked blissfully to bed, and fell back to sleep with a smile on my face once again.

CHAPTER 22

B abies don't sleep that well.

The next morning was crisp, delightfully cold. The smell of fresh eggs drew me to the kitchen, and once there, the filtered morning light and company kept me.

"Morning, Beautiful," Nicholas rang out, making me blush. Roman glared at him, a gesture I was becoming used to. It looked more sinister when he was nursing a hangover.

Gingerly, I sat next to Roman to enjoy the heavenly plate of eggs, fruit and hash browns made just for me. "How are you today?" I asked him under my breath with caution. My voice was the only noise but for the clank of my fork. I was aware of Nicholas's watchful eyes. There was not a trace of the fight on either of them.

Roman folded his hands on the table. "Grotesque. I blame none of what I did on the man I fed from. I'm responsible for being an animal." I tried to interrupt, to tell him I understood, but he begged me not to, unable to look at me. I glanced to Nicholas, but there was no forgiveness in his eyes. "The way I acted, what I did, and almost accomplished—"

"Roman, I won't let you grovel any longer. That could

never be you. There was barely a trace of you there. I knew—
in theory—what could happen, the human residue. I'm sorry
you're living with it."

Nicholas sat down with two cups of coffee. I dared to
go on.

"It's been a little more ordinary than I expected, getting
friendly with vampires. Truthfully, I've been waiting for the
other shoe to drop."

"There are more shoes," Nicholas muttered, but I ignored
him.

Roman finally looked at me. "We aren't used to having a
human so close to us. I guess we've been a bit subdued for
your sake."

The clank of my fork on the plate was deafening. "I wish
you wouldn't be."

Nicholas said gruffly beside me, "Don't ever wish that."

~

Roman spent the rest of the day in his room, as
vampires are wont to do, I was told. There was
silence, which meant he was sleeping or reading, not
drinking. Perhaps the blood's potency was wearing off
already. Perhaps his guilt cut right through it.

I wondered how long it would be until Nicholas fed. Had
he since we met, and I hadn't noticed? A chill ran me
through when I realized that the man I knew may be
nothing like the real Nicholas. No, it couldn't be. I
knew him.

With Roman resting, Nicholas and I had the day to waste. I
was still reeling from the dream sequence of Christmas night,
but Nicholas was steering clear of the subject. He was his
usual self with me, not more reserved like I worried he may
become. I worked at my new expertise of enjoying my not-

exactly-other-half without questioning anything that mattered.

The light of day fizzled as quickly as a Fourth of July sparkler. We wiled away hours delving into hundreds of unrelated topics at random. I relished Nicholas's stories of his mundane humanity, his time in Japan, *Shinigami* legends, of his and Roman's life together. The passion of lifetimes danced in his eyes, his comforting and sly smile. The pearl luster of his skin was luminescent in the dim light. How could I not love him?

I was reminded of that first day he brought me to this house, as the flickering of the fire created the same low light. I chuckled softly to myself.

"What is it?" he asked quietly.

"Oh, nothing. I just remembered the first day you brought me here. It seems like so long ago. To me. For you, it's like the length of a B movie."

He leaned closer to me on the sofa. "Time passes the same for me. I know now that a moment in this world for me is one stolen from death."

I grinned. "You know, sometimes I wonder if there's anything underneath that cool exterior of yours. Then you say things like that."

"You've brought a new vision to this life I lead."

"Oh." I was startled. "Thank you? It's fair to say you've changed things for me, too. I'm jobless now, for instance."

We were both quiet, and I think he was recalling our kiss, by the way he stared into my eyes, his lips quivering into a crooked smile. It triggered a latch on a closed door inside me. It was easy, thoughtless, for me to trust him with the parts of my life that haunted me.

"I don't talk about the things I've told you, my parents dying, how alone I've been, I've always been. I think maybe it actually started while they were still alive, and I blame how I am on them. I refuse to trust people only to lose them." I took his hand in mine. "I won't lose you. It feels amazing."

Unexpectedly, he kissed me in that blur of speed and scent, fast and sweet. "You won't lose me," he breathed.

I sensed more.

He stood, but I pulled him down and kissed him with all of the energy I possessed whenever he was with me. My heart burst through my inhibitions. This was as it should be, and he *knew*, he *knew* it. He didn't pull away.

But he did laugh, with that knee-jerk sarcasm.

"I'm reminded of another night here, a night where we talked forever, and I had something unbelievable to tell you." He swallowed, and for a second it seemed like he had a terrible headache. Squinting, he looked deep into me, and my soul twitched. "Tonight, Eliza, I have something unbelievable to tell you."

I had bided my time, and now he would tell me what I had to know, the entire truth. While I was lost for a minute in my self-satisfaction, I barely realized his complete distraction.

"Nicholas? What's wrong?" He couldn't answer me through the sudden haze that overcame him, like he was watching the best part of his favorite movie in his mind, and nothing would crack his concentration.

I touched his arm and he fell back hard and fast to the present. Sheepishly, he smiled. "Sorry. It will have to wait. I'm on the clock," was his explanation.

The rest of the night passed with Nicholas enveloped in a trance, statue-like and statuesque, eyes wide as though in fear. Sometimes they narrowed in concentration on something I could never see. Occasionally he spoke, the way a person does when they've fallen asleep, but still want to be part of the conversation.

I just stayed quiet, drinking cup after cup of tea. I began reading a dog-eared copy of *Dracula* I'd pulled out of the loft of books over the kitchen. I couldn't believe they even owned it. I realized it may be about a friend of theirs.

It was late, two in the morning, but I was worried about him, and curious. How long this would go on? The darkness was deep when Roman nudged me from dozing and sat beside me, facing Nicholas.

"Oh. Oh, sorry. Hi," I said, rubbing sleep from my eyes.

"Hi. How long's he been this way?" Roman asked, sipping his own tea, eyes glued to his friend.

"Hours now. He said he was on the clock," I told Roman. He smiled, completely at ease, it appeared. He saw that I needed some explanation.

"Sometimes this is how it happens for him."

"He never mentioned this," I said, gesturing to the comatose man. I snickered. "He only told me he knows a victim by Spidey sense."

"Ass."

"I know. Thank you for always giving me straight answers."

"No problem." That encouraged him to elaborate. "I've never had the trance happen, but you know, Nicholas has to be unique in everything," he said, pointing at Nicholas, who grunted in some faraway place. "For that matter, it's not the same every time either. I've seen this happen probably a dozen times to Nicholas. Once, it lasted for almost a week. He's described it to me. He says that suddenly the victim's scent just drowns him, he can't see anything else, or hear, much like he's under water. He's in a heavy fog, walking in his mind he told me, looking for the victim's identity."

"That's…fascinating. It must be so hard."

"He told me it's like trying to solve a mathematical equation with bombs going off all around."

Peeling my stare from Nicholas, I faced Roman. "Thank you for telling me this. It helps so much to know he's not suffering."

Roman smiled at me with pity, I think, but he's a tough one to read. "I'm glad you care for him so much," he surprised me by saying, for I wasn't certain I believed it. "He's a good man, and he's been so alone."

"Some might say the same of you," I said gently.

"I suppose it's part of our plague."

"Was Nicholas always alone? He's never mentioned a… woman." Silence answered me. "Who is the woman in all the photos on your mantle?"

Trance or none, the cold prickle snaked up my spine, and I knew it came from Nicholas, still as stone. The hair raised on my arms and Roman pulled a blanket around me.

"Thanks. Strong reaction there, huh?" I said nervously, cupping one hand over my freezing nose.

"She's the vampire that created Nicholas."

Stab of jealousy.

"He didn't mention her either when we've talked about his past," I said, insecurity softening my voice.

"Nicholas doesn't like talking about her. He doesn't like *her*, actually." Well, that made me smile.

"Then why are the pictures on the mantle?"

"Don't you have pictures of relatives you don't like on your walls?"

"No. No, I don't. Why would I?"

"Well, in this case, Nicholas may not like her personality, but he respects her to a degree." He glanced at me, troubled, unsure. "Just like we're fated for certain victims, the *Shinigami* are predestined to create specific vampires as well. It isn't our choice who we give immortality to any more than it is our choice who we must kill. The call to our *unmei fumetsu* is undeniable, and creates an immediate bond; you *need* to be together."

Suddenly, I got dizzy, hot. I quickly envisioned the pictures of Nicholas's creator—*unmei fumetsu*, I guess she'd be called—at the theatre, and the lake. And they'd needed to be together.

Roman continued. "The *unmei fumetsu* is all you see, until it's done."

"Like you with Lynch."

My eyes returned to Nicholas, pained without cause. Roman made it go away.

"Once the vampire is created, the connection dwindles. The need is sated, and we can go our separate ways, which many do. But when Nicholas was created, the tie was severed quickly. She had to create him, but he didn't have to stay with her. Nicholas's distaste for her harshness, her cruelty, was evident. The blinders had come off, so to speak. Nicholas took to his new life immediately and it angered her to not be wanted. Also, she was quite jealous of the love the Master had for him," he ended with a smirk.

"How do you feel about her?"

He cleared his throat. "Her cruelty grew year after year in her immortality. She's hard and dry. Dead. Nicholas doesn't speak to her now, but he would tell you he owes her his life. Do you understand?" Roman looked deeply at me.

I hated that I understood.

"What is her name?"

"Jenniveve. She lives in Paris now." A chill emanated from Roman, but he quickly controlled it.

"I think I'll go to bed," I said, standing up and putting the cup on the coffee table. "It's been a long—well, it's been long." I yawned and Roman nodded. He'd watch over Nicholas for any change.

I'd crossed half the room when I looked back. Roman was

watching me go off to bed. Nicholas was exactly the same as hours before, staring. I hoped he knew in that maze he was in, how much I needed him here.

"Will I ever know all there is to know about him?" I asked aloud.

Roman didn't answer.

CHAPTER 23

Sleep finally took me as daylight broke. It was uneasy, and rather unwanted. It was hard to settle wondering what Nicholas was doing in the other room. Still sitting, vacant? Dream fragments came in spurts, images of a wild-eyed Nicholas with blood dripping from his chin, or of Christine Simmons, dead in the pond, Lynch watching as she drifted past. But the dream image that catapulted me out of bed was my Nicholas, sitting on the sofa, staring. The light from the window was hitting him just so that a black, charred hole was burning into the side of his neck, consuming part of his jaw.

I burst into the living room, kneeling in front of Nicholas, frantically inspecting his face and neck. Fine. I laid my fingers to his neck, and it was, indeed, very warm.

"Come," I whispered, fairly certain he couldn't hear me, as I tried to pull him to his feet, away from the growing patch of sunlight. "Nicholas, I can't move you on my own. You should be in your room." But only a stare answered me.

I looked around, knowing Roman had gone back to his room. I was a little disappointed that he hadn't stayed by

Nicholas's side, but also knew that that was ridiculous and unnecessary.

The curtains had been pulled as close as they could, but that evil sliver of light still invaded the room.

So, I sat between Nicholas and the light, getting up once at marathon speed for a glass of water and an orange, the fastest food I could see. Hours passed, while I quietly worried about what would happen when Nicholas did wake up. I sat and read *Dracula* out loud, just to keep him company. I would sit all day if I must. There was nowhere I'd rather be. And now that I was unemployed, I could sit here until the end of time if I wanted.

Nicholas's words came to mind:*"Are you surprised to hear that being middle management isn't your big picture?"* I hadn't understood what Nicholas meant, but I knew his end goal wasn't to add me to the unemployment line. What *did* he hope to accomplish by having me "laid off?" What did it have to do with me knowing now that he was a vampire? He'd lived for hundreds of years, telling no one that he was *Shinigami*, and he found *me*, pursued me to tell me…

I jumped a mile when my phone rang on the table. Nicholas didn't move at all. I broke free of my random thoughts to answer it.

"Kat! How was Christmas?"

"Ellie, you're never going to guess what I got for Christmas!" she all but screamed. "An engagement ring! I don't know how he got to Connecticut so fast, but here he was…"

I didn't hear any more. No, no, no. That murdering sonofabitch, what was he playing at? I wanted to shake Nicholas awake as I choked in fear, but forced it down. I had to think about what to do next, I couldn't explode now and lose her, to God knows what lay ahead.

"That's wonderful," I breathed, my eyes swimming as I

stared ahead in shock. "I want nothing more than for you to be happy in life," I said flatly.

"I am, Ellie, really. My dad really likes him, and my mom, of course, thinks he's too good to be true." *How right she was,* I thought frantically, searching Nicholas's face for some sign of consciousness.

"It was like a fairy tale, Ellie. He got down on one knee in front of the tree on Christmas morning, and he looked *perfect,* in an Armani suit, and…"

Christmas morning. Daylight. It meant he'd killed again, right before asking my best friend to marry him. Someone good, that probably loved the sun. My gut curdled.

"…he said since he's met me that he doesn't have to fill his life with things that don't matter. He said he has nothing left to search for now that he's found me."

The snake. "That's sweet."

"I know! He gave me the most amaaaazing diamond, Ellie, and, well, he wants to get married right away. He said it's felt like a hundred years that he's been alone."

Oh, God, I had to work fast. "When? When will you marry him?"

"One month! January twenty-sixth! Ellie, please will you be my maid of honor?"

"Of course. Of course. I mean, of course, that will be great. Thank you for asking me." *Nicholas, wake up!*

"Ellie, who else would I ask? You always want what's best for me, and you, well, this won't change *everything,* but it's important that you be there for the biggest change of my life."

Moving out. With him. They'd be together twenty-four hours a day. While she sleeps and he never does. How could he keep from her that he's a vampire?

What will he do when she finds out?

Oh, Nicholas, please come help me! I got the next best thing— Roman's door clicked open.

"…did you get for Christmas?" Kat asked.

"Unemployment," I replied, in a daze. "Kat, I should go. Let me call you later?"

"Yeah, sure. And Ellie? I miss you."

My eyes welled. "I miss you too, Kat. This is the longest we've ever been apart for the holidays, and it's only been like, three days."

She laughed that little Tinkerbell laugh. Roman popped into frame on the other side of Nicholas, with a smile on his face.

"Tell her I said hello," he said. "I heard her laugh when I left my room."

He wouldn't be smiling when I told him the news.

"Roman says hi."

"Oh! Let me tell him the news! I'm sure Chris will want him to be the best man!"

"Maybe you should leave that up to Ly—Chris."

"Yeah, you're right. I'm just so excited! But you go, be with them for a few more days, then you're all mine for wedding plans."

I gulped. What a way to welcome in the new year.

"Oh my God, I so need to find a New Year's dress! I know we hadn't talked about it, but Chris wanted to have a party at his house. Our house, I guess, on New Year's Eve."

I laughed nervously. "*That* I will tell Roman and Nicholas," I said with a sideways glance. "I think they were hoping for some quiet time," I finished, nudging the vacant Nicholas.

"New Year's Eve is no time for that. Well, I'll let you go back to *Nicholas*," she said flirtatiously.

"Thanks, Kat. I can't wait to see you."

When we hung up, Roman sensed there was trouble, and his face fell. I told him what had happened.

Standing and pacing, he rambled, "Vampires cannot marry unsuspecting humans. No, he couldn't plan to turn her. He can't! He's clearly not going to murder her. Not yet. I mean, he's not planning on it. Eliza, where is she?"

"Still in Connecticut."

In that blur of motion, he was in his jacket, and wordlessly out the door.

"Well, just the two of us, then." I glanced at Nicholas; shadows had crept under his eyes. I frowned, and flipped the TV on to drown out my thoughts.

CHAPTER 24

That night, Nicholas did not move. Nor the next. Only the occasional grunt reminded me that he was real. The shadows under his eyes deepened in those days. His skin lost the alabaster gleam to a sallow yellowness. His cheeks became gaunt, his lips thin, as though he'd grown much, much older. My fear for him had me shaking.

Roman had returned after being unable to find Lynch. It wasn't until the next night that we learned anything of the monster's intentions.

Lynch appeared at the door not long after sunset, a telltale red smear at the corner of his mouth. "Roman, guess what old buddy? I'm tying the knot after all these years!" He strolled around with heady arrogance.

Roman's fury was palpable. "What are you trying to do?! You can't mean to go through with this. And where were you yesterday? I went after you."

But Lynch had spotted Nicholas on the sofa, and flashed to his side, fangs bared with malice that made my skin crawl. He poked his manicured finger into Nicholas's arm, pushing him. "Well, what do we have here? Looking rough! Weak."

"You let him be! Get away from him!" I screamed. I knew he meant ill to the only two people I needed in this life. Then he was in front of me, and I could see the red stains on his inner lips and his teeth, even his shirt.

"What do you think you can do to stop me, cupcake?" he said, that same finger caressing my cheek. "Gee, we'll be like brother and sister now, won't we? Cozy."

Roman was next to me in an instant, the frigid chill of his protectiveness raising the hair on my arms. I saw the stray cat whiz by out of the cold.

"If you don't get away from her, Chris, I will destroy you. You know I can."

Lynch's head spun to face his creator. It seemed as though any charm he possessed, any humanity he did show, evaporated when he slid the ring on Kat's finger. Now here, fresh from a kill, he was ready to take an upper hand.

"Roman! I'm disappointed in you! I come to share wonderful news and look at the way I'm greeted. And you, the most civil of us all." He left me to prod at Nicholas again, and my entirety begged for him to wake up.

Roman took a deep breath, obviously tired of Lynch's games. "You're lucky Nicholas isn't available right now. I hardly think you'll be up to these antics when he is. Is this why you've come here? To show off your idiocy? To threaten exposure of us all? Or to make me scold you like a child for yet another senseless killing?"

Lynch drawled in a low voice, "Did it ever occur to you that my engagement may be genuine, Roman? Do you never grow tired of being alone, *always alone*? All the blood in the world doesn't fill the void." I cringed at the sight of him expressing actual emotion.

In an equally somber tone, Roman asked with evident pain, "Does that mean if we let you have her that the killing will stop? Because, Chris, your hunger never ceases!" He moved closer to Lynch, pleading with him. "Your hunger goes deeper than the thirst, and I don't know if you'll ever stop sating it." His voice cracked, and my heart went out to him again, at the misery this must cause him. *This* was the only child he had seen into adulthood.

Lynch stared with coal black eyes at Roman. "There is no pain in what I need." A smirk twisted his face.

Roman paled. Nicholas was immobile. And I sank further into the sofa, unsure if I'd just heard Kat's death sentence or not.

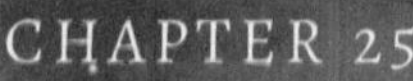

CHAPTER 25

The rest of the night passed in silent worry after Lynch left. Roman was troubled, and I barely left Nicholas's side. Just being next to his body calmed some of my terror.

The rare occasion that I did leave the room presented a problem when I returned. Nicholas's health decreased more quickly when I was away at all, I was sure of it. Continuously, new cracks and black shadows marred his complexion. He looked thinner, more worn, and in such a short time. If this went any longer, he'd be reduced to a corpse. I couldn't allow panic to disrupt my vigilance. If I could provide a fraction of the assurance that he provided me, I would do it.

It was hard to think of Nicholas as helpless, but in that state, he was.

And so, I sat. Reading. Fearing. Thinking. Plotting. Worrying. Protecting. Always protecting him from whatever could possibly threaten us. Lynch was the only thing that came to mind. Nicholas was mine and nothing would get near him.

Roman asked no questions of me, nor I of him. It had been a tiresome enough night. He'd bring me a glass of water or a cup of tea now and again. He forced me to eat a bowl of pasta, which I was grateful for later.

And so another night passed with my silent companion. My heart bled for the ashiness of his skin, and the hollows of his cheeks. Roman had stayed up around the clock, having no need to rest he said. For days Nicholas had been withering away, while I fooled myself, thinking I was doing anything to help. Minute by minute he lost more weight, his skin beginning to hang loosely on his jaw, his eyes sinking, cowering from life.

"Roman!" I finally called. He appeared like a ghost in front of us.

"He's changed?" he asked feverishly.

"No. Nothing good. Roman, look at him. He needs to feed." Roman seemed confused by how obvious that was. "Roman, we need to get him blood. To hold him over until he finds his victim."

Roman shook his head vigorously. "No, Eliza, no. He'll be fine. It takes more than a few days to—"

"Roman, look at him!" I cried out. "He's wasting away, look at him! I can tell you're worried, too." Tears streamed quickly and I was more panicked now that Roman wasn't on board. "I have to help him."

"What do you propose we do? Kidnap someone, bring them back here?" My stare back at him in response unnerved him. "Have you lost your mind? You're so ready to kill?"

"For him. Yes, for him."

The quiet between us was like another person in the room.

"You cannot," he said quietly.

"But you can," I replied. I was the one to move faster than I thought possible to be at Roman's side, holding his cold hands, my eyes pleading with him. "Roman, he must be suffering. He must be. You know this. Please. Or," and I realized it was true as I said it, "I will give myself to him."

Roman's eyes widened, then narrowed with hostility. "Fine. When dark falls, I'll find someone to bring to him."

"You swear? Or I'll get blood for him one way or another."

"I swear."

And with that, he disappeared until dark.

~

When the hood of night fell, I finally took a deep breath. I'd thought over my demand that Roman find someone for Nicholas to feed from. Soon, Roman would come to us, when stars were alight in the sky, and Nicholas would be healed for a while, with blood that wasn't quite enough. And if Roman wouldn't do it, if he changed his mind, then I'd waited as long as I would. I loved Nicholas too much. And he had a purpose in this life, more than I ever would.

I'd had enough time to figure out my loose ends, if I had to offer myself to Nicholas. I'd tell Kat that Nicholas and I had eloped, and decided to stay in Vegas, where we were married. Kat would never buy that I'd just up and leave her behind. Not like she was planning to do to me.

So, it would hurt, but the only way to make a clean break would be to tell Kat that she and I were holding each other back, and I didn't realize this until she announced her engagement. I would tell her of my thoughts to sabotage her wedding, and that the only way for us both to move forward at our ages would be to take a break from our constant togetherness. And I'd disappear. Roman would look after her, make sure Lynch didn't hurt her when I was gone. Eventually, she'd understand that the friendship we shared was but one chapter in her life.

It would be the end of mine.

Roman appeared mystically in the room. I took a deep breath, seeing that the time had come for him to search.

"No movement?" Roman asked, knowing the answer.

I shook my head and swallowed hard. Another cascade of images rained upon me: Nicholas's knee touching mine under the kitchen table, his strong arms around me, his laugh, Christmas day, his lips smothering mine, that intoxicating scent.

My back stiffened. "So, what do we do?"

Roman's always serious blue eyes were so piercing on me, like blue lightning. "If he drinks from you, he'll kill you. We can't let that happen."

"Roman, please don't fight me on this. You know I have to—"

But I never finished my sentence. Nicholas's head cocked to one side spastically, like a hunting dog listening for a rabbit. With a gasp, I jumped up from his sudden movement, backing away.

"Roman?" I said nervously as we both watched Nicholas's eyes dart back and forth, focusing nowhere. His nostrils flared, some scent perking them up, exciting him.

And like a rocket, he bolted off the sofa where he'd sat for too long, and at a lightning run I could barely see, was out of the living room, then the kitchen, and the back door to the woods. The back door swung limply from one hinge, thumping against the wall behind it.

We watched Nicholas's shape dart across the snow-coated ground, the moonlight washing across his body. Then he was swallowed by the towering trees, as tall as skyscrapers, hiding him from my eyes, but not my heart. I knew he would be safe. He would hunt. He would drink. And he would return to me, whole again.

A fairy tale couldn't end more perfectly.

The wind blew a cool mist of fallen snow across my face, the broken door creaking on the remaining hinge. I laughed. Roman messily fixed the door back into the frame, and looked at me, disgruntled.

"Eliza, this is nothing to laugh about."

That made me laugh again. "Roman, lighten up! I mean, I know maybe this isn't cause for celebration, but, well, I'm excited. He's okay! Things are as they should be."

"Fate's purpose will be served, but someone will lose their life tonight. Try not to laugh about it," he said with disgust.

My jaw stiffened. "I'm not glad someone is going to die. You know better."

"Then don't be so tactless."

"Tactless? After some of the things you said the other day, you'll call me—"

"Don't use that against me, not after you've forgiven me, not after you said that wasn't me. How can I believe you now?"

I gulped, ashamed. "Sorry."

"I think you've hardened against death so much that you

don't respect it anymore," he said so softly it stung. I knew he meant it. What was worse, it made me wonder if when I'd forgiven him for attacking me, if *I* had meant it. I was so willing to throw it at him. Roman, in one sentence made me question what I was made of.

The tension consumed us for a while, followed by unspoken apologies for how we felt, and who we were.

"Do you think he'll return tonight?" I asked, taking a seat at the kitchen table. The kettle screeched, and Roman poured two cups of tea. He sat across from me, with a sidelong glance at the broken door.

"I don't know. Who knows how far away he needs to go? But he does have you to come home to. Maybe he'll be quicker than usual."

I rubbed my forehead roughly, unsure why the simple statement bothered me.

"Are you okay?"

"Yeah, yeah. Just a lot has happened, hasn't it?" I said with a nervous chuckle. Hot tears sprang to my eyes, and I sucked them back with a mouthful of tea. Roman's silent gaze only invited me to elaborate, though I didn't want to. "I mean, Jesus Christ! It's only been a few weeks! I'm all but living with vampires, my best friend is marrying one, who's on a maniacal killing spree, she's oblivious to all of it, I've been attacked, lost my job, nearly lost my mind these past few days alone. Why? Roman, why am I doing this?" He just looked back at me, mounting concern in his crystal blue eyes. "I'm not just asking a rhetorical question here. I've come to accept some Japanese vampire design for humanity in a very short time frame. Why am I okay with this?" I leaned into the table, pleading with Roman, for what, I didn't know. "Do you know what Nicholas had to tell me before we lost him the other night? What am I missing?"

I saw his jaw clench. "You can accept what we are, what he is, because you always knew the world was more than what you saw, bigger than us." He sighed heavily. "And because you love him. A person can accept a lot in the name of love."

The door rattled with a gust of wind that found its way to me. I stared into my teacup, trying to decide how to respond, but Roman helped me.

"Sometimes, it's easier to just live it and not diagnose it." He sipped from his steaming teacup.

"Not for him," I said, staring, unfocused into the cup. "He embraces where fate has brought him. He believes in it, and he hates it, and he's proud of it. He owns his big purpose, every part of it, even though it's so hard. It's his soul. I've never seen anything so incredible."

I looked up at Roman, sluggish and reluctant smile on his face.

"Like I said. You love him."

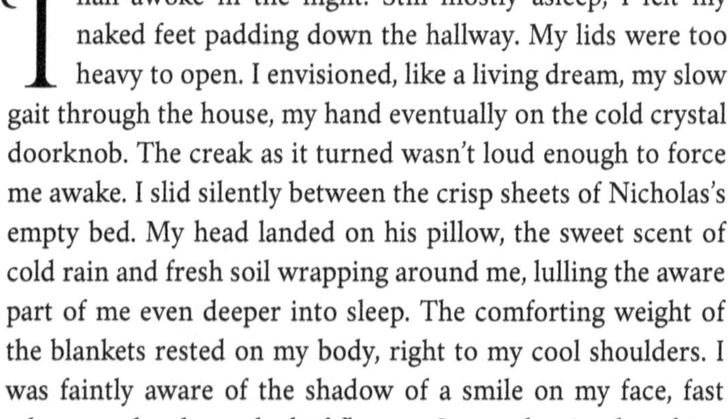

I half-awoke in the night. Still mostly asleep, I felt my naked feet padding down the hallway. My lids were too heavy to open. I envisioned, like a living dream, my slow gait through the house, my hand eventually on the cold crystal doorknob. The creak as it turned wasn't loud enough to force me awake. I slid silently between the crisp sheets of Nicholas's empty bed. My head landed on his pillow, the sweet scent of cold rain and fresh soil wrapping around me, lulling the aware part of me even deeper into sleep. The comforting weight of the blankets rested on my body, right to my cool shoulders. I was faintly aware of the shadow of a smile on my face, fast asleep, my head on a bed of flowers. It was the simplest thing in the world that I should sleep here.

The perfection of sleep in his bed caressed me like a warm

summer breeze. It was right that Nicholas would come to me in my dreams.

For a time I watched with my own eyes, the snow underfoot whiz by, and nearly thought I'd become a bird, but I felt so…carnivorous. The subzero air bit my ears and nose, but I paid it no mind. I was on the trail, and it would take more than a little cold to stop me.

Then I slammed to a halt. My senses slowed to a stop, save my scent, which was alive with the hot, salty blood so nearby. I saw a humble log cabin in my mind's eye, smoke billowing from the chimney, firelight flickering around the windows. A beaten-up blue snowmobile was parked in front.

That's where he was.

And I was a subway train at full speed west into the woods, deeper and quicker every second. Within seconds I was at the cabin, my frigid skin shaking with anticipation and ravenous fever. My hunger screamed for satisfaction.

Then I was watching. I watched Nicholas, an apparition in the single room, claiming the man with his eyes. The man, maybe seventy, sat in a green chair so tattered and old it was a miracle it could still hold him. His jeans and plaid shirt were in near equal state, but he didn't look like a mess, just like a man of habit. I liked him.

Thomas. The name had always been in my head—no, in Nicholas's head—waiting to be unearthed when the time was right.

Thomas looked at his uninvited guest with childlike amusement that didn't fit his demeanor. I couldn't know but I did know that he thought Nicholas was a heavenly creature, an angel, and he was an honest man who deserved to be visited by one. Pity wafted over me, because I knew what was coming.

So did he.

"You've come for me," Thomas said as if in a dream

himself, rising slowly from his old chair. "You can bring me to her." The man blinked for the first time since he'd seen Nicholas. His eyes were welling in what I knew was a rare glimpse of emotion. His words were deliberate, measured. "I..have...missed her," he gulped, "so much." Breaking his gaze, his head fell, like the weight of a thousand years finally slid off of him. "So long, I've missed her."

Nicholas didn't move or look away, or even blink. His chin rested on his chest as he stared menacingly at Thomas with cold, hard eyes; a lifetime of hunger burned behind them. Nicholas's heart shivered and ached with it, but he was still as the man approached him. The vampire's nostrils didn't even twitch with the overpowering aroma of the blood elixir.

Thomas was mere inches from him, smiling, his eyes dancing with excitement. After what seemed like hours, Nicholas finally spoke, his voice heavy with animalistic intent and need.

"Good man, I cannot make you any promises you will like."

Eyebrows wrinkled, lips upturned like he'd heard the most outlandish thing imaginable, Thomas put his hand on Nicholas's shoulder and said, "You, in all your power, sir, haven't learned that by just existing you've answered my prayers?"

Nicholas blinked, unsure, taken aback by the man's kindness. "I can only promise you won't live to hate me." And with that Nicholas was instantly upon the man, his teeth like daggers, draining the faintest wheeze of surprise and anguish from his victim. Only relief showed in Thomas's fading stare. It was the same in his killer's.

When it was over, mere seconds, Nicholas sat Thomas's body back in his chair. He pulled the collar of his shirt over the miniscule twin punctures, noting the pleased, sweet smile on the man's lips.

"I hope you're home," Nicholas said in a whisper, and

licked a trace of blood from the corner of his own, now warm, lips.

~

I awoke in the wee hours, not a hint of drowsiness in my body. I tingled with life, ready for anything. But I knew exactly what I was most ready for.

I swung my legs out of Nicholas's low bed, and grabbing a sweater he'd left in a heap near the door, ventured to the kitchen. The back door still wasn't perfectly aligned, so it squealed as I pulled it open. The work boots Nicholas wore to shovel were at the door. I slid into them like a child playing dress-up.

This was no game. I had no time to waste. He was coming.

I walked out into the crunchy snow and darkness, across the vast lawn that rose into the hills, topped by the larger than life forest. The night was bruise-black but for the immense full moon that appeared so close I wanted to reach out and touch its cratered surface.

Then something more incredible came into view.

He appeared, rising over the hill as he trudged out of the woods. The silver moon illuminated him, a halo around his silhouette of curls and luminescent face. He was shirtless, wearing only the ordinary black jeans from days before, so out of place on such an inhuman creature. His herculean body glided across the snow, radiating power and agility. He was a god, a beastlike angel, moving between worlds in one night.

As he grew closer I realized how I gawked, paralyzed by his flawlessness, and went quickly to him, but he crossed far more ground than I in the short time. He stopped, inches from me. His scent was of blood and earth, like a wild animal, a predator would smell.

It gave me great relief, knowing it made him whole.

His molten chocolate eyes were dancing, gold flecks shooting through them like tiny meteors. The vibrancy wasn't reflected in the rest of his porcelain face, however. He was tired; the fatigue emanated from him, even as he stood staring silently at me, inexplicable ardor alight in his eyes.

"You stayed with me," was all he said. He reached out and encircled my waist, turning me toward home.

CHAPTER 27

Strange, that I should take care of a being of such immense strength. I toweled off his bare torso, tensing at his waist and wondering if he had the energy to change into the cotton pajama pants I'd found. He hadn't uttered another word since I'd gotten him into the house and seemed devoid of energy, though he vibrated with the infused, borrowed life in his limbs.

"Can you do this?" I asked firmly. Expressionless, Nicholas unbuttoned his jeans. I looked away with widened eyes, as if I hadn't ever thought what lie underneath, but now wasn't the time. When he'd finished, I helped lower him into the bed, still warm and indented where I'd slept. Though obviously exhausted, his consciousness sang to me with a new vitality that came, of course, from the good man in the cabin. Thomas.

I pulled the same blankets up to his chin that had comforted me so completely just moments before. I turned to leave as his eyes closed, but he caught my wrist.

"Don't leave me now."

I climbed in on the other side of the bed. Nicholas curled on his side, the ripples of his back rising and falling peacefully.

I wriggled across the sheets to curve my body around his. Breathing deeply, Nicholas pulled my arm around his waist. His skin was warmer than usual, either from bounding through the woods, or from the fresh blood that coursed through his veins. I didn't mean to, but I pulled my hand back a little at the thought. Nicholas, with unnerving speed, pulled my arm closer.

Rolling over, his face inches from mine, he whispered again, "You stayed with me."

"Of course I did," I answered, breathless, my eyes roving his face illuminated by the filtered moonlight.

"I don't deserve your devotion."

"It doesn't matter if you deserve it or not."

The silence filled the small space between us again, as we looked into each other's eyes. The quiet was healing. Had the complete comfort not made me so tired, I maybe would have just enjoyed the silence, but sleepily I said what I wasn't sure I wanted him to know. "I was there with you."

"I could feel you."

The wind whipped against the windows and the house creaked, making me pull the blankets closer. He noticed and misinterpreted.

"Now that you've been there with me... You saw me and the *unmei nashi—*"

"Thomas."

He licked his bottom lip, surely thinking of the taste. "You're afraid? Now?" My mind went to the moment his teeth punctured the man's vein.

"No! No, that's not it. I'm just cold," I exclaimed, waking some.

"You're disgusted. You were too close to that moment, you felt what I felt."

"Exactly. I felt what you felt. You didn't do it without

remorse, and you gave him what he wanted, and you couldn't have done anything else. I am not disgusted."

His eyebrows furrowed and a familiar dart of cold pierced me. I touched a stray curl at his temple. Propping myself up on one elbow, I told him what I'm sure he had to have known already.

"Never in my wildest dreams did I ever think I'd be able to rationalize *murder*. I mean, why the hell would I ever have to, right? But when I look at you, I know that it can't be so simple. I believe in the destiny you have, and I believe in you. And tonight—"

"Tonight," he interrupted, "was not the way it usually is. He wanted that fate too much."

"Yeah, Nicholas, because he saw the alternative! He couldn't be without the woman he loved for another day. Just because the other *unmei* who-whats don't know what awaits them…"

"Neither do I, Eliza! I answer a silent call that centuries-old stories tell me is the right thing to do!" He began to get upset, and his eyes rolled back from the effort in his fatigue. I took his face in my hands, and I looked at him with purpose.

"Nicholas," I said evenly and low. He relaxed, and waited. "I would think in your hundreds of years you'd have learned what I know. Death is inevitable, painful for those it leaves behind, and harsh on everyone. And fate answers to nobody. Not even you."

His eyes turned liquid for a moment, helpless, and finally sleep stole him from me.

❧

I woke up too easily again. I began to wonder if it was another pleasant side effect of sleeping in Nicholas's Zen Garden bedroom.

Nicholas was already up. I was grateful that his immortal body recuperated so quickly with minimal sleep. Flickers of our last words the night before had me hoping the same for his heart. I'd awoken haunted by the abandoned look in his eyes that had sent us both off to sleep. If only he could trust himself the way I trusted him. Despite what was at stake—innocent human lives—I never second guessed him. But then, he wouldn't be the man I loved if he didn't guiltily question his purpose.

Sitting up slowly, I had the immature thought that I had shared a bed with him, and it made me giggle, something I did more easily these days. The sound still was far more normal coming from Kat.

Even though I'd expected it, I still sucked in a breath when I saw Nicholas through the glass doors, practicing the precise, rhythmic martial arts movements. Like the carving of Apollo if he could ballroom dance. He sensed me, and too soon for my eyes, ended his practice to come back to his room.

He was always stunning to look at, but after feeding and practicing, his radiance was not to be believed; as if his skin had been formed of the very snow outside, with not a hint of lifelessness to it. His eyes swam with interloping swirls of caramel, cocoa, mocha, constantly playing together. His tousled curls had deepened to the color of black coffee. And his smile—words haven't been created to give it justice. My pulse leapt at its appearance.

I stood, speechless while he toweled off his hair and body, hoping that when I was one day able to speak again I wouldn't sound stupid.

"You okay there?" he taunted me with a smirk.

My foolish head shook out a "yes." I cleared my throat. "I never look like that after four hours of sleep or so."

"Yeah, well, you didn't have the nighttime cocktail that I had," he joked dryly, and threw on a once-black Blondie t-shirt.

"I walked into that one," I said. "You seem to be in good spirits, too."

Seconds hadn't passed, and he was there in front of me, a woodsy scent clouding around him. He took my cheeks in his unnaturally warm hands.

"Thank you for listening last night," he said softly, "and for the things you said, that you always say. Thank you for being such a soldier at my side."

"Well, you *do* deserve it."

He nodded curtly with a sullen smile, and tugged my forearm toward the bedroom door. I turned him around to say to him that he *does* deserve my love, no one ever has so much, but he spoke first. His mouth opened and closed as he re-thought the impulse to say what he wanted to.

"I can't hide what I am from you. I don't even want to try. I *crave* your attention to me."

The way the word 'crave' fell from his lips implied so much more, and I swallowed hard at the look in his eyes. *Kiss me again, please, please.* I hadn't realized my eyes had closed until his voice snapped me out of it.

"Let me get you some breakfast. You like your breakfast. I don't think I've ever seen anyone eat so much bacon."

My head shook at the tone of this leg of our talk, but that was Nicholas. Hundreds of years still couldn't make him comfortable with showing his depth.

"I don't even want bacon today. I'm not really hungry. Besides, I prefer Golden Grahams."

"Liar. You're such a liar. I'm cooking and you're eating."

So, for yet another cozy morning framed by lightly falling

snow outside, I ate an uncomfortably large breakfast with my favorite vampires.

Roman was visibly relieved to see Nicholas completely restored and then some. Roman's somberness evaporated some and he became talkative, lively. It was fantastic to sit back and laugh as they jabbed at each other. Roman said it had been lifetimes since Nicholas had gone comatose, and my worrying didn't let him fully enjoy the quiet. We joked and swapped stories, none of mine being comparative to theirs, and we were family. Always now, we were family. My heart expanded with every shared smile. Maybe that's why I ate so much; it prolonged the experience. Though the roll over the top of my pants would say I'd been celebrating longer.

Soaking up the familiarity and togetherness made me miss Kat. I both hoped that she was this happy with Lynch, as well as feared and despised him for the lies he was feeding her. And being lied to was the least of her troubles. The danger she was in was almost too much for me to bear. Yet, I had no solution as to how to wrest her away before something horrible happened. From when he had one of his frequent impulses to taste blood. Kat always smelled so good, and her peachy little cheeks were so warm-looking, something was bound to go wrong. Something like what happened to Christine, and countless other women.

"No food coma, Eliza. Only one coma per week in this house," Nicholas sneered. "I think I can rustle up some Golden Grahams if you're still hungry."

I threw a checkered dish towel at him and changed the subject. Not quick enough. Roman caught my eye, and I knew he'd corner me to get it out.

"Eliza, what are you not telling me?" Nicholas piped in.

"In time, it will all be clear to you," I said in my best Nicholas impression, and Roman let out the goofiest guffaw I'd ever heard. Nicholas was deadpan. "Uh, we learned something while you were…gone." I breathed deep enough for it to hurt. "Lynch asked Kat to marry him." The time for jokes was over immediately. My fingers were suddenly numb. I looked down to see them frozen where I gripped the table, which was now coated in ice. My head snapped up at Nicholas.

Anger had frozen his face, like my fingers. His jaw was set, his eyes no longer swimming pools of hot chocolate, but solid and stony. He quickly noticed my alarm and my hands, and softened, warming the room again.

"Roman, is he planning to change her?" he asked, his eyes not breaking from mine. I didn't ask—ever—but it was blatant to me that creating vampires was rare. I knew that it wasn't supposed to happen this way.

"I don't know," Roman said. "His plans are unclear. I don't doubt he's up to no good. Kat has no idea what he is. Or how he kills."

I shivered, despite the frost melting off of my fingers.

"We'll stop him," Nicholas said to me. I wished I could believe him.

Roman planned to go to Lynch that night, but Nicholas said he was able to go out that day due to having fed. We both knew what that meant.

"I don't know, Nicholas."

"No. It's good," I said. "Kat will be there with him today, planning the New Year's Eve party. I bet I can hang with her while Nicholas and Lynch talk. Nicholas, he's afraid of you, this could work. And you could do your bubble-shield-thing, Kat never has to know."

Roman was not as confident. "No. I am his *Shugotenshi*, he's my *unmei fumetsu*. It should be me."

In a soft tone, I said, "Roman, he came here to taunt you about it. He isn't afraid of you."

Nicholas put down his coffee mug with a note of finality. "Fear is the only language the jerk understands. He knows you'll go easy on him in the end, Roman, but he definitely knows I want him dead. I think I can handle it without it coming to that. Depends how hard I try," he said with a smile.

"How will Kat understand all this?" I thought aloud. My head was spinning, now that we finally had to take action. Panic rose from my belly to my chest, to my throat. "We can't just *dispose* of her fiancée without her questioning it! And she'll never believe he's a vampire."

"No!" Roman boomed. "She cannot know!"

No one argued, but Roman explained for my benefit anyway. As if it needed explaining.

"We can't let her find out. Fate's plan isn't to be jostled around at our will, inviting everyone in on it like we're some big club. Who knows what damage it would do? Humans can't know that we exist."

And yet, I know, I thought, and still didn't really know why.

Nicholas spoke gravely. "I'm going to him. I don't need to ask his intentions, they don't matter. Vampires can't risk marrying humans, he knows it, and he toys with exposure already." He drifted, disgusted. "He could never hold the shield up long enough. He'd be careless about what he did in front of her, at best. Then there are few options, once she knows. This is a game to him, but—"

"—it will mean Kat's life," Roman finished. "And the threat of exposing us all if he's as messy as usual." We exchanged a few solemn glances.

"What will you do?" I asked Nicholas.

Nicholas shrugged. "I'll threaten him with death, as I always do. He knows marrying Kat will throw enough of a wrench in our lives that it will have us up in arms, and that's the reaction he'll expect from me." I started to interject, but he knew what I was thinking. "Don't worry, Eliza, nobody can hold up a shield like me, if it comes to blows. I can always make it look like a terrible household accident. I can make it so Kat won't even remember we were there."

"You can do that?" I whispered, frightened, but mostly awed. What other tricks were up his sleeve? What else didn't I know?

"I can't tell you all my secrets." He smiled as he sipped his coffee, but I didn't smile back.

CHAPTER 28

We left soon after I'd finished eating. Nicholas was ready in seconds, like everything else he did. The rose glow about him was still incredibly strong, if not more so. My awe only grew when we stepped outside into the daylight. The sun sparkled on the thin layer of fresh snow that had been added to the never-ending blanket this winter. The glint was blinding.

Nicholas stood on the front step, staring into the sun with the most joyous smile I could dream of. The sun seemed to drink him in as much as he did it. A childlike laugh escaped his lips, and I laughed with him. When the warmth of his hand curled into my own, a shockwave of pleasure shook me.

The slightest touch from him was getting more and more powerful to me. I loved it.

"I'll never get over how soothing the sun is," he murmured. "My senses are so strong, little escapes them, but until you shared it with me…" I was shocked to hear him reference me in this moment. "I never heard the *buzz* of the sunlight."

I stared at him until my eyes stung, until without warning, he transported to the car.

Our pointless banter ended with my sharp intake of breath when we arrived at Lynch's house. Nicholas's eyes lingered on me as the engine shut off. His reassuring fingers curled around my shoulder. A breeze of violet and sugar kissed my senses, but nothing could soothe my dread.

"Eliza, I won't let anything happen to her. You know that, but you're still scared?"

I couldn't look at him. I could only stare at the horribly tasteful mansion that housed the real monster. A calculating, bloodthirsty animal with super-strength and senses, and the charm of a Kennedy. My best friend was locked in there with him. Unsuspecting, unprotected. Signing on for what—death? Immortality with a vicious murderer? Or something worse for her—being married to a liar and a traitor, a joke in her own home.

"Let's go," I said.

"Holy Hades!" Nicholas yelped, swatting the air as a flock of a few crows swooped low by us.

"They're fine, they like me," I said absentmindedly.

"Make sure they leave engagement gifts on his car."

Kat must have seen us pull up. She swung the gigantic front door open, an ear-to-ear grin alight on her face. She was just so happy.

She screamed and smothered me in a bear hug, going on ecstatically about how she had missed me on Christmas again, and could I believe she was getting married?

Tears streamed down my cheeks, because of my own joy at being with her again, and because I couldn't know how long we had.

We all stepped into the oversized mansion, where Lynch lounged on a white sofa in front of an enormous artificial tree decorated in blue. "Oh, what a lovely surprise!" Lynch exclaimed. I could have gagged. He came quickly over to shake

Nicholas's hand, and kiss me on the cheek. I shivered at his too-warm touch.

"Glad to see you so full of life, Lynch," Nicholas said with a sneer. "Engagement looks good on you."

The flicker of fear and resentment I was waiting for shadowed Lynch's political face. Nicholas did know how to get under his skin. I'd been counting on it.

"Well, you two have missed each other, so we'll give you time to catch up," Nicholas offered, motioning to Kat and I. Instantly, he was no longer at my side, but had a hand clasped on the animal's shoulder, turning him out of the room. Kat seemed not to notice. How much could be concealed from the average person?

I guess I'm not the average person.

I held my breath, waiting to hear some ruckus from the next room. Kat pulled me to the sofa, and I told her about Christmas, though I was so distracted. Lynch's proposal took the heat off the topic of my not-so-voluntary unemployment. It was comforting to hear her voice, but so scary to hear her speak of that monster with such endearment.

Then, I heard it. Through my anxiety, I heard in my mind, clearly, the argument beginning, rooms away. It was intense; my ears were hearing Kat's bubbly planning, but my thoughts were wrapped around the conversation between Nicholas and Lynch.

I shook the surprise off, reminding myself that I'd heard Nicholas in my mind before, in Birch Tree Books. Just another little vampire surprise. But he'd been talking directly to me then. This—I was eavesdropping. My eyes focused on Kat. She was oblivious. Good.

Suddenly, like a lightning bolt struck my brain, like someone turned on the TV, I *saw* the scene as well as heard it. The two vampires could have been putting on a play in the same room, for the clarity with which I watched it, even as I focused on Kat.

"I will never let you do this," I heard and saw Nicholas spit at Lynch. *"More importantly, the Master won't let it happen."*

When Lynch finally answered, his voice was deep and menacing. *"I am a flea in his eyes. Why would he care now?"* Then, in a snap, I sensed the psychopath let his mania overrule his logic— he was losing control. He spoke slowly, savoring the words and memories. *"I...have...butchered...and maimed,"* a chuckle burst forth from him, *"and I'm rewarded with immortality?"* His laughter could be heard in the graves of those victims, I was sure. Chills ran down my spine, while Kat sat next to me, tittering about flowers as she flipped through bridal magazines. I welled up, but choked the tears down to grunt in agreement with whatever she said. I could only register her fiend fiancé's voice.

"Some old legend from another country has given me license to do what I do best! And no one stops me! The Master knows who I am, and he thinks Roman will take care of me? He knows better. He doesn't care!"

Nicholas had been silent through Lynch's self-serving rant. I realized there'd been no wave of frost crackle the room, so Nicholas had controlled *his* emotions, and spoke with measure. *"The Master believes you have a purpose, and once it's served no amount of money or charm or whatever you think you have won't save you. You'll pay dearly for what you've done."*

With another guttural laugh, *"So, I'll make the tally worth his while."*

"You know this woman is different."

"Then maybe this will be the one that makes the Master see me for once!" Lynch said through gritted teeth.

Now Nicholas laughed bitterly. *"Is that what all this is about? Because Daddy didn't hug you enough? Trust me, when the 'save the date' hits, you'll have gotten his attention."* He continued to laugh.

"SHUT UP!" Lynch bellowed with such force that my head automatically snapped to the side, but Kat was still oblivious, miraculously. How Nicholas invited me in to see all this…his abilities were incomprehensible to me. I shook my head.

"You think blue is better, then?" Kat asked, pointing to a page full of bridesmaid dresses.

"Uh, sorry, what was the first choice?"

"The green? I like that one, too!" She was sufficiently distracted while I channeled this new trick of seeing into another room.

Lynch was babbling now, trying to rationalize the monster he was, but Nicholas wasn't having it.

"It's not my fault that I can't turn the blood away. It nags me every millisecond. Why not give in? Humans come and go. I remain! I've chosen my piece more carefully this time. And I might keep her! Who knows? Maybe this is what I was designed for. To really throw a wrench in things! I mean, really, Katherine's the friend of someone very important. Otherwise, why would make such a fuss over one girl?"

My head swam.

"Are you done?" Nicholas said, and without waiting for a response, Nicholas slammed both fists into his face and stomach with the power of a bus. Lynch flew across the room, slamming into an expensive-looking vase. It burst into countless bits like it had been shot. Lynch bounced to his feet like nothing had happened. I stiffened as Lynch launched at Nicholas, knocking him to the floor, landing heavily atop him, but Nicholas threw him off fast. Again, Lynch destroyed another antique with an ear-splitting *bang!* Nicholas darted across the room and knocked the monster to the floor, crouching over him like a mountain lion, eyes cold, pointed teeth bared. Lynch struggled against the elder vampire's strength, but couldn't hope to match it. Instead, he laughed.

Nicholas did not. He spoke calmly, countering Lynch's

sputtering and cursing. *"You will call this travesty of a wedding off. You will do it with as little pain to Kat as possible. You will do it, or you know the Master will listen to me and tear you limb from limb himself. And the only thing I'll hear over your dying screams will be my own laughter."*

Time didn't pass before Nicholas was standing across the coffee table that was invisible under bridal magazines. He gave that humble smile to Kat with a sideways glance to me.

"I hope you two have had time to catch up. I need to get over to the book store, but Eliza, you can stay."

No. Not anywhere without him. "No," I said too quickly, jumping up. "I need a good book. So I'll come along."

Nicholas just nodded, but he let out a breath as he watched me get up. Still, he was giving me the opportunity for an out. One I wouldn't ever take, and he was hoping I wouldn't.

He, in all his perfection, still needed me.

My hand gravitated to the crook of his arm. Kat gave me a conspiratorial grin and stood up, too.

"No, totally, it's probably good that we start learning to say goodbye," she said lightly, but I heard the sadness. Saying goodbye to her made me sadder now than ever.

I wasn't one for hugging, but it was always second nature with Kat. I'd never have a friend like her again.

My chest went cold when I realized I was already thinking of her as dead.

"All right, break it up, she's mine now," Lynch said as he returned, unscathed from the hallway. I ignored him, but Kat pulled away, laughing.

"So, you're staying here now?" I said quietly, though I knew the answer.

"Yeah. Are you going home or to Nicholas's?"

I squeezed his arm a little tighter, and saw him smile from the corner of my eye.

"Same thing," I replied.

CHAPTER 29

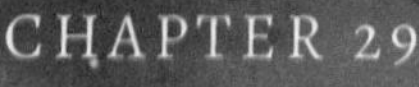

"**Y**ou look troubled. What's wrong?" He slid an old book onto the shelf near my head, a tiny cloud of dust puffing into the air. I hung my head, annoyed that I hadn't hidden my worry better. Nicholas continued to read me too accurately.

I picked up another musty book from the stack and placed it on the shelf as I carefully chose my words.

Turning to face him, I said, "My mind is getting stronger. I'm more connected—to you."

Creases appeared on his forehead. "Meaning?"

Glancing around to be sure no one was within earshot, we leaned in to each other.

"Nicholas, earlier today, at Lynch's…I *saw everything*."

At first, I don't think he knew what I meant, but quickly his eyes widened with understanding. He grasped my arm urgently, and before I knew it we were at the other end of the shop. "You can do that, move like that with me, too?" I gasped, chest heaving like I'd been running. It would be easier to believe I transported than that I'd been running.

Still gripping my arm, eyes trained on my face, he pulled

me onto the window seat, set back into a remote wall that guaranteed us some privacy. "Please explain what that means," he said.

"I knew it! I shouldn't be able to see or hear what was happening in there! I was hoping you could tell *me* what it means."

Now it was his turn to look troubled. He whizzed off to the old coffee maker behind the cash register, and returned with to hand me a cup of burnt-smelling coffee in a moose mug.

I'd figured out on the car ride to the book store that Nicholas hadn't given me the vision of his fight with Lynch, but that I'd somehow *taken* it. Because as much as I hated to admit it, Nicholas was holding out on me still. He never told me the big secret he'd planned to share the night he went into his trance, and Lynch had said I was "important." Nicholas would have known I'd start piecing clues together, and he was chickening out about telling me what I needed to know.

And after hearing him in my head more than once, after all the time we'd been spending together, it made sense to me— the bond was growing between us. And I wanted it. Anything that drew me closer to him was what I needed. And sitting here, in my favorite place, sharing a quiet moment full of new possibility and mystery, was perfection to me, no matter what mystical weirdness came with it.

Nicholas seemed to be thinking the same thing, because he gave me the mischievous grin I loved. His eyes were shot with excitement as he took a gulp of his own coffee.

I told him everything I'd seen and heard; how it was like I'd been split between the two spots in the house while it all happened. I told him I heard Lynch say I was important, but Nicholas breezed over it, shaking his head, an odd look on his face, but not an unpleasant one. Like he could ever look unpleasant to me.

"Never heard of anything like this," he mumbled. "I know vampires without the control to do what you did, after decades or more of practice, and here you are, human…"

"But," I interrupted, "I only have these abilities when it pertains to you. It's not like I can watch Kat do the dishes while I watch TV or something."

"How do you know? Have you ever tried?"

"I just know."

I ached to ask him what *he* knew; what he meant to tell me the night he went comatose, who the Master was, how he really felt about me. I hungered to tell him how I felt about him, and all of these changes, but I still clung to my guard, when I should have had no secrets from him.

"The only thing that worries me," I said with a near-shame of myself, "is that the stronger this—relationship—becomes, the more terrified I am of being apart from you. Ever."

A sad softness took over his face, so tender that my eyes moistened to see it. "The thought of being away from you—" The anguish I couldn't disguise in my face hardened him. I saw his need to protect me from the pain, and I longed for it. I was, as ever, desperate for him to be as freakishly attached as I was.

"Eliza. Vampires, in general, don't make short-term relationships. And I…well, I don't make relationships in general."

"No. I mean, the thought of you being ten feet away in another room. The concept of you in your house and me in my apartment…"

Guilt distorted his face, and he hung his head. I bent mine to find his eyes.

"Eliza, that's part of the vampire's thrall. I didn't do it on purpose. You've been bewitched." He snapped his head up. "Your will is not your own."

To never know if a person was with you by choice or not—it's no wonder he kept to himself.

What a fool he was to think that of me.

"That's not what's happening here."

"Eliza, don't be naïve!" he shouted. Heads turned. In his sadness he forgot to put up his veil to shield us. In a quiet, but no less urgent voice, he went on. "I'm a predator, sweet girl. And you are a far too willing victim."

I couldn't help it. I laughed at him. "So you think I'm a slave, right? Powerless against you? Nicholas, I could get up and walk out that door right now. The pain would be—searing —but I'd endure. I always endure."

"You're kidding yourself."

"Really? Is part of your super-thrall that you're also in gut-wrenching agony when I leave *you*?" He grimaced at my mocking tone and hand gestures, but I could tell he was thinking on it. "And, Nicholas, why would the *thrall*," again with mocking finger quotations, "work on me when your veil or shield or what-have-you, doesn't?" Surprise replaced his shame now. "Nicholas, I can sense so much in you, do you think I wouldn't notice you 'bewitching' me, even if you didn't know you were doing it?"

"You have a point," he said in wonderment and confusion.

"I had many. Nicholas, this connection means something more." Suddenly I became shy and averted my eyes.

Nicholas murmured, "This connection is like nothing I've ever experienced. For once, I'm afraid. And I like it."

CHAPTER 30

We finished our coffee, and went back to work shelving books until dark. The odd jobs were Nicholas's excuse to leave Kat and Lynch, to enjoy something warm and loved that didn't involve a maniac. The familiarity of the musty books, the floating dust, the alcoves and hidden corners gave me security, made me not quite so out of my element. However, sure that Roman was dying to know what had happened with Lynch, we decided to get on our way.

"What will you tell Roman about what happened with Lynch?"

"You say that like I plan important conversations, which I don't."

"Yeah, you could put that on a business card."

He chuckled, a warm, grumbly sound. "Eliza, I did some thinking. I just wanted to say, even before you told me about your 'separation anxiety,' for lack of a better phrase, that I want you to come live with Roman and I. It's already your home, but I wanted to officially ask—again."

My heart pounded, and I breathed out a "yes, thank you," with nervous laughter.

"I'm afraid for you to be alone in that wretched apartment."

"It's not wretched, I love that apartment. Not to mention you hurt when you're away from me, too." Way to stupidly test a good thing by opening my mouth, as usual, Ellie.

He laughed jovially. "Yes, you egomaniac."

I laughed, too, but I don't know how funny either of us found the prospect of agony controlling us like that. Pain or no pain, I never wanted to leave his side, no matter what it cost me. Maybe it didn't even matter if he wanted me—I knew what I had to have. If he never loved me like I loved him, I'd still want to be near him, always.

"Quite honestly, I can't bear the idea of being without Kat in our apartment, knowing where she is now."

"I don't trust Lynch to leave you be. He knows how important you are to me, you've got a target on you."

My rashness surfaced again. I stared at him for a second, and asked, "Exactly how important?"

He looked at me, bemused. "Well, I can't be without you," he said so matter-of-factly that it pissed me off.

"Why not? Because of the pain? Or is it more than that, Nicholas?" Silence. So I pressed on as he wound through the sloppy, snowy road toward my apartment so I could pick up some things. "I pretty obviously am wearing my heart on my sleeve here. Right?"

His fingers curled like iron snakes around the steering wheel, and I stopped asking. His whole idea that this fear of my power over him "felt good" made him as stubborn as a brick wall.

He pulled up in front of the old bed and breakfast. For a split second the image crossed my mind of me slowly closing my apartment door, Nicholas in the dark hall, as I said, "I'll see you tomorrow."

A blade of heat stabbed into my gut. I gasped and doubled over. Nicholas's hand on my knee brought me back to life.

"Let's go get some of your things," he said somberly.

So long it seemed, it could have been weeks that passed since Kat and I separated for Christmas. It was like I was breaking and entering as I turned the key. I walked in anyway, the dark inside swallowing me. When I flicked on the light, my mouth dried up.

Not one thing of Kat's was visible anywhere. Her slippers that were always by the door, her family photos, her pile of DVDs next to, not inside the empty DVD cabinet that always drove me nuts. She'd been erased.

Nicholas cleared his throat from the doorway. "Forgetting something?" he asked.

"What? Oh." He ran his eyes over the doorframe. "Oh! I'm such a jerk! I would like you to enter," I said with weird formality.

He snickered as he glided in, tossing his coat on a chair. "You fell for that! I can't believe it! I've already been in your apartment, anyway."

"Right," I scoffed, grinning and loosening up. I thought how it never freaked me out, Nicholas creeping around in here, through my private things. We shared something more private than underwear and pajamas.

I grabbed an old suitcase from the closet—one that had been here when the bed and breakfast closed. I couldn't bear to get rid of it, something left behind, uncared for—and went to my room to fill it up, Nicholas right behind me. I didn't open Kat's bedroom door. I knew it would look like a dead place inside.

"He did this, didn't he? Clear the apartment of her stuff?" I asked.

"Yes." He breathed in deeply. "Her scent doesn't linger at all. He took every last piece."

A loud sob fled my lips. *"Every last piece"* made me think of dismemberment, falling apart, broken, and I couldn't think of those things in relation to Kat. I was the broken one, Kat was the whole and full one.

A faint *whoosh*, and Nicholas's arms were around my waist, his mighty chest pressed to my back with a gentle strength.

"I won't allow him to take her from you. He won't win this."

I turned into his waiting arms and cried until I thought I would collapse. I cried until the rawness tore at my throat like claws. I cried until finally, my heart slowed and I could hear beyond its pounding again.

Nicholas released me cautiously, his eyes on my chest where my heart drummed.

"You," my throat reeled in pain at that first word, "you can *hear* my heart beating. Or feel it?"

He blinked, the first time his eyes left my heart. "I can almost taste it," he crooned, smelling a strand of my hair.

I swallowed, unsure whether I should fear the vampire or desire the man. His eyes shot to the lump in my throat, and smoldered.

I quickly pushed my lips onto his before he could stop me. My hands pulled the curls on the back of his head to keep him in that kiss, for as long as I could force it.

But I didn't have to. Nicholas's warm, soft tongue idled about mine. He groaned, long and deep, as he breathed in. I felt the weight of his hand on my heart, pounding again, and nearly cried out when it slid gracefully over my breast. A whimper fell from my lips, breaking the lock we had on each other.

"Eliza," he breathed, but I'd already pulled away.

"I know. Not here, not now."

"It's not fair to you."

"I hardly care about fair at the moment," I joked. I pulled the suitcase to standing. "But I know now. That there's more to this story. I can see it in your heart, plain as day. And when it's time for you to show it to me, things will change."

"Or maybe they won't," he added.

"I don't want to be here anymore," I said, but he'd already moved me outside with a brush of his fingers.

~

The sense of finality was oppressive. Kat was in Lynch's hands now.

Nicholas had paid the apartment's rent for the next six months. He seemed to understand my unspoken need to still have the place that was mine and Kat's, to hold on to, just for now. Even so, his enthusiasm about my moving in to the cabin, while simultaneously keeping me safe from Lynch's killing whims was infectious. He talked with lightning speed about how he'd make me more comfortable, with construction ideas to give me more room. I didn't mention my dream of a horror-themed movie theater, complete with massive cutouts of Swamp Thing and the Wolfman at the door dressed like ushers; he'd make it happen. Besides, the creep factor would attract yet more crows, knowing my luck.

Quite seriously, I was praying my little spare room would eventually be occupied by dust only. I had my eye on another spot.

The strength of my connection to Nicholas was increasing all the time. Knowing that the bond we had was—inhuman—I still wasn't fazed. For all the fear and uncertainty the unpredictability my life had slipped into like a new jacket, the "monster" that held my hand made it all go away.

CHAPTER 31

The clacking of my high-heeled feet on the walkway couldn't drown out the pounding of my heart as we approached Lynch's house. My jitters were multi-faceted. I'd be lying if I said none of it was excitement. It was New Year's Eve, and I was actually okay with being all dressed up, arm in arm with His Magnificence. Not to mention that I was electrified by the glamorous affair I knew we were in for. No matter how loathsome the host may be.

I inhaled sharply when Nicholas rang the doorbell. Sugary vanilla encircled my frozen nose as Nicholas breathed in my ear, "Try to have fun. You are with me, after all."

A tuxedoed doorman smiled at us with trained respect. He took our coats and gloves and escorted us into the "Great Room." Pretentious jackass, Lynch.

"Great" doesn't begin to describe the glittering elegance, the sparkling wonderland that had been created for this night. This was a dream New Year's Eve party for Kat if she could afford it. Now she could. I was fleetingly happy for her.

The stuffy, impersonal air of Lynch's Christmas party was only a memory here. Laughter cut through the seductively dark room, lit only by ice blue lights and countless candles. Clinking flutes of twinkling pink champagne took on a life of their own. I didn't recognize the music—like the Nutcracker Suite with sex appeal. The air was fragrant with a hundred perfumes flirting.

A soft, strong sexiness in myself emerged in this environment that nourished it. I traced the groove in Nicholas's hand with my fingertip, and he chuckled low.

A smiling stranger in a silver dress with an apron offered us champagne. Even the way Nicholas smoothly pulled his hand from mine to take the two glasses with a smile of his own set a fire in me. He was such a creature of comfort, but looked as at home as James Bond in his tuxedo, and twice as debonair. How every set of eyes in this misty room weren't on him, I couldn't understand. I watched the silent movie of Nicholas greeting this one or that like an old friend, nodding across the room, flashing a god's smile.

The amused twinkle in his eye flickered out; he'd caught sight of Lynch. So had I. He was telling some exciting lie to an enraptured audience, all of them laughing and *oohing* appropriately. More handsome than he had a right to be in a disgustingly expensive suit, hair smoothed back in movie star style, oozing elegance.

To me it looked as though he'd just bathed in blood, so vile he was with the stench of murder.

And my little Kat, caught up in the laughter at his side, light exuding from her in all her goodness and playfulness. She glistened in an ice blue strapless gown, the queen of this winter palace, in diamonds and sapphires the size of snowballs. Her laugh was the clink of countless champagne flutes.

Not far behind, Roman stood, a polished and stately gentleman as usual, one hand in his pocket, the other cradling a glass. His always thoughtful eyes were trained on Kat, a heavenly guardian to the unsuspecting woman. I breathed a sigh of mild relief. He raised his glass to me when he looked away from Kat long enough.

"Would you like to dance?" Nicholas whispered in my ear.

I looked to the area that had become a dance floor. A dozen beautiful people spun and swirled in a punchbowl of color.

Not enough people for me to blend in, certainly not while dancing with Nicholas.

"Don't pay attention to them," Nicholas said, and whisked me off in one smooth symphony of movement. A nervous laugh burst from me, and soon was accompanied by more and more giggles as Nicholas twisted me around the floor in grandiose motions, made light in his silly, mocking faces. He provided dancefloor commentary in a French accent, a terrible French accent. I loved that he could laugh at himself as much as at everybody else; it put me right at ease. Without so much as a drink, I was tipsy and carefree, in his arms like Ginger Rogers. Fred never looked so good, sophisticated grace and hulking masculinity in perfect pairing.

The scene was a picturesque, enchanting dream. I allowed it to last for a while, spinning and sipping, laughing and flirting, loving the fairy tale time with the stunning prince whose eyes were for me tonight.

Kat and I periodically broke away to a little cove behind the silver and blue monster of a Christmas tree to giggle and gossip and point to this or that stunning person. She was delightful, so clearly in love, she glowed the way you read about in romance novels. I wanted that joyfulness to be real for her, so very much. Guilt crept into my conscience because of how I feared it, how I knew the lies he was feeding her. She was in love with someone that didn't exist.

"What is that look that crosses you? Right there?" She pointed a polished fingertip at my creased brow. She knew me too well.

"Nothing, Kat," I said rubbing her arm affectionately. "I just love you, that's all. I want you to be the happiest person I've ever seen forever."

A slow grin stretched across her face, and I knew that at this silver and blue misty moment, she was.

Her head turned at the instant Lynch's slippery voice broke through the music and chorus of guests.

"Everyone, if I could bother you for your attention, please."

Kat shot me a sideways glance, excitement bouncing in her eyes. She skittered to his side, both of them illuminated in frosty sapphire light that turned glasses of red wine purple. Guests encircled the couple to hear the announcement. I shook.

Nicholas wasn't expecting the public announcement at all. I saw the plan was Lynch's, in his defiantly ecstatic leer, in the way he kissed Kat's apple blossom cheek. He owned his world here. Not even Nicholas would stop him.

Lynch already looked like the tiny groom on top of the cake. "Ladies and gentlemen, friends. First, I want to thank you all for coming tonight, to ring in the new year with us. It never gets old, right Roman?" Misunderstanding chuckles vibrated through the crowd. Roman's face was solemn.

Nicholas was nowhere in sight, but I felt him. If I wasn't so intent on Lynch's words, I would have been able to see him in my mind's eye.

Kat beamed at Lynch's side, his arm embracing her against him. Lynch continued, "I hope to have the pleasure of seeing you all again in one month to celebrate my marriage to this outstanding woman by my side."

Excited gasps burst from every corner, with shrieks of joy or shock. My mouth hung slack. So this was Lynch's way of rebelling, showing he had no intent of doing the right thing. I hoped Nicholas was ready to make good on his threats quickly. My soul reached to find him, desperate for his reaction.

I didn't have far to go. A river of hoarfrost inched up my bare leg, crackled across the marble floor, spreading a film of winter on every object it touched.

Nicholas glided past me on a bitter breeze, eyes fixed on Lynch, who was shaking dozens of hands and lying.

Nicholas intruded upon them all, every one of them seemingly oblivious to the extent of the climate change. A shawl pulled tighter here and there, giving away that not everything could be hidden by the vampires.

Hysteria choked me as flickers of Nicholas and Lynch's prior physical battle returned to memory. It didn't matter that Nicholas was the stronger of the two, my gut wrenched at the danger for him. Surely, that sort of thing couldn't happen now, with all of these people?

I was very wrong. Nicholas's b-line ended abruptly with an explosive kick that threw Lynch into the closest wall, sending an enormous painting clattering to the floor. Kat, inches away from the impact, was tittering with a guest who also appeared to have noticed nothing.

And so it was that way throughout the party, as if a bubble formed around everything Lynch and Nicholas did or touched, even the property breaking. Clinking glasses seemed to erase the violence so close at hand. Nicholas had a spluttering Lynch pinned to the wall, ice in a halo around his head. I was awed at Nicholas's power to shield so thoroughly.

Roman appeared at Nicholas's side, and placed a featherweight hand on his arm, breaking his concentration for a second, one awful second. Lynch bucked him off, and Nicholas cried out as he flew backwards, ever so slightly touching the open flame in the fireplace with his heels.

"Nicholas!" I screamed, and *everyone* turned my way.

So that's where the shield ended. *Fix it, fix it...*

"Nicholas, can I see you on the porch?" I asked awkwardly across the room, in a shrill voice. Two men in tuxedos and a man in a dark blue suit stooped to pick up the fallen painting, unquestioning as to how it came to fall. The frame's scrape on the floor was the only thing to be heard.

"Good, then, yes," Nicholas replied coolly, and strolled with ease toward the porch, straightening his jacket. I expected my heels to sound like dropping bombs across the floor, but the party resumed seamlessly. We left Roman amidst its hubbub, the French doors shutting behind us.

"They named these doors after me," Nicholas said dryly as they clicked closed.

Not to be distracted, I spun on my too-tall heels to face him. "Nicholas! What were you trying to do in there?! All those people? And what if you were…" I couldn't think of anything at that moment except the fire circling his leg like a python. "Let me see it," I said with thorns in my voice.

He made a flirtatiously surprised face when I gestured to his leg, and waved me over. He fell into a nearby chair, and pulled up the leg of his pants, revealing a calf so muscular, so perfectly toned and—alive—I shook my head to focus.

"Pull down your sock, Nicholas," I demanded.

His ankle was charred completely, black as coal. His amber scent mixed with the broken flesh. Tears sprang to my eyes.

"No, no, no," he pleaded, cupping my face in his palms. "Eliza, it will heal when I feed again." He saw how much I wanted that to be true. "Scout's honor."

Smiling meekly, I sat with him and chuckled under my breath. "Do you remember the first time we sat out here together?"

"I remember everything about that night."

"You told me we were kindred spirits," I said. "I still find it hard to believe that someone like you would want me."

The speed and coolness of his words cut me. "Fate takes

choices away, Eliza, and leaves us with purpose." His perfectly imperfect face was nearly touching mine, his breath stealing mine away, eyes a sugary mix of caramel and coffee, boring deep into mine. "Eliza. Your life is not your own."

"No. You own it," I sighed, taking his hand and holding it like it might get away. "Nicholas, these past weeks have been the strangest, but happiest of my life. Something finally *happened* to me." He was silent, and I yammered on, emotion spilling out of me like champagne on the dancefloor. "I mean, I didn't just sit around waiting for something to happen all these years—"

"Yes you did."

"Maybe a little. But I couldn't find…what to do next. Where I was supposed to go to find this *thing* that was waiting for me, that the damn crows are always hanging over my head." I shot a dirty look at a pair of them on the railing, and they flew away fast. "And then you came to me. No more looking required."

"I know you can taste it, smell it, *understand* it. Destiny is waiting to claim you, Eliza."

Anger flared at the misinterpretation of my words, and at the absurd vagueness of his. I threw his hand down and stood.

"I pour my heart out, and this Illuminati crap is what I get from you. Stop doing this! You tell me what you mean! You tell me now what you *always mean!*"

He rose to stand close to me again, a faraway smile showing how unruffled by my outburst he was.

"A new year, and a new life," he said, as much to himself as to me. His eyes were unfocused, silly smile still on his lips, as he brushed a stray strand of dark hair from my forehead. The easy contentment in him eliminated my anger as quickly as it had arrived.

The sound of the huge grandfather clock chiming midnight arrested me from the moment, and Nicholas pulled me back with a baby-soft kiss, drowning out sound, thought, time. Worlds of unspoken need coursed through me, waiting impatiently for him to hear them.

The world came back, screaming, with the last chime of the clock. We parted lips gently to the sound of party horns and noisemakers and singing. Joy, covered me like a quilt.

"Happy new year," he breathed, his hand still cool around the back of my neck.

"Happy new year, Nicholas," I managed through the ruckus in my head. God help me, I *was* happy, no matter what else happened. I laughed out loud, almost inappropriately. I couldn't stop myself. Turns out, I didn't have to.

Nicholas's eyes glazed over, and the neverending storm in them froze. I froze, too.

"Nicholas?"

Not again.

Please, please, not the catatonia, I can't do it again, not if I lived forever...

But his mouth twitched, flashing the tips of his fangs. His eyes returned to their usual motion. "I have to feed again."

My stomach flipped with a gurgle of champagne, but I hardened my jaw. This was the price of keeping his company. "It's okay," I said firmly. "Do we need to leave? What should we do?" I asked, trying to create order, to find my place in this.

"I don't know. Not yet," he said.

The French doors swung open, and Kat ran out in a whirlwind of chiming laughter to throw her arms around me, a trickle of her champagne spilling down my back. I laughed heartily, and she kissed me hard on the cheek before dashing back inside.

Still laughing, I turned back to Nicholas. He was shaking so hard that the legs of the chair danced. His eyes were wide with fear. He could be afraid?

"Nicholas! What is it?"

Before he could answer, I knew.

His tortured eyes moved slowly to me, mouth slack, ready to plead with me. When he spoke the word, acid strangled my veins.

"Katherine."

CHAPTER 32

I think I stumbled backwards, but it was impossible to remember anything except what I said next.

"You stay away from her."

His amazing face became that of a vampire's to me, whether or not I saw fangs. A flood of adrenaline seized me. "You stay away from both of us," I choked out. As I said it, tears in my voice, the pain that had waited to seize me all along grasped me. It needed me to run from him.

The pain wanted me alone, just like death had wanted me alone all this time. Now they were partners, and I didn't stand a chance.

The matching shudder of pain that rippled through Nicholas couldn't matter to me. He doubled over, letting out a cry of shock as he clutched his stomach. That the pain returned with such ferocity to us both told me without a doubt that the little life I'd lived with Nicholas was over.

I had to get away from him, I had to get Kat out of this world of death, and forget it ever happened.

I don't know how I came to be at Kat's car, how I'd made it through the party, or how I'd managed to drag Kat with me. I remember that she didn't understand what I was talking about, babbling as I must have been, terrified and tipsy.

"No one here wants to hurt me, Ellie," she'd said, very calmly, concern gathering in her eyes. I told her she couldn't stay with Lynch, that he was an animal and could never be trusted.

Her face hardened then.

I told her Nicholas wasn't who I thought he was, and that we had to go far away from them both. The hardness in her soft, pretty face became anger.

She spoke very slowly, the anger fueling every word. "Ellie, look. If things aren't good for Nicholas and you, I'm sorry. But things *are* good for me and Chris. How can you try to ruin this for me?" Her cheeks turned hot pink, her voice broke when her sympathy resurfaced. "Ellie, I miss you, too. But my life has changed now. I'm sorry."

She walked away as I called after her. I watched her go like I was seeing her for the last time. One crow perched on the path before me, its own friend gone.

∼

I'd started walking, tottering in the snow without my coat, away from Lynch's house, sobbing. A black SUV pulled up alongside me, and I nearly screamed, thinking it was Nicholas, but a gentle-looking elderly man rolled down the window.

"Miss Morgan, your host has sent me to bring you wherever you'd like to go."

"What? No, that's okay—"

"It's quite all right, miss, several people will be driven home after this party, I'm quite sure. Allow yourself to be one of them," he said.

I choked up at what a nice gesture it was, how kind this

man was, and when he held up my coat that had been on the passenger's seat, I sobbed.

"Miss. With all due respect, where are you going to go in the dark and cold, in the woods, alone? It's not safe, miss."

"It wasn't safe where I was, either," I said, voice trembling. A crow landed on my shoulder, and I reached a hand up to rest on it. Its beak nuzzled against my neck. It wasn't strange; it was right.

The driver blinked rapidly, eyes on the bird. "Pardon?"

"Nothing." I shivered, and he smiled slightly, not wishing to offend, but the offense didn't come from him. I was pissed that Lynch came to my rescue, and that I'd needed rescuing at all. *He* was the monster in the woods.

But he wasn't the only one.

I sat beside the old man and had him bring me to the only place I had to go—the apartment I'd shared with Kat. I didn't want to get out of the car.

What was I expecting? To feel at home? To outrun the pain and the memories and the danger? I just wanted home as I knew it but the heat was turned off, the electricity gone. More or less discarded pieces of furniture still lived here, while the place just existed. I'd have to call the landlord, tell him I was back. Not that he'd care, the rent was paid for six more months. But I would need to get my job back.

The pain strangled me. Making me pay for my stupidity.

I watched the sun rise.

Days later, I watched the sun rise again. Still no electricity. It would have just taken a phone call, but my phone was dead in my coat pocket, and there was no electricity to charge it, and all of that required movement. And I just sat, hurting, shaking. For the first time since New Year's, I truly thought of Nicholas. I wondered if he was sleeping then or if the pain was too harsh.

I closed my eyes for a second and a vision of him threatened to come to me. I willed it away. I refused to see that face. I wasn't sure what it would do to me, or if I even cared. That I did not want to see Nicholas in any way, I knew for sure.

Another thing I knew for sure was that Kat would die.

Time passed. I shook sometimes, my teeth chattering, the tremors adding to, but never replacing the pain.

The only reason I knew my body had not given up, even if my soul had, was the need for water. I concentrated hard on it, to ease the shaking, because I knew that the shaking came with thoughts of Kat. It was much easier not to think, just need.

I clung to the arms of the awful chair, noticing for the first time in days how weak I'd become. The chair was facing our kitchenette, so walking straight to it from my place by the window would be easy.

Standing was agonizing. The ever-present pain relished my weakness, hating me with each horrible step. I couldn't cry. I didn't have the strength.

When was the last time I'd eaten? Or used the bathroom?

Finally, I fell into the counter, and scrambled pathetically at a glass in the dish drainer. I dropped and broke one. The defeat of it was enough to elicit a sob. I reached for another, and my legs gave out from a pain that shot through my stomach and ran up my back like a many-clawed creature. I caught myself by the cabinet door handle and dragged myself back up.

The water ran down my chin, ice-cold on my clammy skin. My fingers were an unhealthy shade of purple with cold.

A wave of nausea heated me for a moment following the water. I still drank another glass, gagging. Suddenly ravenous, I scanned the counter for food. Frenzied, I slapped open the cabinets, and found a box of Ritz crackers amidst cans of food I wouldn't be able to wait long enough to prepare.

Falling to the floor, I jammed handful after handful into

my mouth, scattering crumbs all over the place. With these simple human things done, I was more myself, no matter how much I willed awareness away.

I pushed myself to take a freezing shower, and still had enough old clothes I didn't like in the apartment to keep myself decent. Doing all these routine things here, in this shell of a home, sent pangs of loneliness through me for Kat. The ever-present loom of death around me made my stomach ache for her.

Him, I couldn't think about. The pain that swallowed me with every movement did the thinking for me.

Silence surrounded me here, as I sat, mind blank, on the bed still made as it was that day, so long ago to me now; the day I went home with him, and said goodbye to my home here. Throbbing infused my arms and legs and head with fury. Stinging bile rose in my throat at the thought of him. With morbid curiosity, I wondered what he was doing, and faced the question I'd tried so hard to avoid.

Had he already submitted to the thirst beckoning him?

I couldn't hold the bile back. Dry heaving and crying, screaming, I thought I'd go insane with images of Nicholas tearing at Kat's throat, she as trusting as always, never seeing it coming. Would he put her in a thrall so she'd be numb to pain and regret?

Nicholas told me of the *Shinigami* thrall, one I was certain had no control over me. What if all this time he only toyed with me to get to her? What if all of his bullshit talk of fate was a lie to draw us both in? Were they lies if he told me that vampires cannot be trusted? Did I really need to be told not to trust a vampire?

I was standing now, becoming increasingly more alert and aware of myself. Stronger.

I didn't like it.

A tumult of awful questions about Nicholas, how much of

him was real, memories that were the best of my life, all a sham. Him, luring me in with talk of destiny, ruining my life. I had no job, half-squatting in my abandoned apartment, nothing to look forward to. I should have turned him away the first time he asked me to go outside, but I was stupid to think he knew something about me, that I was something different.

And my only friend...

Was I too late already? What could I do to save her?

The blinding pain sent me crashing to the floor, writhing like a pinned snake. Just in case I forgot that I was alone, there it was, killing me slowly, every second I was away from him.

He'd said this agony tortured him, too.

I could no longer believe him.

He was the one who did this to me.

As if to prove it to myself, I let my mind open to him, something I'd refused to do since the night he betrayed me. The vision blossomed into view beautifully.

Nicholas's serene little bedroom, Zen-like and soft. It was daytime. It was now. He sat, shivering on the floor. As I watched, he clamped onto his head and screamed, long and horribly, deranged in his pain.

A stab of longing to fix it, and guilt tore through my broken heart.

I growled, and shut him out. It was a lie. He made me see that. It wasn't real, like everything else I'd had with him, fake.

I screamed, frustration and anger boiling out of me in fits of pain. I don't know how long I screamed for, only that when it was over, I was hungry again. Darkness had crushed the apartment, with only streetlights outside to give me any sense of life at all.

I couldn't stay there. But I had no one to go to.

"Eliza?"

I jumped with a cry of shock at the sound of my name,

afraid of anyone who would want anything from me right now.

Again, the voice looking for me, from out in the hall.

Slowly, I dragged myself to the door. I had no reason to be scared. I had nothing left to lose.

"Roman."

Shock made him blink too fast, and stutter. "Oh," he finally said, pity in his eyes. "Oh, Eliza." He moved toward me as if to hug me, but my spirit couldn't take it. I flinched away, like a beaten dog. He dropped his arms, and let himself into the black apartment, heavenly blue eyes trained on me, cutting through the dark.

"Eliza, we have to make this right."

The vicious growl that emanated from me in my response surprised us both. "Make it right? How dare you say that? Like I did something wrong."

"I'm sorry," he whispered, barely audibly. The quiet was as impenetrable as the dark. I hated the falseness of it.

"What do you want, Roman?" I spat. "Did he send you here to *collect* me?"

"No, he doesn't know I'm here. Eliza, it's been over a week, and he's fading fast. And the agony he's in, Eliza, you can't believe it."

"Shut up! *His* pain? I can't even... You're lying for him. What I see, it's him, trying to control my mind—"

"No, Eliza, no, his pain is terrible, I've never seen anything so horrific." Then silence. "And, Eliza, if he doesn't feed soon—"

"Get out! Get out, Roman! You're like him, you're making me believe. Stop! And go home! Please."

Scarcely able to make out his distraught face in the darkness, I watched his silhouette as he drifted out the door, closing it silently behind him.

CHAPTER 33

The following few days brought more and more lucidity and survival skill, but not more sanity. While I was able to do things like have my utilities turned back on, and do some grocery shopping, each breath was accompanied by blasting pain. My body trembled whenever I slowed down, whenever it was allowed to concentrate on the agony.

He had done this to me.

The pain begged me to return to Nicholas, every minute of every day. I continually reminded myself that he'd deluded me, and continued to do so in my thoughts; he'd infiltrated. I didn't have to remind myself that he intended to murder my best friend in this world. That is, if Lynch didn't beat him to it.

She wasn't returning my calls. I can only imagine how insane my messages must have sounded, going on about how she was in danger, for her to *really* look at him, that she couldn't trust the abomination she loved.

Every message, I left out that Lynch was a vampire. It's difficult to say whether it was in effort to make myself sound plausible or to protect Nicholas. I hated myself for thinking it could be the latter.

The fifth day after Roman came to plead with me, I allowed myself another vision. Nicholas was gray, the color of old coals. His eyes were dull and bloodshot. He trembled as he moved.

I recognized that shaking. It mirrored my own.

Roman was with him in their kitchen. How I had loved that room in all its country warmth. That restful belonging couldn't have been a lie; it was a *room*, it was a real thing. I grunted with the effort of reigning in my train of thought.

Roman asked Nicholas to please feed, on someone, just to stop the pain.

"It won't help. You know that." Nicholas's voice was guttural, emanating dryness, like he'd just come out of a fire.

"Then you know what you must do, Nicholas. Stop trying to be a hero. Be what you are. You know in your heart that you're not helping Kat." The words were so cold and unlike Roman, I could hardly believe he said them at all.

Nicholas seemed just as surprised, from what expression his gaunt, hollow face could emit. "Death incarnate" took on a new meaning for this vampire now. My heart cried out at the clear pain in his features.

"This," Nicholas spat, gesturing at his shaking thinness, *"is not for Kat's sake! This isn't even about what's right for Eliza, but I don't know how else to keep her, Roman!"* Exhaustion crumpled his face. *"Starving myself, trying to spare Kat's life can't hide that I'm not good enough for this world, and certainly not for Eliza."* The dejected pain and loneliness emptied his voice of life. *"But like any good monster, I'll do anything to keep her."*

I shut off the vision like a light switch, and silence enveloped me. Pain came screeching back, murdering any comfort I may have had. It confirmed what I knew with growing reluctance.

I had to make a move, and quickly. Any change in this situation had to help.

Time was dwindling.

CHAPTER 34

Part of that change occurred with little help from me. Kat came to my door—our apartment door. It was so wonderful to see her face, the brutal pain all but disappeared. She sat in the ugly chair we'd inherited with the place, twirling her fingers around a loose thread in the arm, while I stood. We looked at one another, troubled.

"Ellie, I'm so sorry," she blurted out. "I don't know exactly what's bothering you most, if it's Chris, or Nicholas, or just you and I separating, but I have complete trust in you, and you just scared me, Ellie."

"I know, I know."

"And now, here you are, alone in this place, and you look like you've dropped fifteen pounds, and like you've just…been *rotting* here," she said sadly.

I looked at the floor, ashamed.

"What's going on, Ellie? And please, don't try to protect me like you always do. Please just tell me exactly what's happening, and I'll listen to you."

I couldn't look up. The draw was too great to say it all, just blurt out that they were all vampires, and that now I didn't know which was the most dangerous to her. I ground my teeth.

The disgusting fact was that I knew it would endanger Nicholas to tell her anything of the sort. I knew he meant to kill her, and I still couldn't put him at risk. It didn't matter why.

I silently prayed to a God I'd long since ignored that I hadn't just made a terrible choice. That I hadn't just chosen Nicholas's life over Kat's.

"Nicholas and I aren't together anymore," I said vaguely.

"Were you really together at all?"

"No. No, I guess not. But we won't be seeing each other. That doesn't have anything to do with my feelings about Lynch, though."

"And what are your feelings about Chris, Ellie?"

I took a deep breath. She had asked me not to protect her.

"What if I told you that I know he killed that girl in the park? And that I know he kills—a lot?"

Her eyes grew pitiless. "I'd say you were absolutely nuts."

My head dropped again.

"But," she went on, "you're my best friend. My family. And I believe in you. So tell me what you think you know before I come to my senses."

~

Reliving that day in Singing Pines Park was dreadful. The sight of Christine Simmons, struggling like a doomed doe, the escaped drops of red blood on the snow; it was so very different from my memories of Nicholas and the man in the cabin, and what his death was like.

I sickened myself.

I continued with as many details as I could give her, without telling her about the *Shinigami.*

"How do you know this?" she whispered.

"I can't tell you that. I'm so sorry."

"What do you want me to say, Ellie?" she asked in a low, cautious tone, eyeing me with worry.

Well, if I didn't resign to this now, it would all have been for nothing, a wasted opportunity to change the course of this nightmare. So, I summoned every bit of blind faith I had, and I begged her. I begged her to leave Lynch, for her own safety, my own sanity, for her very life.

"We'll both go, Kat. We need to be away from them both. You say you trust me, and I know you do, so please trust me on this one."

She was quiet, really considering what I'd said, which I give her credit for. But we both knew what her choice would be.

Her whispered words had all the impact of a tidal wave. "Ellie. You've been the most important person in my life for so long. I love you. But the time's come for us to grow up, beyond our jobs and the constant slumber party. We need—*I* need—to pursue this relationship. We're getting *married*. I love him, Ellie. I cannot believe he's a psychotic killer any more than I could believe it of you. I'm sorry. I know you believe the things you're telling me, and you always look out for me, but it's time I looked out for myself. I wish things were as easy for you and Nicholas as they have been for me and Chris, but that doesn't mean you can keep me as your back-up plan."

She'd risen and gone to the door. My body was numb.

"Ellie, why don't you come and stay with us? It's miserable here. I miss pizza night. You're my sister, Ellie."

"I can't be near him, Kat."

And at that, she left.

∽

That night, the nightmares began. They replaced the nothingness of the constant pain. I still don't know which I loathed more. Every night new, always Kat's torture and slow murder. Some nights it was Lynch, but some nights—some nights Nicholas ravaged her throat brutally, grunting like a bear, chunks of her flesh falling to the ground as I screamed and tried to pull her convulsing body away before she was nothing. The words screamed in the air around me; *unmei nashi.*

No fate.

I'd wake up like I'd swallowed razors.

My only escape from the physical agony of my every minute was when sleep stole my consciousness, only to destroy me in dreams. Death, death, death. My thoughts were on constant replay.

I was totally alone. There was no one to help me, not even a job to anchor me to the pathetic world I'd once floated through.

Only the pain was real.

I was without purpose but to suffer for wanting him.

The wedding was getting too close. Kat didn't return. Sometimes I thought I felt some otherworldly presence hovering near my door, but it wasn't Nicholas. Had I been aware of anything but the nails driving into every inch of my body, I would have been curious why Roman didn't knock.

Once in a while, my condition would let up long enough for me to think I could solve this puzzle, any of it. I would think of how Kat was too good to just *die*, and I would think in a second of optimism that maybe Lynch really loved her, and meant to end his killing sickness.

And I would think for a second of *his* face. Of the snow-globe he'd made just for us, safe from the world. Of our private jokes, and of the protectiveness in his eyes when

Roman attacked me. Of him telling me he was a vampire, whether it was fate or his choice that made him kill. I tried to erase those images from my mind before I allowed myself a vision of him, which I now did on occasion, thinking it might steel me against him, help me heal. The pain that the visions caused me only complemented the physical torture I endured for leaving him. Sometimes Roman would be in the visions, pleading with Nicholas to please do what must be done, before he starved and Kat met the alternative horrors that must be in store for her. He sometimes was immobile, like me, encased in pain and hunger too horrible to move. But usually he moved through it, trying to mimic his former existence—going to check on the book store to pitying stares, or forcing his body through martial arts movements, still beautiful despite his obvious strain. My heart threatened to break free of its doubt of him as I watched his bravery while being so gaunt, hopeless, pained.

Now and again I'd see him sit at the kitchen table made by his once-strong hands. He'd stare ahead, unblinking, reminding me a little of Jack Nicholson in *The Shining* when he lost his mind. I knew in those moments that he was thinking of reasons why he shouldn't come to me. I think those visions were the most difficult.

It never bothered me to see him feed. He tried, four times, driven by desperation. He was never healthier or stronger for draining his victims dry. He didn't even pick up any of their characteristics.

Every vision of him cut me so deeply through the screeching torture that I would need to remember that there was every chance in the world that the visions were all just little home movies, made for me alone, and Nicholas was perfectly well, just waiting for me to walk back into his trap. But remembering that was getting harder and harder to do. Such deep-seeded, in-depth trickery, cold manipulation had to be impossible, and yet I wanted it to be that easy—Nicholas was evil, Kat was good. Nicholas *made* me want him, with his "thrall." He could have engineered everything I thought I knew about him, to suit his own needs.

And what if, even if it all was a massive lie, I still couldn't stop loving him? What kind of person did that make me? One who didn't need integrity or trust, who could overlook killing people as a way of life, as long as I was happy.

That made me like Lynch.

Then, there was my answer. I knew what would end my questions, my frantic non-attempts to change this static horror.

It was all I could do to keep from running to the door.

CHAPTER 35

It was dark when I knocked on the enormous front door. The fiend himself answered it with visible malicious glee. It was made worse by the flush of color to his cheeks, the extra shine in his perfect hair.

He'd just fed. Again.

"You?" he exclaimed, his grin widening. "What are you doing here? Kat told me not to let you see her."

Because if she saw me, there would be nothing to forgive. She loved me too much to tell me to leave.

"It's not Kat I need, Lynch. I need you." His face paled, then flushed again. "I need you to kill me." It was the easiest thing in the world to say it out loud, to start the end.

His immediate excitement was tangible. "Come in," he said.

He took me to a library I hadn't seen before. It was dark, gloomy, in stark contrast to the rest of the mansion. All mahogany, bottle-green velvet, orderly shelves of unloved law books, heavy Oriental rug. It was suffocating, rather than cozy, the way a personal library ought to be.

Silently, he was upon me, and past me, to get himself a drink from the minibar. I lowered myself into an armchair with nauseating gold filigree accents. He fed off my discomfort; the grin was still present.

Suddenly I was looking at an empty glass on the bar, and he was behind me, leaning into my hair, smelling me, growling in my ear. The instinctive wave of terror was quickly submerged by my need to end this misery of a life, when I didn't have the nerve to do it myself.

His voice in my ear wasn't the smooth, charming attorney's, but a crude manipulation of it that was worse. "Why should I help you? I'd never do it because you asked nicely." He breathed in long and hard. "The truth is, nothing would please me more than to crush your windpipe in my teeth, to suck every smart-ass, condescending ounce of blood from you, and leave you just far enough from death..." He trailed off, reveling in his own fantasy. "But your pet, Nick, would end me, as much as I hate to admit that he could. And the taste of your bitch blood isn't worth that." He spat his last words, and as the door shut behind him he finished with, "See yourself out."

$\sim$

Roman was sitting in the hallway against my apartment door. *Oh, God, something happened to Nicholas,* was my only thought, but I don't think Roman would have told me if it had. It would have been my fault.

In a blink he was on his feet, looking sadly at me.

"Roman," I said coldly as I fumbled in my coat pockets for keys.

"Eliza." I jumped when his hand tenderly touched my hair.

No one touched me anymore.

He followed me inside, where he wrapped me in a tight embrace, the kind you want to give one of those starving kids you see on TV, I thought. It embarrassed me, and I'm sure he knew it.

"Eliza, thank you for letting me in. We need to talk."

"There's nothing to talk about," I said. "None of us will give up here. I won't allow Kat to be killed, and Nicholas has no choice but to do it." Saying it out loud brought long-dried tears up to prickle behind my eyes.

"You're wrong. You *have* given up. Look at you! And trust me, Nicholas has no hope. If you could see him…"

"I do," I said through gritted teeth. "I still can see him… when I let him in. The vision of him." I clutched the kitchen counter, shaking in frustration that the pain worsened when I talked about him. "Why are you trying this again, Roman? Like you said, I've given up."

"Because *I* haven't!" he bellowed, slamming his fist on the counter, spiderwebbing the cheap tile. "Now listen to me Eliza, because I can't afford to walk away defeated this time!" His voice cracked, and I couldn't bring myself to interrupt him.

He sighed heavily, hanging his head. When he looked up, the depression in his eyes gave me a horrible flash of Nicholas, that same sadness that filmed over his. I groaned.

"Eliza, he's the only family I have. I'm a better man because he's my friend. I can't watch him suffer any longer, and I know you can't either." He paused for me to object, but I couldn't. "The two of you suffering separately is making this so much worse."

My voice was pitifully small, dying with each word. "When I look at him, I see a man I can't ever find happiness with now."

Roman's silence told me he understood. The compassion overwhelmed me, and I fell, sobbing. With his incredible speed, he was over the counter to catch me, and hold me as I cried endlessly.

I had begun to give up the notion that Nicholas deceived me, that I was a victim of his thrall. I wanted to trust my instincts more than that, and I couldn't think anymore about what it would mean if I went to him. What it would mean for us all.

Maybe we could find a way to end this misery together. Or maybe we'd just live through this agony in good company until death claimed one or all of us.

Roman kissed my forehead. "I'll be back tomorrow, Eliza. We can't wait any longer." He swallowed hard. In a saturated voice he said, "He screams your name."

I shuddered, looking down hopelessly.

"There's more you need to know before you abandon him." With those words, Roman slipped soundlessly away.

CHAPTER 36

I tore my teeth out, barbed deep into his throat. He hung in my arms, a line of blood trickling down his chest in a gurgling stream. My ears were tuned to this so much so that all other sound was gone, the pulsing beat of that fluid enveloping me as with bass drum intensity.

I reared my head to the sky, trying not to drown in the blood raging through me, gasping in momentary panic. The need to be *filled* was maddening, filled to overflowing with blood. My mouth hung open, like a lion's in the African heat, the blood coursing through my body, replacing the desperate need. The need for his death hurt deliciously.

Unmei nashi.

Focused on the full silver moon, trying to regain my senses, I watched as a curtain of ruby red fell sluggishly over it, a sickening ooze that coated my eyes. The blood rushed to my brain, my heart, my fingers and toes. I saw nothing without that murky red, the dark sky turning to violet, stars disappearing, the scarlet moon staring back at me, unforgiving.

I leaped from my bed, sweat pouring. A dream. I cast off blankets and stumbled to the window.

The bright moon hung in the sky, powerful and peaceful, untouched by the drapery of blood in my nightmare.

Roman's words thudded in my ears, echoing the pulsing blood of the dream:

There's more you need to know before you abandon him.

And in a snap, I knew. I knew what Nicholas had never told me. I stared at the monstrous moon.

Eternity would never see the end of that moon. Or of me.

It rushed to me in a dizzying flurry, what Nicholas was holding back, what his cryptic words about my fate always meant.

The averageness of your life, Eliza, it isn't you! It isn't what you were meant for.

The thudding in my ears instantly vanished. There was no noise at all. The world had been turned off.

And the all-encompassing pain was totally gone.

I fell backwards onto the floor when it released me. Not a trace of the torture I'd endured, even in my sleep, persisted now. The rigidity of my body relaxed, exhausted.

You can't tell me you don't want more than this. It really doesn't speak to you inside this heart?

I knew my time had come. This life would soon be gone to me.

The *Shinigami* would own it.

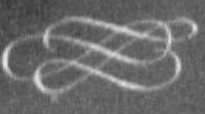

CHAPTER 37

Every second that brought me closer to Nicholas revitalized me. By the time I parked the car in front of the cabin, my spirit was whole again, my body tingling with energy.

I plodded through the snow around the side of the house in the dark, unafraid of the howls and skittering in the surrounding woods, so focused I was. Aware as I was that they couldn't hurt me.

That was not my fate.

My mind could see where Nicholas was, long before I'd stepped into the snow. He stood in the paper lantern light of the fish pond, staring into the semi-frozen water. His back was to me, swathed in a long black wool coat, hands in the pockets. A cold wind ruffled the curls and waves that haloed his head.

When the poetry of him was directly in front of me, it was almost too much for me to stand, but I held myself with fortitude. My knees faltered as I approached him, but I stayed upright. Even when he turned around, and his luminescent face glowed in the night, my tears only fell slowly. They didn't disable me. This was the strong woman I knew, and the one I would become.

Nicholas turned with agonizing slowness, afraid of seeing no one behind him. The relief that heated his hypnotic eyes flooded me with gratitude. I gasped at the sob that broke in his throat.

I'd seen his agony in my visions, had known deep down it was real, but to see such a reaction strangled me.

"You knew I was coming," I said softly. "Can you see me now the way I can see you?"

With a grim laugh, he shook his head. "I've been blind with that *pain* for so long, I could scarcely see in front of me." His lowered head snapped up, his swimming cocoa cream eyes piercing mine with a near-fanatical exultation. "No, I heard you. Your heartbeat. It never left me, all this time. And finally, finally, it began to come closer." He reached out and touched my cheek so tenderly, it was hard to believe he was capable of the terrible things he could do.

That I would do.

His hand still on my cheek, his eyes drinking me in, he said, "You know. Don't you?"

I nodded once. Both deep satisfaction and disappointment wafted over me.

He held out both of his hands to me, and I took them, as I'd been waiting to do for so long. A soft tingling ran from my fingertips to my wrists, and we both let out a sigh.

But I knew what I knew. My eyes were the first to look away.

"I'm your chosen immortal, your *unmei fumetsu*. It's why we can't stay away from each other. You are to be my creator, and I am to become *Shinigami*. It's why you need me here—not because you feel the way I do."

"The way you feel?" Genuine surprise crossed his face. "Eliza, the way you feel about me—you can't trust your feelings, love, you must see that now. Everything's affected by this link we have, and the power I have."

My eyes rolled of their own free will. "The vampire thrall, right? I know, I know. I know all your little secrets, I know them now like I know myself. Just like I know when you feed, you're not completely yourself." More gently, "And I know that you think you're no one, because parts of so many victims have woven into you." He began to turn away, and I grabbed his arm. "No! I know that's what you think, but I know different. Create as much of a thrall as you like, Nicholas, but you can't hide who you are from me behind any of it." I smiled. "I'm looking too hard."

He smiled hesitantly back. With a sharp swallow, I said, "Love doesn't always need the whole truth. I know all of you, and want all of you, no matter what comes along with it. Even if you hadn't been chosen for me."

He looked glum, and guilty, still.

"Nicholas, would you make the same choice? If you loved me, too?"

I expected him to look away, or tell me again that my love wasn't real, but he took a different route.

"Eliza, there's no choice here. I didn't choose to make you a vampire, it is providence. You were chosen, but not by me."

My hurt couldn't be hidden. He took me in his arms, making it worse with their familiarity.

"You know what I mean," he said into my hair.

"Yeah. I think I do." I pulled away from the embrace, my hands lingering on his biceps of their own accord. "Don't feel guilty, Nicholas. It isn't your fault that you aren't in love with me."

"In all fairness, Eliza, you don't know as much about how I feel as you think you do."

The adrenaline rush of being chosen by fate gave me a confidence that was at odds with my confused human heart.

"I'm learning to accept my fate, Nicholas. Would you accept that I'm yours?"

His neverending eyes deepened with sadness. "You are my *unmei fumetsu*, Eliza. That's all. Believe me, your 'love' for me will change when you become like me. You'll see what I am clearly for the first time. Too clearly."

His stubbornness was annoying me. "I thought wisdom came with age. Maybe *you* won't see clearly until I look at you with eyes that match your own. I can wait. It's my fate to wait for you." My certainty grew with each word I spoke. I had no more choice in loving Nicholas than I did in becoming *Shinigami*.

And Nicholas had no more choice than I.

The sadness didn't leave his eyes when his arm encircled my shoulders and he turned us back to the cabin. Wind howled through the trees, sending snow whirling around us. Like magic again, the snowglobe I still dreamed of was an umbrella over our walk home, keeping me safe and warm in a world of ice.

CHAPTER 38

We returned to the amber glow of his handmade kitchen, as we'd done so many nights before, to sit for hours comforted by the close quarters. The aroma of Earl Grey tea from the chipped teacup held me close. The wood-stove purred, not quite covering the mundane sounds of Nicholas stirring his tea and sighing comfortably for the first time in too long.

It would have seemed ordinary to outside eyes. But for that time, we were exactly *us;* no one else with impending doom hovering overhead. We owed it to ourselves and each other to just *be.*

Nicholas's rocket speed had him suddenly slumped like a juvenile delinquent in the chair opposite me, teacup spinning on the table from the movement. He trained his eyes on me, a seductive curve in the corner of his lips.

Like the first time I saw him, he was all I could register in the world, his presence taking over all. I trembled with a hopefulness I hadn't known I was still capable of.

"What are you thinking?" I breathed out, unable to decipher his expression for myself.

Nicholas twirled the cup on the table, and watched me. "I just need a moment to believe you're here."

I smiled sheepishly, and began fiddling with my mug, too.

After a comfortable silence, Nicholas looked away with an odd shyness. "Look, Eliza, I know you want answers, how could you not? But tonight, can we please just—"

"Yes. Let's forget it all. Just for tonight." We smiled in conspiracy, and sipped our tea. I groaned with the warmth that coursed through my still-chilled body.

Nicholas chuckled. "Do you remember when you learned I could still eat and drink?" He laughed again. "You were more concerned with that than when you learned I was a vampire."

"Oh, I don't know about that, but I was surprised, and overjoyed that I could sit down to a hot cup of coffee with you. You know, I'm a creature of comfort, too," I said, echoing his own words to me once. "I like someone to share my laziness with me."

"That I know," he said.

"And I was surprised—shocked—when you showed me what you are. But I always knew you were more than human, better. You were just too *perfect*." I blushed.

"Perfect," he mumbled, shaking his head, eyes downcast. For the millionth time I gazed, probably looking a little dumb, at every contour of his face. Beautifully creamy, smooth, but for distinguished laugh lines and creases that somehow made him more perfect. Except now that I truly looked, they were more hollow than I remembered. And the delicate skin under his whirlpool eyes was gray. His soft, bow-shaped lips were dry, where they were always plump, pink, framing the smile I would die to see.

"You need to drink." Captain Obvious.

He raised his eyebrows, and smiled—not the smile I wanted to see. "I do. I have been," he said distantly. "But it's not what I need, Eliza. It's not what I need."

Kat's name echoed in my head, over and over, as if spoken by God, and I continued to watch the love of my life disappear into all-consuming starvation in front of me. Tears clouded my vision; useless tears that helped none of us.

"What can we do, Nicholas?" Instantly, he moved his chair beside mine. His arms wrapped like a warm blanket, his scent, cinnamon and cloves, tried to calm me.

He mouthed into my ear, "Not tonight, sweetheart, please. I need only to be near you to fulfill any hunger I could have."

Raging desire flooded me, and with speed only he could match, I attacked him with my lips, grunting with my own exertion. My fingers twined into the warmth of his curls, my body curving toward him. I expected him to pull away force-fully, with his usual speech about how I couldn't trust myself, but he didn't. There was a palpable difference in the health of his lips since our first kiss, but that didn't make them any less fervent. He *wanted* me, and there was no mistaking.

He could tell me all he wanted that this wasn't love between us, but words meant nothing now.

I rose from my chair, and sat in his lap, my lips never leaving his. Our bodies melded together as he wound his arms around my waist. My heart must have sounded like a marching band to him.

I guess that was his breaking point. With unbelievable swiftness and agility, he placed me back in my seat, and moved his own chair to the other side of the table again.

"Eliza—"

"Spare me," I said spitefully, but got myself in check imme-diately, afraid to scare him off. "I overstepped. I'm sorry."

"No, you didn't, of course, what else could you think I meant by what I said?" He shook his head in irritation. "It's not that I don't want you, Eliza, but I don't want any mixed emotions tonight. No guilt, no restraint. I only want you *here*. Can you live with that?"

Live with it? I'd do anything just to never leave this room.

"Eliza, if I'd been given the choice, if it was mine—I would have chosen you. I'd want no other to be my *unmei fumetsu*."

I could only smile, trying to consider myself lucky.

Nicholas was up in an instant. "Refill? Better yet, let me feed you." He stopped to look at me again. "I don't have to sleep, and I don't plan on letting this night end anytime soon."

Those words made my smile grew so wide, my face hurt. "Bring it on," I joked, and propped my feet up.

The sun peeked over the horizon, pink and gold through the trees. We sat outside, the intolerable cold unable to touch me in the orb Nicholas projected. It was still an incredible, beautiful mystery, how he could do such a thing, but it was all part of the magic he held for me in general. To be able to sit in the winter night with only a blanket around me, and just *exist* with nature in its private moments, to share them with Nicholas was beyond anything I'd ever imagined. It made my world infinite. It made my fate seem right, in this place.

When the fairy light colors kissed Nicholas's skin, I knew that the snowglobe couldn't even protect him. The shadows in his face harshly reminded me that he was wasting away without blood. And not just any blood, but the right blood. Hers. As glorious as he still was, the hunger had diminished him. I *wanted* him to feed, and knew what it would mean if he did. There was no escaping it.

Fate would destroy us all, even as we outran it.

Nicholas spoke first through a grim smile. "Eliza, I have to go inside. Haven't eaten anyone who likes the beach lately."

"Right." Just like that, I was alone, and our night was over. It had been all we both wished for. Comforting in its impossibility, like our time together in the beginning. I'd been able to forget the horrors that awaited.

Dawn was too bright as it eclipsed the trees. The sun's glare off the endless snow could do nothing to warm me now that Nicholas wasn't next to me, his bubble with him.

As I turned the doorknob, the slightest *pop* evaporated the shimmering bubble around me.

~

Nicholas and I both needed sleep; me after such a long night, he without…proper nutrition. The caverns in his face haunted me into unconsciousness. I dreamed of his burning eyes.

I awoke when darkness fell again. Briefly, I wondered if my sleep pattern would ever be normal again, and realized soon it probably wouldn't make a difference. Sleep would rarely be needed. I shuddered.

I needed to see Nicholas.

Climbing out of the bed that had welcomed me back so easily, flurries of odd thoughts descended, as was to be expected with the turmoil that had become my life. I thought how glad I was that most of my clothes were here, not at the apartment, as I threw on the stolen green sweater over my favorite tee and yoga pants. I thought how I'd probably only changed my clothes twice in my time in Hell, alone in that apartment. I thought how the floor was always cold there, and always warm here. I thought of how Nicholas could spread a frost out in an instant when the vampire came to the forefront. I thought that I may be able to do the same thing one day soon, as I walked to his room.

The serenity of his bedroom never ceased to calm my mind. I breathed deeply as I stood in the darkness, surrounded by rice paper walls, and watched the tiger-like prowess in his movements just outside the doors. Dusk seemed somehow to fill him, not like he was outside in the cold, uninviting night. He wore just a white t-shirt and the well-worn, loose-fitting white karate pants. He shined in the darkness like a candle. His movements were just flickers to my eyes, so amazingly fast and precise, darting through the night. Every few seconds he'd pause, locked in a beautiful, ancient stance that no Kung Fu movie could give justice to. He was perfectly lethal, and completely peaceful all at once.

"He's fast, even for one of us," Roman said, watching Nicholas from beside me. I gasped and jumped, putting immediate distress in his eyes. "I'm sorry. I forget sometimes that you still only have human hearing."

I smiled and caught my breath, looking back with Roman to Nicholas's martial arts practice. Watching him made me buzz inside. "It's not just my hearing. My eyes can't follow him fast enough."

"Neither can mine," Roman replied, laughing. "He's so much more than me. Unique among the *Shinigami*. But as fast as he is, he's still slowing down." Roman shifted to look at me, ready to plead with me for something I couldn't give. I couldn't look at him. "Eliza, you need to let go of Kat if you want Nicholas to survive."

My world went black for a minute as I heard him say the one thing I knew was horribly true, the thing I could never do. I swooned, and felt Roman's hand on my back, steadying me.

"Nicholas will never feed on her if you don't give him permission to. He will die, for lack of a better term. He'll become little more than a skeleton. Eventually he won't be able to move, speak, even blink," he said crassly.

Still reeling from Roman referring to my best friend as food, it was just as gut-wrenching to envision Nicholas as he described. Like a new stab wound, the pain returned. My knees buckled. Roman caught me again. My eyes glazed over as I watched Nicholas slow his practice and come to still meditation. A vision of his meditative stillness dissolving him into a decaying husk assaulted me. The world would be devoid of him. My world. And he had purpose that would not be fulfilled, more *unmei nashi* that would suffer greatly without his mercy killing.

"Are you certain? Are there other vampires still out there like corpses, but alive? Forever?" I asked, hating the answer already.

"Not forever. Eventually their lives return to them," Roman whispered back. Hope poured into me, but was gone just as quickly as it came. It couldn't be that easy.

"When does that happen?"

With a roughness I now associated with his worrying about his Nicholas, Roman gave me my answer. "When the *unmei nashi* meets that other end that awaits them—the worse one –the vampire's life is slowly restored. It will take decades for him to regain the speed and strength he once had, and all the while the guilt will agonize him, that he could have made it easy for her. His will to live will be... Think of suffering what he has and will suffer over this, and think of how he'll want to die at the idea of going through such things for eternity. Only more damage will be done, and it will all have been for nothing, Eliza. Nothing."

Both of us were shaking, he with frustration, me with the silent sobs and streaming tears. Outside, my Nicholas stood in meditation, his strong, well-muscled back now bare.

His shoulder blades jut out sharply.

CHAPTER 39

An hour later, the three of us were in the kitchen. Roman glared across the table at me as I shot him nasty looks behind Nicholas's back. Our sadness somehow made us angry at each other, as if the other were responsible for it. Nicholas hummed happily as he poured three cups of coffee, and smiled when he handed one to me.

I thought my heart would burst into bloody bits.

As usual, I couldn't take my eyes off him. He held the mug in his powerful hands, closing his eyes as he breathed in the steam with childlike glee. A sweet smile lingered on his lips when his eyes met mine again from where he leaned against the counter. There was no hint of his mischievous sarcasm, only a Zen-like pleasure.

Like a dying man ready to meet God.

His eyes darkened as he heard my mug clatter on the table in my shaking hands. In a blink, he was at my side, smoothing my hair. I didn't deserve to be comforted. The harsh set of Roman's jaw told me he agreed.

"Eliza?" Nicholas questioned with horrible unselfishness. Roman thrummed his fingers on the table. "Eliza, aren't you happy you came back here?" Nicholas whispered. I couldn't take anymore. I groaned, looking anywhere but at the hopelessly devoted Nicholas.

It wasn't so long ago that I was demanding more and more of him: more love, stronger ties, the words I wanted to hear him say, for him to say he loved me, no matter how hard it was, whether he believed our love existed or not. Now, I couldn't bring myself to give him the one thing he needed to simply survive—my blessing.

I couldn't be near Nicholas's goodness another second. I ran from the kitchen, but stopped just outside the door, also unable to leave him. Roman's angry voice followed me out.

"I cannot watch this any longer, Nicholas!" I was very surprised to hear that his anger wasn't directed solely at me. "First, you string her along, knowing what she is, but just letting her think you were falling in love with her—"

"*Letting her think?* Roman, you know how I—"

"Nicholas, shut up!" I was shocked that Nicholas did, a testament to how well he wasn't doing. "I watched her fall in love with you, and you, refusing to accept it, like a fool! I watched you both torture yourselves, every way possible to stay *apart*?! Because of what? Guilt? You can't feed, do what you're destined to do, because of guilt! It's going to kill you, Nicholas!" Roman's voice shivered and cracked. I think I moaned.

Nicholas's silence was beyond difficult for me. If he'd been more himself he would have barked back at Roman something snide about him being the Grand Master of Guilt or something, but he didn't have the strength. And what part of Roman's tirade could he deny?

And after all I was doing to him, and the lives on the line, how could I still have the nerve to hope he was in love with me?

My ability to see him in a vision as if he was in front of me was terrible now that I was within reach to hold him, and tell him nothing mattered but his happiness, and that he *lived*. Nicholas's sudden voice brought me out of my own mind to hang on his words.

"Guilt?" he spat. "You must be blind. Everything I do is because I love her. Too much to subject her to this unthinkable thing I must do to her only real friend! Are you so inhuman that you can't see what I'm asking of her? Of course I tried to stay away, but even if I didn't love her, she…is…*mine*."

The last words were said with a power I took more delight in than I should have at that point. I should have been wracked with guilt—but I wasn't.

He continued his fevered speech. "The draw to me nearly killed her when we were apart! You think I'm selfish enough to ask her to see through all this pain and death and sacrifice to *love me*? You think I would let her? It's not even possible for her to see me as I am." His voice became so weak, I don't know how he went on other than that it was harder to keep it in. "You know all this, Roman. I've prayed more to a God I don't believe in these past weeks than I have my entire existence, prayed that the end of it would come, and so help me, I don't care how it ends, so long as Eliza and I are together." His entire being seemed so utterly exhausted, I don't know how Roman didn't reach out to hold him up. "If it means the end of me, I at least have her right now," Nicholas droned, as he fell into a chair, with Roman doing the same next to him, both of them looking every bit as old as they really were.

I caused it all. I'd brought it all on. But I'd be lying if I said I didn't get a surge of sheer joy at hearing some of the things Nicholas said, and worse, I knew that I, too, would do anything to spend eternity with him. That, above all, was our entwined fate. No matter what happened to Kat, Nicholas and I would be vampires forever.

And just like that, I knew what had to be done to stop it all.

CHAPTER 40

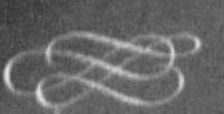

"You're insane. No, you're just ignorant," Roman mumbled, while Nicholas stared at me, wild-eyed.

Roman stopped pacing the kitchen to face me. "Eliza, you don't know how our world works. Not like this, that's certain."

"Yeah, well, isn't *your* world going to be *my* world, too? I have a right to try to help her before just giving up."

Nicholas's eyes never left me as he registered my suggestion. "Make Kat a vampire?" he whispered.

Roman spun on him in a whirlwind. "Nicholas, don't even begin to entertain the thought."

"Why not?" I said, quickly sitting myself across from Nicholas, jarring the table as I leaned on it. "It could fix all of this!"

"NO!" Roman yelled, startling us both. I thought for a second about how gentle Roman was when I first met him. Another thing I'd managed to ruin without trying. "No. We cannot change the laws of our nature to satisfy our own desires, Nicholas, you know in your heart it would be wrong."

Eyes still glued to mine, but with a faint smile to accompany their glint, Nicholas answered with the very prevalent rebel in him. "Why not, Roman? We live for eternity, but we can't change the rules once in a while? Neither of us is happy with them, but we make no attempt to change them." Roman glared at him. Nicholas threw his hands up, but wasn't defeated that easily. "Fine. We'll go to Japan—"

"Japan?!" I blurted. "We don't have time—"

"—to the Master, we'll tell him what we want to do. For me, he'll do this. Who will it hurt?"

Roman sputtered out a grim cackle. "Who will it hurt? How about the unaccounted for humans Kat will kill to survive? She'll have no purpose but to stay fed, no *unmei nashi*! How do you think she'll take it, as gentle and kind as she is, subjected to murder forever? Not to mention it will make Lynch even harder to contain, having a partner to murder with. She would despise us for it. Think before you speak!"

"We're discussing her life and death like she's incapable of—"

"Incapable of what, Eliza?" The anger spilled over in Roman's words more every minute. "Given the choice, what person wouldn't choose immortality over immediate death?"

"Roman's right, Eliza," Nicholas said glumly. "What are we going to say to her? *'You want to join everyone you know in a vampire coven? Did we mention your fiancé is a psychopath that you'll be tied to for eternity? Oh, guess what? If you say no, I'll have to kill you.'*" Oh, Nicholas, such a way with words. "First, we'll go to the Master. We find out if it can be done. You'll be on your way there, anyway." I must have looked puzzled, because he winked and smiled at me charmingly.

Amazing, how that one gesture and today's scent of lilacs and moist soil deluded me into thinking this would all just blow over. For that second, I was pleased.

Roman burst my bubble. "Nicholas, how can you even consider this?"

"Because maybe *this* is my purpose," Nicholas said, leaning forward, his passion so strong it overwhelmed me, and I think Roman, too. "Every *Shinigami* says I'm different, I'm something special, but at the end of the day, we all do the same thing. Maybe I'm the one to change it."

I took advantage of Roman's momentary consideration. "Kat is marrying Lynch in a handful of days. We have no time to waste, not taking action."

Nicholas never took his tornado-like eyes from my face, and I knew it was set in stone.

~

We had no idea how much longer Kat had. Before Nicholas was too weak to take her life, before Lynch did it in a fit of impulse, before the wedding, before she met some other terrible undefinable finish. It was impossible to ignore the time we—I—had wasted, sinking into that oblivion of pain, subjecting Nicholas to the same, in addition to his hunger. But we were pushing our luck.

Nicholas told me Kat was eager to hear about me, and how distressed she was, thinking we could never come back from how we'd separated. It made Lynch jumpy, Nicholas said, like his mood was directly related to Kat's. Maybe he did love her. Or maybe this was just another way for him to feed off of her.

I was incapable of being patient about getting to Japan. Every second we wasted before talking to the Master about saving Kat was a nail in her coffin. Time moved too slow and too fast at the same time.

"You aren't expected in Japan yet," Nicholas explained to me. "I can't just show up at a secluded temple full of vampires with a human, even one who *will* be a vampire, and start making demands."

"Then get on with it, or let Roman contact the Master for

you," I pleaded.

"Only I can connect to the Master's mind directly; he didn't create Roman, and our ability to contact each other through our thoughts is unique to the Master and I. But I'm too weak right now, Eliza. I can't do it."

I rushed to his side. "Let's just *go* please. We'll face whatever waits there for us together."

"The *Shinigami* are exceedingly sensitive to timing, there is a time for everything. I can't stress enough, for me to show up unannounced in Japan with a human, tell the Master that you're my *unmei fumetsu*, and that I'm there to ask permission to change the fabric of reality as we know it in an unprecedented move to save a human would guarantee our failure."

"Nicholas, it's all just stupid tradition."

He drew a deep breath, impatience growing in his widened eyes. "The temple is a place to prepare new *Shinigami*, some quicker learners than others, to control their thirst. We can't show up early without calling and bringing them a fruit cake. Something else to eat besides you."

"So, make the call! Let's get this show on the road!" My feet were tapping with anxiety.

"Eliza, it's an ancient temple on a mountain top that the oldest people in Japan don't know exists. You think they have Verizon?"

Grumbling and rolling my eyes didn't ease the gnawing stress. Packing did. While Nicholas meditated, gathered enough strength to speak across countries and mountaintops to the Master's mind, I would be ready to go.

Roman was sullen, but understanding. He certainly didn't agree with our plan, but he didn't want to give up on fighting for Kat's life necessarily, either. There was nothing to do but be hopeful now. We were making as much progress as I could expect.

Until the unexpected intruded.

CHAPTER 41

Nicholas needed to check in at Birch Tree to put some affairs in order and notify his miniscule staff that he'd be unreachable until further notice, but that his brother would be in town in case of emergencies.

He looked sickly enough to believe he was in for an extended hospital stay.

I anxiously awaited his return to the cabin as a cloudy sunset was absorbed by charcoal night clouds. I knew he would be home soon. I also knew that I was what tethered him to sanity; I could see him rushing through his work in my mind's eye, and I knew it was to get home to me. Without the same ability to see me, he worried, despite being able to hear my heartbeat miles away. Since his confession of love, even if it was to Roman, he'd been different with me—more affectionate, and not so self-resenting. It wasn't a marriage proposal, but we had infinity to spend together, and that was quite enough. I dared a Cheshire cat smile as I finished packing the few things I was bringing with me to Japan, not that I was really even equipped to live in New Hampshire.

Roman had been called to feed not long after Nicholas left

the house, so I was alone. It felt right to be alone here, not like at the apartment.

And then there were footsteps. The *click clack* of heels, light and feminine. Kat! But she wouldn't just walk in here.

Then who?

A fingernail of nerves traced down my spine and I froze, holding an idiotic Yoo-Hoo Chocolate Drink t-shirt in my hands. Who knew the two vampires well enough to just walk into their home? I hadn't even heard the door close. I was completely unaware of any ancient enemies they may have acquired, and me, with a stupid t-shirt.

Panic ensued.

I looked around the room in a frenzy for somewhere to hide. Like any spare room, it was under the bed or in the closet. I threw myself on the floor and rolled under the bed as the door swung open.

Expensive maroon heels stopped inches from my face. Then, her exotic eyes and a gleaming smile took their place as she lied on the floor with a *whoosh* of speed, her dark ringlets spreading across the floor.

"Hello, sweet pea," she purred. Her brown eyes seemed to pulse ever so slightly, like Nicholas's, but without warmth, or humanity. "This is no way to meet a guest."

The photos on the mantle of Nicholas's creator did no justice to her presence. Jenniveve was taller than Nicholas, with legs longer than any model's. Her physical beauty alone was formidable. It wasn't a classic beauty she possessed; her face was perfectly round, her jaw wide-set. Her skin color was rich, but hinted at no ethnicity. Dark spirals of hair with too much luster and movement to belong to a human fell to the middle of her back. Definitely considered "of good breeding," she was well-dressed and poised, sophisticated and condescending.

Underneath it all, she was primal and beastly. Shark-like.

Not one B-movie monster could have prepared me for her. Even if I had words to say I couldn't speak because my teeth were chattering too hard. I clenched my jaw to quiet them as I sat rigid in Nicholas's armchair in front of the empty fireplace. Jenniveve casually paced the living room with a smile that showed too many teeth, caressing the edges of picture frames as she passed. The rhythmic *clack* of her heels echoed like the executioner's shoes walking an inmate to the chair.

"There are no photos of you up here," she made a point to say without questioning why.

"No, I suppose not."

Then she was leaning over me in a soundless flash, caging me into my seat with her arms. She grinned when I whimpered. "And why do you suppose that is?" she sneered.

She resumed slithering around the room, but my shaking didn't end. "Well, I know why," she continued. "He knows when you're turned he won't feel anything for you anymore."

How did she know I was going to become *Shinigami?* I shook harder at the thought. After a second, I didn't care how she knew.

"That's not true," I said assuredly, and her smile disappeared. I held up my chin.

Big mistake.

She was at my throat fast, murder in her eyes, scarcely giving me time to scream. As quickly as she was on me, however, she was gone. When I opened my eyes, I already knew what I'd see. I smelled the sweet vanilla and sugar before he opened the door.

Jenniveve was flat on her back, feet kicking helplessly, with Nicholas crouched over her. His back heaved like a wild animal that's ended a long hunt. Vicious snarling that would send a lion running ripped through the air. But I could hear Jenniveve's relaxed giggle over it.

With an inhuman twist, she launched Nicholas off of herself, and now he was on his back, with her long legs straddling him.

"You've gotten impressively strong over the years, darling," she said, "despite how shitty you look. It's rather sexy."

"Well, I strive for perfection," he mumbled. My blood boiled, and I wished he was as strong as he should be, blood-fueled.

Like a camera speeded up, Jenniveve was on her feet and pacing again, like the scene had been a dream. Nicholas took his time getting up. As frantic as my mind was, I couldn't help but smile at his cockiness. He brushed off his black t-shirt, feigning annoyance.

"Now, what in the hell do you want, Jenn?" he asked, taking the other armchair. He crossed his legs, and looked meaningfully at me. I knew instantly that this was dangerous ground, but that he'd protect me. I'd never allow him to be hurt either, no matter what the cost.

Elbow resting on the mantle, Jenn was totally unruffled by the situation. "I heard you had yourself an *unmei fumetsu*, Nicholas. I wanted to meet it for myself."

"It?" I snapped.

Her eyes were daggers when she looked at me. "You are an *it* to me. As long as the breath of life is in that eating, sleeping, shitting shell, you're just another lesser being."

Well, I'd heard she was harsh.

"You mean to tell me you sought me out after all these years to gawk at my chosen?" Nicholas said, with disbelief. I wasn't sure how much I liked being referred to this way. "Don't you have anyone else to bother? What else do you want, Jenn?"

The woman's mood swings from snide to enraged had to

be record-breaking. Her words were as slow as syrup. "I…don't…need…*anyone*," she hissed.

"Good for you, Jenn!" His mockery of her was bound to get him in trouble here. "So, tell me, how long will you be staying with us?"

What! He wasn't seriously inviting her to stay?!

She never blinked the red rage from her eyes as she said, "I will stay as long as I want."

~

The evening didn't get more comfortable at any point. Jenn wouldn't leave Nicholas and I alone for a second, and we both were on edge. I had questions for him, and he wanted to settle me down. And we just needed to be near each other, alone.

Roman arrived home hours later, in a very friendly mood. I'd long since learned not to ask questions about such things, and Roman was always reluctant to talk about anything vampire-related.

Jenn, not so much.

"Ugh, I always hated the really happy victims. How hopelessly stupid, to be happy until the moment of their death," she said to herself.

"Always the pessimist, Jenniveve," Roman quipped. It was a more laid-back response than he'd have given without a shot of lightheartedness straight to the blood stream. From a person whose life was now over. It was never easy for me to think of those victims.

How many like them would meet their deaths through my own hands?

Nicholas's mood was somewhere in between that of the other two vampires. I'd call it "good-natured caution." Clearly, he was uncomfortable; clear to me, anyway. I wanted to shake him violently for inviting her to stay, but knew he must have his reasons.

"You seem considerably nastier than I remember, Jenn," Nicholas said nonchalantly.

She didn't blink or frown as she examined her dangerously long ruby fingernails. "I suppose I am." She looked up with a sheer, sweet smile that didn't match the malice in her eyes. "I've been taking a little vacation as of late. Hunting in the Amazon." She hissed the words through bared teeth. "The blood of crocodiles is bitter, but refreshingly cold. Followed by a day's sleep under the reeds in the swamp..." Her eyes rolled back as she relished the memory.

"I hear it does wonders for the skin and a bitchy disposition." Way to provoke the time bomb, Nicholas. But she only laughed.

"Darling, you'd benefit from a bit of predator blood flowing through those soft, pink veins. Maybe I could help." And with that, she whirled across the room like a hurricane, and straddled Nicholas, her lips smothering his.

Bile filled my mouth.

When she finally pulled away, Nicholas hadn't moved, neither to indulge or push her off. His expression was unreadable. I'm sure mine was perfectly readable.

He squinted, deep in thought, licked his lips, (making me squirm), and said, "Frog legs. Oversalted."

Jenn growled with irritation and grizzly threat, but left the room without action.

Nicholas's lips upturned in a wicked smile. I laughed until I shook.

~

I don't know where Jenn went, but she didn't return while I was awake. Nicholas and I had time to talk.

"I will *never* leave you alone again," he said, blinking madly. I wasn't sure if he was serious, but it would be fine with me if he was.

"Nicholas, why is she so…" I began nervously, wrapping my arms around my knees on the sofa. Nicholas sat next to me, smelling unlike anything I recognized, but it made me warm and weirdly giddy.

"Nasty?" Nicholas finished. "She's always been a bitch. But when *Shinigami* hunt animals, we take on their traits, too—wild, instinctive. Survivalist through and through. You probably don't want to know what a croc's innermost thoughts are."

I grimaced, thinking of a time at the zoo when I saw an American alligator tank with a bunch of frog carcasses stashed under a log. "Have you hunted animals before?" I couldn't conceive of Nicholas with Jenn's cruelty laced throughout.

He laughed. "I've done my experimenting. I bagged a shark once," he said with a prideful sideways smile that quickly vanished. "I was young. It was fun, but unsettling. That killer instinct, completely stripped of compassion, or any emotion but hunger. Constant, all-encompassing hunger." His eyes darkened miserably.

How much different is it than how you are now? I wanted to ask as my eyes swept over his dark hollows, jutting bones, gray pallor. But then I thought of Lynch, and couldn't think of the two of them as the same in any way.

"Will you be telling Jenn that we're going to Japan?" I asked.

"Oh, she certainly already knows."

"You told her?"

He sniffed. "No, but she has an uncanny knack for

knowing too much. And you were packing when she got here," he said, dripping sarcasm.

"Right. What do you really think she wants, Nicholas? Is she in love with you?" I truly had no idea, and hated not knowing. I hated being so insecure.

Sensing my discomfort, Nicholas was at my side, one masculine, if not a little cold, hand on the back of my neck. The sugary voice was the bandage to an open wound. "She won't come between us. Don't spare her any more thought than you would a jerky high school cheerleader." His eyes pierced mine at this moment, free of turmoil. I kissed him softly. His lips were dry with his thirst, but tasted like raspberries. They lingered for just the right amount of time, sending sparks through my cheeks and heart. As he slowly pulled away, his eyes sleepily opened and blinked. He was unsure of something.

"Eliza, I know you overheard things I said to Roman, about my feelings for you." A chilly thumb caressed my cheek. "I'm too cowardly to say it while these fairy eyes look back at me, but I meant it all the same." His fingers hovered near my temple as he searched my eyes.

I swallowed, and swallowed again, and remembered to breathe. "You don't know how much I needed to hear that, Nicholas."

He smiled wide, dazzling me with his happiness. "Luck is on my side that you still care."

He kissed me again. I don't remember much after that.

CHAPTER 42

"*H*ow *will you survive this trip? Look at you, Nicholas.*"
"*I'm still better looking than you.*"

I awoke in my little bed, with the sun filtering in, but like they were in the room with me, I saw Nicholas and Roman in their armchairs in front of an early fire; it could be cold out there in the morning. Nicholas looked into the fire, but Roman's intense eyes bore into his brother.

"*Don't joke about this, Nicholas,*" Roman pleaded. "*I'm serious.*"
"*Always are.*"

Roman rolled his eyes, but pursued. "*You're too frail. You're dying in front of me.*" My heart stopped. "*The sunlight alone on the plane, it will be too much for you.*"

Nicholas didn't blink. He shook his head, dismissing this as a problem. "*I'll feed first. A nun or something if it will reassure you.*"

Roman ignored the quip. "*Think of what the Master's reaction will be when he sees you this way. He loves you like a son. And because of your love for Eliza, not only are you ignoring the call to your* unmei nashi, *your duty in this world, but you're killing yourself in the process.*"

Nicholas reluctantly faced him and finally answered Roman him sincerely. *"It's true. He won't be excited to do Eliza any favors, but he'll do anything to help me."* Roman shook his head. *"I have to try, Roman. We've been through this."* Now it was Nicholas that begged to be understood.

Roman hung his head for a moment before whispering, *"Nicholas, have you considered the possibility that turning Kat into a vampire might not restore you to health?"*

Nicholas said nothing. He blinked once, and all three of us knew how he felt.

~

Dealing with Jenniveve was a contact sport that I was in no way accustomed to playing. I hated seeing her so early, here in our safe little bungalow, even if it only was in my mind. My visions would need to be a lot more discriminating in the morning if I wanted to continue to wake up smiling every day.

Guilt flooded me as I thought of Kat waking up in Lynch's arms, glowing like the beautiful bride she'd soon be, when I knew what really was in store for her. What right did I have to be happy at all?

I couldn't get out of bed and face Roman and Nicholas after their argument the night before; I couldn't let Nicholas see my worry that Roman could be correct. And I sure didn't want to talk to *her*, long-legged in a black dress not befitting of New Hampshire weather or community, horribly still and staring at Nicholas. The kitchen sunlight didn't touch her, and I knew she'd burn if it did. Nicholas stared back at her with palpable anger. Roman sat next to him, drinking coffee and looking worried, as he always did these days.

"You may be feeding, my love, but not on the right human. The question is, why not?" She tapped her long fingernails on the

wooden table, pulling Nicholas's expressions apart like a puzzle.

"Can't you just leave well enough alone? Once again, I wonder what in the hell you're really doing here, Jenn. I realize it's only been a day or so, but I don't need to point out that you've overstayed your welcome."

"Done with me so soon, baby?" she crooned. *"Is this about the girl?"*

I grumbled at the ceiling, clutching the covers.

"Eliza's not just a girl," Nicholas growled.

Roman glanced at Nicholas with trepidation, but Jenn's face lit up with obnoxious excitement. "She's *the reason you're pushing me out! Which means there's something about her you want to hide from me. And I'm willing to bet it has something to do with why you haven't taken your victim out. And probably why you're begging to go to the Master."*

Shit, how did she work that all out so fast? I bolted out of bed, tripping over my slippers, and took off to the kitchen quickly, not thinking at all what I planned to do when I got there; I just knew that Jenniveve could *not* learn my best friend was Nicholas's *unmei nashi.*

Trying not to look guilty about eavesdropping, I banged the kitchen door open, and stood stupidly in the doorway.

"Well, good morning, sunshine," Jenn said, never stopping the incessant tapping of the fingernails. "You were awfully quick to get out here to your creator, now weren't you?" Damn, she was swift to figure things out, which didn't bode well. Nicholas shot me a wary glance.

"Well, he's nice to wake up to," I said.

"Yes, I remember."

Nicholas rolled his eyes, leaning back in his chair in that delinquent way I liked. "Let's not have a pissing contest, please," he said with aggravation.

Not to be distracted, Jenn turned to Roman. "Tell me,

Mother Hen, why are you allowing your big brother to do this to himself?" Roman blinked, faltering, and I became very concerned.

"Roman," I warned, foolishly.

Jenn shot up and stood too close to me, looking hard into my eyes with her cold, dead ones. "Well, I would love to know what you know about this feeding problem we're having," she purred. "I *know* she knows something," she whispered in my face, but not speaking to me. "Don't you, little girl? Why is it that my Nicholas is starving himself? Tell me."

I was frozen, void of any idea how to handle this, and too afraid not to respond.

"Leave her alone, Jenn. Leave her alone, or get out of my house. Your time here is limited as it is. I can only take you for so long," Nicholas interjected coolly. I stepped around Jenn to sit next to him. He smiled at me, and rubbed my sweatpanted leg in greeting.

"Oh, stop it," Jenn hissed, crocodilian smile glinting. "I can't believe you've fallen in love with this," she said, gesturing at me like she was pushing trash out of her way. "But feelings can be changed, Nicholas." She appeared behind him, rubbing his arms. He rolled his eyes again.

"Jenn, it's a bit early for this, isn't it? For chrissakes, you still smell like swampland."

Her bitter laugh hurt my ears. "It's my blood, Nicholas. You should indulge, instead of just drinking piteous humans. Or not drinking at all." She slapped him lightly in the back of the head and sat down again, her microscopic glare on us like we were a sideshow. I chose to ignore her for as long as I could.

"Are you hungry?" Nicholas asked me quietly, as if Jenn weren't hanging on our every word with supernatural hearing.

"Are you?" she responded out of turn with a little laugh.

"Enough!" Nicholas yelled, shaking the table with a pounding fist. "Jenniveve, you have no right to be here, and you know nothing of what's at stake, so shut the hell up and leave me alone like you've done for decades." Nicholas's temper was still more controlled than I would have expected, given that Jenn was seemingly here only to aggravate and come on to him, with a side of antagonizing me.

"Tell me what's at stake, then," she spat through clenched teeth. She half-crawled across the table, her hands like claws digging into the old wood. "You belong to me, Nicholas, and I will not permit you to cease feeding for *anything*." She heaved and panted with anger and possessiveness, eyes flaring, approaching Nicholas like he was prey to subdue.

"You do not and never have owned me," Nicholas said calmly. He stood slowly, menace bleeding out of him as he leaned over her. "Now it's time to leave. Get out of New Hampshire. Stay out of my life for good. And do not ever attempt to threaten me or my *unmei fumetsu* again."

Something in the way he spoke resonated with Jenn, one dominant animal to another, and she backed off, leaving the room quietly without a second glance to me. I breathed out like I'd never breathed before.

"Are you okay?" Nicholas asked me.

"Are you?"

My answer didn't make sense, but it fell out as if it had been waiting to get out of my head. "I just can't understand why Lynch hasn't done anything yet."

"Eliza, we don't know that he's the one who's going to—" Nicholas whispered, one hand distractingly on my knee. "It could be completely random. A bus."

"Right."

He slid from his chair and crouched in front of me. Searching for my downcast eyes, he dipped his head, and it reminded me once again of every other time he made that sweet, simple gesture. The thought swelled my throat against tears.

This could be so close to over.

"Eliza, I'm going to be fine. Really."

He always saw deeper than what I told him. My eyes met his, and I couldn't hold back the tears. "But we don't know. We don't know." My hand covered his, its surface chill a mask of the warmth underneath. "Nicholas, I love you." My voice splintered, and I averted my eyes.

"I wish that were enough to save us all."

Neither of us noticed that Roman had left the room.

CHAPTER 43

Starting the day that way was disarming to say the least. If nothing else, Nicholas's fury with Jenn and his worry for me gave him enough strength to meditate and contact the Master. He came back to me sweaty and even paler, needing sleep. He told the Master he would be arriving with a human friend, but that was all his energy would allow. We would leave for Japan within the day, as soon as Nicholas could walk upright again.

Firelight danced around the grooves and shadows in Nicholas's face. Both of us were lost in silent thought for so long that my voice cracked when I finally spoke.

"I guess I should thank you for getting Jenn out of here, since it was kind of for me," I said.

"Oh, no, it was just as much for me. I hate her."

"Then why did you let her stay at all?"

Nicholas breathed a little laugh out of his nose. "With Jenn, you have to give in a little bit or she'll destroy everything in her path to find out what she wants, get what she wants."

I shoved my hands into my hoodie pockets. "Did you and

she ever have a relationship?" I ventured to ask. I was already in a mood I couldn't come back from.

Nicholas didn't even blink. "Nothing that mattered. Why do you ask?"

"Seriously?"

"Yeah, seriously. I told you she wouldn't come between us. What does it matter?"

"I don't think we need to go into it, do you?"

"Clearly you do think we need to go into it, or you wouldn't have asked. So let's get into it. Creator and chosen have a connection, so we were connected. After I became a vampire, I was only an annoyance to her. I saw her for what she was; we just didn't bother to leave each other alone. It was easier to be together, for a while, but we really hated each other. Still do. So please don't worry that she'll win me back with her sweetness and charm."

I chuckled, but it was dark. "You've gotta be able to see it my way, even if she is a bitch and a half. She's so exotic and powerful, and I'm kind of a mess a lot."

"Would you stop it?"

"Nicholas, I know you say you…love me…but I also know that I'm the one who got the prize here. I hope I'm a little more exciting as a vampire."

"You're plenty exciting now, and you'll be even more exciting as *Shinigami*."

I turned on him with passive aggressive irritation. "I'm mediocre, you've told me so yourself on countless occasions."

"Eliza, you've led a very forgettable life, but you are a very unforgettable woman."

"That was a whole new category of backhanded compliments."

"Unbelievable," Nicholas huffed, slumping further. I wished I hadn't exhausted him so much, but I was a pretty exhausting person, as it turned out.

"I'm a pain in the ass, sorry," I said, sitting next to him. "I'm just so worried." My hands were fists waiting to hit something or someone, and it didn't help to catch sight of Kat and Lynch's wedding invitation lying on the mantle. "I was pretty much told that my entire life is worthless, and only my death that matters. *This* is the secondary news, and I haven't had a chance to deal with it... And I have to hope that I do better with eternity than I've done so far."

"Eliza, are you so afraid to fail that you'll talk yourself out of your destiny? I won't let you. You *insist* that you're nothing, but *you* are chosen! Everything happening around you, to all of us, it's because *you* are so important. You're filled with a power that you're blind to because you're so damn worried about what you aren't." Fire in his eyes, waving his hands, exasperated with me, roaring with passion... I loved him like this. "You have this bravery in you, and you're so intelligent, and there's nothing you won't do for the people you love, and you're thoughtful. Such determination, and common sense..." he trailed off. "You're a hero *now*, Eliza," he ended in a throaty voice.

Tears prickled behind my lashes, and I threw myself in his arms where he sat, kissing him hard and desperately. He laughed as his lips molded into mine.

"Is that your response to all compliments?" he asked with a smirk as I sat back, still on his lap.

"Yes. It's how I got that prestigious job. And my apartment. And all my clothes."

"Well, you deserve a better wardrobe then."

"Hey!"

He laughed, still a full-bodied sound, at odds with the frailty of his thighs underneath me. "I like the way you dress," he said. "No frills. Just you."

"Man, those heels of Jenn's, huh? What were they, ten inches high?"

He pulled my afghan off the back of the chair and wrapped it around us. I snuggled into him, breathing deeply of his mint chocolate scent. "I don't want to talk about Jenn anymore. She's gone."

I frowned. As he said this, our foolishness hit me medicine-ball hard in the stomach. How could we think it would be that easy to get rid of her?

"Nicholas, where exactly do you think she went?" A second passed and his body stiffened. "Nicholas, would she pay a visit to Lynch? Where's Roman?" The questions poured out like a tidal wave, and Nicholas couldn't answer them.

He looked quickly out the window, where dusk was falling. "We need to go," he said, and we were both on our feet as fast they could carry us.

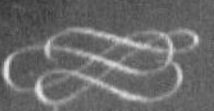

CHAPTER 44

Nicholas slammed the SUV into park, skidding in Lynch's slushy driveway. A morbidly cold drizzle soaked everything. The white house loomed ahead like a mausoleum, a giant albino monster threatening to devour us as we approached. Grim, black windows stared at us, eyes hiding the depravity inside.

I knew Jenn was here. I knew this would end things. I knew it would be horrible. I knew it like I knew that I would be a vampire one day. Any uncertainty was obliterated by the line of a hundred or more crows dotting the mansion's roof, all eyes on me.

Nicholas was a man walking to his death beside me. We didn't speak. We didn't touch. We only trudged forward, toward the towering front door, neither of us ready for what we'd find behind it. Nicholas didn't knock. The door wasn't locked.

Please, God, let Roman be in there, let him protect her from those two things. Hope burned in my gut, which felt bruised like I'd been beaten. I was thankful that I didn't have the ability to see visions of Lynch, or Jenn, or both, attacking defenseless Kat. I think I would have thrown myself from the car.

I retched when the door swung open. Nicholas fell to one knee on the doorstep.

A smear of glistening blood made a path across the marble floor. It ended in a gruesome puddle, with tendrils of Kat's fiery hair trailing into it. She was bent over backwards, as if being dipped in a romantic dance. Her eyes bore into mine as she hung upside down, alight with disbelieving fear and betrayal. I tried to utter her name, but a choked gargle came out, matched by one of her own. A shimmering red bubble of blood popped on her neck wound.

My eyes dragged up her wilted body to the demon ravishing her, shaking her form as the last drops of life were sucked dry. I fell to my knees beside Nicholas when I saw that it wasn't Jenn's cascade of curls falling around my dying friend, or Lynch's perfectly styled black hair, but golden blond locks.

Roman?

The vampire and his victim fell to the ground, Roman still clamped on to Kat's neck, grunting with the end of her breath.

"Noooooo!" The scream erupted from deep inside me. I crawled to the spot where Roman and Kat had collapsed on the floor, making sounds I didn't even know in nightmares. Roman's head shot up, blood raining off his chin, dripping from his fangs. He heaved with the exertion of the kill. He met my wild stare, but said nothing to answer my senseless babbling. A sob broke from Nicholas behind me.

"Roman, God, what have you *done?!*" Nicholas scrambled along the floor, past me to Roman, pulling him off of Kat, but I knew, I knew she was gone. A stream of blood snaked over my fingers on the floor, and soaked into Nicholas's pants as he crawled through it. The despair rolled off him in waves as he clamped a hand on the killer's shoulder. Roman scuttled back, sprawling messily on the floor. "What have you done?" Nicholas repeated, head hanging.

"What God should never have asked of you, Nicholas." Roman's voice was thick with her blood, it gurgled in his throat. I let out a screaming sob.

Roman floated to standing in a single inhuman move. I watched his feet pause near me on the floor where I stroked Kat's blood-caked hair. "I'm sorry," he said. My tears fell into a puddle of blood, turning it a sickly pink.

Roman walked to the still open door, pausing once again to turn around, his eyes avoiding me to look to Nicholas.

"Roman, we are still brothers."

Roman's voice grated, "Until time ends, brother."

I put my head on the floor and closed my eyes.

CHAPTER 45

Dear Nicholas,

This cannot be a letter of apology. Apologies are reserved for mistakes and regrets, of which this was neither. I am saddened irrevocably by what I have done, but I will not apologize for taking away your choice. It was the same difficult choice that will keep you alive.

Even still, I don't know what I intended to do when I came to Chris's tonight. Jenniveve was already here. The two of the fiends confronted me, demanding I confirm what they'd theorized, that the only reason you wouldn't feed would be for Eliza's sake. Lynch wanted to know what Kat had to do with it, and I was too shocked by how quickly they worked it out to deny that she was your *unmei nashi*. Lynch broke down, terrified you might get to Kat, and Jenn turned it to her favor in the blink of an eye. She convinced him that they had to finish both you and Eliza to ensure of Kat's safety. Jenn's psychotic way of taking back what's hers. Lynch begged me to stay here to protect Kat. I'm shocked, as I am sure you are, that his feelings for Kat are real.

I wish there had been some other way. I'm certain that you wouldn't want to survive at all without your chosen by your side.

Your loyalty to Eliza is too strong to take this friend from her, who means as much to her as you do to me. Your plans to go to Japan were admirable, but we both know that it was a pipe dream. You'd not have survived the trip, and most certainly would not have made it back to the States to feed on Kat.

You won't be as strong as you once were, and it will take time to get back to your former self without having fed like you should have, but weakness is a small price to pay when you consider the options.

I pray that you do not try to find me. I cannot handle the hatred in Eliza's eyes.

Please, Nicholas, know that I have done this, and would do anything, for you. Your love for Eliza is worth the end of our friendship. It is all that either of you need.

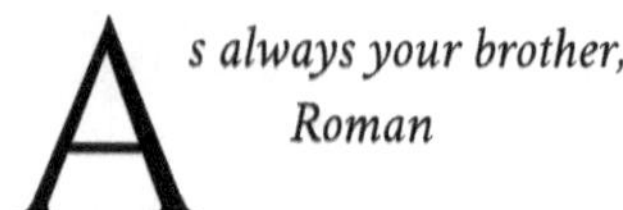

As always your brother,
Roman

CHAPTER 46

To say I was in shock was far too delicate a phrase.

It didn't matter that Kat and I hadn't spent any time together recently. The loss of her ripped me to the core. It wracked me with guilt, but there could be no real comparison to the anguish of leaving Nicholas, whether because I loved him so, or because he was to take me from my pitiful life into a better one. Not even now, in losing the only friend I ever needed, who'd shaped part of who I was. Even now, when I wasn't sure *who* I was anymore.

I no longer existed underneath the suffering I'd caused, endured and run from.

Kat was all that had rooted me to humanity. With her gone, nothing tethered me to this aimless "shadow of a life," as Nicholas called it. To leave it behind was only to abandon the overwhelming losses of those I loved. When I turned my back on life, it didn't feel like I was running away from the misery it had become—it felt like I was running home, finally. I no longer had to try to create significance in a world that was never meant for me.

What direction I did have pointed to Nicholas. I was a fool

to think I had any choice in my fate, or in the lengths I would go to in order to be with him. The endless circle of blame in my head was akin to the seven circles of Hell: Lynch, for dragging Kat into the world of vampires, Jenn for being the catalyst that ended it all, Roman for doing the dreadful deed, or Nicholas, who just escaped the cruel hand of fate.

I blamed myself for knowing that really, I'd chosen Nicholas's side all along.

My captor rested his hand on my shoulder from behind the chair in which I sat, staring at the bowl of Golden Grahams I would never eat. Automatically, my hand rose up to cover his. I leaned my head against his wrist.

"You all but thanked him for killing her." My voice was dry, dead, scratching at the air.

Nicholas's sighed, relieved, I assumed, that I could speak at all. He said nothing.

He knew what I knew. None of this mattered now. I was born *Shinigami*, and I was his, willingly, forever.

"I'm ready."

PART II
RUNNING AWAY

CHAPTER 47

K at's death turned me into a haunted house. The lights were on, but nothing good was home. Inside, was an infestation of hornets.

I sat at the handmade kitchen table in Nicholas's log cabin, watching the first clear day of the new year out the window. It was dead calm, quiet. Lifeless. Even the birds didn't know what to do without the constantly falling snow we'd had that winter in New Hampshire. Nicholas put his hand on my shoulder from behind me. Instinctively, I leaned my head into it.

"I'm ready to go to Japan."

Nicholas sighed. "Eliza, you're not."

"You showed me my fate, but it doesn't mean you get to call the shots. I say I'm ready, and I am."

"You only think you're ready to become *Shinigami* because you feel so horrible right now."

"I barely feel anything now!"

"Eliza—"

Rage coursed through me, propelling me out of the chair. "No! The reason everything's horrible is *because* it's time for me to become a vampire! I've been stripped of any reason to go on alive, in true *Shinigami* fashion! Right? That's how the world you know works, right? Some hand of fate does everything it can to make sure I have nothing to live for, that I'm all alone? Nothing ties me here anymore. I have no job, thanks to your well-thought gift of getting me fired, my apartment is gone, everybody that ever cared I existed is conveniently dead, and now my best friend, my only true friend—gone. We were together every day!" Acid tears ate at my lids, my voice was broken glass. "Kat is dead. *Your* best friend killed her. And if Roman hadn't, you would have. Despite that, I still love you more than I thought possible. Do you know what that does to me?" Like gasoline mouthwash. Like a bed of nails in my brain. Like termites in my gut, cockroaches in my heart. A flesh-eating disease.

Pain crossed Nicholas's beautiful face, but he couldn't deny my words.

My voice evened out, fueled by crude determination. "My whole life has been a tool to make sure I would have nothing left. It's my fate to be alone, except for you."

I approached him slowly, like he was some scared rabbit, and took his hand. It was as limp as I felt.

Softly, I said, "I cannot survive another day like this, knowing everyone around me will be destroyed, will be ripped apart, away... I'm a cancer here. I don't belong. It's time for me to go to Japan. We've got the tickets, our bags are packed. It's time for me to become a vampire."

CHAPTER 48

I was as lifeless as the cold, gray morning that Nicholas and I left for Japan. It was miserable boarding that plane, early so that the sun wouldn't burn Nicholas in his frailness. He missed the sunlight; I could see it in the longing, Jesus-like stare upwards through the plane window. I pictured his skin bubbling and turning to ash in the morning light. Since Kat was killed, the continual cloud of death that followed me had nested inside me instead, giving me morbid visions. I was too empty to be worried about it.

Nicholas held my hand in both of his on the plane. I looked over to find him staring at me, a panicked look of worry about him. He'd been doting on me like some worried grandmother. It was getting on my nerves.

"Eliza?" Nicholas whispered, like he was talking to a child he just found in the woods.

"Yes?" I whispered back.

I studied his face with detachment. He still looked rugged, even though he was gaunt. His lips were paler. His chocolate eyes weren't the inhuman, ever-swirling storm of caramel and cocoa; they were still, as if they didn't have the energy anymore. His cheeks were hollow, his skin dry. His dark hair, a mix of well-groomed and tousled curls, fell across his forehead, limp. Denying himself the blood of the human he'd been fated to kill had diminished him. It happened to all *Shinigami* that dared defy the call of fate. It didn't seem right that Nicholas had to play by those rules, but I saw him decaying before my eyes. Roman was certain that Nicholas wouldn't survive the plane trip to Japan, but that was before he took away Nicholas's remedy. Before he killed my best friend himself.

I wasn't so sure he'd make the trip to Japan either. Only that realization shocked my feelings into play.

Nicholas was all I had left. And he was destined to make me immortal; I was his *unmei fumetsu*. I didn't feel much like *his Eliza* just now, only Ellie Morgan. I was the teenager again, abandoned in a world without anyone to love me but a ghost of decay that clung to me like a leech.

He leaned closer, murmuring, "You should try to sleep. You haven't slept since Kat—"

I cleared my dry throat. "Oh. Really?" Sheer pity emanated from him. Glaring, I turned away. The last thing I wanted was pity. I was the reason Kat was dead.

Nicholas kissed my hand, and held it to his clammy cheek. "Eliza, I don't know how to make this right." His voice broke. The thought of him suffering should crash like a falling boulder into my heart, but not this time.

"Well, Nicholas, you've lost your best friend, too." I couldn't control the spite in my voice. I didn't want to.

"Roman isn't gone for good; Kat is. It doesn't matter who drew the blood, the guilt is all mine," he muttered.

Volatile as I was, I couldn't let Nicholas take all the blame. My spine stiffened as I told him with cold calculation what I knew was the truth. "Kat was *unmei nashi*. No fate." The words stung like poison through my gritted teeth. "She was doomed from the day she met me. It's my fate to become a vampire, and the only way that can happen is if nobody misses me. It's why everyone around me dies. Why I'll be forever alone if I stay human." I squeezed his hand. *"Not your fault. It's not even Roman's fault that he killed her. He only did it so you wouldn't have to."* I swallowed. "He was trying to do us a favor."

Nicholas's sharp bite of breath substituted for his disagreement. He knew better than to disagree with me, and on this point, what argument could he really make?

A flight attendant with bouncy hair like Kat's stopped by our seats.

"Can I get you—"

Her question ended abruptly when she saw my face. To look so truly frightening that you can stop the essence of perkiness mid-sentence with the slightest of eye contact must be the worst superpower a person can have.

"Miss, I'm sorry to bother you," she said quickly and quietly, and moved on to the next passenger, ignoring Nicholas completely.

I put my head back and went to sleep.

I let Nicholas tote me through the crowded airport to switch planes, jostling obnoxious people coming down from vacation highs, all brightly colored and loud and pushy. There were so many people bustling about, they became a blur. It wasn't hard to tune them out.

Nicholas bought me a coffee for way too much money, and we found our way to a quiet spot that had been overlooked by the masses. I watched the boards change times and destinations. I sipped the coffee. I tasted nothing.

"Eliza?" Again he stared at me with unmasked worry. He

shifted in the seat next to me so he could hold my gaze, and make me pay attention. Kat used to get my attention by giving me food. "I want to talk about what you'll come across in the temple."

Nicholas's eyes burned with the discomfort of thirst and guilt. Rage bubbled inside me again, that any of this was happening, and that I couldn't be more kind to Nicholas now that he needed me. I needed too much and had forgotten how to process the void of losing everything.

"What do you need to tell me?"

"The temple is completely off the map. It technically doesn't exist, but is actually at the top of Mount Daisen." He paused to rub his forehead with his palm. "A lot of vampires call the temple home. *Some* of them are well adjusted," he said with a crooked smile, "but most are dangerous. They leave only to feed, and have no interaction with humans besides. The humans that are chosen to become *Shinigami* are reluctant exceptions."

I was surprised to find myself interested. I hadn't bothered to think of anybody else in the temple, vampire or human; I had no intention of making friends. It was interesting to think there were other people who repelled companionship the way I did, though.

"Tell me more."

He smiled tightly, the only way he really could now that his lips were so constantly dry and cracked. "The vampires there are the most primal of us. Don't expect a fruit basket. But you need to be there."

When I realized that was all he had to say, I got up the energy to respond. "I don't want a warm reception. I just want to leave my life behind."

∼

The Kyoto airport held staggering amounts of tourists buzzing with energy. I longed for Boston, where you could get lost in the crowd on purpose, and nobody made eye contact. Despite the bustle, nobody here bumped and pushed and grumbled. Some of them nodded politely, acknowledging that I was real. It felt like everyone was watching me. I had no right to be there.

The train looked like it should be robot operated. It was a city that someone made up but hadn't gotten quite right. Landing in Japan was like falling into a video game, where there were vending machines for everything, and glaring lights, pulsing music, but the buildings looked like they were too old, and too clean. It wasn't the opposite of Ossipee, New Hampshire, it was a different planet. In Ossipee, everything felt familiar and warm; but that town didn't want me anymore, if it ever did. So, now I helplessly allowed Nicholas to navigate me through the train and bus routes that would bring us to the base of Mount Daisen.

When we began traveling through the countryside, when the strangeness began to fall away, I allowed myself to slowly attempt to repair. I didn't deserve peace, but the world of snow that greeted me was too like the New Hampshire winter for me not to fall in love with it. A fire was put out inside me as I took in the streams, hot springs, and mountains that belonged in a fairy tale. Snow-covered pagodas perched on hillsides, overlooking skeletal forests. Tiny villages spotted the landscape, and I could imagine families inside around their tables, together. Forest animals fearlessly showed themselves in this place.

For the first time, I felt like it hadn't been only desperation that made me ready to come here. I was *unmei fumetsu*, chosen to be immortal, a vampire, *Shinigami.*

"Amazing, isn't it?" Nicholas asked me in a low grumble. I'd almost forgotten he was with me.

I looked at him, really looked at him like I wanted him to see me, too. I wasn't afraid for him to see the wretch I was, because being here, I knew that the feeling would end. "It's the most beautiful place ever."

He smiled, and a pang of missing him swallowed me. My eyes swam with tears that I'd held back too long.

"You'll be okay, Eliza." He pulled my hand into his rough, warm ones, and smiled more. "This is where you'll be okay."

The tears fell as the train skidded to a stop. Two more hours until arrival at the temple.

~

Yonago Station was surreal. At first, I thought I must have dozed off on the train, and this was one of the half-dreams I'd been suffering. But it was too pleasant. Boston's stations were muted burgundies, grays and other dirt-encrusted dull shades, the worst of New England fall colors plastered to dirty city things. Here, my eyes couldn't stop moving from the vibrant hues that painted every surface. Drawings of Japanese families and royalty in traditional robes that belonged in a museum covered the buses, the walls, the tiny shops, every sign and window. There were even standups with holes cut out to put your face into for photos, like you'd see at a carnival. The colors came to life in the people here, all of them wearing tulip yellows, deep sea greens, sunset pinks, blending like flowers in a colossal garden. Simple, sweet, harmonic. I'd walked into a children's book.

The bleakness in my heart edged off, letting a little of this light in. For the first time in days, I noticed Nicholas's scent from beside me. Today, it was fresh fruit and cinnamon that complemented this incredible place.

I wished I wasn't a pock mark on its beauty.

"Eliza," Nicholas whispered in my ear. His breath sent the first rumblings of desire through my body that I'd gotten in a while, but the black hole in me consumed it.

"This place is so alive," I hissed, yearning and contempt kicking the seeping warmth from my body, beating each other in my heart.

Nicholas sighed and leaned his forehead on my shoulder. I leaned the side of my head against his, trying not to crumble. "I can feel the pain throbbing from your heart, and Jesus, Eliza, I want to heal it for you, would do anything to heal it for you. The death in you—it's killing me."

"Nicholas, I love you." My voice was hollow. I meant it, I knew it the way I know what the state capitals are, but I felt nothing.

"Your love for me chokes you, and I don't know how to fix it."

I stared straight ahead into the blinding colors of life.

CHAPTER 49

Daisenji Temple was perched on the mountainside like it had been there since the dawn of time, emanating serenity and power, but welcoming. Nicholas smiled wide when it came into view.

I was afraid of it.

The fear invaded all my other warring emotions, making itself real more real. Nicholas didn't notice, thank God; it was embarrassing, and he was babysitting me enough.

"Let's go," Nicholas said, and started up quickly, tugging me behind.

He took his boots off at the door, motioning for me to do the same. As soon as I did, I wanted to run away.

The peace inside the temple punched me in the face. A Japanese woman with the hint of a smile was silently adding incense to an urn, and it made me want to cry with inexplicable anger. Only the terror that stung my chest prevented it.

"You look like you've seen a ghost. What's up?" Nicholas said.

"I want to leave."

Nicholas shook his head in disbelief and ran his fingers

through his hair. "Okay, let me pay my respects quickly, and we'll go." I tried to stay still and not fidget like the devil in church as I watched him place incense in the burner, nodding a quiet greeting to the woman before him. My stomach turned as the subtle scent assaulted me.

"You must go."

I gasped, spinning around to face the owner of the voice behind me. A tiny man in brown robes stared up at me, his face solemn. I could only think one thing.

This man can see inside me.

"Grief consumes you. It burns everything in its path. Your fire is impure. You must go. *Aitou.*"

Mourning. I knew the word in my heart. I was panting in fear, shaking as this man's soul peered deep into my own, and nothing should be in there, nothing.

"I—I'm sorr...sorry."

I ran barefoot from the temple out into the snow, desperate for that place to be behind me, away from me and the spirit of death that haunted me. A half dozen crows met me, black ash marks on the snow.

Nicholas appeared at my side like a stream of energy, making me yelp with shock, my nerves were so electrified. He grabbed my arms, and I struggled, whimpering, but couldn't match his strength.

"Sssshhh, Eliza. Eliza, it's okay." He smoothed my hair, and bent at the knees the way he always did when he wanted to look deeply into my eyes. He calmed me like that, like a wild horse back from the brink of a destructive panic. My breathing was so erratic that it hurt as it slowed down. Hot tears poured down my cheeks as I tried to erase the temple in my mind, screaming at me with its tranquility.

Nicholas pulled his gaze from mine with a long breath. I answered his raised eyebrows with a nod, that yes, I was settled. Only then did he kneel to put my boots on. Like a little kid, I let him. The crows watched his every move.

"Your feet are soaked, love," he whispered, drying my numb toes them with his coat.

Standing back up, the snow crunching under him, he pulled me close, smothering me with his arms and chest. His scent was like home, our home; cinnamon and chocolate, vampire-tailored to suit my needs and make me his, but it wasn't working.

"God, I'm sorry. I should have known," he murmured.

"Known what?"

"People in mourning don't belong in a temple. Here, grief is an impurity of the soul." He shook his head, his fists clenched. "Your heart hurts too much right now."

Cold stung like bile in my throat. "I have no heart now."

The incident at the temple left me emotionally scorched. I sat in the snow with Nicholas, the image of the old man's eyes burned into my mind. This stranger that was repulsed by my frozen soul.

Nicholas rubbed my back like my mother used to when I couldn't sleep. His touch made me hurt more. I wanted nothing good near me, no one else to touch me that I could ruin. But Nicholas was no better than me. His mere appearance in my life brought the destruction of it, gave a name to the death that I created just by existing; *unmei fumetsu.*

"There's an inn not far from here. Let's head there so you can rest."

My head was an anchor that I had to pull up out of the sea just to meet his eyes. Nicholas was emaciated. "You need to feed, Nicholas."

He ran his hands through his hair. "I won't get any weaker before we get to the temple."

"If you fed, you'd be stronger, though."

"Not right now. Anything but *unmei nashi* right now won't be enough anyway. Waiting until I have another one won't hurt."

Silence sat in the air while I thought, *So Kat just gets replaced then, by someone else to kill.* "Where do you think Roman is, Nicholas?"

He sucked in a breath. "He doesn't want us to know. What difference would it make? Kat's still dead, and we are still this."

CHAPTER 50

Crows circled overhead at the inn. They must have known I was coming.

The burning in me subsided as Daisenji Temple vanished from sight, and my fear with it. It left me drained. Grayer than Nicholas looked.

He led me to a modest little inn hidden by trees, that looked like part of the mountain itself. The fresh smell of the place was so different from the heady scent of incense in Daisenji that I breathed a sigh of relief. There were vegetables being cooked nearby, and a fire was burning strong and bright to welcome us.

"I'll find the inn keeper," Nicholas said, and left me waiting. He headed to a back room like he knew exactly where he was going. I could hear him speaking Japanese with a man over the sound of pots clanging, followed by laughter from them both. It felt like home, home with Nicholas and Roman, where I could rest. Finally rest my soul.

I wasn't sure I wanted a soul anymore.

Nicholas came out of the room with an old smiling man clapping him on the shoulder. The man easily was two feet shorter than Nicholas, his back hunched. He walked with a cane that looked like it had been cut right out of a tree, probably by his own hand. Happiness filled me when the old man looked up with the most beautiful toothless smile.

"This is Ayumu," Nicholas said. Ayumu smiled up at me, now so close that I could smell the scent of the kitchen on him, and of the earth.

"*Konnichiwa,*" I said, bowing, but Ayumu grabbed me in an embrace with more strength than I thought his tiny body could muster. I blinked back tears from the simple humanity of it.

When he pulled back, I was surprised to see him still grinning. He took my chin in his gnarled hand and said, "*Unmei shinsei.*"

I looked at Nicholas over the old man's head.

"Chosen for new life," he said quietly.

I looked back down to the little inn keeper, and this time I embraced him first.

~

Our room was dim in the fading afternoon. A low table in the center dominated it, covered in a pale blue blanket, thin enough to reveal a glow from underneath. It promised warmth to my aching muscles and freezing limbs, and pulled me in fast.

"Put your legs under the blanket," Nicholas said as I sank to my knees in front of it. Sure enough, it was heated underneath. I could have crawled inside. I groaned, closed my eyes, and put my head down on the tabletop.

I sat up what I thought was moments later, but the sky was dark. I'd been woken by a soft sound at the rice paper door. Nicholas emerged from behind an ornate room divider at the rear of the room, wearing black sweatpants and a gray thermal shirt. In an instant he was in the doorway, bowing to a young girl and taking a tray from her hands, though she wanted to bring it in herself; he knew I couldn't see anyone. Not yet. A delicious scent wafted towards me.

"I'm ravenous!" I belted out.

Nicholas grinned, a hint of his former self shining through. "There's my girl."

The prospect of food coupled with a nap changed my attitude quite a bit. It's the little things, sometimes.

"I like you better when you eat," Nicholas said.

"Mmmph," I mumbled as I shoveled fish and steamed veggies in my mouth like I hadn't eaten in a week. Actually, I wasn't sure when the last time I'd eaten was. "I'd still kill for a box of Funny Bones."

"I could give you horse shit and you'd eat it right now. For your first victim I'll try to arrange for a Hostess factory employee."

I laughed hard, choking. "Come on!" I said, wiping tears from my eyes. "That shouldn't be funny!"

"You eat like a starved bear, and it's really sexy."

"What every girl wants to hear."

"You're not every girl."

"If I was every girl, there'd be a lot more stomachs being sucked in all around the world." It was hard not to sing the Oprah theme song, but I wasn't about to stop eating.

"My God, it's good to hear you laugh again." His voice thickened. "I miss you, Eliza."

I stiffened. "Well, Nicholas, I was always here." The cold fire crept out in my voice, refusing to be forgotten entirely.

"You haven't been and you know it."

"That's not my fault. It's one thing that's not my fault."

We ate in silence for a few minutes, but a couple of glances over the table confirmed neither of us was ready to let go of this peace. My belly wasn't churning and screaming, finally.

Nicholas watched me, the cream and coffee spinning of his eyes as warm as the heat on my legs. He looked so tired, so pained, but beautiful, flickering in and out of existence in his worry. He reached across the table to tuck a black curl behind my ear. My momentary contentment and that single touch stamped down my rage and sadness; I leaned into his hand, surprising us both. Nicholas actually took a sharp breath.

"Eliza," was all he said, but it forced a sob out of me as my former self broke the surface of the despair I'd ingested. He was around the table, holding me from behind, and rocking me, but I was already still. I had no tears left.

His lips grazed my ear through my mess of curls. "I promise you, I'll make this better—"

"You can't."

Nicholas stopped moving. "You'll be *Shinigami* legend, Eliza. One day, you'll see there's nothing more important." He stiffened, betraying his fear of saying what he'd say next. "This life that you're leaving behind was never really yours. And you never really wanted it."

I wasn't offended by what he said—he'd always said what he wanted to, and I knew it was the truth. It was the deadbolt on a door I'd already locked.

CHAPTER 51

Never had the sun sparkled that way, until I witnessed it kiss the snowy cherry blossom trees surrounding the temple. My own steady breaths were the sole sound to interrupt bird songs. The world breathed a sigh with a cold wind ruffling my hair.

This was the place I would die.

Nicholas inhaled deeply. My heart jumped to my throat to look at him. I hadn't seen his face in the sunlight in so long, it took my breath away. I tried to see him as he'd been, before all the death that crushed us. The close, bouncing dark curls had a tint of gold here. I loved how his eyes were the most dominant feature on his beautiful face; they were at their widest staring at the temple, and their warmth encompassed me over the distance. The ever-present five o'clock shadow was rugged, but managed to make his face even fresher against peach pearl skin. Subtle furrows framed the berry lips that I dreamed of, still plump like a child's, smooth and inviting.

Even wilting like he was, he was spectacular.

He caught me out of the corner of his eye, and flashed a smug smile.

"Home," was all he said in his lion's growl.

My world was coming together.

Climbing the stairs embedded in the mountainside, Nicholas told me about the creature who waited at the top inside the temple.

"Records of the Master date back over 1700 years, but still no one knows when he was made, or how."

"What? Hasn't he ever told anyone? Not even you?"

"He's too old to remember." Nicholas shrugged.

When the only the sound was snow crunching with our steps, I blurted out, "I'm scared." I hated that it was true, and shocked myself by saying it out loud.

Nicholas stopped and turned to me. The mountain wind carried the scent of peppermint and brownies to swirl around me while his cocoa cream eyes looked into mine; sedative made just for me. I pushed the emptiness, anger, and fear away as hard as I could, and let Nicholas comfort me.

"He's fierce, but kind, and he'll be pivotal in deciding the rest of your existence, so, yeah, be nervous. Nothing surprises him, nothing escapes him. But he'll show you the way."

Nicholas's admiration and love rang clear. It must have shown on my face how it touched me, because Nicholas bowed his head shyly.

"Oh my God, you're like, overcome with emotion," I said like a jerk.

"I'm not."

"Are too."

A smirk twitched his lips, but it faded in his sincerity. "The Master saved me from myself. He took me under his wing while all vampires were under his care, he took care of *me*. I owe him everything." He swallowed, and his eyes never left mine when he said, "Without him, I wouldn't have you."

I tried not to let the emotional door slam that I'd built recently. "Nicholas, you were fated to be my creator whether the Master existed or not. You don't owe anyone for what we have. Nobody made this happen, not even him."

"He made me believe there was more for me. And that's you. So stop arguing with me."

"You're still happy you found me?"

"Happy? Yes. Yes, I am. Tortured, disturbed, but happy." He looked at me harder. "You're not happy you found me?"

I was pinned, motionless by this all too simple question, even though I was the one who brought it up. How the hell could I be *happy* to have found him, after my life and Kat's and everyone's had been destroyed because of it? I suppose if the Master wasn't responsible for what Nicholas had become, Nicholas wasn't responsible for what my life had become.

Bells clanged at the top of the mountain, and it sent a flurry of birds flying. Not crows, for once. I was lying to myself if I said I wasn't happy to be here. I was happy to know what I was meant for. I'd spent my entire life wondering what it was. I wasn't fool enough to think I got a higher purpose in life for free. There had to be sacrifices.

Mine was my best friend, and I made that sacrifice to save my own destiny, and Nicholas; they were one in the same.

"Silence is answer enough for me," he said, more ice in his voice than under my feet, more cold coming from the frost he gave off than from the cold wind around us. His brownie scent was gone. He didn't want to comfort me anymore. There was nothing but hurt and anger from him to match my own.

Finally, we felt right together again.

～

Once inside the temple, I understood right away that the vampires I knew in Ossipee, even the psychotic Lynch, were refined and humanized. This place was as primal as it came, closer to the Earth and Heaven than anything I'd ever imagined, bare of anything except soul.

The temple itself exuded a life of its own, formidable and ancient. I was shocked to feel as though it was wrapping its arms around me, but I shouldn't have been; this was the only place that welcomed death.

Flames flickered in orange lanterns lining the walls in the womblike darkness. They lit a path along the red runner down the enormous length of the place to an altar sitting atop a short flight of stairs. Incense created wisps of smoke, shrouding the sole figure.

For as singular with the Earth as the temple was, the creature before me couldn't have been more otherworldly. He was so still it gave the disconcerting illusion that the ground was moving. His presence defied his slight stature. A force of silent will, he emanated power that filled the hollow hall, seemed to shake the very walls. He wore a simple white robe with his hands tucked into the bell sleeves. Waist-length white hair with matching mustache gave the impression that he'd never been young. And his eyes—they bore into me across the length of the temple. They were a glowing, colorless shade of milky white, no pupils. At once, I realized I shouldn't be able to see such details so far from him, and gasped at a disarming sensation that he was standing right in front of me, like he was in both places at once. Goosebumps sprang up on my arms under my layers of shirts and coat.

"Holy hell!" I screamed. The Master was in front of us with not so much as a flicker or the flash I would see from Nicholas when he moved with vampire speed. The Master was up there, then he was down here. My head spun like I'd been put under a spell.

"Shhh," Nicholas hissed at me.

The Master's face was smooth as glass, but rippled inhumanly with joy as Nicholas bowed to him. I followed suit. Ignoring me, the Master pulled Nicholas upright to embrace him.

"Nikorasu," the Master said in a voice rich with age and love. "I've missed you. And now you only come on official business." The Master focused his eerie eyes on me, and I smiled. My discomfort was like another person in the room, it was so overwhelming. "Ah, but *she* is not all business," the Master said into Nicholas's ear, milky eyes never leaving mine.

Nicholas pulled gently away. "You see too much sometimes," he said to the Master.

The old vampire continued to stare at me, and my soul squirmed.

"It is simple to see the death in her," the Master said. After a cryptically long pause in which I realized that vampire pauses are longer than regular ones, he finally looked back to Nicholas. I was able to exhale.

"I'm ready. I'm ready to be done with my awful life, and to see how *you* can somehow make it all better by teaching me karate? I guess?" I spat.

"Eliza," Nicholas started, but I turned on him. Being sized up didn't suit me.

"Shut up, Nicholas. I won't be censored. I'm here on good faith, and I have every right to—"

I didn't get to finish. My teeth began chattering, and I shook like mad, attacked by cold. The kind of cold Nicholas gave off, that I was familiar with, but intensified to a dull ache. It came from the Master.

I squirmed, sending needles to my head that morphed into

a throbbing eye pain. I forgot everything except how afraid of this ancient vampire I was. He glowered at me, and Nicholas had been right; all I saw was a god, beyond human or animal.

"Master," Nicholas pleaded quietly.

Warmth flooded me so quickly that I buckled in half like a dropped marionette. I sucked in the cold air, wincing as it stung my chest.

Point taken. Don't mouth off, and don't screw with Nicholas on the Master's watch.

CHAPTER 52

The Master left without explanation, just vanished, leaving a cold mist in his wake. I'd never seen anything move like him.

Nicholas and I were alone. I dreaded looking at him, but I did it.

He was deathly serious, the lines around his mouth making him look sadder now that he was so malnourished. But as I watched him, he burst into laughter that echoed up and down the long space, and had me looking around like we were going to get caught.

"What the hell, Nicholas! Shush!"

"You're not the boss of me," he said, lips trying to stay still.

I tried not to laugh with him. "What's so funny?"

"What's so funny? You! What were you *thinking*?"

"Yeah, yeah, I know I shouldn't have yelled. We just met. Yelling should wait for a second or third meeting."

Nicholas ran his fingers through his hair, and shook his head. "Eliza, nobody talks to him like that." He laughed again, and it was beautiful. "Who the hell do you think you are?!" I hadn't seen him laugh so hard in a long time. His now-bony shoulders shook with it.

"I'm screwed, right?" I said, holding back laughter.

"Yeah, you so are," he wheezed.

I crouched down, suddenly very tired. It might have been from the emotional exhaustion but more likely because of climbing a million stairs. "What now?"

Nicholas recovered himself and crouched next to me. "You're going to learn."

"Karate?" I said skeptically.

"Martial arts are a way of life defining the most enlightened people in history. And the Master," he said, his lip twitching again to a smile, "has been *the* Master as far back as martial arts are recorded. Trust me when I tell you, he has plenty to teach." Nicholas glanced around. "He's waiting for me to talk to him. You stay here, I won't be long. Then we'll get you fed, get some rest." And he was off with that *crack*, leaving a streak behind him.

The silence enveloped me. I'd have burned the place down for a nap, but I stayed awake, cross-legged, alone, in this strange place—and it was right. No matter how scared I was, this was right.

Then, the feeling filled me, like it had never done before. It seeped through me like oil, into every limb and thought. It was different, more intense than ever, and I recognized it as soon as it entered me. That shadow of death, the thing all too real, like an old friend that nobody wants, but the only one I ever really had. It was always with me, after my parents' death, the rest of my family. It left me after Roman killed Kat, but by then, I'd already knew what it was; the *Shinigami* coming to claim me. The ever-present chill down my spine that was fate itself.

I breathed slow and deep through the presence of death

overcoming me, catching myself *smiling*, smothering the oppression and guilty that had ruled for so long...

A shadow flickered impossibly on a wall already too dark for shadow, behind a column. Finally, after all these years, a body to go with the presence of death invading me, embracing me. I wanted it, and wanted to hit it, and was so happy to see it was a real thing. I didn't dare move.

The shadow moved again. A person, but death. I couldn't understand.

"Hello?" *Real smart.*

The shadow darted out of view, giving me a glimpse of a bare chest, loose white pants, and waist-length black hair. Human? I stayed still and waited for more, but nothing and no one came. Only Nicholas.

"Someone was here," I whispered.

"Okay."

"You left me alone."

"Not really."

"Was I safe?"

"Probably not. But you could handle yourself until I got back."

I just gaped at him. He'd left me to be vampire fodder. "Thanks, Nicholas. You just told me the *Shinigami* weren't going to love me, then you left me for dead. I was feeling awesome already."

He smirked. It pissed me off. "I'm not into your ill-placed mockery."

Nicholas looked unfazed. "The Master did it on purpose. He wanted me to leave you to your own devices."

I should have been mad that Nicholas was amused by it, but instead I was just irritated that I'd acted like such a girl in the face of the challenge. What did I do, call out *hello?* Me, horror movie buff—I pulled a Classic. Then bitched at

Nicholas about it. I should have gone to check the shadow out. I should have confronted him—it—but I chickened out. Fail.

There could be no failing here. I had to get over myself if I wanted to be rid of this life that didn't want me. I had to see things the way the *Shinigami* saw them if I was to be ready.

"Nicholas—" I started, looking back to where the shadow had been. The presence of death had gone with it, leaving a vacancy in my chest.

Though Nicholas was beside me, I smelled nothing from him—which meant he wasn't trying to be close to me, to capture me. It hurt me more, and I had no right to be hurt, not the way I'd been treating him.

He waited, looking at me distantly.

"I saw someone over there," I said, pointing to the column, "and it felt like death. Like the feeling I always had, but more."

Nicholas was completely still, emotionally, in every way, and I grew more disconnected from him as I realized he would never know that specter that haunted me. No, that belonged to me alone.

"I imagine death will find you a lot more now, Eliza, so get used to it."

Hot-headed as he was, Nicholas's odd anger threw me for a loop when he got up and walked away. I glared at the place death had been, and followed Nicholas; my own path was too dark to forge.

Nicholas walked ahead of me until I asked him to slow down.

"Where are we going?" My feet ached, and my eyes were crossing with exhaustion.

"Where you'll live."

My eyes snapped open with that one.

"Where *I'll* live? Not you?" I hadn't thought about where I'd be staying, but I wouldn't have thought alone.

"Not me. I have my own place here. You need to find yours."

"Shit, don't say I have to go on some scavenger hunt."

He stopped and hung his head in front of me, something I'd gotten used to seeing him do. Here he was immortal, and I was making him old.

"This is a place for you to be alone, as much as you can," he said quietly. "You don't need me as much as you tell yourself."

I swallowed. "Good, because I think I lie too much."

It was dark, and I burst into waking frantic, with no idea where I was. But there were sounds.

"Nicholas? Nicholas?!" I whisper-shouted.

Noises again, and worse, I got the sense of something. Not just anything—death again, lurking, as invasive and comforting as always.

My limbs shook when I flung off the blankets and threw my legs over the side of the bed, only to discover the bed was on the floor. The noise of my feet hitting the bare floor made me gasp. My small room, alone, on a mountain top.

Japan, I'm in Japan, and in my own room. Nicholas isn't here.

Eyes adjusting, I saw nothing in the room but for the bed I'd been in and a few very pieces of simple furniture. Shadows flitted across the walls from outside, the trees swaying in the winter night. I steadied my breathing, knowing I was alone, and knowing anything could be waiting for me. The vampires had kept themselves hidden during the day, and now they were out, looking for blood.

No. These are Shinigami. They're not horror movies.

I wanted light but couldn't find anything and didn't want to draw attention to myself. Hide from the dark in the dark. Try to deny that you *are* the dark.

"Perfect time for some crap karate test, Nicholas, for the love of—"

A branch snapped. Two thin walls framed a sliding paper door to outside, and there was enough snow on the ground that a branch would have to be stepped on to snap.

The silhouette of a man appeared on the other side of the door, inches from my face, and I screamed, stumbled backwards, and fell onto the bed.

He didn't move. Didn't try to run or come after me. He waited. Like death itself. The death that always knew I couldn't resist. The only horrible thing that was familiar to me here. It owned me. When I stood and moved to the door, I never doubted I should open it. Sliding the screen door open, the figure made no movement, didn't even blink. The full moon illuminated him.

He was breathtaking in his darkness.

The night made him brighter somehow. A full head taller than me, bare-chested with only thin white karate pants, the same crispness as the snow. Perfectly chiseled, smooth, strength in every pore. Beautiful and fearsome. He looked down at me with onyx eyes, shining black hair falling around his cheeks and chest, the front held up in a traditional knot.

He smelled like red wine and roses. Rich, heady and slightly nauseating. The scent of looking into something beyond.

The smell slapped me with memory, one I hadn't touched since it occurred. I knelt at my mother's casket, eyes on my father's next to her. The room felt too heavy, stagnant. Wine heavy on her breath, the scent of withering roses succumbing to it from too many wreaths and bouquets, my grandmother leaned close to me.

"There's shadows all around you," she'd whispered in my ear.

My mouth was opening and closing, no sound coming out as I stared at the man in front of me.

He was *Shinigami.* And he was looking at me with as much wonder as I was him, all in his eyes. The rest of him was rigor mortis still. Until a *crack* resounded, one I knew all too well, and the Japanese man was gone. Scared away.

I slid the *shoji* screen shut as snow drifted in over my bare feet, and turned to run back to the bed, only to smack into Nicholas.

"You're late," I muttered when I'd stopped my scream of shock. I breathed in his cinnamon plum scent. A mix of New Hampshire and my new home, Japan.

"Who was that?" he asked, like I'd answered the door to Girl Scouts, not a vampire, and like he'd been here the whole time.

"The same vampire from earlier."

Nicholas flashed to the doorway and looked out, but we both knew nobody was there.

I collapsed back onto the bed. I didn't know what day it was, or what time it was, but I knew that Nicholas was in the room with me, and that I wanted him to stay. "Please stay. I know I've been a pain in the ass to deal with, but, please."

His shoulders either relaxed some, or they sagged. I had both effects on him these days. I didn't see him turn around or come to me, but he was there, kneeling at the edge of my bed.

"I'm not a man who needs apologies for everything to be all right."

"Good. Apologizing is awful."

He sighed heavily, his eyes glinting in the moonlight. "But necessary. Look, I didn't want to come here tonight, I wanted to be alone. Because I've nearly killed myself for you, Eliza Morgan, and you resent me for it. Feelings don't die any faster than I do, and it's agonizing trying to kill them."

"What are you saying?"

"I'm dying, and you're spending the time we have hating me for something I had no control over."

I stopped breathing. This spite towards me—I didn't know what to do with it. And I didn't know what to do with the notion of Nicholas being gone from this world, from my world.

"What is it, Eliza? All the times you said to me 'it's not your fault, this is my fate,' you didn't mean it? You seemed so sincere."

"Your sarcasm isn't making this easier."

"Nothing is easy! *Nothing!*" Cold nipped at my legs and feet under the blanket, and I wanted to die. I was terrified that he was calling my bluff. I was terrified that I'd pushed him too far. But I was pissed that he was treating me this way, knowing what I'd seen, what I'd been through, and what I was leaving; my life.

"I lost my best friend," was all I said.

"And so did I. I spent my immortal life with Roman. Until you. Do I hold it against you? No. Because it's not your goddamn fault. And for the number of times you've said to me that it's not my fault, it's yours, maybe I started to believe you. You and I both know we need this to be somebody's fault."

The wind was knocked out of me. It felt like I was losing him, and of course, I was. He was melting into nothing because Roman took Kat's life and he hadn't. And I was pushing him away. All this death for nothing. No explanation except that there was no choice.

"I think we both need to remember what it's like to be alone," he said, and in a sickening flash, he was gone.

The only scent that lingered was red wine and roses.

CHAPTER 53

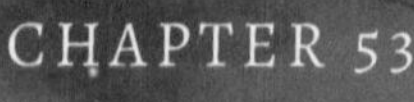

The silence was heavy, the room warm when I awoke, despite the rice paper walls and the snow that was basically a notebook's thickness away. There were woods behind those doors, close, just like New Hampshire. The trees were different. Dead of winter, no flowers on them. And this room —it should have been colder, with such simple texture and sparseness, but the lack of clutter made *me* uncluttered.

A plain, white wraparound jacket and baggy pair of white pants hung from a hook on the wall. I wished I knew who left them. I was sure people were watching my every move here but I'd only caught one.

Where was everyone? How many vampires were here, at the temple? Were they hiding from me? I got the distinct impression I was the rabbit on the racetrack.

A bucket of clear, cold water was next to a basin on the floor, and I washed up in it. "This hotel sucks," I muttered to myself.

Today I had to get my bearings, gain myself back. I wanted control again, as if I'd ever had any.

The karate clothes were not me. I sighed looking at my

cargo pants and hoodie. Time to give up a little bit of me. A little bit more.

Still nobody was visible when I went outside into the snow, and looked around at the other little dwellings like my own. No shadows moved behind those walls. No noises came from within. I didn't know where I was going, and nobody was going to help me.

And I didn't need any help.

A flashback of the strange night before with Nicholas made me shudder, but I wasn't letting go of him that easy. I needed him. Not because I was a stranger in a strange land, but because I'd woken up believing something.

I believed Kat's death wasn't my fault. And I needed him with me, to feel the same way.

I should never have said I didn't blame him when I did. I shouldn't have told him it wasn't his fault, like some bitchy wife trying to get her way. I was ashamed, but had to put that away. I couldn't change it. I had to let myself *feel*.

Unable to give up my Converse All-Stars this morning, I walked on winding boardwalks with overhung trees and iced-over fish ponds. Breathing in the mountain air, I knew what this place was; magical. Heavenly. A gift to me.

If I wanted to share it with Nicholas, I had to find him. Wandering aimlessly wasn't working.

I stopped in the middle of the boardwalk, closed my eyes and listened to my own breathing. It had been a while since I let myself *see* Nicholas this way, to watch him in my mind. I tried to brush off that part of my brain and wake it up by just standing there, concentrating on nothing else, and I wasn't surprised when the picture of him snapped into view.

But I *was* surprised by what I saw.

He was in the snow, in the morning sun, wearing a pair of black sweatpants. His bare back was so bony, he didn't look like the same rugged man I knew that could build a house in a month, who looked so strong just moving.

He was on all fours, retching blood into the snow.

His agony was my agony, and it drew me to him, running down the boardwalks, slipping and falling all over the place. Finally, I fell into the snow at his side, my feet moving too fast for the rest of me, and was almost sick myself over the stench of regurgitated blood as it pooled and clotted in the snow.

"Nicholas, Jesus Christ!" His back was slick with sweat, but it was covered in a frost that came from within him. Hunching over to look in his face, I saw his lips were blue. Frost clung to his eyebrows, and the stubble on his sunken cheeks.

He tried to answer me, but all that came out was a grunt that sounded so painful, tears sprung to my eyes.

I pulled him to me, wishing I had never let go of him before, and rocked him like he'd done to me so many times, always taking care of me when I didn't deserve it, always loving me when I didn't deserve it.

He could tell me all he wanted that his thrall drew me to him, or that it was the unbreakable bond between *Shugotenshi* and their chosen, but we needed each other every way there was.

"Cold," he said through chattering teeth.

"Okay, okay, let's get inside."

I pulled him to standing with effort. He was the weight of a corpse and about as much help in getting up. He stumbled more than I did, and all but fell through the paper doors of his room, which was thankfully heated by a fireplace. We struggled to cross the small room, falling with a thud to the floor.

"What happened?" I asked, as I searched the room, knowing he had a thermal shirt thrown somewhere, he always did. When I found it at the foot of his bed, I threw it at him to put on as I pulled all the blankets off of the bed and dragged them across the room.

"Just f-f-ed."

He was still wiggling into the shirt when I sat with him. Every movement was molasses-slow when he should be able to do this simple thing before I even noticed. I wrapped myself and the blankets around him, hoping my body heat would help restore him. But this cold came from inside.

"This happened from just feeding?" I asked him quietly, rubbing warmth into his hands.

He nodded. "Not m-mine. Not my *unmei nashi*. I can't t-trick my body anymore." His teeth smashed together with every word, his body trembling while mine sweated. "E-e-eliza, I don't th-think I have l-l-long. My b-body is re-rejecting blood."

My throat hurt from sucking back tears. This was the most hopeless a person could be. The kind where you knew you could have done better.

"What can we do, Nicholas?" I sobbed, rocking him like a baby, my heart turning black at how small he felt in my arms.

He only shook his head, though I could barely tell the difference from his spasms.

"I'm going to the Master. He'll know what to do for you."

"He won't," Nicholas croaked.

"He's not going to let you die, or become a vegetable or..."

"This is my fate. I f-f-found you, but—p"

"Enough. You called me a hero once, and goddammit, let me be one."

Sweat dripped from his frost-coated hair as he lifted his head to look at me.

"Let me taste what a hero is."

His cracked lips parted, and slowly his fangs protruded while his eyes stayed on mine.

"Nicholas?"

"Ssshhh," he said. The shaking was gone, the sweating stopped. His eyes glazed over, as if he'd seen an answer in me.

He put his hand, still clammy, on the back of my neck and pulled my lips to his. Once his lips met mine it was like a hot cup of tea after a long, cold day. The scent of him enthralled me, and I couldn't get away from it.

That's when he bit me.

Right under my jaw, just lightly, and then another further down, and then a deep, forceful one on my jugular. It had purpose, and it was selfish; draining, and fulfilling. I couldn't get away from the slow poison of his lips and tongue and teeth, pulling the very life from me, wrapped in sugarplum chocolate scents. If I were to die right then, it would all have been worth it.

He grunted, winding my mess of hair through his fingers and pulling my neck closer. The blood running out—I savored every drop. Ecstasy. I could let him drink until there was nothing left.

But he drew back, leaving me gasping for air, stars swimming in front of my eyes, heart pounding erratically. He smiled, the grin that sang of confidence, happiness and sarcasm, and licked blood off his teeth. I took a sharp breath.

"That was worth near death," he said, and wiped a drop of blood off my collarbone with a rough thumb.

I nodded dumbly. "You're not shaking anymore." My voice sounded too far away.

"Nope," he said, and shot up. He stood straight, something I hadn't seen for a while and not even realized it.

I stumbled to my feet, dazed, and dizzy. Nicholas became a blur of beauty in front of me, catching me as I fell.

"Sitting down is great. Let's sit down," he said, and put me on the bed gently.

"Oh, man. This is why I don't donate blood."

"You do now."

My head cleared up quickly with that statement. "Do you think drinking from me will fix you?"

He sat next to me, hard. It meant he wasn't himself, that existing still hurt. He needed the right blood, and I'd thought it could only have been Kat's. It's what we both thought.

What if we were wrong? What if another's blood could restore him? There was more than one kind of right in this world.

"Your wheels are spinning. It's hot, but scary. What are you thinking?"

"I need to go to the Master."

"What for?"

"Because, Gatekeeper, I need answers and I want them from him."

He ran a hand, now steady, through my hair, and did the thing he always used to do, before I took myself away from him and anything that wasn't sadness. He put his finger under my chin to lift it up, to make my eyes meet his.

"Feeding from you was great, but I don't think it's permanent, and I don't think the Master will like it at all. Wouldn't have stopped me, but he wouldn't like it."

Seeing the beauty restored to his face, knowing it was my blood that did it, made me angry that we hadn't tried this to begin with. And I was angrier to think that the Master wouldn't want this for him.

"What's not to like? Look at how much healthier you are!"

"Your proposal is to be my blood donor? You're here to become a vampire, not exactly conducive to donating blood. We're more takers."

"I don't have to be *Shinigami.* I don't need anyone to tell me what my destiny is. It's you, and if I can save you—"

He absentmindedly ran his thumb over my lip, sending shivers down my arms. "Your fate isn't to save me or serve me. It's not what you're for. You're bigger than this."

All the emotion I'd held prisoner since we left New Hampshire escaped in my voice. "I. Am not. *Strong* without you."

He bit his lip, and smiled through it. "I'd tell you that you're stronger than me, but you'd tell me to shut up. I'm glad you need me again. I've needed *you* all along."

I kissed him hard, winding my fingers through his thick hair. He needed my blood. But he needed my heart more. I rested my forehead on his, tasting my own blood as I pulled from his lips, and I breathed our salt in deep. "Don't you ever forget that I love you. However lost I get, when I drift away, it's always you I need. Nothing else. No one else."

He tilted his head and took my lips again. The scent of oranges and cinnamon made me ache.

"I love you," was all he said.

"Then let me take care of you. While you need me."

He nodded, and I was out the door.

CHAPTER 54

Guided by an inner sense that had only awoken in Japan, in this temple, my mind ran as fast as my feet, over boardwalks and bridges, down stone steps and snowdrifts. I reached the top of stairs overlooking a clearing between elaborately carved pagodas and doorways straight from a Kung Fu movie.

"Holy hell."

Dozens upon dozens of vampires. They sat in an enormous circle, quietly watching two others sparring in the center.

What the hell had I been thinking, running around Vampire Village, knowing I was being spied on by at least one of them in the middle of the night? What, was I just going to go say hello? What a clown.

But Nicholas needed me and the Master was down there. I took a deep breath and started down the stairs. The Master stood straight and tall, no matter how small he really was, with a long stick-weapon-thing, watching the fight. I kept my eyes on him as the eyes of the mass of *Shinigami* stayed on me.

Breathe steady, suck your stomach in. Don't be a wuss.

The Master slammed the bottom of the stick on the

ground when I reached the clearing, and the fighters stopped at once, turning to bow to him. He bowed back, before turning his cloudy eyes on me.

"Master," I said awkwardly, and bowed.

I heard vampires making noises at the sound of my voice, predators forced to sit like nice, quiet pets. I sucked in my stomach again.

"Eliza Morgan," the Master said. "She belongs to Nikorasu."

The murmuring stopped, and only then did I dare look around me.

The *Shinigami* all looked up at me. They exuded a cold mist that chilled me and made this already foreign world a little more foreign.

But I belonged here, and they knew it. I could see it in all of their eyes. Some gritted their teeth, fangs protruding, but I didn't move. I might as well have been naked behind a podium while they all waited for me to talk. I didn't let my voice betray how unsure I was.

"Master, please may I speak with you?" *Stupid and formal and ridiculous sounding.*

With one nod of his head, the *Shinigami* were silently on their feet with not a hint of movement. They bowed in unison, and were gone with flashes, cracks and bangs like colorless fireworks.

And I was alone with a vampire so ancient even he didn't remember where he came from.

He barked out a Japanese word, making it very clear I was to come closer. I did, reluctant though I was to let him know I was afraid and would probably have done anything he said.

"Nikorasu has fed from you," he said with a voice as cold as the snow underfoot.

"Yes," I sad breathlessly.

"It is not to happen again."

So, Nicholas was right. Shocker. Wasn't he always?

And yet…

"If I may, why not, Master?"

"Look at me, *onna*," he said, ice in his voice. With a magnetism that reached into my head and wiggled around, I was made to pull up and look into his blank eyes.

"You are here for you. Not for him. His path is his own. Yours is yet to be seen. Do not turn from it so quickly."

His words were gentler than I expected, and they pierced my heart. It was like a stroking of the soul.

"But I can heal him, I think. The others' blood is killing him, faster than before."

"It is his path."

"No."

He didn't move at my boldness, but the chill in the air became a little colder. I continued.

"It doesn't have to be his *path*. We can fix him, we can bring him back. He doesn't have to suffer."

"He has chosen to suffer."

"He didn't! Roman—" I took a deep breath, steadied myself before my emotions ran me over. "Roman fed on Nicholas's *unmei nashi*. Nicholas never chose that."

"Nikorasu chose to allow it by not attending to his destiny."

"I won't believe that. It's a cop-out." He stiffened, and my breath caught.

"*You* would teach *me* what fate is?" he said, bemused.

I gulped. "You can't know everything. And forgive me, but I don't see how learning karate is going to help prepare me for being a vampire, and I don't see why I should want to if Nicholas isn't with me."

He pounded his staff on the ground again, and a shock-wave rumbled through my feet.

"*Baka!*" he bellowed, but I heard it in my head in English; *fool.* "You question the need to learn, no matter what the subject matter? Ignorant American! To think you cannot grow simply from the act of learning. Or did you not think of that at all? Your lessons begin today, and let this be your first. *Learning is change, and change is the only thing that can save us.* Shut your mouth if you don't understand. There is such a thing as a stupid question."

The wind had been knocked out of me with his vehemence. When I finally found my breath, shutting my mouth was not a problem. I'd solved nothing except pissing off an ancient vampire and Nicholas's father figure. He turned his back on me, and even I knew it was meant to be an insult.

A prickling across my scalp and down my spine, as if darkness itself had run its fingers over my skin, and it loved me. Death, back again, to defend me this time.

The Master spun back to me in a lapse of motion, and something rippled across his terrible eyes.

So, you sense it too, I thought.

The Master's mouth worked up and down, and I could have sworn he was *scared.* I let the dark sensation wrap around me and hold me. There was little else it could take from me. It was time for that lurking death spirit to pay me back.

"You feel it?" I said to the Master, in a voice from deep inside me, that was inhabited by something else.

"It can't be," the Master said dreamily. He spoke in Japanese, but I understood. He looked like a little old man then. Not a god among men; a man. Until, in his fear and hostility, his fangs found their way between his lips.

They were so long they touched his chin, and they were matched by two more on the bottom, like a viper. I had no doubt he could move as fast.

I took advantage of his slight senselessness. "There's more to me than just blood, and fate. I'll take care of Nicholas until there's nothing left if that's what it takes. Neither of us wants to lose him."

The Master paled, lips quivering around those gruesome teeth as he stared over my shoulder. I knew he was seeing the man who came to me in the night. I could smell his wine and roses, could feel the death of him like hunger pangs.

The Master nodded absentmindedly, like an old man in the home who doesn't know what he's agreeing to. It was enough for me.

"I will not become *Shinigami* for as long as my blood helps Nicholas." My voice sounded like stones dropping, final and hard, and I had no more to say. I bowed low and deep, one hand covering my fist, and waited for the Master to turn away from me before I exhaled.

I needed more strength before I turned to face the man behind me, and the presence he had inside me.

"Who are you?" I asked, my back still to the man of death. When he didn't answer me, I spun on him. I prayed he wouldn't be gone, or the feeling that came with him—that everything was about to be taken away, and I wanted it to be.

He stood in front of me across the clearing, topknotted hair whipping furiously in the wind that I barely noticed, like the storm was his alone. His bell-shaped black pants and flowing white sleeves billowed around him, but he was as solid as stone, staring back at me. Crows circled above him.

"How did you find me here?" I whispered to myself, though he'd certainly be able to hear me, even from his distance. Did I really think I could have escaped the spirit of death by leaving New Hampshire? I'd known I was coming to meet it all along. I could never leave it, and it could never leave me.

We were the same.

"I cannot find what is not lost," he said, and I jumped at the softness of his voice. Powerful and gentle. Mournful.

"Who are you?"

"I am the space between heartbeats and the breath at the end of things. I am living shadow and lamented life. Izanagi."

He burst into the space in front of me, leaving the air torn like paper behind him.

Silence echoed around us. The brown-gray sky seemed bigger suddenly, and Izanagi dwarfed me with the power of his being. Human in stature, heavenly in proportion. He was the height of mountains and just as immoveable.

"Eliza," he said, leaning close to my cheek, tendrils of his hair tickling my nose. "Take death by the reins."

And he was gone but for that scent of death. The walls of the mountains threatened to swallow me, and I ran back to Nicholas to try to stop death again.

CHAPTER 55

Nicholas was asleep when I got back to his room, the crisper version of his log cabin in Ossipee. It was warmer than my place here, not just because of the fireplace. The wide mattress on the floor ran almost the length of the wall, pillows all over it. Nothing hidden here, everything close. Zen, fresh, and of the Earth. The peace followed him into his sleep, his chest rising and falling quietly. The hollows under his eyes weren't as deep. Already, he was better. I ached to give him just a little more. Anything to bring the man back I needed.

My thoughts went to Izanagi, and what he'd meant when he said *take death by the reins.* Nicholas and I, we might have done it.

My fingernail bled where I'd been biting them with nerves. I'd been at the temple for one day, and had more questions than I did answers, and the answers I did have weren't wildly supported by the powers that be. And as much as I wanted to feed Nicholas forever, I knew it was impossible. I wouldn't outlive him as a human, and like Nicholas said—it wasn't my job.

I would become *Shinigami.* But I would do it in my time, on my terms; no one else's, fate's included.

I looked at the blood on my finger, and slowly slid it between his parted lips. Squeezing my fingertip, blood dripped into his mouth. He closed it around my finger, sucking gently. Nicholas rolled his shoulders over, and clutched my arm to his chest, sucking on my finger like a wounded animal, getting more and more intense. He groaned, making me groan in response.

His eyes popped open, heated and searching for me. Pulling my finger from his mouth, I kissed his wet lips, and for a minute we were back in New Hampshire, being just us, not afraid. It seemed now like we were always afraid.

My hands found his bare back cold underneath his shirt as I caressed his ribs and shoulders, down his spine, stopping at his waist when he moaned, but not for long.

I was tired of waiting for everything to happen *to* us.

Nicholas pulled my hips closer to his, and kissed me forcefully. "Eliza."

"Don't stop, Nicholas," I breathed in his ear, my hair falling into my face, the same color as his, our curls winding around each other, our limbs winding around each other.

He grunted, pushing his hardness against me, his rough fingers dimpling my fleshy arms. He took my hand, and lightly pierced my fingertip with one fang, making me pull back for only a second before I pushed it in further. The thin stream of blood left me, deliciously slow.

"Sorry?"

"What?" I said. Confusion scrambled me at a third voice, in my head, followed by a fast vision of a man I didn't recognize. I didn't know where he was, or why the hell he was in my head. I sure didn't love vampires in my head, and certainly not now.

"What?" Nicholas grumbled.

Then Nicholas's head snapped up as the voice sounded, out loud this time, at the door.

"Sorry?" the voice said from the other side of the door. This was déjà vu of the worst kind, where nothing made sense and I nausea bubbled in my gut.

Had I just seen the future a second before it happened?

"Shit!" I said, scrambling to straighten out my clothes under the blankets.

Nicholas was up like a bolt of lightning, pulling aside the *shoji* door as I struggled with the blankets. I grinned that he'd been so caught up in me that he hadn't heard the third person approaching.

I was still smoothing down my hair when I made eye contact with the young man at the door over Nicholas's shoulder. He smiled sweetly, his ice blue eyes piercing me.

"Sorry to interrupt," he said shyly, looking at his feet. His was the same voice I'd heard in my mind.

"Get the hell over here, kid," Nicholas said, pulling our visitor into his arms and clapping him on the back. "Eliza! This is Paolo!" like I was supposed to know who that was.

Paolo was still looking at the ground with an embarrassed grin.

"Well, great to meet you, Paolo," I said, trying not to sound resentful or give away that I would much rather have met him another time. Almost any other time.

"I-I'm so sorry to interrupt," he said again, looking anywhere but at me. I ran my hands over my messy hair again, in case I was scaring him.

Nicholas leaned into his ear, one eye on me. "Been a while since you've seen a pretty face around here, has it?"

Paolo laughed too loud, wildly, refreshingly awkward.

"Sit, kid. Tell me what I've missed around here. It's grim as hell, like nothing any good has happened since I left." Nicholas was so much like *himself,* before he began melting into nothing. My heart swam with pleasure at it, and any resentment I had was gone. For anything. For our interruption, for the tension between us since Kat died. I only needed him to be Nicholas French.

As Nicholas sat cross-legged at the low, dark wood table with Paolo on the other side, I answered when a shadow appeared at the door.

"I asked for tea," Paolo said quietly. "The good kind."

I opened the door to a young woman. "Hi. You know, *konnichiwa*." She bowed, averting her eyes. It was weird. I was the one who didn't look at people.

I realized she was waiting for me to ask her inside, so I moved, allowing her to glide in gracefully at human speed. Her kimono shuffled making the sweetest swishing noise. I wanted to hug her for being a person like me, but I would have given her a heart attack.

And no person was like me.

Nicholas and Paolo chatted and laughed as if they'd just seen each other last week, though the both stopped to thank the girl as she poured their tea.

"Thank you," I said as she left, head bowed.

"*Hai,*" she replied before running off.

"It's funny when you scare people," Nicholas said. Paolo still hadn't looked at me for more than a second.

"I'm honored to meet you, my lady," Paolo said, an accent now clear.

"I'm happy to meet you, too," I said, eyeing Paolo. It was his scent; I'd never smelled anything so fresh and *empty*. He smelled like goodness and freedom. So calming, and Jesus Christ, did I need that. I waited for Nicholas to tell me something about him, but knew the pain in the ass was waiting to see what I could find out on my own.

"We've missed you around here, Nicholas," Paolo said, his accent getting thicker as he became more comfortable. Italian.

"It has been a bit dull. *I've* missed you." He spoke so plainly, no mincing words. "I've been aching to see you fight again."

"Sure, sure. I have a little healing to do before I see myself in the ring, but you'll get front row when I do."

"Nicholas is all but a celebrity at the temple. We all wait for him," Paolo said to me with a grin.

"Some more than others," Nicholas answered, throwing a tea towel at Paolo, who caught it without movement.

"Yes, I've heard, and met a few of his *admirers*," I said, my mind needling in images of his creator, Jenniveve, the heartless bitch. And Roman, of course.

"Wait until you see him out there, Eliza," Paolo said. To hear him say my name was like the purity of churchbells. The man was extraordinary. So humble, unassuming, with this clarity about him that made him a white light of a person. Or vampire. My eyes sought Nicholas's to let him know I expected to hear more about Paolo, but Nicholas just waggled his eyebrows at me and drank his tea. Paolo watched every move he made. He was a *fan*. Nicholas had *fans*.

I wondered what that made me.

"I admit, I'm pretty anxious to see what everyone else thinks the fuss is about," I said, nudging Nicholas with my elbow.

"Oh, he's legendary," Paolo piped up, eyes wide, finally really looking at me. Excitement glittered in his eyes, lit up his young face. "What I've learned by watching him—"

"Kid, you're better than me in the ways that count, with the humanity and closeness to God and all that."

"You guys worry about being close to God?" I asked.

"You know I'm not really a God-fearing kind of guy," Nicholas said, leaning his elbow on the table.

"I was a priest in life," Paolo said with a humble smile, silencing me. "I was deemed a man of God at a very young age, and my studies began immediately," he said, sensing my questions.

Nicholas uncovered a basket of bread in the middle of the table, and leaned back with a huge piece. "Paolo was more than a priest. He was very nearly a saint," Nicholas said solemnly.

My head swung to take in Paolo. There most certainly was something about him that was *higher*. It made sense. Nicholas was right.

"A saint?"

Paolo looked down. "Many believed I was destined for sainthood, yes."

My confusion came out as irritation. "But the *Shinigami* know their destinies. *This* is our destiny, how could there be two of them?"

"Paolo was turned by mistake." Nicholas shoved bread in his mouth and raised his eyebrows at me.

"Mistake?" I whispered. "How can that be?"

"I wouldn't say *mistake*," Paolo said, shooting Nicholas an apologetic smile for disagreeing. "The Lord knows the path we must take, and fate is part of his will. I am this because it is what was meant to be, from the hands above."

Nicholas watched him intently. "You don't resent being turned at all?"

"Resentment changes nothing. *We* change everything." That was *Shinigami*-speak if I ever heard it.

"Cut it out, kid. This is me you're talking to."

The wisdom in Paolo's young face was, indeed, heavenly. "I mourned my life. But this life is eternal, and the good I can do with it is still His will. Had I been deemed a saint, would that not be another form of immortalization?"

Puke. "But, you were so devout, and now—now you kill people."

Nicholas went dead still.

"Yes. I do what the Lord asks of me."

"Or what the Master asks of you?"

Nicholas made a shocked noise and jumped to the defense of his Master. "*Unmei nashi* have no fate. The Master's just a guide for us." His eyes flashed with irritation. I didn't care. Answers didn't come easily here, and I would find them all, kicking and screaming, before my life was taken away from me, as pathetic as it may have been.

"Good talk," Nicholas said, finishing the conversation as he put down his tea cup. He stood, and looked stronger in stature than I'd seen him in weeks. "I'll make my grand appearance tomorrow, but now I need rest."

With calm fortitude, Paolo asked something that would probably be on the minds of many *Shinigami*. "Why do you need so much rest now, Nicholas?" He sipped his tea and waited.

Nicholas shrugged. "Long trip."

"That's not the rumor, my friend."

"Always listen to rumors, Paolo. They're always right."

"In this case, they are," I said. Both men looked at me. The mouth I usually shot off at home seemed to have purpose here. I went with it. "What? Why hide it, Golden Boy?" I turned my back on Nicholas and looked in Paolo's swimming blue eyes. "My best friend was his *unmei nashi.* But he couldn't do it."

"Is it true that Roman took her life?" Paolo asked with a pleasant firmness. He spoke with the certainty of a man who never doubts himself. I nodded. Silence filled the room, trapped by the paper walls.

"Nicholas, not feeding on your *unmei nashi,* it will be the end of you. It's a miracle that you're not worse off."

"Not quite a miracle, kid," Nicholas huffed, throwing a meaningful glance my way.

"What is restoring you, if I may?" I definitely thought Paolo knew the answer.

"You already know," Nicholas said.

Paolo looked at me. "This is not how things are supposed to be, my dear."

"I don't like how things are supposed to be," I said with a stiff jaw and a raised chin.

Paolo smiled, like someone would smile at a particularly strange child. "You're strong, Eliza, but we are His sheep."

"I am no one's sheep." And it was as if Izanagi were with me, his astounding power fueling my words.

"Certainly no debating that," he said with a tip of his head and a grin.

"What rumors are there about Eliza?" Nicholas asked. The room got a little colder with his question, but I was warm from his protectiveness.

The boyishness returned to Paolo's face in a huge smile. "She is an instrument of change for us all. The buzz is everywhere."

"And the Master? What does he think of it?" I said.

"The Master keeps his opinions close. He is closer to the gods than any of us," Paolo said, then laughed. "But I've got a hunch you'll have a way of getting them out in the open."

It was beginning to make sense to me why the *Shinigami* had chosen victims; their prey held something they needed, something they were missing. I wanted to dig into it more, the importance of it screeching at me to figure out the riddle. It could be the answer to making Nicholas whole again. Maybe it would give answers to a lot of the *Shinigami*. They deserved them. They deserved to know why things weren't in their control, no matter how powerful they were.

"Eliza, may I walk you back to your room?" Paolo said, since Nicholas had implied we were done talking. The snow had begun to make drifts against the bottom of the door.

"Sure," I said, but I really just wanted to crawl into bed with

Nicholas and keep him strong, never be without him. There was nothing I wouldn't do to keep him strong.

If anyone had the strength to live forever, it was Nicholas French. I hoped I could keep up.

I kissed Nicholas good night as Paolo put on his wool trench coat. It made me think of Nicholas standing in the snow at home, though this trench was older, speckled with holes, and thinning. Nicholas's coat was in good shape, but at any moment Nicholas himself could be speckled with holes, thinning. I kissed him again, wrapped my arm around his waist to pull him into me, bit his bottom lip, swooped my tongue deep in his mouth, anything I could do to show him that I was all in, that I would never let go. It left his lips hot pink and puffy when I was done with him. He raised his eyebrows, swollen lips parted, and mumbled something about things done in front of a holy man.

"Quite all right," Paolo said shyly.

"See her back safely," Nicholas told him.

The night was pin-pricked with stars through the falling snow, and there was no wind for the first time I'd been out on the mountain. Paolo took my arm in his like an old fashioned gentleman, which I suppose he was.

"I'm glad we talked," I said through the silence.

"The pleasure is all mine, Eliza. I've certainly not met anyone like you in my long life."

More silence.

"So, you are romantically involved with Nicholas, yes?"

"Um. Yes, we are. Plainly." I laughed the nervous laugh Kat always hated and would kick me for if she was within range. *No longer in range.* I shook my head at my inner crassness.

"Do you not find your relationship to be a bit dangerous?" Paolo asked with not a hint of judgment.

"Everything about us is dangerous," I replied.

"Indeed. Do you think you tempt fate too much?"

"Fate can kiss my ass. Fate has done nothing except give me that man, and a reason to not be human."

He stopped. "Is this also the way you feel about God?"

"With all due respect, I have enough on my plate without worrying about God judging my choices. He lets me make them for a reason. He doesn't like them, he's the one who gave them to me, so… And then the *Shinigami* tell you that there are no choices. So, I'm inclined to do whatever I want right about now."

Paolo only blinked, slight smile on his lips. Unreadable. "I hope you find your way, Eliza. Your way will carve the path for the rest of us." He turned and began walking again.

First the crows landed in my path, and then I got the familiar jolt of him, Izanagi, near me. Through me. I couldn't see him anywhere in the woods surrounding us, but a flicker of darker than dark shadow between snowflakes.

"You have a big day tomorrow, my dear," Paolo said, putting his hands on my shoulders, like he was so much older than me, which I guess he was.

"I do?" I said.

"Tomorrow Nicholas will make his appearance, with you by his side. Tomorrow, you begin to become." He kissed my hand, a salty ocean scent mixed with cherry blossoms folding over me as he did. And he flashed out of sight, leaving me alone.

Not entirely alone. Izanagi was there, behind the trees, I sensed him; not like the prickle on the back of my neck, but like a hand in the soul. He had something I needed, and it unnerved me to know it.

"I know you're out there," I said quietly, certain he could hear.

Something opened in me. It let me see Paolo before he got to his door. It was the beginning of a purpose. I could feel it here. And it's the thing that drove me to look for Izanagi with my vision. The presence of death I'd known all my life lurked in the woods, real and with answers for questions I couldn't put to words, that had formed my life.

I crouched down to the birds, who met me with one hop forward. I reached out and laid my hand on the one closest to me, stroking the spot between his eyes with my thumb. "Show me," I said.

It was me that zeroed in on that spot, far out into the mountainside, and it was me that reached for Izanagi's death scent of wine and roses. But it was the stream of crows that fled into my vision in a thick straight line, that led me to him.

There he was in my head, a shadow deeper than the blackest night, darker than the murder of crows. There but not quite there, a presence as light as the snow.

And he could see in my mind's eye, too.

My breath caught painfully in my throat, my knees went weak, and I got dizzy. Eyes that had seen unfathomable darkness stared into my thoughts. I would have hit the ground if he hadn't suddenly appeared in the form I knew, to catch me. I was close enough to look in those depths, and see that the Hell in his eyes didn't come from within—it was a reflection.

He'd seen things only a god could live with, but never understand.

"I'm okay now," I said while I got my feet under me. He didn't let me do it alone, putting me upright before I realized we'd moved.

"Yes, you are," he said, still locked on my face, so close I could see the lines in his lips, see where his teeth had dimpled them. He was still looking *inside* me. And he was worried about me, despite telling me I was okay.

"I am. Izanagi, don't leave me with the horrible mystery that vampires seem to love. Tell me what I need from you. You have something for me, to help me. Don't make me fight for it."

With a quick bow, he vanished like they all did, leaving the trail of death incarnate in his wake.

"Goddammit." Destroyed and revitalized all in one day, over and over. "Japan is exhausting."

The bed was on the floor, making it easy to crawl to. I dreamed of death.

CHAPTER 56

"I can't believe I let you near all those vampires alone," Nicholas said, shaking his head like a madman.

"You weren't yourself." Still wasn't. Or wasn't again. The hollows were back under his eyes. His cheeks were sunken. As quickly as my blood had revitalized him, it was used up it seemed, left him emptier than before.

"I had to be drunk. Did you get me drunk? You're a bad enough influence without getting me drunk, too."

We'd been back and forth over it since Nicholas dragged himself out of bed and realized what exactly he'd given his consent for me to do when I went to the Master. I'd wandered the temple alone, among hundreds of vampires that only wanted to kill humans, not hang out with them.

"They didn't know who you were yet. Any one or fifty of them could have attacked you and nobody would have batted an eye."

"I made sure they knew who I was quickly enough."

"Wait until they see what you can do. Who you really are under that stunning face and smart-ass mouth."

I smiled. "I think you just called me 'ass mouth,' but thanks?"

"You're better than them all. Every last one of them."

"Pretty sure you're still drunk."

He was at my side in an instant, tipping my chin up with one finger, making my heart stop, making my mind race back to the times when I was too numb to know what it meant to be so close to him. When all I could think of was how he'd taken things from me. Her from me. I was still losing him in one way or another, all the time. His fingers shook as he touched me. I hated that it was with as much physical weakness as with emotion.

"That was an incredibly brave thing you did. For me," he said, taking me by surprise with a swift kiss that lingered like a bee sting.

"Um. Sure, I guess. You would have—"

"Don't do the self-deprecating crap, it was amazing and you know it. You knew the danger you were in. You did it anyway. Thank you."

I kissed him that time, making the dryness of his thirsty lips softer with my touch. "I would do much worse for you."

He leaned his forehead on mine, hands wound through my hair. "I could test that out."

"What, make me walk on broken glass or something? Lift up a burning urn with my bare arms, Kung Fu movie style."

"Yup, that's what I was thinking. As soon as I stopped thinking of you naked." He kissed me hard, wrapping his arms around me, still stronger than life. My will flooded out of me, and I was his to do with as he wanted.

What he wanted was to tease me. This was getting painful.

He pulled away and kissed my nose. "Time to make our great appearance."

I whined like a candy-deprived fat kid. *It has been so long since I had anything but healthy food.*

Smiling, he started digging through my clothes, which were in the process of being unpacked, and probably always would be. They were currently all over the place, hanging from the screen at the back of my room, on the floor, in stacks, in the old suitcase. Unpacking sucked.

"You need layers. We'll be outside a long time." He threw gloves at me, and a hooded sweatshirt. "Put these on under your *gi* top," he said, throwing the white karate uniform at me. And socks. And another thin shirt. Then the green sweater I stole from him.

"What exactly are we doing?" I said, getting bulkier by the second as I pulled more shirts over my chest. I looked huge. Huger. My boobs were planetary. "Nicholas, do I really have to make an effort to look more like the Michelin Man?" I twisted and turned trying to loosen up my arms, but gave up fast.

"You don't look like the Michelin Man," he said, still nose-deep in my suitcase, inspecting a red bra. "Sexy Stay-Puft Marshmallow….Lady." He looked up long enough to waggle his eyebrows. "We're formally introducing you, presenting you, in fact. Watch some training. Maybe do some. But it will be cold, and my shield isn't strong enough to contain you in my pathetic weakness."

I was reminded of Nicholas encasing us in a man-made shimmering snowglobe to protect me from the wild storm, making me untouchable in the backwoods of snowy, windy New Hampshire. It was magic. He was magic. The night was a fairy tale.

Everything was real now. He was dying.

"Nicholas, feed from me."

"No." He zipped up the suitcase.

"I can already see you losing your strength. Let me help you."

"Nope. Thanks."

"Nicholas! We know it won't really hurt me. What's the harm now?"

"The harm, *Eliza,* is that you're human. And whether you're *unmei fumetsu* or not, you're still human. This isn't the Red Cross. You'll be needing your blood." He winked as he passed me into the snow.

Dressed to Nicholas's overbearing specifications, we began the walk to the clearing I'd been to the day before. My nerves fluttered at the idea of seeing the hundreds of *Shinigami* again, but they weren't going anywhere, and neither was I.

"Nicholas, I have something to tell you," I said, as we walked, my head down, his head held high.

"Shoot."

"My visions are different now."

"How?"

"They happen. Not about you."

He didn't break stride. I was, as usual, impressed by his coolness. "Have you had any before that weren't about me?"

"You know I haven't."

"Don't worry, I don't think they're like wet dreams. I won't get jealous."

My sigh was probably insulting. "I saw Paolo come to the door before he did. Seconds before, but still. *You weren't in it.*" I swallowed. "And then last night, I looked for someone with it. And it worked."

That furrow between his eyes. I wanted to kiss it. "Who were you looking for?"

"Izanagi," I blurted.

"Izanagi. The guy from before?"

"Yes."

"Stop clenching your fists. It's okay. You found him?"

I nodded, breathing in through my nose. I knew I looked guilty and nuts. Nicholas's smirk told me.

"That's really something," he said, and started walking again.

"What do you think?" I said as I ran to catch up with his too-fast feet.

He shrugged. "Probably because you're here now, where it all began. You're with *people* like you. You'll flourish even faster."

"That makes sense," I mumbled. I was looking for a little more excitement from him, and didn't know what it meant that he was brushing it off like this. But I knew one thing: when Nicholas kept secrets from me, they were important. Things I needed to know. And I didn't like having information doled out to me in rations.

I grabbed his arm and he let me turn his body toward mine. He could have stopped me if he wanted to, but he knew there was no stopping me in the long run.

"Nicholas, tell me who this man is. Izanagi."

He swallowed hard. "I'm not the man for that job."

I raised an eyebrow.

"Since when do you care whose toes you step on? I trust you, there's nobody better to tell me secrets that have to do with the rest of my damn life."

"Nope, not my story to tell." He walked ahead.

"You'll make me figure this it out on my own? Right? Initiation crap?" I caught up to him again, and we were suddenly staring down at the arena, or whatever it was. With him by my side, it seemed smaller. But it wasn't my fight down there today.

"Tell me what you know, Nicholas French. Nothing gets kept from me in the interest of sparing my fragile little mind anymore. This is my story. Tell me how it goes."

He breathed in so deep his chest rose like a balloon was inside. "Maybe you're right." He looked at his feet, cracked his knuckles, and began.

"The Japanese god who created all the other gods, who created Japan itself, is named Izanagi."

"Okay."

"Nobody knows who you're talking about. I've asked a few, and this guy who only you see, he doesn't train here, or live here, or do whatever here." He ran his fingers through his hair fast. So he was troubled. "I think you're seeing a god."

"Jesus Christ, what?"

"Yes. I'll tell you his story tonight at the ceremony—"

"Ceremony?"

"Yeah, there's always a ceremony around here. But I'll tell you then. Right now, we have a date." He nodded toward the crowd below. "Ready? All look, no touch today."

He gave me that face that shows he's proud, but also shows he thinks he had something to do with it. "You're really not scared, are you?"

"No, really not. I'm ready for whatever." Even to find out I was seeing gods. Emotion that I'd just started to let back in took me over, and images of Kat and Roman exploded into memory. "I'm ready to not be part of *that* life anymore. I want a reason to exist. I don't want this limbo anymore. I want to put the world behind me."

He pulled my chin up to face him, and I held it there, finished with hiding. It was time to own this thing I was to become.

"Let's go, my love," I said. And I started down the stairs.

CHAPTER 57

We descended the steps to the watchful eyes of all below. Everyone stopped, the sparring in the center ceased, and a throng of vampires stood to face us. Some wore karate uniforms, billowing and black, like pictures of samurai, others in slimmer fitting and less showy white *gis* like mine. But every one looked distinctly not of this world. And of course, the Master was the most ethereal and intimidating of them all.

Nicholas walked down the steps at my side, our bodies touching with every movement. His scent was powerful, like cardamom and cloves, and I could see his chin cocked out of the corner of my eye. He was an arrogant bastard, and I loved it.

When we got to the bottom, the *Shinigami* parted to let us through. They didn't make a noise as he passed. He made eye contact with a few, all of them bowing their heads to him with respect. He was so much stronger here, no matter how frail. He was a god himself. Pride made it impossible for me not to smile, and I was cool with knowing all the vampires saw it. Pride and respect went hand in hand.

"Master," Nicholas said as we approached, and put his fist into his other hand, bowing. I did the same. All this bowing was unnatural to me, but Nicholas had told me the value of respect here. I'd read a book or two, I said, and I'd argued that not bowing didn't necessarily show my lack of respect, but I had no leg to stand on. I was being arrogant, and I knew it. Even here, totally out of my element—in theory—I didn't want to let anyone have the upper hand. I couldn't afford that attitude here; I had to let myself give in, let go of my defensiveness. The Master's haunting eyes searched me out, rather than Nicholas, and both of us noticed, acknowledging it with a glance to each other.

"Nikorasu," the old vampire breathed. "And our Eliza."

Our *Eliza is an endearment, not an insult.*

It was cold outside, and colder still with the vampires at my back.

"Thank you, Master, for having us," Nicholas said. I'd never heard him hand over authority so easily. He was always the one in charge. Ironically, it made me want to protect him from whatever dangers there might be here.

"Thank you for bringing us this gift," the Master said, fathomless eyes on me.

"Are there any other humans here, Master?" I asked, apparently out of turn.

His white eyes grew cold, and I grew colder. I knew he was doing it to me, like he'd done before when I didn't know my place. This time, I wouldn't cower, or let the frost forming between the Master and I stiffen me. Keeping my attitude in check was just too hard, and who knows—that attitude might keep me alive at this temple. I stared back, refusing to even grit my teeth against the cold he was wrapping me in, until Nicholas gently squeezed my fingers, and I relaxed. The Master loosened up as well; the lines of frost from his hands and feet to me wound their way backwards like tentacles to his body. I stood tall.

The Master didn't speak to me, but reached out fast as a whip and spun me around to face the crowd of *Shinigami*.

"Eliza is Nikorasu's *unmei fumetsu,* but she is more than that. You all sense it. You have all been speaking of it. But not a one of us knows what her great gift is." He turned his head slowly to me. "We begin to find out now."

The silence of the creatures staring back at me was unsettling, their stillness chilling. I bowed in the awkward silence, and they all answered in kind simultaneously. *Yes, got that one right.* I could feel them breathing me in, smelling me. Their scents were all jumbled and mixing, a white noise of smell. But Nicholas's cut through them like a knife.

"Sit with me," Nicholas leaned over and whispered in my ear. Simple words, but they sent a shiver down my spine.

We sat cross-legged on the small set of steps where the Master continued to stand, facing the vampires who returned to sitting as well.

Only one continued to stand. He leaned, James Dean-style against an intricately carved doorway, ankles crossed, hair mussed up, days-old stubble roughening his cheeks. He squinted like he was looking into the sun as he took a last drag off a cigarette and flicked it into the snow, burning a hole in the clean whiteness. He wore jeans and a black t-shirt, faded tattoos peeking out of the short sleeves.

"Nicholas," I whispered, leaning over. I caught him rolling his eyes but with a bit of a smile, also looking at the only man dressed like he just rolled out of a bar.

"Kieran."

"Right, am I up then, boss?" this Kieran said with an Irish brogue that made every woman in the crowd sigh. If Nicholas hadn't been next to me, I might have done the same thing.

He swaggered to the center ring, looking more bored than

a derelict at the police station. As he passed, he swung his eyes at me, burning with a sultry glint, and winked. I couldn't breathe. Nicholas made a haughty noise, and I squeezed the frost off his fingers with a smile.

Kieran looked up, and pointed lazily at a raven-haired beauty with her arms around her knees.

"Blue, me and you, lass," he said, and turned his back to the crowd.

This Blue was suddenly on her feet, with that non-movement the *Shinigami* threw in my face. She was tiny perfection, a total bombshell with more strength in her petite, voluptuous body than any woman I'd ever seen. She made the loose-fitting dark blue uniform look dramatic and sexy. Black hair shimmered in waves down her back. Her eyes were wide, but piercing, and her lips were rose red, full, but not childish. She was exquisite.

I stole a glance at Nicholas, who couldn't take his eyes off of her. My eyes took on a heat of their own when I watched her glide to the ring, to face Kieran as he stared her down, arms crossed, chin down, the tip of one thumb in his mouth. He was making me blush. He was completely focused on Blue, like he wanted her, or wanted to eat her alive.

The tiny woman and Kieran faced each other, Blue's back straight, all business; Kieran's slouched like he was just as ready to pick up a beer as fight.

"*He's* going to fight *her?*" I whispered to Nicholas.

"*Hajime!*" the Master barked, and Blue moved like the wings of a hummingbird, darting and flitting, knocking Kieran flat on his back. He sprung back up, still looking like he had somewhere better to be.

Blue was a tiny tiger circling him. Kieran's lips quirked like he was watching the best part of a porno. She moved in on him again, this time flipping over his head and kicking him from behind so that he landed on his knees halfway across the ring. He let out an *oomph*, and laughed.

"Give me more, Blue, baby," he said. It made Blue growl and run at him again, this time slowly enough that I could see her steps, and her bared teeth. She was more predictable in her anger.

The Irishman stopped her solidly with his forearm, but caught her in a dancer-like dip before she hit the ground. He kissed her with an animal ferocity that had more than one gasp coming from the crowd. Blue wasn't swayed. She pushed him off; he landed on his ass in the snow, still laughing. Blue marched back to the center of the ring, bowed to the Master, and went back to where she'd been sitting. Fury was all over her face. But when she met Nicholas's eyes in her scan of the crowd, she smiled wide. A blazing, brilliant thing.

"She's pretty amazing," I said into Nicholas's ear.

"Sure," he said, waving to her.

"Kieran likes her."

"Kieran is the peanut butter to the jelly of every woman here."

Kieran was leaning back in the doorway again, lighting up another cigarette.

"Kieran," Nicholas said loudly. His voice carried and echoed, silencing the crowd's murmurs.

"Frenchie!" Kieran called back. "What's cracking, mate?"

"Frenchie?" I said.

"Give me a try," Nicholas said, ignoring me, and stood.

I tugged on his pants leg, and he looked down at me, knowing what I was about to say. "Eliza, don't worry about me." That Nicholas smile that made my heart stop, and told me I was in for trouble. "This'll be fun. Hair of the dog that didn't bite me."

"Wha—"

Nicholas strode to the center of the ring, forcing the

Master to hide his surprise. Nobody was expecting this. *Shinigami* pointed and nudged, and if I didn't know better, I'd say they were placing bets.

He told me we were just watching today. He wasn't strong enough for this.

Kieran met him in the ring, and they did some handshake thing that looked like they'd met for a beer. So they were friendly, then? That was a relief. I didn't need him to have any other battle to focus on besides getting better.

They bowed to the Master, Nicholas deeper and with eyes down, Kieran like he'd rather be smoking.

Nicholas straightened up, still strong as hell, but not what he was. Kieran was well-muscled, lithe, as if he'd fought on the streets of Ireland his whole life. He shuffled a little, readying more than he had for Blue. The pin-up girl on his arm winked at me like she knew a secret I didn't.

Kieran moved first. He was brutish compared to the cat-like silkiness of Nicholas's movements or the darting beauty of Blue's. He was all means to an end, with the least amount of show and the most scrappiness. Nicholas didn't flinch, but met Kieran's swift punches with equal blocks and artful strikes of his own.

But he was tired.

The more Kieran came at him, all punches, no kicks, the more Nicholas backed up, moving slower, even if he was the fastest thing on two feet. My teeth hurt from gnashing them together.

When Kieran hit him with an uppercut that lifted him a foot off the ground, I jumped to my feet. Nicholas didn't recover fast, and Kieran kept on him with another blow to the gut, then one to each side of his beautiful face, the second knocking him to the ground. Nicholas spit blood.

And that son of a bitch, Kieran, looked up at me with a smirk on his face like he'd pissed on a national monument.

"He can take it, lass," he said to me. My lip curled back, and I growled out loud.

Nicholas's fingers dug into the snow from where he lay on the ground, and it froze underneath them, creating a crackling spiderweb of ice that raced across the ground toward Kieran. I'd never been so pleased to see Nicholas angry.

He was on his feet in a whirlwind of snow and ice, making the closest vampires gasp and cover their eyes. Nicholas was on his opponent, invisible in his stormy flurry of movement, but the snapping of Kieran's head and the buckling of his body made it clear what happened.

There was blood in the air, frozen droplets suspended around them.

"*Yamete!*" the Master yelled, banging his staff on the ground. Nicholas and Kieran both stopped to stare at the Master with wide eyes. Apparently, his anger wasn't something they were accustomed to. They both bowed low to him, to each other, and left the ring to stunned silence all around.

Nicholas fell to the ground when he reached me.

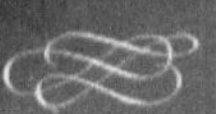

CHAPTER 58

"What the hell is wrong with you?" I shouted at Kieran, as I tried to pull Nicholas to his feet. Blood splattered the snow.

Kieran's eyes were wide with alarm, puppyish despite his roughness. He put his hands up, to tell me to back off. "Easy, love. He came after me, remember?"

Nicholas fell again to the ground, making me groan with disappointment in myself for not stopping him. I turned on Kieran as he approached us.

"Get away from him or I will end you one way or another."

The Irishman stopped in his tracks, and I couldn't look away; his thrall was working on me, a smoke that traveled through my body. Nicholas said that the thrall was unintentional, but I wasn't sure if I'd believed him. Still didn't.

The scent from Kieran wasn't enough to lure me in, but it was just dangerous enough to make me want him, ever so briefly. Campfire, smoke, burning leaves. Heat emanated from him, melting the snow under his feet, making waves in the winter air around him. Wisps of smoke drifted upwards from his hands and hair. And his eyes….. From this close I could see flames dancing in the autumn brown.

"I didn't mean to—"

"You didn't care!" I shouted at Kieran. "Now look at him."

Vampires watched us from all sides, but Blue was the one who caught my eye because she was looking at Nicholas, crumpled on the ground.

"He's mine," I hissed in a feral cavewoman voice as I hovered over him, shocking myself. But what else could I do to keep vampires away from him at his weakest? Celebrities are only loved until they're at their worst.

Nicholas struggled to his feet, and once again the crowd parted for us. We left tradition and honor behind as we climbed the steps together.

"I'm sorry," Nicholas said, his arm heavy across my shoulders.

"Don't be."

"Good, because I'm really not."

We were quiet for the rest of the walk back to his room. All I could think about was healing him, and to what extent he'd go to prevent me doing it.

He fell on the bed face first. Crashing after that short bout, where a month ago it would have him strutting around with his shoulders back...it hurt to watch. I thought of his constant battles with Lynch, how invigorated he was after. I was constantly battling not to lose Nicholas like I had everyone else, but there was never a break, never a promise that I would ever get to stop. He was slipping through my fingers and I'd have eternity to live with it.

"What the hell got into the Irishman?" Nicholas moaned, rolling over.

I chuckled. "That's what I called him in my head, too."

"Picking off the biggest guy in the yard isn't his MO. Really excited he decided to change his mind today."

"Why did you?" I spat.

"What?"

"Why did you change your mind and fight? Today wasn't your day, it was just a meet and greet. I didn't do much meeting, since you were so amped to get your ass kicked."

He put his hands behind his head and looked at me, standing there in my absurd layers. He was still god-like to me, and he knew it.

"I don't like having my footprints stepped in."

"Stop being obscure."

"I know no other way."

Sweating under the bulk, I struggled to peel off clothes, barely able to move under them. Nicholas watched my pitiful strip tease with amusement as I grunted and pulled all the knotted layers off. I wiped my hair out of my face and turned my attention back to the weakened thing that was Nicholas.

"You can't laugh this off," I snarled, but softened up when he didn't deny it. "I think we both know what you need right now."

He groaned, and bit his lip with a sexuality that only Nicholas French could pull off. The laugh lines around his mouth wrinkled, his swirling eyes quickening. "God, I hope you weren't thinking of waffles, or a nap."

I wouldn't let him distract me.

"Nicholas, you need to feed from me. Don't be shy. I can handle you taking more than you did before, but you can't handle not doing it."

"I'm going to live forever," he said with a regal wave of his thin arm.

"Right, you'll live forever looking like hell and feeling worse, so sick you won't be able to make bad jokes."

"Well I never!"

"Stop it, Nicholas. Do you think I'll be any better off when you're rotting away, or do you agree I could stand to lose a few pints now? I'm not exactly underfed, Nicholas."

"Trying to make me to tell you you're not fat?"

"What? No. Look. I'm healthy—"

"—Healthy is a good way to describe it," he said, looking at my chest. I sighed.

"*You're* not. If I was the one dying, you'd do anything you had to. And I'd drink from you because I trust you."

"One day, that's how it *will* be."

"When you turn me, I drink your blood? Dracula-ish?"

"Something like that. I don't have a harem. Yet."

"The rate you're going, you won't be *able* to change me. You'll have to outsource." Deep breath. "Maybe I could get Kieran to do it instead, if you'd rather put off getting back to yourself."

He pursed his lips. "Sonofabitch."

He got to his feet with a single movement; faster than human, but not his usual. He pulled his shirt over his head, revealing the still strong body of a man who you'd see chopping firewood, but bruised. I'd kill that Irish bastard.

Those shadowed eyes never left mine as he crossed the room, his confident swagger making my heart pound. Orange and cinnamon waves lapped over me, leaving me heady—and when he kissed me, the seductive richness of it was over-whelming.

His fangs pierced my bottom lip before I could even gasp, and hot, salty blood filled my mouth, making me sway. Nicholas wrapped his arms around me, and gently sucking the puncture. I tingled and writhed through the starry sensation, losing myself as he groaned and pulled me closer. I took his cheeks in my hands and pulled away just to regain my fleeting consciousness and see how he looked, what I did to him. He let me stop him, so I could see my blood drip from the corners of his mouth, down his chin. The swirling of his eyes was chaotic, and he heaved, cheeks flushed, desperate for more of me.

I wanted him to have it all, to take away all my memories, the pain and crushing responsibility. I wanted him to own every last drop of life in my body, to take my soul and make it his.

So this was the vampire thrall in action, then.

With a bear growl, he sunk his teeth into my neck without warning. My knees buckled in shock, but he caught me. He always caught me. The fight-or-flight fizzled away in that orange cinnamon sugar rush he brought with him, and I was his, never wanted to be anything again except his.

No fate, just blood.

My flesh tore. The room was a haze, the crimson streaks on Nicholas's chest, the red stains on the floor, the only color in the gray static. The crudeness of it made my head swim, and I retched. My head hit the floor with a *thunk*. Nicholas picked up my head, apologizing, as another wave of nausea rolled through me.

That was when it happened.

I saw him.

Roman.

"Eliza," Nicholas whispered.

"I'm okay." Knee-jerk answer that wasn't true. I got up on one knee and fell to my side like a jackass. Nicholas was a spinning blur. The vision of Roman was the only real thing for me then. His self-loathing throbbed in my mind like a fresh bruise. It was reflected in his eyes; glaring and animalistic. And he was alone. Alone, and full of hate at the wonderment he felt and the happiness he'd stolen.

Kat's blood popped like champagne bubbles inside him, an effervescent, energizing brilliance that he'd taken. Her goodness swam in his painfully bright eyes.

"Eliza, I don't know what to do," Nicholas said, panicked. I'd never heard him not know what to do before. I couldn't get Roman out of my sight.

"Air."

I managed to get to my feet, even if I fell into the shoji screen and heard a rip. Nicholas opened the door, letting me stumble outside, wearing karate pants and a tanktop. I shivered from nausea and the cold, and sank to a crouch on the boardwalk.

"I have to get you blood. You need blood," I heard Nicholas thinking out loud to himself.

"I'll be okay," I said through dry heaves. Roman was fading.

"What in the hell did you do to her, you nutter? I can smell the blood a mile away!" Kieran's firery scent cut through the mix of bile and blood. I was suffocated by Nicholas's too-warm smell, poisoning me with its false comfort and intent, no matter how much I'd asked for it.

Hands on me, rougher than Nicholas's, but not stronger.

"Your particular brand of salvation isn't needed here, Kieran. She's mine, and don't you forget it." Nicholas's voice was chilling, resounding. He was his old self.

My blood was bringing him back. It might kill me yet.

Kieran pulled me closer, my body burning with his touch.

"You were killing her, man!" he said in his brogue. The worry in his voice touched me; so unexpected from the jerk that basically put us in this predicament to begin with.

Nicholas was silenced, and I had to speak up for him. Shaking my head to clear it, I looked into Kieran's eyes. "I'm fine, Kieran," I said quietly. "I can pull it together now. Thanks."

The scent of ashes surrounded me as he pulled me to standing. "Anytime, love." My vision was clear enough now to see the sexy smirk on his lips as he ran his eyes down my body.

Nicholas growled like a kicked tiger, and the air began to spin with thickening hail around him. Nicholas's frigid anger mixed with Kieran's lusty fire wrapped me in another world, and I swayed, wobbly again.

"Looks to me as if this girl needs to start taking care of herself a little more, and letting you do it a little less, if you know what I mean," Kieran said, inches from Nicholas, eyes alight with a defiant blaze.

"Guys, stop," I said, sounding weak, despite my brimming power. "Kieran, I wanted him to feed from me." Nicholas groaned with irritation.

"You're just a hum—"

"I am not *just* anything," I blurted.

"My mistake," Kieran said, his voice barely a murmur, that accent making it sound like something out of a dream, the overly intimate smirk back on his lips. "You, my dear, need to look after yourself more than you look after anyone else." He said it with such a gentleness, my heart skipped. I wanted him to look out for me. There was no other way to put it.

I wanted *him*.

I backed away, to Nicholas.

"Thanks for your concern, but I think we've got it from here," Nicholas said, wrapping his arms around me from behind. The air shimmered around us, and became a solid thing, the shield that he created like a snowglobe separating us from Kieran. I breathed out, the warmth and safety of it holding me close. The cold disappeared, and Kieran's burning scent was replaced with the peppermint brownie of Nicholas's. My mind flashed to my mom in the kitchen, back when I had a home—and then to Nicholas's cabin in the woods. All of the places where I felt safe, but none as safe as in his arms. Still safe, no matter how much he took from me.

"Aye, well, I'll leave you to your destiny then," Kieran said with a pointed look at me, and turned away.

We turned back to Nicholas's room, but not before I saw Izanagi lurking in the trees.

I'd seen Roman.

I stayed awake all night wondering how in the hell it had happened. The more blood I gave to Nicholas, the more I envisioned. If I took control of it, I could find Roman. *Something* wanted him found, something connected to me.

In the middle of the night, I dragged my exhausted limbs out of bed, threw on my puffy coat and boots, and stood outside. I couldn't lie there anymore, my mind working and reworking answers it didn't quite have. I walked, to find somewhere away from the only two rooms I knew, somewhere I wouldn't be a kept creature. My new, self-induced anemia made me colder. Shaking, I walked and thought, until I didn't know where I was or how long I'd been drifting.

"Well, this is how horror movies start," I said, looking around the woods, the night sounds making me feel small.

There were things in the night that knew better than to make noise.

Under a canopy of skeletal trees, I found the remnants of a garden, long ignored before it had been covered in snow. Instantly I was transported to the pond in Nicholas's back yard, shimmering in pinks, blues and purples in the sparkling winter night. This place was too beautiful to be wasted, in its broken down antiquity. It had to have a purpose, but it was misplaced, half-useful.

It meant something to me, at least.

I brushed off a rickety bench that had been barely visible under snow and vines, and sat, huddled into my jacket. There was so much to see; the roots of things, mosaic tiles, smashed by the wildlife growing between them. A birdbath filled with snow so high I couldn't believe it didn't topple over.

Beautiful things driven to the dark. The best kind.

"Lass, you smell more like the flames than I do."

I almost fell off the bench with surprise.

"Jesus Christ, what are you doing here?" I blurted, catching myself.

Kieran stood in the snow, same black t-shirt and jeans, same disheveled look of wrongdoings. Blood tattooed his chin, stubble and throat.

"Call of the wild, dearie," he said, running a thumb under his lip; it came off red. "I think you have a bit of the same." His eyes glittered, and could have melted the snow.

I pulled my jacket over my chest tighter, only making my boobs more of a spectacle. "I had thinking to do. It couldn't be done where I was."

He growled as he smiled, making my chest burn. "Well, you do have a bit of the dark inside, don't you?" A new smell of heat came from him, a secret burn, something sacrificial.

"Yeah, well, darkness follows me around," I said, glaring at him. He chuckled.

"I wouldn't call your Nicholas dark. Bit of a shining light, that one." He pointed at me. "I can help with the cold," he said. His eyes narrowed and an assault of heat, like a blast from the fireplace took me in. The air bubbled around me—a shield, like Nicholas's, but different. Sheer orange, red and yellow danced across it, like glass being heated and blown into shape. To protect me from the outside.

"Oh my God," I breathed at its fiery beauty.

Kieran sat beside me, crossing one ankle over the other knee, and threw his bare, tattooed arm over the back of the bench. He motioned with one curling finger for me to come closer, looking like sitting in the freezing night was the most comfortable he'd ever been.

Maybe the cold soothed his fire.

I did it. I inched over to him, the bubble of fiery glass moving with me. I was unable to take my eyes off of the trails of smoke that rose from him where the snow touched. The bubble grew to hold him inside with me. I leaned back, eyes on his, his hot arm behind my neck.

Nothing could touch us, nothing that we were *supposed* to be.

His eyes called to me like moth to flame, their combination of doe-soft brown with thick black lashes, and the jumping silhouettes of flames you could only see up close.

There was more turmoil in him than in me, and I needed to be close to it in a selfish and mystified way.

"How does the fire not burn you?" I asked, thinking back to the time when Nicholas's foot slipped into a fire, rending it black.

He licked his lips. "I take strength from what consumes me."

Didn't expect that from him. "What's your story?"

"My story's a wee bit long, with not a lot to say, love."

"That's not a fair answer."

"You just don't want to tell me about yourself."

I kicked the snow at my feet, slushy in this bubble of warmth. "I wouldn't know where to start, and I definitely wouldn't know where to end."

He looked at me harder. "Nobody knows *your* end, dearest heart, do they?"

His riddles weren't so hard to figure out as Nicholas's. And Kieran was just so—out of the box. Different. Welcoming in a way that even Nicholas wasn't for me, in a way that I couldn't put words to. I guess it was obvious that Kieran was no stranger to slumming it, and I felt a little slum-like, with my *higher purpose*, and my trail of dead people, and my pimping out of my blood to keep my lover alive, and my running from everything I was.

"Everyone thinks I have this amazing gift to change things, some untold future here, and all I want to do is just not be this half-thing anymore. And tonight, when Nicholas fed from me, I saw—" I cut my rant off, and tried to ward off the guilt; I'd not been caught doing something wrong.

"What did you see?" he said, taking a strand of my hair in his fingers with assumed intimacy.

I swallowed, mentally said *screw it*, and told him. "I saw Roman."

"Aye, okay."

"We don't know where he is, he left the night he—killed my best friend. She was Nicholas's *unmei nashi...* Anyway, that's why Nicholas was so easy for you to beat," I said, elbowing him, but unable to keep up the air of amusement. "Roman was so real in my mind, and it was because Nicholas drank my blood."

He ran his hand through his hair, like Nicholas did. When Nicholas did it, he came away looking more put together; when Kieran did it, he looked like he just rolled out of bed with some girl, and was ready to drink. Leaning forward, resting his elbows on his knees, I could see all of the lean muscles in his back and shoulders. I tried not to look.

"All right then. You have visions of the vampire that drank the blood Nicholas was supposed to drink. You get them when you let Nicholas drink from you." Kieran was talking more to himself than me, but it was a relief to have someone apart from me say it out loud, try to piece it together.

"There's a connection," I said. State the obvious, why don't you.

"I don't listen often, but I don't think this has happened before." He rubbed his scruffy chin. "What do you think it means?"

"I was hoping you could tell me. What am I supposed to do?"

His smile was brilliant. "What the feck do you care what you're supposed to do, love? Do what you want with it."

For a heartbeat, a jagged saw threatened to slowly cut me in two; the pain that Nicholas and I endured when we were too far apart. *Do you feel it now, Nicholas?* Guilt overwhelmed me and I let it rather than go to him. It intrigued me a little, actually. Being here, in Japan, next to the rebel with plenty of cause, made me want to question everything. This tie between Nicholas and me, between creator and chosen, if it was so strong, why did it need to lord over us a hideous, agonizing pain to remind us we belonged together?

And the pain disappeared as quickly as it reared its ugly head. I laughed, too loud. "What are you talking about? Fate, destiny, my entire life, yours too, we're all shaped by it. This is what we're meant to do. But I don't know what *this* is yet. I don't know how these visions fit in."

"Not *these* visions, Eliza. *Your* visions. They belong to you. Don't let anyone tell you how to run your life—it's still yours."

"For now."

Kieran took me by the shoulders firmly, and I thought he would kiss me, but he just looked hard into my eyes, searching. God, I wanted him to kiss me, and hated myself for it. But the burning in him—it felt like hitting the self-destruct button. Sometimes, that was all I wanted to do.

"Eliza, do you want to become *Shinigami*?"

With him looking at me like that, the fire burning in and all around him, so full of vitality and willpower, I didn't know. I didn't know if I just wanted to run from my life, or if I really wanted to be something else forever. The *Shinigami* came for me, and I never bothered to look for another way out of the world that didn't want me.

His face was so close to mine now that I could capture the heat of his breath if I tried.

"Why did you let him drink from you? I can smell him," Kieran said, distantly.

"He needed to. He needs to. He's dying." I said it with cold calculation because saying the words brought something to the light that I didn't need to see.

"He'll never die, Eliza, no matter how much you fear it."

The flames in his eyes jumped higher, and the smell of cinders called to me until I looked away.

"Everything can be taken away. Nicholas is this way because of me. I'll never turn my back on him."

Kieran let out an irritated sigh. "Have you wondered what would happen if you just said screw it to what you were supposed to do, and just did what you want to?"

"Should I wear a t-shirt and jeans to train tomorrow? Is that what you're telling me?"

"What I'm telling you, love," he breathed into my ear, making my stomach clench in a vice grip, "is that the wolf in sheep's clothing is still a wolf. Don't turn from the wrong fangs."

"Nicholas is no last resort, and he's no wolf. He's exactly who he is, and has no impression to make," I finished, eyeing his overt sexiness.

Kieran sprang to his feet, hands in pockets to make him look disinterested. But the look in his eyes was one of such a deep intelligence and emotion that it was impossible to believe he was as laid back as he looked.

"You owe him. That's what you think."

"A little. Doesn't mean I don't love him."

"He hurt you."

"Everyone gets hurt, Kieran. That's what life is."

He belly laughed, and it echoed through the trees. "*That's what life is to you? No wonder you're so quick to end it! But why in hell would you want to make it last forever?*"

I was starting to see a little fire of my own. "Fate cornered you, too, right? Let you have nothing in life so when the *Shinigami* claimed you, you'd have nowhere else to go. That's how it happens for us." I hoped he didn't have a different answer than the one I knew.

"I always had somewhere to go," he said with a hint of mournfulness. "I have a place because I make one."

"You're braver than me, then. I know my role, I'm not looking for another." The words came out without my allowance. I was going to be a vampire, and Nicholas was going to be with me. There were doubts in everything in this world, but this… This I knew.

Was it only because I was too afraid to find my own way?

Kieran said, "I'm not brave, I'm resourceful. But I don't let anyone use me for their means, and I don't like to see it happen to a woman like yourself."

"This is just another way for someone to tell me what to do, if you look at it that way."

His dark, intent gaze was heated from inside. "I'm not one to mince words, Eliza. I find you very attractive, and I don't want to own you. Perhaps it's time you let your eyes be opened." Inches from my lips, the scent of brimstone danced between us.

"Kieran, your pick up lines are solid, but—"

"Not a pickup line. I mean it. Maybe it's a little bit of a

pickup line, but you're not afraid of directness, and you're not a follower." He licked his lips. "Come with me for a while, and I'll let you take the lead."

I was short of breath. "Are we talking about the same thing?"

His lips parted, a glint of his fangs behind them. "Wouldn't you like to find out?"

CHAPTER 60

Kieran walked me back to my room. He was all the questions I hadn't known I'd wanted to ask come to life.

And if I was being honest, I liked the way life looked on him.

"Well, here we are then," Kieran said. I looked up, and indeed I was looking at my door. I'd been running over and over in my head what I was supposed to be doing with this vision of Roman and barely registered anything but snow and heat. I picked up my head too fast and got dizzy. Too little blood, too little food, too much mayhem.

"Holy hell, woman, get inside," Kieran said, and steered me by the elbow into my room. He led me to the floor in front of the fireplace, leaning close enough that the stubble of his cheek brushed my own smooth one.

"Watch this," he whispered in my ear, his voice the growl of a barely tamed animal.

His fangs emerged slowly. I braced myself for the waves of frost that I was accustomed to, but instead, a thin line of flame came from where he stood and went straight to the fireplace logs, flaring them up. He turned his head to me and grinned. "Brilliant, right?"

My mouth hung open. "How?"

"The same way the rest of them make things cold, I suppose." In a ripple of motion, he was on one knee in front of me, the devil's grin alight with the flames behind him. "The burning in me begs to be let loose," he said, and kissed me swiftly on the cheek with soft, hot lips. I thought I might pass out. "Now, my pet, you stay put. I'll be back with something to take away that death pallor."

A gust of cold wind came in as he left me to sit and wonder what in the hell I thought I was doing.

I nodded off and dreamed of Roman. I was awoken by a gentle kiss on the top of my head.

"Mmm, Nicholas."

"Not this time, love," the Irish brogue said, and I sat up, my cheeks hot.

"Sorry," I said.

"Here you go," he said, sitting cross-legged by my side. He put a bowl of bright red strawberries in front of me, and the sweet scent of them made my stomach growl. I wolfed down one after another. "I hope they bring back a little life in those cheeks," he said, and brushed a finger down the side of my face.

"Kieran—"

"I know. Your heart belongs to Nicholas French. So would mine, were I a woman." He held up another strawberry. I took it in my hand, though I think the intent was for me to eat it from his.

"Then what are you doing here, with me?" I said, eating another strawberry.

He looked at me, and no matter how much of a black sheep he was, and how tough, his eyes were just a little boy's. "I don't know, truth be told." Trouble—he sensed it, too. "But I think you're lost here, and this is where you should be found. I don't want to see your life cut short to save one of us, even Nicholas French."

"I *am* one of you." Our voices were barely above whispers, our skin so close that the heat fizzled and popped between us.

"Not yet." His breaths were shorter, his voice a rumble. "I want to watch you get there, see you play by your own rules."

"I will when the time comes."

"Eliza," he said. "I think I should go."

I didn't want him to. I sickened myself with it, and he could see it as I looked down at my lap. Nicholas and I belonged together, and here I was, running after the first hot Irishman that looked my way.

I nodded. "Thanks, Kieran." Sucking in a breath, I met his eyes. "I loved talking to someone that doesn't want me to just —I don't know—just be what they tell me. We had no choice in being this, and I don't need more people telling me what I have to do. God, that sounds juvenile."

"But right. Juvenile, but right."

We laughed, and the pleasure spread from my head to my toes, overtook me.

"Right, then," Kieran said, and ran a thumb along my jaw. I sucked in my breath, watching him follow the trail of heat his hand left on my skin. "Sleep well now."

He pinched my chin between his fingers, longing in his eyes. With that, he was up and out the door, his smoky scent lulling me into a sleep right there on the floor.

～

My eyes snapped open, heat from the fire on my face. Weak and alone, I wished I didn't want Nicholas to make me stronger. Nighttime did things to me here that made me wonder if I'd run away to the wrong place.

I dragged my feet to the door, more tired from confusion than anything else. There was no shame in wanting help from the man I loved, I'd put myself entirely in his care in coming to Japan, and yet I still... I slapped my hand against the door frame and swore.

"You need something."

I screamed.

Izanagi faced me from the woods.

"Do you live in the goddamn woods? You're always hanging around me, I thought I was up here to be alone. I'm sick of being surrounded."

He didn't move, just watched me, pissing me off more. I knew why he appeared when I was alone, why nobody else saw him; he was a part of me.

"You're missing something," he said.

"Yeah, I usually am."

"We need each other."

This was too much. Too many personalities to contend with, and me, alone with them all after spending my adult life close to only one woman, who was now dead—

No. Don't go down that road again when you're already coming apart at the seams.

"Thanks for trying to help," I said to Izanagi, not masking my sarcasm, "but I'll deal with Nicholas, and Kieran, and my visions on my own. Alone."

"I've always been there. You've never been alone."

I shivered, not from the cold.

A snap of air, and he was inches from me, wrapping me in

that all too familiar wretched funeral scent. I held my chin up. I was tired of being run down by death.

"I am what you need."

"Cryptic. I never get that these days. Look, I'm so tired I could die. I've had the blood drained from me, watched Nicholas get beaten into submission, and Kieran—" What to say about Kieran? "There's too much happening, but all *I've* done is talk and get pushed around. I'm ready for action." I realized that was true as I said it. I didn't try to hide from death all those years just to turn into its puppet. I wanted power.

I'd never wanted power before.

The wind whipped Izanagi's long hair, making black slash marks against the snowscape behind. "When the visions over-power you, when you're empty and no one can help you, you will drink from me. I will calm the storm."

As if on cue, Roman materialized in my head again, a clue in a scavenger hunt given to me too slowly; I was losing the game. I got dizzy, seeing the world outside spin through my haze of people who weren't there, and the god who was.

"I have to stop talking now," I said.

"I will be close," Izanagi said, and was gone.

As sure as I knew death, I knew he would be.

CHAPTER 61

"I'm so mad you didn't tell me I was doing this today."

I was all gussied up in a black silk kimono that showed off my chubbiness really well.

Nicholas looked straight ahead. "There'll be food there, and beer."

"And the other humans. And a lot of vampires. And me in this." I tugged at the waist, envisioning myself bursting the seams when I sat down.

"You're a princess. Now shut up."

A dark wood table ran the length of the temple. It was dim, only orange lanterns lit the walls, casting a comforting glow over us all. I was anything but comfortable.

"I want to punch you so hard right now," I whispered into Nicholas's shoulder.

The Master sat at one end of the table, glaring with those awful eyes, making me want to crawl in a hole and die. At his side was Blue, a china doll in an elegant midnight blue kimono. Paolo sat beside her, smiling, laughing. He was the only one who waved to me, like I had a place at the high school lunch table and wouldn't have to huddle in the bathroom eating my meatball sub. Vampires lined the table, none attempting to welcome me, either staring at me like I was a sideshow, or ignoring me altogether. I breathed a sigh of relief to sit down so everyone wasn't staring at my chest. This was reminiscent of one of Kat's endless cocktail parties, and it hurt that I didn't miss them one bit.

"There are your new best friends," Nicholas whispered to me, nodding, giving me brief rundowns.

They were only two other humans. I don't know what I was expecting, but these two weren't it. Arthur was exactly like you would picture an Arthur. Glasses that made him look like a mole, thinning hair. Despite his soothing British accent and bookish appearance, he was actually a pompous, shallow ass. I'd been watching him as he looked Blue up and down, elbowed supernatural creatures in the ribs, and made a general monkey of himself. Nicholas watched him, bemused, forehead slightly wrinkled, eyes wide as if interested in everything he had to say, sarcasm just oozing from his pores.

I kept hoping for Kieran to appear at the table, but he didn't. He would have ripped this guy to shreds.

"I don't care that I'll have to kill people," Arthur was saying to one of the vampires that wouldn't look at me. "What have people ever done for me?" He threw back a sip from a flask, and looked around for a reaction.

His creator, his *Shugotenshi,* sat next to him, looking like some French cartoon with a thin mustache and American-hating upturned lip. Attractive to look at, but his physical beauty was secondary to what a jerk he seemed to be. The condescending disgust for everyone around him made him the perfect nightmare match for Arthur. Jesus, I hated them both instantly.

"Do you know Arthur's *Shugotenshi?*" I asked Nicholas as quietly as I could, but of course, the vampire could hear me from across the table. He briefly glared, and I met his eyes, forcing myself to be unafraid.

"Pierre," Nicholas said. The French man's lips quivered into a sly grin full of malice and distaste. I forced my heart to slow down, determined not to let him sway me; he was working a thrall smoothly on me, I could *see* it, but for what reason I couldn't possibly discern. Nicholas's calloused fingers laced through my own under the table.

"To live for eternity without regard for life will be somewhat of an empty existence, don't you think?" Paolo asked Arthur. Pierre made a haughty noise that Paolo ignored.

Looking at Paolo like he was the kid who didn't want the candy, Arthur said, "The *Shinigami* don't need to have regard for life; a death god that sympathizes with its prey is a weak god indeed." He looked over sweet Paolo, like he was *better* than him.

"And you think there's strength in being a self-important ass?" *Why do I say this stuff?*

Arthur's paunchy cheeks reddened. "I won't hide behind humble lies, and I certainly won't deny my nature to spare my *girlfriend's* feelings," he spat, looking at Nicholas. My blood boiled until I could barely see straight through my own heat. The table fell silent. Nicholas squeezed my knee under the table.

"That's spectacular relationship advice, did you hear that advice?" Nicholas said, looking around the table, wide-eyed. "I'd deny my inner child a goddamn lollipop if it meant keeping this woman on my good side."

"And your nature means nothing if your soul is nonexistent," I said angrily.

The Master sat silently, weightless somehow, as if made of air. So powerful that he had too much presence to be distracting.

Paolo was looking at me thoughtfully. Eyes were on me

from everywhere. *Way to make yourself the center of attention.* I sucked in my stomach. The other human girl smiled at me.

Her name was Leann. She had pieced-together beauty that said she'd been too many places, most of which were in her head. Thin, with long, tousled blonde waves, she was a fairy of a girl. Confident, quiet. She had these wide, but sultry eyes that gave away her cynicism, showed her damage. I'd keep my distance.

"Who's her *Shugotenshi?*" I asked Nicholas.

"It's Kieran," he said.

I took in a sharp breath. I wasn't sure if she was being quiet and observing anymore or if she was so lost she had no words. "Why isn't he here? She's alone."

Nicholas swung his eyes to me, shades of cocoa rolling over and over in them. "You know he's not one for tradition." He raised an eyebrow. "What's that? Eliza Morgan, you're blushing."

"So?" Real mature.

"He's made an impression on you, too?" The hand Nicholas held suddenly ached and tingled with cold; out in the snow with no gloves on kind of cold.

"Nicholas," I gasped. The Japanese vampire across from us grimaced. I'd been trying to ignore him due to his extreme creep factor, but when he responded with a blast of cold from his own hideously long nails that shot across the table, I jumped. I suddenly longed for sweatpants and for once, anything but horror movies. Especially *The Ring.* Or *The Grudge.*

"Sorry," Nicholas muttered, reminding me of his icy fingers. He took his hand from mine; the ache was worse that way.

The other vampires took his cue. It seemed they did that often, even the most reclusive of them. They all relaxed a bit, the chill dissipating. The Master raised his hands and the air warmed instantly.

The room breathed a sigh of relief, and Pierre ruined it. Obnoxious.

"You truly care for each other, no?" he said, gesturing to Nicholas and me. Disguised innocence made it seem harmless, but he was trying to provoke us. All eyes were on us, but Nicholas just sipped his wine, while I squirmed.

"You don't care for your *unmei fumetsu?*" Nicholas replied after a hearty mouthful. My heart faltered some when he didn't just answer that I was the woman he loved.

Pierre leaned forward, clearly happy to talk about himself. He and Arthur were a truly nauseating duo. "He is a fulfilled purpose for me, of course," he replied. "But we will both be pleased to have ourselves back, without this *need* to be near one another. It is one side effect of our relationship that we could both live without."

Arthur did nothing but stare at the vampire. It was impossible to imagine him experiencing the pain I felt for Nicholas when he wasn't with Pierre. It couldn't be. My curiosity got the better of me. "Arthur, do you have visions of Pierre when he's not with you?"

Arthur and Leann both gaped at me like I'd stepped off the mother ship. "No. He's in my personal space enough. I don't want him in my mind."

I pitied him.

CHAPTER 62

"Thank Christ that's over," I said, eyeballing Nicholas on the walk back to my room.

"That wasn't the usual fly on the wall game you play in groups," he said, glancing at me with something like pride. "What gives?"

"If ever there was a time for me to open my trap, that was it. Arthur and Leann—"

"Are dull. The both of them. I was worried how you'd react," he said, matter-of-factly. "I mean, they aren't blank canvases entirely, but I didn't want you to think that *Shinigami* were only created from the saddest of the gene pool. I knew you'd apply it to yourself and make me spend hours telling you how wonderful you are." He popped a piece of gum in his mouth from a hidden pocket.

"Is *that* why we sat so far from them? I might as well have been at the kids' table at Thanksgiving! I'm still pissed you didn't tell me what was going on tonight, by the way. A little preparation would have been nice."

"You would have argued with me to get out of it. Then

you'd have freaked out, worked yourself into a frenzy and come anyway. I cut out the middle step."

"I wouldn't have argued," I said under my breath.

"Even you don't believe that."

I laughed. "No, I don't."

The room was warm, and I wanted to curl up with a book. I missed that.

"You were pretty magnificent tonight," Nicholas said, closing the door.

"I couldn't shut up." I dropped my huge coat and looked down at the black kimono, dying to get it off, and not sure where to start.

"Right, that's what I like. I like to see you becoming who you are here, in the minds of all of these vampires." He ran his fingers down my arm, raising goosebumps under the silk. Watching his hand move, he pulled the sleeve down, revealing my soft upper arm underneath. My breath quickened.

"I don't feel like anyone yet," I said, closing my eyes to his intensity, wishing my bra strap wasn't as wide as a highway. "I'm ripped in so many directions, and I have all these questions that I make up the answers to, none of them right. Arthur, Leann, they might be dull, but they know what they're here for exactly. Exactly."

"Look at me," Nicholas growled. I had no choice but to do it when that voice told me to. "Everyone else here is an extra in the movie that is you. Don't get caught up in them. They can put your fire out too easily."

The mention of fire made my cheeks flush. *Kieran.*

"Nicholas—" I started, nearly telling him about the vision of Roman, but I stopped. It had the air of a secret, and yet Kieran knew, and Izanagi; my other secrets.

"What is it?" Nicholas said, suddenly stopping me. With his face so close, the light in his eyes so strong, I couldn't lie to him.

"Izanagi came to me again. He knew something about my visions." I still didn't say I'd seen Roman. It would hurt him, make him long for things that I couldn't give him.

Nicholas raised an eyebrow.

If only he knew I'd told Kieran all my deep darks.

"He said he could help when the visions became too much," I said, my lip quivering. I left out that he said I would drink his blood. Not that I would need to, but that I *would.*

Nicholas looked like he was waiting for me to break, or wanted to break himself. "I feel you slipping from me," he said out of nowhere.

I gulped. "I belong to you more now than I ever have, Nicholas. You're my future."

"That's it?" he said, lip curling up, a chill running down my spine. "I'm a game plan?"

"You know better. You're my fate."

He bowed his head. Once again, I'd saddened him.

"Eliza, how can I make you into a vampire when your blood is the only thing keeping me alive?"

I hadn't heard him admit it before, that we'd been backed into a corner. It was time for me to figure out what fate's next trick was before my cards got crumpled in a ball and thrown away. I needed another vision.

"Speaking of which, you're looking a little grim right about now."

His eyes went dark and still in his sadness, but he couldn't help licking his lips and looking at my chest where my heart was. He lifted his hand to touch it.

"Your heartbeat haunted me when we were apart in New Hampshire. I could hear it like a band playing. It killed me but I couldn't die. Now, I'm supposed to make that heartbeat stop forever. What a torture to endure." His eyes were so faraway, I just wanted to tether him here, with me, and yet I was doing so much to keep him away.

I swallowed hard, my emotion strangling me. "Taste it now, while you can," I whispered.

He brushed my hair aside, and without further ado, sank his teeth into my neck. Nothing more intimate, making it all the more intimate at the same time; no pretense needed.

My head swam, but I stared at the paper wall before me, forced myself to stay conscious and will the visions to come to me. They had to give me an answer, if I just looked hard enough for it.

Nicholas held nothing back, didn't try not to hurt me or take too much, giving in to his own weakness. Maybe he figured out I was strong enough to handle it, even if that wasn't altogether true.

No visions came, and so I gripped Nicholas by the back of the neck and pushed his head closer. His lips clamped down and he groaned, wrapping his arms around me. The blood came faster, and then the vision hit me. Not Roman, like I was waiting for.

Lynch.

Chris Lynch sat on his white sofa in his giant white house, with his head in his hands.

Jesus Christ, he's crying.

A wave of nausea passed over me, but I stifled it the best I could, and I watched.

Lynch stood up, looking every bit the successful, dapper attorney he was. *A ladykiller*, I thought angrily. But I forced thoughts of Kat out of my mind as the blood was forced out of my body. Just one more wall to put up, that shouldn't be too hard. Clarity was too important now for my pain to interrupt.

The attorney paced frantically, tears streaming, before flashing across the room out his front door into the night.

Nicholas pulled away from my neck, making my body buckle. The vision became a vacuum in my mind, sucked out and leaving me empty, as Nicholas heaved with exertion.

"That's enough," he growled, my blood coursing down his chin onto his chest.

"No," I growled back, and pulled him to me again. He pushed me off hard, and I landed on my back on the bed.

"What are you doing? You'll die, Eliza!"

"I need this, and I'm fine." My heart raced from blood loss, a hot flash skipped over my skin.

Nicholas cocked his head at me, swirling eyes narrowed. "What do you mean, you *need* this?"

Screw it. Man, I was saying that a lot. I sighed, running my hands through my blood-soaked hair, fingers catching in the knots. "When you feed from me, I have visions." Clenching my fists, I said the name I didn't want to say to him. "I saw Roman, Nicholas."

He became more still than I'd ever seen him while conscious. "Do you know where he is?"

I shook my head. "But I've seen Lynch, too. He's still in Ossipee. I don't know why I'm seeing either of them, but the answers are in me, and only you can draw them out. Nicholas, this is no coincidence. You have to feed from me for me to show me the way. I know it in my heart."

"And if I kill you?" he spat.

"You won't."

"You have no idea if that's true."

"So what? There's more at play here than we know, and we have to dive into it headfirst, Nicholas, or who knows what we're missing? The things I can see, the way I can *call* Izanagi to me without even trying—"

"I don't know…" he mumbled, shaking his head of ringlets and waves, droplets of blood flying.

"Well, I do. Nothing happens by accident for us, and you know it. If I die while you feed from me, that's the way it's supposed to be. But we both know that I mean something here, and things are changing all around me, *because* of me."

"You've been talking to Paolo. This sounds like his divine providence double-speak."

"No, it sounds like mine. You've drilled into me that I'm meant for more. Let me look for it."

His eyes drilled into me harder than his fangs ever could. He wanted to protect me, but there could be none of that anymore. I needed to become the thing I was meant to be, before it was too late for Nicholas.

"Okay," he grumbled. "You're more than this. I have to let you become it. But I hate taking from you selfishly this way."

"I'm the selfish one. I need you." In a wind of peppermint brownie, the first and warmest scent I knew him for, he pulled me into his arms. "We're both so weak," he said into my hair. He felt like home, smelled like belonging, sounded like my future.

"We know what we need. That's all."

He sunk his teeth into me again, and I waited for magic to happen.

CHAPTER 63

I sprang to life from a puddle of my own blood, gasping, trying to move rigor mortis-stiff limbs. I slipped in the wet thickness and fell. Sobbing, confused, I cried out for him.

"Nicholas!"

With a *whoosh* he was at my side, covered in blood himself.

"I passed out," he said apologetically, pulling me to him.

"Me too, I guess." I shook in his arms, blood everywhere.

"You're trashed. We need to get you cleaned up, not in a bucket of water," he said. He lifted me too fast, and I wished I would black out to escape the dizzy heat wave.

"Nicholas, please."

"Sorry. I'm stronger than I've been in a long time," he said. "Thanks to you. I'm high. I'm trembling."

I couldn't respond; I had no energy to do anything except be carried to wherever he was taking me.

Nicholas put up a shield around us, as strong as it should be from him. The air solidified in a glass-like arch. He carried me, safe from the elements, lulling me, until I heard a door swish open.

"What's this?" A woman's voice.

"This is my *unmei fumetsu*," Nicholas said, slapping me on the butt that was pointed in the air.

"Why is she here?"

"You have a shower."

That made me pull myself up on Nicholas's shoulder, and struggle to get down. A shower sounded to me like sex must sound to prisoners.

Once he'd set me on the ground, I was looking at Blue. Then I looked back at Nicholas. Because he knew she had a shower.

Why the hell did he know she had a shower?

Blue saw jealousy bubbling in me. Her gorgeous, wide brown eyes shot to my chest where my heart was punching like Mike Tyson. She gave me the prettiest kissy smirk, and I wanted to rip her lips off. "I have the only shower on the mountain," she said softly, with a British accent I hadn't noticed before.

"Ah," I said, putting my head down to hide my embarrassment. "You must have vampires beating your door down."

She leaned forward with a conspiratorial smile. "I also have quite the reputation for not giving it up." She turned away, Nicholas and I following.

Blue's room smelled like farm fresh apples, and felt like *her*, not like a girl stuffed into a Japanese room. The rice paper walls were hung with pink silk tapestries from floor to ceiling. There were old, bound books everywhere, in piles, not a shelf to be found, like in my own room. Open CD cases littered the floor in one corner, near a stereo that had perfume bottles lined up on top, in reds, pinks, blues and purples. All color, all decadent.

Best of all, her low-lying Japanese bed, covered in a rich purple silk bedspread, had Peanut Butter Cup wrappers all over it.

I laughed, making Blue turn around, smirking like we had

an inside joke. I liked her so much, it hurt. It hurt the Kat part of me.

Nicholas was looking at me like I'd just eaten a spoonful of Tabasco sauce.

"Are you all right?" he said out of the corner of his mouth. "You laughed."

"Yeah." I smiled to reassure him, or me. Blue was in front of me in a heartbeat and a burst of Red Delicious.

"You're soaked in blood. It's rather disgusting. You can use my shower this time, but don't make a habit of it, American." She winked at me and put a fluffy white towel in my dirty hands.

Turning to Nicholas, she said, "I'll make tea for us. But first, get the poor girl something decent to wear."

~

The water was the hottest I'd known in weeks, and it had some serious pressure. The blood pooled around me in the drain, and I just stood there in the dimness of orange lanterns.

I could hear her and Nicholas chatting in the adjoining room, only separated by a silk screen with ornate carvings in its ebony frame. Her Tinkerbell laugh was so like Kat's, tears sprang to my eyes to be washed away with the rest of the past.

When my pale skin was beet red and I was sure the rest of the residents of the mountain would need to liquefy snow if they wanted water, I forced myself out. As soon as the water shut off, a pair of karate pants and a long white jacket were thrown over the top of the screen with some panties, a t-shirt and a bra. I caught them as they flew at me.

"What time is it? Is it...the next day?" I asked Nicholas from the other side of the screen.

"Yeah, it's the next day all right."

Blue piped up, "You both have some expectations today, I believe."

"God, no, come on," I groaned to nobody in particular.

Nicholas came around the screen, making me cover my chest for a second. Then I didn't care. I pulled my shirt on over my bra, and started putting on the jacket.

"There will be training today," Nicholas said gently, holding one side of the screen and looking me over unashamedly. "But I'll make sure they go easy on you."

I fastened the jacket and lifted my head high. "No. We have to move forward, and I refuse to be treated like some spineless girl who needs special attention. I have to learn."

Nicholas glanced behind him, and leaned over to me. Our little secret. "Eliza, what did you see last night?" he whispered.

Until he mentioned it, I hadn't remembered. But the reappearance of the vision made me cry out loud and fall back.

"Shit, Eliza!" I could hear Nicholas, could hear the screen fall over, saw my body moving wildly, but couldn't answer.

"Is she having a seizure?!" Blue screeched. Her apple smell enveloped me, fighting with Nicholas's peppermint brownie. I only know my body slowed because Nicholas's grip loosened. Gasping like I'd been drowning, I looked back and forth between the two faces over me, both so worried and terrified.

"The vision is strong with this one," I said in my best Jedi voice.

Nicholas fell back on his butt, and ruffled his hair. Fidgeting became him. "What the hell just happened?" he blurted.

Blue was still over me, looking down, her hair falling on my face. "Can you move?" she asked.

My limbs dangled, heavy and tingly, and Blue seemed noticed. With her delicate arms, she managed to pick me up like I was a child, and carried me to her bed in a blinding movement. "Maybe you should tell me what's happening in that pretty little head of yours," she said, sitting with me, tiny body not even wrinkling the comforter that all but groaned under my weight.

And without question, I did. She served me cup after cup of tea in a grandmotherly, unabashedly doting style, pairing her exotic beauty with maternal warmth. Between the blankets on her bed, Blue's comforting and Nicholas's brownie scent, I'd talked for hours before even realizing it. I'd told the whole story; *my* whole story to her. Everything from the ever-present feeling of death replacing my parents when they died, to how Izanagi was the living, breathing version of it. I talked about Roman, and Ossipee, and Kat. I talked about the pain of Nicholas and me, of not knowing how he really felt, while he watched me with glistening eyes.

Blue was a rapt listener, nodding when she needed to, sad with me when I needed her to be, hugging me when I didn't know I wanted it.

Kat would have loved her.

"God, I'm hungry," I said. I really needed a watch—for someone who couldn't be accused of missing meals, I did it a lot on the mountain. Blue rang a bell that brought a young girl to the door. They spoke quietly to each other.

"Nicholas," I said while Blue was away, "when are we supposed to train?" What a nightmare to think of doing anything physical. On my best day I wasn't running any marathons—right now I felt like The Blob, but with less conviction.

Nicholas smoothed my hair, the muscle in his bicep leaping. He looked so healthy again, and I'd have given every drop of blood to keep him that way. "I told the Master it had to wait until tomorrow."

"But—" I protested, even though hearing that was akin to

hearing that I didn't have to go on one of Kat's blind dates, or watch any movie with that British romance guy in it that everyone loves. But I didn't want to be seen as weak, would have pushed through anything to prove I wasn't.

"But nothing. You've been talking a Blue streak," he said with a grin, "and still nothing about your vision. We're staying here, for as long as it takes. You needed this, and neither of us knew it. You want to talk, finally, and you found someone you can do it with."

I'd not had one of the rare long talk-about-our-feelings nights since I was falling in love with Nicholas, and Kat demanded details. It was tranquilizing and energizing at once to curl up, warm, fresh and clean, with hot drinks, the snow drifting against the door. It was wonderful to relax, to be with people who wanted me.

I nodded. "Okay. I guess it's not a terrible idea to take care of myself a little today. This is really good, actually." I smiled over at Blue, still talking politely to the servant girl. "I've missed having a friend like this."

Nicholas's face darkened. His brow wrinkled. God, I was stupid.

"I'm sorry, Nicholas, that was stupid to say."

He quickly kissed me on the forehead. "I don't expect you to avoid the subject of friendship forever just because Roman is gone. I'll be fine. Always am."

Blue joined us again. "There's food on the way," she said with a sweet smile. "Now, I hear talk of Roman. Let's hear about this vision, shall we? Let's try to fix this."

With one more glance to Nicholas, I let her rip.

"I saw Lynch," I said in a breath, my voice shaking already. "He had two girls pinned to the ground by their throats. They were young, really young, like teenagers. And he—" I stopped to breathe, "he leaned down and ripped a huge chunk out of the redheaded girl's breast, a big chunk of it came off in his mouth with her shirt—"

"Dear lord," Blue whispered.

"Then he just tore into the other girl's throat, and drank and drank, while the red-haired girl kicked and sobbed. He killed them both, I watched the whole thing."

"God, he's worse than ever," Nicholas said.

And the worst of it was still yet to come. "But before that, I saw him—*crying*. He was a wreck. He misses her so much, Nicholas, our hearts were one in the same, his was mine—" I pleaded, for what I couldn't say. I couldn't come to terms with the idea of asking for mercy for the abomination that was Lynch. "I hurt for him. With him."

"No, Eliza, you can't."

"You can't tell me how to feel, Nicholas. It never works." He smiled sadly back at me.

"So," Blue said, breaking the moment, "Lynch is back to his tricks."

"Lynch's tricks are piss poor and he's always at them," Nicholas told her, their faces close. I didn't even get jealous. Nope.

"Then what's different this time?" Blue asked.

"Well, I know he's doing it now because he's so grief-stricken," I said. "Not that the motive makes it okay, it's just he's in pain, and..." And what? He can brutally murder people because his girlfriend's gone? If I thought of it outside of Kat —no, it was still inexcusable. "I'm no psychiatrist, and it's confusing to know why he does what he does."

"Great," Nicholas muttered. "Now he's got reasons to be a unconscionable monster, and nobody's watching him. Jesus, he has nobody keeping tabs on him." He pinched the furrow between his eyebrows.

"That's not all," I said.

"What else, then?" Blue asked.

"I know something about Roman." How to do this without hurting Nicholas more? I hated even saying Roman's name. "His depression. It's all-consuming, such heartache, sadness like I've never felt in my life, and that's saying something. I don't know where he is, but he's alone. I don't know how my visions of Lynch and him are linked, or what it means to me and you, but I intend to find out."

CHAPTER 64

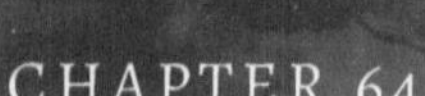

G od bless Blue, she managed to get me a cheeseburger.
"You need iron," she said with a wink, and handed me the plate. I devoured the thing in three bites and looked for more. Blue was laughing hysterically, holding her stomach.

Nicholas lifted the lid on the tray with as much flourish as a magician. A half dozen more burgers were underneath.

"Eeeeee!" I squealed.

"How are you getting this food?" Nicholas asked, eyes narrowing at Blue. "Cheeseburgers don't grow on this mountain. This isn't Cheeseburger Mountain."

"Nicholas, a girl like me gets what she asks for," Blue said, biting her lip.

"You do have all the comforts of home here," I said, eyes roving over the luxurious room.

"This *is* my home," Blue said with a mournful beauty that made her a kitten amongst lions. "I don't leave the mountain —much."

Nicholas studied her, weighing whether to open his mouth or not. Obviously, he did. "I've heard that you don't even leave to feed," he said.

Her face paled. I was so confused, I stayed quiet before I asked something dumb.

"Well," she said, chin tipped up with dignity, "you've been asking some strange questions, then, Nicholas."

"Just looking out for you, that's all," he replied.

Exactly how much was he looking out for her?

She sighed. "Don't worry, Kieran takes care of me. I'm afraid of being away from here." Her smile was apologetic, like she owed us something. "So Kieran brings me my victims. He doesn't like to see me scared."

To be so powerful, and so trapped…it had to be gut-wrenching at times.

"What happened to your home before?" I asked her. The kind of fear she spoke of I knew well; it came piggybacked on loss.

When you lose enough of something you cling to what's left as hard as you can.

"Fire," Blue said. "I lost my whole family in a fire. And when Kieran found me, the burned-out thing that I'd become myself, he took me with him to Ireland. And a fire took our home there, too. It wasn't until then that we found out he was to be my creator."

"You were his *unmei fumetsu*, too?" I breathed, glancing at Nicholas. He shrugged. How many *unmei fumetsu* could one vampire have? How did Leann deal with that? I didn't like thinking of Nicholas being close to anyone but me in this singular way, this mystical and horribly magical way.

And it was glaringly clear to me, the one connection that nobody was mentioning: All the fire in Blue's past—it had to be indicative of the fiery vampire in her future. The very one who was to take her from life took everything around her with a stamp of his own.

Secrets were as deep as the snow in Japan.

"How long have you been a vampire?" I asked.

She smiled sadly, like she had something to be embarrassed about. "A mere fifty-two years," she said.

"So young, and so strong," Nicholas said.

Blue looked at me, a glow of knowing in her eye, a message. "The circumstances made me strong. The time it happened is inconsequential." Fate strengthened her, but she was strong to begin with.

My fate as *Shinigami* gave me the visions, but the fighter I already was had to make sense of them. That was my *choice*, not my problem to solve. I just had to choose to do it.

"Nicholas," I said, turning to him, begging him with my eyes to trust me. "Figuring out what to do next is in here," I said, tapping my temple. "I'm strong enough to survive another feeding, I know it. And you're both here to help me, take care of me." Suspicion pinched Nicholas's face, and Blue was blinking like crazy.

"What are you saying?" she asked.

"I know this seizure and the blood loss is scary for you guys, but I'm okay. I want to keep pushing to discover what my visions mean; how they can help Nicholas. I know I have the answer, and the blood-letting is when I find the pieces of it."

"No way. You think I'm going to drink from you again tonight? You're crazier than you look."

"Izanagi won't let me die."

Nicholas's jaw clenched, and the familiar cold shook down his limbs, spreading across the carpeted floor at the mention of the god's name.

"Nicholas, stop it. Izanagi only wants to help me."

Closing his eyes and cracking his neck, he said, "I just don't know him, and I don't like him near you when I don't know him. No strangers allowed."

With a tight-lipped smile I went to him, standing for the first time in hours. I willed myself not to look as dizzy as I felt.

Touching Nicholas's arm gently, I looked into those eyes that exuded something unearthly that wanted me for its own.

"Izanagi's not a stranger to me, Nicholas. He's death to me, *my* death, the death that always hung out and made me different." Nicholas gave me a look that I deserved, because nobody wants death to hang out. "I didn't know what I was when my parents died, when my grandmother died. I hated death, but it was constant at least, the only thing that was. Izanagi is what being *Shinigami* means to me. He's good, I promise you. And he'll be there for me when I need him. When we need him."

Nicholas pulled my head to his chest with one hand, and kissed my hair with a lingering love, wrapping his arms around me.

"Seeing you suffer for the sake of helping me sucks. But you trying so hard to become what you're supposed to be is the most beautiful thing I've ever seen."

"If you're going to feed from her, do it here. I have better resources," Blue said, waving her hand around. I nodded and smiled. Then I did something I barely recognized as my own action.

I hugged her.

She was warm, and smelled so much different from Kat that it made me hug her harder to escape the loneliness and help me blink back the tears that came with the memory.

"Thank you," I whispered in Blue's ear.

She pulled back some, still holding me with the strength of a large man, a funny smile on her rosebud lips. "My pleasure. Have another cheeseburger," she said. "You're going to need it."

CHAPTER 65

"I need to go outside," I said to them both, shocked that they listened to me so readily. There was a desperation in Nicholas's eyes, but they were letting me call the shots. *I really am something special to the* Shinigami. *They listen to me.*

Standing out there in the cold, tiny snowflakes flurrying around me, I was able to breathe, to be me. Me, who'd eaten too fast, whose head was swimming. I closed my eyes, and imagined this to be my home in Ossipee, facing the mountain-side full of trees, Nicholas and a friend just a step away.

And I reached out to find him.

"Izanagi," I whispered as I called him into my mind's eye. There was a drunken pressure in my head, but I pushed further. The flutter of wings against both my palms at my sides didn't come as a surprise. I didn't need to look to know that a pair of crows were loitering with me.

Faster than last time, he was there.

"Izanagi," I said again. There, in front of me, but not quite real. Hair blowing as always, black streaks in the night, his head tipped down in a slight bow so only his eyelids were visi-ble. *Gi* jacket and pants flapping in time with the gusts of wind. A vision of black and white on a background of the same, part of the world, yet removed from it.

"Eliza," he said, his voice ethereal, like death breathing down my neck in the most comforting way. Inevitable, we were. Tied forever.

With one shaking hand, I reached out and touched his arm. Lifelike, but like a carved thing as well. A being of another place and time.

"Fate has given me a way to carve the fates of others," I said, images of Roman, Lynch, the girls he killed, and Nicholas, coming to me in rapid bursts. "It will take a lot from me." I raised my hands to his cheeks, smooth and soft, and I tilted his face up to look at me. "You will help me when I need you?"

His dark eyes bore into me, as soulful as the Master's were chilling. He put his hands on mine where they held his face.

"By all the devils of Yomi, I would destroy this world to help you."

I pulled my hands down slowly, the crow feathers brushing my fingertips again. "What are you doing here? What can I give you?" I knew he needed something, as much as I did. We were one in the same.

"Salvation from this place. I created this place, and it has become something different. You can free me, all of us."

"I don't understand."

The air stilled, bowing to his words. Words that held a weight of centuries, and words that came to me simply, without riddle. "My wife, Izanami became a thing of Yomi, that shadowy land of the dead. My beautiful wife…" His dark eyes glinted with a swordlike edge. "A coward, I left her there to decay and rot, abandoning my honor and my love in my fear of the devils of Yomi. Izanami was a creature of great passion, sharp intent, and with pride as deep as Yomi itself. In her rage over my betrayal, my beloved vowed to destroy one thousand people every day in this world that we created together. And so, I vowed to give life to fifteen hundred."

"You," I breathed, heart skipping madly. "You created the *Shinigami*."

Mournfully, he continued. "I created the *Shinigami*. Bound to this mountain, I create beings to never die by her hand, a new god to balance what we had done to fate. And now, we need saving once again."

"I am no god to help—"

He put his finger to my lips. Such a human thing to do. "You have just begun to cast pebbles on this path. All becomes clear with blood."

Izanagi looked over my shoulder, and I turned to look with him. Nicholas and Blue stood, watching us. They could see him this time.

Their mouths hung slack with his magnificence, and he was a part of *me* somehow.

"Go," he whispered over my shoulder, and without a look back, I went to drain myself again.

~

"He was there. I mean, barely, but there," Blue said, eyes wide, staring out into the night.

"That was Lord Izanagi," Nicholas said in a haze. "He rang through my bones."

"Told you," I said, as I picked up a burger, still warm from the chafing dish, and waggled my eyebrows at Nicholas. With a roll of his eyes, he turned to Blue.

"You're sure you want to be here for this? There's blood," he said simply.

She batted her lashes without a thought to how stunningly feminine it made her. "I'm fine. Kieran just paid me a visit."

Thoughts of Kieran throwing an unconscious body on the bed and Blue attacking it made me blink extra hard and refocus on the task at hand.

"Izanagi chose *you* to speak to," Blue said, shaking her head, one hand on my shoulder. "It's a miracle."

I bit my burger and thought about whether or not I should tell them the things he said. More secrets.

"We should tell the Master," Nicholas said.

"No!" I yelled without meaning to, startling them both.

"Why not?" Nicholas asked.

"Because if Izanagi wanted to involve him, he would have," I said. I realized that the Master could see Izanagi. Memories of that day at the sparring arena came to me; the Master was afraid because of what he saw behind me. Of *who* he saw.

My suspicion of the Master grew. I glanced to Nicholas, who was watching me eat with a little smile, but his eyes were sadder than they should be. It left a bitter taste, to tell the man I loved to keep secrets from his the man he thought of as a father. But this was not my secret to let go of.

I felt Izanagi breathe a sigh of relief from the woods outside.

I finished off the burger, thankful that I wasn't wearing jeans, and straightened my spine. I had work to do.

"Now," I said, clapping my hands to rid them of crumbs. "Drink from me, Nicholas, before I get too tired. We have training tomorrow, and a long night ahead."

CHAPTER 66

The visions swarmed me like angry bees trying to get inside, and fill the emptiness I'd known for too long. Nicholas sucked long and hard at my throat, and when that puckered and pained, he went to my wrists. Blue stayed close, holding my hand sometimes when I whimpered or let a cry out, or slipped away.

And there were many times I could have slipped away to unconsciousness, but I didn't want to go to the place the visions were taking me.

Not even if it was once my home.

I saw New Hampshire, Lynch again, and so many images of the women he'd killed that it angered me through my stupor. The metallic scent of my own oozing blood kept me present, and I forced myself to make sense of what I was seeing, and why. Izanagi was out there, in the woods, urging me on. Urging Nicholas on.

Why am I seeing all of these murders?! I shouted in my head.

Light flashed in my mind, blinding me. And just like that, I knew what needed to be done; and I knew what would be asked of Nicholas the following day.

"The Master is going to ask you to return to Ossipee, Nicholas," I heard myself say. I felt nothing.

"He's going to what?" Nicholas's voice was an echo in my bloodstream, reverberating through every cell, not heard, but breathed inside me.

"To take care of Lynch. He needs handling."

"I won't leave you," he growled into my soul.

"Lynch needs watching more than me. I can't see past you enough to know what to do next." My heart pounded. "My mind needs to be clear of you."

It was an arrow through my sluggish euphoria to say such a thing. Nicholas's hurt wove into my own blood before he pulled his mouth away, air flooding my skin; it felt like the agony between Izanagi and Izanami.

"You want me to leave?" he whispered. Blue left the room, though I was certain she hadn't heard any of the words that passed between us; it was all through my blood. My eyes fought to regain clarity.

"Nicholas, of course I don't want you to go. Do you think these are my *feelings* driving me to do this?"

"Your *feelings* are why you give me your blood. Now this, this is something else."

I swallowed, and clung to the bed for stability. "Something is in me, struggling to get out, and the *Shinigami* need it. You need it for me to restore you completely. I need it, to find out why the hell I'm alive, why I have to die to be someone! I need you to trust me. This is me finding my way. Let me be *Shinigami*." What had begun as a way to soothe Nicholas ended with me struggling for my identity. That escalated quickly.

"This is you having other options."

I almost fell on the floor with that one. "Excuse me? You think I want you out of the picture so I can play college freshman with some vampires?"

"Don't be ridiculous, you didn't go to college."

"Your sarcasm sucks." The thinning blood in my body was boiling. I closed my eyes and called to Izanagi. It had become that easy. With every drop of blood I lost, we were closer and closer.

He appeared next to me with no time lost, the door left wide open.

"I need your blood," I said to him.

Blue had returned, shifting foot to foot in my peripheral vision. The room became that level of cold only Nicholas could inflict upon it in so short a time. I tried to soften up when I said, "You've made me want to be more than what I was. What I have to do—"

"—is drink Izanagi's blood," Nicholas finished for me.

My heart ached for Nicholas, angry or not. I had done this to him, was always doing something to him. I took his face in my hands; his cheeks were ice, his eyes the cold chill of old coffee.

"Tell yourself you have to do this for me, because that's what I'm doing." His voice broke, and my heart with it. "I'm not angry," he added. "I'm just not ready to kick you out of the nest."

I pulled his face to mine, and kissed him hard enough to show him he belonged to me. Resting my nose on his, I said, "We're building a new nest."

~

"Do you have fangs?" I asked Izanagi.

He smiled serenely, and shook his head. He was human in so many ways, just a man, who'd been thrown into a vacuum because of being afraid, being in love, having choices that weren't really choices, more fated occurrences. He was *human*.

And one day I would become as inhuman as he had become.

"You're not a vampire, you just make them," I said with a grin. He cocked his head at me like a child trying to understand.

A rush of intoxicated air, and his body was so close it could have been as much a part of me as his heart was.

It was time.

He held up his hand, and looked at his wrist. A gash opened up on it out of thin air, making me cry out. The god looked at me slowly, willing me to calm down, and I did. "This pain," he said, corner of his mouth twitching at the gushing wound, "is nothing compared to what I live each day with my wife a shadow that I can never touch and would leave me colder if I did. This pain is nothing compared to waiting for you to come."

Trembling, I put my lips to the wound, knowing that I was about to drink *blood*. Knowing that something was about to happen that was written in stars, knowing that this choice would change my life into something it hadn't been.

"This won't make me *Shinigami*," I murmured against his pouring blood. Not a question, something I knew. This wasn't how I became a vampire; Nicholas would do that. Only Nicholas.

"You have always been *Shinigami*," the god whispered, loud as thunder.

I drank, and it tasted nothing like when you instinctively put your finger to your mouth when you cut it with a pizza slicer once a week. This blood was tingling, alive, the taste of constellations and oceans. It didn't fill me, but *replenished* me, revitalizing every sensation, every memory, every dream as it coursed through me with dizzying speed. His potent mix of wine and roses enveloped me, death mixed with life mixed with death. One in the same.

The visions lost their aggression, and became more cohesive, until they melted away entirely, leaving me feeling stronger. So much stronger. *Haunted* by strength, like it was the remnant of someone else, inhabiting me.

"My god," I said, wiping my clean chin. I didn't miss a drop of that ecstasy.

"How did it taste?" he said simply.

My eyes let me see what wasn't there yet.

I sucked on my lip for one last hope of a drop. "Like a world of death at my fingertips."

CHAPTER 67

I tried to stand still in the cold break of day, mind whirring like an engine, my body bursting with an inhuman energy. The sleep I'd had after drinking Izanagi's blood was more peaceful than Sleeping Beauty's, despite being filled with dreams of things I didn't understand; demons, devils, spirits of Yomi. And her face—Izanami.

The peppermint brownie essence fanned across me before Nicholas was in sight. My vision told me he was coming, even while I slept. I woke up and put on fighting clothes, ready to go before the sun rose. I would face a vampire, I knew it like I knew my own name. It was supposed to intimidate me, toughen me up Navy Seal-style, but the Master didn't know what I had now: the blood of a god.

I'd touched death with my lips, and nothing scared me.

"You're up? Not like you," Nicholas said, appearing in front of me. With my heightened senses, he was even more irresistible. I grabbed him by the arms and pulled him into a kiss that would have bruised a human man.

Nicholas drifted away after, licking his lips to savor the taste of me and said, "That stuff is good." I smiled while he looked me up and down. "You look different, too. Oh, I know, you're dressed like you're going to the Vampire Human Resources Barbecue. Aren't you cold?"

I looked down at the lightweight white cotton *gi* top and thin, loose pants that matched. They did look brand spanking new compared to the worn-in ones that the other *Shinigami* lived in. My bare feet were invisible under the newfallen snow, and only then did I realize how crazy that was.

"I guess the blood warms me up."

"Pretty sure you can still get frostbite."

"Maybe." I looked at him, to see what I could see. What he'd done the rest of the night while I was with Izanagi.

"I'm okay, stop worrying. Jealous of another man touching you, sure. But he doesn't touch you the way I do. And it wasn't your choice."

"Nicholas, don't think I'm some victim. I decided to drink his blood. I'm not a puppet."

"You're telling me he didn't mean anything to you?" he said.

"I'm telling you that it isn't a tie like you and I have. And I'm also telling you that we didn't touch any other way except for me to drink from his wrist. I don't want anyone that way except you." A flame of Kieran flickered into my head, and I just as quickly snuffed him out.

He sighed and smiled the winning, egotistical smile that I loved. We were okay. "How do you feel today?" he asked.

Grinning, I said, "Like nothing can stop me."

"Frostbite can stop you. You're barefoot, you lunatic. Go put socks and shoes on, I'll wait." He put his hands in the pockets of his hoodie and stared at me as I pulled my frozen, bluish feet out of the snow and wiggled the toes.

"Ha. They still move," I said. I looked at everything in a dream state, like I was stoned. "How did you know I was barefoot?"

"I smelled your feet. No, you're boots are by the door."

I bypassed the boots and put on socks and the wooden nightmare shoes I'd been given, highly impractical for snow, and sparked the vision of Nicholas the night before. Like snapping my fingers, as easy as blinking. I saw a fraction of a moment of Blue and Nicholas sitting on her bed, talking low, and I thought steam would come out of my ears. Their fingers were nearly touching, their eyes trained on each other. I didn't know what they were saying, and I was glad not to. It would have boiled my heart inside me.

I willed my hands not to shake, and my voice to remain even. "All right, let's go," I said, tottering with as much dignity as I could muster in these shoes on the boardwalk ahead of him, toward the sparring ring.

I was becoming used to the order of the sparring ring. Hundreds of *Shinigami* in a crowd around the open center, with the Master standing at the head on his little stone step, just always that much more important than everyone else. I spotted Blue where she'd been the last time, on the ground cross-legged with a few other female vampires. They all watched her, listened to her. I still liked her, despite my vision. It was then that I became aware I could *feel* the air between her and Nicholas, how powerful their connection was, the both of them. My heart warmed, oddly more toward her than it did toward Nicholas, who held my hand firmly at the top of the stairs.

"I know what's going to happen today," I said, my voice hollow, borrowed, as I stared down at the *Shinigami*.

"What?"

"I'm fighting a vampire. That one," I said, pointing to a young man in the crowd that sat motionless, staring at the empty center like it had his favorite toy and he wanted to take it back with the most violent means possible.

"Him?" Nicholas said, incredulous. "Wait, how do you know this? You know you're fighting today? And who—because of what happened last night?"

I merely nodded, unable to put words to the experience of having not new senses, not heightened ones, but different layers of understanding, new dimensions.

Nicholas shook his head. "He looks a little mental, that one. I don't like this. Do you know what happens?"

Relaxed, I shrugged and shook my head, Izanagi's blood a drum beating in my bones. "No, but I want to find out. Let's go."

"I mentioned I don't like this?"

The Master watched every step I took, and I didn't take my eyes off of his. The blank cloudiness of them didn't bother me.

Nicholas started towards a spot at the inner edge of the circle, with vampires making way for him fast and excitedly. Some were saying, "Hi Nicholas," like he was the quarterback of the football team and they were the Mathletes. Nicholas smiled at them all, the perfect class president.

I took my hand from his. "Nicholas, I'm going that way," I said, motioning to the Master whose eyes were still trained on me. He wiggled his long-nailed fingers at his sides, like he was trying to cast a spell.

I was making the Master nervous.

"Okay," Nicholas said, confused.

The vampires at my feet bowed their heads when I walked by, without willing themselves to, a magnetism from Izanagi's blood. As if the obscure promise of what I was to become to their race wasn't enough. As if being Nicholas French's *unmei fumetsu* wasn't enough. My chin lifted higher, my back straightened. I didn't need to suck in my stomach or fiddle with my hair.

I couldn't wipe the smirk off my lips when I bowed low to the Master. I was totally out of line with my sense of superiority over this *Shinigami* god, but I couldn't lie to myself as much as I could to Nicholas; there was something about the Master I didn't trust, and that Izanagi trusted less. Something about the man that Nicholas all but worshipped that I thought had ulterior motives.

When the Master tangibly relaxed in response to my show of respect, his momentary ease tingling down my spine like a drip of warm water, I sensed that he *did* trust me. He didn't want Nicholas to choose between us and knew he one day would. Thank you, all-knowing blood of Izanagi.

"You have changed, Eliza," the old man said.

I stood to face him. "I have. And you know who's touched me this way. Don't you?"

The eyes of hundreds of vampires were on my back, and of course, they could hear every word I said, no matter how far away they were. It was okay. If the Master was all Nicholas said he was, then he'd welcome a little effrontery. Maybe it would remind him fondly of taking Nicholas under his wing, but I didn't necessarily care. For once, I didn't need to hide behind the fear that I might get called out on being strong.

The Master didn't answer the question, but he didn't need to. He felt my power. It was juvenile and robust; growing, waiting. The Master's fear of me was a blanket upon it, willing me to go forward and become more.

I leaned forward to his ear, watching the anxious clench of his jaw, and I whispered, "Wait until I'm a vampire."

With a short bow, I walked unhurriedly back to Nicholas's side in the circle, every set of eyes on me. I caught Kieran's as I sat down, and he gave me a wide, defiant smile that warmed me like the campfire. Nicholas's hand chilled me to the bone when he put it on my knee.

"What was that?" he said.

"What was what?"

"All that with the Master? It's like you were calling him out or something."

"He can probably hear you."

"He's not listening, and if he were, he'd be glad I asked you what the hell you were doing."

My grin disappeared as I turned on Nicholas. "Sorry, I didn't realize he was so untouchable that he couldn't be spoken to. Is he not supposed to be a mentor? And you were the one who wanted to tell him about Izanagi. Think of it this way; I just did."

Nicholas got colder, but it didn't touch me. "He's like a father to me," he said, full of hurt.

Pursing my lips, I took his icy hand. "Nicholas, I know you love him, and that's important to me, really. I want to love him, too. But I can't give up *me*."

"This isn't you," he said with a mirthless laugh and not a little condescension. "This is Izanagi talking, and maybe a little too much Kieran."

Kieran heard it, and noticed my head snap in his direction, if he'd ever looked away from me at all. And leave it to the troublemaking bastard, he winked and smiled. My hand froze stiff in Nicholas's.

I'd had enough of the pettiness. A volcano of unease boiled in me, and I needed to *do* something. At that very moment, the Master pointed his staff at the vampire I'd spotted earlier, the one I knew I would be fighting. And knowledge hit me, hard, with unfaltering certainty.

I was the one who decided to fight the vampire. Nobody chose for me. Nobody made me do it, not even fate itself.

I stood fast, turning the heads of every vampire around me. "I would like to spar with him," I said solidly.

"Sit down, Eliza," Nicholas hissed.

I looked down at him and smiled, a happy smile, not an angry, defensive one. "I want this."

"You've never done anything like this in your life. You've never even thrown a punch, have you?"

"Sure I have, and don't worry about me. You won't let me die or anything. You think my super wonderful purpose here is to die in the ring? I don't think so."

A heavy sigh from him made me smile more, but he was freaking out.

"This is the worst idea I could never have come up with," he said. "This is Kieran-worthy of a bad idea. Don't think I don't see it."

There was the anger I needed.

I stalked to the center circle, more self-assured than I had any right to be. This was madness, and I had not an ounce of panic in me. Standing there, with hundreds of vampires judging me, I wasn't scared.

I wasn't even scared when the wiry vampire with too-wide eyes began bouncing around the ring like a meth addict ready for his next score. I swear, he was salivating. What purpose could *this* creature serve? Fate chose *him*? I immediately felt like a jerk for thinking it. Just because he looked like a disaster, didn't mean he was useless among a fleet of nearly perfect vampire peers.

Maybe we weren't so different.

The Master barked, *"Hajime!"* and I threw Nicholas a reassuring smile.

A second of hesitation too long.

The vampire struck me in the jaw with the back of his skeletal fist, and I hurtled across the ring, falling into a snow mound.

I expected to hear noise, besides the ringing in my head. Noises like you'd hear at a chicken fight or something, hollering and whooping. I heard nothing. But the blood inside me sensed something—concern. From several of the *Shinigami*, not just Nicholas, Blue, Kieran and Paolo. From ones I'd never spoken to. From strangers.

They wanted me to win.

I righted myself, pulled myself up and went back to the ring, one foot in front of the other, just like I'd gotten there to begin with. Blue and all her following were smiling wide at me from behind my opponent. It gave me strength, more than the considerable amount I already had.

The Master didn't look at me with the questioning eyes of a referee in a boxing match. He just signaled for us to go again. Without thinking, I lunged at the vampire, hitting him with a girly punch to the chin; artless, but with strength behind it. In dreams, I thought of punching people I was afraid of over and over, but my fist had the impact of feathers on their face. This punch had impact. His head snapped back. I hit him again, both fists at once, one to the face, one to the stomach, with all of my might, surprising myself. He stumbled backwards. I threw a kick like I'd watched Nicholas practice, landing it in his belly as he fell back, propelling him backward faster. Nicholas yelled encouragingly from out of my vision.

This was happening. I had power.

The vampire came at me fast, but inspired by my own tenacity, I rushed at him too, throwing a flurry of kicks that I had no idea I knew. I landed almost all of them somehow, as he spun and flitted like a sickly hummingbird around the ring. It wasn't until I knocked him down that I was too overcome with exhaustion to continue anyway. I swayed on my feet, and in that instant the vampire had a new light of anger in his wild eyes, and he swung back like a wrecking ball, hitting me on the top of the head with a hammer of a fist.

I felt Nicholas suck in his breath. The Master showed no sign of concern. Kieran was burning inside, and Paolo had stilled like fetid water. All of these things I felt in my core as the world spun.

Eyes closed to the maelstrom of color outside, I struggled to get up. When I opened my eyes, the vampire was in front of me, slack-jawed. Shaking his head, he put his hand up and said in a remarkably normal voice for such a wretch, "I give up. This one's yours."

I heard Nicholas breathe a barely audible word: "Amazing."

CHAPTER 68

I huddled against Nicholas's chest, drifting in and out of
sleep before the sun set. My bone-crushing aches were all
too human, but easily forgotten in the safety of his arms—
arms that were back to the hulking, wood-chopping things I
knew before his emaciation set in. I'd done that for him. Now,
his cinnamon and springtime scent drugged and healed me to
a perfect state of pleasure, and I smiled to think of what I'd
done.

With his lips on my hair he mumbled, "I can't believe what
you did out there today."

"Me either," I said, slurring with heavy, comfortable
exhaustion.

"It was stupid."

"Totally."

"It was eerie. That was nothing a human being could do,
stand up to one of us like that."

"Are you talking about the meth-head vampire or the
Master?"

He snickered. "Both. What are you trying to do to him,
anyway?"

"Nothing, I don't want to give him more meth, if that's what you mean."

"You know what and who I mean."

I sat up with great difficulty. "Come on, I didn't really do anything. If he's who you say he is, as a person, he won't mind. He's not a dictator."

"What difference does it make to you, though?" he said, bristly.

"It needs to be done. Part of it's for me, part of it's for the rest of the *Shinigami*. And part of it is for Izanagi." Nicholas stiffened, but didn't get cold, so I went on. "There's something between the Master and Izanagi. Something old, more important than us, but a part of us somehow? Standing up to the Master is something I can do for Izanagi. I want to."

I expected Nicholas to get a little irritated by this, but he softened, his eyes running over me, the warmth of them matching the scent that rolled off him like a newly opened oven. I loved this man for all of these things; he brought my heart to life. He ran his hand through my hair, his touch instantly making me want to fall asleep, and my body slackened more.

"It's okay to go to sleep," Nicholas murmured. "I might do the same, actually. I'm tired. This day has been—a little more than I was expecting."

I'd exhausted him and given a breath of life to him, as usual. My blood churned in a half-dream state, and another sense told me there was one more thing to do that day.

"Nicholas, drink. Just a little. Let me dream my visions."

"El…"

"Do what I say, I'm right."

"You're an obstinate bitch, too."

I smiled, even if he meant it. And I smiled again when he opened the vein.

~

Known only to me, Izanagi hovered outside as I fell asleep, a deeper calm than I'd known in a long time. Nicholas was drinking from me slow, slow, and it was actually *relaxing*, even as the visions of Lynch appeared.

Half-conscious, I saw the Master. He was outside the door, looking in with his blank eyes. I was too exhausted to open my eyes and see if it were true, but the presence of such a man was overwhelming, even in my sleep. Nicholas got out of bed with barely a movement, and I knew what would happen next.

I saw the scene in the room as if I were wide awake and watching. Nicholas flashed to the door in a burst of baking scents, and the Master hovered there, cold and ghostlike, a presence that filled the room before he entered it.

"You have a duty to perform," he said in Japanese, but I understood.

Nicholas bowed. I disliked seeing him in supplication to the Master, even if he did create their race.

Wait.

Nicholas thought the Master was the creator of the *Shinigami.* It was common knowledge among them all. It only occurred to me in this vision that it wasn't true. Izanagi created the vampire race, and the Master made everyone believe otherwise. It had to be part of his thrall. He was so incredibly old and strong, he could make them all believe whatever he wished.

I connected with Izanagi in the woods, saw him as plain as I was seeing this scene, all at once. He felt me, too, and the realization I'd come to. And I was right.

How could I tell Nicholas? I couldn't, I just couldn't.

"So Eliza was right," Nicholas said, moving aside so the Master could enter.

The Master gave my sleeping body that frighteningly

empty glare, full of anger and judgment. "Yes. It seems she is right frequently. You know what I'm going to ask of you, then?"

Nicholas sat, sprawled out on the floor, leaning lazily against the table. It was comforting to know he was still this much himself with the Master, reminded me that they were family. We expect family to disappoint us, in the end. But it wouldn't make it easier to tell him that their history was a lie.

"Eliza had a vision of you asking me to go to New Hampshire." He looked over at me with love-filled eyes, and I drifted more comfortably into my deep sleep.

"She's correct. You know why, then. What else does she see?"

"Lynch is on a killing spree. He's hurting over Kat." The simplicity of his words cut through me with their obviousness. It was still hard to think of Lynch as capable of love, a serial killer dubbed "the Abomination" by the *Shinigami*.

"Roman needs you to repay the favor he did for you."

"Favor," Nicholas said quietly, eyes downcast. I'd said to him so many times how hurtful it was that Kat's murder was a *favor* between Roman and Nicholas. Killing my only friend brought them closer together, even if Roman was nowhere to be seen. And I was alone, without her.

"You alone can keep the Abomination in line. It is only you that he's afraid of."

Nicholas nodded. "What of Eliza? What happens to her while I'm gone?" They both looked at me, and I saw myself through their eyes, my side rising and falling where I lay curled in a ball like a sleeping cat.

"She'll become what she must. Then everything will change."

Nicholas looked at him sharply. "Master. Nobody else can turn her. It has to be me." He breathed in through his nose, eyes drilling into the old vampire. "Nobody else can have her that way."

Both reacting to the other's anxiety, the two vampires put up glassy shields, which immediately crystallized around them in domes of ice. Two grim smiles showed through the shields like fun house mirrors. The Master's fell away like it had been in my imagination the whole time, while Nicholas's exploded into millions of fragments and disappeared. So like the men themselves; one a complete illusion.

"Of course nobody else will touch her, my boy. Do you think she would allow it?" For the first time, I agreed with him.

But Nicholas's neck twitched, and I knew he thought of Kieran, and maybe a little of Izanagi. He stared at me in the bed, shoulders stiff. "I want to change her before I leave."

I was awake.

In the woods, Izanagi clenched his fists.

CHAPTER 69

"Stop pretending to be asleep," Nicholas said as he slid into bed.

I rolled over and slid my hands over his shoulders and back. So robust again. After feeding from me the solid jaw and cheekbones under the five o'clock shadow didn't look fragile.

"I heard everything, saw everything," I said.

"In a vision?"

"Yes."

He released a troubled, sad sigh. "I was hoping you were wrong and he wouldn't have me leave."

"We've been over this," I said. "What I'm more afraid of is what happens to *you* when you leave. I won't be with you to feed from me."

He didn't want to admit that worried him, or that he would just plain miss the taste, and the intimacy. He swallowed hard. "You're overlooking that I want to change you before I go."

I had no words. Nicholas had to leave, it was part of fate's plan, *my* plan to save him, and I was terrified to become a vampire before he was cured. The idea of taking away the one thing that made him whole again chilled me. The time

431

between me deciphering the visions and Nicholas withering away without my blood couldn't be avoided. As certain as the death that owned us.

Nicholas wiped tears from my cheeks with his thumb. "Trust yourself, Eliza. You're afraid of what will happen to me, but you're doing it *for me*. I don't doubt you, and if this is the end, if we're wrong, you have given me Heaven here and I'm ready for Hell."

Only one question remained. "How soon do we do it?"

His eyes bore ferociously into mine. "Speaking of things we've already talked about, are you absolutely certain the way you feel about me isn't just the pull of being my *unmei fumetsu*? This thrall thing, and the scent… Once you've been turned, the illusion is gone, all that goes away—"

"Don't."

"You may never remember what you saw in me." His jaw tightened, and he went still, the way people do if they are very, very afraid and don't know what to do. "You could be so disgusted by this existence when you see me through eyes like my own, that you'll feel you could never love anything again." My soul ripped when he tore his eyes from mine.

"First of all, you're in love with me and I accept it. Why can't you do the same?"

In that nonchalant way he had, he said, "Oh, I regret every day the time I spent denying that I was hopelessly in love with you."

"No regrets. And we don't question it again. End of story."

"The problem is, it's only the beginning of our story."

"Sorry, that's a problem how?"

Fear of what unknown thing he might say next chilled me to the bone the way the icy woods of New Hampshire or Japan could never do. He ran his fingers through my hair. "Because, beautiful girl. I could *ruin* you. Make you something you're not, damn you for all eternity. Loveless, cold, trapped seeing the world and me too clearly through superhuman eyes."

I grabbed his hand in my hair, angered by his ridiculous despair. "Is there going to be a time you don't think I'm a moron? This *thrall* you still think you have me in, well, people do it all the time. They fall for someone and can't explain it, because of the way they smell, or some look they can give. You're not so special." His lips puckered, and I was encouraged that maybe he understood my logic. "I can explain exactly why I'm drawn to you, Nicholas. It's that you're *you* no matter what human residue gets left behind in there. It's *your* emotional walls, *your* sarcasm, *your* generosity and your laugh, and the way you're just so good at everything." I choked back some of my own emotion. "Those things and so many more things that I see in you is why I'm forever in love with every curl on your head, and every pain in your heart. Can't you trust that the more clearly I see you, the more I'll know how worth loving you are?"

His eyes glistened. "We can be like this forever," he said.

"As long as you don't think eternity is too long to have the same girlfriend."

He propped up on one elbow. "No. I think probably every-thing—slows down. Takes on new meaning. Not just once, but over and over. Probably all the things I saw before will become clearer when I look in your immortal eyes, so I'll think maybe I never *really* saw anything. And I think those times when nothing matters, when time is my enemy because it won't stop, I bet that doesn't happen anymore. I bet time is on my side again, when I never have to turn from you. I bet I'll be glad that time won't end. I bet I wouldn't be able to stand it if it did. Not that I've put any thought into it."

Through hazy grins, we dreamed of when eternity would start.

～

My visions followed me into sleep, where I was dumbfounded to see Leann. Of all people, the other *unmei fumetsu* was the last person I expected to see, so little an impression she made on me. I woke up eager to get training, though from the aches and pains, I knew I wouldn't be volunteering to fight that day.

"Nicholas, wake up," I whispered, shaking him hard.

"Why are you whispering when you're shaking me like the human earthquake?" he groaned, his face in the pillow.

"We need to get ready to training. Right now."

"Right now?"

"That's what I said."

"Bossy." He got up with a dancer's ease, his bare back rippling, his thigh muscles flexing, revealed by only boxer shorts.

I literally rolled out of bed to a crouch on the floor. Jesus, I was sore. And covered in bruises. I'd put on a long sleeved black t-shirt and sweatpants, and the bruises still peeked out from under the sleeves and cuffs. I couldn't let Nicholas see. He wasn't looking, but stepping into his karate pants and grabbing a Star Wars tee with Japanese writing on it.

"Cool new shirt."

"One of the young ones gave it to me," he said, smoothing his hair fruitlessly after pulling the shirt on. God, they showered him with gifts.

Was that going to be me one day?

After rubbing his eyes and grimacing either at the taste in his mouth or his breath, he really looked at me.

"Holy shit."

He crossed the room in one motion to touch my cheeks with tentative fingertips.

"How bad is it?" I asked him. "Is it like, G.I. Jane bad?"

He pursed his lips, with a pained frown. "Yeah."

I smiled, the skin tightening around my eyes where they must be bruised. "Progress. Outside hurts heal, it's the inside ones you have to worry about."

"That's a heroic thing to say."

"It's how I feel."

He kissed me with featherweight lips on the cheek, and it still stung. I pulled my hair into a ponytail, stifling a sharp breath when I touched the top of my head. "Hero turned vampire. That will be perfect. But we knew that. Now we have training to attend to. I guess? It's what the boss says."

I kissed his lips hard, not caring that I had bruises around mine. "Thank you for blindly listening to me."

"Your eyes are fresher than mine, and your mind knows more. I'm dying to see what kind of ride you take me on today."

"Something is happening with Leann today, but I can't see what."

He looked faraway for a minute. "You can see her now, too?"

I shook my head. "She just popped up. It wasn't as clear as my other visions, but it's definitely a real thing that's going to happen."

"Should you tell her?"

"What could I possibly say?"

Nicholas made me lie down while we waited for breakfast to arrive. He just watched as I devoured eggs and fruit, and looked for more.

"Still think it's sexy when I eat?" I said through a mouthful.

He curled his lip back, animal-like. "I could devour you."

I choked, and pictured myself black, blue and yellow, food on my face, chewing like a goat. He smoldered looking at me, and I tried not to get distracted. We had to go.

The walk seemed shorter all the time, even being all

banged up and in awful wooden shoes. It wasn't long before I'd planted myself next to Leann on the outside of the circle, hoping not to be pointed at. I could've used a day without being the center of attention.

"That was pretty ballsy of you yesterday," Leann said, hugging her knees, not looking at me.

"Or pretty dumb. Look at me." I said it, but didn't mean it. I felt goddamn good. I could take on the world, and all it could do was bruise me.

"Did you train before that at all? Like, at all?" Her face was full of unhidden skepticism.

"Not so much."

"Then why did you volunteer to fight a vampire?" She smirked, like she was talking to someone stupider than her.

She wasn't the one who had visions so clear she could taste the air in them. She wasn't the one that had Izanagi's blood bubbling in her veins. She wasn't the one who had Nicholas French in her bed and in her future.

This superiority wasn't like me, but it was. It was like the new me. *Shinigami* ran deeper than the rest of me. Leann may be on her way to becoming a vampire, but I was something more.

"I wanted to do it. What have I got to lose?"

She squinted, sizing me up. I didn't like it. *This is my place.*

"Where do you come from? What's your story?" she said, not really asking me, more wondering out loud.

"New Hampshire. Story is death took over and all that. You?"

"Pretty much the same."

"You're from New Hampshire and death followed you, took the world from you so as to make you its slave for eternity?" God, what a bitch I could be.

She laughed, eased by my unease. "Yeah, something like

that. From Ohio. An orphan. Never had anyone, so nobody I cared about died. We're not so different."

I sniffed at her. She was nothing like me. I was a jerk for looking down on her, but I did. I just did.

"Are you afraid?" I asked her, without intending to. They were words from within me, from that place that gave me visions. Maybe they came in part from the place where I was misinterpreted and alone, too. Possibly I just wanted to hear someone like me say out loud that yes, she was afraid, and that she didn't have everything under control.

But Leann's malicious sneer didn't offer me any comaraderie. "Of course I am," she spat at me, like I was a complete imbecile for asking.

But I was the one who knew she was becoming a vampire that day, not her.

"Do you know how it's done?" I asked her, because I didn't know *everything*. Kieran was alone, smoking. She shrugged and looked away. "My—Nicholas—only told me it's very personal, and hard to explain, because he's never made a vampire before." But Kieran had, with Blue.

A bolt of lightning-filled jealousy shot through me as an unsolicited vision of Kieran's naked silhouette came to me.

With *her.*

I stared at Leann, forcing the image of her nudity beside Kieran's out of my mind, and she looked back at me with actual fear in her eyes.

"What's your problem?" she said.

"What's yours? I'm a useful one to have on your side, seeing as Kieran clearly isn't interested." Izanagi buzzed inside me.

"What is it with you and your *Shugotenshi?* You two are so attached," she said, like it disgusted her.

"And you and Kieran aren't. Sucks to be you, huh?" I snapped back.

"Nicholas is nothing like you. Kieran is nothing like me. We aren't meant to be together."

"You don't have the attachment we do?" Genuine curiosity. Kieran paid her hardly any mind at all. The pain would have slaughtered me in every way.

For the first time she looked at me like a person, like someone with actual emotions who wanted to trust and be trusted. I just think she didn't know how. "I hurt all the time," she said, voice cracking. "I couldn't take it if we were *together*, like Nicholas and you are."

I'd never thought of it that way. Like it was harder to care for each other. I'd never had the choice. And from the look on her face, I don't think Leann did either. She blistered with emotion so much that it was nearly invisible until you knew what to look for.

"What makes you think Nicholas will stick around after you turn vamp?"

Gulping, I had to fight off every cell in my body that wondered the same thing. Would I be the same for him when vampire blood roared through my veins, or when I took on my victims' traits after draining them? When I acted more like a dead person than myself? I had to believe it when he said it wouldn't change anything.

"We were meant to be together, it's there, every time he looks at me," I said.

Leann's eyes narrowed. "Yeah, good luck with that," she muttered.

In the center of us all, Kieran and Nicholas ignored us to good-naturedly batter each other with fire and ice.

~

"Tonight?"

Nicholas was sweaty, something I found amazing when it occurred. He swatted my hand away when I put a finger on a burn mark on his arm.

"Holy crap, is that from Kieran touching you?"

"It will go away soon enough," he said, pulling his arm away. "So, tonight. I don't know if she's ready."

Leann would have to be ready. Our training was different, every one of us. She'd been at the temple for months. Sometimes it took years. Arthur had just barely arrived when I did.

Nicholas was deep in thought, cracking his knuckles as we walked. "The Master asking me to leave, Izanagi showing up, all this centers around you. I wish to Christ I knew why."

As if he'd heard the Lord's name used in vain, there was Paolo, keeping pace with us.

"Eliza," he said, nodding quickly with a smile for Nicholas. "Eliza, there's a haze all around you. Do you need to talk?"

I was so taken aback by this, I stopped completely, and so did Nicholas. Paolo kept going. "Realizing your higher purpose requires a lot of soul searching. Your soul is troubled. Do you need to talk?" he repeated.

I looked at Nicholas, who looked back at me, bemused.

"Eliza's not really a woman of God," Nicholas said.

But the idea of having someone to talk to about the conflicts in my heart had certain appeal. Paolo noticed me considering it. His peacefulness flowed over me like beach waves.

"When you need me, I will be ready to listen," he said.

"Th—thank you, Paolo," I stuttered. I was uncomfortable, not because Paolo could see my soul changing, but because Nicholas could not.

"Nicholas, a true pleasure to watch you and Kieran today.

You're such an artist," Paolo said, bowing his head in reverence.

Nicholas bowed back. "Thanks, Paolo. Now come have a drink. We could all use a stiff drink."

"Oh, I don't know about that."

"Luckily, I do," Nicholas said, cuffing the younger man round the back of the neck. "Come with us. Loosen up."

CHAPTER 70

P aolo's skin was flush from attending the sparring matches in the bright sun. That meant he'd fed on a good person, someone with a good soul. And he, a man of God.

He caught me looking at him as Nicholas poured sake. It was barely noon.

"What wracks your lightning-quick brain, Eliza?" Paolo said.

My cheeks got hot. "Sorry. I just was thinking of all the vampires out in daytime."

"I fed last night," he said, with the hint of a smile. "As all God's creatures do."

"We're drinking, this is no place for God," Nicholas said, downing his sake. We sat around the table once again. Like a family.

Kat and Roman would have loved it.

Blue appeared at the door. Dragonfly presence; shimmering blue kimono top against black hair, a tiny stature that didn't threaten, but was fearful all the same. Dark beauty. "I want in," she said, grinning. Her presence made me lighter.

She sat next to Nicholas with a decided plop and looked at us all. "What are we talking about?"

Paolo smiled wide at her, as charmed by her as the rest of the world.

Nicholas answered first in the way only he could. "Talking about how a man of God consumes the blood of the innocent and walks in their daylight and still considers himself holy." He grinned at Paolo, who grinned back.

"I fulfill a purpose, and I'm happy to do His work. I'm more concerned how Eliza is feeling about coming into her own." He pinned his eyes on me.

May as well be honest. "I'm feeling a little pompous about it, actually. Weird."

"You've been hanging around me just the right amount, then," Nicholas said.

"The visions are stronger, aren't they?" Blue said in a whisper, turning it into a secret between friends.

I nodded. "I can call them up, and sometimes now I get these…premonitions, I guess." I glanced at Paolo and Nicholas. "I know Leann is becoming a vampire tonight." Paolo smiled, but Blue paled.

"Kieran will change her tonight?" she asked, voice thick.

"What's wrong?" I asked. Nicholas didn't look at me, only at Blue, wordlessly showing disturbance.

"I—I, um, just wasn't expecting it. But I should have. She's his. Too," she said, sentences broken, eyes on her hands as they twisted in her lap. I wanted to hug her. I couldn't imagine how hard it must be to see your *Shugotenshi* sharing that intimacy with another.

"There's nothing between them, you know," Nicholas said quietly, meant only for her.

"There is and there isn't. Nothing…lasting. But it's still not easy to think of."

"It doesn't mean Kieran's going to have sex—" Nicholas started, but Blue gave him a withering look.

You only had to take one look at the Irishman to know he most certainly would be having sex with the girl. All the girls. Nicholas put his hand on Blue's back, and she smiled at him sadly.

"That means there will be a ceremony tomorrow night," Paolo said.

"So many *ceremonies...*" Nicholas moaned, rolling his head back. Great. Dressing up was imminent.

"We celebrate our own," Paolo said.

"It's beautiful," Blue said, cheering up a bit. "You'll love it."

"It's a lovely thing to see someone who was mere flesh and blood become one with their destiny," Paolo went on.

I wondered what it would be like for me. It wouldn't be long before I found out.

"Pour me some sake," I said to Nicholas.

〜

Nicholas and Paolo went off to practice *katas* together, a prospect Paolo was absolutely giddy about. It was still funny to see Nicholas treated like such a celebrity. The *Shinigami* were starstruck by him so often, it threw me, but I was equally happy to see that everyone recognized his splendor the way I did.

Blue stayed with me to drink more sake. It was probably a bad idea, but slurring and laughing about the room being so blurry made me not care that much. Blue was an open book, so willing to talk about her feelings for Kieran. She didn't think she was in love with him, but she didn't know, and she was sure he wasn't in love with her, or anyone.

"Nicholas denied we were in love for a long time, too. Thrall this and that. Chosen ties, blah, blah."

"They're still men under it all, aren't they?" Blue said softly.

I reached out and held her little hand. "I wish there was something I could say to make this better for you."

She looked into my eyes, and asked, "Is it happening right now?"

"Not yet. It will be dark."

"Thanks for telling me. It makes it easier, just a little."

We sat quietly, leaning against each other, watching snow squall in circles.

"I can see them outside in this weather, right now," I said, closing my eyes and smiling. "The snow is wild, and Paolo and Nicholas are fighting in it."

"Is it hard for you to be human and see what he is? Are you afraid of killing?" Hearing her talk about it in her singsong voice was surreal. To remember her fighting, and to think of her ripping someone's throat open, it was somehow *beautiful* to me.

"It shouldn't be so easy for me to think of people being killed. Of being the one to do it."

"No," Blue said, looking desperately into my eyes. "I felt like I was becoming a monster. I wasted too much time thinking how awful I was. Maybe that's why Kieran doesn't love me—he knows what I thought of him then."

"It's not your fault. Kieran feels how he feels, nobody has to be at fault for it."

She threw her arms around my neck without warning. "How are you so wise about things that are so terribly simple, and so terribly complicated?"

I laughed. "Because I'm something—else."

CHAPTER 71

Darkness brought the return of Nicholas, and my own dark with him. A bleak sense of overwhelm writhed in me and I was alone in it. Blue wanted to cope with Kieran's next move by herself. Thank God she didn't have the visions I did of their naked bodies.

"You drank like a drunk, didn't you?" Nicholas said. "Impressive. Manly."

"Sssshhh."

"Headache already?" He put his cold fingers on my temples. It nearly lulled me off to sleep standing up, and I would have welcomed it. Too much was happening too fast, and yet not fast enough for me to react to it. I wanted out for just a while.

"Paolo's a big fan of yours," Nicholas said, leading me to bed by the hand. "You may be the new icon around here."

"That bother you?" I sounded drunk.

"I'm your biggest fan."

"Creep."

"The worst kind."

He covered me up as I lay on my side, and moved in behind

me. Sweat and cinnamon overtook my senses. His hands ran up and down my arms, his nose nuzzled into my neck, and if I hadn't been so comfortable, I would have turned to kiss him.

I sat bolt upright when the heat in the pitch dark reached me. A sudden blast of inexplicable warmth, waking me out of a sound sleep. Nicholas slept like a porcelain god next to me, hands folded on his chest, sleep-puffed lips parted. A vision was skirting the edges of my mind, but couldn't quite find its way in, fogging my thoughts up. I almost woke the peaceful beauty at my side to have him drink from me, so that I could let in the images that wanted to be mine.

I was becoming an addict.

Frustrated and groggy, I got up, throwing on my heavy coat and Nicholas's boots by the door; old things of habit. It warmed me to think that he missed the place where we'd trudged through the snow together. He missed New Hampshire.

The blustering wind hit me hard when I opened the door, and I looked around for the source of the heat that was warming me when I should have been freezing.

The Irishman sat on a rock only feet away, his head in his hands. I rushed to him, wanting nothing more than to make help, his despair was so evident. Waves of heat shimmered the air around him, regardless of the icy wind. He was boiling inside.

"Kieran," I said, putting my hand on his shoulder. How the heat emitting from him didn't burn the black tee right off his body, I didn't know.

He didn't lift his head. "Leann's a vampire now," he said.

I gulped. "I know."

"Right," he nodded. "What if she wants more from me?"

"That, I don't know."

He looked up, smoldering tears in his eyes, the remnants of

earlier ones smoking on his cheeks. I gasped, not expecting to see such emotion in him. I'd thought he bottled it all up to let it out in every self-destructive way he could.

"Kieran," I breathed, dropping to my knees in the snow next to him, the cold a welcome change next to his incessant burning. "Why are you so upset about this? She's your *unmei fumetsu.*"

"Aye, but I don't want her."

I blinked dumbly over and over.

"Does she want you?"

He looked at me with those sweet brown eyes, eyes that betrayed hurt that he so successfully hid from everyone. "Not like Blue does. And I don't know what to do with either of them."

It strangled me to see him so conflicted. It hurt like when Nicholas was hurting, or when Kat was crying. It hurt like I cared a frightening amount.

"You must be freezing, love," he said, that accent melting me more than the fire in his eyes and heart.

"Not next to you," I said. God, did that sound like I think it sounded? I glanced back at the doorway, where Nicholas slept not so far inside. A disgusting guilt overcame me, and vanished when Kieran put his hand on mine.

"It looks like you've got as much trouble as I do. I could see it from you a mile away. I wanted to be near you."

This close to him, the simplicity of those words, I felt stripped. My eyes tore from his. "There's a lot going on in my head. And—" Should I tell him this? Catching myself mid-sentence, I looked at him, scared. But I had nothing to be scared of.

"And what?"

"And Nicholas is leaving."

"Leaving?"

My throat tightened inside an invisible fist. "He has to go back home, but nobody knows yet."

"Except you. You knew first." I nodded, and he added, "Our Mr. French is leaving you with no one? Hardly seems right."

"I'll be a vampire before he goes, and I can take care of myself. You made Leann one, what, twenty minutes ago?"

"You're a hell of a lot different from Leann."

"Different, but still afraid."

The sweltering heat of him wrapped around me in cuddly bear hug. I'd never felt anything so soft and warm in my life, and he hadn't even touched me.

Then he *was* touching me, his tattooed hands holding mine against his chest. "Don't be afraid. I'll make sure nothing hurts you."

My heart crumbled. Part of me wanted to be weak and taken care of, was so tired and bored of being different. There was no end to how strong I had to be, and sometimes it was just easier to fail.

He pulled me to his chest, wrapping his arms around me tight. No one had ever made me feel as understood as he did at that moment. We were alike in that moment. It hurt like rubbing a bruise.

I swore I could hear Nicholas breathing from inside.

"Kieran, I don't think I should be out here."

He let me go, and the wound I didn't know was there opened up again.

"What do you *want* to do?" He held a strand of my hair up to his nose. The slight tip of his head bared the dark stubble on his throat, its straining tendons, intensely sexual. His voice was guttural, lustful. I couldn't move, the burn of him holding me captive there. "What Nicholas gives you is part of the vampire package, love. Don't let it tell you what you want."

That sent a chill through me, and I leaned away. "Nicholas

and I are in love, and we would be whether I was his chosen or not. He's what I want."

Eyes on mine, Kieran put a cigarette coolly in his mouth and lit it with the touch of his fingertip.

"Then it shouldn't be such a distraction to come with me for a while?"

In Nicholas's boots, my pajamas under my big mess of a coat, still tipsy, I went with Kieran. Maybe he was right, maybe I just wanted to do something that wasn't expected of me. He was the devil on my shoulder and I found myself all too willing to listen.

"I didn't know about this place," I said as we walked into a dark, decadent tea room. Smoky under purple lantern light, I saw vampires lounged on black pillows around cherrywood tables. Their shadows on the walls seemed more real than they did.

"We don't talk about it in polite conversation, love," Kieran said.

"Like you know polite conversation," I muttered, looking around. I wondered if Nicholas knew of this decadent, dirty little hideaway.

All the vampires here were alone, even if they were together. The secrecy simmered in a haze of saccharine-sweet smelling booze and whispers, hid in violet-hued corners, flaunted in glimpses of skin and teeth.

The serenity of Japan was becoming unsettling to me, and I

welcomed this place that hid a little rebellion. Zen gardens and gently tinkling music, cool, calm colors and meditation areas; all for us killers. It didn't always sit well.

Walking with a derelict grace, Kieran grabbed pillows from every empty table and threw them all on the floor against a floor to ceiling window. He sprawled across them, hands behind his head against the glass, and I sunk down with him. The air around him tasted like flames.

When the serving girl brought us tea, Kieran gave her a wink, making her giggle into her hand. My eyes rolled of their own volition.

"Is there a woman here you that isn't hot for you?"

He swigged the tea, and then bucked his hips forward to pull a flask out of his back pocket. "I can't get the deaf and blind girl to touch my biceps."

I drank my tea, but pretended it was something stronger. The hour approached when the shit would hit the fan, and my buzz was wearing off. I needed some desensitizing to this intuition telling me that too much was about to be revealed, too much would occur in one day. I wasn't ready for morning and drinking would help.

I took the flask out of his hand and tossed it back, as he watched with a surprised grin.

"Feel the burn, baby," he said.

I winced. "Jack is no gentleman."

"Gentlemen are no fun. Now tell me why you're here."

"You made me come?"

With raised eyebrows, he gave me a chastising finger point. "You need to stop doing what everyone tells you."

"Including you?"

He leaned forward to take the flask back, and finished it off. "I'll never tell you what to do, even if you beg."

I thunked my head against the window behind us. "I'm still a little drunk and I want to drink more. I agree with you, it's time I had some fun. This ceremony tomorrow's gonna get ugly, and booze makes the ugly go away."

"Eh, not always. What's that brain of yours showing you now, Miss Morgan? Is it Leann?"

I blinked, and she flashed in my head. A femme fatale of a vampire, on the temple steps. Visions of red. The sting of betrayal and surprise and lust for blood. It disappeared as fast as it came.

"Eliza!" Kieran was crouched over me, holding my back off the ground. "Eliza, what just happened?"

"Whaaa—" I couldn't speak for the mouthful of my own saliva, and it was running down my chin. A seizure.

"Christ, Eliza, this is how visions treat you now?"

"I sure as hell hope not," I said, rubbing my eyes.

"Your body is kicking out the human," he said under his breath. "Only *Shinigami* could handle a power like this."

He signaled to Giggly Girl, who was quick enough to know we wanted alcohol, not tea. My body buzzed with aftershocks, my ears rang, the room was too loud. Kieran waited for me to drink a hearty mouthful before he did the same, his concerned eyes helping to slow my heart as it pounded an arhythmical beat. Kieran's strong, working hands were on my cheeks and he was looking hard into my face, too close, full of worry.

"You keep me on my toes, woman," he said, rolling back on to the pillows against the window.

"Good thing, looks like I'll be falling down a lot."

He took the shaking cup out of my hand, our fingers touching for a pulsing moment. "You need water, a clear head. Whatever you just saw knocked you on your arse."

I put my head in my hands to slow the whirring room down. "These visions are too strong for me, they're coming faster and harder. And when they don't, they still want in and the only thing that makes them come is letting Nicholas drink from me, and that makes me weak and—"

"Sssshhh," he crooned, lifting my head gently. My hair hung in my face as usual, and he brushed it aside. "I don't know how to help you, but I'll be here. I'll hold your hand tomorrow if you need."

"Something big is going to happen. More than one big thing. Lots of big things. They're like ants crawling in my brain."

"Tomorrow will come soon enough. Then some of it will stop. I think." He ran his hands up and down my arms, every movement the smell of a freshly snuffed flame. My mane of hair hid us from what little light there was, and we were alone. Two things that weren't what they were supposed to be. "Why do you feel so much like mine, Eliza?" he breathed in that small space, his breath as heated as his words.

I tried to object, but my lungs collapsed and my heart stopped working. My brain screamed and everything in me stopped doing what it was supposed to.

"I won't kiss you if you don't want me to," he said.

I moaned, not the kind he was probably looking for, but one of crushing defeat. Flashes of Kieran and Blue, Kieran and Leann, Leann in red, Nicholas and Izanagi, Roman, Lynch, blood. And Nicholas again. But so much blood.

Kieran leaned his forehead on mine like Nicholas had done so many times, relaxing me the same way. "I won't pretend that I don't want you, Kieran. I do. But I'm his."

"For once, do what you want, Eliza."

I pushed him off as nicely as I could, and the subtle darkness of the room filtered in again.

"Jesus, what am I doing to ya?" He rubbed his hand over his jaw. "I'm sorry, acting without thinking. Truth of it is I don't know what I want, either."

"What sent you my way tonight?" I asked. "What about Leann? Blue?"

"Ah, those two," he said with a grim laugh. "I don't know

how I got blessed with two *unmei fumetsu*. I don't deserve them. They sure as hell don't deserve me."

"You mean well," I said, touching his arm soothingly against my better judgment. God, could I please drink more now?

"Intentions will be the end of the world one day."

The fire was all around him. He couldn't survive without it. The fire reminded him of the bad thing he was, even if he wasn't.

"Kieran, I don't believe you're a bad man because of all this," I said, waving my hand at his fading tattoos, faded t-shirt, faded jeans, faded conviction. "There's something so much more real about you than the rest of them. You've got more fight in you."

"Only because I'm a walking mistake. Once you're one of us, my unique flavor wears off."

"It hasn't for Blue."

He winced, stung, but I didn't regret saying it.

"Blue lets her fears turn her into something she's not. That woman doesn't need me."

"Seems to me you two are kind of perfect together."

"Perfect isn't perfect for me." His voice was becoming more agitated. He squinted, taking the last drag off his cigarette and putting it out in the cup in his hand. "Tell me you don't ever feel a little less than perfect with Nicholas French by your side."

"I don't need to be perfect to be right for him." Nicholas never made me feel like I wasn't good enough—maybe just not right for a lot of things. But Nicholas did feel right, so right that I often wondered how I survived so long without him.

And yet here I was. With another man.

"I think I'd better get back, Kieran. Got to sleep this off, be ready for Leann's ceremony, whatever in the hell's in store tomorrow." Disappointment spread across his face. "Where is Leann, anyway?"

He looked out the window, like he might see her there. "Dying, being reborn. Forgetting the world she never really knew."

CHAPTER 73

Light woke Nicholas and I at the same time. Having him next to me in bed never lost its shine.

"Where'd you go?"

No good morning, just wondering where I went while wearing his shoes.

"Just outside," I said. Then I realized that wasn't true, and I hated myself for going on, but I had to. "Then I went with Kieran for a drink." Shit, that sounded bad.

"Oh. Of course. That's exactly what I expected to hear."

My eyes shot open to see Nicholas making that face, where I couldn't tell if he was serious or just a lot more fluent in sarcasm than I was.

"R-really?"

"No. No, it's not. That's what I'd expect to hear from a homeschooled teenybopper with daddy issues. Not from you."

"Well, if you'd let me go out once in a while, I wouldn't have to rebel, Dad."

With a gasp and a hand to his chest as if to say he was mortally offended, he burst out, "*Dad? Let* you? I didn't realize

I held the reins too tight. Or at all." Then, more seriously, "You're right, I'll back off."

"No, no. You're right. I snuck out like I was grounded. I didn't want to wake you, and me and Kieran just—talked." I knew I was blushing. I wanted to cover my head in the blankets, but Nicholas would feel my heart beating fast from under them.

"Kieran doesn't ever just talk. Nobody with an Irish brogue does. They entrance and take advantage. It's fascinating, really."

"Nicholas, I was born at night, but not last night. However, I know someone who was."

Leann was a vampire now. Meaning this was the day of the ceremony, and all the *other* things that I could sense, but not quite see.

His lips darted onto mine, and were gone. "I don't ever want you to feel like I own you. You're stronger than me, I'm a fraction of a thing without you." He smelled like dreams feel; billowy, marshmallow and cookies, not quite real. Like what I wanted for us. Soft, easy, cloud-filled days.

I put my hand on his face, the five o'clock shadow he always had, different from Kieran's leftover stubble from forgotten nights. Nicholas was rugged and in control, strong. I wanted him to stay that way, and I knew I could help.

"I love you for all of it. You have your possessive side, Nicholas, but so do I. I want to belong to you, so it works just fine."

He kissed me without hesitation or seduction, a full, growing thing. Like the world would burst with the strength of it.

"I know the best way you can possess me," I said, closing the inches between us.

"Frisky minx. We have things to do, places to be," he said.

"That's not *exactly* what I meant, though I wouldn't turn you down."

His pupils dilated, and he stared at my chest, heaving with heavy heartbeats. He wanted it as much as I wanted to give it to him.

"Are you ready for me to drink?"

"Do I look like some fragile little flower? I know what I can take." What I couldn't take was the fringes of these visions that wouldn't quite come to me, but lingered and tickled and scratched at my consciousness. He could help me as much as I could help him.

"I want to drink you dry, but I'll settle for your taste." A growl of darkest intent. I bared my throat to him, brushing my hair over my shoulders, waiting for the pinch and sting.

He licked a long lap up the length of my throat to my ear, biting my lobe ever so slightly, letting the stab of his fang linger. Blood beat through every inch of me.

"I crave every part of you to the point of insanity," he whispered. "Stop me when I go too far."

"Impossible." I was panting, squirming, a wild animal with his slightest touch.

With light kisses to my collarbone and behind my ears, he teased the blood to the surface, and when I didn't think I could take another minute without his hands on me, he plunged his fangs into my neck, making me squeal. Then groan. Then go black for a moment, a moment filled with stars and the sweet sensation of becoming lighter in an all-too heavy world.

"Nicholas," I breathed, wanting to pull my shirt off, pull his shirt off, have only the heat between us.

Heat. Kieran.

As if he'd read my thoughts, he wrenched my body just enough to remind me who was stronger.

Digging in further, the visions trickled in, filled with too much power. Nicholas's sucking grew painful with them, and I found myself just trying to suffer the moments to see what would happen next.

Try as I might to call it, the ceremony wouldn't appear. Instead I got Roman, brooding Roman, and I *tasted* how he missed his only brother. Roman had just fed. I tried to sort through the foreign blood in his veins, to see where it had come from, but the distraction of the barbs in my throat and my desperation overtook me.

"Eliza, oh God," Nicholas said, frantically patting at my neck with his fingers while I tried to hold my eyes open. Hot flashes soaked my clothes, making me nauseous. How much had I bled?

"I need to sit up," I said, not actually knowing what I needed. "Wow, I'm getting tired of passing out and stuff." He helped me to a sitting position, and the movement made a stream of blood squirt from my neck onto the blankets. My hand flew to my throat—more gushing there.

"Nicholas," I said, and then I was out.

My limbs ached with cold. I woke up to see Nicholas standing over me, and next to him, the god himself.

Izanagi.

"Leave us alone," Izanagi commanded Nicholas. Pink tears stained Nicholas's cheeks. If I'd had the strength to speak, I would have told him it was my fault, that I hadn't almost died, and that it wouldn't matter if I had, as long as he was okay.

But none of that was true.

Nicholas bowed his head, and with the most defeat I'd ever seen in him, he walked into the snow with nowhere to go.

I knew he would go to the Master. He needed his god like I needed mine.

Izanagi knelt at my side, a gesture I didn't want him to make. He smiled, of course knowing my thoughts. "Gods are but men," he said.

My body began to shake, convulsing with a primitive need for Izanagi's blood. I tried as hard as I could to stay still, but my throat swelled for the life in him.

I grabbed and clung to his wrist for dear life. Exactly like I remembered, the very essence of life rippled into me in a scarlet gush. I tasted oceans and Heaven, ancient things and things the world had never seen. I laughed as it ran down my chin and the warm thickness of it drenched my neck.

The intake of air when I'd had enough gave me something.

Not a vision. Knowledge. A lead weight of something that was so true it was a presence like me, like Izanagi. A thing that could not be argued or doubted. Real.

Tears mixed with the blood on my face as I gazed at the god. The missing piece had been revealed to me because of what he'd done for me.

"Izanagi," I sputtered, my voice thick with blood. "I know what has to be done."

Izanagi stood, larger than anything I could imagine, reaching Heaven and Hell at once.

"Tell him what he must do," was all he said. And he was gone.

Every organ buzzed with an electric life, making it hard to settle enough to clean myself up. I wiped the blood off my face, neck and chest with shaking hands, and tried not to laugh at the knowledge I had, and the promise of the beginning of things, a new leaf on an old bud. Knowledge that belonged to me, and to all *Shinigami*.

But it started with only one *Shinigami*.

"Nicholas!" I shouted into the woods.

He was at my side in a blinding snap of air and light. "Christ, tell me you're all right. Please tell me you've never been better than you are right this second or I'll find a way to end this life of mine." His teeth were clenched, his eyes blood red.

I pulled him to me. He was so weak, limp, and yet I was tethered to the strength I'd infused him with, waiting for its time.

"Nicholas, baby, I'm fine. I swear. I know I wasn't, but I am now. I promise." I kissed him over and over on his face and lips, wanting nothing more than for him to feel the roots of all life growing inside me through the blood of a god. "And Nicholas." I pushed him back to hold him at arm's length, half holding up his body. God, I was strong now. "I know what to do for you."

"You don't have to do anything for me. You have nothing else to do. What are you talking about?" The rattle of confused words made me laugh, confusing him even more.

I said the words that I hoped he would understand as deeply as they ran in every molecule of my body. "Nicholas, if you feed from Roman, you'll be back to normal. Never weak. You'll never need to drink from me again."

His mouth opened and closed, and he fell back against the screen that I feared would break under the weight of him. "Jesus, why didn't we see it before?"

"How could we? We don't know if this has ever happened before." And right away, I wondered if it had, We'd never questioned it since coming to Japan. With another surge of pure knowing, I could see the Master's thrall and just how far it extended. But why?

"We have to tell the Master," Nicholas said, upright and frantic.

"He'll find out. Relax." I rubbed the contours of his arms, and hoped I looked as relaxed as I was telling him to be. "I see so clearly, Nicholas, like a world on top of a world. You have to go to New Hampshire. I can find Roman and get him to you." Everything was so simple. How thick was the cloud the Master had created? What was he hiding?

Could Nicholas bear to hear?

"We make you a vampire before I leave."

"Yes." Not an agreement, something I knew.

"How soon do I leave you?"

Something about those words and the undercurrent of things I *knew* made me sick to my stomach.

"You. Don't. Leave *me*. You just leave." The scent of wine and roses took shape encircling me, a burgundy shadow that wasn't just in my mind. Nicholas's eyes grew to saucer-sized, scanning the air red mist that billowed around me. Wisps of scarlet smoke circled my body in a translucent shield of funeral scents.

"Okay," Nicholas shrugged. "Maybe you should just breathe for a minute, and stop scaring the piss out of me."

I blinked madly, trying to unsee what I'd created, and it was gone. This cloud I'd surrounded myself in felt like a connection between Izanagi and I that I'd harbored all along. Ours. It poured out of me like a part of my breath and aura.

I cleared my throat. "You've got your little Mr. Freeze trick. I guess I have this."

He swallowed hard, his Adam's apple plummeting down, and pointed at me accusingly. "That. That felt like death walked in the door and wasn't leaving."

I thought of Izanagi and the ever-presence of death, the shadow that never left me and drove everything else away. It hadn't been just my companion; it had been inside me waiting to be released.

Nicholas reached out to me tentatively, as if to pat a mythological beast he wasn't sure would bite him or not, and touched his fingertips to my throat, to my collarbone, to my heart. His eyes followed his hand, carefully averting my face. "What kind of vampire will you become? What sort of thing that we've never seen before, and what will you do?" The words came out like he questioned a prophecy—with a tinge of fear.

I covered his hand with mine, and counted my own slow heartbeats through them. Steady. Unafraid. "I'll be me, no matter what," I said softly, and hoped I meant it.

He sighed and bit his lip thoughtfully, making me shiver. "You're going to change everything, Eliza Morgan. Things we didn't know even needed changing. There's so much hope here," he said, his hand still on my heart. His forehead wrinkled as he debated with himself whether or not to go on, but Nicholas didn't debate with himself for long. He knew he was going to say what he wanted, whether anyone wanted to hear it or not.

"There were times," he said, low, fearfully, "that I thought I would never see anything except ache and emptiness behind those eyes ever again. When I looked at you, I saw a ghost of the woman you were meant to be. Kat was always in your eyes. And the lost choices you never really had—they tortured the life out of you." His hand moved, lost, over my shoulders and arms, slow and circling. "I thought I broke you without even trying."

I couldn't answer. He was right; I *was* broken. I'd been put together poorly to begin with.

"A phoenix from ashes, you are. You're brilliant, more glorious than even I saw you could be." Tears glistened in his eyes, and I was never so happy to see it. His voice thick with everything he wanted to express when I wouldn't listen, all that time I could do nothing but mourn, he said, "You will make *Shinigami* a name that the most wretched of us will be proud of."

Lynch. The word *wretched* brought his miserably handsome face into my mind.

There was so little I could say. "I'm sorry that I—was gone. Knowing that I'm going to be something special isn't enough of a reward for enduring the isolation fate slapped me with. Getting the grand prize in the end isn't good enough consolation for taking everyone from me, or for making me a placeless thing half my life. I'll never have peace about what happened with Kat, or Roman, even if it was to better the entire race of *Shinigami,* or the entire world. It isn't fair that there should be such a price to pay for something I never asked for."

He licked his lips. "But I know you. You wouldn't give it back if you could. You wouldn't want to be a regular person, no matter what it cost you."

Goddammit, he was right. I hung my head in shame.

CHAPTER 74

A red silk tube laid on the bed next to a package wrapped in light pink tissue. Beautiful things that filled me with dread.

Opening the soft package, I knew what I was in for. Nicholas thought of everything. Here we were, on the top of a mountain that the world didn't know existed, and he'd gotten me a gift. I'd worked at a gift shop back home and still knew nothing about buying gifts.

Folds of rippling pink silk unrolled in my hands, the same as the package it came from. So this was handmade, I figured. God, he knew what to do. A kimono the color of my cheeks in the cold. He loved that color on me, said it made me look like Snow White. The gray trim grew into black towards the bottom, like dusk turning into night. The white silhouette of a winter treeline embroidered against the black hem instantly transported me to the dark, wintry nights in New Hampshire, standing in the snow with Nicholas. Japanese words were sewn on the inner draping sleeves of the beautiful gown, and I could read them, like Izanagi could read Japanese characters. *Unmei shinsei* on one sleeve. *Unmei wo seisu* on the other.

Chosen for new life.

I control my destiny.

I held the cool fabric to my chest. I was pretty easily impressed with gifts, given my thoughtless nature when it came to giving them, but this was stunning no matter who you were. I cringed inside when I thought how beautiful Kat looked in pink with her red hair, and how she would have jumped up and down to see this.

Night was creeping up on us. I looked at the elaborate invitation again, all beautiful Japanese symbols written in blood red. And at the top, *"The Shinigami Grow."*

Time to get dressed. In an hour we'd see what growth meant.

I could barely take my eyes off Nicholas long enough to walk. We were completely absorbed in each other dressed like this. My kimono fit—well, like it was made for me. For once, I didn't need to pull at it to cover up my chest, or wiggle in the fabric to mask my fuller curves that weren't so much curves as little rolls in a lot of places.

Actually, I was more comfortable dressed like this than I would have been a month ago. Oh, right, when I ate pizza and cake all the time and considered myself a decent eater because Golden Grahams has iron in it.

"Let the record show that I'll stare at you all I want," Nicholas said.

"Well, me too," I said. Nicholas looked incredible in traditional *hakama* pants, black, with a white silk kimono trimmed in smoke gray. He needed nothing extra. The silken shimmer made his skin glow like a pearl, and his smile was so radiant it was hard to look at.

"How did you figure out the right size?" I asked, tucking

my hair behind my ear. It knocked some of the flowers out of it that Blue pinned at the crown of my head. "Crap."

Nicholas laughed. "How did I know? By this." He stopped walking and put his hands on my waist, looking into my eyes, full of mischief and intent that I wanted to make reality. "And this," he continued huskily, his hands running up my body to graze the sides of my breasts. "And this," he growled, putting his hand on my lower back, and running it down, cupping me in it. I was riveted there, trying to breathe. It was fruitless when he nipped my ear. "Your blood isn't the only delicious part of you, and you're mine forever to taste, *saisai*." Beloved.

"*Mugen ai*," I whispered to him, winding my fingers through his hair. Infinite love.

"Party time, lovebirds!"

I jumped at Blue's intrusion, but Nicholas merely lifted his head slowly, as if he planned to anyway. "We *were* having a party."

Blue was a vision in a bright red kimono with gold phoenixes on each side. She was pure fire, and I wondered if she did it for Kieran.

"You fed from Izanagi again," Blue said. I didn't ask what tipped her off. I checked the vicinity for my red gas or whatever, but there was none. The god's blood was written on me like ink on parchment. "Let's go," Blue said, taking my hand, Nicholas trailing behind.

The great entryway to the temple which was always sparse and holy-feeling was glowingly elaborate. Hundreds of white candles lined the long walk to the altar, showcasing dozens of goth-lipstick-maroon roses scattered all over, turning the rice paper runner a carpet of soft red. More red roses hung in bunches from the eaves, but the scent of them didn't make me grit my teeth as it once did. This didn't feel like a funeral, and the kinship with Izanagi had...changed me. Scarlet paper lanterns hung from the high ceiling, showing dozens of black paper crows that would have been otherwise invisible in the moody, macabre beauty. Crows were *mine* more than Leann's; I felt possessive of them, rather than haunted by them now. The sound of drums and chimes was more eerie in the gothic elegance in the temple, and I'd fallen in love with it instantly.

"This is unbelievable," I said, taking in the decorations while I taking in as many of the guests as possible. Every resident of the temple would be here. The invitation was more a command than anything else.

I was fully aware that Arthur and I were the only beings with living blood among hundreds of vampires.

"I didn't want to scare you," Nicholas whispered out of the corner of his mouth, looking around, "so I didn't tell you how this ceremony can get a little—well, office party out of control."

Both of us still looking and smiling at his adoring onlookers as we walked through the crowd, I said, "Will you ever tire of holding information from me until it's nightmarishly too late?"

"Maybe. Depends what else I can hold of yours," he said through his golden boy smile.

Some of the *Shinigami* clearly hadn't fed in far too long from their gauntness and sunken eyes. Others were robust with the blood they'd feasted on. It was like looking at a swimming pool full of sharks and diving right in.

"Anything I should be doing? Not doing? Running from in particular?" All said through my best politician smile.

"Never leave my side," he growled. His arm around my waist tightened like a corset.

"Easy enough," I said, turning my eyes to him. He wasn't looking back, however. My eyes followed his menacing stare to a gangly vampire with bone-chillingly pale skin and something to prove. The wraith stared at me with such intrinsic animalism that it sent a chill down my spine even before the wave of frigidity radiated from Nicholas, leaving my teeth chattering. A grizzly bear growl rumbled from Nicholas's belly. The emaciated vampire sensed it too, a good twenty feet away, but he didn't look away fast enough for Nicholas.

I gulped down my frozen fear and leaned into Nicholas, putting my hand on his cold chest. Tomb-like waves of cold shivered up my arm.

"Nicholas, I'm okay. You're here. He won't do anything."

"Goddamn right he won't."

"Don't make a scene if you don't have to, Captain Dramatic. These vampires will be my—family, I guess, and I can handle them. To a point."

The vampire took Nicholas's endless stare and my words as a challenge, and I had to wonder just how stupid he was. In the short time it took me to make my little speech, the ghoulish vampire had closed the distance, and stood face to face with us. He grinned at me, showing decaying teeth and a lack of self-preservation.

Nicholas didn't need to move; Izanagi's blood surged through me like whitewater rapids.

I hissed long and low, releasing from the red, hazy swirl of smoke from inside. It curled around the lanterns and crows above. I leaned forward, my face inches from his, radiating Izanagi's wine and roses scent, now my own, overpowering his acrid decay.

"Run while you can," I spat at the creature through clenched teeth.

I wasn't surprised when he did just that.

Nicholas was angry. It was clear in the way his shoulders were thrown back, his head angled away from me, lips tight, churning coffee eyes slow and deliberate.

"You. Are still. Human," he said.

Shaking with violence, fangs bared, Nicholas flashed across the room where the vampire had escaped to. They were yards away, but with a blink I was next to them in my mind's eye, my vision showing me what transpired as though Nicholas was still close enough to breathe in my ear.

Mad with fury, he growled, "You take your thoughts and eyes off of her forever, or I will tear out your throat like the jaws of Hell itself."

My breath was prisoner. The vampire, who'd thought he was in the clear when he fled from me, made the idiot mistake of turning, wide-eyed with fear, to look over his shoulder at me. While I took this as a question of *what the hell is it with you two*, Nicholas took it as his threat not being quite powerful enough.

He twitched forward, grabbing the vampire by the throat.

I didn't realize I'd whimpered out loud, but all the nearby vampires did. All around me were things that spoke like humans, dressed like humans, but they wanted to consume me. Countless predatory eyes bore through me. The earth stood still.

A flare of hungry heat screeched to my side, a venomous burst of fire that had every vampire in its path crying out, hands shielding their eyes. Kieran, of course. I already knew. I knew by the licking flames at my feet and the inner sigh I breathed, filled with the ashes of guilt.

He glared around him in a quickly widening circle, as *Shinigami* fell back to get away from him. Every muscle in his body was taut, veins straining like he might burst, and the only way he could relieve the pressure was to let out a deafening roar that sent everyone into terrified silence. The air crackled with the electric heat he wrought.

Nicholas glared at him from where he stood, arm shaking with the wriggling vampire in his hand, its feet dangling midair, and I swear I could see more fire in his eyes than in the fire spirit next to me.

And in an instant that would never end, the most compassionate, thoughtful and genuine man I'd ever met snapped the neck of the vampire he held.

All the dead eyes turned to the delicate snapping noise. The tension didn't leave, just shifted.

And grew.

"She's not yours to protect," Nicholas growled at Kieran, his voice an earthquake.

"She's not anybody's," Kieran said with a coolness that defied his fire. But I knew he felt different.

Why do you feel so much like mine, Eliza?

"This party's turning out awesome, right guys?" I said loudly to them both.

To add to, or detract from the flurry of activity that made me want to crawl in a hole and die and take everyone with me, another figure weighed in.

Leann appeared at the head of the room on the altar platform, scanning the crowd of immortals while they measured her up; the youngest pack member. What certainly would have been fear shivering through her yesterday was nothing but curiosity this night.

Physically, she looked the same. It was the fluidity of every small motion that set her apart. Her timidity and utter indifference that made her forgettable in life, made her superior in death. The appearance of boredom transformed into a quiet pensiveness, allowing her to take in her new world at her leisure, rather than shun it.

Vampirism suited her.

The throng of *Shinigami* drank her in, as I did. It seemed like hours ticked by, the lack of thrum from undead hearts unsettling mine, alone among them.

Alone.

I pushed my vision to the surface easily, searching for the only other heartbeat in the crowd, terrified that I had to look so hard. Then I found it; slowing, faltering. The rhythm of it peaked and jumped, and was sickly, stolen. My head tilted to the sound, a dog to a whistle, a sound I ought not be able to hear.

Arthur.

"Nicholas," I yelped, my head on a swivel, dizzy with the scents all around me, but not one of them of human flesh, not one. Nicholas flashed to me without question.

"What is it?" He bent at the knees to meet my eyes, to bring me back.

"Nicholas, where is Arthur?" I said as levelly as I could manage.

Ghoulish laughs, hisses, rumblings around me.

A frenzy was beginning.

Nicholas's nostrils flared. His pupils dilated. His head swiveling frantically. He didn't have to say it; I smelled it, too, with Izanagi's infused senses.

Blood. The faintest whiff of blood, winding like a snake in the ripe evening air.

Leann's head snapped to the side demonically fast, painful-looking. I could *feel* her need for that first taste of blood, the emptiness behind it. She had no *unmei nashi* yet, nobody waiting for her to finish their life of "no fate." And anything else she drank would leave her craving more; a mirage.

I couldn't help but look at Nicholas with a deep pang of sorrow and guilt. He was half empty.

Eyes focused where Leann's were, Nicholas grabbed my arms, and propelled us both with sickening speed to a spot hidden by a pillar, where a blonde vampire woman sucked on Arthur's fleshy neck. The scene, the odor of newly gushing blood made me go blank, seeing only flashbacks of the huddled vulture that was Nicholas's friend, my friend, Roman, murdering Kat. The sound of flesh tearing, the darkening of his eyes, the river of blood down his neck when we surprised him, drinking the life out of her gorgeous, rosy face.

Nicholas pulled the vampire woman off of Arthur, her blonde hair whipping back. She'd been looking up at me as she drank from Arthur's neck, just like Roman had. I couldn't stop seeing Kat on the ground, her face pale, disbelief the last look in her eyes. I saw Kat, but it was only Arthur there, and he was just as dead.

"He's dead," I said, but it was clear. I peeled my eyes from the body that had been one third of my peers, and looked to Nicholas at my side, unsure of what I'd see there.

A mixture of fury, shock and shame clouded his swirling eyes. "I'm so sorry, Eliza," he said.

"For what?" My voice sounded too tinny, too much like it had in all the time I mourned Kat and pushed Nicholas away. Too much like me when all my softness died with that red-haired beauty. I was afraid to ever be that thing again, to fear the crows circling overhead.

"I'm getting you back to your room—now." He swept me up into his arms as if to carry me across the threshold, and belted like a subway train from the celebration, across board-walks and through courtyards and gardens to my room.

The last thing I saw before leaving the gathering was Leann's too-bright eyes searching wildly for the blood source. Her desire was so desperate it felt alive.

Nicholas set me down fast and smoothly on my bed. "The Master needs my help at the temple, I'll be back soon," he said, his worry unmasked. He glanced behind him to the open door. "Can you sense Izanagi out there?"

I tried, but I didn't. And I was a little more afraid than I had before.

Nicholas held my arms and looked into my eyes. "Right. Back."

"Hurry," I said.

He nodded and dashed out the door, taking my breath with him.

CHAPTER 75

My mind raced, waiting for Nicholas to return. What was he doing? Was Kieran okay? Blue, Paolo? Was everybody—else—besides Arthur—okay?

When it was my turn, would I be blood-crazed and dying to hunt like Leann was?

Would images of Kat's death haunt me in spasms every time I took a life? For the rest of my impending immortality?

The prophetic dream I'd had of becoming a vampire back in Ossipee sprang to memory; another Eliza Morgan, teeth barbed into a man's throat, blood pounding like bass drums through my every pore, until it deafened me and made me see a blanket of red cover the moon above. Blood intoxicating, overtaking. Becoming.

My heart quickened at the thought. I swallowed back a panicky excitement. I understood the desire for the succulence of human blood. Being human, I should have been sickened by it.

If I were, in fact, only human.

If I hadn't drank blood before and reveled in it.

I paced the floor madly waiting for Nicholas. What the hell

was going on at the temple? I imagined vampire bats flying through the night, searching out blood like monsters, not like chosen heroes, the Master yelling after them to stop and wait for the call of their *unmei nashi* as they screeched in the sky.

My vision begged to be let out to watch Nicholas trying to help control the frenzy, but I would not. I would not. I could picture what he'd say: "*I* don't even want to see what's happening out there. You've got plenty of time to be traumatized. Immortality loves trauma," he would have said. "A vampire riot sounds cool, but it's probably not."

The crowd of vampires had become just that: a riot, a mob. Any pretense of my importance to the grand scheme of things, any fear and love of Nicholas they had wouldn't make them spare me. Put a steak in front of a wild dog and he's going to eat it. Thinking of myself as meat made the air on the back of my neck bristle.

Or was that the hair-raising feeling of being watched?

My vision blasted into my consciousness, but I didn't need it. In the corner shadows, I could saw a pair of cold, cruel eyes.

"He won't miss you for long," a rich, familiar voice said. "He'll understand I needed it."

"Jenniveve," I gasped.

"Don't!" she yelled, and my bed didn't creak or move under her added, unearthly weight. "Don't beg for your life like a fool!" The dead chill in her eyes had been replaced with a madness for blood. She was a reptilian thing, and there would be no reasoning with her. I cringed, like it would do something to help me.

She bared her teeth at me, a primitive monster with Victorian beauty. I closed my eyes.

But when I did, I saw myself in the courtyard, defeating that vampire.

I leaned back as she lunged at me, and met her chest with a powerful kick, throwing her backward. She shook her head, as if she could make what happened disappear, and in that moment, I leaped at her and connected both fists, one to her belly, one to her sculpted, exotic face.

She flung me back with brutal force, a dragon growl behind it. I hit the wall, hearing it rip and splinter. Blood trickled into my eye from my scalp, and she was on me again, and God help me, she was *laughing*.

That was more than I could take. The red vapor rose from my body, the unexpected appearance of it making her cry out with fear. No, more than fear— *it burned her.* Blazing pinpricks all over her face that she clawed at, shrieking, making them worse. I shuddered to watch it, but I did watch, thrilled. Because this fiend had done everything she could to ruin Nicholas. The mist lashed out at her, but stayed close to me, a fearsome protector.

The mist swaddled me instantly when I yelled in surprise: the Master was hovering, terrifyingly silent and ghostlike, behind Jenn, his long, yellow fangs bared. Milky eyes full of rage, he grabbed Jenn in one hand by the back of the neck. Her feet kicked at the air as she continued to scream, writhing, though I couldn't say if it was from the burning of my scarlet mist or if she was trying to see what held her, dangling in midair.

I scrambled to my feet and held the Master's gaze, to tell him I was fine, if he cared. Slowly, he pulled the struggling mess that was Jenn to face him, lifting her effortlessly to eye level while she whimpered and cried. My mist had let her go, and she could see the Master now. I think he horrified her more than the unknown attacking substance from me.

"Give me a reason not to destroy you for your—indiscretion," he said.

Gasping, she whispered, "Please, Master, I was drunk with the scent of her." She managed to roll her eyes to me, veins popping in the whites. "And she's come between me and Nicholas."

The Master shook her once, making her yelp, apologizing over and over. I loved seeing the volatile thing so terrified, as she'd terrified me so many times.

I stepped forward until I was inches from her, and the Master made no attempt to move her away. Her eyes focused on me when she said her next apology; but even now, so helpless, her hatred was deep.

"You're only sorry you didn't get the chance to kill me," I said quietly, "and you're sorry I'm going to be one of you."

The Master snarled, his eyes on her trembling face.

"She," he said, nodding toward me, "is more important than you."

The simplicity of that statement shocked us both. Jenn's eyes darted to me, fearful and plotting.

But, in the flicker of an eye, the Master held only Jenn's head.

I didn't even make a noise at the unimaginable thing I'd seen. My heart didn't even speed up. She was dead, and I was glad.

Nicholas crackled into the room like an electric current, mouth agape, eyes flitting from one of us to the other.

The Master turned to him, lowering Jenn's decapitated head to his side.

"Wow," Nicholas said. Always the wordsmith, that one.

"I imagine you settled the others with less finality," the Master said to him.

"Yeah, that's pretty final," Nicholas said, snickering and stealing a glance at me. Jenn's body was crumpled on the floor underneath the dripping head. Nicholas cleared his throat for dramatic gesture, and smiled. "Yes, I calmed down the rest of them with a myriad of interesting threats. Then I sent off a hunting party with Leann. They were controlled, and she needed it."

The Master dropped Jenn's head on top of her body and lowered himself to the ground, Superman-style. "I'm disappointed in them all. The last time such an outbreak occurred, all the *Shinigami* ceased to exist not long after." With blank eyes on me, he continued. "The blood of the *unmei fumetsu* is pungent. You are very lucky that Nicholas didn't seem to notice Arthur's."

"No, I didn't," Nicholas said quietly, looking at me. "But you did."

"Yup. Where was Pierre? Why wasn't he with Arthur?" I asked.

"He had a calling," Nicholas said with a roll of his eyes.

"Ridiculous," the Master spat. "Unacceptable. Selfish. There is no excuse not to accompany your *unmei fumetsu* to an event with so much meaning for them both. He will be dealt with." The air throbbed around him with his angry energy, and the room was quiet.

Nicholas, of course, broke the silence. "I didn't know Jenniveve was here," he said, staring at the body in pieces.

The Master seemed taken aback, his energy dissipating and returning like a lightbulb flicker. "Jenniveve has always wanted to be near you. She may not have loved you the way you love Eliza but she didn't know how to do anything the right way."

I blushed to hear the Master speak of our love for each other.

"Ah, morbid curiosity about my girlfriend choices. Jenn always loved making a spectacle of herself, and hated having anything taken from her," Nicholas said.

"Eliza, I'm sorry you were in fear for your life last night."

the Master said, voice filled with more emotion than I thought he was capable of, at least for me. Sure enough, the sun had risen and I'd not noticed. "Rest now. You have training this afternoon."

And he was gone, leaving Nicholas and I holding hands, staring at the dead vampire staining the floor.

CHAPTER 76

B efore I could ask how we were to dispose of Jenn's dismembered body, two mild-mannered vampires arrived and gathered her up on a bamboo stretcher.

"Thank you," I said cheerily as they left. Nicholas gave me a mocking smile. "What? It's only polite."

A moment of pregnant silence rested between us.

"I'm sorry she's dead. She meant something to you," I said.

His lips turned down in that way that dismissive way. "You're not sorry, and I don't blame you," he said, still looking at the bloody spot on the floor. "She created me, and I think I thank her for it. But she was a pitiless thing besides." He turned to me, jaw clenched. "But to give me immortality only to gouge out the part of me that I live for—" It took me a second to realize he was talking about me. "The Master killed her quickly. I wouldn't have."

He pulled my face to his roughly and kissed me with a force that took my breath away. Groaning, he stole his lips from mine, leaving them stinging with their absence. He looked *different*, stronger and weaker at the same time.

"Nobody has ever loved anyone as much as I love you," he whispered huskily.

"I know an exception," I managed to say through my own short breath.

His eyes were wild pools of chocolate mousse and melting fudge. He was panting, bearlike, lustful and fearful together at once. The powerful blood inside me vibrated, a volcano ready to erupt. The small space between us thrummed before filling with my red mist.

"So that doesn't just happen when you're threatened?" Nicholas panted, mouth running all over my cheeks and lips, down my neck.

"I dunno." Red deathly desire swarmed me and I couldn't think.

"You're ready," he said, his fingers a whirr of motion.

"Always am."

He pulled back, revealing his fangs.

"Oh. Oh, you mean for—"

He nodded.

If the world exploded then, it would have been less dazzling than the heat between us. My blood grew hot in return, my body quivering with need for his.

And there was something else. A black energy that spoiled the air, a crackling lightning that shoved us together, leaving trails of steam. We collided in a burst of sparkling darkness, terrifying and pure. My lips flamed upon his, swollen, ready for all he could give me. Static electricity stung my fingertips as I ripped his t-shirt over his head, my breasts skimming the hair on his chest, my nipples screaming. His flavor over-whelmed me, his tongue caressing mine with vanilla and spices I never knew. His hair in my fingers was too soft to endure. I needed solid strength, everything hard, able to handle the power budding in me.

Nicholas groaned, grabbing my waist with one powerful

hand, my breast cupped in the other. I leaned into it, squirming out of my top, breaking the snaps on my bra to wrestle free into his frantic hands. Swirls of a new, black mist swam around us, glittering, glinting, magic come alive. The air whispered and bit when he bent to pull down his pants unfalteringly fast. His nose brushed my navel, my hips arched to touch his face.

There was a chasm, a void we were the midnight center of, howling with primitive desire. A wild thing drove us, our connection as *unmei fumetsu* and *shugotenshi*, bursting to life, begging for death. The same presence that followed me my entire life, that death that was alive, that death that was waiting to have me alone.

The dark stirred in me. I grabbed the back of Nicholas's head, yanking him forward into the pulsing between my legs. His fangs pierced the skin of my thigh without warning, and I screamed. I screamed in pain, and I screamed for more.

I wanted blood. Dripping, squirting, oozing.

His.

When I couldn't take anymore wanting, I pulled him up to my face, so he could see how desperately I needed the essence of him, what lied beneath.

"Blood," I moaned through the rich scents and sparklingly poisonous colors flurrying around me, and through me.

I was becoming something new.

"Give it to me," I hissed, my entirety screaming for his touch, the taste of him.

Nicholas threw his head back as if ready to howl at the moon, then dove into my throat, and sucked hard, pulling my skin viciously. He squeezed the flesh of my upper arm, another hand on the back of my neck to keep me close, letting not a drop escape. Black torrents of liquid air rushed around us in this not-quite-real reality, and for just a second, I was jealous that Nicholas was tasting Izanagi's blood through me.

That power was mine.

With a violent efflux of strength, I laced my fingers through the decadent dark curls on Nicholas's head, making him moan with need. I pulled his head back, exposing the pulsing vein in his throat, and plunged my own, still-human teeth into it.

He bellowed an indistinguishable word, causing the magical stars around us to scatter, and simultaneously held my naked body against his own. Fear and desire, clutching power and letting it go.

My body heaved against his while his blood invaded me, blending with Izanagi's, with my own that was something *more.* The world belonged to me. All the isolation, the loneliness, the fear and resentment became something I owned, became an iron thing in my core that blood wrapped around and fed.

It still hurt. But now it was mine.

Seishi. Keieiichinyo. Izanagi's voice in my mind: Life and death. Inseparable as form and shadow.

"El—" Nicholas started, but his voice was gone. Then *he* was gone, but still there, invisible to me. A blinding black flash swallowed the stars and mist, swallowed *us.* We'd been absorbed in each other in every way, and now the world was absorbing us, too.

There was nothing except the blood racing in me, sending me quivering with pleasure and rage, power and consumption.

When I did feel someone else again, it wasn't Nicholas; it was Izanagi. He wasn't there in the room, but he was close by, and he knew what I knew.

That when the dark let me go, I wouldn't quite let it. I would be *Shinigami.*

CHAPTER 77

"She's reacting…differently," I heard through the darkness. The stars still swam, and Nicholas's blood tingled on my tongue. That flavor was all that mattered.

And the power. Raw. Power that begged to *take*. Power like mountains, power like fairy tale monsters, power of agony and ecstasy and everything in between. God almighty, it tasted like dreams.

"She's not like the rest of us," Nicholas said. I couldn't feel him, couldn't see him. Even my visions had deserted me.

He felt so *gone*.

"No, I suppose she's not," Paolo answered. I knew that he was leaning over me, inspecting me, I sensed it, but I couldn't smell his oceany saltiness, or get the tingle of his non-breath. I was swimming in the world, a bodiless thing.

Trying to envision Nicholas through my blind haze brought up a different sort of energy.

Blood came together in my veins like the most perfect puzzle: mine, Nicholas's, and Izanagi's. Not enough was Izanagi's. The god didn't take well to his blood being second best, his blood told me so.

With a full body roar, I exploded back to this plane, with an anger not all my own. My inner vision returned first, and it was Nicholas's face I saw. I cooled to see it, but Izanagi grew angrier outside, and inside me. My eyes fluttered open, and the world met them with brutal light and life.

I was floating near the ceiling, looking down at Nicholas and Paolo.

Nicholas looked up at me, unblinking, hint of a smile as he tossed popcorn into his mouth. He twitched his eyebrows at me.

"That's new."

Paolo was slack-jawed, eyes bulging. "Only the Master does that," he whispered.

"Nope," Nicholas said; popcorn tossed in the mouth.

Anger swelled in me at the mention of the Master. My red mist surged, swarmed the air, darkening the room.

I was glad I wasn't on the ground. I wanted to be high, where I was strong.

Nicholas and Paolo looked around themselves, unnerved, and moved closer together, as if a gang was closing in on them from all sides.

"Hey, Eliza?" Nicholas said, eyes still sweeping the room. "Maybe you could come down from there, and you know. Cut that out?"

I was scaring them. The shroud of blood-red mist surrounded me, my arms stretched to either side in a Jesus Christ pose, my hair floating around my head and brushing my cheeks like some evil mermaid. Yeah, that was a little weird.

They watched as I slowly lowered myself to the ground, becoming more like a regular person with every inch I came closer to them. Aside from the *sounds* of everything; the wind outside that had a voice, the singing of the *tatami* floor, the hush of the mountains, the rushing of the blood in their veins.

And the sound of a million fates all around me and nowhere near me, watching me and waiting for what I'd do next. *Waiting for what I would see.*

I'd never be alone again.

This was what being a vampire was? This uber-awareness of everything, even things that weren't there?

"Eliza," Paolo whispered. "Are you all right?" He'd forced himself to look into my eyes, his waves of calm barely touching me. He needed more settling down than I did.

I smiled, and even I could tell how creepy it was. He took his hand away.

Nicholas breathed in deep through his nose. "Well, glad that's done with," he said with a dramatic grin. "You freaked us the hell out there, El. Nice vampire thing you've got there," he added, waving his hand around at me.

"What did I do." It was the first thing I'd said since I came to. It sounded like bricks moving.

Nicholas shook his head at me quickly, eyes bulging, and looked at Paolo like *can you believe?* "You have no idea," he said, running his hands through his hair.

Eyes moving, taking it all in, their movements under their movements and what they meant, the hum of motions so miniscule they didn't matter. But they did, everything did.

"What did I do," I said again. I was asking, but it didn't come out as a question, I was too solid, too controlled. I could tell I was unnaturally still, my hands at my sides, my eyes trained on them when they weren't darting to see the next thing to see.

Nicholas sniffed, with impressed shock. It was Paolo who spoke. He said softly, "You made us feel so alone."

"Like we'd been abandoned and nobody would ever come for us again," Nicholas said, his self-assured lightheartedness disappearing.

"You both experienced it," I said. Not a question. They nodded.

I take strength from what consumes me.

"What was that?" Paolo said.

"I didn't mean to say it out loud."

I looked Nicholas in the eyes, and he twitched. "I once asked Kieran how his fire didn't destroy him. And he told me it was the thing that consumes him, and the thing that gives him strength." But it was so much more than that. Kieran's burning was alive, assaulting me where I stood. It pained him constantly, and it was a force more powerful than fear.

Nicholas ran a hand over his stubbly chin. "Makes sense."

"How do you mean?" Paolo asked him.

"The thing that consumed Eliza now gives her strength," Nicholas said, shrugging, unfaltering stare on me, ready to catch me if I fell. Ready to stay with me when everyone ran.

"And that is?" Paolo asked.

"Isolation," I said quietly.

As I said it, the room became *void* again. Vacuous. The darkness in the witch's woods.

How I'd felt most of my life.

Nicholas held me. I wasn't sure I was ready for that, but I gave in because I didn't want isolation to consume me anymore.

Not when I could turn it on the world.

"Eliza, you're doing it again," Nicholas said into my ear, and kissed me quickly on the cheek.

"Sorry."

"You okay? Are you hungry? Do you want to be alone?" Paolo asked me in a flurry. It wasn't stifling, because his concern was so real.

Concern, and something else.

"Stop cocking your head at Paolo, it's weird. You can't eat Paolo."

My laugh rang high and strong, dissipating the oppressive aloneness of the room. So, I had the power to take the aloneness away, too. That was a new thing for me—to be the one the party started with. I'd always left that up to Kat. I smothered the red mist of my anger and solitude this time.

"Where's Blue?" I asked.

Nicholas blinked rapidly. "I can find her."

"Please," I said. "Paolo, go with him. I need to be alone." My voice was so different now, and not just my voice, but the person behind it.

Paolo gave me a reassuring, sweet smile. "Very good," he said. "We won't be long."

Nicholas kissed me with supernatural swiftness, but I saw every single move now. My eyes could detect the flexing of the muscles before they moved.

"Say you love me," I said. Monotone.

"I. Love. You."

With a nod from them both, they were out the door, and I was alone with myself, the only feeling I recognized. When they were gone from my consciousness, I looked to the door with a slow, measured movement. Everything I did was that way in this form.

But I wasn't really alone anymore.

"Izanagi."

I wasn't surprised that now, more than ever, Izanagi and I were one artery, and the blood had nowhere to go until we were together.

What did surprise me was his wide, brilliant smile and boisterous laugh.

"You've arrived," he said, like I finally showed up to a family reunion that I blew off every year.

He threw his arms around me, making me gasp first from the gesture, and next from the onslaught of *everything*. Visions crowded for space in my mind, but I wasn't overwhelmed by them. I could see anyone I wanted, if I wanted. Their lives were there for me to pluck like cherries.

And I could see myself, the way he saw me.

My curly dark hair had an inhuman vitality. My skin was the same, smooth and fair, but my eyes—the green had a fury in it, the way Nicholas's had a warmth. They were bursting with it, like the reflection of light off of a rough emerald. Like the aurora borealis. They positively glowed.

And underneath what he saw on the outside, he saw prom-ise, layered under a glimmering ferocity. He saw death incarnate. A fearsome, wild supremacy that he, himself possessed in my own eyes.

He saw the future of the *Shinigami.*

"Please, let me drink from you, Izanagi," I whispered.

The god *wanted* it, but he didn't need it. He wanted my blood to swim with his own. It was vanity.

Taking my hands in his, he looked into my eyes, quelling my restlessness. "You do not need it now, nor do I. But you will, as will I. I will be there then. Every time."

"But I don't understand these feelings, I need help." My throat constricted. "I'm too strong, and *evil*—"

"Not evil. This is not a world of right and wrong, it is a world of harmony and power. You will find yours and use it the way it must be used. Do not let your beliefs about good and evil follow you here."

I trusted his words, and though I wanted to taste his power, I knew I had enough of my own. It would drive me insane to have more so fast, the narcotic that he was.

"You have an *unmei nashi*," he continued. "Tonight."

"Already?"

"Yes. It's why you sent for Blue."

I hadn't known why I needed her, but now it was crystal clear.

"I'll be waiting for them," I said.

B lue looked at me from the doorway with a fear that didn't become her. Or me.

"I don't want people to be afraid of me," I whispered to no one.

Nicholas brushed past her into the room, eyes lingering on me. "Sorry, doll, but fear is your middle name now."

Blue pushed him away from me. "Oh, shut up, Nicholas."

"I always wanted to say that. *Fear is my middle name,*" he grumbled.

"You mean *my* middle name," I said.

"Nope. It's my middle name now. You're too pretty for it." Nicholas leaned against the wall.

"Miss me, did you?" Blue said, in such a Kat-like way it was like arsenic in my heart.

I held her arms, looking hard into her eyes. "I can't explain it, but I need you here."

"You all right?"

"I—well, you know how I am. Nobody's made words for it yet, but we'll live long enough to see the day they might."

She smiled wryly at me, and turned to Paolo and Nicholas. "I'm glad to have this woman on my side. Can you imagine having a brain like that against you?"

"I don't want any brain against me. But I bet hers would be even grosser." Nicholas smiled at me, and as usual, I just shook my head at him. He narrowed his eyes in response.

"Izanagi was here, wasn't he?" Nicholas said, and all the vampire eyes in the room looked to me.

"Yes."

"Did you drink from him?"

"Does it seem like I did?"

"No."

"Well, there's your answer, then."

Blue cleared her throat. Paolo stood silent. There was too much stillness here; it was murdering me.

"What do we do next?" I asked the group. "I imagine we should tell the Master I'm changed."

"Already done," Nicholas said.

"Of course." And as much as I resented the ancient vampire, I was still hurt that he hadn't come to see me.

Nicholas reached out to brush a strand of my hair. "He knows you'll send for him when you want him. He knows you're taken care of and need time to yourself." He smirked. "And he knows you probably won't want him here at all."

I was surprised how smug that made me. That the man believed to be the creator of the *Shinigami* gave a crap about what I thought, or that he would listen at all. It made me even more suspicious.

Was he too afraid to see how powerful I'd become?

"So, that's the thing you're talking about," I heard Blue whisper to Nicholas. I'd zoned out, and they were all three staring at me, Blue bent to Nicholas slightly, their arms touching.

"What are you whispering about?" I said in that dead voice I now had.

"You're getting misty, my love," Nicholas said.

And sure enough, there was the red mist curling in tendrils around the vampires in front of me.

"I can stop it," I said, emotionless. I looked about me, at each tendril of the red cloud, truly seeing it, and must have looked like I was trying to communicate with vapor, but hey, clearly I was weird now. *Stop now*, I thought at it, but the mist stayed.

And it began to take a shape.

"You guys see that, right?" I said, but they were dumbfounded.

The mist formed the silhouette of a woman, and though she was made of smoke, she looked to me as real, as defined as Nicholas. I knew her. So much of my life was smoke and mirrors, it was recognizable to me now.

"Crikey, what is that bottomless pit I have in my stomach? Is that—*you*—Eliza?" Blue asked with shivering words.

"Mmmhmm. That's our girl," Nicholas said, eyes on me, fascinated.

"Quiet," I said, as I watched the shadow woman move. She was washing dishes. It was the silliest thing to see in such an unnatural medium. Her name was Clara, I knew it like I knew my own. I was watching a life in progress, in a red puppet show. She was whistling, though only I could hear. She was so happy to just do dishes, because they belonged to her, and she'd had so little.

"What's happening to her?" I heard Paolo say, but I couldn't take my eyes off of the sheer burgundy image.

Nicholas would want to understand what I was going through, but I couldn't tear my eyes away to tell him. The magnetism between Clara and myself entranced me.

"Nicholas, she isn't moving."

"I know, I know."

"What's happening?"

Voices melded together as Clara dried the dishes, ran a hand through her hair, wondering why she hadn't washed it that morning.

"This happens to me, sometimes. Something like this. Scares the shit out of Roman." Nicholas.

"Roman." That was Blue's voice. It struck me in the head, as if she shouldn't be allowed to say the name.

"Nicholas, how long do you believe this will last? She's shaking, it's very worrisome."

"Should I get the Master?"

"No."

"No." My own voice that time.

The mist vanished, but the thread that tied me to Clara remained, singing with tension, a tightrope dying to be cut.

"What happened, El?" Nicholas said, searching my face.

"I have my first *unmei nashi.*"

CHAPTER 79

"I don't need a hunting party."

Paolo insisted I wait on the *unmei nashi* until the Master assembled a hunting party. Goddamn tradition.

Paolo put his hand on my shoulder, his eyes lingering on it. If I hadn't known of his commitment to God better, I'd have thought he had intention of letting it wander.

"It's too difficult a task to undertake on your own, so new at this as you are. The emotion, the sheer distance you may need to cover. Do you know where she is, your Clara?"

"London."

Paolo smiled, such a sweet smile he had. "And she already knows," he said with wonder in his blue eyes. "We will help you get there. It can be rather exhausting, and you need guidance to comprehend it when so young. This world is very different now, your place in it, very different."

Paolo and I sat on a high wall overlooking a snowy garden. I could see the sun-colored koi under the pond's frozen surface. I was trapped like they were, waiting for feeding time.

"Fine. Then we leave. Me, you, Nicholas, Blue and Kieran. That's it."

"I thought you may want Leann to come along."

"Why?"

"She's a newborn like yourself."

I had no reason to take offense. Doesn't change the fact that I did. "We aren't alike in any other way. We'd not be any comfort to each other."

The saltwater scent of Paolo washed over me.

"Getting ready to impart some wisdom, are you?" I said through a smile. He returned it.

"Eliza, all I mean to say is that you don't have to be alone anymore. There's no need to keep yourself apart. You've arrived, my dear. God has taken enough from you, and now you've been rewarded with eternal companions. Enjoy them."

My fingers curled into the stone underneath me, shocking me when they dug right into it. I struggled not to let my new signature red death mist scare Paolo off in my annoyance. "Just because some mystical fatal force has decided that I've been *good* enough to be granted friends doesn't mean I'm ready to embrace the goddamn world. I have a heart of my own, it can't be made soft again just because I got the cheese at the end of the rat maze I was thrown into."

"I didn't mean to imply—"

"No, please, don't apologize. I know what you mean. But I think I've been scarred too much to start looking for play-mates now. I can't *work* at it, and Leann, well, she's too much work. I have you," I said, trying as hard as I could to give him the peacefulness that he gave me. "I have Kieran, and Blue. And I have Nicholas. I don't need more."

A dismal look simmered in his eyes, one I couldn't understand.

"What about Izanagi?" he asked.

Suspicion. I hated it. Hated having it, hated being on the receiving end of it. "What about him?"

"What does he mean to you?"

I cleared my throat, nerves propelling me into an answer that I wasn't ready to give.

"Maybe he's a bit of what God is to you. He saves me when I need saving."

"And what do you give to him?"

I narrowed my eyes. "What do you give your God?"

His bright smile wasn't the guarded kind of a man under attack. It was full of admiration and enjoyment, and made me smile along with him.

"Eliza Morgan, I can't decide if you're a rebel or unrelentingly loyal."

I laughed, my laugh, not the creepy, flat vampire one I'd picked up. "I guess depending on whose side you're on, I can be both."

With his gentle hand, he took mine, making me smile still. "There doesn't have to be sides, you know," he said, a mournfulness lacing the waters of his calm.

Sadness crept in. "I'm learning."

"Nope, no hand holding," Nicholas said, edging between us, making Paolo chuckle. "Whatcha doin'?"

"Just talking God. God talk, with Paolo and Eliza," I said.

"So sorry I missed it."

Paolo laughed, and the snow seemed warm afterwards. "You are not, Nicholas. He can see you, you know."

"I make myself known, He doesn't even have to try."

After we all had a good laugh, I dove right in. "What's the Master have to say about Clara? I want to be free to make my own hunting party choices."

The same kind of piousness that I saw in Paolo's eyes came alight in Nicholas's. "The Master thinks you should wait to feed until after your ceremony tomorrow night."

"Woah, woah, woah. He still wants to have a ceremony for me? After what happened to Arthur?"

Nicholas glanced at Paolo, the sarcasm just screeching to come out. "But—we all hated him."

"It doesn't matter, he was supposed to be one of us. I can't believe you don't see it. There's a reason he was supposed to be *Shinigami*, now we'll never know what it was, what he might have done."

Nicholas wasn't giving in that easily. "How do we know Arthur's fate wasn't to be killed here? Maybe he was going to turn out like Lynch. Maybe he was going to irritate us eternally. What happened, happened, and there's no way to know what might have been."

"I'm not comfortable with taking the cards dealt us. It isn't an excuse to do what we want, that we had no choice. That vampire, all of them had a choice. Just like Jenn did. Just like Roman."

"And just like me, right?" Nicholas said.

Paolo stood, sparkling blue eyes riveted on me. "There's nothing here to argue about, my friends. A higher power gives us paths, and we take the best one we can. Right now, my path is to get a good workout in. I can't take being so sedentary."

We said our goodbyes, and Nicholas and I were alone. The first time we'd been alone since I was changed. I was scared.

All of Nicholas's sarcasm and egotism was gone as soon as he had no one to perform for. His concern for me was all I could see when I looked at him, even though I'd been so spiteful. It was so reassuring I wanted to cry those watery blood tears.

"You know that what Jenn said isn't true, right? That I'm not finished with you now because you're a vampire?"

I hung my head, embarrassed by my show of weakness. "Leann said it, lots of people say it. And sure, it scares me." I picked my head back up, desperate to prove myself wrong in his eyes. "They say there's no connection anymore, but that's not how it is for me. I can still have visions of you. And I don't feel like you've kicked me out of the nest, I don't feel like you don't love me. But—" My throat constricted, and emotion tore through me. Impossible, to hold this much feeling back, it had color and teeth in my vampire form. "But, I don't feel like the person I was anymore. I mean, I feel *good*, like I have a reason to be someone, anyone at all, but I'm not the same person you saw at Birch Tree Books that day."

He turned to me more, so I couldn't get away from his gaze. As if I'd ever want to, especially now when I could see the invisible flecks in his eyes, the life inside them. I touched the stubble on his jaw, and he took my hand.

"What you are now is unlike anything I've ever seen. What you were before was unlike anything I'd ever seen, too. I want to see what's next with you until the end of time, do you understand that?"

I tried to nod, but the emotion in my throat was too thick to let me move. He took my chin between his thumb and index finger, a gesture so familiar from him that my shoulders relaxed and everything in me heaved a sigh.

"As Ellie Morgan, gift shop employee and sarcastic, passive-aggressive—"

"Nicholas, tell me this is going somewhere good."

Heartbreakingly charming smile. "When I learned who you were under that, you made me think of abandoned castles you see in documentaries. Gloriously beautiful, but cold, empty. Waiting for something to fill it and make it as magnificent as it was created to be. Stunning in its emptiness..." He stared dreamily at my lips, my forehead, anywhere but my eyes. "I always want some dying billionaire to buy those places for a bunch of orphans or a huge, poor family, then fill it with all the incredible things it once held. Think of how much more heavenly that castle would be, renewed with such purpose. Reborn."

Finally, his eyes met mine, and my haze of blood-tinged tears blurred him. "I understand," I choked out, and threw my arms around his neck. His warmth even in just his thermal shirt in the falling snow, was Christmas all over again. Every bit of comfort I ever wanted, mine for eternity.

"Nicholas?" I said into his ear, his arms holding me until my wild heart slowed down.

"Yes?"

"I know we don't need it, but could you make your snow-globe for us now?"

The shimmering bubble softly came into being, enclosing us inside, sheltered from the flurries of snow.

"Our castle," I said, and sunk against his chest.

~

My world had transformed. A light was in everything, and a life to everything. The world was aflame to welcome me. Thank God for that. I needed something to distract me from the constant waiting.

When Kieran showed up at my door, I jumped.

"Jesus, get in here, I'm so restless and bored I could die."

The smoldering fire that was Kieran stood in front of me, the smell of cigarette smoke lingering behind him. "Hello, love. Look at what the afterlife has done for you," he said, his arms crossed, the tip of one thumb between his teeth as he sized me up.

"Ah, cut it out, Kieran."

"Can't. Look at ya."

He was a welcome distraction. All I could see was Clara, the sweet, but not simple thing she was. The life that bubbled in her, the hardships she'd endured.

I wanted to kill her like I'd never wanted anything in my entire life. It fed from me like a leech.

"Kieran, I have to get out of here. I need to tell the Master that there isn't going to be a ceremony."

"It's on for tomorrow, yeah?"

I nodded. "I don't want one. As if it isn't bad enough that I have to get dressed up for a bunch of vampires to stare at me, we were just *at* one, and Arthur was killed there. It's horrible. I think he deserves a *little* respect."

"And you have to feed."

I studied his face. "How did you know?"

"I can smell the need off of you," he growled. I flushed so hot, I thought I would burn like he did.

"The Master won't let me hunt until after the ceremony." The whiniest thing I ever heard.

"Won't let you?" Kieran said through a grin. "Immortal, the savior of us all, and taking orders from an old man." He tutted at me, and without warning, wound his fingers through mine with one hand, then the other. "Time to start making your own rules, love," he said with a conspiratorial smirk. "I'll be the first in line to play along."

My mind hurt from seeing Clara, drenched in my scarlet mist, smelling of life and the impending loss of it. I was her deliverance. Chess pieces ready to make their moves.

I was hungry for her.

"Fine. We go. Just you and I."

Kieran blinked several times, and I smiled wickedly at him. "You're sure about this?"

"No. But I know I didn't become a vampire to have a leash put on me. I won't have my fate given to me in rations."

I may have meant the Master, but having Nicholas hold out on me when it damn well suited him, I let it hurt for once. Emotion as *Shinigami...* it had fingertips, blood, a will of its own. It couldn't be denied, forgotten about in my brain's attic corners.

"You have to know our Mr. French certainly won't like us sneaking off into the night together."

"This choice is all mine, and Nicholas will have to understand. Now, how do we get to London?"

CHAPTER 80

Clara was the lighthouse in the middle of my ocean. I was lost between my heightened senses and the infiltrating voices begging to be heard in my head, but she glowed and drew me to her.

"Wait till you try this," Kieran said with a glint in his eye. He stood in the snow, snakes of smoke rising from his feet, and then there was nothing but black ashes where he'd been.

I closed my eyes and pulled him up in my vision, opening the file of Kieran Coughlin. He stared into the darkness, eyes a fury of flames, waiting for me in a thicket of trees. I wanted to be there with him. And then, I was.

"You found me," he said. He simmered around me with a magical heat, enveloping me as I appeared in front of him.

"I wanted to."

His heat was too much, the buzz of moving in this world without moving was too much, the urge to drink from her, too much.

I grabbed the back of his head with brutal need, and kissed him so hard, I thought I'd break his teeth. He met it, unsurprised, pushing back, wrapping his fingers in my hair. His tongue burned with passion. If I never left that moment, there in the dark snowy woods, I would have been happy.

If only there was blood.

"I'd like to say I'm sorry, lass, but—"

"You're not," I said. I swallowed down my guilt, and tried not to see my Nicholas in the back of my mind. "I don't want to be either." Eternity would be unbearable if I held myself back. I was not made immortal to hold back.

Briefly, I wondered if Lynch felt that way when he murdered.

Kieran's arms around me, fingers splayed on my back, darkly warm, had a different strength than Nicholas's. I don't know that I'd notice the difference of if I was still human. It held me up, and let me go all at once.

"Let's go," he said in his gravelly voice.

I let the red glow of Clara take over Kieran's cinders. Arms still around each other, we flashed again, and left that moment behind us.

～

"You don't pull punches," Kieran said.

We stood in pitch black, staring up at the Bethlem Royal Hospital of London. It was enormous, and cruel-looking. It may have had a makeover, but its horror was a steaming cloud hovering over it.

Pure evil.

"I know about this place," I said, reaching for his hand. I'd read a lot of everything, looking for reasons to go to Birch Tree Books to see Nicholas.

If you wanted to lose your soul, the Bethlem Royal Hospital was where you would never find it again. Where the rich once made side shows of the mentally challenged and the poor for the sake of tourism. Where people were chained to walls, sleeping on straw under holey roofs, bared to the elements, hungry, wondering whether the next torture would come at the hands of the staff or the other patients.

The moans and screams lingered, looking for a way out that they'd never find. They were dead and gone, but their cries were as loud as the crows cawing overhead.

My Clara was in the middle of it all, washing dishes even as we spoke.

"She's in there, and she doesn't know I'm coming," I said.

Kieran turned to look at me, eyes searching me for any sign of emotion. I didn't have any. I only had need.

"Are you ready?"

The words may have been gone, but the blazing light of them was a ghost over the gaping mouth of a door, written there decades ago by someone who never escaped.

WELCOME TO HELL.

I didn't have to nod. This was all I'd ever been ready for.

~

It was as dark inside as out, perhaps darker with the fluorescent lights casting a sickly glow on the halls.

I wished Izanagi had come for a moment, but his kind of death didn't belong here. There was no poetry to the death in this place.

"Jesus Christ, this is horrible," Kieran said, cringing from a passing orderly. I remained fixed on the hallway in front of us, so I wouldn't see anything else, but it was hard to miss the wandering patients in pain of one kind or another, or the staff in white uniforms that only showed how decayed everything else was. Bethlem was a place that nursed pain only so it would be promised more.

We were getting ever nearer to Clara, and my blood burned to take over hers, and be free of it all.

"Eliza, dearest, put your teeth away," Kieran whispered in my ear as we walked. I hadn't noticed the little barbs because my mouth was open. Holy hell, I was panting like a tiger in the sun.

"Oh my God," I said with a little laugh I was sort of ashamed of. "I didn't know. I'm glad the mist didn't come out."

"You're a Stephen King book waiting to be written, woman," he said out of the corner of his mouth, nodding at a matronly nurse who looked like she could use a little mental help herself. "I'm impressed with how you're holding yourself together."

I tore my eyes away from the doors at the end of the hall, suddenly curious about him. "What was it like for you the first time you fed?"

The scent of old smoke from him. I wondered if it was consuming him or giving him strength.

"I didn't want to do it, the man I killed wasn't ready. He didn't want to die." He was quiet, but the fire in him blazed so much I thought it might singe me, too. I couldn't believe the expressionless people around us were oblivious.

With a droning, foreboding buzzing noise, the double doors at the end of the hallway opened to a battered and bent sign for the kitchen. It was all I could do not to run there, leaving every questioning staff member and Kieran behind. I wanted Clara more than anything in the world.

"You knew the man," I said before I realized I'd said it. I was transfixed on the kitchen doors, my fangs impossible to retract.

"I did. How did you know that?"

"I just know things now. I'm sorry you had to do that to your friend. It should never happen that way."

The kitchen loomed ever closer.

"You're creeping me out, love," he said, but I couldn't look at him to see how much he was kidding.

We'd arrived at the dingy white kitchen doors.

"Do you want me to go in there with you?" he whispered.

Clara was whistling from the other side. I put my hand on the door, and fought back tears.

"Yes, please."

The door creaked when I pushed it open, Kieran at my side.

The hospital kitchen was a jail cell in itself. Water-stained walls brought shadows of metal pipes to life, industrial puppets clanking and banging from within. Cracks littered every ceramic tile on the walls. The sink and stove were as discolored and rusty like the slop basins and trash barrels around them. The cabinets would never be white again, the window never quite clear. One wall was cement, blackened in spots with age. Every corner beneath the rusty metal work surfaces was brown with leakage and dirt that could never be hidden, with grunge seeping onto the floor. It was vacant of scent, like no kitchen should be; no soup was boiling, no cooking meat wafting through the air, certainly not cleaning fluid. A sadly spinning metal fan was in the window high near the ceiling over the sink. Too high to cool the room or shed any light; high enough that an inmate couldn't reach it to escape.

And under that streaked window that looked out to nowhere, a gleaming presence in the yellowing disease of this place. Clara's back faced us as her body shook with the scrubbing of dishes. She was humming. Stacks had already been done, stacks more waited for the same. And still, she hummed, amid the hopelessness and filth.

"Clara," I said, not with a whisper. There was nothing to hide from her.

She spun on us, the whites of her eyes the brightest thing I'd seen in London.

"Oh," she said, with a welcoming smile. She dried her

hands as she walked towards us, her shapeless skirt swishing around her, and wiped a tendril of orange-ish frizz out of her eye. "I wasn't expecting any visitors. Can I help you find your way?" Her simple happiness was too good for the hospital, and yet so desperately necessary.

I hated what I was going to do, and wanted it even still.

"We aren't really here to visit, Clara," I said, looking as hard into her eyes as I could while her heart still beat. "And I have found my way."

Her eyes slid between me and Kieran. Panic set in, and she backed away. God only knew the dangers she'd faced herself in this place, just delivering meals to the patients. But I would be the last danger she met.

"What do you want? I don't have anything," she pleaded. Kieran was shuffling his feet in my peripheral vision, rubbing his fingers together, surely wishing for a cigarette. Her fear should have repulsed me, but it made my breath quicken.

"Don't be afraid," Kieran said. She laughed at him. She may be sweet, but she wasn't stupid. Kieran himself was afraid.

But within a beat of her heart, her shoulders relaxed, and she stopped backing away. Her eyes landed on me, lessening in fear until there was none at all. In a puff of red smoke I was at her side. Even Kieran gasped, but Clara's eyes remained steady.

"That smell—" she muttered.

"What do you smell?" I asked. So, this was my first thrall. Designed especially for the future dead.

She breathed in deep, momentarily closing her eyes. "Peonies."

I went cold at the mention of Kat's favorite scent, the perfume she wore no matter what the season or event. Clara reminded me of her; the decided obliviousness to the cruelties around them. That light they embodied, creating happiness wherever they went. Tears sprung to my eyes, and I touched

Clara's hair, remembering Kat's red locks, and thought Clara's might be that beautiful if she had the mind to bother with it.

"Clara, I'm so sorry for what I'm about to do."

Her eyes welled with tears, and I wanted her blood more for it.

"My mother wore peony perfume," she murmured. It was hard to say who was more mesmerized, her or me. "And when she smelled just like that," she said, pointing her finger at me, "a mix of lemon pie and peonies, I knew she had something bad to tell me. It didn't happen often, but when it did, she put on a squirt of her perfume, and made me a lemon pie. She hated that pie, said it wasn't sweet enough. I told her I had all the sweet I needed when I smelled her perfume and saw her smile. We were alone, and she was so sick. I loved her more than anything. Even when she had to tell me bad things."

I couldn't bear to shed the tears that strangled me for her. I wanted to hold her, and kill her.

"You have bad things to tell me right now, don't you?" she asked, entranced.

I closed my eyes ever so briefly, and hoped she had wonderful love in life. I hoped she wouldn't remember how awful I was in her last breath. I wished it wasn't all my fault. *Kat, I wish it wasn't all my fault.*

"I forgive you," she said.

And with a roar that deafened only me, I plunged my fangs into her neck.

CHAPTER 81

Blood is something so familiar, and so alien all at once. It's not meant to be stolen, but when it is—it smooths out all of the heart's rough edges; the things that don't make sense, all the wrongs that need righting, they each fit neatly into the slots they're supposed to. That first taste of human blood, when it slid down my throat, was the last glimpse of an ugly world, and a new vision of one that I would make my own, one death at a time.

This was what being a vampire meant to me, when I sunk my teeth into Clara Borden.

I tasted the love she had for her mother, the way she smiled at the staff when they brought her dishes to wash; the way one old man smiled at her when she snuck him an extra grilled cheese. She desperately craved strawberry ice cream, and stopped on her way home from the hospital twice a week or more for it. There was a flavor to the way she sang along with the radio, when she didn't know the words.

When I was done drinking her, I would carry that away with me. I would sing along with every song I heard, even if I didn't know it. Her residue. And I would carry away her forgiveness.

I was buried in her in a million ways.

When I thought I'd disappear in her blood, I tore my mouth from her, breathing in the second-long difference in taste of her blood as it hit the air. There was a crimson haze over the kitchen, over Kieran.

"I dreamed this once," I gasped, still heaving with the imaginary need for breath.

"Don't talk," Kieran said calmly. He leaned against the work counter, arms crossed, watching me. I was fixated on how surreal he looked, doused in red, until Clara twitched in my arms. In *my* arms the way Kat had hung from Roman's as he bled her dry.

"Alive," I moaned. Once again I sunk my teeth in, eliciting the smallest squeal from her.

My knees buckled and our bodies hit the floor. I consumed, drinking the last beat of her heart, wanting it so that she wouldn't have to endure a fate worse than death at my hands.

With this rush of blood, I saw things. Not the things she'd done, or the person she was, but something much more painful and powerful. I wanted to scream until my throat was dead and gone like she would be.

Visions unveiled themselves to me as I drank my *unmei nashi*'s blood. I struggled to be aware of the floor beneath my knees, to keep me present while I saw the other end that had awaited her.

The vision showed Clara screaming and screaming, here in the kitchen, back against the floor, with a monster doing exactly what I was doing to her now—drinking her life away. A flop of dirty blond hair hung over her attacker's face, thin arms pinning her to the ground. A hospital gown fell open at the back, revealing his every vertebrae.

I pulled my mouth away from her long enough to scream, the same sound I'd made when Roman held Kat's dying body in his arms.

Now, I was seeing him kill again.

Clara fell to the floor when Roman's face appeared in my vision; gaunt, empty, sad, needing, more alone than I ever thought a person could be. Not a drop of blood pooled around Clara's head on the grimy kitchen floor. There was none left. My tears hit her shirt. Confusion roiled in me, but only at what I knew could have been.

Kieran knelt at my side, and pulled my head to his chest. "Sssshh," he said, rocking me. He smoothed my hair, and lifted my face to look at his. His eyes burned me, they were too much. "You're okay, Eliza. In through the nose, out through the mouth. It's over now, whether you want it to be or not."

I swallowed hard, the last taste of Clara Borden's blood washing down my throat, and with it, the last piece of undeniable knowledge that only I knew. My head pulsed wildly.

"Kieran. I know too many things. It hurts."

"I know how it is. You know everything about her now, don't you?" he said, a rhetorical question, as he kissed my forehead. I wished that kiss could take away what I'd learned.

My eyes rolled upwards to the stained ceiling, focusing again, dripping water as we spoke.

"Roman is in the hospital."

~

We left her there. It disgusted me to do it, but we left her there, on the floor.

We raced down the hallways, through double doors, into elevators, looking, but never knowing where to look.

"I saw him, but it was *her*. I saw the other death she would have had if she wasn't my *unmei nashi*."

"Roman killed her?"

"Right there, where we were."

We bolted through door after door, aimlessly rushing around the hospital, as it crushed us with its oppressive sadness, Kieran following my pointless lead.

"But—but—that's the same thing— She wouldn't be any worse off if Roman killed her in that kitchen."

"I know. I was confused for a second, too." The other end a chosen victim would meet if the *Shinigami* didn't take their life was always fated to be a horrible one, something that could never be repaired. We were the better option.

"She couldn't have been chosen for more than one vampire? Or he just killed her, no call to do so. Wait a minute, wait a minute." Kieran stopped, mouth gaping. "*You can see her other fate?*"

I stopped, but hated it. My head was moving too fast to want to stop. "Yes, yes. I saw it, plain as day, but then...."

"Then what?"

"Sorry, I'm a little—lost in my mind right now. I realized that first I saw *her* fate, but she was a—supporting actor. It was Roman's story, she was just a part."

"Dear God," Kieran whispered, falling back to lean limply against the wall. "Dear God." He looked so small then, like a little kid afraid of his first day at school.

"Don't be afraid of me. I don't like it."

"Not exactly afraid..."

"Convincing."

"Eliza Morgan, do you realize what you're saying?" He crossed that space without moving and held me by the arms, shaking me a little. "You can see what no *Shinigami* has ever seen, no one at all has ever seen. You can tell us what might have been."

If I could see what the alternative was, I could decide whether or not to feed on the victims fated to me. I would have choice.

And for all their power, the *Shinigami* had never possessed choice.

"Why would you want to know what might have been?" I asked him.

"You can be the first of us to decide on their own who—"

"To kill? Why would we want the power to choose who to kill? Sure seems a hell of a lot simpler on the conscience to let fate pick for you."

He was smoldering, a delicate smoke rising off of him as he struggled with it. "I'd want to be in charge of my own choices. If I could. You have that power, Eliza. One sip, and you can decide if you want to finish their lives for them, or give them another chance."

"I can play God."

His fire nearly burned out with that. "You don't have to play at all if you don't decide to. The rules are gone now."

"But it was Roman I saw, too. If I wanted, I could have seen what his fate holds for him."

"No more guessing at what our purposes are," Kieran said, eyes glazed over. "Everything is different now."

Orderlies were gawking, so we moved on. More pointless searching.

"Should we ask one of them where we can find Roman?" Kieran said.

"No, I can find him."

"Maybe—"

I stopped again and spun on him. I knew what he was going to say.

"Maybe what, Kieran?"

"Woah, slow down, gorgeous. I know you're bright enough

to have thought that if Roman ran away, he doesn't want to be found. Maybe."

"He can cure Nicholas, and he's here. This is Nicholas's chance to be whole again without me."

Something gray passed over Kieran, a ghost of a feeling. "Remember, just because you know these things now, doesn't change the fact that Roman left you both. Your knowledge doesn't change that."

I kissed his lips quickly for the things he didn't say then. But this was Nicholas's life, and I wasn't about to give Roman the option of leaving him for dead.

"Kiss me again," Kieran said, his breath hot.

I pulled him to me by his shirt, and kissed him, longer this time, vampiric emotion and strength and sensitivity to every breath fueling me. I lived every second of it like reading about someone else's life in a book I couldn't put down.

When I pulled away, my determination was even stronger. "We have to find him right now. Enough of this running. I can see him if I let myself."

Kieran held my hands, while smiling at a pretty nurse walking by. I closed my eyes, and without even having to try, Roman popped into my mind. He felt so alone every time I saw him, my heart cried out to him, despite what he'd done. What he'd taken from me.

"He's in the attic."

"Christ almighty, woman, could you make this creepier if you tried?"

We had to backtrack, and it pissed me off that I'd wasted time running, afraid to see something I didn't want to see. My entire life was about seeing things I didn't want to see.

What consumes me gives me strength.

I'd been made for this, to shape my own world using what fate had given me. This was my purpose.

Pulling open a door where no orderlies bothered to look,

down a hallway that nobody bothered to walk, I paused, and made a choice again. I put my hand on Kieran's shoulder, and turned him toward me. I let everything be slow for a moment, so I could kiss him as deeply as I cared for him, my hands squeezing his bare arms, breathing in his fire.

"Well," he said, licking his lips when I pulled away. "That was a wee bit like a goodbye." His eyes took on that puppy quality again, too vulnerable to resist.

"It's not. It's a thank you."

He grabbed me by the waist with one hand and yanked me into another fast kiss. "You don't owe me anything."

"You helped me make my own way. But that isn't why I—it isn't exactly why I feel like this about you."

He looked at the floor, giving me a view of his messy, spiky dark hair. "What do you feel for me?"

"I can't give it a name, Kieran, but I need you with me. You ignite something in me that nobody else can."

"Not even Nicholas?" he said, looking up at me again. Beautiful. Rebellious and strong.

"Not even Nicholas." I shriveled inside to say it.

Kieran saw my reaction to my own words. "Don't worry, Eliza, I won't turn you against him. I won't tear you away."

My eyes welled, a pink cloud over them. "I'm already torn." My voice cracked. I looked away, and put my hand on the door handle, taking myself out of Kieran's grasp. The door squeaked. Nobody even tried to make it look like this part of the hospital was taken care of.

We would find more of that in the attic.

CHAPTER 82

Cobwebs hung like ghosts from the ceiling, threatening to descend upon us. The wind roared through the loose boards and decrepit roof. The remote parts of this hospital that the public didn't see were ignored to decay, left to die like so many of its patients.

Like Roman was trying to do.

His despair stabbed me as I drew closer to him. It was no fresh vampire sense, only the utter silence and darkness of the air that told me he wanted to die.

I'd poked my head through the opening at the top of the stairs before Kieran. It was enormous, and ice cold. Bats flew from rafter to rafter. Snow blew in from a broken octagonal window at the far end of the cluttered area. A single crow waited for me on the sill.

Kieran came up behind me on the stairs, and let out a low whistle as he looked around. "Ah, for fuck's sake, woman," he mutters.

"Sorry, we had to."

As agile as we were, our footsteps echoed. Silent, heads

spinning, we walked through paths of rusty metal tables, outdated medical equipment, chairs with restraints and ripped seats, and something that looked like a cage. Jesus Christ, I prayed it was something else. Spiders skittered when Kieran picked up a tool that looked suspiciously like a cattle prod.

The attic was a graveyard, the space proof of the mental hospital's history of depravity.

"I hate that Roman's here," I whispered, kicking aside an open trunk filled with what looked like gas masks.

We turned a corner, and I cried out when I saw him.

Roman, hunched like a beaten animal, on a yellow-stained naked mattress, his forehead against the wall.

He was trying not to see anything.

"Ro-Roman?" I said, my voice creaking like the floorboards.

He didn't move. I glanced at Kieran, whose eyes were wide like a twelve-year old's breaking into an abandoned house. With raised eyebrows, he motioned with his head for me to go to Roman.

If Nicholas's life didn't depend on it, if it wasn't so *wrong* to let Roman suffer this way, I would have remembered that this was the bastard that killed sunshine for me the day he drank Kat's blood.

My feet were in quicksand, but I dragged them to Roman's side. The closer I got, the clearer was his deterioration. His golden blond hair was stringy, bedraggled, greasy. His body shook, sending whiffs of filth to my oversensitive nose. And he was mumbling to himself. *"Walking death, walking death, walking death...."*

It may have been Nicholas that was withering away, but Roman disappeared when Kat died.

"Roman," I said, my hand on his shoulder. I don't know which of us was shaking harder.

He jolted away from me, slamming violently into the corner. I screamed at the speed of it. Once again, I said his name.

And when I did, I remembered the humble quietness of him, the liquid warmth of his scent, the way he never complained about lording over Lynch's sick obsessions, his face when reminded of his family in life, his eye rolling at Nicholas's terrible jokes and egotistical witticism.

I remembered how much he loved Nicholas.

I remembered how much he loved me. And how much he loved Kat.

"God, Roman, what have I done to you?" I hung my head, ashamed. "Why would you come here?"

I can't bear to see the hatred in Eliza's eyes. He'd said it himself in a letter to Nicholas. The last we'd heard from him.

"The ghosts here are louder than mine," he whispered.

I was punishing him, stealing his life away. Walking death. That was me, not him.

"Roman, Jesus Christ, I'm so sorry," I said, tears of diluted blood splashing on my arm.

His shaking slowed, then stopped. With painful slowness, he turned his head, forehead scraping along the wall, making me wince. The blue of his eyes was a sad storm; more empty, lonely ocean on a cold day than the warming, lifegiving one that I once saw in him.

"Eliza?" he croaked.

I threw my arms around him, completely aware of the filth he was coated in. It was my fault. His decay, was all my fault.

"Roman, I can't let you stay here, you need to come with me. We'll make you better—"

"No," he said, clearly and with backbone. "I stay here."

"No, no, you can't. You can't! This place will kill you!" And the vision I'd had as Clara's blood flooded my own slammed into mind with a destructive brutality. I fell back, and Roman caught me.

"Eliza Morgan, why have you come here?" he said.

My tears came faster, and I Kieran's warmth crept up behind me. He ached to come to me, but left me to Roman.

"Roman," I said, head hung. "I can—see the other ends we could meet, Roman. What would have happened, if we didn't feed on our *unmei nashi*. For both them and us."

He came back to himself, then, instead of sinking into what he'd become. What I'd made him.

"You're *Shinigami* now," he said.

"Yes, that's not important. What's important is that I know what would become of you." My throat constricted. "The worst fate I can imagine, Roman. *This.* You'll never feed, never take the lives of your *unmei nashi*. You'll become a ghost of this place, and those humans will suffer hideously for what you won't do. Hundreds of them. I can see them." His blue eyes became clearer, pupils dilating. "And you. You'll never die, and you'll be this thing, that you are. Forever."

His face didn't change. "What I do makes everyone suffer, anyway. I'm powerless to do anything but ruin lives, then end them."

"What if I told you that Nicholas will never be healthy without your help?" Please let that be enough to convince him.

"He will be restored with time."

"If he drinks your blood, he'll be whole again, immediate-ly." Not enough. "Roman, Nicholas needs *you*. You're his brother. I can't make him happy enough, he misses you too much. You're his home as much as I am, and without you, we're falling apart."

It hadn't dawned on me until I said it. I never wanted to admit that Nicholas and I were drifting from each other, slowly, like the earth moving, imperceptible until the seasons die. But Kieran behind me was as much proof as I needed. And the clinging to me, the utter owning of me that Nicholas wanted these days—it spoke volumes that he was missing something. I knew who it was.

"He'll repair. You both will. But I never will, and I don't deserve to."

"Stop the pity party, Roman. I get it. You're in agony because of what you did, but you did it for us."

"I snuffed out a light so bright, I never want to see blue skies again."

Me, crying again. I hated it more than words could say. "Nobody understands more than I how much it hurts that Kat's dead. But think of how you feel, and that's how Nicholas feels without you. You were his light for so long, and now you've left him. He thinks it's his fault, I think it's mine, you think it's yours. We're monsters together, Roman, but we're worse apart. Please, come with me. I'm begging you."

He clumsily rose to his feet. It was so sad to see the struggle in someone who'd been so angelic. He wasn't meant to be destroyed.

"Say it's true. Say I can help Nicholas. He'll never look at me the same again."

"Too bloody bad, man!" Kieran piped up out of nowhere. "You can fix wrongs here. You owe it to yourself. You weren't meant to live like this."

"I've done all kinds of things I wasn't meant to do," Roman said through a sneer.

"No, you did one thing you weren't supposed to do, and you only did it for me and Nicholas," I said. "You've made your point. Enough is enough."

He turned on me, snarling at me like a feral cat backed into a corner. "Stop trying to convince me I can do some good now."

I was getting nowhere.

"Fine," I hissed, my red cloud rising around me in my

anger. "Sink into yourself, hide up here and think you can't change anything. I can tell you one thing—you've just proven that Nicholas French is a better man than you."

Roman sunk to the floor again. "You tell me nothing I didn't know already."

CHAPTER 83

Leaving Roman made me feel like the biggest failure and the worst person that ever lived.

"You didn't give up," Kieran said. "You did a great thing."

Snow melted in heavy drops all around us; I could hear it as much as see it. The rebirth of spring, coinciding with my rebirth into death. The crows circled high overhead, not wanting to come near me.

"What will you tell the golden boy?" Kieran asked me as we approached the mountain in leaps in bounds, envisioning ourselves closer and closer to the temple. If only I could envision other things, things that could actually help.

"Don't call him that. I'm not telling him about Roman."

"Lying to him?"

"No," I spat. "But I won't tell him I saw Roman that way, or that Roman refused to save his life. I won't tell him I failed. I'll tell him when I've succeeded."

"But Nicholas is leaving for New Hampshire."

My blood ran cold at the thought of him leaving me alone with this new power, and colder with the idea that he'd be without my blood to keep him strong in another country.

Roman was supposed to heal him before he went to Ossipee, that was the perfect plan. My failure to bring him back didn't change that Lynch was out of control, or that I needed to breathe without Nicholas.

I needed to be alone to remember how much I wanted Nicholas French.

"Nicholas won't leave me if he senses that I need him. If he knows that I'm seeing things like this… He has to go."

Kieran was quiet as we moved, slower now, the temple and the surrounding dwellings in sight. Neither of us was ready to go back yet.

"Will you be telling him about us, then?" We stopped, looking hard at each other. He looked so hurt already.

"I can't."

There was so much guarded vulnerability there, hidden under tattoos and stubble and cigarette smoke, and he'd let *me* in. I'd wronged both him and Nicholas.

"I know you can't, lass," he said with a sad smile and a quick kiss on the cheek. "I'm not the kind you bring home to your family, and he is."

Ice formed around us on the melting grass. "I have no one to bring anybody to, Kieran. I make no apologies for caring about you, but I can't do right by anyone right now, and I certainly shouldn't be pulling you into my mess."

"I want to be here." He took both my hands in his, fire burning under his fingertips, ready to touch me and leave their mark. "Maybe once Nicholas is off babysitting the Abomination, you'll be able to see what you want more easily." His lips on mine were unexpected fireworks, his fingers knotted in mine like he was afraid to fall.

I know I was.

He pulled away, smoke trailing from his lips between us.

"Now, time to report into the powers that be, before they come looking for us."

~

Like a solid shadow in the disappearing snow, Nicholas looked into the sky like it was going to answer his questions. I could see him without even trying in my vision now. The connection we had that was supposed to fizzle out was stronger than ever.

He looked sharply northwest, where I was, like he could feel me, too. I wondered if he could still hear my heartbeat miles away as he had when I was alive. I wondered if my heartbeat meant anything anymore.

Without warning, I couldn't find him in my mind, only the space where he used to be. It hurt, that sudden emptiness. Then it *really* hurt, a soreness that grew into a throbbing, that became a stabbing, then a scratching of healing skin around wounds. I doubled over with the intensity of it. I knew this pain like I knew death.

"What's wrong?" Kieran asked.

"Nicholas," was all I could say, shaking my head, not knowing what else I could say.

"I'm here."

Kieran took his hand off my back, and I straightened up to see Nicholas next to me even as I smelled the peppermint brownie scent.

But the pain still wracked me, and I could see it was in him, too.

"Oh, God, Nicholas," I gasped, and threw myself into his arms. He was a deliciously warm blanket wrapped around me, all I needed to make me whole. "It felt like I lost you for like, a minute, and I wanted to die," I said into his ear, his dark waves brushing my nose. I could never die if he was gone, I would suffer it infinitely now.

He pushed me away before I was ready, and my shoulders slumped as he held them tight in his hands.

"How do you think I've felt since you took off on me?" he said with tense frigidity. My shoulders grew cold as the ice waves rolled from his fingertips. The ice in his eyes was worse.

I was stammering, looking at my feet, when Kieran came to my rescue.

"She needed to feed, and was tired of waiting."

"Well, thank Christ she has a womanizing Irishman to take advantage of her needs," Nicholas said, true to form.

"Maybe if you could get your head out of the Master's arse, she wouldn't have come to me at all."

"Maybe if—"

"Shut up!" I yelled at them. I pushed down my nerves and looked Nicholas square in the eye. "I'm sorry I left you like that, but you would never have let me go. I couldn't ask you to defy the Master and come with me."

"But you could ask *him*," Nicholas said, glaring at Kieran.

I looked at Kieran, too, hands in jeans pockets, chin on chest, eyes looking up at us, wide with innocent defiance.

"Yes, I could. He doesn't ask questions," I said.

"Is that where I've been wrong, then? Should I not question you, challenge you, treat you like a grown-up?" The ground was a solid brick of ice at Nicholas's feet.

"You shouldn't *doubt* her, man! She's more powerful than you or I will ever be, and was before she became a vampire."

My mouth gaped at Kieran, the sincerity of his words.

"Thank you, Kieran," I said quietly. He winked at me.

Wrong thing to do.

A sheen of shimmering frost filtered down Nicholas's body, chilling the air around him in slivers of ice. He growled low, teeth gnashing, fangs glistening. He was a wild animal, hunched over, broad shoulders rising and falling as he panted.

He was staring at my heart.

"Nicholas, calm down," I said slowly. He'd become more of a Mr. Hyde than at the most esteemed vampire among us.

"I spend my existence trying to convince you that you and I, this is forever. I've done everything I could to show you that you can't lose me, Eliza. I'm the one thing in your life that will be here always. Nothing can take me from you." His chill warmed up, and he looked so exhausted, so pained, so old. I'd done this to him. "You're the one running from me, Eliza. You're looking for a way out."

With one last sad glance, he left me with Kieran and the crows in the

woods.

CHAPTER 84

It should have been easier to leave Kieran's side then. I should have run from him, telling him he was a bad influence, that being close to him was putting another brick in the wall between Nicholas and I.

But I needed him. He never judged me. Sometimes guidance was more like pushing.

Don't push me.

"I'm sorry, Eliza," Kieran said as we stood in front of my door, the sound of snow melting all around. The in between stage between wintry death and the life of spring.

"Nothing to be sorry for, Kieran." I sighed, afraid to go on, but I had to say it out loud. "Things are hard between Nicholas and I right now. You helped me in a lot of ways. This wedge between us was there before you were."

"But—" he struggled with the choice to speak. "But he most certainly is in love with you."

"And I'm in love with him." Slow, measured words.

"Love is the thing that makes you fear too much, make you so afraid that you run from it, when it's the only thing that speaks the truth." He looked off into the distance.

"Who are we talking about, Kieran?"

He dragged his long-lashed eyes back to me with a grin. "Ahhh, quiet, woman. It frightens me when you speak the truth, too."

"What the hell do I know about truth?" Tears strangled me, but I wouldn't let them out. I wasn't sure why they were there at all, and that made it all the worse.

"I should probably be alone now," I said, motioning to the door behind me. "I don't think I'll have much time alone before the Master comes." Dread seeped in.

The fire in Kieran's eyes burned black this time. He was full of hunger, but for what it was difficult to say.

"I won't kiss you again," he said before he turned to leave me. "I want you to be alone with how much you want it."

And then he was gone, too.

I'd barely sat in front of the fire before Blue was beside me.

"I can't believe you just *left* like that," she said with no small amount of admiration in her voice.

"I have no patience for being told what to do when I know what to do."

"Why did you ask Kieran to go with you?"

I looked at her, but she wouldn't look back. She would have seen what we'd done if she had. And I was ashamed to admit that I hadn't thought of her at all when I kissed him.

"You know Kieran better than I do, Blue. He won't tell me to fall in line like a good little vampire. I needed that."

"I wouldn't have told you to fall in line," she said softly. It hadn't occurred to me that she wanted to be the one to run off to London.

"Oh, Blue, I'm so sorry. I *suck*." Just when I didn't think my body could contain any more guilt. Vampirism: Day One. "Of course I would've wanted you with me, but I was so restless, it happened so fast... And I know—"

"I know, I know I wouldn't have left the mountain anyway. I'm not sure I even could anymore." In a blur, she stood. "I'm tired of being afraid, El," she said, pacing the floor in her miniature royal blue slippers. "I'm crippled here."

"Blue, what if you just told Kieran he didn't have to bring you your *unmei nashi* next time? What would happen to you if you just *went*, by yourself? Or I could come with you, if you want me."

The half-smile on her face was disconcerting. "So that's how it feels, then?"

"What?"

"To be babysat like a child?"

"That's not what I—" *You're the one who has her meals brought to her in a mountaintop hotel suite, Princess,* I thought viciously. *You pretend it's a palace but it's a prison.* I sighed at my own thoughts, squinting my eyes as if I could dispel them and what a terrible person I was that easily. "Yeah, that's what it feels like, I guess."

She put her hand on my arm, an apologetic smile on her lips. I couldn't look her in the eye. "Don't worry. I have my creator bring me back food like a baby bird, right? Nobody can snap me out of this fear, especially not myself."

I swallowed hard. "Does any of your fear have to do with Kieran, himself?"

"Meaning?"

"Well, I just wonder—I wonder if your fear of leaving the mountain is really your fear of leaving Kieran. Maybe this is your way of holding on to him?"

Suspicion crossed her face, making her just a little colder. "Are you looking for me *not* to hold onto him?"

"I'm either being interrogated or psychoanalyzed, but I

can't decide which," I said, anger surfacing, the red mist not far behind. Always, so much anger.

"Join the club, Eliza."

I had no right to be angry at Blue, no right to resent her or blame her, but if there was one thing that pisses me off it's when the solution is *right there* and excuses are so much closer. Kat and I would argue about why I didn't talk to people, why she was always looking for Prince Charming, why we bought cake instead of fruit when counting the minutes until pay day. Then we gave up and did the things we were doing anyway.

Blue and I couldn't do that. Because if we gave up, it could be forever.

She brushed her gleaming ebony hair back, closing her eyes. When she was ready, she opened them again and said, "Kieran is a crutch. Until I saw you and Nicholas together, I didn't know. You're so much yourselves, and don't stop each other from anything. Kieran and I hold each other back. But I don't know how to be without him."

Connections forged by fate, and ripped apart by humanity.

I brushed her hair back on the other side, and said, "We'll live forever. We don't have to learn to be without each other."

CHAPTER 85

I went to the Master for two reasons: I wanted to throw in his face that I'd disobeyed, and I knew Nicholas was with him. Nicholas's desperation was like rusty nails down my back. He was ashamed of it, because he didn't think the feeling was mutual, but he was afraid to be without me now.

And he still needed my blood, no matter how hurt he was.

I entered the temple with the intent of a storming army, silk kimono swishing around my legs. The Master sat at the altar, the king on his humble throne, with Nicholas by his side. I was a little surprised to see Paolo with them. He looked so much stronger than Nicholas there, young and wiry, and clear-headed.

The Master's opaline eyes glinted, waiting for me to speak and put my foot in my mouth, but we both knew I wouldn't back down. I was, after all, Nicholas's *unmei fumetsu*, if not the woman he loved.

"I fed. It's done. Now if you want to have the ceremony, I won't stop you. But I don't want it."

Staff in his lap, the Master stared at me, as if trying to take me apart with his eyes. A few months ago, it might have worked. "I am not disappointed that you disobeyed me," he said in that controlled voice of his.

Nicholas cleared his throat and leaned over to the Master, eyes on me. "You're not?" he asked the old man.

The Master smiled in a warm, fatherly way. "I am not."

Nicholas pursed his lips to keep from smiling, but Paolo was unreadable. I tried not to pay attention to either of them, though Nicholas's mere presence made my undead heart race.

"Eliza is a singular woman, *Shinigami* like none before. She defies tradition. She makes fate eat from her hand." With a *crack* he stood in front of me, staff resting on the top of my foot, waiting to smash my toes if I did or said anything that didn't fit his plans for my rebellion. I didn't flinch, and he didn't expect I would.

The swell of blood in my newly immortal body told me things—and it told me now that my actions were part of the Master's world; he'd let me play my hand, but he was the dealer. I knew something else, too.

The Master was intimidated by me. It was all I could do to keep from laughing.

He'd seen the blasphemous look on my face, and my hands and feet went numb. Then my legs, my arms, my neck, as he searched inside me for something that I didn't want to let go of. My latent power was a slippery animal in my mind, trying to slink away as the Master closed his fists around it over and over.

"You know what your power is," he murmured, not hiding his surprise.

I held up my chin. "I know the beginning of it," I said.

"Eliza, what's going on?" Nicholas said. Fresh pain stabbed him, making his head twist unnaturally. A matching pain seared into my stomach.

Eyes still on the Master, I said, "I'm learning about myself, that's all, Nicholas."

Nicholas materialized between me and the Master. "Please don't shut me out," he whispered.

Nicholas took over the moment, like that first time we'd met, when he inserted himself in the middle of me, Kat and Lynch, when everything I knew was eclipsed by what he brought with him.

I was a new vampire, different from the woman he'd come to know, but he was with me. Our connection wasn't perfect, but he was still here. He ignored the Master behind him, as entranced by me as I was by him.

"You've been so far away, I can't stand being *me*, without you." Unblinking, steel in his words. "Eliza, don't let me go."

"Never."

One swift motion had me nestled in his arms, looking over his shoulder at the Master, who gave me a warm smile. I closed my eyes to eliminate anything but Nicholas.

"Please forgive me for everything I've done, Eliza," Nicholas murmured into my hair. "And don't say there's nothing to forgive, that's not what I need to hear."

I swallowed back the urge to tell him it wasn't his fault, none of it, like I'd done so many times before. But this had to be different. It had to be true.

I eased out of his grasp so I could see his face register what I would say. "You blame yourself for Kat's death, and I blamed you, too. I blamed myself, and Roman, and Lynch, and Jenn. I forgive you for bringing all the dark forces that came with you. A thread connects you to Kat's death, but you weren't the beginning or end of that thread—you were caught in it. And there's nothing to forgive you for when it comes to me. I never wanted the life I had. This, I want."

"Thank you," was all he said.

"Now, I believe you should tell us about the things you've done and seen," the Master said, turning his back on us to walk unhurriedly to the altar—a show of apathy that I wasn't buying. Paolo waited for the old man, watching in stillness. His eyes met mine, and I looked away, ashamed without reason. Like God was right there judging me, ready to send me to Hell. I gasped to realize that Paolo was *doing* this, making me feel this way. He was doing it for the Master.

"I don't know enough myself yet, to give away all my secrets," I said.

"Tell us what you can, Eliza. This isn't an FBI debriefing." Paolo sounded clinical.

I'd been entirely betrayed.

Nicholas took my hand and we faced the Paolo and the Master. Pretending would be as good as me cowering and sobbing *I don't know anything* while they threatened me with a hot poker, like a deleted Tarantino film scene.

"My visions now are more...specific, and not limited to Nicholas."

"That's not new to us," the Master said.

"I don't have to tell you everything, do I? You're a dictator, not a teacher, if that's the case."

Nicholas squeezed my hand in warning, but I was done watching my words and actions.

"What do you have to hide?" Paolo said.

I coiled on Paolo, ready to strike. "What do you?"

He blinked rapidly, from guilt or fear. Either one reminded me that I needed to be less trusting.

"If Eliza doesn't want to talk about what she's seen—" Nicholas started.

"—then she shouldn't have come here," the Master finished.

I looked down to see that my feet had disappeared in a blink under the flaming red mist. It wound up my legs, around my waist like a secure arm, avoiding Nicholas's hand as it snaked up my chest and billowed around my head like a cobra's hood. My words came from within, channeling a depth of power from someone else. Maybe I was; Izanagi was never far.

"I'll go where I like. I came here because I was expected, and I won't play games. I face what challenges me, Master. I'm not afraid."

"You have no reason to be afraid," he said, unconvincingly. I saw right through him; he planned on using me for something and nobody but him knew what.

I rose from the ground, dropping Nicholas's hand, the mist hissing faintly underneath me with a life of its own. Paolo watched in awe while the Master's jaw clenched and his eyes followed me into the air.

"You would reduce to trickery to intimidate me?" he spat, saber-tooth fangs protruding. "Now, tell me what you see! Tell me what happened when you fed!"

"Or what?" I said coolly.

"Eliza," Paolo interjected. I snapped my head in his direction. "There doesn't need to be secrets here. We're here to support each other."

"Paolo, the temple isn't a goddamn support group, or Arthur wouldn't have died here."

"We're a sanctuary," Nicholas said, "which means we don't force each other to do anything." I lowered myself beside him, the red mist dissipating only when I held his hand. "Eliza will choose anything and everything she wants."

Looking at Nicholas, I knew that meant a lot of things for us both.

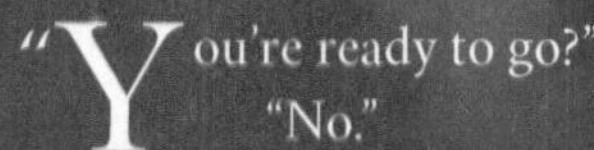

CHAPTER 86

"You're ready to go?"

"No."

Nicholas was as warm as an Olive Garden bread basket, and just like one, I never wanted it to be gone. God, I missed real food. I anticipated crashing Blue's room to indulge in her endless stream of human, non-secluded world treats when I broke down over Nicholas's departure.

I wouldn't let him leave me without drinking my blood as I was now: immortal.

"Taste me before you leave me."

In a needy moan, he said what had to have been weighing on him. "You'll have visions about me, and us. Our futures…"

"I refuse to be afraid of something in my own head," I said.

I opened a vein for him, or maybe for me. If I could have crawled inside his skin, I would have. Wanting him to go and wanting him to stay created jagged edges in my heart, a sensation of both giving up and truly *starting* for the first time. It warmed me, and left me skinned alive.

When we were finished with each other, a pink sheen of

watered-down blood covered us both from sweaty curls to naked feet.

"Are you crying?" I asked him, touching the half-moon circle under his eye. It wasn't dark anymore. I'd done that for him.

"I don't know," he said with an embarrassed laugh. "I do know I'll miss this like—like—"

"Like I miss pizza?"

He glowed with that laugh. A full sound, one of a man missing nothing. But the sudden lightning bolt of Roman in my brain, screeching through me like a missile, reminded me quickly of what he was missing.

"Eliza?" Nicholas said softly, his hands over mine as they held both sides of my head, trying to keep it together.

I was immortal, and this pain was a sliver of what I would know.

Shards of silver and black streaked across my vision as I opened my eyes and forced Roman out of my mind. God, Roman was in more despair now than before. I'd added to his entourage of ghosts, people he'd lost and given away.

"The visions are harder on you as a vampire when I drink, aren't they? Why am I sensing something bad's about to happen?"

"I have the same feeling," I said with a mirthless laugh. "And it's not just because you'll be withering faster with human blood that's not mine, on the other side of the world."

"My cryptic has worn off on you. Spit it out, beautiful."

"*I'm* going to be—different—when you do come back."

"So I will be able to come back eventually," he said with a deep sigh. "You let that one slip out. I won't be gone for good. I won't always be a crippled thing over there."

Crippled thing. Reminded me of what Blue had said.

"You'll be okay." *Better than okay*, I thought, and a flash of Roman slammed through me again.

"But you won't be," he said. Not a question—a statement. He'd caught on. I'd given too much away.

Another deep breath. "It will be hard for me without you, yes. But I need them to be. With you here, Nicholas—I can't see past you to know my own next move. Something is coming for me, something I have to be ready for. And whatever it is, I need it. Please understand that I can handle suffering, it's why I'm *Shinigami*. I need it to get to next."

He ran his palm over his face, like an angry father would do right before he said he wasn't mad. "It's enough for me to know that I'll be back for you," he said, his voice molten and dark. "No matter what state you're in or what you think you've changed into, it can only be more of you."

"God, Nicholas." My voice cracked and I fell into his arms once again. Every time I closed my eyes, I wanted to see him, in that translucent bubble we knew, where death didn't touch us. But I was assaulted by weakness, rained upon with horrible images, and tired. So tired.

Nicholas, my life and the very one draining the life out of me.

"I need Izanagi," I whispered, ashamed.

~

"He's leaving you today."

Izanagi's words were robotic, exactly what I needed. Less emotion, more blood. Less loss, more growth.

"He'll be back," I said.

"Are you in pain?" the god asked me.

Pain like holding a glass that shatters in your hand. Pain I caused myself, but it was still somehow done *to me*.

"No. I'm not."

"This will help you when he goes," he breathed, his voice as ancient as the mountain breeze behind it. My mouth watered at his fresh death scent of wine and roses, and I sunk into him. His blood tasted like all the things I'd lost and all the things I wanted. It took away Roman, and left me with just enough Nicholas to keep me sane.

When I was filled, but wanted just another sip more, I took it, and my penalty was more than I could handle.

I pulled away, panting, the world moving in light speed. Simultaneous slide shows of past, present, future, worlds that didn't make sense together or apart, assaulted me from splices in the air that weren't there before.

I didn't know I was screaming until Izanagi whispered above the noise for me to stop, his voice the only thing that could penetrate the din.

"It is over," he said once. And so it was.

"I'm so sorry, I'm so sorry I took too much, I didn't mean to do it."

"Quiet. You did nothing wrong. The blood of gods doesn't lend itself to restraint." His words were an elixir for my panic. I took his hand and squeezed it, unable to speak for the overwhelming quiet in my mind.

"I didn't know how much the visions took of my mind until it was quiet. You quieted me."

He was having one of those milliseconds where he seemed almost human. "While you screamed, I saw through your eyes. Parts of my lifetimes, and worlds I do not know. The things that you will be and do, the lives of the fateless that you will touch, and many that you will not. Not but a god can see these things and expect sanity to survive."

He would save me in the treacherous weeks to come. I didn't know what they held, but I knew that without him, I'd be reduced to an animal.

"Thank you, Izanagi," I said, bowing low. "You honor me. The peace you give me now is more than I could ask for."

He said, "You did not ask for it, and it will not be yours for long."

Nicholas and I walked like humans in the cold, early spring rain, going through the gardens, woods, well-worn walkways, bridges over half-thawed ponds. It had the tone of a date, but this was anything but a date.

"The Master wants you to have dinner with him in his room after I leave," Nicholas told me. I made a gulping noise and a face to match that was probably on the lines of pelican-ish. I didn't want to go to the principal's office, and yet, that's where I was going.

"What else did he tell you?" I asked suspiciously.

"He thinks my leaving will be too much for you."

"Why does he care?" The rain became a pelting, driving thing. I raised my head to let it soak my face.

Nicholas stopped to look at me with a disbelieving grin. "You're so smart, and so dumb. More dumb than smart maybe."

"Shut your mouth. Tell me what you're talking about."

The rain ended, or so it seemed; turned out I just wasn't being rained on anymore. I looked up to see our snowglobe surrounding us, the rain cascading down its sides in blurry waterfalls. Translucent gray streams, never touching us. Maybe it was the proximity of his scent, the dark quiet that closed us in, but I wanted nothing more than to go home, wherever that was, and not be the future of anything.

Nicholas dropped his tattered duffel bag. It looked and smelled like Rocky Balboa's castoff, making me like it more. I smiled as he stepped closer. The world handing me a plate of brownies.

"Two reasons why the Master gives a crap about what happens to you when I leave," he said, holding up his index finger. "You're going to change everything. You've already started. Whether he likes it or not, it's his thing." Then another finger. "He loves me, and wants to keep you safe for me. It's that simple."

I smirked. "He doesn't like me. He's only doing this for you."

"And because of what you mean to the *Shinigami*. You're the first thing resembling change we've seen in countless years."

"But you didn't say he likes me."

He shrugged, cocky and dismissive. "How the hell could he? You've been a pain in his ass since you got here."

I toed my Chuck Taylors in the slush. "I'm not *that* bad."

Nicholas needled me in the ribs, laughing. "Are you serious? Even look at what you insisted on wearing today."

"I look perfectly fine. Like myself." No stuffy kimono, no torturous wooden shoe-things. Me: cargo pants, black Converse, and a hoodie. None of the hidden pomp and formality of the Japanese temple.

I was a vampire, and I was Eliza Morgan, and I was done trying to be anything else.

"I'm not trying to fit in. If I'm—if *we* are going to move

forward as a race, we should be comfortable in our own skin. This is my skin."

Nicholas leaned over and sniffed me with a sly smile. "You smell of Irish rebel."

"Kieran's one of us for a reason. And I think what you're smelling is Japanese god."

Nicholas lost the smile, and looked deep into my eyes. Izanagi's blood in me made me able to look past the entrancing mocha concoction, spinning like Nutcracker Suite dancers, into the man behind.

"Nicholas, don't be afraid of what's behind my eyes now. Izanagi lets me see clearly. No voices in my head, no other destinies fighting each other in there. He's elevated me."

He put his hands on the side of my head, pulling my forehead to rest against his. His mind whirred, working, his admiration and jealousy plain as day. "How can I not be a little afraid of you? Your existence threatens the only father I know."

I yanked my head back from his fast, electrified, the utter truth of what he said resonating in me with the weight of an entire race of creatures.

"Oh my god. You're right."

He did the rapid blinking, wide-eyed thing he does that says he's surprised, while not too surprised to be sarcastic. It was familiar enough to help me not panic.

"I'm right?"

I looked at him like I was confessing to murder. Non-negotiable apology. "This is all his making," I said, looking around, stating only a half-truth. Izanagi made the *Shinigami*, the temple, the reason for our existence, even the mountain. But the Master claimed it as his, and had made the temple something else. "If I change all this, what else does he know? He doesn't even know his name."

The rain poured down our shield, and when Nicholas's shoulders sagged, a few drops broke through, hitting the ground with a sound that pounded my eardrums. I couldn't be sorry to Nicholas for the threat I was, for who I was. I couldn't be sorry that fate would have me take away from him someone so close.

Kat.

God almighty, fate knew how to twist the knife then throw hot coals on it and laugh in your face and say, *see? Could be worse.*

"An eye for an eye, my love," Nicholas said, eyes darting to avoid mine, to expose the anxiety there. Rain penetrated the globe more, drops hitting us with ferocity.

I pulled him to me and squeezed as hard as I could, for what I would do, for taking from him what I shouldn't, but had to. The shield he'd made over us weakened more.

I held his head to my chest and gazed up into the rain bulleting through the shimmering wall. I breathed in deep through my nose, smelling the fear of loss in the air around Nicholas. Closing my eyes, I imagined it seeping into me, a real thing that I could drink, eat, breathe.

His abandonment issues were edging in, and nothing had even happened to the Master yet. Nicholas's fear of losing the Master was worse than death.

With a roar from deep within, I consumed Nicholas's fear, letting it soak into me like the rain that punctured the snow-globe. My eyes snapped open, focusing on the places where Nicholas's shield faltered. I watched my red mist, thicker than I'd seen it before, rise and seep across Nicholas's shield, covering it from the inside, reinforcing it. The rain ran down outside again, the streams now pink through the red mist and the globe's shimmer. Rain and blood.

Nicholas's back straightened from the hunched position it

was in. He looked above to the slithering mist that filled the space of the dome.

"Once again, getting all my strength from you," he said, smiling meekly.

I kissed him on the forehead. "I have plenty more where that came from." I picked up his duffel bag and we walked on.

CHAPTER 88

The Master's bungalow was greatly removed from the rest of the vampires' homes, like any leader would do. Establishing himself as one of them, but just a little apart, ever so slightly better. He loved leading the *Shinigami*. He loved his people, and he loved Nicholas. And he loved power.

Izanagi's blood was a hissing snake of knowledge in my veins.

Soundlessly, the door slid open to reveal the Master just inside. "Master," Nicholas said with a bow that I mimicked. The Master bowed back, his hands in the bells of his sleeves, and turned to go inside. Nicholas followed, stopping to remove his shoes. I took off my Chucks, determined not to be embarrassed by my holey socks.

Though the Master's home was more solid than any of the other homes at the temple, it was still extremely humble by any standard. Built of large stones from the mountain streams, and of a wood darker and thicker than what I was used to. A kettle was boiling in the fireplace. It was obvious this was the fireplace that inspired the one Nicholas had built in New Hampshire. This was home to him, too. The firelight flickered on the walls, illuminating weathered scrolls that hung there. The Master's home was cozy, cave-like. With the warmth and the rain tapping on the roof, it felt a little indulgent, something I'd been missing for a long time. I wanted to curl up under my afghan with a cup of tea in my sweats, a book from Birch Tree in my lap.

That afghan was still folded in my suitcase now, and I hadn't read a book since I got to Japan. I wanted that comfort now. I wanted all the parts of myself to be one.

The Master went about his business, his back turned as he tended to the pot over the fire. Nicholas walked past into a hallway, looking over his shoulder at me, beckoning me along.

That look could make me follow him into Hell.

"Your new room, if you want to stay here," Nicholas said.

"What? Stay here? Why would I—"

But the comfort of the room took me in right away. Smaller than where I'd been staying, and darker, it lent itself to hiding under the covers on the low bed, never looking out to see what new surprise I had coming my way. Never having to see that Nicholas was gone.

I swallowed back tears that pricked the corners of my eyes. I would not make this harder on Nicholas. But there was no hope of it not being hard on me.

"I'll think about it," I murmured, looking down.

A living apparition, Nicholas moved so quickly to be in front of me and hold my hand that I forgot I was just like him for a moment. He was golden, good, soft as he touched me, my sadness reflected in his churning eyes. I didn't have the strength to erase it anymore.

"I trust the Master with you implicitly. I need to know the one I trust above all else is taking care of you." He swallowed, and blinked. It made my heart race, the emotion of the one second. In a pleading growl, he said, "I need your heart, soul, your blood, all of you to be protected. The thought of you being alone—unimaginable. Unimaginable."

I crumbled against him. "God, Nicholas, I'm afraid of the pain when we're apart. Not mine, but yours."

"I can handle the pain. It means you're still there." Another agonized swallow. "I love you," he said through gritted teeth, like the pain had already claimed him.

"I love you, too. If you need me to stay with the Master, I'll do it. Anything to make this easier on you."

His hands on my cheeks, he smiled, purely happy. "You'll be happier here than you think," he said. "He'll be here, but you'll still be alone. I know you need that." He kissed my forehead and turned.

"Blue," he said.

I looked over his shoulder to see Blue standing in the hallway, wide-eyed and trembling. I pushed past Nicholas to go to her and hold her hand.

"What's wrong?" I said, searching her eyes. Surprisingly, she smiled back.

"I've made a choice," she said. The hairs on the back of my neck bristled.

That's when I noticed the bag she held in one hand.

"Where are you going, Blue?" If I'd been human I might have hyperventilated. I needed her here now. Her eyes were on Nicholas behind me.

"I've thought too much about this, and you can't talk me out of it, El," Blue blurted, dropping her bag and pacing in two-step bursts, eyes on the floor. "I can't stand being afraid anymore. I'm going to New Hampshire with Nicholas."

I spun on Nicholas, waiting for an explanation.

"Eliza, I don't know what this is."

"Not really the explanation I was looking for."

"He didn't know," Blue said.

"And what is it exactly I should know?" Nicholas said. "Because I get the impression I'm swimming in trouble for it."

"Nicholas, I want to go to New Hampshire with you. You make me feel like I can leave this mountain, and experience this world, and I want that so much."

Jealousy stabbed me in the chest when Nicholas's face softened toward the tiny girl in front of him. She shuffled from one foot to the other, so vulnerable, but so powerful. Seductive.

What a mess I was next to her.

Please say no, Nicholas. Please.

"Okay."

"What?" I whispered.

They both looked at me like they'd forgotten I was there.

Nicholas flashed to my side. "She wants to do this, finally, and I could use the company."

I sneered. "Oh, could you now?" *Well, so could I,* I wanted to say. I wanted to say that I needed someone to have pizza with, someone who would let me cry with them when it was all too much, someone who would give a crap when I told them I missed *Saturday Night Live* and moose crossing signs and going to work at a dumb tourist shop, and having coffee and nothing to do. I wanted a friend, and she was leaving with the man I loved; the same man who took friendship from me. Who'd lost his own friend, and the trust of his lover...

My mind ran away so easily since being imbued with vampirism, but it always came back to the same feelings I'd known in life: *Abandonment. Guilt. Anger.*

"Eliza," Nicholas said, lip twitching. "Are you actually jealous?"

Kieran would still be with me. I smiled as convincingly as I could at Nicholas. "No. No, I guess not. I just—miss you guys already."

Blue was on me with a hug that might have killed me. "I'll call this hug the Gorilla Killa," I squeaked out.

"Thanks for helping me get here," she whispered in my ear. "I can come back anytime I—can get up the nerve, you know."

"I know," I said. "But while you're gone, I'm using all your stuff."

CHAPTER 89

The agony that ripped through me at the sight of Nicholas walking out the door with Blue at his side had me bargaining with God or Izanagi, anyone who would listen, to please let the torture keep going for as long as he was gone. The pain that we shared when apart was how I knew I was insurmountably his.

He'd lifted me off the ground, his hands dimpling my fleshy curves, murmuring into my ear how much he loved me, how much words could never say it, how painful it was to let me go. I wanted to remember every syllable, but could only remember how it felt.

I longed already for the little signs of his presence. Hearing him open a drawer when my eyes were still closed in bed. Watching him sort through a half dozen black thermal shirts just to choose one that looked exactly like the rest. The sound of his old china cups clinking as he poured tea. The beauty outside the door that offered me silence, stillness, closeness to Heaven if there was one, was all just cardboard scenery next to sitting at a table with him.

I'd sent him away on purpose. This was a solitude I'd asked

for. He left me with a creature that I didn't trust, and I all but begged him to do it. Asking for what plagues me.

Take strength from what consumes you.

I fell onto the bed that was mine for the time being, and curled up in a ball. My stomach was wrenched with the beastly pain that had been lingering out of sight, just waiting for a moment like this, to remind me what being human felt like when I'd had nothing to look forward to.

A strange coolness wrapped around me as I lie there, comforting me and making me feel both like I was outside in the budding spring, and held close in a warm blanket. I popped my eyes open to see my red mist embracing me.

"You're staying."

I leaped off the bed, chilled by the Master's silent approach, when I could hear anything, everything. So much for making myself comfortable.

"Are you offering or is this really Nicholas imposing?"

The Master smiled, but only a little. "You're important to us all for different reasons."

I stood, though there was plenty of effort involved in it. He needed to see that I could do this, face my choices on my own. Even if I couldn't.

"Did you see anything when you came in?" I asked, chin held high.

"Your mist is quite unusual, isn't it?" he said with a tight smile.

"I suppose it is. It makes me strong."

His face softened. He seemed just like a little old Japanese man then, one hand on his staff, treating it more like a cane, slightly hunched over. I sensed nothing behind his unexpected kindness, just that he knew I hurt. "It is quite difficult to see the one you love walk away," he said.

I laughed inappropriately, and my hand flew to my mouth. But he laughed, too, a rattling, pure sound.

"I'm sorry," I said. "I never thought of you…"

I saw why Nicholas loved him. It confused me that I'd not trusted him, and it confused me that I was giving up my suspicion so easily. His power thrummed through me with every false breath he took. Was it just that I was so desperate for companionship? Then again, wasn't that how he lured every single *Shinigami* to this place, isolating us all then giving us something to live for?

"It's hard to think of a strange old man like me doing anything except being strange, am I correct?" He was still laughing, and my shoulders relaxed. My head bowed, and I let out a deep breath.

The Master was next to me, hand on my shoulder. I gasped with surprise, but didn't pull away.

I wanted to give him a chance, whether it was his thrall or that I wanted him to love me like he loved Nicholas, like family.

I whimpered. The Master squeezed my shoulder, and I leaned against him. He laid his hand on my hair. Like calming a wild dog, the whole situation could be volatile at any second, but I didn't care.

"I will miss him, too," he said. "I'm sorry you're in pain."

"Thanks," I whispered.

He gently pulled my head from his thin chest to look at my face. "You can overcome the pain to grow into yourself. You are frighteningly strong. You quite frighten *me*, in fact."

Grinning, I said, "I know."

No sooner had I woken up than I found myself clung to the ceiling like a big, freak spider, a spray of scarlet around me like a—well, like a vampire shield. Even in sleep, my exhaustion couldn't keep away the emotions that were even more powerful than my senses, my strength. My mist had taken care of me in rest, and the pain didn't grip me until I felt Nicholas's absence again. I only feared for a moment before I opened my vision to him, desperate to be close.

Nicholas huddled in a dark seat, afraid to look anyone in the eye. His heart beat irregularly, each throb a stabbing pain. He could still feel my heart beating across all that distance.

He hurt worse than I did. Not one bit of him had wanted to leave.

Blue sat at his side, one hand on his back, staring straight ahead and biting her lip worriedly. Her worry made my own worry multiply about how fast my blood would wear off, how quickly he'd return to his former state of decay. My stomach buckled, and I crashed from the ceiling to the floor.

The Master crouched to help me to my feet by the elbow, saying, "Shhh, shhh, you're all right." It gave me another jolt of wonder at why I'd been rebellious since the minute I'd come to Japan, his home.

Then I thought of Izanagi, a hazy memory in the Master's sanctuary. The Master's thrall was so subtle, so enduring that it dulled even my senses.

The Master pulled me along to the main room and sat me in front of the fire on a stack of pillows. I groaned when he wrapped a blanket around my shoulders, and when the cup of tea was placed in my hand I thought I might pass out from the comfort it brought me.

"You're being so good to me," I breathed. I was apologizing, really. Jesus, I guess I should say sorry, then? Every second I fought with myself whether I was under thrall or genuinely reconsidering, or if I just missed Nicholas so much that I'd do anything to make my life easier.

He sat cross-legged next to me. "Why wouldn't I be?"

So, he was going to drag it out of me then. "I've been snotty and rebellious. I've second-guessed you, and challenged you and treated you like a mountain to climb."

He chuckled and sipped his own tea. "You have acted like no one that has ever set foot on this mountain. I would expect nothing less from Nikorasu's vampire."

Staring into the fire, I said, "I belong to Nicholas, but I am my own vampire."

That chuckle rose from his chest again. It was boisterous. *Loving.* "That you are, my friend, that you are."

I looked at him, trying to see inside, but only able to detect traces of his emotions through the pulses of power. It showed me nothing of what he really was. Izanagi was restless in the woods outside.

"Do you trust me?" I asked him outright.

Long white hair rustled as he turned his head to study me through blind eyes. "Trust is an emotion that I have tried to forget."

"But you trust Nicholas."

"And for that reason, you are still alive," he said with the same warmth he'd been speaking with all along. He rose and left me to watch the fire burn.

CHAPTER 90

The Master came and went as though I didn't exist. But for the pain, I might not have been sure I existed either. The longer I went without Izanagi's blood, the more I was attacked by visions of fates I knew nothing about. Surges of dread, restlessness, helplessness; the same dense despair when I stood in front of my parents' caskets and knew I was totally alone. The scent of wine and roses synonymous with death itself, with Izanagi, now a crouching predator waiting to slide itself into my thoughts.

These pictures in my mind were bits and pieces that belonged to other people, maybe other vampires, and I needed to find their owners. Nancy Eliza Drew, putting the clues together.

I threw on my hoodie and cargo pants with vampire speed and slipped outside, the Master nowhere in sight. The sun flooded my every pore, momentarily chasing away the dull, sightless fog the visions left me in. A pang of sadness came with my sigh of relief.

I could only stand the sunlight because I'd killed Clara Borden.

Nicholas loved the sunlight. It made him glow even when he was at his most gaunt and lifeless. With a deep breath, my mind opened up. Within a second I saw him carrying a stack of paperbacks with wrinkled bindings in Birch Tree Books—he avoided the windows. No sunlight for him then. I could smell the familiar must. The dust motes danced around the windowsill, the too-strong coffee from the old pot on the register, the peppermint-brownie of *him*, all things that sang of home. Nicholas looked up, his eyes dimmer than I liked, but still full of strength.

So my blood was potent in him, still.

"You're a shoddy replacement for Roman, the eternal babysitter, Nicholas. You can't make me check in with you like a grounded teenager."

"A grounded teenager wouldn't check in because he wouldn't be going anywhere. Keep up, Lynch."

Lynch showed up behind Nicholas in the vision, angry, fists curled. Nicholas didn't even turn around.

"You'll be happy to know my fangs haven't come out to play once today," Lynch said. He *was* checking in with Nicholas, like it or not. This wasn't the headstrong psychopath I knew.

This was a lost man looking for direction.

"Nice job. You can live to see another day." Nicholas stacked books on a pile of more books, his hands around them to keep them from falling. They fell anyway. Nicholas turned to Lynch, who glared back.

"You won't kill me," Lynch said. *"I'm your only company,"* he added with a sneer. *"It wasn't enough for Roman to be errand boy for the great Nicholas French."*

Nicholas's eyes narrowed dangerously. The playful wit vanished, and his hand closed on Lynch's throat, fingers tight on his windpipe. A bead of sweat trickled down my own back as I watched Nicholas's lip curl in an animalistic snarl, his breath making puffs of cold smoke, frost crawling up Lynch's throat from his fingertips.

"It takes more than a lapdog to keep you alive, you ass. You should have thanked that man every day for your miserable existence. I would never have let you keep it. If not for Roman, the Master would have turned the other cheek long ago for me to stop this life of yours. If that's what you call it." Nicholas pushed Lynch back by his throat, leaving him gagging and smiling, as his personality dictates.

"You need me to focus on, or you'd have nothing," Lynch spat. *"But don't take it out on me that Roman deserted you. He didn't murder the woman you loved first."*

I shuddered, shaking the vision away, stomach rolling. The combination of Nicholas so far from me and Lynch showing actual emotion was painful.

"You're here," I heard from behind me.

I spun to find the only person on the mountain I wanted to see; Kieran. His eyes were red-rimmed, his five o'clock shadow a full beard, shoulders slumped. Reminiscent of Nicholas, actually.

"Kieran." I wanted to wrap my arms around him and kiss him with all the energy I had left. "You don't look—like yourself."

He stepped towards me, hands in his pockets, head focused on the grass below. "I thought you'd left, woman," he said with a hint of shyness that made me groan inside. He looked up at me when he was close, the dull fire in his eyes flickering darkly. It seemed as tired as he did. "I am very alone," he said. And he put his forehead on my shoulder.

I put my arms around him, squeezing him as close as I could. "I'm so sorry, I've been, I don't know, mourning I guess? I'm sorry to have left you alone. I should have known you'd be like this, with Blue gone, and Leann, and now me—"

He pulled his hands from his pockets and placed them on

my upper arms, head still resting on my shoulder. "Everyone else is so boring," he said with a grim laugh. "That Paolo boy has been all over me, and my God, I can't stand it."

I laughed, squeezing him tighter, then reluctantly letting go. I picked up his head by his fuzzy cheeks, and smiled to see the glint of fire in his eyes brighten.

"You've been staying with the Master?" he said, eyebrows furrowed.

"Yeah, actually. It just sort of happened. Nicholas asked me to, and when he left—well, I kinda collapsed in there and, well —I've fallen and I can't get up."

His mouth fell open, eyes blinking, incredulous. "It's been weeks, Eliza. You haven't been out of there for *weeks*. We all thought you'd left, too." He ran a hand through his spiky, messy hair that was in need of washing.

Weeks? How was that possible? My mind couldn't wrap around it, I had just fallen asleep, and vampires don't need to sleep that long… I had to change the subject, had to learn more without bringing Kieran into it anymore.

"Kieran, how have you been without Blue?"

A grimace that turned into a sad smile. "Don't worry about me, Eliza, I always burn on."

I squinted into the grass trying to replace the vision that popped up. Jesus, but they were frequent and without warning.

"What do you see?" he whispered, his fingers brushing my arm.

"I don't know. They hit me from all sides, and I don't know who or what—I don't know." With those visions taking me over, time was surreal, undefinable. Could I really have been in the Master's house for that long? Weeks, with Nicholas thinking I was…was…just fine without him.

He cleared his throat. "Rumor has it that you took off with Nicholas and Blue to hide your visions from the Master."

"Where did this rumor come from?"

Kieran glanced sideways, like he was waiting for the cops to break us up. "It seems to me Paolo knows something he shouldn't."

I'd been surprised by Paolo's sudden closeness to the Master when I returned from Clara. The way he'd turned on me when the Master was watching, it hurt me, but it was Paolo. I trusted him. We all had secrets, but we were still ourselves.

"No, no way. He's too loyal, if not to me, to Nicholas." With a snort, "And to God. Rumor-spreading isn't in his nature."

Kieran licked his lips, a darting thing that was full of warning somehow. "No man is above his nature, woman, and no vampire can be tamed. Remember that. There's always something inside pushing out, wanting to prove itself. Paolo wants to be more, just like any one of us."

I found myself shaking my head at the beauty of his words, the darkness and heat of him. He was a remarkable creature, and waking from my slumber to him was like opening my eyes in a museum.

"So, tell me, gorgeous. Why are you hiding your bits and pieces from the Master?"

Kieran wouldn't have spoken a word about what happened that night with Clara to anyone. I believed this more than I believed in anything. He wouldn't want me to give any more of myself to our *cause*. Telling the Master that I could see the other fates of the *unmei nashi,* of the *Shinigami,* would be like putting a leash on me.

I wondered how long this dog could hide under his roof.

"I'd be the center of attention here, a sideshow. My purpose has to be *mine* for now."

Kieran swallowed, shuffling his feet. "The Master will make a slave of you if he finds out, Eliza."

My fangs splintered into my lip and the grass in front of me grew red with as my mist spread across it.

"He can try."

~

K ieran and I went back to my room, my *real* room, in the plain light of day, to the surprise and hissing of some of the *Shinigami* we passed.

"Their tunes change without Nicholas around, don't they?" I said with a mean-spirited grin towards a hulking beast of a vampire.

"They don't know if you're predator or dictator, dear girl. They know you have power, and they're more afraid of it than envious."

"Monster!"

I spun on a small group of vampires shying from the light in a doorway. They huddled together, hissing at me like the witches in *The Clash of the Titans*. The one who spoke stood a little taller, but still looked like an animal dragged through the dirt in the dark.

A whirlwind of red wound around my legs, spiraling up my body in a tornado of decay, the scent of wine and roses. The world emptied of emotion as I raised my hands up to the sky, as if I could make it grow to the clouds, and I rose from the ground like I was ready to try.

"You don't know what monsters are," I hissed at the quivering vampires below. They flashed away in shadows, leaving me to return to Kieran's side.

"Putting on a little show, are we, lass?" he said with a smirk.

"I won't let my power be bigger than me, and I sure as hell won't be intimidated."

He growled under his breath, and it arose a stirring in me

to match. I snarled like a primal thing, and Kieran responded with an electric scent, eyes flashing when they met mine. Nature at its wildest.

Shaking it off, I tried to regain my humanity. These momentary bursts of unbridled force were addictive, and I wouldn't let them control me.

Kieran ran his fingers down my arm, a path of sparks left in their wake as they touched my skin, a sizzling clue to our magnetism.

"Eliza, we need to reel you in." He was panting, eyes following the jumping sparks on my skin. "It's like you fell asleep and woke up with a little extra magic. More than a little magic."

My power took over, and a blinding vision of Roman, shivering in the same spot I left him weeks, or months before, pulled into my brain like a train from Hell. I screamed with the intensity of it, the odor of dirt and neglect, the creaking of the floorboards from the wind outside, and him, a golem without the sense to hide from the horror. He flickered out of sight, reappearing at the door of a patient's room. His fangs came out, and he went inside with a deadly purpose, yet not one that called to him. Not his *unmei nashi.*

"Oh. When the hell did that get here?" I said, swatting my mist away. I flashed an insecure smile at Kieran, who didn't return it, just stared at me with grave concern.

"You have less control of yourself than I thought," he said.

"I was born yesterday, pretty much, and then was….what? In a coma or something for a few weeks? I'll get it. I'll get it." Of course I would.

He ran his hands through his hair a bunch of times, the pinup tattoo on his arm dancing with every movement. "We're missing something. These visions are getting stronger, and so are you, but it's like you're on two different frequencies."

I gritted my teeth and said, "They're incessant now that I'm *Shinigami.*"

"And when you drank from Clara, you saw not only her other fate, but Roman's as well." His eyebrows furrowed, and he groaned as if it hurt to think. "What if we experiment a bit?"

"I don't like the sound of that at all."

"Hear me out, now, you know I won't let anything hurt you. What if you drink a *vampire's* blood? Not Izanagi, he's..." He licked his lips, eyes filled with excitement. Such a child with a box of matches.

"I drank Nicholas's blood."

"Could you see anything?"

"I wouldn't let myself."

"So you *can* control this some." He breathed in deep through his nose. "You said when you drank from Izanagi that everything was clear. The longer you go without blood, the more muddled your mind becomes."

"It's more than that. These visions are missing pieces, waiting for me to find the right person to connect them with. But they aren't my *unmei nashi.*"

"Jesus, where is Blue when I need her wares? I could really use a beer."

I laughed, for what felt like the first time in months. "We could go to the, uh, *tea room.*"

His lips spread in a wicked grin, his arms crossed over his chest. He put the tip of his thumb in his mouth and I nearly passed out. Kat would have fallen over for sure.

"Eliza, you just woke up from a three week nap. You need a night out carousing with me? Or do you need to figure out what it is that ails you?"

"Maybe what ails me is that I need a break."

He crossed the room in one motion, the scent of burning embers following him. "Let's break some rules."

~

The tea room seemed more like a bar this time. Vampires were laughing, lounged out on the floor and being more social than I knew them to be. The music was less traditional, more sultry, like it hid secrets of its own.

Kieran slapped his hands together, rubbing them greedily. "Now this is more like it!" His whole body relaxed, a strut replacing his protective hover over me. I watched him walk ahead, body equal parts lithe and rippling musculature, confidence a cloud of smoke around him. There wasn't a woman in the room who didn't have eyes for him. I kept myself from hissing.

"He doesn't belong to you," I whispered to myself. He glanced over his shoulder at me with a look the devil couldn't copy, and I bared my teeth in response. An animal's reaction, but the only emotion I was capable of showing.

We sat in the same place we'd been before, and a girl came right over with a pitcher of something that smelled like cranberry and heat. A low growl emitted from me. "What is that?" I said in a voice I didn't know to Kieran. He poured us both a cup, and my mouth watered, fangs tingling.

"Blood and beer, love. Can't be beat." He handed me the cup at eye level, eyes glinting.

My hand was too fast for even my eyes to follow. I grabbed it and chugged it down, throat filling with bloody, hoppy perfection. It dripped from the corners of my mouth; I wiped it with the back of my hand, then licked it off. I didn't stifle my grunt when I said, "More."

Kieran threw his head back with a gorgeous, sinful laugh, and did indeed pour another. I waited for him to tip his first back, slower than I had, and then we both gulped the second fast.

The room got lazy for me, the scene slower while my mind got sharper. An amazing contrast, the blood making me hyper-aware while the beer calmed me. I never wanted it to end.

"You've picked your poison, I see," Kieran said, leaning over the table. God, he smelled good. Fire and brimstone. Like everything that held me back, burned and left behind. It was simple now, to see what he was to me.

He incinerated everything I was told to be. He was my birth by fire.

I met him halfway across the table, the rich scent of blood beer wafting up between us. I grabbed him by the back of the neck and I kissed him like he deserved to be kissed. Like he was my savior and fury, passion and freedom. Like he was the smoke of burning villages and fired cannons.

He apologized for nothing and slipped his tongue inside. Every rule that shouldn't apply to me, broken.

"Well, aren't we friendly with the all the wrong people?"

We both looked up to see Leann standing there, like a spoiled brat kid catching her older sister with a boy.

"Leann," Kieran said throatily. He leaned back. "Haven't seen hide nor hair of you. Where have you been?"

She crossed her arms and tapped her foot like a real bitch. "It matters to you, *shugotenshi?*" she spat. "You've been occupied with someone else's woman." Her eyes on me were meant to be harsh, but they felt too empty, and I felt too full.

"Yes, it does matter to me," Kieran said. "I created you. I want to know that you're well."

She looked well, all right. The colors about her that seemed drab as the hidden human she'd been were vibrant now, defiant. Bright blonde hair, deep dark eyes, lips with an erotically pink pucker. So full of resentment and ferocity, she resembled a fallen angel.

My eyes were stuck on her jugular. I shocked myself with

need to taste her blood.

A sneer revealed her sparkly new vampire fangs. "You did your job, Kieran. I don't need you to hold my hand in the afterlife, I'm doing just fine on my own."

"Then why are you so bitter to me, woman? Did you want something else?" he said huskily. Without looking, I knew he was running his eyes all over her.

"Don't flatter yourself." Her lips turned down with a child-like sadness. She shook her head a little, ready to regret saying what she would say next. "I don't want anything from you, and holy Hades, is it ever liberating to not have that *connection*, without supernatural handcuffs holding me to you, but it would have been nice if you hadn't cast me off so fast. If you showed you even *liked* me, even once. That I wasn't a chore for you."

That vein in her neck pulsed. I sipped my drink to keep myself from looking at it, and watched Kieran over the top of my cup.

He sat up, losing some of the rebel he'd been. "Neither of us wanted to be best friends. Neither of us wanted that blasted invasion-of-the-body-snatchers brain itch. You were as happy to be rid of it as I was. There's a reason you were chosen for me—we'll see it in time. Until then, we have our lives back. Easy come, easy go."

She looked away, making the tendons on her neck stand out even more. I shivered. When she looked back, she was smiling a tight smile, but the abrasiveness was gone.

"I guess I can live with that." She turned her body to me. "Why do I have the feeling you want to drink my blood?"

Kieran looked at me with surprise, but I only had eyes for Leann. When the words came out, I knew they were true, and that fate showed itself at the strangest times and in the oddest ways.

"There's something in your blood that I need."

CHAPTER 91

"You want to drink *her* blood?" Kieran's voice squeaked, and I laughed, but my gaze remained on Leann, whose eyes were darting, equal parts disbelief and scared rabbit.

"Where can we go?" I said to neither of them in particular, ready to imagine myself there and be there faster than any living thing could do. This was my world now:

I saw Kieran chug the rest of his blood beer out of the corner of my eye. "We go to Blue's," he said over the clank of the cup on the table, the liquid still thick in his throat. "Nobody will look for us there."

I dragged my eyes off Leann, as if being released from a hypnotist. "You're coming with us?"

He opened his arms, Jesus-style, giving me a look that was like Nicholas incarnate. "Like I'd miss this?"

Grabbing them both by the arms, I envisioned the three of us at Blue's, and we got there fast. Leann was screaming as if I'd brought her on a roller coaster, and Kieran doubled over, hands on his knees, muttering that he was tired of Eliza surprises. I couldn't concentrate, Leann's blood singing a morbid chorus.

When he recovered, Kieran walked into Blue's room like he lived there. I had a gut-punch of jealousy that I willed away quick, replacing it with guilt.

Blue's place looked like she never left, and I missed her. There were still peanut butter cup wrappers on her otherwise sumptuous bed. The bathroom door was open and a fluffy purple towel lay on a heap on the floor.

Leann walked past me and sat on the bed.

"Dear lord," Kieran said beside me. I rolled my eyes.

"You're sure you can let me do this?" I said to Leann. "Because I think I'd do it anyway."

I *liked* the fear in her eyes. "I don't think I could stop you," she said with a reluctant sniff of laughter.

The hint of challenge was enough to make the red mist start to bubble around my feet, creep like eager fingers up my calves with a sickly warmth that begged me to do bad things. My sharp grin felt sinful, and I indulged it for a second before I willed it away to do what fate needed me to do.

"No, Leann, you probably can't stop me. So, enjoy giving in while you can."

With a movement that even I recognized to be a little too much like something from *The Ring*, I was leaning on one knee over her, pushing her back, her eyes blank in their trepidation. Kieran groaned behind us, but I couldn't pay him any mind. Leann's blood was a magnet for me, and I dove into her throat like a murderous machete.

Her scream was too far away, underwater. The instant I tasted her life source, I was nothing but an animal, with no more thought but how to get more.

Until the image swooped on me, and it was all I could do to keep myself from echoing Leann's lingering scream.

I forced myself to continue drinking through the horror I saw. Leann's undead blood was decadent, an exquisite dessert when you'd had too much. Every mouthful was heavenly, but the path to the gate was lined with razor blades. I winced as I swallowed until I couldn't bear it another second.

With a thrust, I jumped off of her, my red shield in angry swirls. I hovered near the ceiling, as far from Leann as I could get, but never would I get away from what I'd seen. Never.

"Get out," I hissed at her, the words erupting through the shield like a bullet.

She sat up like a drunken sex toy of a girl, hair in her face, sticky with her own blood. "Wha—what?"

"Now."

She gaped at Kieran, who said nothing, before disappearing into the night, leaving the door open behind her.

I lowered myself to the floor, my eyes on Kieran, who was pale and shaky. Again, I should have been ashamed that I'd instilled fear in someone so strong, but it felt so *right*. This was how I was supposed to be seen.

It gave me temporary reprieve from what *I* had seen.

"What in blazes just happened, Eliza? You're making me doubt my own sanity."

But now that I was settling down, and the singular image stood in my brain like the Grim Reaper waiting for that final moment, I couldn't look Kieran in the eyes.

"I think should talk to the Master," I whispered.

Softly, he said, "I think you should talk to me first."

I stared at our feet, inches apart, and I let my eyes travel up his body to his face, a mixture of sadness, puppy dog vulnerability, and fierce protectiveness.

I became a little more inhuman in that moment. A little more beaten.

"What did you see in there?" he asked me, head cocked to one side.

My chest could cave in with the weight of my words.

"You. I saw you."

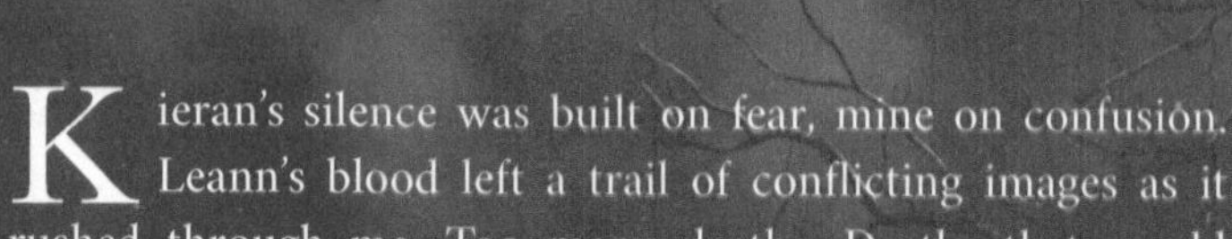

CHAPTER 92

Kieran's silence was built on fear, mine on confusion. Leann's blood left a trail of conflicting images as it rushed through me. Too many deaths. Deaths that would cripple me with loss, fear, and helplessness. Again.

"I wish you'd tell me more about my starring role in your vision before you tell the Master, who neither of us trust or even like." Kieran whispered this in my ear as we stood outside the Master's home, waiting for nothing. He knew we were there, I could feel it.

The Master appeared out of thin air in front of the closed door. "Why say the same thing twice?" he said. "Come inside."

I looked to the woods before going inside. I wanted Izanagi to be there, and he wasn't. Even the original death god ran from the war raging inside me.

"You must start at the beginning," the Master said, pouring tea. "Tell me everything."

I had no choice but to look for guidance, and the Master was it. Izanagi was who I wanted to lead me, but the Master was the one I had to have.

Short version. No time for pomp. "When I drank from my

unmei nashi, I could see the other fate that awaited her. Another vampire."

The Master stiffened, milky eyes growing colder. He nodded, urging me onward.

"And I saw that vampire's other fate, too. What would happen to him if that fate was realized." Still, silence. "I can see the alternative for both *unmei nashi* and the *Shinigami.*"

The Master stared, the cold chill of him radiating around him. He took a sip of tea.

"Why the urgency to tell me this now?" he said a second later.

I gulped, the taste of Leann still in my throat. "Because I just drank from Leann."

"You drank from the young one? A *Shinigami?*" The Master's anger caused the rays of white cold around his body to shiver.

"I did. That's not the problem. The problem is that…" Jesus, was I really going to let this go further than my own mind? I wanted to chain it up in my head and take control of it.

"Tell us, please," Kieran said. I was reminded with perfect clarity why I needed help.

The image jabbed my mind, bursting through the constant stream of swimming visions that I'd learned to block out. But not this one. Not this one.

"I saw Kieran," my voice cracked, "burning. In a pillar of fire, his body consumed in it so all I could see was his outline, bright, brighter than the flames." I could see nothing in the room, only *this.* "He's in there, perfectly still, waiting to—to be *gone.* He doesn't even scream, but his pain is—unthinkable."

Kieran put a hand on my back, soothing *me.*

I couldn't look at him. "There's more," I said to the Master across the table. The world stopped. "Leann is there, just watching. She just watches him burn."

"Her blood showed you that," Kieran said in a small voice.

"Nicholas is there, too, watching," I said, ashamed.

"Nikorasu?" The Master's back straightened even more, the shock in his voice palpable. "He has such power with the cold, but he doesn't stop it?"

I nodded, looking down into my teacup.

"They want me dead," Kieran said.

My head snapped up. "No, I don't think that's—entirely—true." The maliciousness in the vision, a snapshot of jealousy and venomous rage shook me, but it was so strong it was impossible to tell who it came from. I shuddered to think of that kind of hatred coming from my Nicholas, but the memory of him murdering that vampire at Leann's ceremony was vivid. "Anyway, you're safe as long as Nicholas is in New Hampshire."

"Ah, woman, you underestimate me."

"Never." I kept to myself how unnerved I was that Kieran didn't put up a fight in my vision.

He wanted it.

The Master stiffened, opaque eyes cruel. "Nikorasu is the most supreme of death gods, the best of us all. He would never allow himself to be reduced by such cruelty." The cold around him reached for me like icicle fingers. "And I am disappointed that you would believe it possible."

Guilt. More guilt. "I can't believe it either," I said. "But you asked me to tell you everything, and I did. It doesn't have to become truth, but you'd be foolish to think we aren't all capable of that level of viciousness. You're a greater being than that, to be so naïve."

The Master flew to his feet with an icy blast, rage shaking his body.

"What now?" Kieran said out of the corner of his mouth to me.

I rose to my feet, too, but kept my red mist at bay. This was not a time to intimidate.

"Master, you can't admit I'm right because you'd be wrong. Every one of us can change, and the world will change with us, one way or the other. If you aren't a part of that, then the world will eat you alive."

The air between us electrified with our tension, but the Master's chill subsided, leaving a small, ancient man standing alone.

Kieran's warm hand closed around my calf, shooting heat up my leg.

"What is it?" I asked, looking down at his puppy eyes.

"*Unmei nashi.*"

"You? Now?"

Kieran widened his eyes at me. "Yeah, right now, woman. I have to go."

"Can't it wait?" I hissed. But I saw the hollows under his eyes, and knew it couldn't.

The Master sat again. "He must go to his calling, and you must stay here where I can protect you."

"Me? Protect me from what?"

A surge of prideful anger welled in me as I answered my own question.

Leann.

CHAPTER 93

K ieran bolted off with such speed that it burned a black spot into the floor where he'd sat. The Master leaned over the table, and looked at the still-smoking stain.

"Hmph," he said.

I bit my lip to keep from smiling.

After several long moments of me wondering what to do next and figuring out just as fast that I didn't know, I realized that the Master was probably waiting for me to ask him.

"What do we do next?"

His thin shoulders jutted out as he tended the fire, long white hair dangerously close to the flames. "Do you need my help, Eliza?" he asked. Thank God I couldn't see the smirk on his face.

"I do. It's why I came." I had to take my own advice and be willing to change. I went to the Master for help and now I was irritated to have to ask for it. Childish. "I won't let Kieran burn."

The air froze behind him in his movement to me. He stroked his long beard. "Things become clear in battle. We train."

"We train? Now? Will there be a montage? The timing seems incredibly poor."

He ignored me. "You need to shed this shell and see what must be seen. It comes clear when the warrior kicks in the door of civility. You must fight."

I looked down at the clothes I'd been wearing too long. Such things just didn't occupy my mind space as a vampire.

"I'll need to change."

❧

The sparring arena was laid bare, no longer under heaps of snow. As troubled as I was, I was taken aback by springtime newness jumping at my vampire senses like the pirates in that Disney World ride. Enjoyable, but disarming.

The falling petals from the cherry trees had a shushing sound all their own, as loud as the birds singing and the cry of my crows. The silence of the flowers bursting to life was deafening. The brilliant red roofs and intricate scrollwork and symbols that adorned the temple walls wriggled with sentient energy. Wind chimes carried a scent of life that mingled with the scent of death I carried, creating a blissful home where I was both stimulated and comforted.

But there was no time for comfort as I stood toe to toe with a hulking *Shinigami* man, who stared at me like I was an alien. The muscles on his muscles had muscles. His fresh soil skin boasted black symbols tattooed on his neck and bald head. Gold hoop earrings hung from both ears.

And his fear of me was evident in every twitch of his fingers and musculature.

Pink and white petals rained around us. The Master slashed his hand through them silently, signaling for the fight to begin.

I'd never received formal training. I knew none of Nicholas's *katas*, had no long and drawn out smashing of my arms on a wooden dummy or carrying of water buckets for miles. For me, that would all have to come later, if at all. I was different, and my need was urgent. And Nicholas had once told me that to be good at form one had to be good at fighting, but not necessarily the other way around. I didn't question the Master's choice to pit me in a fight without training; I learned best when faced with the impossible.

We bowed, and my opponent began circling me like a wildcat. I mimicked him, curious to see if he would attack first.

His movements were fast, but not as fast as mine, which shocked me, frankly. It's not as if I was physically fit, even with the sparse diet of fish and vegetables. But I blocked one front kick, and a second, before he caught me with a jumping back kick, leaving me sprawled on the ground at least fifty feet away. With an ache in my gut that was definitely going to stick around for a few days, I grunted pulling myself up, only to be pounded back down with a powerful fist.

You really do see stars when you're hit that hard.

I shook it off, but my vision was blurry. My dead heart pounded in my chest with anticipation of the next bout of blows, and my legs ached as if I'd thrown countless kicks, but I don't think I'd thrown even one. I swayed, the multicolored world spinning sickly.

To my horror, the Master barked out the order to continue fighting.

The dark blur came at me, and I threw a wild punch, catching him on the jaw. He stumbled back, giving me a second to regain my sight, but only just. As he tripped over himself, I followed up with a roundhouse kick to his kidney that made my thigh muscles scream with exertion. I knew the names of these kicks, the basic ones, because of Nicholas, but had no idea how to *throw* them. Nonetheless, they worked. The monstrous vampire fell back more, and with every last ounce of power in me, I leaped into the air, the dizzying colors and sounds making my stomach turn, and spun myself into a contorted kick that only an inhuman thing could manage. It landed on his face, knocking him out cold.

When I fell to the ground on one knee, I was seconds from sobbing. Every bone in my body hurt from our brief match. I'd been broken. Lost. Suffering like I'd known when Nicholas and I had parted in New Hampshire, when I couldn't bring myself to eat, or sleep, care that I was cold. Despair that dwarfed my physical agony. Failure. This was one millionth of the pain I'd suffered in my life, made worse because Nicholas wasn't here.

All becomes clear in battle.

That this pain is only a fraction of the pain I had felt in my life and would know in my eternity.

That all my suffering was for a purpose.

That being alone was my strength.

That no amount of suffering was too great if it helped my Nicholas somehow.

That pain was the way I learned and saw what was next. I was destined to suffer for that which consumes me gives me strength.

"Dokkoudou." Izanagi's voice, only for me, from a place deep in the woods. The words reverberated through my bones: The path of aloneness.

I stopped panting, because being out of breath was in my head. My opponent was stirring on the ground in front of me. I knelt by him, and wiped dirt off of his smooth skin, relishing the sensation of every pore under my fingerprints. *So alive, even now...* His eyes flickered open, and he looked at me with an admiration and fear I was growing accustomed to.

"You're terrifying," he said, his voice a booming, thunderous thing. His wide grin made me grin in return.

It felt ridiculous to offer my hand to help up such a giant of a man, but I did it anyway. He laughed and accepted, rising to his feet and shocking me with a bear hug.

I stood beside the Master as we watched my new friend flash out of sight. When he was gone, my knees buckled, and the Master threw one bony arm around my waist.

"Have you seen what you need to see?" he asked softly.

I met his eyes that scared and magnetized me, and knew only respect for him. "Right now, the only thing I need to see is a bed."

~

The pain of Nicholas's absence and my mind-melting visions drove me through more rigorous training over the next few days, much of it with the Master himself. I didn't need to sleep, and was hungry to do something, anything. I stretched when I wasn't sparring, meditated when I wasn't stretching, and watched sparring in between. It took my mind off of Kieran, who I hadn't seen since my confessions to the Master, off of Leann, who was nowhere to be found, and off of Nicholas. But on the fourth day, the battling visions in my head came to the forefront again, wearing me down as much as the physical aches.

"You are pained today. Differently." The Master appeared next to me at the door where I looked out at the fresh life sprouting on the mountain. I breathed every creature's breath in those woods.

Where was Izanagi?

I cracked my neck in an unbecoming way. "I'm just tired," I said.

"Tired and weary are different things." He put his hand on my shoulder. It touched that place inside where kindness makes pain worse. I held my breath to will the tears away.

"Do not fight off how deeply you love," the Master said. His words made my tears spill over. "No one can abandon you as much as you abandon yourself. Do not let Nikorasu become less to you because he is not here."

I turned to him, captivated by how he could read my soul through the chaos of my mind. "I miss Nicholas so much."

"As do I. I always do when he's not here." He sighed, looking out at the rustling leaves, and gave me a rare, endearing smile of uneven teeth. "Few understand what an ancient thing like myself can be passionate about."

"Honestly, I expected you to say something ancienty, like, 'We all share the same Earth and never truly miss each other.' It's nice that you just miss him like I do."

Without a reply, he disappeared and returned with the afghan out of my suitcase. I hadn't taken it out the entire time I'd been in Japan; it felt out of place. But when someone offers me my actual security blanket, it changes things.

"We miss our loved ones most in times of growth," he said as he sat me down on a stack of pillows. "And grow, you have. You've thrown yourself into your training with heart. It is clear you're learning more than just how to fight."

"I have much to fight for," I said quietly. Never mind that the ones I fought for also fought each other.

"You must sleep," the Master said, brushing the hair that fell out of my ponytail away from my neck. I didn't know he could be so loving, and that I could draw such strength from it. But I suppose, had I listened to Nicholas, if I'd seen what he'd tried to show me, I would have known.

"I don't want to sleep," I said. I'd loved a nap in life, but it was such a waste of eternity, and I'd rested plenty. Falling asleep with the warring visions, without Nicholas, hurt like a punched bruise. The pain already gathered in a knot at my throat, and my hand went to it. My companion watched, knowingly.

He said not a word as I ambled to my room in the back of his home, and soundlessly slid the door closed.

CHAPTER 94

Vampire sleep is like drowning in the dark. It took me over, smothered me, until I wanted it.

The Master came in to my room to wake me, silently handing me a glass of water, which I drank with eyes on him. I appreciated the crisp cold of the mountain water as much as blood, so vastly different it was than the tap water in New Hampshire; and *that* water was from a mountain.

There was no way he was getting me to fight. Vampire stamina coupled with *Shinigami* training was doing little for me, it seemed. I'd been death-ray blasted with exhaustion and I needed to sleep forever.

"You have a visitor," the Master said with a little smile.

Kieran.

I shouldn't have wanted him to come to me as much as I did. But Kieran didn't want me to be anything I wasn't, or wasn't yet, or was supposed to try to be. I needed that. I always would.

The Master left my room, and I pulled the blankets up, even though I was fully dressed. I slept fully dressed all the time now, a testament to how much I didn't give a crap about clothes, I guess, or was just so exhausted I didn't care. I watched the door, patting my disastrous hair down, and waited for Kieran.

But it was Paolo who walked in. I hadn't seen him since I returned from feeding on Clara Borden. When he'd all but turned on me to side with the Master.

He gave me a sheepish smile as he closed the door behind him. He'd unnerved me at the temple, digging for information that I didn't want to give, and I sensed an ulterior motive. I hated ulterior motives. Now, he was the boyish, pious, peaceful young man that I'd warmed to immediately upon my arrival. The one that Nicholas had taken under his wing. My trepidation disappeared instantly.

He whisked across the room with more of a whisper than a *snap*, the way Nicholas did. Paolo worked alongside this world, while Nicholas exploded into it. I loved the difference between them, and the friendship they had in spite of it.

Sitting on the end of my bed, he blushed, and dipped his head. We laughed at his shyness together.

"Eliza, I apologize for how I behaved at the temple," he said, his Italian accent more pronounced with his earnestness.

"I was pretty irrational, in your defense."

"And frightening."

"I was not," I said, throwing a pillow at him.

"Oh, yes you were," he said, catching it. His smile turned down, his eyes still on mine. "You must understand, Eliza. You're the closest thing I've seen to a miracle in my existence. I want to be part of it. I want to know what happens next, what it means." His blush returned. "What *you* mean to us all." The gold cross around his neck glinted in a stream of sunlight. He didn't shy away from the beam, like I did.

"Paolo," I said quietly, suddenly shy myself. "I'm hardly a miracle. I'm just different from what you know. And I'm not afraid to be different."

He smiled with infectious hope. "Change is miraculous when you've gone this long without it. You're a symbol of freedom for the *Shinigami* that we were unaware we needed." Springtime came alive in him as he spoke, the cherry blossom scent in the air lifting from his pores, the sunshine from his eyes.

Things were changing because the *Shinigami* wanted them to. I was the change they wanted. So, I told Paolo what I could do, the things I could see.

"Why didn't you tell us after you fed that first time?" The softness of his lips, his smile and demeanor was a comfort I needed.

"It was too raw, too much at stake. This is something in my *soul*, this ability. It's hard to let anyone, you know…see it."

He reached his hand across the bed and held mine, the priest in Paolo clothing. "Part of your gift is in the releasing of it," he said with a gentle smile. "This is your time to let the world see what you're capable of. Your anonymous days are over."

"I'm going to need a beer."

I drank a lot of beer. Not blood beer, Budweiser. I hated Budweiser, and the headache that lived inside the bottle, but it was what the Master brought me.

"I can't believe you drink Budweiser," I said to the Master, the fifth one going down easier than the first four.

The Master took a sip of his own. "It seems in my everlasting old age that only terrible flavors tend to linger."

"Thanks, Master," I said quietly, trying not to hate the vulnerability this showed. "For letting me stay here, for taking care of me."

His eyes didn't seem so terrifying as he looked at me then.

Almost like he had pupils under that creamy haze. "Thank you for seeing past your fear of me," he said.

"I wasn't afraid of you."

Paolo stiffened. So, I'd said the right thing.

"Are you certain that's true?" the Master said with a sideways smile, showing his old man vampire teeth.

"Do you want it to be? Is fear the way you run the show?" I smiled back, the challenge accepted.

"Fear is not a sign of weakness, Eliza. Not admitting it is."

"I don't need to admit what isn't true. You unsettle me, but I'm not afraid." My smirk was jerky, and I shouldn't have done it probably. "Are you afraid of not being feared?"

My heart ached as I pictured Nicholas making a comment about me being better looking, but not as well-spoken as Yoda.

The Master didn't falter. "I am feared by all. But it is change that I fear."

Even I know when to shut up.

I don't know how long the three of us were together, but I do know that I fell asleep with a soundless certainty that didn't trouble me.

Until I woke up.

The Master hovered in my room again, glass of water in hand, smiling pleasantly. So why did I tremble with the fear I said didn't exist for me? He sat on the end of my bed, where Paolo had sat the day before. I'd become no more than an invalid getting hospital visits. "Eliza, you've made me think about things I've not had to consider for a very long time," he said.

Dread snaked into my bloodstream, raced through my skin.

"What exactly might those things be?"

"That those who do not accept change accept death into their hearts. I cannot make that mistake. We will move forward together, Eliza."

"Ooookay."

"I believe you should drink from another *Shinigami*. Let us see what you can see."

The churning of my mist begin inside, ready to create a shield around me.

"I guess I could? But I haven't had any *draw* to anyone since Leann. They only seem to call to me if they have something to show me."

"Eliza, I'm going to ask you a question and I do hope you will answer it. When you fed on the human, did you see which vampire would take her life had it not been you?"

I looked away fast, scared he would learn where Roman was, but I couldn't say why.

"Your apprehension tells me this is your secret to keep. You'll know when it's important."

I had the painful urge to get out of bed and run as fast as I could, run like a human being so every pounding footstep reverberated through my legs, and find Kieran. But I stayed there, not because I was paralyzed with nerves. Not because it was my duty to listen to the Master. Not because I had good reason to trust this man now, if I hadn't before.

I stayed because I wanted to know what exactly the Master had up his sleeve, and how deep the rabbit hole went.

CHAPTER 95

"I 'll leave you to ready yourself for your guest," the Master said.

"Um, yeah. Okay, thank you? I mean, thank you." God, this weird scenario was making me trip over my words and sound like a moron.

Where the hell was Nicholas when I needed him? Right. Babysitting a psychopath.

I washed up in cold water, and opened my mind's eye to Nicholas. It seemed so long since the last time I'd seen him. The cacophony of visions that I couldn't piece together grew louder when I saw him, as if I opened a door to a mob in my head. But I needed him.

His woodsy warmth seeped through me, his peace and strength, his perfect unrest with thoughts of me. He was cutting wood in his massive back yard, out of sight of the cabin. Alone.

I'd spent half my life alone. It wasn't lost on me that once I had Nicholas, I pushed him away, and resented that I'd never be alone in my own head all at once.

I dug a pair of yoga pants and Nicholas's old green sweater

586

out of my spilled suitcase, taking a second to breathe in his scent. I'd washed it out a dozen times, but as a vampire, I could smell him in the fabric faintly again. Peppermint brownies. My whole life breathed a sigh of relief. He wasn't far, no matter how far he was.

Wet hair hanging down my back, I went out to the fireplace where I knew the Master would be, with whoever he'd chosen as my *guest*. They both turned to me as I entered the room. The vampire by the Master's side was full of suspicion and contempt. I didn't know him, and from the way he looked at me, he didn't want to know me.

"I'm Eliza," I said solidly, loud.

"Victor," he said, staring into my eyes. He made me think of truckers in horror movies, if they were glamorized a little. Like a hot actor playing a trucker. Same untouchable attitude.

"Okay, Victor," I said. He didn't flinch when I appeared next to him in wisps of red smoke. "Why you? What do you need from me?"

His Adams's apple rose and fell, and he blinked a few times. My mouth watered at his minimal show of emotion, his vulnerability.

When had I become a predator towards my own kind?

"I need to get away," Victor said, voice like crashing rocks. "Be my drug to get away."

I think he was meant to be *my* drug, but I understood his plea. He needed escape that he couldn't find anywhere else.

I nodded, choked by the sadness in this strong man. His shoulders relaxed, only to tense again when I sunk my teeth into his neck without warning, unwilling to prolong or intensify our friendship. I knew more about him already than I wanted to, frankly. Death god or not, I had only so much capacity for pain.

His blood was oil-thick and *fast* somehow, the speed of a bullet in every molecule. It overwhelmed me with its sheer need in my mouth, like it always needed to be somewhere else, was always looking for the next thing, the next place, the next step away from where it was. Nothing in my life could compare to it.

Grunting with the labor of keeping up with its swiftness, I coughed against his skin. A torrent of blood cascaded down my throat, and as fast as his blood was, the visions he gave me came even faster.

A girl, of course. It was always a girl, wasn't it? *Foster.* Her name was Foster. Blonde braids, running-in-flower-fields fresh, and madly in love with Victor. Her heart nearly exploded as Victor mouthed an apology, and plunged a shard of wood into his chest, eyes locked on hers, not a tear shed in his own. Triumphant, he fell to the ground, his immortal life spilling out of him onto the tile floor. All joy evaporated from the girl's face as she fell to her knees, sobbing, screaming. The screams became groans, the groans became whimpers, and all were replaced by a vengeful howling that spelled revenge, and the souring of a ripened heart.

I didn't have to see her lap up the blood he'd spilled, declaring she would do anything to avenge him, to know that she was able to unleash immense darkness. This was what fate could look like.

Victor slumped in my arms, all his tension gone like I'd given him a massage instead of sucking his blood.

All of his angst had become mine.

I fell back, flat on the floor, living the moment of Victor's death and the blackening of the girl's heart over and over dozens of times a second. The wild images of the anonymous fates that plagued my visions for so long faded, leaving only this perfect image of agony seared my soul.

"What the hell is that?" Victor said, clearly startled.

"Her shield," the Master answered.

"It's fucking weird."

I couldn't see anything, but felt my mist rising, the coolness of morning rain. The sheer crimson enveloped me in a familiar isolation.

Death, my only comfort when left blinded.

"You are not blind. You see with new eyes," the Master whispered in my ear.

"How—"

"Ssshh," he breathed. "You're safe here."

I went cold with the falseness of it.

My internal clock was powered by blood. The only thing that mattered past the abuse my mind took from the visions of Victor was that my body was stronger. My heart had a hummingbird whirr, begging for my body to move anywhere, everywhere. If I could have, I would have imagined over and over all the wonderful things my new immortal body could do, but inside my head fate and death held the reins, and I was lost.

Every. Second. Hurt.

"She's so beautiful."

I was paralyzed and blind, but sensed eyes on me. To be so strong inside an immobile shell terrified me.

Fingers on my cheek. "A beauty of fairy tales. Like Snow White in her glass coffin." It was Paolo.

"She has been this way for two days." The Master. He put down a pitcher of water on the table next to me, I could smell it. My senses were alight, even in this state. But all I could *see* was Victor bleeding out in front of the woman who loved him.

Paolo's breath on my face smelled of waterfalls. "What must she be thinking in there? Look at her eyelids flutter. She can hear us."

"I have tried to hear her, but I cannot. Her mind is a maze with no way out."

The Master left the room, his scent of earth and ancient stones going with him. But Paolo stayed.

"You are not lost, merely finding your way, Eliza," he whispered to me. "*You are* the light at the end of the tunnel."

~

The days came and went, though I only knew because my heart quieted when the daytime creatures went to sleep and the nocturnal ones burst into life. My skin vibrated with every molecule of the world for miles, but Victor consumed my mind, more real than the vampires in my presence. It was only ever the same two; Paolo and the Master.

To push Victor and Foster out of my head was like performing a self-induced lobotomy. The only other thing I recognized was Paolo holding me down, his tears splashing on my cheeks. It was the only thing that made me aware I was still part of something outside of Hell. In tortured desperation, I waded through the quicksand of my brain to pull out a vision of Nicholas.

When I was finally able to scrape back the scar tissue that was my connection to Nicholas, his pain came to me first. It was ever-present, always a dull ache; he needed me and I was too far. He sat on the sofa, feet up on the trunk that served as a coffee table, coffee mug on the sofa arm as usual. Gray sweatpants and a black tanktop with the elegance of a tuxedo, watching *Three's Company*. I missed *Three's Company*. I missed all reruns. I missed leaning against Nicholas's bare arm.

"*Ha. Furley,*" he said with one shake of his head, and sipped his coffee. Old coffee mug, from some other time. The man drinking it from some other time, inserted perfectly into this time.

Just as perfect, the delicate beauty that was Blue swooshed through the kitchen door in a flannel shirt and jeans, carrying her own steaming coffee mug. A movement beyond her caught my attention. That's when I saw fingers clutching the arms of the shabby chair by the fire, holding on like it might get away. Lynch stared into the flames. A never-before-seen five o'clock shadow was almost as dark as his eyes. His hair was disheveled—another first—and he wore *jeans*. Sloppily.

Blood stained his ripped t-shirt, and he was crying.

I wished Nicholas would go to him, sit with at the fire as he would with Roman, but he just watched television. Blue ignored the Abomination as well, sinking herself next to Nicholas, laughing at Jack Tripper.

Their perfection stabbed me, heedless of the blemish across the room, but my pity for Lynch subsided fast. Jealousy bulleted through me, of Blue and Nicholas's comfort, of their togetherness, of their ignorance to the pain so close to them. Jealousy so strong, it drove my mind through the sea of visions to the surface.

"She's waking up!"

The Master joined Paolo at my side.

My eyes stung from lack of use, but I could see again. Paolo pulled me up into his arms. "I prayed every day you would come back to us, and I've been answered."

Leaning back to see his tear-streaked face, I let his purity shove my agitation aside. "Paolo, I heard you when I was—in there," I said. "You helped me not drift away."

He smoothed my hair, the knots rising against his hand. "You cannot drift away. Our miracle."

The Master appeared next to me in a burst of cold energy. "What do you need? How can I help?" Concern had the corners of his mouth turned down, and he was actually fidgeting.

"I think I'm okay," I said, smiling. My face hurt to smile.

"Right now, there's nothing in my head." I laughed awkwardly and couldn't look them in the eyes.

The Master tried to keep me down, but I was desperate to get up and move. "What did you see, Eliza?" he asked, his hand ice cold on my shoulder.

All he had to do was ask, and there it was again, brain-jacking me into a screaming convulsion. Victor, his blood in a pool, and Foster, becoming some other thing, a thing made of revenge and fury. And lurking behind it all, Nicholas, Blue, Lynch.

"No!" Paolo yelled, grabbing me by the shoulders. But the damage had been done. The wild mess of faceless images of fates returned, making a mush out of my thoughts as I tried to weed through them and find something familiar, something I could use. A pigpile of fleeting horrors, overrunning each other, then brought to an agonizing pinnacle by one of Roman, howling with his own madness.

"What do we do for her, Master?" I could still hear Paolo's panic, but nothing was stronger than Victor's blood pulsing through me in electric shocks.

I hoped they could hear when I moaned for Nicholas.

CHAPTER 96

The Master's answer for my madness was to bring me another vampire. And another. And another. Their blood would relieve me momentarily from the deluge of visions, replacing it with only one. Sometimes I found the strength to whisper the details of their fates into their ears, the worst secret there was. The secret that could change their eternity or leave them as powerless as I was.

When I was too weak to speak, the Master found a new way to divulge my thoughts. The gift was inside me, swimming in my blood and heart. And he found his way in.

He drank from me countless times, needling into my veins with his four snake-like fangs, leaving me captive to the horrors in my mind. Singular images of my latest feeds would be replaced once again by random ones in time, and then with those of Roman, and then back to feeding on another of the *Shinigami*. One torment replacing another over and over.

I could hear them sometimes, speaking about me like I wasn't there, the Master and the latest vampire who wanted me to open me like a fortune cookie. I'd always known, I *knew* it, that the Master would use me, and I'd let him do it.

My transformation to vampire made me a sideshow, the bars of my traveling cage my own mind.

Sometimes I heard Paolo, in the low tides of my visions. They ebbed and flowed, letting me hear just what I was missing in the real world, as if the torture wasn't enough. Paolo held my hand, brushed my hair, and for the love of God, he bathed me like an invalid. I could only make animalistic noises to let him know that I recognized he thought he was helping me, but this humiliation… I'd let no amount of kindness cripple my rage, no matter how desperately I needed it. Paolo was the only one who could stop this *torment*, but he didn't. Man of God or not, he didn't.

I wished for Nicholas, that he would sense my anguish across the world. But I learned that this was where our connection met its limit. Kieran's face would blaze in my mind's eye, but not for long. Nothing lasted long in that spiritual and mental chaos. I hoped that Izanagi would come to my rescue again, when I could hope. If I'd been remotely human, rather than that knot of turmoil, I would have missed them. There was no sense of time for me. Days and weeks may not matter when you have eternity, but stealing from the rich is still stealing, isn't it?

"Paolo." The word sounded like a curse, it was so thick and raw on my tongue after my silence.

"My God, I thought I'd never hear you say my name again."

My eyelids fluttered, shards of light blazing into them with each pass. "Why—why can I speak today?" I managed to say.

Paolo's breath was on my cheek as he said, "You have refused to drink in several days," he said.

My eyes stayed open at that. And when they did, I was able to acknowledge the relative quiet in my head, my own presence in it.

"Paolo," I said again, and he smiled, angelic as always. "What do you mean, I refused to drink?"

He stilled, unblinking, breath held. His words pounded like a monster up the stairs in a child's nightmare.

"You have attacked and shielded yourself against all of the *Shinigami* the Master has brought for three days now. You simply would not drink."

My blood sizzled with fury. And my mind was as clear as a crystal stream.

"You mean to tell me," I said, my voice gruesomely threatening, "that I was *fed* vampire blood until my *unconscious* body rejected it through my goddamn coma. You're telling me—that even though I pushed *one* away, that you. Kept. Bringing. Them. To me."

"Not me," Paolo said in a trembling voice. "The Master." This was no saint in front of me, this was a man, who feared for his very existence because of me.

I showered in his terror.

My body rose into the air, my shield pungent with the scent of wine and roses, and the same color. An ache for Izanagi made me angrier. Where was he? Why had he let this happen?

Or had my captors done something to stop him?

I howled with animalistic pain as Paolo cowered from me, backing out of the room.

"No running," I hissed, gathering mist to my chest into a miniature wall. I willed it across the room to stop him in his tracks, dropping the semi-solid wall in front of him. A vibrating, scarlet cube, like a chunk of gaseous blood. Horrifying, and mine. The wall became more liquid in front of Paolo. Droplets of red fell from it to the ground, and with each passing second, the wall transformed more into an erect barrier of pure blood.

It made me buzz with vitality to see.

Paolo's eyes met mine. "Eliza, you don't understand what's been happening here."

"Make me understand," I growled.

He spoke to me like he was pleading with God. "You have suffered for your people immeasurably," he said. "And in your blindness you have opened their eyes." His own eyes glistened with tears, rendering me speechless. He let his fear dissipate, and I understood this trust in me, as vengeful as I was.

I had become his God now.

I pictured myself standing with him, and I was, leaving a path dotted in blood behind me from a dripping shield. He didn't flinch. The Master's outline stood in the door behind Paolo, and I thickened the red wall with a fast focus of my eyes, to keep him where he was.

Paolo took my hands in his own; I stiffened at the touch. "The vampires of this mountain can see their options through your blood. You've given us choices we have never had."

My thick, misty shield faltered around me, dulling to a shade of weak pink.

My gift was to give options to the rest of my kind. And to take my own away?

"The *Shinigami* can see what will happen if they don't kill their *unmei nashi?*" I asked.

Paolo nodded, eyes welling more.

"I've given them the ability to be judge and jury. Nobody should have that kind of power."

"But you do. This is what you were chosen for, because you alone can lead us down the right path!" He swallowed hard, eyes spilling over. "Show us the impact of our blind decisions. We see the path in front of us. Because of you."

"And those who are choosing not to feed? Are they sick?" Pictures of Nicholas made me close my eyes. Nicholas's shoulder blades jutting out from under loose thermal shirts. Nicholas's eyes ringed in black. Nicholas's hair, dull in the sun that he had to shy away from. A race of withering gods, all because of me.

Paolo let out a laugh that reeked of disbelief. "They are not! They are as well as they ever were! It's a miracle, Eliza."

"What?" How could that be? How had I done that? The answer dawned on me behind a sickening red glare.

The wall of red that held the Master out, the most powerful vampire of us all, fell to the ground and disappeared in evaporating droplets of blood. The Master came inside, his soulless eyes on mine.

"It's been you, all along," I said. "You made them believe they had no choice. And when they saw another way, you lost your power over them."

Paolo and I watched the old man expectantly.

"Is this true, Master?" Paolo asked.

"The *Shinigami* needed a leader. I am that leader. You need someone to guide you, your powers are too great to be left to your own devices. I am that guide. You needed a deity to rest your faith in and give you meaning. I am that deity."

The mist boiled around me as I spat, "Izanagi is that deity. He created the *Shinigami.* Where is he?!"

The Master didn't answer, but Paolo did. "You needed to be alone."

"*You* saw Izanagi?" I asked. Things became clearer and clearer, and I hated it. "When you trusted in me, more than him," I shot a look at the Master, "Izanagi showed himself to you." I seethed with anger, wondering who else had been kept from me. "And Kieran? Has he been trying to see me?" I almost asked about Nicholas, but if he wanted to find me, nothing would stop him. Nobody could.

"Kieran is an upstart who has no place with you," the Master said icily.

"And I suppose my place is here, in a coma, being experimented on to see how much I can take?"

Paolo answered. "The Lord will not give you more of a burden than you can handle."

The room pulsed with my anger, the walls buzzing. "*The Lord?* You'll put your faith in anyone that doesn't make you accept responsibility for your own choices, won't you?"

He gaped, his heart pounding. I could feel it in my own, how deflated he was by my words. I meant them.

"I accept one thing," he said, tears thick in his voice, shoulders sagging. "I would follow anywhere you led me."

My knees grew weak, but I held myself up. This could not be my undoing. "You would want me, diminished, weak, barely alive, Paolo?" I said, shaking my head.

"I would want you any way I could have you," he said levelly.

"My God," I said. What else could I say?

The Master snickered, an ugly thing.

"When Nicholas finds out what you've done, he'll find a way to kill you," I said, snarling.

"Still a fool," the Master said with a laugh. "Nikorasu loves us both. You are the one who would make him choose. I have kept you alive because he needs you. He'll see that through your hatred of me."

I thought the Master had begun to care about me. I still saw it now, despite his cruel words, his terrible actions.

"You have your own reasons for keeping me here," I said softly. "Please, just let me understand what the hell all this is," I pleaded, blood tears masking my eyes. I couldn't hold them in anymore. The things that had been taken from me, the things I'd caused. "I don't want to disappear in my own head anymore," I said, my voice barely audible through the cracks.

The Master waited a long time to answer, and Paolo was dying to speak, I could see his jaw working. How hard was this going to be to hear?

"Shall I tell her or will you?" Paolo said, staring at me, through me. "I cannot see her suffer her ignorance any longer." And no matter how depraved, a rush of love for him flooded me at that moment, for the suffering he'd endured in his own way.

The Master sighed, and flashed across the room to sit in a chair by the window. The sun lit his face up, making him almost translucent. An ancient man with too many secrets.

"Nikorasu is my son in my heart. Everything I do is for him."

I nodded. Because I knew love could make a person do ugly things.

"Jenniveve came to me this winter," he said. I sucked in my stomach. I'd never wanted to hear her name again.

"Go on," I said. Paolo took my hand, but I pulled it away.

"She was a terrible creature, and more terrible with age, but she loved Nikorasu as much as a soul like hers could love anyone. She was desperate, and still my child. I couldn't fathom her pain to see Nikorasu, as filled with light as he is, taken away from her. She's never known anything but the darkness of her own heart." He focused on me, and the room went cold. I pretended not to notice. "Her pain at seeing you in his home, what you meant to each other, spun her into a world that no one should have to endure. I could not say no to her, my creation."

Mother of Christ, if I didn't despise myself for understanding.

"What did she ask you to do?" I asked. But I knew.

"Kill you, of course."

Paolo sat in the middle of the floor, drained. My heart went out to him. Compassion for people who would torture me.

"I was aware of you from the second Nikorasu found you, you know," the Master went on. "When you didn't know what you were, I did. I knew you would change everything I'd created." He smiled, and I smiled back. I still can't believe I did it. "I am a god to these people, but I am just an old man, Eliza. I fear change."

His admission sent more tears cascading down my cheeks. Emotion I'd held back in life knew no restraint once my mind had been opened, once I saw too much.

"Jenniveve and I both only wanted things to stay the same. I know no other life than this one. I would fight for it until the end of time. So, Jenniveve stayed quiet as long as she could, and—"

Paolo's sob broke through the Master's sentence, stopping my own tears. I was wracked with suspicion. Conspiracy.

When Paolo spoke, he could only look at the floor. "I didn't ask why they wanted my help," he said, trance-like. "I'm not one to question my God, no matter what form He takes. When the Master asked me to find a way to end you, I saw my purpose here, finally. But fate's plan for you was bigger than me." He looked up at me, eyes dry, but his heart broken. "You were invincible in my soul. How could I resist such a miracle? I love you," he finished with a sad laugh.

I fell to the floor next to him, unable to fight with myself anymore. I held him and he held me back like I was the only thing that mattered in the world. For him, I guess I was.

Looking over his shoulder at the Master, I asked, "Why did you kill Jenniveve, then?"

The Master cocked his head. "Because even I know when I am wrong."

CHAPTER 97

I asked to be alone, and they both left in silence. Seconds later, a heat emitted from the other side of the door so strongly that I pulled the blanket over my eyes, like that would stop me from burning. The shoji door went up in flames, incinerating in seconds. The door frame smoldered, the metal lamp near it melting into a deformed thing. My heart nearly exploded with hope and more joy than I thought I would know again.

Kieran was coming for me.

He appeared in the smoking doorway, his eyes a rippling orange, his skin vibrating with a radioactive energy that resonated in my bones.

"Eliza." Words in a wisp of smoke, Irish whiskey-scented longing.

I exploded across the room in a magician's burst of red death clouds, my emotions strangling me. I threw myself into his arms, our skin sizzling, a hiss between us.

I would heal from that. I could not heal without his arms around me.

He buried his face in my hair, I wound my fingers into his.

We held on like both of us would burn forever without this moment.

"I'm so sorry," he whispered in my ear. My stomach clenched at his unnecessary guilt.

I moved my head as much as I could from his grip. "What could you possibly be talking about?"

"I left you here to find my *unmei nashi*, for god forsaken *blood*, and I couldn't get back to you." He held me so tightly that I could feel burn marks on his skin under his t-shirt. I tried not to cry. What had he done to himself? "Jesus, Eliza, I'm sorry I wasn't strong enough to save you."

Running my hands over his back, the heat jumped under my fingertips, making sparks. "This had to happen to me. Fate led me this way," I said.

He took me by the arms. "Don't let them own you any more than you have to."

The Master appeared behind him, and I glared over Kieran's shoulder, clenching my teeth at the onslaught of visions that came with him. I spoke over them, doing all I could to hide the pain.

"I will have this time with Kieran. You've kept him from me long enough." I held Kieran closer. Holding Kieran at that moment was as good as taking my life back, whether or not it gutted me with guilt.

Kieran released me and spun on the Master, smoke rising from his shoulders, his t-shirt growing holes where it burned. "She is no puppet. She's not your second coming, and she won't be your salvation. She is a woman with more fire in her spirit than you deserve to be witness to, and I will not be kept from her again."

The depth of Kieran's feelings for me came to life in his words, and my soul ached to hear it. Partly because I knew it would never become anything, and partly because I felt the same way.

"You are the embodiment of destruction that cannot be allowed to touch her," the Master said.

My anger might burn me alive, too. "Why not, Master? So you can *protect* me?"

"You need no protection, Eliza," the Master said. "He needs to leave you because you belong to Nikorasu."

An image of Nicholas, meditating in the spring sunshine by the fish pond in New Hampshire blazed in my mind. But I could still see Kieran through its vibrancy.

"I don't care what your reasons, I won't be enslaved for you or any greater good. You'll be lucky to survive my leaving here." I squeezed Kieran's hand and we brushed past the Master.

"We can't just walk out, Eliza," Kieran whispered.

"Why not?"

"Well, lass," he said, scratching his head with his free hand, face scrunched up. "I amassed myself quite a crowd on my way over here. Seems the townspeople knows their princess has awoken."

Sure enough, outside the door a throng of vampires stared back at me. Some cheered, some hissed. Others cried tiny rivers of blood.

"What the hell—"

The Master stood beside us, looking out at the *Shinigami.* "They need your guidance, Eliza. You're here to provide them with it."

"I'm not their leader," I spat. "You are, right? Self-proclaimed."

Kieran cleared his throat. "Leaders are chosen, Eliza. You've done something for them that the Master can't undo," he said, nodding to the crowd.

I looked at the *Shinigami*, really looked at them, all of the faces I'd become familiar with. Others that rarely came out of the shadows of their mountain dwellings. They all wanted the same thing from me, even the ones that resented me for it. They all wanted to know what happened next.

The recognition of their need caused a volcano of a rupture inside me, an explosion of fates. All at the same time.

I screamed, digging my fingernails into the sides of my head, and so help me God, if I could have ripped my brain right out, I would have. Kieran's arm held me up, searing me with its heat.

Fate would take this last person from me—myself. Not part of this world, but a conduit.

"Bloody hell, Eliza, can you hear me?"

"Kieran, get the vampires away from here," the Master said.

"You get them away from here. I won't leave her side."

The Master's presence left the room, but it would take more than that to dispel the *Shinigami* that wanted me.

Not me. My visions. They didn't care if *I* lived or died.

"Crooooooows," I groaned.

Through my closed lids I saw the swift shadows descend the instant I needed them. The vampires cried out in alarm, my senses clearing as they sought cover.

"Well, okay then," Kieran said. "We'll fix this, Eliza," Kieran breathed, his hand under my head as I lay on the hard floor. "I won't let you get lost again." He kissed my forehead, searing and tender.

I wished I could scream for Nicholas to come. Then through my selfishness, I remembered that when Nicholas came back, my vision could become reality; Kieran would burn. And here I couldn't unburden myself of this slide show of images that meant nothing, when I needed to help what did mean something.

As the visions dragged me under again, I wished I could burn in Kieran's place.

CHAPTER 98

As long as Kieran held my hand, I could sense the world around me, but as soon as that warmth was gone, so was I; inside the nightmare world fate had built for me, plagued with lives I couldn't control.

The nightmare outside of my head didn't seem to be much better. Kieran would only ever leave my side to fend off *Shinigami* trying to force me to drink from them. Dozens of them, thundering in my brain before I heard them. Each one had a calling to an *unmei nashi;* and each vampire wanted to know if they were killers that made things better, or just killers. Vampires, waiting for me to make them heroes or monsters. Their faces swam in front of me in a scarlet haze, with a backdrop of hellish images of death: rape, torture, dreams unfulfilled, terrors unleashed because one death god made a choice. I was glad I couldn't hear my own screams.

Every time Kieran returned to me and took my hand, the world flooded back, adding to the things squeezed into my mind until I prayed for my existence to end, any way it could.

Only one could calm my butchered soul. When he arrived,

I couldn't be angry that he didn't come before, my need for him was too great.

"Izanagi."

His name was a sigh of relief on my lips, the only thing I was able to say.

"Jesus, you spoke," Kieran said. "I don't know where he is, Eliza, I can't find him."

"He's here." My voice sounded scorched, like I'd been burned at the stake. The people's heretic.

"What? Oh! Mother of Jesus!"

My old friend, death, in the flesh. Wine-soaked sorrow, wilting roses, the end of things, here. The one thing I knew better than anything else—loss. Tears dried on my cheeks as the scent enveloped me once again.

That which consumes me makes me stronger.

Izanagi whispered in my ear, words with the impact of an avalanche. "You are not what fate would make you."

And life inundated me with a deafening rush of his blood, washing away the poisonous images at once. He tasted of overripe fruit and the beginning of the world. A musty richness of something that has lived too much life, and is more beautiful for it.

Izanagi's blood took away the hateful roar that made me nothing, and brought back the god in me.

I flew to my feet, my heart thundering with blood, a sheen of silky red over my eyes. I wanted to see nothing but Kieran and Izanagi. Kieran, perfect in his imperfection as always. Dirty jeans, plain black t-shirt, twenty-four hour shadow, knuckle tattoos bared as he clenched his fists with worry. Izanagi didn't belong in the same room, and there was nowhere better for him to be. Pristine *hakama* pants, bare feet, bare, smooth chest. Glistening midnight hair in a topknot, sword hilt visible behind it. One sob broke free of me, and I grabbed Izanagi first, holding him to me like he wasn't a supreme being, but a man. A man who'd known me when no one else did. A man who would always understand when I was disintegrating, and would bring me the darkness that completed me.

"I failed you," Izanagi said into my ear.

I pushed him off to look into his black eyes. I didn't ask why he hadn't come before, I didn't need to know. "My life isn't yours to save. You came when you could." I kissed him on the forehead, like an equal.

Kieran stood hunched a few feet behind him, hands on his knees, looking at the ground, panting like he'd just finished running. My Kieran, always running.

A ghostlike flood of red swarmed around my feet, propelling me towards Kieran. No time passed before my hands were on his warm, stubbly face, our lips brushing. I squeezed my eyes shut against the thought of him invisible in a nest of flames.

He rested his forehead on mine, hands on my cheeks, and we were alone. Without regret, without future or past. "Thank you, Kieran."

"Never thank me for my selfish needs, woman. I needed to be here more than you needed me here." He cast his eyes to the floor, one hand knotted in my hair, like it was the only thing that kept him from fading away.

"I'll repay you, Kieran. What I saw won't happen. I won't ever let you burn."

I hated what I saw in his eyes. The thing that happens before defeat, that voluntary hopelessness.

The two of them looked so utterly *inferior*, like they'd accepted failure. Two of the most magnificent beings I had ever known.

"Both of you, look at me," I said slowly, red mist a raging tornado around me, holding me steady while the world trembled. "You've been unerringly loyal to me, and if you think I'll let you wither into some depression because you didn't get to me fast enough, you're goddamn wrong. There's more than one way to be by my side. Because of you both, I'm stronger than I've ever been. Fate will try to destroy us from the inside out, all three of us. It doesn't stand a chance against me. I won't let either of you down. Just like you've never let me down."

Something was consuming them both, and I prayed I wouldn't have to choose between the people in my vision to save them.

All becomes clear in battle.

"Now. I need to fight."

CHAPTER 99

I needed to fight because immortal or not, love could always be taken away from me. I needed to fight to understand who I was fighting for and against. The image of Kieran burning alive, the realization that Izanagi depended on me, the distance from Nicholas, all of it fought with my own changing heart.

I needed to fight because the person that might let it all go was me. All it would take was one…wrong…move. One second of hesitation. One poor choice.

My blood senses awoke the world for me. The sparring arena was filled with more springtime beauty than I wanted to see; none of it was on fire. I wanted that fire. I wanted to face it in real life, not in my head. I was ready for it to pick on someone its own size. Instead I was faced with a flurry of falling cherry blossoms and singing birds, while in my mind were burning trees and screeching crows.

Its timeless peace warred with the change that was coming, and it felt like a lie.

In the center was Paolo, meditating, trying to grasp a higher meaning I wasn't sure existed. My higher meaning stood next to me, stronger than the mountain itself, the god who created it all, while Kieran leaned against a pillar, pulling a crumpled cigarette from his back pocket. I grinned at how much he looked exactly like he had that first day I saw him, right in this same spot.

With a smile, I left them both to watch me. I flashed across the arena, and sat cross-legged with Paolo. We didn't look at each other.

"Kind of a shitty day. Want to spar?" I said.

He laughed, a despairing thing. "Love to."

We stood in a single motion, and faced each other. My breath caught. With Izanagi's blood in mine, Paolo's eyes were warmer and sweeter than usual. So full of faith. In me, in God. A trust I longed to have.

This was one vampire that was more dangerous than I'd realized.

We bowed, our friendly smiles never leaving each other. My speed dizzied me as I bolted across the ring and threw a series of punches and kicks in a blur. I was stronger than before, but Paolo's unhurried strikes nearly matched me. We laughed, reveling in each other's strengths, and it felt like diving into cool water to be with him. This was what balance felt like. I never wanted to stop until I finally crumpled to the ground dramatically, exhausted, sore and sweaty with a pink sheen on my skin. I tapped the ground.

"I'm done," I gasped through a smile, my hair spreading around me in the dirt. "You've made your point."

Paolo laughed heartily. "What was it?"

"Eliza weak. Paolo strong."

He sat next to me again, full circle. "You're far from weak, my dear," he said, rubbing his chest and wincing. "I've been too afraid to spar with you since you arrived. Nicholas was right—even as a human, you could have laid me out." His face was as friendly as the first time we'd met, like we were at a wedding or something, not like we'd just exchanged blows. Not like he wanted me for himself. Not like we were just showing each other that everything was okay between us despite that he'd helped trap me, that he was challenging his own faith; not like everything was going to change even more than it already had. He was still an ointment to my emotional wounds. The odd part was, even with all that had happened, I still seemed to soothe him, too.

He stood and pulled me to my feet with an outstretched hand. We stood face to face, two priests of different churches.

"I don't want to change anything except the ability to change," I said, a meaning that came from the blood inside. "It's all any of us really want." I glanced behind me at Izanagi, and saw to my surprise, the Master not far behind him. I kept my eyes on them as I said, "We're death gods, Paolo. We shouldn't only be able to change, we should initiate it. We should not be denied choice."

My own choices were ganging up on me, but I refused to be powerless against them.

Kieran swaggered over to us, flicking the cigarette butt and incinerating it in the air with one look. *He could do that?*

Kieran didn't stop until he'd pulled me to his body and kissed me with a fervor that I didn't think I could survive. His hands on my hips, bending me back, not questioning if I was his to have, the taste of rebellion on his lips, complete control of his lack of control.

I lost myself in his lips, my heavenly blood coursing into every sinew, to take in every molecule of his love. Letting him know I was filled with it, too.

It lasted for as long as I could stand it. Eternity isn't for all of us. I pulled away, aware of Paolo's eyes on us, but Kieran pulled me back again, his fingers digging into my skin.

"This," he said into my lips, "is what love feels like. Letting go, and taking back. A burning inside that won't stop." He pressed his lips to me harder until they stung. "Burn with me, Eliza, until I'm all you breathe."

I nipped his bottom lip, tasting a speck of blood that made my dead heart pound. I groaned, and pulled away, afraid. A predator with a heart as full as mine was the worst kind of animal.

A white glimmer appeared in the air around Kieran, distracting me. I squinted and watched it hover by his shoulders, cling to the tips of his mussed up hair, then to the dirt at our feet. I got a chill and saw it on the sleeves of my shirt.

Frost. Sticking to me, melting right off of Kieran.

Hair whipped into my mouth, across my eyes, as I tried to find the only thing missing. My mind's eye opened to search for him. Gasping and sobbing, I focused, desperate to find where he was in the real world.

I spun to see the top of the great stone stairs, and found Nicholas. A white flurry raced around him in his own personal hurricane. His dark curls, black wool coat and swirling eyes were just visible to my own preternatural ones behind the storm from inside him.

In a white streak, Nicholas was inches from me. Traitorous wretch that I was, I threw my arms around his neck, inhaling the smells of home. He was so cold to the touch, and stiff.

He didn't return my embrace.

"I couldn't stay away any more," he said dryly.

I pulled back, ice snapping from my arms. His caramel and chocolate eyes that I'd dreamed of, that I couldn't bear to see in visions, were sedentary and sludge-dark. His neatly trimmed beard didn't hide the clench of his jaw, lips pursed, chin up, shoulders back.

"Nicholas," was all I could say.

He swallowed, but didn't blink. Didn't falter. "I hated every second. Every second of my life without you. I listened to your heartbeat from halfway across the world." He punched his chest, breathing in through his nose. "It never left me, no matter how far I was."

He didn't have to say any more.

"Nicholas, I'm sorry."

"There is such a thing as self-fulfilling prophecy. You never believed I could want you forever, and you worked your hardest to make it true, didn't you?" he spat, turning on me to look at Kieran.

"No, God, no, please."

The image of Kieran burning crashed in my mind, making me stumble. But goddammit, I would not take my eyes off Nicholas.

The Master appeared next to me, and put his hand on my shoulder, holding me up with his infinite strength in this small gesture. It snapped me back.

"Nikorasu," he said. "You don't know what she's been through."

"She made me leave!" he shouted, pointing at me.

"It was necessary. She couldn't breathe enough to see what she needed to see. She needed to see it alone."

"She wasn't alone much," Nicholas said.

"Watch it, man," Kieran said, raising his hand up. "That woman's heart beats only for you."

I squeezed my eyes shut, itching to close myself off, my heart stiffening against Nicholas's accusations. "That's not true," I said.

When I opened them, all eyes were on me. It was then that I saw Blue and Leann at the edge of the ring. I wanted to cry out and throw my arms around Blue, but her face showed me it wouldn't be welcome. She shook her head at me in disappointment. And the idiot I am, I was blind with jealousy that she'd been with my Nicholas, when I hadn't been. Leann stared at me blankly, as unknowable as ever.

"Nicholas, my heart bleeds with how desperately I love

you. But Kieran," I glanced at him, the innocent rebel that he was, "sees me another way. He helps me break free. No desperation. I love him for it."

The heat from Kieran was the only thing to stop the world from freezing when Nicholas heard those words.

"And Nicholas," I said, crawling inside myself with every revelation. "I know where Roman is."

"No," he said, shaking his head. Blue rushed to his side and took his hand when it looked like he would lose control. My sharp look at her was enough to make my shield extend from my open palms and the bottoms of my feet, fluid like blood, light as air. I didn't try to reel it in.

"You'd keep that from me?" Nicholas whispered.

I wasn't going to say I had to. It was my choice. "I did. He didn't want you to know, Nicholas, and if I told you, you wouldn't have gone to New Hampshire."

"Why are you doing this?" Blue said, squeezing Nicholas's hand tighter. The mist became a solid thing.

"Because now that Nicholas is here, I can see what happens next." The swarm of visions that plagued me were gone, and now with him here in front of me, I saw what they'd covered up. "You have to go to Roman, Nicholas. You have to go, and I can't come with you."

The Master seemed to grow bigger in my peripheral vision. "You will not leave Nikorasu for *this*," he said, nodding his head at Kieran.

"Tell me how you really feel," Kieran said.

"Blue is going with him," I said.

It was Nicholas's turn to look apologetic. "Eliza, things aren't like that with us, and you know it."

"I do know it," I said with a sad smile for him. "But Roman needs you, and I know he needs her, too," I said, smiling tightly at her. "I'll be waiting for you, Nicholas. But our paths have to part again. Not just because fate says so, but because I need to work through my own heart." The mist swirled around me, wrapping me in its comfort. Blood welled in my eyes, tears I couldn't hold back.

"No!" the Master roared. We all stared at him, unsure which of us he was angry at. Big surprise, it was me. "You will not send away the only one who knows what I'm worth here! You will not take over this place, *my* place! You will not stay here to replace me and destroy what I have built. You will not stay here to abandon Nikorasu for the Irishman! You will leave, and you will leave with the man who loves you."

"He's right," Kieran said. "You belong with Nicholas, and as long as I indulge your finer tastes, you won't love him the way you should."

"This isn't about you, Kieran," I said gently. "I've seen the alternative, and this is what has to be done. Nicholas leaves. Blue goes with him."

"It doesn't matter what you've seen, dear heart," Kieran said, next to me with his hand on my cheek. "I see your heart, and I cannot live without it. You may leave me, but I will never leave you."

Nicholas was to my right. Leann had found her way to my left. Kieran between them both. When he stepped back, it would be exactly the way I'd seen it. Fate's fingers were clawing down my back. My vision was coming to life.

"No," I whimpered, blood tears thick on my cheeks.

"Ssssh, lass," Kieran whispered, kissing me swiftly on the lips. Cold blasted me from Nicholas's side. "If I had a purpose in this life, it was served the moment I found you. There's nowhere for me to go from here, Eliza. I can't let you go, and I won't watch you stay."

"You listen to me, Kieran. You told me that which consumes you gives you strength." I swallowed, but the pain was still there. "If your love for me consumes you, *let me give you strength.*"

"Keep giving and you'll have nothing left. Don't do that again," he said with a grim smile. He took his hands from my face, and backed up, eyes still on me, but all I could see were the flames waiting to engulf him.

Cinders crackled under his feet, and I sobbed again. They licked up his legs, his arms, tore through his body. He made not a sound.

"Nicholas!" I pleaded. "Please, stop him!" But Nicholas's fury had him staring back at me blankly. In a billow of red mist I rose from the ground and flew to him, grabbing him by the shoulders. "Don't let my choices keep you from doing what's right. Please," I begged.

"How much betrayal should I take before you don't ask me for favors?" Nicholas said to me. Of all the coldness I'd seen from him, never had I been so frozen. I turned my back on him.

"Leann," I said as calmly as I could while Kieran's body burned to ash. "Show me why you're here. There's a reason."

"What reason do I have to save someone who wants nothing to do with me?" she said, sneering.

"He's your *shugotenshi!* Please, don't watch this happen. Make something better happen."

"I owe you nothing."

"Please!" I screamed, but nobody was listening. I looked at Paolo, who looked back at me with wildly anxious eyes, shaking his head. Nobody could or would help, and Kieran didn't want it anyway. The orange streaks reached for the clouds, the air crackling around Kieran's body, invisible in the inferno.

A deep hum filled the air out of nowhere, and Izanagi materialized in front of the flames with an electric blue shield around him that pulsed with bolts of ice cold lightning, freezing the ground instantly and the feet of all those who stood on it. The trees above turned glassy with ice.

The flames around Kieran dimmed ever so slightly. This was what hope looked like.

"You!" The Master howled through the air at Izanagi, knocking him to the side with his staff, letting it fall to the melting ground, while the flames grew. The two *Shinigami* erupted, becoming what gods of death were meant to be; enormous, too terrifying to look at. They took to the sky, their bodies assuming translucent shapes, cloaked in the apparitions of dragons that consumed the sky, too otherworldly to look at or understand. Shimmering, thundering, ghostly fire poured from their mouths, their monstrous claws shredding one another. Destruction greater than time.

And Kieran burned.

The red mist wailed like a possessed tornado, lifting me higher into the air than I'd ever been. I twisted my arms in a circle over my head in an ancient dance that I couldn't know, spinning red mist like the twirling scarves of a bellydancer. Izanagi battled with the Master, and I summoned his blood inside me, feeling it bubble, rupture, until it spouted from my fingers, twisting blood streams into the raging red wind. Rivulets of blood splattered the sky and hung suspended, until there was no more mist, only a whirlpool of pungent blood. Airborne over Kieran, the blood rained upon his flames.

His fire hissed and bit at the sky, dwindling.

Kieran's face, scorched black, looked up at me from beneath, more afraid of me than the flames that destroyed him.

"Don't leave me," I whispered through my storm.

The notion of losing him, of losing anyone else, plowed into my heart, and my fountain of blood overwhelmed the sky, cloaking the spring newness in my abandonment. My very own gift of isolation, working my will. The Master and Izanagi stopped tearing each other apart with ghostly claws.

When my power exceeded both of theirs.

The wretched *aloneness* ate through me as the embodiment of it fought his own battle with the Master, his presence the most comforting threat that I loved to despise. I screamed, and mist the color of warfire, the odor of wine and roses, poured from my mouth, taking with it all of my horror at being left without Kieran, without Nicholas. Being *me*, alone. The red cloud tore itself apart, like my heart, the explosion of it transforming into hundreds of blood-sculpted crows, blind and screeching. Their liquid wings created a deafening wind, pouring my life's desolation into the air with every beat. I spread my arms wide, torrents of blood thrashing around me, and with another scream I felt my skin stretch, blood being ripped from it like hooks into my flesh, curdling into another flock of bloody crows, taking my emptiness with them.

Fueled by the desolation that lived in me, their wings pounded the air, and nothing could be mightier. They would all feel how I felt.

Kieran's flames of self-destruction extinguished below.

The Master recovered from his shock when he saw, and sped towards Kieran, his dragon form dissipating into the hellishly determined vampire, leaving Izanagi behind in my recoiling shield.

Leann flashed to the ring of embers, screeching like an eagle, and met the Master with his own *bo* staff, driving it into his heart, straight through his body. Impaled, and sputtering, he asked for only one thing before his body stopped moving.

"Nikorasu."

And then he vanished, like the ghost of the world he'd made.

CHAPTER 100

W hen you hunger for the death of things, and it gets delivered, you think it will be a weight from your conscience. A wintry kiss on scorched skin that brings newness by utterly destroying the ruin that came before it.

I didn't know it would show me how much I'd decayed.

We weren't heroes. We were birds of prey, and the world was our carrion.

Nicholas wouldn't or couldn't speak to me. He'd try, in an empty monotone, but never finished a sentence. I couldn't know what trumped what—his disappointment and anger at me, or his grief for the Master. It was an awful reflection of myself not so long ago, and the hollow that Kat left inside me.

Maybe Nicholas was just like the rest of us; afraid of what would come next.

Two days had passed. With the Master gone, I expected the birds to be quiet, the trees to stop moving, but apart from the silence of the *Shinigami*, spring bloomed as usual. Vampires left the mountain to pursue *unmei nashi*; I refused to exchange blood with them, to give them a choice.

What had choice ever done for me?

As a matter of fact, I was making another bad choice right at that moment. I slid open the Master's door, noticing immediately how *missing* he felt. But the place wasn't empty.

I cringed as I sat next to Nicholas in front of the fire. I could only see Kieran's face in the flames.

"You pulled me apart in so many ways, I don't know if I can put myself back together," Nicholas said.

I straightened my back and looked at him, even if he couldn't look back. I'd deserved no better than to watch him unravel.

"You deserve more than apologies, but the only other thing I have to give you is my blood. You need it for your trip," I said.

"I can't go anywhere, and I don't want to taste you."

My heart stopped. "Nicholas, I get that you don't want to let him go," I said, motioning to the room that was all Nicholas had left of the Master. "But I've seen what you need to do, and there are reasons for the choices I make."

"You had a reason for Fire Boy, did you?"

"I have a reason for most things," I whispered.

He turned to me with a set in his jaw and a darkness in his eyes I didn't like. "So, tell me, prodigy. What plans have you made to get me out of your way this time?"

"It's not like that. Exactly. Look, I needed you to leave because I felt as much as you did that we were waiting for something to happen. I didn't know that the something was going to be me imprisoned by the Master, or that Kieran would be the one to come for me. But if I've learned nothing, I've learned that fate guides us, but it's up to us to decide what to do with it."

"And what you decided to do was push me away. You *took* from me. You knew where Roman was. You took the Master from me. And you took you."

"All true. But I won't apologize anymore, it's what I had to do. Not because it was written in the stars or whatever...but Nicholas, before you I went my whole life without feeling, and then, then..."

"When I had to do something, I didn't. I didn't because of what it would do to you."

"You're going to make this about Kat?"

"Isn't it always? She's all you see when you look at me. Now you'll only see that I would have let Kieran burn."

My mouth went dry. "That's in your heart, not mine. You have to go, Nicholas. It all falls in place like the world's suckiest puzzle," I blurted. "We need to heal from what we've done to each other, and we can't do it holding hands. You can feed from me first." *Please say you will.*

He put his head down. "It can be a terrible thing, when your taste lingers," he said slowly, like each word hurt. "Like waiting for the world to end one second at a time." He looked up at me, eyes filled with sorrow. "You've made me wonder if change is the worst thing that can happen to us. Just looking at you makes me think of what we've both lost. We've made monsters of each other."

My throat constricted, and the pain I'd long since forgotten, that connection between us, threatened to take me.

"You told me you'd love me after I became—*this.*"

He looked at me, and I knew he was seeing the blood and the crows, the storm, and that he didn't recognize me. "It's the person you were already that hurt me this way."

I hated being ashamed. "I'm sorry about Kieran." My voice cracked. "My reasons don't always make sense, even to me, and I won't blame my choices on fate. Fate gave me options, but my choices were mine." There was no more for me to say about the things I'd done and hadn't said. It was time for change. "You have to go to Roman now."

"Roman," he said, running his hands through his hair. As much as he didn't want to leave the Master's place behind, he desperately wanted his brother. The notion that I could be successful in making him go was a debilitating success. So, I continued.

"Roman's blood will restore you once and for all, and fix his mind in the meantime. And when he's done fixing you, and needs a new reason to hide and brood, Blue will be there to drag him out."

"Blue?"

I nodded, smiling weakly. His heart pounded, reminding me of all the times he gazed at the spot where my heart beat for him. I took his hands, and held them over my heart, hoping he would feel how much it belonged to him no matter what came between us.

"I'm yours forever, and nothing will change that," I said, tears choking me. "But I have somewhere to be, sweetheart," I said.

The man who held my heart pulled his hand from me, and turned away.

~

"It's been two bloody days. Nice of you to show up. He's been asking for you."

"I know, I'm sorry."

Blue left me at her open door, and I followed her in. Her frustration with me was clear, and I was eager to talk to her, but all thoughts stopped once I saw the black ash that was Kieran lying in her satin bedding.

I ran to him, putting my hand on his forehead like it would do something, and pulling it away as it seared my skin.

"Right, don't touch him," Blue said. I rolled my eyes at her, cradling my wounded hand.

"Woman, look what you've done to me," Kieran said in a hoarse breath.

"Yeah, I've heard that already today," I muttered. "I'm sorry I didn't come sooner, I didn't know what to say."

His charred skin split as he turned his head to me. "You came to say goodbye."

"What?" Blue said, coming to my side. "Where are you going? You can't leave the *Shinigami* now! The Master is *gone*, they'll all be looking for you and Nicholas to show them what to do!"

"Exactly," I said. "They'll never make choices on their own as long as I'm here, and Blue, you're leaving, too. With Nicholas."

Kieran and Blue blinked at me, wide-eyed, mouths agape.

"I won't leave Kieran like this," Blue said, shaking her head, black hair flying. "And neither should you."

"Blue, if Eliza says you have to go, you have to go," Kieran said. "You can't say she has to lead us in one breath, and deny what she tells you in the next."

"Who will lead *them*?" Blue said, looking out the door.

"Someone who can rise from his own ashes," I said quietly, looking at Kieran.

Kieran stared at me, white eyes in black ash. "Woman, Izanagi's blood has made you mad. The *Shinigami* don't trust me, never have. I'm no leader. Look at Paolo for that."

Blue's voice was so small, it barely existed. "Paolo—"

My heart froze with dread. "What about him?"

It scared me more when Blue softened, her anger subsiding. "Paolo is a man of faith. The things that have happened… they've taken it from him."

"Where is he?"

She licked her lips, held her breath. Jesus, what could this mean?

"He went to the part of the mountain we never see; the Master never wanted us there. And when Paolo came back, he was *dark*. He drank from bad things there, and now he can't come outside, he can't look me in the eye. The only one he'll talk to is Leann."

"Sounds like he went looking for a little slice of Hell," Kieran said, his voice smoke-dry.

Falling dominoes, every one of us. And I pushed the first, second and third one. "Paolo will work his way through his faith. He and the *Shinigami* have been sheep long enough. They need to make their own way, guided by someone who isn't afraid to find his own path. That's you, Kieran."

He craned his neck to kiss my wrist. "You're just afraid to do it yourself."

"I'm not afraid of anything anymore."

Kieran sat up, his skin crackling as he moved. "You're afraid of being alone now more than ever, it's all over you. You're afraid I'll leave you, but I'm the one who should be afraid." He held my hands, steam rising from between them. A thin layer of red mist wrapped itself around our hands, and he breathed a sigh of relief. "Don't tell me to fall down the rabbit hole and leave me to do it alone. I want you by my side. That rabbit hole has teeth."

I smiled at him, kissing his hands. "Kieran Coughlin can climb out of that rabbit hole bloodied up to hell," I said, laughing. "But I have to go. Something's calling me," I whispered. "Something is begging me to burn who I once was."

He put his head back against the wall. "Is this because Nicholas doesn't want you now?"

I gasped, and Blue appeared at my side.

"Don't listen to him," she said, glaring at Kieran, patting my hair. "That's not true."

Red tears blurred my vision. "No," I said, my voice far away, but my words close to me. "It's true. You both saw what I became. I'm something different now. He doesn't want this. He doesn't want me."

Kieran sat up fast, pulling my face to his in a kiss that made me sizzle with a hundred emotions, all of which hurt. His hands on the side of my head, he looked into my eyes. I don't know whose hid more in their flames, mine or his.

"He'd be blind if he didn't see what a magnificent thing you are. It's time for a change, for you, too. Don't let anyone decide who you're going to be." He rested his forehead on mine, burning my skin, leaving his mark. "Get away from here, from me, from all the things that would hold you back. Only death and fire live here, Eliza. Time to burn it all down."

CHAPTER 101

The woods were dark, but not dark enough to hide the murder of crows, perched on every branch. The only thing darker was the god who stood among them.

"Your mind is in a turmoil that I cannot save you from," Izanagi said as I approached him.

There was something incredibly different about him. My blood cooled as I reached for his mind, still so connected to mine.

"But yours isn't," I said.

He smiled, wide and bright. The crow closest to me cawed. "Tell me I had something to do with this. Did I do something besides cause a goddamn catastrophe here?"

"Do you know why you were brought here, Eliza?"

"To make my own path. To take back my choice," I said before I knew I'd said it.

He smiled knowingly. "And because my wife, Izanami, wanted it to be so. She wanted you to give me the same." He looked at the crows surrounding us. "These are her creatures," he said with a smile, reaching out to one of the black birds. It nuzzled its head into his fingers. "And now they tell me to leave here."

"What? I don't understand."

A stream of images from Izanagi's mind trickled neatly into my own as he told me his story. "I created this mountain, and it created me. There is a place on this mountain that leads to Yomi, the gate of Hell. I left my Izanami there in a moment of mortal weakness and fear, and in her vengeance, she vowed to destroy one thousand men each day. I vowed to create the *Shinigami*, a breed that would not die. My first vampire creation was what I wanted to be, to have given her. Strength, stability, for nothing to change."

"The Master," I whispered.

He nodded once. "But we were blind to how destructive never changing can be. When you believe something for so long, it becomes real. The *Shinigami* believed many things that the Master believed."

Pictures of Nicholas, losing his strength. "That they would wither away if they didn't feed on the right humans," I whispered. And with pain I could barely fathom, that dwarfed all the other agony I'd been through, I realized the truth. "That they would be in agony if they didn't turn their *unmei fumetsu* into vampires. That there was no choice in any of it." The pain of separation from Nicholas; it wasn't real.

"The choice you are about to make, Eliza, is one that you can refuse. All of your choices are."

I didn't have to think about it. The churning temptation deep in my gut, the screeching need in my blood rose to the surface, clawing into my consciousness to feed it.

"Fate has shown me the way. It knows what it wants to do with me, but it can't tell me who I am." The ache in my heart told me there was more to know. The same sensation when Leann's blood called to me, imploring me to drink and see what I could see.

To give me the gift that would make me a hero or an abomination. Blood sang to me now, of truths and pains, and a life unled.

Lynch's blood.

"I choose to go to New Hampshire," I said. Izanagi nodded solemnly.

Smiling felt so strange.

PART III
CRAWLING BACK

PART III
CRAWLING BACK

CHAPTER 102

The crows followed me back to the woods of New Hampshire, and I was met with the form of living death that I despised.

Chris Lynch glowed with life, even behind the cobwebs in his eyes. The tragedy of Kat's death was all over him, but there were others. So many others.

"Time for some emotional sword swallowing. Can I come in?" I asked as I pushed my way through the door.

The Great White Mansion appeared darker through my vampire eyes. Or maybe through any eyes—clearly he'd dismissed any cleaning staff he'd had. The cobwebs weren't only on his soul, if he still had one, but on the high crown molding meant for mimicking classic elegance to lure in easily-impressed victims. Dust rolled across the marble floor as I came in. I'd never noticed until they'd wilted and died, but Lynch had always had fresh flowers in big, expensive vases on tables nobody ever used. Lilies, I think. Now they were corpses.

Trailing my finger over one of the crunchy petals, I knew

without question that it had been Kat who kept the fresh flowers.

I'd have known it without the lightning-flash image of her carrying in an armload of them, kicking the door shut behind her, striking me with an electricity that burned in my brain.

Pink dress. Then jeans and my stolen Batman T-shirt. Then green raincoat.

Layers, prisms of pictures of her smiling, arms loaded with the blooms. Something a person would do in a *home*, not at this miserable castle. But everywhere Kat was had felt like home.

I whipped my fingers away, holding them to me as if burned, my heart instantly scorched by the vision that jumped into my psyche without warning.

Never before had my mind's eye given me a vision from a mere touch, and of an inanimate, dead object. I fell back against the wall, panting. Me, the most frightening and unpredictable of the *Shinigami*, frightened. My eyes shot to Lynch to see if he'd noticed my reaction, but he toured the room aimlessly, a ghost in his own home.

"Do you even wonder what I'm doing here?" I asked him, more gently than I'd intended. Abomination or not, he was still *cracked*. To attack him now would have been horribly cruel, though I couldn't say why I cared.

"Why aren't you with Nicholas?" Lynch monotoned as he roamed the cold room, eyes never resting on me.

"He doesn't want me there right now," I said. To say such a thing to this monster, to open up to him so easily didn't feel as foreign as it should have, as it would have before his blood called to me across nations and oceans. His blood had something to show me, and I was okay with giving a little to take a little. Or a lot. He was, after all, the man who undoubtedly loved my best friend, and we'd both lost her. The light of both our lives, snuffed out.

The Lynch I'd known would have taken that opportunity to make a vicious comment, but this Lynch was too far away, too lost to feel vicious or anything else. Anything but sadness, pain. The vision that dragged me here, of him crying in this very room, tearing at his hair, then rushing out the door, letting it hang open behind him as he sought a woman to kill burst into memory.

This was a man who was more dangerous when he was sad than when he was angry.

"Lynch, sit down," I said quietly, and with only the urge to be there, I was suddenly beside him. Moving more quickly, Nicholas had said once in Japan, than any vampire he'd ever seen. I put my hand on Lynch's elbow in his wrinkled shirt. Nothing about him was as polished as it had been. The look he gave me, wide-eyed, shocked and afraid, made me lean away, but I kept my hand on his arm. It was as if he'd just realized I was there. I steered him toward the sofa I'd always hated, *Miami Vice* white leather, and pushed him onto it.

"You came here," he said, utterly blank. "Why would you come here?"

"I have my reasons." I shook my head, and sat beside him. "Sorry. I won't pull a Riddler on you. We'll save that for—" My throat constricted. I couldn't say his name, didn't want to think of it anymore when he was so close and so far away. *Nicholas.* "I came here because your blood called to me from Japan."

For the first time, he really looked at me. The supple skin, the healthy shade of his lips—it didn't match the utter madness of his eyes, the hollowness of them. I could only imagine the vitality of the woman he'd stolen this latest glow from—

…how her blood must have sparkled on the tongue.

I growled at myself, the way my thoughts became so gruesome with the blood craving. How could I condemn this man whose own kind called him "the Abomination" for acting on urges I was barely controlling myself? I'd found that since leaving Japan, since knowing that I was my own higher authority among the death gods, since confirming that I had a choice in who I killed, that I saw everyone as a potential victim.

Lynch still had his eyes on me, waiting for me to speak more. Again, a new trait for the forked-tongue attorney who'd been too quick, always assessing, always on the hunt. This waiting…this was a new hunting tactic that I recognized as a vampire, one of his own kind. Subtle, intimidating in the most calm and cautious way. He didn't even know he was doing it, which made it even more blood curdling. Even to me, a dead thing like him, in so many ways.

I thought of myself as dead in that moment, but in truth, I felt completely alive. Unhindered. Strong. Purposeful and determined. Invincible. I was *Shinigami,* wandering this world as I saw fit, like a bird of prey, swallowing down every sense, every bit of knowledge, every taste with renewed vivacious-ness. I didn't feel dead. I felt, for the first time, entirely my own. Not owned by the lingering spirit of death—I *was* death. Not beholden to the shadows to avoid humanity—I owned them, if I wanted them. Not tortured by a mystical connection to the man who delivered me to this fate—it was my choice. For as much as I loved Nicholas French, it felt damn good to not feel owned by him. And I'd known it as soon as I'd gotten to Japan; my path was mine to carve and I needed to do it alone.

Dokkoudou, Izanagi had called it. *The path of aloneness.*

I drink the blood of a god, I thought, and found myself sneering.

"You're a vampire," Lynch said as I let my mind wander into its own depths. I found I was far more inclined to dig deep into my subconscious as a vampire, that one second of thought suddenly became the unlocking of a treasure chest I didn't wait to explore.

"I'm a vampire," I said back.

"I'm sorry," he replied.

"Wha—what? What?" I stuttered, unable to comprehend his words. "Why are you sorry?"

Blood-tinged tears glinted pink in his bloodshot eyes. "To live forever without her…"

I took his hand in mine, and waited in silence with him for darkness to come, when we could wash away the haunting of Kat in someone else's blood.

CHAPTER 103

I didn't ask where he was going; I already knew. Another Eliza, a human Eliza would have had a pang of sadness for the life—or lives—he would take this night, but the Eliza who had a world of choices opened up to her didn't. Human Eliza would have been racked with guilt over the loss of an innocent life, convinced it had something to do with her. But *Shinigami* Eliza saw all too clearly that it wasn't a matter of when, but how a person would die.

I could be that death.

Lynch could be that death.

I'd spent most of my life thinking about death. Now as a vampire, my mind moved so fast, thought so deep, I thought of all new aspects of death. Probably not good for me. No wonder Nicholas had been so torn apart when we met. A thinking man with too much time to think. I'd never concentrated on what Lynch did to his victims, how he delighted in and drew out their murders, hardly any of them having been "fated" to die. Because I'd seen how short-sighted even the *Shinigami* had been under the Master's leadership. They'd blindly followed a calling to kill with the knowledge that the human's alternative fate would have been worse for the whole of humanity. But not once did the vampires question what the fates of those who *weren't* chosen would be. Certainly there were horrendous tortures, deaths, enslavements and the waking nightmares people suffered every day. Unless some higher power told his vampire clan to do it, they weren't supposed to drink from anyone else, even though any one of those victims could be suffering every minute of their lives, in their own minds for that matter. It was for the better of *humankind* that we drank. That's what the *Shinigami* told themselves. Gods indeed.

If I was to be a god, I would be the death god I was meant to be. One that didn't follow senseless orders, or let fate decide for me. If I wanted to be a humanitarian that sucked blood, I'd do it with the mindset that everyone suffers, and suffering is a detriment to humanity in all its forms. Even vampire.

Kieran Coughlin would have stood cheering at this most recent foray into my subconscious. He would have burned as brightly as the sun.

While Lynch hunted to take his mind off his own suffering for as long as he could, I wandered the mansion, taking in all of its quick decay. In such a short time, he'd let the home he'd taken such arrogant pride in deteriorate. I could hear bats, birds and squirrels in the attic. I felt the pungent wetness of mold, the dryness of the balls of dust. The smell of dried blood and sweat in the piles of clothing in his bedroom reached me in the great room where he held parties, where he "lived." My vampire senses didn't need to give me *everything* in high definition.

My fingers hovered over the dead flowers I'd touched earlier, and they shook wildly. As much as I wanted to touch them, see what I could see again, I abhorred the thought of glimpsing a living Kat just to have her taken away again. I should not have to relive that over and over.

The unfairness of it made me want to take a victim, let someone's loved ones feel the pain I would feel for eternity. And that thought didn't make me feel guilty either. Misery loves company is right. But Nicholas wouldn't agree. Nicholas would look at me like a stranger if he knew what I was thinking, how I felt. It stomped all over the ideals he'd been raised as a vampire on, the ideals of a power-hungry ancient liar that stole the *Shinigami* from their true creator, Izanagi. Left him alone for eternity again.

I plunged my hand into the center of the flowers forcefully, petals crumbling to the floor. I howled in rage when I saw nothing. Nothing. Where before I had seen her, felt her, now I came up empty, and I hated...*hated*...that I didn't control this new sort of vision. I hated not knowing what I would see next and when.

Aggravated, I envisioned myself upstairs, just to get away from this room and all its memories. I'd never been to the second floor of Lynch's house, and he wouldn't care if I was there now. He cared about nothing now. He hadn't even said goodbye when he left the house to hunt as he pulled his hand from mine.

Upstairs was the wreck I knew it would be from all the things my senses showed me before. It was hard to imagine the sharp attorney that had so enchanted my best friend living in this hole. Standing on the white carpet, now stained with filth and blood from coming in after haphazard hunting, a new fear welled in me.

What would I see if I touched the things in here?

Morbid curiosity got the better of me, and I perched on the very edge of Lynch's bed. It was also gross, and I didn't really want to touch it. The blankets were in a ball, the pillowcases stained, and the worst of it all—the fitted sheet was coming off one corner. Placing my palms on the mattress on either side of me, I let out a long breath. But I saw nothing. I did the same thing on the chair in the corner, and the ottoman at my feet, but saw nothing. The knot in the pit of my stomach unwound as I realized that I wouldn't be assaulted with memories of Kat everywhere she went—but when would I? When I least expected it, of course.

Memories. The place held memories. That hadn't been a vision, when I touched the flowers—it had been a memory. But surely there were more in this mansion where she'd spent her last days. Why would I not discover them everywhere, in everything I touched that she'd touched?

Again I let my mind delve into hidden possibilities, losing track of time and forgetting the space I was in. Two things stuck out for me—two things that I probably wouldn't have picked up on in my human life, and for a second I reveled in my abilities. First, Kat had personally brought those flowers into the house. They were there because of her. And second?

They had been alive.

I don't know why it troubled me so, made me grit my teeth and pant until the protective red mist that shielded me seeped into the room from my fingertips and toes, taking over until it was the only thing that mattered anymore, soothing me. I don't know why I would be so goddamned *afraid* of the idea that living things Kat touched held a piece of her memory.

I was one of those living things she touched, and I held her memory powerfully myself. Too powerfully. Though really, I was no longer living, I was no longer that emotional corpse I'd been in the days following her death, before getting to Japan. The kinship I was feeling with the dead flowers in my home-town showed me how much I'd changed.

How little was left for me here.

The marble floor split with a *crack* when I ground my feet into it, as if rooting myself there, refusing to leave, to be forced out. Not when blood called me there, back to my home, not when death itself turned me in this direction.

I screamed, stomping the cold floor over and over, shattering it like an earthquake, shaking the walls.

"It's MINE!" I growled, hunched over, wraith-like, waiting to defend myself against the world. But the world wasn't coming after me. I wasn't prey any longer. This was my home, New Hampshire belonged to me, and unnatural thing that I'd become, I still had the right to come home.

"I'm home," I whispered to the white walls, the decaying room. And I pounded the floor once more. The door fell off its hinges.

~

He stumbled through the door, banging his head on the frame and falling to one knee.

He didn't even swear. Not once. I would have sworn at least three times. That's how I knew he was dead inside.

I glided to his side instinctively, as anyone does when a person needs help. "Lynch, what happened to you?"

He raised his face, blood wet on his chin and throat, ruining his already filthy shirt beyond repair. His eyes were blank, emotionless. "Nothing," he said, voice guttural. *Nothing.* He'd drunk the blood of a living, breathing, complex creature, and felt nothing.

The mess that he'd become sent me a memory of Roman in that asylum attic, withering away in every way he could. Then to Kieran, black as ash, only partly hopeless; the part that knew I loved Nicholas. And Nicholas, alone, a flash away, may as well have been in the next room for as fast as I could get to him, and still...alone. Immortal, all of us, the eternal gift of life, and we'd squandered it so young. We were all still so *young.*

Eternity promised a lifetime of hurt, but infinite time for redemption.

I led Lynch to the stupid white sofa as easily as a kitten to milk. The sofa wasn't white anymore—nothing was pristine around us. I'd hated this man with every breath in my body, blamed him for the end of my friendship with Kat, known what horrors he was capable of, felt the deaths of those who hadn't deserved it, having seen through his eyes in my visions. But now? I felt only pity.

Pity for this vermin. Soulless murderer, the Abomination to his own kind, the only family he knew.

My dearest friend had seen unparalleled beauty in this despicable bastard.

He sat immobile, but he was listening. I sensed the tiny hairs in his ears moving ever so slightly. But he stared straight ahead as I faced him at his side. "I'm not here to kill you, though I'm sure that's what you think. I don't think you'd care if I did. I always hated you, from the moment Kat told me the crap you spewed to her while trying to...*date*... her. Before I had vampire senses I knew you were a monster —I just knew. Given the chance then, as confused as I was, my whole world changing around me, I wouldn't have killed you. You symbolized everything I knew being taken from me, but I wouldn't have killed you. Now? Now I could kill you in the blink of an eye, less than the blink of an eye. And I don't want to."

"Why, then?" His voice crackled with age, as neglected as this home he'd built. Everything about him was surface, so easily ruined, despite its appearance. The thinnest of skins. "Why are you here when you belong in Japan?"

"Your blood. I need to drink it."

He looked at me, incredulous, the first real feeling I'd recognized in him since I'd arrived. "I'm a vampire, just like you," he said simply.

We are not alike, I ached to say, but stopped myself. Now was not the time to lean back on my human resentments.

"What use could my blood have to you?" he said. He hung his head, surely thinking that he was of no use to anyone. I'd felt that way for too long, before my purpose was put before me like a home-cooked meal to the starved.

"Let's find out," I said, fangs protruding, dimpling my bottom lip. Fear flickered in the wells of his eyes, riling my not-so-inner predator. I pulled him to me by the arm with one swift tug, and buried my teeth into his exposed neck where his shirt was torn. He was silent as I wrenched my head back and forth to get the vein right where I wanted it, though the pain had to have been extraordinary. My eyes unfocused and rolled back with the first deep drink. Moments passed like years as I waited for knowledge to fill me with every drop of blood.

The first mouthful caught me unawares. It wasn't Chris Lynch I tasted, but that of a girl—always a girl with him—visiting the slopes for her last snowboard run of the season. She had a creaminess, a soft vanilla flavor, pure but rich. But there was another personality deep in her recesses, one she didn't know yet. One that would torture her for the rest of her life. One that was capable of hellish things that this brilliant young lady would never dream of; until she did. *Shayla.* Shayla's recessive personality was a dark, terrible thing, one that she hid from without knowing it.

When I'd drunk her story, I pulled away, wiping the wetness from my chin with my sleeve. "Nothing!" I roared, mist flooding out of me as red as Shayla's blood. It churned for a moment, confused, upset, before mummifying Lynch, straightening his body and covering every inch of him but his face. I relished the panic in his expression. I wanted him to answer for whatever he was hiding.

"Eliza, what is this?!" he whimpered. Coward. The mist constricted more.

"What are you covering up, Lynch? Huh?"

"I don't know what you're talking about!"

"Stop squirming, the mist won't let you go. I saw nothing important just now, no reason for me to be here, drinking from you, what are you *hiding*!"

"I have nothing left to hide, Eliza! I killed the girl, it didn't help! I don't know what you mean!"

Calming my panting, the anger swelling in my throat, I unclenched my fists and the mist dissipated, releasing him. He lay gasping, holding his arms around himself in a hug that didn't comfort him.

Pacing, running my fingers through my hair, getting it caught in a knot on one side, I rambled. "Your blood *begged* me to come here, it had something to show me, and I listened, of course I listened..."

"I don't know what you're saying!" he screeched in a panic. I stopped and spun on him, and he leaned back as far as he could into the sofa.

"I can see your fate if I drink your blood. Human, vampire, I know what's going to happen or could happen, and I get visions of things that matter, but this... Shayla's life story wasn't what I came here for. You have something *in there*," I hissed, leaning over him and pushing my index finger hard into his forehead. "There's something in there that you're keeping from me, and I want it. Do you hear me? I want it, Lynch."

Gently, he pushed me away from him, and with a sad smile said, "I have nothing to give you. But maybe you can do something for me."

"What? No. I'm here for one reason, and then I'm gone."

He closed his eyes. "Do you remember coming to me, asking me to kill you?"

"Not the sort of thing you forget."

"I wanted to do it, but I wouldn't because I hated you so

much. Your reason for being here is to torture me, and finally kill me. I deserve it, but because I *want* it, you won't do it. Even if it's the real reason you came here, you won't do it." He wasn't making much sense, and it made me wonder what someone so confused could really show me.

What if my visions, the call to feed, all of it had failed me? What would my purpose be then?

"I'm not here to do you any favors, Lynch. One of these days, your blood will give me the answers I need, and I'll act on whatever it tells me. Until then, sulk, rot, cry, do whatever you need to do, but keep your self-pity away from me."

I left his house slowly, letting him hear every footfall that would leave him alone once again.

CHAPTER 104

The idea was preposterous, that Nicholas was the equivalent of footsteps away for me, and that I was trying not to go to him. No matter that we left on terrible terms, or that I told him to go away for so many reasons. No matter that Blue was living with him at that very moment in the cabin that was *my* dream house, with my dream lover. No matter that the pain we'd both suffered when apart was an elaborate thrall that the Master had managed to create. Pain was endurable. But this… I missed him. I missed him too much to stay away.

No sooner than I'd thought about it, I was in the woodsy front yard, fully aware of how terrifying I would appear to human eyes. Standing unnaturally still, staring at a little cabin with eyes full of fire and red mist and ice, betraying my feelings. My confusion.

The sun was coming up. Barely touching the trees, but I felt it on my neck, my back. It reminded me of being alive. My mind went down one of its whirlpools, remembering the beach and how fast I'd burn, how I'd refuse to go to the beach again until Kat begged and I'd burn all over again. I'd worry about skin cancer, and Kat would make me go to the doctor but there was nothing to worry about. I always worried about the burns until winter anyway. Winter, when I met Nicholas and it would turn out the burns wouldn't matter anymore.

The thoughts came so fast and plunged so deep, the sun burning holes into my flesh, my scalp, hotter than when I'd been alive. Vampirism and vivid memories—vivid everything, especially pain—but it was a memory.

Except it wasn't a memory. I stood in full view of the big bay window, horribly still, my reflection in the glass screaming as I burned.

Terrified, and stupidly stubborn to admit I'd done something so careless and *while* going to blubber about missing Nicholas, the screams tore from my throat, but I couldn't move. Hoarfrost tickled my fingers where the prints had certainly burned off. Cold brushed up my arms, across my throat, a personal blizzard engulfed my feet, but I could see nothing, only feel. Cold battling the fiery sun, my body the killing field.

All at once the unbearable touch of the slightest breeze on my body, as if I was naked to the elements, flesh burning and freezing, my veins surely exposed with my skin eaten away—

"What the hell were you doing out there!"

Nicholas. Nicholas. Nicholas. I could say it over and over in my mind until that burned away, too.

The scent of the cabin took over the scents from outside and the merciless searing of my nostrils. Old wood and freshly cut wood mingled, traces of dirt tracked in, the wool of the blanket on the back of the sofa, the mustiness of the books in the loft. And the flowers that were my friend, Blue. Better than any of it, the peppermint brownie I needed. I needed it more than blood. But when my eyes healed from the sunlight, I saw Nicholas, and I wasn't ready—the sight of him hurt more than the sun.

He looked healthy enough. Dark, tousled mess of gorgeously styled hair, lips pinker than any other man's in the world, laugh lines and perfect creases framing the eyes that swam with mocha and cocoa and cream in a constant vortex. But it was his inner health that shocked me. I sensed it, felt his peace just by laying eyes on him.

He was happy. And I was crushed and confused by my own head.

"I said what the hell were you doing out there?" he repeated calmly, running his fingers through his hair. Tendrils of steam rose from them where my fire had met his ice moments before. "What are you doing *here*?"

"You…you look great," I murmured, my voice hoarse from the heat.

"Yeah, thanks, but no thanks," he said with an angry confidence.

"I needed to see you," I said, my voice as tremulous as his was strong.

"Why?"

Blood tears formed in my eyes, the pink sheen making me feel weaker than the sun ripping my body to shreds. I looked to the floor. "Didn't think I'd need to say why."

His silence gave me hope that he'd soften toward me, but it ended soon enough. "I think you should get a hologram of me, Eliza, for when you feel like seeing me. And then you can just, you know, blink it out when you're in a mood."

"It's not my fault—"

"Don't say that!" he shouted, surprising me into looking at him, and God help me, he was *smiling* this scornful, wicked smile. "What can you possibly expect to say isn't your fault? Actually, I changed my mind. Say it. Finish your sentence, I need a good laugh." He raised an eyebrow in that genuinely amused way I'd loved, always loved. Until now.

"You said yourself time and again that I would be different

when I became a vampire—you had no idea how different, how could we ever predict *this*?" I rambled, gesturing to myself. As I looked over my pants and plain T-shirt, I noticed there was no sign whatsoever that I'd been on fire when the sun rose. My clothes were unaffected, but my body was covered in sores underneath. I laughed. *Just like me. Okay on the outside; inside, an open wound.*

His chin was still tilted up in that condescending, snarky way I loved, but his eyes were glassy and his smile gone. "I would have loved anything you became."

"You don't now?"

"You. Sent. Me. Away."

What was I now, really? Who? I resembled nothing of the girl I'd been. Sitting on this couch, watching horror movies, talking books, sucking in her stomach and noticing the bulge of second-boob over the top of her bra. I was nothing now. No one.

"There were so many reasons for that. I'm pretty new at this, Nicholas, and I think I'm doing okay! I don't know which path to follow—"

"You were crystal clear when you told me to go. You needed to be alone."

"I know what you're thinking, and it's not true!" My voice cracked, the blood tears flowing freely, hissing where they touched my cheeks. "Now that I see through eyes like your own, you think I don't want you. That I think you're a monster because—because I'm one, too."

"You could never be a monster," he said, certainty returning to him instantly. "Even if you were, you'd be my monster. I would always love you." Blood tears streaked down his own cheeks now, and I sobbed at the sight of them. "I would always love you, Eliza Morgan, monster or not."

I was in his arms, making him stumble backwards as I bowled him over in the rapid movement of my body. I was more confused than I thought a being ever could be. My mind reached to depths as a vampire that I was totally unprepared for, reminding me of the patients at Bethlem, drowning in their own mind disease. But there was no confusion to the utter satisfaction of feeling the heat of my body hiss against his coolness, of his arms around me, the scent of Christmas kitchen enveloping me. This was where I belonged, fated or not. I couldn't restrain myself any longer.

"I'm sorry about what happened with Kieran—" I said.

"—what you *did* with Kieran," Nicholas snapped.

"Yes. What I did with Kieran. I'm sorry I betrayed you, because that's what it was. I called it a lot of different things, but that's what it was, no matter how I *felt*. No matter what I needed."

"I'm barely a good man, let alone perfect, El, I can't—"

"Neither of us are. We don't even have to be good, really. We aren't human. We just aren't."

That went a different way than I'd expected. And once again, feelings from a place I was just beginning to discover erupted in words I didn't want to mean. Nicholas was clearly taken aback, head tilted at me as if he wanted to run, but was afraid to.

"You don't mean that."

"I don't say anything I don't mean. Please, don't give me that face, and don't be all silent. I have to be able to say things to you that aren't...perfect."

Something sank in him that brought down his face, his eyes, his spirit. "You keep me human. If I lose that in you, my heart can't survive."

The tenderness vanished quickly at those words, dissolved into anger at being given such a responsibility as to keep him grounded for eternity, but even more so...

"You made me a vampire! I am *not* human, I am *not* the same as I was. I don't want to be loved *despite* that, like I did something wrong by becoming what I was meant to be.

Finally, I have my place, and you want me to stay the same as I was? Dull, chubby Ellie who bored you to tears?"

I only saw red. Felt red. Anger, venom, rage, rage, rage.

My head felt every fiber of the ceiling's wood when I rose into the air, propelled by my crimson mist; my protector, my lifeline, my instrument, my emotions come to life. The smoky tendrils wound around my legs and I felt all traces of the sun's burn disappear. I sighed with relief, relaxed into its arms and let it heal me, even as the anger boiled from inside, threatening to incinerate me.

Anger at Nicholas. Nicholas French.

Memories of him beside me at the pond in his backyard, of the pain that connected us, of sharing the shield bubble with him in the growing sunlight, of his lips, of the teacup in his hands, of his T-shirts and his laugh and the way he balanced a mug on the arm of the couch instead of the table, and of him petting the stray cat that moved in. Of his *katas,* how he made the fighting movements into a work of art, how the *Shinigami* adored him, how he put everyone at ease, how he carried me in every way through the mountains of Japan, how he nearly became nothing but ash to spare my feelings and my best friend…

I hit the floor, the red mist retreating into my soul with a hiss, Medusa's snakes recoiling. I lay there, my cheek sensing every particle of soil beneath the cabin, the rings on the worms moving them along.

I was going mad.

And Nicholas didn't come to help me up.

I got to my feet like a human, clumsy and pained. I brushed my hair out of my face. My boots felt too heavy, my clothes like scraps wrapped senselessly around me. But it felt real, like me. Like I was. And I wasn't that anymore. There's some comfort in being imperfect and powerless, lost and with death chasing me down. But I left that mediocrity behind when

Nicholas French entered my life. I took death by the hand when it offered me a place by its side. And the comfort I'd had was gone. I had to create my own all over again. It had to come from within me, not dependent on Nicholas, or Kat. I was *Shinigami.* Death god. I'd been trained and acclimated to this afterlife by the oldest death gods in Japan, the creator of vampires himself. I was given the means to a fount of strength that only martial arts could infuse me with. I didn't need anyone to make me feel valuable, powerful, myself. But I wanted Nicholas there.

I met his eyes. I saw his hurt and his fear, but more than that I saw his love and concern. It entwined with every whirl of cocoa and cream. He remained rigid, waiting for what I would do next. Because things didn't *happen* to me. Not anymore.

It was me that changed everything for a race of vampires.

The blink of thought of my hand in his, and it happened. I grinned when the speed of it made even Nicholas jump.

"You are such a wild creep," he said, combing his fingers through his hair with his spare hand.

"Oh my god, all I want to do is watch a Rob Zombie movie right this minute, now that you said that."

With speed matching my own, his fingers were in my hair, his lips hot on mine, his hips pressed against me, and we were one.

He pulled away too soon. "That," he said, "is the humanity I'm talking about."

CHAPTER 105

House of 1000 Corpses was halfway over before Nicholas and I even looked at the screen. Red sparks and puffs of my crimson mist erupted every new place I touched on him, followed by trickles of blood as we fed from each other in love bites. My body healed along with my heart each second, wholeness overcoming me like a tsunami.

Nicholas's hair was soaking wet as he brushed it off his glistening face, eyes wild, chest heaving with breath he needed only in memory. He collapsed against the arm of the sofa, head hanging back. "God, I've missed you," he said.

I crawled on top of him, our flesh sin-slick against each other. "We haven't been apart very long," I murmured, running my fangs along his jawline.

"But we have been far away."

"Too far away," I agreed. As he put his swollen lips to mine again, I pulled back snarling, whipping my head back and forth, searching. I leaped up, throwing a stray hoodie on and pulling on my panties. "Another," I hissed, the animal in me taking over.

"Another what?" Nicholas gasped, unsettled by my sudden alertness after the sleepy urgency of our lovemaking.

"Another vampire." I'd reared back on my haunches, crouched and ready to pounce, no thought whatsoever in hindsight, only instinct.

A shadow slipped past the window, jerkily, graceless. I was at the glass in a scarlet burst that disappeared immediately so as not to give me away. My armor, my guard. I zeroed in across the distance, through the trees, everywhere my mind wanted to see at once. I felt the unknown creature. It was still now, and I saw nothing.

Wheeling around, I caught Nicholas's expression: terror. Once again, I was terrifying him. But there was no suppressing the soul of the thing I'd become, a *Shinigami* unlike anything else.

The Japanese god of creation's blood still flowed in mine, forever there like the very marrow. Beyond taming.

"Eliza, what's out there?" Nicholas asked.

"Vampire," I hissed again. I couldn't have formed a sentence if I'd tried. I was not a person then.

My head spun at the pulse of the creature on the move again. Closer. "Closer."

"Jesus, El, I think I'll take my chances with whoever's outside," Nicholas muttered. I ignored him.

The front door burst open, and a cobalt ball of material rolled inside, steaming and shrieking. *Weakened. No match for me.*

The creature unfurled, waves of heat emanating from its body as it came to standing.

"Blue!" I cried.

"Gah, Blue, for crying out loud, you made Eliza turn scary."

Even I was shocked as I came back to lucidity, when I found myself at Blue's side, sniffing her all over like a hyena. I met her eyes, this seemingly delicate flower of a woman, yet such a powerful fighter, so fiery. Also the same vampire who'd been terrified to leave the mountaintop to hunt her own fated victims, leaving it to her creator to bring the *unmei nashi* to her, worms to a fledgling bird.

I saw nothing of that complex woman here.

Her cheeks were sunken, raven hair in knots, rosebud lips curled back and trembling. Blue's dark, inviting eyes had become fathomless, *evil*. It snapped me back at once to who I was, hoping to find who she'd been.

"What's happened to you, Blue?" She gazed at me with a crushing hollowness. I was hyper-aware of the vampires I knew, even ones I'd spoken with briefly at the temple—but Blue was utterly unrecognizable to me. I hadn't even known it was her soul outside the cabin, when before she'd had the aura of exotic flowers and polished gemstones. It broke my heart to see her as such a shell of herself. Blue had been the only friend I'd made among the *Shinigami* whose vitality and warmth reminded me of Kat. This was not the same vampire. "You don't even smell like you."

"Oh. Yeah," Nicholas said, feigning boredom. "Blue's been feeding on real bastards."

Human blood leaves a residue on the *Shinigami* soul. An essentially good person gives us sunlight, love, happiness complementing the fullness of their blood. But drinking from the broken, the wretched, the cruel and vicious left us the same. Left us in darkness in every way.

Nicholas continued as Blue and I stared at each other appraisingly. "Some of her personality quirks have been really exciting," he said, dripping sarcasm. "Our little Bluebird tried to poison my coffee...what was that? Thursday?" he said mockingly to her. But Blue only stared at me, shivering occasionally. I winced at her state. She was so *lost*, not a hint of her refined fierceness apparent. I wanted to touch her, hold her to me and let my mist wrap around and heal her, but one snarl from her was enough to stop me.

"What happened to her?" I whispered. "Why would she do this to herself?"

Nicholas approached her easily, took her hand and disappeared with her down the hall, certainly to the room that had always been mine when I stayed here. So long ago. Moments ago.

"She's acting out," Nicholas said, suddenly beside me like a warm cup of hot chocolate I'd waited too long for. He plopped on the sofa where we'd been alone, before I saw what Blue had become. Nicholas rubbed a hand over his face, a dad lamenting his troubled teen. "It started with one *unmei nashi*." He saw my eyebrow rise when I heard it. When I'd become one of the *Shinigami,* I brought to light—or more accurately, took away—the illusion of having victims fated to be ours. The entire idea was created by the Master, a thrall he put the *Shinigami* under to keep them in his control. But when the Master was destroyed, his influence wasn't. Not for all of the vampires who'd been reborn and raised with him. And not for Nicholas, his most trusted and trusting. Truly, his son.

"You know *unmei nashi*—"

"A figment of our imaginations, yep," Nicholas said with a huff. "But imagination has been pretty good to me. A little imagination broke you out of cashier land."

"Don't. Start," I warned, sensing the oncoming critique of my mundane former life as gift shop lady. I smiled, the memory of all those conversations warming me despite myself. "Imagination is a powerful thing, I know." In truth, I was becoming more and more certain that imagination and the *unmei nashi* were a self-fulfilling prophecy. The *Shinigami* believed in them, and so it became real. Wasn't that the start of anything great? An idea that turns into truth?

The irony wasn't lost on me that my truth, the purpose I'd always searched for by hiding where I didn't belong, was to take the purpose from those who *did* want me. Unmei nashi *aren't real, and the man you consider a father is a fraud, and you're not just a murderer, but now you're a murderer with no higher reasoning to blame.*

I missed not knowing my purpose.

"Earth to El." Nicholas's eyebrows were raised.

"I slip away sometimes." Vampire thoughts wrapped around me, enveloping me and dragging me away.

"Don't get lost in there. Anyway, Blue had one *unmei nashi* that was really dark. She wouldn't talk about it, just spent days in her room—your room—silent. When she came out she just sucked all the light from around her. I've never seen a human leave a residue like that, turn someone so vibrant into a Dementor."

I snickered. We'd missed too many Harry Potter weekends on the Freeform Channel recently. I hoped Freeform would exist for eternity.

I sat with him on the couch, throwing my legs over his. My vampire senses felt every sinew, the blood pumping through his veins, the blister on his toe. "So after that one dark human she drank from, she went looking for more." I knew. I didn't have to ask. Dark called to dark. Someone as buoyant as Blue would fall, trusting the darkness to show her something wonderful. She'd come to New Hampshire without a plan, her excitement leaving her open to every new experience, every new feeling and side of herself. She'd been lost as soon as she'd left Japan.

"She'll be okay," Nicholas said, patting me on the leg with one strong hand.

"We don't know that she'll be okay, sweetheart." I almost said, *You didn't see Roman in Bethlem. You don't know what it looks like when the bulb burns out in a loved one.* I recognized my own arrogance right away; Nicholas had lived through the Master's death.

And he'd been there with me those long weeks after Roman killed Kat, leaving me as good as dead.

Blue was a sister to Nicholas. They were so much alike, and different in all the right ways. If their relationship hadn't been so clear and magnetic I might have worried that I stood no chance of him loving me over her. I'd thought that for a time, when her effervescence was so overwhelming that I couldn't see myself in her presence. But Nicholas did. Always. As reassuring as it was, it left a lot for me to prove. A lot that I couldn't handle.

Darkness called me even now. The stench of death was wine and roses to me, and I longed for it as much as I'd wished it away when I was alive. It was something I wouldn't share with Nicholas, not if I ever wanted him to see me as this human he insisted I was.

If only either of us knew what I was capable of, maybe I could have been saved.

CHAPTER 106

It was all too easy to avoid talking about—anything—for days. Blue hadn't come in the house more than once in her dark state, preferring to prowl the woods with the wolves and bears. Though uneasy when we knew she was peering in at us sometimes, we felt alone in the cabin. The more Nicholas and I touched, the more my mist encircled us, the more my burns healed and the living tissue strengthened. In that short time my body became even stronger, my skin still fair, yet toughened like a lady who'd seen one too many tanning beds. I'd never entered a tanning bed in my life and if I ended up with second-hand leather skin I'd be pissed.

I'd like to say those days were blissful, but they were merely pleasurable and ignorant. Bliss comes with a certain carefree peace. We were immune to such things. We hadn't earned it and we'd never get it now. No, those stolen moments in the cabin were just that—stolen. Ignoring all the things that forced us apart. The roaring god blood inside me begging me to be alone as a vampire, to find myself like some underage hippie. The same blood that showed me Nicholas was supposed to be here with Blue, and I was supposed to be with

Lynch, and that was the only way Roman would return to us. And I so needed him to return to us and allow Nicholas to feed from him. That alone would restore Nicholas to his complete health. But all these mystical elements had very little to do with the problems in our relationship. Problems that we needed space to sort through.

It didn't change how much we loved each other. It didn't stop our wanting and needing and hurting and obsessing and hoping.

We'd been curled under his old afghan for hours. So many times we'd wiled away hours on that couch, surrounded by the scents of Christmas, the blinking tree lights, the hush of the snow on the windows, the clinking of tea cups, the feel of his old sweater that I'd stolen on my arms. Some of my favorite human memories.

Then Kat died.

"You got up," Nicholas said with surprise. "Get me a cookie?"

I shook off the memory of Kat, the hole that she'd left. "I'll never not love that you still want cookies," I said.

"Yeah, got that sleepy craving for something sweet, so it's cookies or I eat that pharmacist downtown."

My laugh came out as a sudden bark, one of those that hurts a little because it's such a surprise. "Oh my god, how can you say things like that?" But I was grinning.

"If I can't say it to you, who can I say it to?"

I relished the familiar feel of my feet on the wood floor, the creaks and groans. Nicholas had left as much of the knots and roughness of the bark as he could when he built this cabin. He said he wanted to keep nature on his side and leave as much death as he could at the door. Through a battered, red swinging door, the wood gave way to black and white kitchen tile in need of a polish it would never get. As I unwrapped the cellophane on the cookie plate—chocolate chip—and glanced at the coffee pot. It was unnatural not to have coffee, to pick up that pot every time I was in this room with its wood stove and the memory of the black stray cat curled up in front of it.

"Where are you now, kitty?" I whispered. We'd left for Japan in such a fog, wrapped in ourselves, we'd barely given him a second thought. I twisted my face in disgust at myself, that I hadn't even wondered about him until this moment.

I returned to Nicholas with three cookies in one hand and one in my mouth, and handed him two.

"I didn't say *you* could have one of my cookies," he grumbled.

"Two, and then one more in the kitchen."

"Which means you ate two more in the kitchen in Eliza Cookie Terms. Why that face?" he asked, wagging a finger.

"Where's the cat?" I mumbled.

"I don't know." He sighed. "I was hoping he'd be here when we came back. Ships passing in the night, we were."

"No. He loved it here. He loved you guys." The trouble it gave me that the cat was alone again, abandoned after he'd found security and happiness, made me nauseous. "If we can't keep one damn cat safe, what hope do we have for eternity as do-gooder murderers?"

Nicholas rolled his eyes. "The cat was never this existential whenever we talked."

"I'm not kidding," I said, elbowing him. "We have to find him. He picked this house, you and Roman"—Nicholas winced —"for a reason. We owe it to him to take care of him."

"Okay, let's find him," he shrugged.

"You said you tried."

"I did, but you didn't. You have super aura-ra-ra powers, so use them."

In the heat of a late night or early morning in front of the fire, Nicholas asked me if I'd found any less torturous vampire abilities since we left the temple in Japan. I tried to tell him about the sensing of auras, knowing no other way to describe it. I hadn't noticed it at the temple; being enslaved by an all-powerful ancient vampire and subjected to visions of thousands of humans and inhumans alike hadn't left me much room for dawn-of-the-dead exploration. But once I left that place and knew I wasn't going back, I saw colors around everyone. Not just crayon box colors, but hues from other planets, from times more ancient than the Master himself. Colors of tastes and memories, and heat and light. The hues were smoky as campfire around some, as clear as stained glass windows over others. They tasted like dungeons and carnivals and the first breath of life and violence that throbbed like a bruise. In my growing ability to control the visions that had assaulted me mercilessly, I gained this glancing sense of people and I reveled in it.

"You think I can find the cat this way?" I hadn't noticed the aura around animals yet.

"Yeah, I do." The way he looked at me, as if I were some storybook character with a crystal ball sent my heart fluttering. "I think you've found ways to do the most incredible things, stuff I never even dreamed of, and finding a *cat*," he grinned, "is one more thing we can add to your afterlife resume."

"I guess I should get to it, then," I said, smiling.

"Right now?"

"Sure. Why not?" I walked, human walking, to my favorite window, the one where Nicholas had put his green sweater around me so long ago.

I tried to breathe through ignoring everything around me, but it was sorta tough when I didn't actually need to breathe. Ended up concentrating more on that than focusing on the cat. When I stopped thinking of breathing or the cat, everything else piled on top of me—the memories. The things I wanted away from.

"I can't do this. I'm focusing on the wrong things."

"Then stop focusing on the wrong things," Nicholas said with a shrug.

"Why are you this way, who do you think you are?" I said, shaking my head slowly, forever unable to believe that he was always so right when he was pompous like this.

He watched me expectantly, a scientist waiting for his beaker to bubble.

I concentrated on shoving the errant thoughts and memories away, clouds of red crowding them out until there was only the crimson sea and my own non-breaths.

And I noticed. I noticed the aura of the spring-fresh trees, as old as time and promising of futures. Tiny, flitting auras of gold and berries that were the hummingbirds around the feeders Nicholas had carefully hung. When I looked to the soft ground, I saw beats of light where life grew underneath in worms and moles and grass seeds. I saw the very air's brightness as more than sunlight now, but something else entirely; what Heaven really must look like.

I could always see, and I could recently see better than any other vampire, but now I let myself notice. Nicholas had given it to me.

"He's there," I murmured, awed by the ease in which I found my mark. Instead of taking in the glory of the air surrounding every good and evil and gray matter, I gave it mine. I let my own aura, venom red and mourning gray and forest green and buttermilk yellow; warm, vanilla-scented and tinged with spiders and sharp crow claws. I pushed it forth like a peace offering, a request, and the world gave back to me what I asked for.

"You found him?" Nicholas asked, flickering to my side like a firefly. "Already?"

"You were the one who said I could.'"

"Yeah, but come on. You're so *weird*," he said under his

breath, searching the woods outside through the window, then shaking his head when he saw nothing.

The cat ran across the yard, fast like he was chased by something terrible, right to Nicholas at the window. Nicholas put his fingers to the glass in disbelief and the cat meowed at him.

An imperceptible movement, so fast it left Nicholas's mumbles about weird cats and women trailing behind him, and he was outside, lifting the cat in his arms and back in the door before a human could have seen. But I saw. I saw his lips nuzzle the cat's fur, the twinge of his smile as he held the cold kitty close, the sigh he let out at its softness.

I felt like the Grinch; my heart grew three sizes that day. I loved this man so much.

And just as fast that feeling soured in my stomach and a heat replaced it, a vengeful heat that told me I had no right to such innocent pleasure. "*Shayla,*" my insides hissed at me. I gasped at the foreign name, only barely recalling that it was the name of Lynch's last victim.

Now her blood ran in mine, in its briefest traces. It wasn't her residue I felt, not some endearing little habit of hers that joined my own as a last tribute to her life. No, this was a second-hand blending of that innocent girl's life and Lynch's perversion of it, the vitality he stole for his own. Together, they created a torturous combination of base elements, a simultaneous Heaven and Hell where nothing made sense except ripping things apart. An implosion that made an explosion. A *hurt.*

"What's with you?" Nicholas said, shaking me back to earth.

"Um, I have to feed, I guess."

"You guess?" The fear of me had returned to his eyes, his very being, and he clutched the cat closer like a little boy would, for security. I hardened more.

"Yeah. I guess. I have a feeling."

His jaw tightened, the little muscle jumping near his ear. "You scare me," he said, not in the cutesy way he would say before I was a vampire, or when I showed some crazy ability as a newborn. There was no hint of love in this statement ; it was a subconscious release of anger on his part. He was angry that I'd become something so frightful. Not a trace of humanity left in me.

He said he would love me no matter what I turned into. That we were the same no matter what.

I stifled a growl.

"I'm going," I said. And I brushed out the door, leaving him behind with his cat.

Darkness became part of me as I bolted through the wet streets of New York City, searching for the depth of black blood that wanted me.

Nicholas was a distant memory as I raced, nothing more than a wind to the throng of people around me. None of them were horrid enough, angry enough, hateful enough, inhuman enough. Not for what I needed.

I needed to take in a monster and feed it to my own.

An alley. Wasn't it always an alley, where the dredges lurked? I stopped so fast that wind hit the back of my head like a brick, but it didn't faze me. The people closest to me on the street stumbled out of my way, one falling to her knees. I didn't help her. Nobody did, actually.

Panting with starved anticipation, I turned sharply, air slicing at my sides, and rushed down the alley, the dripping of the gutters pounding in my ears like thunder—or was that my own blood?

Thinking of blood, Izanagi's bubbled up in me. *He would be so ashamed,* I thought. And pushed the thought away.

I found a feral thing crouched behind a dumpster, shaking

with cold. I cocked my head at it, trying to read its mind, its heart.

"What are you?" the woman croaked.

"Certain death. You?"

"Nobody. I'm nobody."

"You don't feel like nobody." Surging anger, screeching banshee blood, a need to hurt things that nestled in deep, so deeply that it was comfortable to her, protective. This was the animal I wanted. One that had been hurt and hurt others so much that she owned it and liked it. It was all she knew.

"You want to kill me?" she said, rasping. She scrambled to her feet. "Think you'll be doing someone a favor?"

"Lady, I don't care about doing favors. Do I seem like the type to do favors right now? Stalking you in an alley?"

The woman smirked. "You don't know what I was doing before you got here. Seems you might change your mind about what a favor is."

I killed her fast, not wanting to savor it in my mind, no matter what my blood screamed for. And if I was being honest, it was what my *soul* screamed for—to torture her. Ruin her more than she'd ruined herself. Take her black heart and keep it, darken it, make it mine. I was so *needful* of evil that I turned my own stomach, but the power of that need was too great to resist, even if I tried.

I was so tired, always, of trying. Always trying to be something more, something else, something better, something different... It was exhausting. And this bleak nothingness, where dark would hold me close with slippery bat wings in my heart, it felt so wrong it was right.

A lone crow cried out at me from the top of the dumpster as I dropped the woman's skinny body to the ground. I didn't feel bad. Not for her. I reached up for the crow, hoping he wouldn't try to pluck something from the body I'd left, but he backed away from me. Crows never backed away from me.

"Maybe I should start looking for bats," I said. And left the city.

~

Passed out cold on the sofa that had once been white, Lynch looked like a drunk who'd finally had enough to drink.

"God, you're a mess," I said, immediately huffing at the realization that I was covered in blood, still recovering, at least emotionally, from the burns I'd received on Nicholas's lawn. "If Nicholas could see us now."

I fell beside him on the couch, eyeing him as he didn't move, thinking for a second that maybe he had found a way to end his immortal life. I nudged him with my boot. Twice. Finally, he snorted and picked his head up, a line of drool streaking his chin. Not much classier than my own streaks of blood.

"Eliza," he croaked, and turned away.

"Yeah, I came back," I said. "Happy to see me as always, huh?"

"Why do you keep coming here?" he spat.

My gut wanted me to throw some snappy comeback at him, but that wasn't what the moment called for. He was more than lost, more than in pain. He was a dead thing without direction. Chris Lynch was a mass murderer, a monster that could undo generations, and he was so *sad*. This Lynch was far more dangerous than the charmer with composure, grace, and egotism on his side. This beast was pitiful and had nothing to lose.

"Why?" he said again, voice cracking, head falling to the side.

I reached out to him. He flinched at first, but then he gave up and let me take his hand. A tear splashed onto my index finger—a human tear. Not tinged with red like all the vampire tears I'd seen and felt. A real tear. My eyes narrowed as my head snapped up to look at him. "How are these real tears?" I said, more to myself than Lynch.

"Residue," he whispered.

I zeroed in, looked harder. His aura was empty. Dried up.

He'd been feeding, but took no life from it. Even his dead heart felt shriveled to my *Shinigami* senses.

I didn't register when my body curled up on the sofa with my legs tucked under me, and faced him with rapt attention. Something was *here*, something I needed to understand. The answers pushed toward me through his skin, drifting from his pores like ash from a volcano. "Why aren't you more...?" I waved my hands around in a stupid gesture that in my head meant "animated." "It's like you haven't fed at all."

He hung his head, without answers. Without life. "Why are you here?" he said a third time, his lips twitching into a frown to hold the tears back.

"I know you don't want me here," I murmured, trying not to break him worse than he was, "but your blood called out to me, and I listened. I can see fates when I drink—"

"The Master must have loved that," Lynch muttered.

I blinked fast, making Lynch a moving picture behind my lashes in my shock. That Lynch would think of such a thing, that he would know the Master would exploit me as he had. I hadn't thought Lynch considered anyone but himself...and Kat. "Yeah, he thought it was a great old time to mess with me, mad scientist himself all over my head."

"Terrible wording, Eliza."

I laughed, wild and loud. He smirked, but the tears still fell, every one of them crystal clear and without a tinge of death in them.

No death in them.

"Holy hell. You're not killing them."

Lynch didn't move, didn't react at all.

"What are you doing with these girls, Lynch? Lynch!" I smacked his arm in a way that as a human wouldn't have done a second's worth of damage, but Lynch fell over on the couch and scrambled away, afraid of what more I could do. The fear filled me with happiness that I had to shove into a hole in my gut.

He lifted his head, looking me in the eye finally with his own flat black ones. I straightened my back at the hint of his old self, the ruthless monster who did nothing without himself in mind. I knew the answer before he said it.

"I'm making vampires."

My knees buckled with the vision that hit me—a slideshow, really—of two, then four, then six girls, all the same as his victims ever were. Young, bubbly, sweet. Kind. The usual revulsion rolled through me, and then it stopped. Right before the young ladies' hearts would stop, right before that climactic horror, the senseless murder, the disgust disappeared. Because these girls didn't die. I felt it as they did: the last beat of my heart. The hitch in my throat with the final breath. The darkness when I wondered why I was dying. So different than when I became *Shinigami;* these girls were sure death was theirs. The apologies they would never utter, the kisses they'd never give. The things they'd never learn. The dreams that turned to dust. In that split second, they were forced to accept it.

And then in the next unexpected breath, it was all in their grasp again.

Jealousy coiled in my gut like a viper, but it had no one to strike at.

These girls got a chance to not only see what they'd missed, but the chance to correct it, and to try harder. My chances looked much, much different. My chances all hinged on that moment of giving up. I hadn't had any chance until I'd died.

Like a gentle arm, the red mist embraced me on the inside, pulling me back. The time for me to lament my mortal life was over, and certainly not the problem right now. It wasn't even *one* of the problems right now.

"You turned them, and then you just let them go?" I asked, incredulous. For all I could see, I couldn't see *why* Lynch would do such a thing. "What's in it for you?"

He didn't hesitate to say, "I was lonely."

"But you left them!"

"I was lonely and I was afraid. I'm still the Abomination, am I not? I don't owe you reasons, Ellie."

His resignation turned my stomach more than the senseless killing—or not killing—of all these women. His acceptance of the monster he was…

Why can't I accept it that way? Why do I always have to try?

"No. You don't owe me reasons why you're creating vampires and leaving them to kill half the world, or die in the sun, or whatever. But you have to fix it. I can help you." *What was I saying?* As if it wasn't bad enough that I was there, spending time with this shark in shark's clothing, whether it was long past washing or not, I had this sudden compulsion to offer him my help? The Eliza who despised him before she became a vampire, before Kat was killed, wouldn't recognize me at all.

Maybe that wasn't a terrible thing.

But it was a terrible thing that I'd been cursed—or cursed myself—to connect with goddamn Lynch, of all people, when the love of my afterlife was a blink away from me with vampire speed. So much was separating us, and also nothing. And yet when I was with Nicholas, I couldn't get to the bottom of the divide between us. One thing I didn't need to question, though, was that I loved Ossipee, and all of New

Hampshire. I would not let fresh vamps ravage it, and I needed to be with Lynch to stop him turning every pretty girl immortal.

"Look," Lynch was saying, inching toward me, a remarkably clear look in his soulless eyes, dirty palms turned up in supplication. "The truth is, I don't know why I'm turning them into vampires. I haven't wanted to admit it—I don't know about that either—but I've had this urge to do it, a new urge. Not like my urges before."

"Yeah, you don't need to go into detail, I've seen the remnants of your *urges.*"

"Of course. It isn't as if I've had a sudden change of morality and I can't bring myself to kill any longer. That kind of pathetic salvation is far beyond me. But a new feeling has overcome me to give them blood, to bring them across and make them immortal. As if it's my—"

"—purpose." My dead blood chilled at the thought of fate actually having a hand in the Abomination's existence. The Master made it all up: the *unmei nashi,* the alternative fates of the victims, the wasting away of the *Shinigami* who didn't feed on their intended, all of it. And yet, there was an undeniable force at work in the *Shinigami* world, and it was impossible to ignore. That fate felt very real.

I still found it hard to believe that Lynch had any greater purpose in his miserable life, and I regretted having anything to do with it. But it also felt like taking a correct turn in one of those newspaper mazes in the *Ossipee Gazette.* Like I was getting closer to the end. Completion. Everything worked together so smoothly, I wanted to race to the next turn.

If only I'd known then what was around that next corner. What terrors and atrocities I'd commit in my foolish plan to "help."

～

"You can sleep in here," Lynch said, pushing open a white (of course) door on the second floor.

"Your room is right over there," I snapped, not really knowing why I was snappy. I wasn't worried he would try something on me, or that he'd try to kill me in the night. It was just being *close* to him like that, able to hear his dead heart if I tried, saying "good morning" to him as we both emerged from our rooms. "This isn't a frat house, we aren't roomies. I don't want to be here."

"So why are you?"

"You keep asking me that…" I grumbled, looking away, rolling my eyes.

"And you tell me you have to be."

"Right."

He was quiet after that. I think he was waiting me to say something else, that I wanted to be there because I just *wanted to be there*. And I felt terrible that he had no one who cared to spend time with him. That for all his success, at least before Kat, and his charm and good looks and intelligence, he was alone forever. Truly alone. Even Roman hadn't wanted to be anywhere near him, and he was the one who made Lynch a vampire.

Now Roman didn't want to be near any of us. But that had to change.

"Okay," I said. "I'll stay here." *Did I imagine his shoulders relaxing?* "You can keep the east wing empty still. Unless you've got a dungeon over there or something."

Lynch did a thing then that I didn't know he was capable of. He let out a howl of nervous laughter, doubling over with shock. When he stood up his eyebrows were near his hairline, I swear, eyes wide and glistening, mouth open to show his still gleaming white shark teeth. What struck me most was the way his hair fell softly across his forehead, brushing his brows, messy like some eighties cult classic movie star. This Lynch was vulnerable and…*endearing.* I'd never seen him so human. I didn't think it was possible.

"You're smiling," he said, lips upturned.

"Don't get used to it, huh?"

"Good night, Ellie."

"Eliza, please."

His eyes darkened. He knew that only Kat called me Ellie once I'd become part of the vampire clique.

"Of course. Good night. Eliza." He smiled at me humbly, lips soft but tight, eyes dark but not quite as cruel or hurt as they'd been even a few minutes before.

"Good night," I whispered to the air. He was already gone.

~

Vampires don't need to sleep, not often. But we do get weary. Mental and emotional exhaustion follows us into immortality. Awesome, right?

So it was with great pleasure that I fell into the king-size bed with fresh sheets scented with lavender. Though things had fallen into disrepair, just like the master of the house had, the mansion was still brand spanking new; must and dust hadn't taken the place over yet. This was no ancient, abandoned castle—it was a new place without life to it. Squatted in. Soulless before, when I called it the Great White Mansion, and now it was just *vacant.* So different from Nicholas's cottage, where the fire always crackled, the teapot was always whistling, laughter was always heard. Those early days where I'd stayed in the spare room that had become mine, when Roman and Nicholas were the closest of brothers, were some of my favorite days in my life.

It never did feel quite right without Roman there.

Rolling over in the massive bed, the sheets swishing against my body, I tried to fall asleep but thoughts of Roman kept me awake. Not of Nicholas. But of Roman.

Why was he *so* adamant about keeping away from us? I wouldn't go so far as to say all was forgiven, but Nicholas, me, we'd done things we weren't proud of, too. And we loved each other still. We loved Roman still. Fate had handed us all a rotten deal, cornering us all and forcing us into solitude in more ways than we could count: Roman, his wife and child ripped away from him. Nicholas, adored and proud, but restless and ashamed underneath. Me, with death by my side— my parents, my grandmother, never even able to keep a damn dog. But when Kat became Nicholas's *unmei nashi*, fate had destroyed us all. And what fate hadn't done, Roman finished.

Death gods.

The old stories of the tortured relationships of Greek mythology sprang to mind. The *Shinigami* weren't so different. Gods indeed.

I heard the moaning first. No question who it was, of course. A short scream followed, like Jack Nicholson in *The Shining* when he has the nightmare about killing Wendy and Danny.

"Shit."

I threw off the covers like a human would, the blankets snapping. To go or not to go? If I went to Lynch—who was still making strangled screaming sounds—everything would change. We would be friends. No other way around it. A person didn't wake another person from a nightmare unless they cared. What would he do when he woke up? Would we "talk it out" and have a nice midnight—or whatever time it was—chat?

He's not my friend.

Then why was I down the hall at his door, hand raised to

knock and knowing I should just go inside when I heard the sob?

"Shit," I said again, and turned the knob.

I couldn't go to him, I couldn't. "Lynch," I said loudly. He continued to thrash sporadically, kicking off blankets, revealing his nearly-nude body. Shit, again. "Lynch!" I called to him over and over, louder all the time, but finally I faced that I had to go and touch him.

His skin was slicked with icy sweat, his face ghost-white with a sickly shine. "Lynch." I shook him hard, but his own movements were more forceful, I was just white noise. *Buck up, you frigging baby.*

I gripped him by both shoulders, leaning over him like he was an *unmei nashi* and I was saving him from his own worst ending. "Lynch, wake up."

"Dead," he said.

"Lynch—"

"Dead. Dead." He said it over and over, his jaw so tight I could hear his teeth rubbing together. The tendons in his neck looked ready to snap, I could *feel* them straining with my fresh senses, see the blood pulsing through bulging veins, not his own. I put my fingers to them without thinking, drawn to the way they stood at attention and reached out to me.

Lynch's hand shot up and grabbed my wrist with more force than I could ever have, even at my strongest, squeezing until I cried out. That sound woke him immediately—a woman's cry of anguish. Naturally. The beast.

"What are you doing?" he spat, and pushed my body away with just the force behind that one hand, sending me stumbling back with a totally human lack of grace, like the old me in a pair of heels.

"You...you were having a nightmare," I said, rubbing my wrist, rattled and afraid. God, I hated being afraid, but he took me by surprise, and being a vampire didn't change me enough to erase my fear of Lynch completely. But I had forgotten it for a while.

Never again.

"I don't remember it," he said angrily.

"Well shit, *sorry*. Next time I'll let you freak out all night. I should have slept on the third floor like I wanted…"

"No," he said, his entire demeanor changing. A trick. He wanted me near him for a reason, he had to.

"Why not? You know, I don't have to stay here—"

"And go where, Eliza? Face it, you have nowhere better to be."

He was right. Being with Nicholas and Blue felt wrong. Thinking of their names together wrenched me, even if I knew there was nothing between them. That it wasn't just always "Nicholas and Eliza" boiled me. And I had nowhere better to be, just like Lynch said. No one else who wanted me around, not even the death god who'd followed me my whole life. They were all gone, and I was alone.

As usual, I hadn't noticed the red mist that erupted in protective billows around me, slinking its way around my limbs and purring to me with a sound that only I could hear. It lifted me just off the ground, as though telling me it could take me far away from all of it. But as comforting to me as the mist was, it was a thing of nightmares to everyone else, and Lynch was no exception. I think I was worse than the nightmare I'd woken him from. He looked at me with a freshly sweat-slicked brow, more terrified than he'd been in his dream state, I felt his stomach clenching inside him.

"I won't hurt you," I said, my voice tinny through the crimson haze. Lynch didn't believe me. Why would a man so thirsty to hurt others believe such a thing?

"You couldn't," he said. And I think that hurt worse than anything else I'd heard from him. I lowered myself, the mist dissipating, replaced with a sadness I couldn't explain.

"You don't have to be this thing you are," I said. "You don't have to give in. You can change."

"I can't. And I have no reason to." When I didn't reply—because what could I say to that, when I knew all too well what it felt like to have nothing better on the horizon—he continued. "Aren't you going to tell me that it's the right thing to do, to stop killing for fun?"

"That's the reason you should fight the urge, right there. Because you're looking for someone to tell you to."

I'd found my way to sitting on the end of his bed somehow, and cursed that vampires could move so fast. I hadn't even thought about it and done it. But when I realized I had, I didn't move away. I stayed with the same creature who'd horrified me a moment before, who I'd despised from the minute we met, and who was speaking of murdering like it was simple and normal. I suppose for him, it was.

And hadn't I felt that way myself after drinking his blood? Before I'd killed that woman in New York City? Hadn't I craved to do it again?

"You're thinking about blood right now. Aren't you?" Lynch asked.

"How did you know?"

"We share the blood, remember?"

"But I can't feel…"

"Can't you?"

I did feel it before, Lynch's ache to cause terror. But what did it *mean?* I couldn't believe I was brought to Lynch's doorstep so we could bond over murder. I didn't want to share blood with him, not his own, not his victims'.

"I did feel a…rush…earlier. More savage than I ever was. I think." *Why was I sharing this with him?*

"It's not so awful, is it? You see why I go back for more?"

I shook my head wildly, bubbles of red behind my eyes. "No, this isn't the lust for blood that drives you, it's straight vicious, cruel… You kill because you hate them, you want to feel their fear. You don't think anyone can stop you. You were this way in life, and you're this way as a vampire. Now you just have the tools," I said, showing my fangs.

"Then why was I made a vampire, huh?" He rose to his feet in a heartbeat, his mood shifting from sullen and sad to brilliantly angry in the same amount of time. "We all had a purpose for being made, right?"

"Yeah, about that…"

"I know what you think. I know about the Master, and the *unmei nashi*, Nicholas told me. I never believed any of it. I don't know why the *Shinigami* are all woven together. Some higher power decided we all need to be miserable and inbred, but I do know that someone, somewhere had a plan for me." His lips were taut, eyes pleading but determined. "I was meant to be a vampire, too many events have worked together to make me this way for it to be chance. So what reason do I have to exist, Eliza? Do you know?"

In that moment, I saw that Lynch wasn't so different from me. We were both drifting, and being prepared our entire lives for a fate that had been withheld from us. I was working through my own destiny, but Lynch was just stuck. Stuck with less of a reason to live than ever, now that Kat was gone.

"I don't know, Lynch. I don't. But I know one way to find out."

With a *crack* of air, I was at his throat, pushing him back on the bed, and sinking my teeth in hard.

Drinking blood both invigorates and exhausts me, turns me inside out in such a way that I don't know if I've done something right or torn myself asunder. But drinking Lynch's blood wasn't confusing like that. His blood was a straight arrow, pointing at nothing at all. Nothing. It wasn't rich blood, metallic, like all of it. Not full of history and promise like every other. It was empty. He was empty. No potential, only nothing.

I wanted nothing. But nothing was not what I was there for.

"Aaaargghh!" I screamed, tearing at my hair and elevating off of Lynch like a ghost. I squeezed my eyes shut, hoping to see something I'd missed before, but found only a thirst for more blood. I felt Lynch's constant hunger to have more, without any reason or expectation. It was pure. So blank that it felt like falling into white cotton sheets and blocking out the world. No visions warring, no wrongs to right. I was jealous that this was a feeling he knew well.

"Why do you do this?" he cried out, hand clutching his neck, scrambling backwards across the bed, against the headboard, eyes wild and afraid. "Why did you come here to do this, is this my punishment?"

My eyes shot open, my hands still tangled in my hair. "What? You think this is *your* punishment?" I sneered, disgust rippling under my voice. "Being here with you, needing to drink your blood, and *liking* it, memories of Kat all over the place, and never knowing why? *Your* punishment… You're the most selfish monster I can think of," I hissed, still afloat, now wrapped in crimson clouds. "What the hell am I being punished for?" I cried out to no one. "Why does nothing come easy to me?"

I sank back down until my feet touched the floor. Solid ground. No white bedding to catch me, only my own two feet.

Lynch looked like he'd never stop sweating. I'd come in to relieve him of a nightmare and brought him a reality far worse, though I couldn't say if it was worse than the one he'd always lived. I walked away, with nothing more to say. Once again, his blood hadn't revealed any mysteries to me, and I was beginning to believe my own truth that fate and *unmei nashi* and everything our culture had been built upon was nonexistent.

But like everyone else, every other *Shinigami*, and probably every human, I was too afraid of what believing in nothing would leave me with.

"You don't have to stay here," Lynch said faintly behind me, in a voice dripping with sorrow.

I kept walking, my feet touching the earth, my head under those imaginary white blankets.

CHAPTER 108

For days we avoided each other, but I couldn't bring myself to leave. Not for good. When I left to feed, I returned to that broken castle, a queen of horrors just like its master.

I'd grown into a beast with Lynch's blood in my veins, and the feeling of something more, some*one* more lingered behind it, like a shadow whispering secrets. And yet, I still knew that extra presence was not what I was looking for. God, I was so tired of searching. It was hardly fair that my prophetic ability to see alternative fates led me to the vision but then wouldn't give it to me. And in the meantime, I was just stuck. Just here.

I approached the Great White Mansion in the sunlight, the rays puncturing my skin, but warming me inside. My last victim—she'd been a good person. All the gloom and doom in me this time was my own, and the residue she'd left made the sun dance delightfully on my skin, no matter how damaging it was to me. Her residue also left an odd need to climb trees. I'd never climbed a tree in my life, and this girl hadn't looked a whole lot like a lumberjack, with her wisp of a body and heels. But this was a memory from her childhood, slipping into me like shots from a bottle, of her climbing the trees in the woods behind the school for some peace and quiet—school was so *loud* to her. The trees gave her cover from the abrasiveness of her life.

Passing Lynch's house to the backyard, past the porch where Nicholas had once come to realize that it was his "fate" to murder Kat, I stopped dead short.

The once-manicured lawn was overgrown, a forest of weeds and storm-strewn branches, long grass and dead patches. Abandoned.

Except for one very new addition.

The tree house—it could be described as nothing less—had been built so recently the lumber still had the earthy, rich and fresh scent. *Where did this come from?*

A handmade hidey-hole of a cabin, carefully crafted of seaside green, robin's egg blue, cherry blossom pink (*just like Japan!*), and nuclear family white. It abounded with rivets and reclaimed wood, barn door latches, weathered wrought iron, and was surrounded with pink roses. As if they'd been planted there for years. Smoke billowed from the smallest chimney I'd ever seen. Both beachy cottage and forest den. As if the place had been made...

For me.

The whitewashed stairs creaked in all the right places up to the wide-open barn doors. Holding my breath, I peeked inside, knowing that this had been made for me, thrilled and afraid at the same time.

It had been a long time since I'd been nervously excited about something not blood-related.

But nothing comes without some expectation.

The woodland nook sang of springtime—just what I needed after the world's longest winter. My stomach churned with the mere thought of the winter's impossible number of events. I banished the memories and took in the here and now.

A daybed beckoned, loaded with blankets to help with the shady chill from the open windows. If I wasn't cozy enough, I could plant myself on the rug in front of the tiny fireplace with a book. Empty bookshelves lined the walls, waiting for me to fill them. The fluttering in my stomach was reminiscent of all the times I went book shopping when Nicholas and I first met. I'd have read just about any piece of crap to have an excuse to go back to that simple time. But the thing that put the biggest smile on my face was the coffee pot on the windowsill, empty though it was. Tucked into a private spot, but still central.

Just like at Birch Tree Books. My place.

Our place. It became Nicholas's too.

He made this for me, even if he doesn't agree with why I'm not at the cabin.

My entire body relaxed, calm as I entered, just as gray clouds rolled overhead. A cool spring rain came in through the open windows, sudden and sweet, and I held out my fingers to feel it. Sinking onto the floor by the fireplace, I thought without guilt that Kieran could have lit it in a heartbeat for me. I smiled. I didn't stop smiling when Lynch came close, through the woods behind the house, smelling not of blood, but of flowers. He appeared at my doorstep, brow furrowed, tentative.

"I know, it showed up out of nowhere, right?" I said, grinning. Not that I should have been surprised—Nicholas had built his own cabin out of the New Hampshire trees by himself basically overnight. "He's—something," I said. Sensing Lynch's discomfort, I offered, "Come in."

He entered hesitantly, as if expecting the floor to fall out from beneath him. Even more hesitantly, he sat on the floor a foot away from me, and that was when the smell of the peonies wafted across.

Peonies. Kat.

"You like it?" Lynch asked, eyes darting around.

"What's not to like?" I asked. "It'd only be better if the coffee was already made." I elbowed him playfully, more relaxed than I'd been in forever. "Seriously, go find a coffee girl to drink so you can get barista skills for a few days."

He actually *blushed*. A hot pink tinge that didn't come from his own blood—but blood I wanted nonetheless in that instance, with the violence of springtime bursting to life.

Whipping rain gusted into the windows more fiercely, the *shush*ing of the leaves whispering across each other became a slick slapping. Tiny creature feet pounded in my ears as they scuttled into knots and burrows, a cacophony of life and destruction, and I sank my teeth into Lynch's wrist before he ever knew what happened.

Every sensation disappeared except the ocean waves of hot blood flowing through him and into me, spilling over my lips. I felt Lynch's other hand on the back of my head, still as hesitant as when he'd entered the cottage, despite the intimacy with which I'd stolen his immortal life force. Groaning, I took a long pull from his arm, the rush making me dizzy, the world turning blacker than black...

Then it snapped back, hard, fast, with a woman's scream approaching me like a train.

I don't know this woman, I thought, my anger blossoming like a bruise.

Her face approached mine, and the clarity didn't help at all. Straggly blonde hair, thinning even. Dull eyes the color of a murky lake, thin lips. Blood trickled neatly from her throat. So, another one of Lynch's playthings. My compassion dwindled more and more for these victims with every vision, seeing only another one, and another, and never what I came to see, never the things I *needed to see.*

A cry curdled from Lynch's throat—I tasted it, the flavor of raw hamburger. I'd bitten him again, a new spot inside his arm, and it was sloppy. I saw myself tear the skin, shake my head side to side to sink both fangs into the one wound—I saw it in memory, having done it so quickly, the time had passed.

And I was screaming into his skin.

Blood bubbled around my lips. Lynch shook, trying to free himself. I held down one thigh, my other hand pushing down a shoulder as I bent over him and drank in gulps so enormous they hurt my throat going down. Or maybe it was the muffled screams coming up. But it was what I needed. It worked.

Roman, finally. Roman.

And Kat. No, I didn't need to see this, I'd seen this already, watched him murder her. What pointless—

Then it was another time, another moment that I hadn't known. Roman and Kat together, without me or Nicholas nearby, and she's telling him something. What is she telling him? Why is his face twisted, but happy, and she's smiling but—

"Get off me!" Lynch screamed, finally wrestling free of me in my confusion. His shirt was drenched in blood, more in his hair, on his pants.

"I'm sorry," I whispered. But he just stared at me in horror and shock. "I didn't mean to—"

He rushed out, away from that cottage which had been so lovingly built, and was now just another place to kill things. I wanted to go after him. I felt bad, I really did… But how many people had he inflicted pain like that upon and never given it a second thought? Doing it for attention from a Master who wanted nothing to do with him.

But the fear on his face.

It had been pretty close to the fear on that roughed-up

blonde woman I'd seen before Roman appeared in my vision. Another victim I had no connection to, just leftover blood from Lynch's last kill. Another puzzle that I was getting sick of trying to solve. But the one common piece, the one that kept getting lost and turning up where I least expected before disappearing again, *hiding* again…

Roman.

~

Bethlem was…unpleasant…the first time I'd come. For my very first feeding. The smells, the bland and filthy colors, the howls and whimpers came at me like bullets, but I could see beyond them for the gleaming, screaming purpose of my visit.

My *unmei nashi*, Clara Borden.

As violent as her end was, the connection we felt, the residue of her life that ran through my dead veins after I'd killed her burst with a romantically sinister intimacy that I couldn't deny. We shared destinies.

I looked back on that first time *fondly*.

Jesus, I'm grotesque. I long for that closeness again. I'm disgusting.

Worse, after spending such little time with Lynch, I was *less* disgusted by it than I should have been, than I would have been a month ago. I understood the need more, like I'd been looking for an excuse to justify the serial killer mentality. This atrocious, crumbling, shit-soaked house of horrors was where I deserved to be.

This time, without an *unmei nashi* to guide me, my vampire eyes showed me too much. With my new strength stolen from so many victims, from Lynch, from Izanagi… Now it was an overlapping mix of timelines, one more degrading than the next, the worst of each of the hospital's eras, all assaulting me at once. Inmates in a hollow, flickering blood-red haze, brought to me by my own traitorous mist shared space with solid flesh and blood patients, ambling through and across one another never aware of the other. Ghosts and man-made ghouls, decaying together. So alone. Looking closer, I not only saw the physical anguish of the sores and wounds, but the actual medications, warring inside them, dehydrating them, crushing and weakening them, tearing their organs apart. Their thirst was my thirst, their desperation was mine to get to the wooden cistern in the overgrown courtyard, demonic watering hole that it was. A single, glorified bucket surrounded by dirt. The "lunatics" crowded around it, kicking up dust as they pushed their way in with hoarse moans. The ones who'd already overfilled as much as they could huddled mere feet away. A handful of them, unable to hold the pitiful amount of dirty water they'd gulped down too fast. Some retched, but most fell to their knees with filth trailing down their legs—the drugs I could so plainly see flushed every ounce of moisture or sustenance from their bodies. The complete *dryness* coupled with the stench of bile and shit overwhelmed me.

Shaking my head too fast, the world blurring around me, my red mist shot up from my feet to protect me, taking me away from the overload of this place. But it couldn't take away the knowledge that Roman brought himself here deliberately. This was where he felt he belonged. The man Nicholas called his brother.

And like it had with the cat, the mist reached out, extended fine tentacles all over Bethlem, quicker than even my eyes could follow.

Then *Slam! Slam! Slam!* The tentacles coiled back into me from every direction, punching me all over my body until I gasped, buckling, flinching. I coughed, struggling for air I didn't breathe, and with a great breath, the mist wound into my throat and gave me what I really needed.

"Roman."

Brushing past dumbstruck and whimpering patients and nurses, I fled to him.

He sat at the bedside of a man who spoke to him excitedly, bony hands gesturing, laughing. And Roman laughed, too.

He *laughed.*

My breath caught as I watched, having just motioned myself through the doorway, to see Roman enjoying something, some*one.* He took the man's hand as it waved through the air, and squeezed, smiling with all the charm he ever had. Our Roman. Nicholas's Roman, who exuded goodness, community, thoughtfulness, sincerity. He was always better than the rest of us.

Even when he killed Kat. He did it with the saddest song in his heart.

Roman rose from his seat, bidding quiet farewell to the man, who finally saw me and smiled gently—though his eyes narrowed. He pursed his thin lips, bunched the blanket in his hands, and nodded to me as if we shared some great secret. One that neither of us wanted to know.

Pushing past me out the door, Roman didn't look at me. He only muttered, "Let's get this over with."

I followed him without speaking up to his same subhuman nest in the attic. "I see you did something with the place," I said. He'd swept. Cleaned and repaired the corners where before there had been rotted holes and cobwebs. The disgusting mattress was gone—replaced with a rocking chair. No bed for him to rest on now, and I supposed that was an improvement. That mattress was a haunted thing, a magnet for self-loathing. It spoke of suffering more than any piece of furniture should. He'd brought up a lamp as well, a glued-together old mess of two amber-colored glass orbs. It made me smile. I could picture it having belonged to one of the patients here, one that Roman took a liking to.

He sat in the rocker, and in the same movement, pulled up another rickety little chair to face him. I sat, and I got up the courage to look at him.

Some color had returned to his cheeks, and his eyes weren't dead anymore. The brilliant ocean-blue hadn't returned, but a shadowy sea was there, full of treasure waiting to be brought to the surface again. His hair had been brushed —golden again—taken on the color of the sun, where he'd spent some time recently, I was sure. His lips had plumped, but his neck, his arms under his button-down shirt, were still thin. He was no longer as unkempt as he'd been, worse than the patients in the beds below.

He was getting better.

"I'd offer you tea…" he said absently.

I smiled, just a little. This was far more like Roman than he'd been the last time we'd seen each other. "You aren't drinking much tea these days, are you?" I asked softly. He'd been visiting with patients, making friends, moving with a little more life, but he wasn't his old self. He would deny himself the comfort of a cup of tea or hot chocolate from the kitchens.

Actually, that was a lot like the Roman I knew. Selfless to a fault. Self-flagellating.

"You've come back," he said. "But I told you—"

"I know. You won't come back."

"No."

His voice was that gentle thing with the slightly gravelly undertone that I remembered. So warm, unlike any other voice I knew. "I don't believe that anymore, Roman. I look at you now, and I see how you want to get better. You *are* getting better."

He looked away, covering his mouth with his hand, as if

afraid to agree. "I couldn't survive any longer as I'd been. I wanted so much to let the pain and the guilt consume me, but it couldn't in the end. It never really turned me into one of them downstairs. Some of them are so far gone, I can't even see remnants of who they might have been, but others..." He looked back to me, and he smiled. I couldn't help it—I let out a sob of happiness. He was still so sad, but he had hope. I felt it. "There are some patients here that aren't gone yet. Nobody visits them, though. They're left here, but I *feel* the spark in there, for some of them. Just some of them." He scooted to the edge of his seat, steepling his hands, elbows on his knees, eyes alight, as muddy as they still were. "And I started talking to a few of them in the night, when they were the most alone. I watched them get better. Then some of the ones that had been written off as little more than animals, they began to speak, too. I was doing some good, El. And it did good for me."

"You always did good, Roman, always." I took his hands in mine, squeezing as he'd done to the patient I'd found him with.

"No," he mused kindly. Still worried about how I felt, even after all he'd been through. "Nobody is good all the time, Eliza. Not me, not you, not anyone. But we show it differently. We let it show differently."

"You always let it show. So many others..."

"Don't."

"...let it goooo, let it go. They aren't nice folks anymooooore..." I sang.

He laughed. The same laugh that had warmed me more than the fireplace, the cat at my feet, the Christmas light glow on the snowy nights, the hot chocolate balanced on the tattered couch arm, the wood stove in the cabin's kitchen. All those memories and not a one of them complete without that laugh, of Nicholas's brother. My friend.

"Come home, Roman. Your blood will heal Nicholas

completely. He'll be his old self again, and we miss you. We just miss you." The absence of his spirit left a void in New Hampshire. We all darkened without him.

But Roman's face hardened, not angrily, but shielding him from hurt. From rejection. I felt his fear so strongly it choked me.

"I know something that will change what you think of me, even now. Something that will make you forget that I killed Kat and hate me anew, with a greater, deeper resolve. I could never look you in the eye again."

Those words—that he could never look at me again—he'd written it in his letter to Nicholas when he left. It pained me to think he stayed away because of me, how I'd feel.

"It doesn't matter. I don't know what it is, so it can't hurt me, right?"

He opened his mouth to object, but shook his head, dropping it to look at his lap. And he gave in to me, finally. *Finally.* "All right," he said, clear and strong.

I felt something break inside him—a barrier. An inner hatred. And I saw his acceptance take over.

But acceptance of what?

CHAPTER 109

"You're staying with *who?*"

Roman's mouth hung open, all his pointy pearlies showing, and the first thought I had was, *Wow, he kept brushing while in the insane asylum.*

"Yeah, I know," I mumbled, nervously scratching my hair as we walked casually through the center of North Conway. Perfectly normal, this, two vampires in broad daylight, touristing in a tiny tourist town. One thing that never ceased to amaze me was the way drinking blood affected us—good guy, all the sun we want. Not so good guy, and we're hiding in the darkness. "Not by choice. Not really. I'm not gonna say he's changed, but he's definitely chang*ing*. I don't know into what, but…"

We rounded the corner to Birch Tree Books, and if I'd had breath, it would have been stifled like a chihuahua in a handbag. Nicholas had no idea we were coming, that Roman was coming. It had been so long.

"It's crazy to say, but I missed Lynch some. The Abomination. I missed him."

"Well, straight outta Bethlem, I guess it's not too far-fetched. Are you ready?" My words were slow, but my dead heart pounded fast, fast, fast.

Roman glanced at me, meeting my eyes in that old Roman way—just looking at me, but always understanding me, appreciating me. It was a thing that only he could do; it changed a person. "I don't think 'ready' is a word I'd use, but let's go." His lip quirked, eyes sparkled, and the bells on the door handle rang as we entered.

His back to us, Nicholas balanced a stack of books in his arm with a steaming cup of coffee on top as he slipped one onto a high shelf. The man would do anything for attention, even when no one was around.

"Came to stalk me, like the good ol' days, El?" he said, chin on the coffee cup rim.

"I come bearing gifts," I said.

He spun around, coffee not even sloshing, and looked from me to Roman with an unreadable expression. He was so good at being indecipherable and yet wearing his heart on his sleeve at the same time. "Here to see me practice my new circus act?" He pulled another book out of the stack, coffee cup barely moving. But we were all too familiar with his vampire skills, his totally *Nicholas* skill at just about everything, including his poker face.

"How have you been, brother?" Roman asked.

Swirling eyes trained on Roman's, he paused before saying, "Brother, huh? Brother, as in eternally connected, blood thicker than water even if it's not our own blood, that kind of brother?"

"That kind. Yes." I felt Roman tense beside me, more like a flicker of fear. Not horror movie fear, but fear that everything he ever did was wrong, and all leading to this point.

Those eyes never moved away, stared Roman down in challenge and sadness. "No. A brother doesn't run away because he's afraid of what he'd already done. Not my brother." Amazing how his words would cut to the core, but he'd say them as if they were a fly on his shoulder, merely brushing them off and it was over. He turned away, back to the bookshelves.

"I'm sorry," Roman said.

"'Bout what?" Nicholas shrugged.

"Nicholas, don't make him do this," I said quietly. "Don't make him answer for his choices. He's been doing it for so long."

A human might not have noticed, but the air chilled, a ghost of anger breezing between the musty pages of books.

"Really, Eliza? You'd know. What it's like to answer for every little decision you make until the big ones don't even matter anymore. Right? Guilt yourself long enough, and suddenly everyone has to forgive you."

I gritted my teeth, willing the red mist to stay at bay. "Can we not be an immortal Jerry Springer show right now? This isn't about Kieran, or me. Roman is home! Roman is *home.* You've missed him all this time, been half of yourself without him, and now you're giving him a hard time for coming back. Shut up for once, Nicholas! Shut up and be happy to have your family!"

"Eliza—" Roman started.

But Nicholas cut him off, having set down the books and the coffee in one fell swoop and embraced Roman more tightly than any human could have endured. Eyes squinted shut, one hand holding his brother's head close so he could tell him all the things he needed to.

Not to toot my own horn, but I felt pretty responsible for that happy mini-ending. The Nicholas I'd met an eternity ago would have kept Roman on the wire, strutting about his business with shoulders back, dropping one-liners through an arrogant smirk until he could barely stand himself anymore. I'd had some influence in his life.

"El, you wanna flip that sign to 'closed,' please?"

"But it's the middle of the day—" Roman started.

"Like I care," Nicholas said, sinking into a dusty green armchair that I didn't recognize.

"New?" I said, gesturing to it.

"You're asking if this," he pulled a tuft of stuffing out of a hole in the arm, "is new? I took it from this guy's house. It needed a new home."

"Ah, gotcha." Reading his expression, I knew. His victim had an attachment to this chair, and the residue left Nicholas needing to hold onto it. I went to it—to him—wanting to be a part of it too, to be a part of whatever Nicholas had been doing without me. The distance between us was too great. I felt too much like we were starting over every time we saw each other. Sitting on the arm of the chair, I put my hand on his bicep. He dropped his head against me, our bodies magnetized.

If there was one thing that vampire-dom had given to me, it was this unending connection to my maker that left no questions. It wasn't only that we loved each other, as if that weren't enough. It was more than feelings. Memories, promises, fates, enigmas of a future…

Me, alone without my family

Wine, roses, death all around me

Surges of knowing I possessed a destiny, just out of reach

Nicholas, bringing it all together, and so much more

Nicholas, betraying me, called to kill Kat

Death sneaking in and taking both of them from me in different ways

The agony of denying our connection that nearly killed me before I could die…

"Eliza! *Eliza!*"

Sprawled on the floor awkwardly, one leg still hooked over

the arm of the chair, I'd banged my head when I fell. It pounded, but the blood in my veins pounded harder.

"Nicholas?"

"Yeah, right here." He crouched over me, concern swimming in his hazelnut eyes, the peppermint brownie scent seeping through my red mist as it grew around me like a bed of roses.

Roman sat in the chair, leaning over to be with us both, but I still didn't know what had happened. As if reading my mind, Nicholas said, "You started telling a story, you said something about a girl who died."

But I was thinking about me, my *story, and Nicholas. Kat. There'd been no vision, only feeling...*

I couldn't stop the tears that burst forth, unable to comprehend why they'd appeared.

"This is too much like when I first started getting visions," I said gravely. "They took over—even before the Master enslaved me—I couldn't tell what was real." I choked on the words. "They interfered with who I was. It won't happen again."

I got to my feet, forcing my head clear, moving like a vampire, like *Shinigami.* Not some victim of death or blood, but the master of it. And I twisted my mist with my hands like clay, shaping it as I channeled that blackout moment on the arm of the chair, and I thrust the half-formed haze into the air. Where it did exactly what I wanted it to.

Just like the image of my *unmei nashi,* Clara Borden, my very first kill, the mist showed us a moving red picture, bloody shadows of a life that was to end. Beautiful, terrifying, a moving death omen.

"What in the hell is that?" Roman said, jumping out of the chair, either in awe or fear.

"Eliza's super freak mist? The Kit to her Hasselhoff, but with weird, bone-chilling abilities. Watch."

The mist still hadn't shown me much more than the vague shapes of two people, a man and a girl, but it gave me no *feeling,* no knowledge. Not like with Clara, where she enveloped me and her story became my own memories.

So I pushed harder. And I *took.*

"Oh goody, she's doing the soul-suck," Nicholas said, sinking into the green chair, clutching his chest.

"Nicholas. Nicholas?" Roman was saying, backing into a bookshelf, sending it banging to the floor in a heap.

Wild-eyed, Nicholas looked at his brother and forced out, "What consumes her…makes her…stronger." He shut his eyes and composed himself, sitting up straighter, leaning forward to put his elbows on his knees as if this were a casual thing. But it made him feel more like *him.* "Emptiness, death, they drive her and destroy her, and now she uses them and it makes her stronger." He shrugged, having said it, and sat back, letting it happen.

Roman blinked hard at me. And I understood that he was giving in.

Rising into the air, the mist propelling me from underneath, I shuddered and ate up all the fear in the room and the fear that lay beneath—the fear of loss from both of them, Roman and Nicholas. Afraid of losing each other, and me, of losing their immortal lives that they hated and loved at once.

And the vision became solid.

More than shadows, but not quite real, a man and a young lady spoke in a shroud of crimson. They stood close together, not lovers, but not far from it. He reached to her, and she took his hand. He leaned in, kissed her deeply, darkly, and the mist deepened in color to a near-purple. Then he bit her. He drank, but didn't drain her—though when she had nothing left to give him, he forcefully put his wrist to her lips, pushing until she had no choice but to clamp on to it, tear into it with her teeth. And she in turn, drank from him. She fell back, both dead and alive. And he left her.

"What am I seeing, Eliza? What are you seeing?" Roman said.

I turned my cold gaze onto him, and he shrank back more.

"Next *unmei nashi?*" Nicholas guessed.

"No," I said, my voice that hollow thing that felt like the blood pouring from the elevator in *The Shining*. I shook my head, not wanting to be that terror right now, and lowered myself to the ground, pulling the mist into me again; its job was complete. I looked to Roman, Nicholas, and smiled, trying to show them it was just me again. "It was Lynch. And that chair," I said, nodding to the mildewed green chair that Nicholas sat in like a throne, one leg thrown over the side.

Nicholas turned a suspicious eye to me, cocking his head like I was trying to pull one over on him. "Noooo, nope, no Lynch here, just me."

"Not you, and not your victim. Lynch fed on your victim's daughter. In that chair."

"Creepy," Nicholas said.

Roman said, "But why would *you* see that…this way? Why does it matter to you?" The regret showed on his face as soon as he said it. Because Roman cared about every victim, felt the pain of each one. They all mattered to him—and for him to imply that they didn't matter to me… Well, it hurt.

I debated it in my head for a split second, whether to tell them, either of them. Because I knew exactly why I'd seen it.

"Eliza?" Nicholas said quietly.

"Um, yeah, I think I saw it just because of the like, power of the chair, you know?"

"The…power…of the chair," Nicholas said in that incredibly condescending yet likeable joking tone.

"Yeah, you know. Humans carry residue through us—the

chair carries a residue with me." Sounded good. "It's pretty close to home, you know? And I *am* all-powerful-like."

"I should never have told you you'd be a vampire of legend."

"Probably not."

Nicholas joked, and he didn't press me, but he knew I was lying.

I'd added another brick to the wall between us.

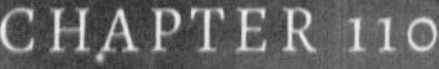

CHAPTER 110

"Where is this girl, the one you killed in the green chair?"

I'd stormed into the mansion, ready to drill Lynch.

"The girl in the green chair..." he trailed off.

"That one. Well, you didn't kill her in the green chair—you didn't kill her at all. Where is she, have you seen her since?"

I'd left Nicholas and Roman at the bookstore to catch up on the very strange events of their time apart. I didn't want to be around when Nicholas told Roman about me and Kieran, or how the Master was dead because of me. I didn't want to be there when Roman told Nicholas about Bethlem.

I didn't want to be there when Nicholas fed from him.

The idea of that much pure emotion and so much drudging up of the past, all the *talking*, the memories, I couldn't expend that much of myself. And the warmth between Nicholas and Roman just couldn't include me right now. I didn't belong there.

You don't belong here.

I had to push the mist inside, wrap it around my heart

then. Those words, being back here…coming home and real-izing maybe I never had one.

The thought wrenched my heart in a way that reminded me of being human. Vulnerable, constantly searching and never finding. *How could I continually miss what I never had?*

But I had belonged once. With my parents. With my grandmother. With Kat. Missing them didn't make me any less annoyed with myself for being a baby about it. I'd spent so much of my goddamn life mourning them and fearing death.

I would not let it happen to me in my immortality. I might have eternity, but I had no more time for moping.

Being the third vampire in that room with Nicholas and Roman gave me such a sense of being *other*, especially the way I life-sucked everyone now. I couldn't let my own self-pity ruin what I had with them. But I had something else to do.

Stop thinking. Confront Lynch about the girl in the green chair, why she's important.

And she was important. She had to be for Nicholas to be called to feed on her father, the strings of fate tying her so tightly to the *Shinigami* that it bled over into her family. Even knowing what I did about the Master, our origins, I still believed in fate's ties to the *Shinigami*. I think that people can believe in something so deeply that they make it come true. And I believe that we determine our own fates—it all worked together too powerfully.

I believed in it like anyone believes in a higher power when they just have no other words to describe the eerie reality of being.

"I haven't seen her," Lynch said, setting a glass of bourbon on the table with a *clink*. So casual, so painfully disconnected. I stormed through the place right over to him, ready to Force-choke him if I had to, get him to tell me everything he knew. Snarling, I took one look in his dark eyes, and I was disheart-ened to find the truth.

He didn't know a goddamn thing.

I was the one who knew everything important when it came to the girl.

Lynch showed not a hint of fear. That sadness of his, it was so *sticky,* clinging to every emotion, every move and thought of his, he couldn't see past it.

"Never mind," I said calmly. No need to frighten him into doing something stupid. Stupider. "I know all I need to." I turned away to go somewhere I could figure out my next move—because the next move was completely mine. This girl…she was unfinished business that needed sorting by the only vampire who held the keys to vampire future in her hand. Lil' ol' me.

"Wait," Lynch said behind me. "Please, tell me what you're talking about."

Strange request.

I turned slowly back, hesitant to involve him in anything, but too interested in *his* sudden interest to back away.

"Well…" I started, realizing that I was telling Lynch what I wouldn't tell Nicholas or Roman just hours before. I told him about the green chair, that Nicholas had been called to the man—the man who was Lynch's victim's father. I told him how I'd created the vision-mist. "I know what happened. You turned the girl into one of us. You weren't her *shugotenshi,* she was nobody—until you turned her."

"Why would you think that?" Lynch asked, mesmerized.

"Think what?"

"That she was nobody. Why would you, of all people, think she was nobody?"

Well, that stopped me dead in my tracks.

"Um, I mean, she wasn't anything to us, like, she wasn't supposed to have anything to do with vampires."

His sneer was something I was more accustomed to than

his sadness. "Still buying into fate and destiny even after you've destroyed it, are you?"

Wow, he really must have been a good lawyer when he was sane on the outside. Making me stumble across my own very opinionated nature, even now that I was all-powerful. I gulped painfully that he saw me so easily.

I'd been nothing. Or so I thought.

Nobody was nothing.

"I do believe in fate a little. At least a little. And because Nicholas *was* called to her father. There's no other explanation for the connection. He was Nicholas's *unmei nashi.*" And a sort of pride swelled in me for Lynch, because I saw a beginning, one that I in part was orchestrating at that very moment. My voice became an urgent whisper, my senseless breathing fast. "Lynch, *you* changed fate's direction. You *forced* it to change. You created a vampire, and *then* fate decided it wanted her. That's why Nicholas fed from her father—fate wanted no ties left behind. *It wanted her alone.*"

"Like we all are."

I nodded slowly, taking his face in my hands before I could help myself, a glee filling me that I didn't recognize, the opening of a closed door that I'd just discovered. "This is your purpose, Lynch. We all have one, and this is yours. It's in my skin, I feel it." Red mist firework bursts and bubbles puffed up between us with my excitement, had me wiggling my fingers, laughing in fits.

"But," His eyes glistened with tears, a zealot looking in the face of his god, "there have been others. She's not the only vampire I've made. What makes her special?"

And so it came full circle.

"Like you said—nobody is nothing."

J ust like that, Lynch and I were a pair, a team, with something new between us aside from our hatred and anger and sadness over the woman we loved. We had a mystery to solve, one that *we* could determine the end of.

The Abomination was about to find out why he existed. Why he, of all murderers and narcissists and sociopaths would be chosen for immortality. I was the one who would hand the knowledge to him.

And I was racing toward the purpose that had always been waiting for me. One that stole my parents, my grandmother, my best friend, replacing it with the presence of death I'd only recently come to know as a real being—Izanagi. I was a legend. I'd been told this for as long as I'd known Nicholas, and I had powers no vampire before me had—but they weren't the reason I was different. Those powers weren't the end of my road; they were stepping stones.

One thing I'd learned in the journey toward becoming Eliza Morgan, *Shinigami*, was that the road wasn't straight with a beaming light over the finish line. No, becoming a vampire had the same path as grief. When I thought I'd finished with it, it popped back up. I'd feel better, then worse; alone, then haunted, then myself; I'd be nothing, then I'd be everything. And there was never really an end to it, not like I thought.

This girl, she held something that I needed to bring my fate to fruition.

And I was perfectly fine knowing that once I found her, my journey still wouldn't be over. There would always be something *more*. Immortality didn't come with an expiration date. Vampirism is a job with endless perks and endless responsibility.

The best part was that I could find her in a heartbeat. An

instant. But for some reason, I wanted Lynch to do it for himself.

I *cared* that he was finding his reason for being.

Maybe it would stop the senseless murdering he'd committed his entire existence, before and after death.

Maybe it would help heal him from Kat's death. Because as much as I hated to admit it, I wanted him to get better. This depression that he couldn't escape, it was too terrible to watch. It wasn't him. It wasn't the man Kat fell in love with, and it hurt my memory of her to see him deteriorate so completely. Some of me wanted that shark back with the gleaming smile, the raven-black hair styled to gleaming perfection, the charm. Even the morbid ulterior motive feeling I got every time he spoke. That Chris Lynch brought me back to a time when Nicholas, Roman, Kat and I were together, a family, as dysfunctional as we were.

I never had been a fan of change.

"Lynch, she's your *unmei fumetsu*. You have a connection to her."

"I feel nothing for her," he said. I believed it.

"You've turned more than just her. Do you not feel any of them?" In a trace of energy through the air, I'd brought him by the hand to my new tree house out back. I wondered for a split second what Nicholas would think about me sharing it with Lynch. But if I was going to pursue this new journey with him, I needed to let him in. I had to open up.

Whether it be to Lynch or anyone else, opening up, getting close, seared me inside. A challenge I'd rather not accept. It was worse than dying; the stakes were higher.

There were plenty of places to sit in my treehouse, but we sat crisscross applesauce on the braided rug, facing each other. No escape from one another.

"Uh..." He couldn't get a hold of himself with the sudden

change—or maybe it was the question he didn't want to answer. "I've changed a few. More than a few."

"You don't know how many vampires you've made?"

He shook his head, eyes downcast.

I took a deep breath. "I'm not judging you. I'm not—disgusted—by you." Ellie Morgan would have been disgusted by him. Eliza *Shinigami* was not. "It was just a question."

His breath was deeper than mine. It endlessly amused Nicholas how we breathed so much when we never had to take a breath. "I don't know, Eliza," he said, voice relaxed, sad as always. "I never bothered to count. I only do it to pass the time. There's so much time with *nothing*. I just want something to happen…but then I don't care anymore just as quickly." He shot his eyes up at me. "I leave them all, I don't care what happens to them or anyone they touch. It feels *good* to do something so cruel."

Lynch never was one to mince words.

"I understand." I did. He hurt, and hurting felt good. I realized it always had been that way for him. He'd hurt when he'd killed as a human, and he hurt when he'd done it without need as a vampire. With him, it never felt tragic to me. He'd been so self-possessed, egotistical, a lawyer for crying out loud. It's not easy to feel bad for someone like that. Which is why he felt bad for himself.

"Why do you understand?"

"It's a test. How much you can hurt the world without anyone ever caring to stop you."

He *smiled.* That old Lynch smile—warm, but had once shaken me to the core. He was feeling my power, trying not to let it scare him more. "You're very astute as a vampire. Unnaturally observant."

"No, I feel it. I don't see it, I feel it." Here I was, opening up again. "I sense your greatest fears and I grow stronger with them. The more afraid you are, the more I can feel about you. I can even have visions when your fear is at the forefront."

"You'd be a fantastic lawyer," he said.

"Eliza Morgan, Vampire Lawyer."

We laughed, and he leaned back on his elbows, stretching his legs out in front of him. With the scruff and the messy hair, he reminded me of Nicholas, but he was too lithe and far too emotionally distressed.

"Lynch, I want you to stop shutting your *unmei fumetsu* out. All of them."

"I'm not."

"You're lying."

He gave an angry shake of his head and looked away from me. "I don't *want* to know them."

I dug in. I kept the mist minimal, a tinge of red underneath me, seeping out like smoke, like my pants were on fire. Lynch was mumbling to stop it, to get out of his head, but the more afraid he was, the more I wanted in, the more powerful the vampire in me became.

"Stop!" he screeched, clutching his ears as if I were needling into his brain through them.

"No," I growled without intending to. My reasons for bringing Lynch here had changed, and the death god in me was taking over when the *Shinigami* legend should have been in control. I was meant to be a leader, not a predator. "I'm sorry," I said, drawing myself back, squeezing my eyes shut. "I'm still new—"

"No you're not," Lynch said forcefully, angry now that he'd gotten his strength back. "Just because you aren't as old as the rest of us doesn't make you new. That word implies weakness, vulnerability, of which you possess neither. You're a predator, make no mistake." He swallowed hard. "But no one is safe from you. Not even the rest of us."

I chuckled. "Who's the abomination now?"

That glint returned to his eyes, that inhuman element that showed the killer he was at heart. Whatever heart he had.

Trying to reconcile that monster with the man who'd been ripped apart by my best friend's death was where I was stuck.

"I didn't mean to invade like that," I said after a shared silence between two villains. "I did mean to maybe, but I shouldn't have. I sense fear underneath this wall you've put up between your and the vampires you've created. You've done this yourself, the connection is effortless—you made this obstruction, this barrier. And it was that fear which called me to you—you're terrified of, of..." I couldn't say it, it was too close to home, same as my own nightmares, my reality.

"What is it? What do you think scares me, O Legendary One?" he spat. Aggressive like any cornered animal.

"You're afraid of caring about any of them. You know forever can end just like anything else."

The words were bitter in my throat, oozing their truth into my mouth, a blistered sore infecting everything around it.

"You would know," he said huskily.

There he was, the little boy turned monster. The tragic creature that made sure he was unloved. The one who'd lost everything. Who'd driven it away. The one who Kat saw past to the gentle heart underneath. The soul of the soulless.

"I would know," creaked out of my throat.

I embraced him, burying my face into his neck—not to feed from him.

But to love him.

CHAPTER 111

I could find her in an instant, and it killed me not to.
Lynch needed to take this new vampire under his wing, needed to open up to her and let himself get attached. I couldn't do it all myself, not if this fresh vampire was what I thought she was for me.

A new beginning. A new order of vampire.

I had to give Lynch the room he needed—or maybe I just told myself that because I missed Nicholas.

NICHOLAS.

Blood, thick, dark, pungent, curtained my eyes, turning all I saw into a sheet of pure blood.

His.

Nicholas's blood, *but he should be feeding from Roman.*

My heart clenched, stopped, and I gasped. I choked, the blood disappeared. I gagged, doubled over, head swimming.

And I was there. At Nicholas's cabin.

Not a vision. Physically there.

I fell to one knee on a stepping stone, facing the front door as my roiling stomach settled.

Deep breaths.

But all I breathed in was blood.

No deep breaths. Feel the heat on your back. Feel the dirt under your fingernails, the stone hard against your knee. The feathers against your arm.

What.

I opened my eyes to find a crow nuzzling against me, beak tilted up so I could look into his eyes. The darkness there and the *knowing* brought me back to myself. I laid my hand on his downy back. "Thanks," I said. He screeched—I winced—and he flew off.

Just as I got to my feet I was blown across the yard by a boulder, barreling into me at a speed nothing so heavy should be able to travel, the air howling in its wake.

I smashed into a tree. With a great *crack*, the tree split in two, crashing down on me like an axe, pinning me to the ground with my arms and legs splayed out on either side of its thick trunk.

Eyes glazed over, I blinked hard to see what could have done this to me. The force of the initial blow would have crippled a human, let alone what the tree would have done.

"Blue?"

My sweet friend, the impish, otherworldly beauty made of jewel tones and sugar, crouched like a feral animal. Smoke rose from her hunched shoulders where the sun pierced through holes in her ragged black shirt. Truly, her usual modern fairy tale-esque clothes, sleek with crochet black, doily-ish lace and pops of rich color, hung in tatters around her, making her wraith-like, just as her matted, overgrown hair had done. Her pale face showed through the curtain of knots, too brilliantly, too inhumanly, as she snarled at me.

She growled hearing her name and limped off into the woods, leaving me stunned.

Crimson mist rose around me like bubbles in a bathtub, lifting the tree from my body. Spots of black popped in and out of the red froth around me: crows, bobbing around like rubber duckies, to soothe me once again.

With a fair share of grunts and groans—because not even vampire strength could make *that* not hurt—I got up, brushed myself off, and came face to face with a dismayed Nicholas and horrified Roman.

"What in the holy—what the—"

"Wow, Nicholas French at a loss for words," Roman muttered, but his eyes were glued to me, assessing the damage.

"Was this Blue?" Nicholas asked, head cocked, brows furrowed, swallowing hard.

"It's okay, Nicholas," I said, seeing his struggle between shock that our little Blue could do this, and fury that *anyone* would do this to me.

"What has happened to her?" Roman said.

"She should never have left the mountain," Nicholas growled.

I couldn't help but agree. If she'd stayed in Japan, she wouldn't have been out in a world that terrified her. When I left Kieran had been in no shape to go hunting for her, but he would have taken care of her, would have healed quicker just to do it. He always found a way to make sure she was okay.

Nicholas could barely take care of himself. He was no babysitter, he wasn't the type to hold hands and do everything for a vampire who was as strong as Blue in every way.

Why on Earth did she ever leave Japan? What was she thinking?

Of all times to leave her home, she chose to go with Nicholas, to leave Kieran alone, to try to find herself in such a tumultuous time for all *Shinigami*. Why would she do it?

But I knew the truth. Her aura told me, the blankness that it had been when I first saw it had given way to a ripped and skewered, violent mass that begged me to read it.

Blue *wanted* this.

"Eliza, come back," Nicholas said, putting a hand on my

arm, the only one who could snap me out of the think-hole I'd fallen into. His hand felt bonier, older.

"Did Roman feed from you?" I said, more accusingly than intended. "I smelled—"

"I just cut myself, El." He pulled up the leg of his jeans to reveal a jagged, half-healed cut that ran the length of his shin.

"That should have healed already."

"Yeah, but it didn't. And I'm okay," he said. But we both knew that if he just drank from Roman it would be better, not just now but for good. We were pretty sure, anyway. "Besides, you're the one that just got tossed like a salad in the wind."

"I'm fine, Nicholas. I'm more worried about Blue."

"And me. And who else are you worried about?"

"Lynch," I said without thinking.

We both glanced at Roman who turned and stalked to the backyard of the cabin.

Nicholas took the moment to dip his head, force me to look into the mesmerizing eyes that I could tear myself away from even less as a vampire than I could as a human. Their motion was slower, sluggish, and the color dimmer, more like Autocrat coffee milk. I loved the color but the man was suffering—and therefore, I was too.

"El, I need you not to worry about my condition, and *don't*" —he expertly cut off my impending objection—"say you have to. You don't." His *it's that simple* face almost made me believe it. "You put the wheels in motion, you went and got Roman to come here. Right? Didn't you?"

"Yes," I answered reluctantly.

"You worry enough. And whatever you're trying to figure out with Lynch, that's your problem. I'm not trying to solve it for you, am I?"

"Well, no, but—"

"Nope, no, uh uh. I'm not solving it for you. And you don't have to solve this one for me." A little more softly, he said, "I'm telling you that you came here to do your own thing *for us.* You didn't forget me, and I didn't forget you. Now I'm doing *this* for us. Eliza, we don't need to be joined at the hip, we're in this forever. Maybe too long, you don't know. I'm on board, babe."

"That—that's awesome," I said, and holy shit did I ever mean it. His words brought it into simple perspective. The *it's that simple* face was followed up with actual logic, at least this time. We had eternity. No way would we be able to deal with each other for every second of it, and if there weren't periods where I had to pursue something for myself, what kind of eternity would that be for me? For him? We were still ourselves.

"You get it," he said, smiling, showing me those gleaming teeth, the fangs just visible. "I think we both just want this, us, to not feel so damn fragile."

"Like everything in the world is against us just having a goddamn normal day, you mean?"

"Yep. That's what I mean. And we forgot for a minute there —well, a vampire minute—that we can *do* the apart thing and it doesn't mean we aren't together. Eliza Morgan, our love is not a fleeting thing. We don't have to treat it like it is."

Red tears clouded my eyes, and I blinked them away. Hoarsely, I said, "Yeah. I know. I love you, too. So, whatcha building?" I traced Roman's steps around the back. The smell of lumber permeated the air now that the figurative dust from the attack had settled. "You're on a streak, huh?"

"What?"

"Building. You've been building a lot."

"I don't follow."

Just walking into that backyard brought on an avalanche of emotion, the stimuli too much, the memories too much. That hill, where I'd seen Nicholas come home to me after his comatose state, fresh from a kill. When Roman and I waited for him, together in our love and need for him. The way he surrendered to me, so utterly energized and drained at once.

Nicholas turned toward me, and his eyes went to my heart. Just as they had when we first met, at Lynch's party. He was hearing and feeling my heartbeat.

"It was yours then. It is now."

Nicholas blinked and shook his head.

"You heard me," I thought.

He nodded, and let out a deep, troubled breath.

Well, that's new.

"What's the last thing you heard from me?" I asked him aloud.

"You heard me," he said.

"Not 'Well, that's new,' you didn't hear that?"

"What did I just say?"

So I can control it, too.

"Hey Nicholas. I have a new power that you don't."

"You don't know I can't do that," he said with fake nonchalance.

"I have another thing you don't," I teased.

"I can build stuff you can't," he said.

Nicholas jumped onto the new platform in the backyard like the wild man that he was, landing with a *boom* in a super-hero pose that suited him too well.

"I am Iron Man," he said.

"Yeah, I know." I grinned.

"Building a place for Blue," he told me, gesturing to the deck of a new cabin.

I looked into his head, past the place I'd read his mind from, and a red blanket of foggy knowledge bled into me.

"You didn't build the tree house, did you?" I said.

"Tree house? What, you've got a secret clubhouse now? I'm not in the club?"

"Lynch built it," I said. I'd never even entertained the idea. "Jesus, he was just trying to make me feel at home."

"Did it work? This She-Shed he made you?"

"It's not a She-Shed, and yeah, it did actually. Well, no. Yes and no. It's not easy living with Lynch, not how he is now."

"You think it would have been easy before?" Roman said from across the lawn.

"Stop eavesdropping, this is a secret club meeting."

"Nicholas, there is no secret club."

"There is too a secret club," Nicholas said to Roman, not me. "But Eliza says there's not. Wait," he said, turning my way. "Is *Roman* in the club?"

"I love you," I blurted, laughing.

"I know."

"You did an Iron Man, you cannot do a Han Solo. Pick a theme."

He pulled my face lightning-fast to his, smothering my lips with his, stealing my breath and keeping it in his heart.

There was nothing else. Nothing to forgive. No monumental event to erase all we'd been and done. Just this one little backyard moment and the life we'd made for ourselves and together. We didn't need anything else.

"All right, take five, worker bee," Nicholas said as Roman slammed his shoulder into two tree trees, shoving them together like Lincoln Logs. "You probably should get me, I don't know. A sandwich. Not just a sandwich, a *sub*."

Roman glared at him half-heartedly and left the two of us alone.

"There's something he doesn't want me to know," Nicholas said matter-of-factly, Sherlock Holmesy. Nothing accusing in how he said it, just a detached statement that I knew meant more to him underneath. "I tried, El," he added with a sigh, cocking his head in apology to me. "I know you wanted me to drink from him and you'd come back today to a sparkling refurbed Nicholas, but he was so twitchy, I couldn't do it. He was a mouse in a trap."

"He's just afraid, Nicholas. I don't think he's got anything to hide—I think he's done plenty on the surface to be ashamed of. We might be over it, but he's not."

"We aren't over it, Eliza."

"Yeah. No, I guess not." *Roman killed Kat.* "It won't go away. But you think there's something else?"

"I know it."

When Nicholas French *knew* something, he was never wrong. Infuriating sometimes, but handy where I could be oblivious so much of the time.

"So what happened when you tried?" I felt like one of those intrusive friends in some John Hughes movie who hounded for every detail of a date down to what his breath smelled like. "Like, did he…"

"It was a 'no means no' scenario, and I won't push him just so I can have perfect health for another few hundred years. I get it—he just came home, he needs to settle in after being in Bethlem for so long. Maybe he doesn't want that kind of responsibility." He threw his hands up. "Nope. That's not it. Roman loves responsibility. It's like, his favorite."

Nodding, I answered, "He's hiding something that his blood will reveal."

"Right, creep. You and your 'let me drink the blood and see what I will see' thing. He'll come around." Nicholas shrugged as if this were the most casual conversation. "He'll see me fading away little by little and let me drink because that guilt on top of his just-being-Roman guilt will be too much for him."

"Worst. Friend. Ever," I said, poking him in the still-muscled arm. He'd been feeding enough to keep himself burlier than the average man, but only his brother's blood would restore his vitality, bring him *back*. Everything about him was just a little slower, a little duller, a little…weaker every day. Eventually he would die like any old human would. But he deserved so much better than that.

We sat on the platform that was the unfinished floor of Blue's new cabin, the open air inviting us to stay. I'd never paid much attention to birds singing, or the springtime blooms, the difference in the forest when life returned to it. For me, the crows drowned out the tittering of sillier birds, and the darkness of winter dwelled inside me on the brightest of days. But there in the stillness with Nicholas, there was nothing between us, nothing that hated us and wanted us for its own in those woods.

"I'm glad we're all back," I said without thinking. I didn't think I'd ever get over *not* saying how I felt. Words just came out with Nicholas, in a way that they hadn't even with Kat.

"Me too. It feels right here for us."

"I don't miss Japan," I said.

"You wouldn't."

I did miss Kieran though.

It was a reversal in time, he moved so fast. Nicholas had me on my back, kissing me as if he hadn't seen me in a year, hands in my hair, feet twined around mine. "I love you," he breathed into my hair, against my cheeks, my lips. "Never leave here again. There's nothing for you out there."

I smiled against his lips, and agreed.

R oman took a long time with those sandwiches. Subs. He went out to the place that looked like a barn, and probably was a barn, but man they could make a steak and cheese. Swinging our legs off the edge, we ate our subs in a line on the platform like a bunch of construction workers.

"You got roast beef, didn't you?" Nicholas asked him. "You know it's not real meat."

"It is too," Roman said, taking a huge bite.

"Is not."

The best part is that if Roman hadn't been there, Nicholas would have gotten roast beef, too. I laughed to myself at their ten-second arguments. This was the way home soaked into the skin, rode in on a wave of burnt-orange calm and honey. I laughed thinking of all the times Kat would tell me to "stop talking that way," and to "talk that other way I talk." I think this was exactly what she meant, but as a vampire, I couldn't know another way. Feelings take on life as a vampire, a life that keeps the undead going.

Nicholas took my hand with his free one, shoving his sub in his mouth with the other.

"Hey Roman, seen Lynch yet?" Nicholas asked, knowing goddamn well what the answer was.

"*No,*" he replied, "and you know it. I suppose you think I should go for a visit."

"You said it, not me."

Roman looked to me, and I met his eyes, unafraid of his questions, shocking myself at how willing I was to defend Chris Lynch.

"He could use your company, Roman," I said softly. Pleadingly, if I'm being honest.

"Tell me what he's been doing. Because I've neglected my duty to him."

Nicholas's head lolled back. "Ughhhhh, stop it. Your duty is only to yourself, et cetera, et cetera. Besides, Eliza murdered the Master, so there's no such thing as duty anymore."

"Holy shit!" I screeched, eyes nearly popping out of my head. Birds raced away from my booming voice. "You just throw that into casual conversation over lunch?"

"Eliza, you know I'm too good for casual conversations," he

said in mock accusation. "Maybe I'm *extra* good at casual conversation because I find all subjects casual. Speaking of which, hey Roman, tell me what your not-so-little secret is. I know you've got one and I want it."

Roman didn't crack a smile, which was the thing that Nicholas French counted on when he put someone on the spot like this; that his unique charm insured him against refusal or grudges.

"I can't," Roman whispered to his hanging feet. My heart went out to him, to have this vulnerability exploited by Nicholas in such a good-natured way. A violation for his own good. I knew the feeling all too well. But Nicholas was also the master of making anyone feel comfortable revealing their deepest, darkest secrets without feeling like they've done anything to be sorry for.

"Your secrets are our secrets," Nicholas said, leaning close to his brother. "You have nothing—*nothing*—that you need to keep from us. From me."

Blond hair too neat to truly obscure his face, Roman couldn't hide from his brother's eyes. His voice was so small, like a thoughtful child's. "I need to keep this one to myself for a while."

I wanted to yell at him that he already had, all those months in Bethlem, that keeping his secret from Nicholas meant keeping his blood, too, and his *life.*

Nicholas patted his brother on the knee and sat up straight again. "Well. I'm not building anymore until you tell me," he said lightly. "Which means you're sleeping on the floor. If you choose to sleep. Goddammit, I can't make you tell me, can I? You're so annoying."

Roman chuckled, and Nicholas didn't press any further, though he wanted to. When Roman said no, it was with a heavy heart. He never did anything to hurt a person unless necessary—and yet somehow he was always the one to do the hurting. He committed so much more deeply than the rest of us, always willing to take one for the team, to his own detriment. I'd think it would ruin him, but he always survived, overcame, went on. He was stronger than us all, probably.

I put my hand on his shoulder and sighed, wishing I could do something to make it easier in his mind.

He smiled at me, more with those kind blue eyes than his lips. "I'm going to see him now. Lynch. I owe it to both of us."

I smiled back, warmth flooding me. "He'll be so glad you did, Roman."

Roman's angelic face darkened inexplicably. But there's always an explanation for a vampire's turmoil, and I knew that better than anyone.

We let him go, Nicholas grumbling the whole time about how Lynch had a new babysitter, glaring at me but getting no reaction.

"I wish I didn't like Roman so damn much," I said. "He's being obtuse about letting you drink, when he knows how much you need it. You'll never be healthy without it, he's the only one who can help you, it's in *his* blood—" I stopped myself before saying because he murdered the woman Nicholas was supposed to murder. My friend.

Nicholas's eyes trained on me with an intensity we both felt in our blood. "I'm not his responsibility."

I shot back, "Right. You're mine."

"What the hell kind of screwed up logic—"

But I cut him off by slicing my neck open with a fingernail, sharp and fast. He went deathly still at the sight, the smell that even intoxicated me, and clutched me close to him, drinking in deep gulps, moaning, writhing against me. I actually felt his muscles thicken from the inside out, his skin tighten, his cheeks become fuller, the tender skin around his eyes puff up from their dark holes. His very ligaments grew taut and I knew the sensation was mine.

That was when he pushed.

At first it was a poke in the brain. Testing the waters, looking tentatively for a way in.

Then it was a stab.

Then a rumbling of frustration when my mind didn't give.

"What the hell are you doing?" I yelped, pushing Nicholas off me.

He didn't deny it, just ran his hands over his face, coming out from under them with the impatience of a teen delinquent's dad on prom night. "I wanted what you had for a minute, okay?" he said in that condescending and yet still charming tone. It might've been funny if it didn't make me feel like he was accusing me of catching him at something. Pure Nicholas, unlike anyone else. Endearing and aggravating as hell.

"You wanted to see what I was thinking," I barked, tapping my temple. "I'm glad you can't do what I do, you clearly wouldn't do anything nice with it."

"*Nice?* Since when do you care about nice?"

"Since you tried to not be nice to me!"

The eye roll. I think his eyeballs traveled the earth and came back.

"You can read my thoughts now if I let you, and that is enough. Stop being such a greedy baby."

"Nothing babyish about *that* statement," he muttered.

My mist tickled the soles of my feet, aching to emerge as my protector from the violation. But I didn't feel as threatened as it did. I understood. I would have done the same thing if the power to see into heads wasn't mine to wield.

Come to think of it, it wasn't as if I regularly got permission to dig into minds.

"Sorry," I said, sitting back down. "I don't need any barrier with you, I just wish you'd asked first."

"I should have. You know me and choices; the good ones

aren't any fun. No excuse—I had no right. I'm sorry." His fingers twitched, and I knew he wanted to pinch the bridge of his nose, but wouldn't take his eyes from mine. This was how he punished himself, by facing the person he hurt. I loved that about him. I, on the other hand, wanted to bolt like a rabbit, and I hadn't done anything wrong. Well, not in the last few minutes.

I leaned against his shoulder. "We both just want to see more than we do. I'm getting nothing from Lynch half the time, and the other half it's like zombies piling up to push me over, all dead and grabby."

"Nice zombie analogy."

"Yeah, you know me." I shrugged.

He bit his lip, and it ran right through me like it always did. "We do this to ourselves." He turned to me, excited. I half expected him to come at me with like, "let's go to Six Flags!" But it was better. "We can just *stop it*. We can do all the other stuff later, if we feel like it. For now, you move back in here, we forget this crap with you needing to drink Lynch's blood, find out some elusive secret to change the world… Our world doesn't need changing, Eliza," he pleaded, grasping my hands. "You did enough. The *Shinigami* know the Master made it all up," he said, freeing a hand to wave it around his head. "All made up. They've got the choice of who to kill if they want it. They know Izanagi created them. They have the Irishman to lead them now—if they want a leader. You freed them. You don't have to do any more. And you and I," he said, bringing my hands up to kiss them, "we can learn about and from each other, do what's good for us for a change."

The grin spread across my face, I felt it open like a flower from the inside, unleashing life. Nicholas smiled in return, this gleaming, startlingly warm smile. *That* was my home. That was the home I deserved, that I needed.

"I could, couldn't I? Move back in," I said, looking to the

towering trees. They'd always felt like a hood over me here, the roof of a cuddly nest. Now I could look down on them from a wave of red mist in seconds, freer than they'd ever be, rooted where they were for decades. "Take my own advice, stop giving in to archaic feelings of *duty*—"

"You said—"

"Yeah, I know I said *duty*." I sighed. "But I do feel this *need* to uncover something with Lynch, and it can't wait. The difference is this isn't just some responsibility to an invisible force of fate, or even Izanagi. This is my choice. I want to know what Lynch's blood is trying to tell me. I want to follow this path, see where it leads. I do feel like it was meant to be, but I'm good with it. Good will *come* of it." My turn to plead, I guess.

"So optimistic," he said, pushing my hair out of my face. "It's unlike you."

"I am too an optimist! Tough to seem like it when you've got a goddamn flock of harbingers following you around," I said, glaring at the forever-hovering crows.

He took my cheeks in his hands in a sudden bout of seriousness. "Eliza, we need that. We need you to be optimistic. With me—dying, I guess—" I started to protest but he cut me off. "We don't *really* know Roman's blood will fix me. Right?" he said in this premature *I told you so* mode. "We've got Blue going off the deep end, you and me apart, and the worst one of all of us with some frigging secret, but probably not the same secret Roman has. We need you, Fresh Meat, to make it all better."

"No pressure then."

"Oh, all the pressure. But you've got this, El. You've got this like nobody else could."

"Please. Someone else could. You could. You could fix it all if you wanted to."

"There it is," he said, pointing at me. "You want to. I don't. I don't care about Lynch, I barely care if I fade away into nothing. I've lived long enough. It's you that keeps me here more than anything."

"That's not fair. Don't make me your reason for living."

"No, no I don't mean that. I just mean that I'd let go a hell of a lot easier if I didn't have you in my corner. I want to see what happens next with you. You're a wild card."

"I'm a sideshow for your amusement," I said, grinning.

"Yep. And I'll sneak into the big top as much as you let me."

Little did he know how fast this circus would burn down.

"He's coming, I can feel him. What did you tell him?" Lynch came at me like the grownups had driven up in the middle of our teenage house party.

"Roman? I didn't tell him anything." And no, I hadn't. It was our little secret that Lynch was making vampires and leaving them around like a scavenger hunt for bad choices.

"Why didn't you warn me he was coming?" Lynch whined.

"You knew faster than I could tell you; you're connected. Besides, it's good for you to see each other."

"How do you figure?" Lynch muttered.

Then Roman glided into the doorway behind me without so much as a smile. It had been so long since they'd been face to face, it almost hurt that they couldn't be happy to be together. But Roman would always see Lynch as the greatest mistake he was forced to make, and Lynch would never stop making him suffer for it.

"Lynch," he said in awful greeting.

Chris turned away and sat on his couch, the only piece of furniture not covered in dust. It pained me unexpectedly that Lynch didn't even snap a viperish comment at Roman, taunting him as he always did in his rebellious way. It shocked me even more that Roman didn't seem affected by the change in Lynch's demeanor. He was the most compassionate man I knew and the obvious state of disrepair that Lynch was in didn't bother him.

How that must feel, to be so abhorred by your maker that nothing you did would turn his heart your way.

"Tell me what you've been doing while I've been gone," Roman said robotically. I recognized that he dreaded the answer. I felt his fear in my heart, and the vampire I'd become wanted to drown in it, drink it, let it power me.

Not now, not now, not now, you monster.

"Eliza?" Lynch said, fear creeping into his voice, too.

I gulped, vision darting between the hollows under his eyes —*he's tired*—the pallor of his skin—*and weak*—the quickening of his breath—*afraid. Afraid, afraid.*

My throat went desert dry. I heard myself panting, couldn't stop it, my eyes drawn to Roman with a jerk of my head while the rest of me was paralyzed, rooted in my hunger, desperate to devour their horror which filled the space more and more with every passing second.

I dropped my jaw wide, wide, wider than humanly possible.

I'm not human.

And it made sense to me that I would do monstrous things, that I *should.*

The cold fear rose out of Lynch, an unfamiliar chill that surprised and wrenched through him as I dragged it from him. It pierced out of him, making him tremble, suck in his breath. Though the sharp green ice was only visible to me, only real to me, only meant for me. Sheer, crystalline daggers the size of small mountains tore out of him to me, and my mouth gaped, became a cavern the length of my body to engulf them.

I faintly heard Roman screaming my name, but I belonged to the fear now, and it became me, told me... It told me...

Almost there.

Spinning on Roman, I threw my arms out, willing his fear to evacuate his body and fill my own with all its wisdom. My mist gunned for him in streams, pulling him toward me, though he struggled against it. And he was afraid, yes he was, but not quite enough.

"Eliza!" he called out. Not a scream of terror, but pleading, not just with me but for me.

"No!" I screamed back. Their fear together, the two of them, could tell me all I needed to know, I was sure of it. *Imagine what Nicholas would think of me now*, I thought.

It was the one moment of clarity that allowed Roman to break free of my mist, and to stop me from sucking their souls free of fear.

The power gushed out of me, the shards of Lynch's fear I'd been devouring exploding into a thousand slivers and disappearing.

I fell to the floor, hiding my head in shame. Roman's eyes would be too kind, and too impossibly understanding. But his scent surrounded me, crisp ocean breeze and farm-fresh apples. He put his hand on the back of my head, that gentle touch of his making me shudder.

And then Lynch's cold steel scent joined Roman's. Lynch's fingers ran over my own where I clutched my hair.

"It's okay, Eliza," Lynch said. "We're all monsters here."

But the words didn't hit me in the heart the way I know he intended. Because all I could think was: *Not a monster.*

A god.

The thought struck me and stuck, sending my head spinning, and my heart reaching out for Izanagi, a better god than I could ever be. I was nothing, and he was a legend.

"You killed a legend."

I screamed, and Roman and Lynch held me harder, enveloping me in their arms as if to comfort me. But they couldn't comfort me this time.

Because those words in my head weren't mine. They weren't Izanagi's, stretching toward me through our shared blood. Certainly not Nicholas's.

I didn't know who they belonged to.

Eerie, ethereal, pure energy, indistinguishable and utterly unique at once. The voice lit me up with a desire to learn and know that I hadn't felt for a very long time. A need to absorb as much as I could, like sitting at Birch Tree trying to figure out which books to buy because I didn't make enough to buy them all. I wanted to drink them all in, own them.

I pulled my arms out from the ball they'd been wrapped in, held tight by Roman and Lynch, and I drew the two of them close in an embrace. The red fog emerged, enveloping the three of us as we reassured one another.

"We'll figure this out, guys," I said, incredulous that *I* was comforting *them*, these two vampires who'd lived so much longer than I had, both so different. All of us killers. "We just have to trust each other to handle all the secrets we've got."

And the voice invading my mind said, *"Never."*

The voice was partly right—I couldn't say it would never happen, but our secrets stayed with us for the night. Whatever Roman was holding back remained right where it was, torturing him. Brightness colored his eyes, but his aura was diminishing. Like one dot removed from a mountain-sized Pointillist painting, it withered a speck at a time. I saw it. Withering. Slowly eating away, while Lynch's riddles ripped and mended in a flurrying madness.

My secrets—Lynch's rampage, and now the voice in my

head—weren't going to be the first to come out, that was for sure. And those were just the topmost ones.

When we eventually got up from our heap on the floor, we were all too relaxed for once in our immortal lives to even try to delve into the mysteries around and within us. Instead, Lynch and I showed Roman the treehouse that wasn't in a tree.

"This is some solid woodwork, Lynch," Roman remarked, running a hand up the wall.

"Thanks. It felt good to do it, and actually be creative for once."

Creative was not a word I would ever have associated with Lynch in any respect except maybe his torture tactics.

"Do…do you have a creative side?" I asked, wishing I hadn't right away.

But he laughed, and Roman joined in. "I actually liked to paint once," Lynch said with a touch of golden energy trickling into his black, blank mess of an aura.

"I never knew that!" Roman exclaimed, making me smile but quickly hide it, afraid they'd stop being goddamn normal if they caught on to how strange it was.

"Yeah," Lynch continued, actually swooshing his foot back and forth across the floor like a shy teenager. "Surrealist usually, but it was the Renaissance that truly fascinated me."

I wondered if Kat knew this about him. I figured I should try to learn.

"Learn," confirmed the voice in my head.

As the guys laughed over some memory, I took the moment to slide my hand over the smoky blue paint right where Lynch had. *This is so stupid,* I thought, but I tried to reach through the paint itself, to another time and place where Lynch had paint on his hands, to see what I could see, to find a memory that belonged to him.

I pictured different shades of blue.

Canvas rather than wood.

Delicate brushes rather than a roller.

Lynch, younger, before he was terrible, painting some Dali-esque weirdness.

Nothing.

So stupid. What a dumb idea.

"Not a dumb idea. An experiment."

"Oh my god, just shut up," I said, exasperated.

Obviously both Roman and Lynch looked at me like I was the biggest jerk in history.

"I didn't mean you!" I blurted out.

Lynch's eyes roamed around looking for who else I could possibly mean, while Roman's wouldn't peel away from me.

"The crows," I lied. "They never shut up."

Oh wow, is it the crows talking to me?!

"Not exactly," said the voice.

I knotted my fingers together, wishing I could rip the voice out of my damn head because if there was one thing I did not need, it was more unfamiliar shit in my brain. Never again would I be host to hordes of unknown voices and visions for everyone else's benefit and my detriment.

"I'm here for you and you alone."

"El, you don't look so good," Roman said, taking my hand off the wall. "Why don't you lie down over there, we'll make ourselves scarce, okay?"

I resisted the urge to say I was fine, because everything was blurry—something I hadn't experienced since the last party Kat dragged me to, and certainly not something I'd experienced since becoming *Shinigami.*

Something was wrong.

Trying not to trip over my own feet, I curled up under the blanket on the little sofa Lynch had managed to furnish my treehouse with and before my two friends had even left, I was asleep.

~

Maybe not asleep. Unconscious, more like. Taken over by lack of awareness is even more accurate.

Used for my brain activity, even.

I'd been shut down by that voice. It used me, like every vision ever had, like the Master had done when he learned what I could see. The voice knocked me the hell out, like I'd been roofied, and violated.

The "dreams," if they could be called that, inundated me. But not like a flood—no this was a carefully unfolded series of events that made little sense but were the teaser to a bigger story. The manipulative bastard in my head was setting me up to *want* to come back for more. The idea of it crushed and nauseated me in that nearly-peeing-my-pants way that happens when the whole body turns against a feeling. The utmost lack of control.

The dream began with a laugh.

A laugh that said *I got you* without saying it. I was trapped and wasn't looking for a way out.

This place it brought me reeked of hopelessness. Things moved, but nothing was visible, not even glowing eyes. Only heat. Body signatures, but nothing I wanted to drink from. Blood flowed in these beings that I wanted no part of.

A baby crying.

Then everybody crying. So many tears it washed away the darkness to reveal skittering things, running from the light. One was left. A crouching, animalistic and primitive, hurting body. Its suffering pierced me like a thousand knives.

My own voice, saying, "Blue?"

But it was Paolo who spun on his heels, his vampire teeth showing, his once-holy eyes haunted and lost.

I pleaded, "No," over and over again, and tried to get to him but couldn't. That alone was torture. As a vampire I could move in the blink of an eye, and more recently *teleport...*

"*That was a gift to you, from me,*" the voice boomed over everything else in my dream.

"You? You're giving me powers?"

There was no answer, only me trying again to get to Paolo, every motionless step sinking me into my own hell—because I'd left him, and he'd fallen apart. I selfishly deserted him, and he'd disappeared to—

"*Yomi,*" I gasped.

And when I did, the darkness of Purgatory lit up in a blaze of blinding heat, and all the devils of Yomi screeched at me as one. They pointed their howling faces at me from above, below, every side. Their demon horns crashed against each other, their lionish vampire teeth jutting out of squared-off mouths, wild eyes round and ferocious, brows knitted together in sheer fury.

Paolo, in this cruel light, curled in on himself, shaking in terror of the *oni.*

"Paolo!" I cried out, aching to go to him and comfort him, protect him. No man as pure as Paolo should endure fear like he was showing.

FEAR, I thought.

Even in my dreams, my spirit breathed only to feed on the fear of anyone I could suck it from. And nowhere had I seen such unbridled, liquid horror as I did at this moment. Fear of what waits in the dark.

"*Such a simple fear for a simple man,*" the vampire voice inside me cooed. "*Imagine, a man of the cloth trapped in Yomi.*"

But wait. Was that *my* vampire voice that had made me draw the fear from everyone I knew to gain strength from it? Or had it been *her?*

"You're Izanami," I said out loud. "Why are you coming for me?"

With a clap of thunder, Yomi blacked out again.

Izanami's face was inches from mine, hissing fetid breath on me as real as summer wind. The white paint on her face dripped in rivulets, and in their wake left maggots, wriggling down her cheeks. Black hair was piled high on her head, held in place by bloody bones. And when she spoke, spiders formed her words, running down her filthy *kimono*.

"Because we are both Izanami," she said in a voice like ice breaking.

"What? No. That makes no sense."

The cracked lips turned upward grimly. "Do you believe there is sense in this nightmare?"

She turned away with creaking bones, but as she did, I saw only the once-stunning woman she'd been. A royal goddess in shining splendor and humility and a smile like a pink crescent moon.

"Wait!"

But she kept walking in the pitch black—and then I saw what she was walking to.

A baby with flaming red hair.

CHAPTER 113

"Shut up, I think she's moving."

"I didn't say anything."

"I said shut up, what's wrong with you?"

"She's not moving, it's the mist. It's vibrating."

Nicholas, Roman, and Lynch.

I snapped my eyes open and found nothing but a crimson sheen. I could see only their shapes, the men in my afterlife, and I couldn't move, didn't want to…

"I see her eyes, she opened her eyes!" Nicholas said. "She needs to get out of there, El, get out of there!"

Out of where?

"She's struggling! Why won't it let you go, Eliza?"

Panic in Nicholas's voice made me struggle more, but I couldn't move, only moan in frustration and fear. *Where am I? Is this Yomi?*

No, there was nothing black and blinding here. Only warm, red, all-encompassing.

My mist.

I was trapped in it like a goddamn Jell-O mold.

Bursting out in a flurry of crimson fireworks, I sucked in a breath. Rubbing the red from my eyes, I concentrated on Nicholas's hands on my arms, the realness of them, the solidity of them. Nothing like Yomi.

"Cough, I feel like you should cough," Nicholas said, brushing the hair off my face.

I don't know why I listened, but I did feel like I'd been found in a river, and so I coughed.

"Nicholas. What is that?" Roman said tentatively.

"What, what's what?" Nicholas hovered over me, Roman not far behind.

"Eliza, open your mouth please," Roman said.

I opened my mouth, a vision of that gaping maw of mine eating their fears alive threatening to overpower me, but instead I coughed again. Nicholas peered in my mouth as I did, horror written all over the lines in his withered face.

He put his hand on the back of my head and I didn't ask what he was doing when he reached into my mouth.

And pulled a long black feather from my throat.

"You mean this?" Nicholas asked, handing the wet thing to Roman while Lynch gagged.

As I sat in the remnants of a red mist that had betrayed me, tried to keep me like Snow White in her glass coffin, and I watched the men look over the crow feather, I knew what was real and what wasn't.

The mist was mine; it was not from Izanami.

The crow feather, the crows themselves, no matter what Izanami wanted me to believe, were not her doing—they were her husband's.

I also knew that there was truth in what she said about us being the same. And it was one more tear in the fabric between me and Nicholas.

"What happened to you, Eliza, where did you go?" Nicholas blurted, rushing back to my side.

"I…it was just a dream. I didn't go anywhere."

"No, you flashed in and out like a goddamn disco ball in a swamp, and you came back here in a bar of glycerin soap with half a bird down your throat."

"So dramatic. It was one feather. I wasn't in a bar of soap, it was just…a Jell-O mold, and I'm weird and do weird things and we all know it. This is another one."

Again, I didn't want to tell him the particulars. It was becoming a habit.

But Nicholas French can read just about anybody, and me even more so. He wasn't buying it this time.

"El, don't hide from me. Please."

I hung my head, willed my mist to disappear completely and let me be just *me*, not Eliza Morgan, Vampire Freak. Roman asked if I wanted him and Lynch to go—but I didn't. Not only because they comforted me, and I needed to feel like they were on my side, but because I didn't want them talking too much without me.

This was not the time for Roman to find out that Lynch was creating vampires and abandoning them in his latest psychotic break.

"Okay. Maybe you can help me figure this out. It's gonna sound total *Twilight Zone*, but I went to Yomi. Kinda."

Nobody said a word, not even Nicholas.

Japan was a sacred home for the *Shinigami*, and the Master had been a god among them. Their creator, they'd believed. But I had brought to them a real deity—Izanagi, the actual origin of the *Shinigami*. And Izanami, his wife, had become the goddess of Yomi, trapped there for eternity. To think that I once again had crossed the paths of ancient gods of myth and legend was more than a little overwhelming. To see the shock on these vampires' faces solidified that. The fact that I'd now gone to their underworld, basically… It raised a lot more questions. Not the least of which was, *How far would I go? Where did my own power end?*

Now that I'd said it out loud, I wanted to keep going.

"I saw Izanami—"

"Who?" Lynch butted in.

"Izanami. You know, just the wife of our race's creator, no big deal. Lynch, don't you know anything about the *Shinigami?*"

"You just learned it yourself, Ellie, don't get started," he retorted. "You killed the only maker we ever knew."

"You never cared about him either," Nicholas said. "So shut up and let *Eliza* tell the story we asked for, would you?"

Glaring at Lynch, I went on. "I saw Izanami there. And"—I didn't want to say it, I really didn't—"I saw Paolo too. He looks just *craven*, a shell of who he was. Nicholas," I said, red tears filling my vision, "it was just horrible. Why did he ever go there? Why would he go to a place that would do that to him?"

Without meaning to, we both looked at Roman, who met our eyes and made no apologies. Bethlem had made him even more steadfast. As strong-willed about his own choices as he was for everyone else that he loved.

"Izanami said that she and I were the same. That we were 'both Izanami.' What can she mean?"

"Nothing I want to find out," Nicholas said. And again, his eyes betrayed him.

He was genuinely afraid of me.

I didn't mention the baby. Not exactly intentionally, but it could wait for a later time. I had so little idea of what it meant, and couldn't drop that potential bombshell on top of all the other ones. I'd just add it to my list of withheld information. Also on that list: Izanami claimed to be giving me these new abilities, these gifts that other vampires didn't have.

I wasn't sure I believed her. I couldn't trust her, that was for sure. But why would she claim to have done that? She certainly didn't come across as the giving type, and Izanagi had craved freedom from her. What was she kissing my ass for? If she was giving me these gifts, what did she want me to have them for?

"We are both Izanami."

Christ, I had to figure this out.

My mind ran through a hundred scenarios and followed a thousand threads of thought in a matter of seconds. Now, I'd always been a quick thinker, but this… *Did all vampires think this way when they put their mind to it? So fast, so clear.*

Or was it another "gift" from Izanami?

Not that I had much to go on, but first impressions were everything: Izanami wanted something from me. And she was not the type to have a half-cooked plan. The woman—the *deity*—who reigned over Hell, had eternity to make things happen. Whatever she wanted, she'd have had all the time imaginable to come up with every worst-case scenario, to try and fail as much as necessary to achieve her ends.

No, whatever she wanted, it was endgame material. And I was in the middle of it. But I couldn't quite get my head to fathom what that was.

Izanami could give me powers, what else could she do to my head? Could she keep the truth from me?

Brain rushing in every direction, meeting dead ends all over, I became drained, beaten, in a matter of minutes. Weak, even. I had to feed, and I had to do it fast. My mind was becoming fuzzy, my trains of thought crashing painfully all at once.

Early morning would hurt to go hunting, but I couldn't stop myself, I was salivating. My fingers were shaking. I needed a fix, and I'd take it from the first warm body I could pin down. The muscle memory made my teeth gnash.

I wanted to kill and drink and I didn't care from who.

I wondered if Izanami was the reason why I had so much less compassion for the victims I took. Or had I done that to myself by hanging around Lynch? Might have been nice if my cruelty wasn't my fault. But then again, was Lynch's his?

If Nicholas could come with me, keep me in check, it would be wonderful. But he couldn't know the measure of my brutality when I fed now, and besides, he was too weak to keep up with me, let alone stop me. Roman needed to just goddamn give him what he had to have. What kind of brother would withhold life's blood just to keep a secret?

Good question, Eliza. I wonder how far you'll go to keep your own.

Shaking off my philosophizing, I left the treehouse as calmly and casually as possible, trying to be somewhat civil. But the sunlight stole any civility I might have had. My skin screamed beneath my clothes, burning like a boiling lobster.

There wasn't enough goodness left in me to let me stand the sunlight. Was that it? I hadn't paid enough attention to my kills recently to read their auras, see if they were more good than bad. I'd been relentlessly fast, barely taking any pleasure from the feeding—just *doing it* was what I needed, the feeling after, the fullness and warmth that I hadn't had since I was alive.

Turns out having purpose doesn't really keep a person warm at night.

Keeping to the shadows of the trees, I bumbled through the forest, trying to escape the sun.

Grunting nearby—or vampire-nearby, which could be almost anywhere.

Blue was running alongside me, a wolf waiting for the right time to close in.

I was a predator, too.

"What do you want, Blue?" I growled under my breath.

Fleeting glimpses of black hair, black rags, running on all fours.

I don't have time for this, I thought, my throat begging me for blood. And I used my gift from Izanami to get myself the hell out of the sunlight and into a vein.

~

I didn't mean to end up in Japan. I sure as hell didn't want to be there.

On my knees in an unusually clean alley in Tokyo, blood pouring from my chin and all over my clothes, I could finally think clearly. Cleanly.

Three men and one woman sprawled around me, more blood shooting from their throats in geysers, all convulsing in varying stages of death and dying. I felt nothing for them. I didn't know who they were, I didn't remember their faces and couldn't see them now as they twisted and twitched on their backs.

I couldn't even be disgusted with myself, even though I wanted to be.

She'd done this to me.

Izanami. Of course, it had to be.

God, it was easy to believe it was all her fault, and that I wasn't just growing more and more inhuman.

I swaggered out of the alley into the Tokyo night, having spent the day poaching citizens and feeding on them. In Tokyo, everyone was too busy to register me, immersed in activities I couldn't understand. Nothing seemed to scare them. I barely got a second look as I strolled down the street, debating what I should do next. Where I should go. I knew, but I wanted to pretend I didn't. I wanted an excuse to wander through a crowd of prey, knowing what I'd done over and over again.

When I felt like it, I rooted my feet as firmly onto the slick black street as I could, I threw my head back and howled to the sky in that bustling square, and with more purpose than I'd put into transporting before, I let myself loose. I embraced that power from the Empress of Yomi. The air sucked me in, made me fold in on myself, then double, then expand and reach, until I was where I wanted to be.

At a long-forgotten garden bench on a mountaintop.

"What in the bloody fuck, Eliza Morgan?"

"Hi Kieran. You look really good."

Fully aware of how frightened he was that I'd burst in on him, that I was soaked in blood, that I looked more like a sadistic golem than the woman I'd once been, I waited until he could gather himself. He still sat on the bench, but loosened his shoulders up again and patted the seat beside him. We'd come here often once. He took a deep breath, finally un-rattled. No longer did I want to eat his fear like a fresh, raw steak. That was a hunger I controlled now.

This was what it must feel like.

To be Izanami.

"Woman, you look like Hell itself coughed you up."

"I look a hell of a lot better than that, come on."

He laughed, that thick Irish brogue laced with eternal cigarette smoke that set hearts to fluttering. "I suppose you'd look like a queen no matter what you'd been crawling through, love."

It softened me fast, melted me like butter on toast. Like guac on a burger.

I was human in an instant. That pudgy, fleshy, flawed and perfect woman I'd once been that fell—for just a while—in love with Kieran Coughlin.

"I've missed you," I said, in my old voice, the one Kat hated. Not at all the vampiric goddess voice that had weaseled its way in. It broke, and I sobbed suddenly. Looking down at myself, I was ashamed. Superhuman and completely apart from anything that made me *me*. I was coated in the blood of multiple strangers. Kieran was fresh and smooth in his white T-shirt, sleeve rolled up over a pack of cigarettes like some greaser. The stubble that never went away. The mussed hair, the squinting eyes, sizing me up. "I missed you so much, Kieran." The tears fell freely now, and I did nothing to stop them.

"No, no, there there, beautiful."

He didn't care about anything but helping me and making me feel better. His hands in my snarled hair, he held my face right in front of his. His eyes... I'd forgotten how flames constantly burned there, a flicker of the heat inside him. Nothing could ever give justice to that fire in him. He blazed with passion in every movement he made. When he spoke again, it was with the scent of campfire and chocolate and almonds. "Eliza, I've missed you more than you know. I didn't want to do this all alone, love, and it's safe to say that alone doesn't suit you either."

"I'm sorry I left you," I blubbered. For every second I hadn't been human, I made up for it twice in the most humanly messy way. Tears, wet lips, runny nose and all.

"You had to, you had to do that," he pleaded. "You weren't created to be a nursemaid in the immortal burn unit, Eliza dear, now were ya?"

Laughter burst out of me, ugly and wet, but I didn't sniffle it back. "I love you," I said through the gross laughter.

"Yeah, yeah, I know it."

He got me to calm down as only he could—drinking straight from a bottle of rum and laughing at pretentious vampires who had no Master to listen to anymore.

"They look at me and all they see is... Well, I don't know what they see, but they don't like it, I'll tell ya that," he said, chuckling. "They don't exactly listen to me, right? But then again, I have nothing to tell them." He was the strongest vampire I knew. Laughing the whole time he said this, making fun of his own lack of leadership. "They're grown vampires, for chrissakes! I don't need to tell them what to do! Feed, don't kill each other, they know the drill."

He passed me the bottle again, and it was mixing really poorly with a belly full of blood. But I took it. "Kieran, there is nobody—nobody—I would want to see put in charge if I were them. They needed the exact opposite of the Master, and holy hell did you give it to them." I fell onto my side, laughing as messily as I was crying before, and it felt so powerfully loose and unplanned. I loved it as much as I loved Nicholas. I loved it the way I'd never loved being human.

"Your Golden Boy still treating you well?"

I knew that was coming.

"Of course. I mean, things are strained, but aren't they always?"

"And Blue?"

Sighing, I squished my face up, scratched my forehead, did all kinds of awkward gestures that I thought would help me avoid answering, but Kieran wasn't buying any of it.

"Eliza Morgan, tell me about Blue."

Forcing myself to meet his eyes, I told him. "Kieran…"

"Now, Eliza!"

"She's gone feral. Wild, like an animal, we don't know why, but she's not okay. She's not."

"And why am I finding this out now? How long did it take for her to become an animal? What the hell are you doing out there?"

"Calm down—"

"Like hell, woman! That's my girl." He choked. "Eliza, that's my girl, and she's in trouble, and I was stuck in this—" With a deep breath, he looked hard at me. "What am I doing here?" He threw his hands wide. "They don't need me. I don't need to be here anymore, I'm *well*. And I left her."

"No. No, Kieran, she left you. How long could you support her, feed her, hunt for her? Just like you said, they're grown vampires. So is she."

He nodded, but smoke was accumulating beneath his feet from his rage. I went on.

"She's grown, but she needs our help all the same."

The agony in his eyes when they met mine was immeasurable. Unfathomable. Blood tears danced on his lower lashes—and when they fell they became ash. "She was never meant for this world, Morgan. She's never been strong enough, and she suffers because of me," he spat, jabbing his thumb into his chest. "I stole her from life and forced her into this life of death that she cannot survive. I destroyed her and she'll never escape it."

I couldn't take my eyes off him, riveted to his suffering, aching to ease it. Black ashes cascaded in front of him, pink cherry blossoms cascading behind.

Well, if that didn't sum up Japan. Death on one side, picturesque on the other.

"Wait. I think I know what happened to her, Kieran. Not exactly how, or what…but *who*."

"Paolo looked, acted, just like her when I saw him in Yomi."

"In what now? How in the hell?"

"I wasn't really there, but Izanami—you know who she is." Kieran nodded. "She came to me in a dream." I told Kieran all of it, including the baby. Which raised questions, as expected.

"A baby, in that dreaded place," Kieran said, shaking his head.

"She wanted me to see the baby, I just don't know why. But that's not the point, not now. Kieran, she got to Blue somehow. Izanami got to her, drove her crazy, just like she did to Paolo. Goddammit, I won't let either of them turn into one of her devils."

Kieran always listened well. He didn't judge, and he didn't dig. He went for the solution.

"If she came to you in a dream, she's giving you these gifts… She wants you to come there."

"Well…no."

"What do you mean 'no'? We can find a way right now, Eliza."

"So, your plan is to literally go right into the trap she set. That's the strategy you're opting for?"

"I wouldn't call it a *strategy*. I would call it 'taking initiative.'"

I rubbed my eyes hard, pinched the bridge of my nose, trying to make his idea disappear. When I opened them, he had a glass of beer in each hand, the blood mixing inside a welcome sight. I didn't know where this blood came from, and I wanted it to wash away the murders I'd committed in Tokyo.

The first sip traced a line of heat down my throat that made me moan.

"Don't make noises like that, woman. Now I need a cigarette." He plucked one out of his shirt sleeve and lit it with a snap of his fingers.

"New trick?"

He winked one devilishly dark eye. "I'm full of 'em."

"You're unbelievable." I laughed. The man could always make me laugh in the direst of situations—of which we'd seen many together. So, I should have probably listened to him this time. But that wouldn't be me. "Izanami is wicked smart, right?"

"Wicked smaht," he agreed in his best Boston accent.

"And if she went after Blue and then—released her—back to New Hampshire, she had a reason for it. Why Blue?"

Every time I mentioned her name, he stiffened. It was clearly torturous for him to hear about her. I couldn't imagine if he'd seen her, been attacked by her like I had. Hell, she'd tried to poison Nicholas. *But why?*

I answered my own question. "We all love Blue. We all want to protect her, there's no question of our loyalty to her. That makes her someone we'll fight for. We'll do anything to help her."

"Which sure gives Izanami a lot of leverage if she's the only one who can do it."

"Same for Paolo. Such a good man, it kills me to see him suffering like that. She wants me to owe her, and she wants power over all of us."

"Holy shit, Eliza, that's it. She wants power over all of us." He flicked the cigarette onto the ground, amidst others between the broken paving stones, and stomped on it, which made my teeth grit even now, but I was too enraptured by his line of thinking to yell at him. "She's a goddess. And she's trapped there, with a bunch of little ghouls—"

"And a baby," I gasped.

"Listen to me," he said, frantic. "The Master is dead, Izanagi is gone, Nicholas isn't well. I don't want to be in charge, and you're the most powerful vampire in the world now, Eliza. Don't say you're not, you know that you are."

I shut my mouth, ready to protest. I'd never put it into words before—but he was right. I was the most powerful vampire in existence.

Of course it was me that Izanami would appeal to.

Of course it was me that she'd claim to be equal to.

"Oh my god," I choked out. "She wants to trade places with me. She wants out."

CHAPTER 114

Kieran knew I had to leave, but I don't think my going helped him worry less about Blue.

Izanami was in my head, she'd gotten into Blue's—who was far less stable than me now—and that made her a threat. The goddess hadn't just created leverage, someone we'd all fall over ourselves to save, possibly fight amongst ourselves to save. No, she'd created a secret weapon, one I'd discovered.

To destroy the life I'd died to have.

She'd taken Blue away from me, and my biggest fear was that now she'd use Blue to take away Nicholas, Roman… Blue alone could destroy all of Ossippee. My poor, sweet friend. Poisoned.

Desperate to get to Nicholas, I all but evaporated from existence to travel the distance to him. Entering his world from the one in Japan was like passing between two different planets; one rooted in ancient prophecy and responsibility, the other in comfort and the life I wanted. I didn't want to be part of both.

"El, Jesus, you ever just knock?"

"Nicholas." I fell into his arms, squeezed my eyes tight.

"Hey, hey," he said, patting my hair down. "Where'd you go? You okay?"

"Japan."

He pulled me away from him, gently, but there was a suspicion behind it. "What was in Japan?"

"We don't have time for that right now, I need to know where Blue is."

"I don't know. She doesn't punch a clock with me."

"And I do?" I said, passively aggressive because I did not like to be questioned, regardless of how important that information was. And I was more than a little embarrassed, I suppose.

Warily, eyes wide, chin down, he said, "I just wanted to know where you went. Casual question for someone who disappeared."

"I need to know where Blue is, she's not in control of her own mind, Nicholas. She's being used and she's going to do something—"

"Whoa, whoa, she's not a threat right this second, okay? If she shows up in the next five seconds, we'll deal with her."

"I don't know that we should be reactive and not proactive about this one."

"Well, I am," he said smoothly with a reassuring smile. "If she's working for someone, if she's coming for us, then *she will come for us*, and we'll be waiting. What are we going to do if we go out there and hunt her down, El? Chain her up? Drag her back here and make her talk?"

He had a point. I had zero plan. Just confront the issue and think later, really. I nodded my concession.

"Now please, just tell me what you've been doing and why you think you need to keep it from me."

"Hunting. Nicholas, I've been hunting," I blurted. "A lot. Often and—and more than one person at a time."

I don't know why that was my leading statement. The first of many confessions I'd have to let go of.

"How do you mean?"

"You know how I mean."

He searched my face. "Like a killer," he said. Not a question. I just nodded. "How long?"

"Since we came back."

"You mean since you've been palling around with the Abomination, right?"

"Now isn't the time for…whatever that is."

"The truth?" His eyes apologized to me, and he was right. It was the truth and I didn't want to hear it.

"Yeah, I don't feel like hearing the truth. Tell me something else."

He took my hand. "Come on," he said.

Through the swinging red door into the kitchen with its cracked tile and old wood stove. He knew I needed to feel at home. Comforted. Even if I didn't deserve it. He put the tea kettle on, muscles flexing with his every move—but not as much as before. It struck me whenever I saw him how much less alive he was by the day. He turned around to lean against the counter, crossed his arms, and we just looked at each other. Happy, but troubled, but happy? For at least a minute.

"Water doesn't boil at vampire speed still," he said. "It's aggravating, really."

Silence stretched between us as we waited for the distinct whistle. Even though I kept looking over my shoulder, like Blue might jump out at me, slasher-style. The cat jumped down from the top of a high cupboard and curled up at Nicholas's feet. It wasn't even a comfy spot, it was right in the middle of the floor. But he so needed to be near the man who'd taken him in.

I knew the feeling.

When tea had been poured—that sloshing sound always

made my shoulders drop and everything loosen up—Nicholas set mine in front of me. Same chipped teacup. He sat down, legs splayed in front of him, leaning back like a school delinquent. "So. Eliza goes a' huntin'. What's that like?"

I wrapped my hands around the cup, tried to channel those first moments in this kitchen when Nicholas told me—showed me—he was a vampire. I'd loved him enough even then to know that it didn't matter.

"I get this like, screaming inside me. Nothing can stop me. And the more I go out, the less satisfied I am to take just one life. Yesterday?" I couldn't look at him—but I forced myself to. "I killed four people yesterday."

"Whoa. Four. Four? In Japan?"

"Yes. I don't know—well, I didn't know why I went to Japan, but I do now."

"Kieran?"

No judgment in his eyes, no irritation in his whipped cream voice. Just looking for understanding, and to be there for me.

"I saw him, but he's not why I was there. I was there because..." *Why can't I say it?*

"Izanagi?" Nicholas guessed.

"Close." I laughed. "The wife."

I told him about the dream, and the "gifts" Izanami had bestowed upon me.

"I can't imagine you'll be sending a thank you note for her thoughtfulness."

"I actually think she'll come to collect it in person."

We drank another cup of tea while I told him our trading places theory. I wish Nicholas hadn't so readily agreed.

"Eliza, can you please explain why ancient monsters like to hang out with you so much? Are there more after this one? I think you covered them all, at least vampire-wise. Is there a boss level I should expect?"

"Well, I think the boss level is really my problem, while you'll have to be on the distract and extract front. Because Izanami will have thought this out, she's had all that time in Japanese Hell."

"Purgatory. Yomi is Purgatory."

"Uh, yeah. Okay. Anyway, Nicholas. She has Paolo. And worse, I'm pretty sure she's responsible for what's happened to Blue."

He squeezed his eyes shut. His fingers flew to the spot between his eyes that he pinched to make everything go away for a second. The thing about being *Shinigami* is that you could close your eyes to it all for decades and nothing ever went away. All those horrors waited. All we can do is try to be scarier.

Opening his eyes wide, blinking away the stars, he said, "She's in her head? That's what you're saying, right?" I didn't have to respond. His jaw set, he put his shoulders back, still stronger than any one of us. He focused on me, zeroed in. "You have to take her out."

"Whoa, what?" I mean, I thought at least it would have been a *we* have to take her out, or a plan, or *I know a guy*. But it was none of that from him. "Nicholas, she's the goddess of creation, and of Yomi. She's not... How? I can't do that. Look at what she did to Blue, look at the abilities she's given me. Think of what else she can do!"

"Think of what *you* can do!"

"This is no time for a motivational speech, Nicholas! We need a plan!"

Infuriatingly, he smiled. A big toothy one, amused by me. I could have strangled him with my mist, drawn blood and drained him—

That's not you thinking that, dammit, get control of yourself, Eliza.

Fiddling with his teaspoon, he said, "Remember at the

temple, when you fought that mountain man, like, our first day there?"

"Yeah. Seems so long ago now."

"Not that long ago. You were human then. You fought—you beat—that goliath as a *human*. Zero difference from you as a death god fighting an older god. You were powerful then. You're powerful now. Not so much has changed."

A memory of Kat popped into my mind. We'd been young, just moved in together. It was a blizzard, had raged for days, and we were running out of food. Nobody with a conscience would have considered calling a restaurant for delivery on the off chance any were open. So naturally, I said I'd go out. I'd shovel as much as I could, warm up the car. If the car was frozen, I'd boil water to thaw it. If I had to walk through the storm, I'd stop any place I could go indoors along the way to warm up. There might be people who needed help I could check on as I went. There'd been no electricity for two days, and in New Hampshire that could be deadly. As I'd strung together my plan, Kat sat stunned.

"You can do anything, can't you?" she'd said without a hint of a smile.

I actually didn't think I could do much of anything. I couldn't button my jeans. I couldn't cook. I couldn't do laundry without turning something a new color. I couldn't stand anyone long enough to get a job outside of the gift shop where at least I knew the people would go away. But this? This was just survival.

"You'd do it if you could," I'd said to Kat.

"But I couldn't," she'd said. And we'd left it at that.

"She was right, you know," Nicholas said, interrupting the memory.

I shook my head. "You heard that?"

He pointed above my head to a red cloud, and the silhouetted figures fading away within it. "I saw it," he said.

"I miss her," I blurted.

"Yes. You do. Every day," Nicholas said, with a single nod. A statement as clear as my name. Like a promise.

Like the air I didn't need to breathe, like the pain I didn't need to wince from, like the food I didn't need to enjoy. Missing her became a habit that I couldn't let go because I didn't want to. But if any of those things made me sick or hurt me, I would stop them. Wouldn't I?

Wouldn't I?

If humanity had taught me anything it was that missing my parents and my grandmother could steel me into an impenetrable fortress. It ached on the inside—that fear of dying, and of losing anyone else I loved. It squeezed my heart until the *Shinigami* claimed it for their own. I kept everyone away because the inevitability of them being torn from me by that same beast, Death, was too imminent, no matter how long it gave me. Until Death was all I had left.

And so I made a choice.

I had lost Kat, yes. But missing her could not consume me any longer. I had given in to Death—and it had given me something in return. Pining for those I missed would never bring them back. And I would not endure eternity shying away from all those other lives I missed out on because I'd been eaten alive by my feelings.

Lynch had been sent to me. What he was doing now was for *me*, I could accept it now.

Turning those girls into vampires, leaving them scattered to find their own paths, he was looking for Kat every way he could and never finding her.

And he was losing *them*. As if they had nothing to offer. As if they had no purpose.

I had a mission. A plan. A path of healing.

A coven of my own.

And Nicholas would have to be a part of it.

"Nicholas, there's something I need to tell you. I probably—"

Then Roman slammed his way in, shaking the entire cabin like a leaf. When he came through the kitchen door, he wasn't even walking—pure fury held him aloft, floating him in. Any deadness behind his eyes before was purged with this anger. And I had a feeling I knew why.

"Eliza Morgan, what have you done?"

"Oh hey Roman, whatcha been doin'?" Nicholas didn't even raise an eyebrow as he threw an arm over the back of his chair.

"You have no idea what she knows," Roman said, still hovering in the air. I'd never seen him so viciously angry, and *accusing*.

"Well, I don't know, I'm learning some stuff," Nicholas said, nodding at me as if to say that we were really getting somewhere.

"Roman, calm down," I said, which is the stupidest advice for anyone having a serious meltdown. "I mean, please let's talk."

"Let's talk?" he screeched. "You're no better than Lynch!"

"Whoa," Nicholas said, getting to his feet in a move faster than light. "Back off her, right now, or it will get ugly." He put his hand on Roman's chest, and Roman blinked long and hard before lowering himself to the ground.

"You don't know what she's done, Nicholas," Roman said in little more than a whisper.

"Why don't you tell me, hmm? Come on, sit down. This is Eliza we're talking about. We've probably seen worse together."

But Roman's glare said he disagreed.

While Roman and I sat down as if we were facing off over a chess board, Nicholas made his brother a cup of tea. And he brought a pie out of the fridge.

"This is my favorite *Golden Girls* episode," he said as he sat with us. "Where the ladies talk about life and death and morality over banana cream pie. Okay Roman, go. What happened at Lynch's?"

Roman, to his credit, picked up one of the forks Nicholas tossed on the table, and took a bite straight from the pie. "Lynch is turning women," he said simply. "And Eliza knew. She's been letting him. Encouraging him."

"Turning women? What women? Where?"

So this was it. I'd kept it secret for what, ten minutes? This was what I got for not being totally up front. Since when did I keep secrets and not, often stupidly, face the uncomfortable stuff head-on?

"Everywhere," I told Nicholas, drawing his attention from Roman. "He's not..." I almost said Lynch wasn't right in the head, but that would be a poor argument. He never had been.

"He's pollinating the world with vampires," Nicholas said, lips turned down, raising his eyebrows in a familiar unsuitably-impressed look. "I mean, when you're a serial killer and you want to step up your game, I guess you make more killers."

Again, I had to stop myself from defending him.

Roman gave me reason to throw fuel on the fire though.

"Eliza knew he was doing this, Nicholas," he barked, pointing a finger at me. "She was there with him the whole time, and she let it happen!"

Fury filled me, right or not. "What would you have me do, Roman? Huh? What, should I talk some sense into him? Is that how you reform a next-level serial killer? Maybe you're the wrong guy to ask, seeing as you not only knew he was a murderer, you made him one for eternity."

Nicholas sucked in a breath and looked away.

Roman had the cleanest, clearest blue eyes I'd ever seen.

When I said this to him, they muddied, not in anger, but like a pure thing turned forever wrong, a violated beauty.

"I know," he said, all his anger gone, along with his spirit, his love of life.

But not his fear.

His aura still held onto it, a gray-brown, focused mass like a disease around him. And I knew then that while Roman wore his shame on the outside, almost saintly in his humbleness and compassion, he also harbored a secret. A terrible secret that he'd never let go of.

And being me, I was certain I wouldn't stop until I uncovered it.

The somber air around us was thick, and we had nothing to do but acknowledge it and move on.

"Okay," I said. "We're all clear that none of us is mistake-free and error-proof, yeah?"

"*Yeah?*" Nicholas mocked me. "Channeling your inner Irishman?"

"YEAH," I said more loudly at him. "We aren't error-proof, *as I was saying*. But we have forever to fix things."

"I suggest we don't take that long," Roman said with a sad laugh. "We have to stop him."

I nearly said that stopping Blue was a far bigger problem, but I just could not get into that with Roman now, not when he was so upset with me. He was good at rationalizing evidence against whoever he was angry with.

"What do you suggest?" Nicholas asked Roman, but I didn't hear much after that. I was busy in my own head, reasoning out that I wasn't so gung-ho about stopping him.

I wanted to make a coven of my own. It was there, in front of me, waiting.

"No," I said, more to myself than either of them.

"This'll be good," Nicholas said.

"Just listen for a minute. A Stop-the-Abomination plan focuses our attention on the wrong issue."

"What other issue could there possibly be?" Roman asked, incredulous.

"That there's already a bunch of newborn vampires out there, flailing around in the world, maybe so many that we can't get to them all before they're lost forever. And I mean, *really* forever. If we don't focus on contacting those women and helping them, we could truly be creating serial killers all over the globe."

"She's right," Nicholas said.

"But we have to do both," Roman said, shaking his head. "Stop him and start with them."

"Our Stop-the-Abomination plans *suck*, though," Nicholas said. "They never work. For as heartless a beast as she was to say it, Eliza's right—we can't just talk the serial killer out of being a serial killer. We don't run a rehab. But we *can* run an Avengers-style Vampire Camp."

"I am *not* a heartless beast, but I like your idea. We gather them up. Bring them here. Lynch has room for some… I don't know how many there are, guys. But I'm like…well, I have a fine ability to sorta teleport these days," I said. Roman raised his eyebrows. "We keep them close."

We make a coven, I thought. It was all working out.

"Okay," Roman said. Which shocked both Nicholas and me.

"I'm sorry, did you say 'okay'?"

"Yes. I think it's a good idea."

I ran with it. "We give them a purpose." Before either of them could butt in with the *Shinigami*-esqueness feel of that, I bowled them over with logic. "One thing that has worked all these centuries is that the *Shinigami* had a common place to feel grounded in Japan. A home made for them. We can do that."

"Yeah, but El, giving them a purpose sounds sorta culty, don't you think? Like we're starting a religion," Roman said.

"It could be, sure, but it won't be. We'll be organized. And we need to give them *some* direction or they'll fall back on the one thing that always feels good—blood."

Nicholas cleared his throat, which meant he was actually going to be completely serious. "And what *will* we tell them about blood? We've got no Master to manipulate us into... Whoa, *we* were a cult!"

There it was. An entire species following the teachings of one man who turned out to be lying all along.

While we were all dumbstruck, Nicholas said, "I need to write a tell-all. *Vampire Cult* by The Golden Boy."

"I can't believe you haven't written a book yet, Lestat. It was a matter of time," I said, getting a hearty laugh from Roman while Nicholas struggled to argue that he wasn't self-aggrandizing. Then everything lightened up.

Because yes, there were going to be challenges, and problems, and we were rounding up killers before they knew what they'd become, but we were doing a good thing, and together. Starting as a family.

A family with one extremely unstable son named Chris Lynch.

CHAPTER 115

I was getting what I wanted.

Difficult to say, how often I actually got what I wanted completely, let alone handed to me with little struggle. But here we were. I thought I'd need to drag Nicholas kicking and screaming into the idea of starting my own coven. I hadn't thought of Roman's role in it at all. I never considered that they'd actually listen to me and think I was right.

Was there actually a chance of this turning out *well*? It seemed impossible. It was a winning lottery ticket that multiplied.

Chris was a wild card, there was no getting around it. I never saw where the problem really routed from, but goddammit, I should have. It's something I'll never let myself live down.

We planned, we *created*, made all the trappings of an organized mess until we were exhausted. Three tired vampires was the sign of a job well done, Nicholas said. And so we all went to bed, though there wasn't much rest in it for the two of us.

Even though we were in this together, even though it was obvious to me that he was excited, I couldn't tell Nicholas how much I wanted to do this. The words wouldn't come. We showed each other instead.

I'll never be like the Master, I thought when I could think, but I didn't want to think, only feel, and be there with Nicholas.

It's not a myth that vampires have heightened senses. Supernatural abilities. Well, they could be natural for *us*—we're a different species. Some can see every minute detail of every little thing in existence. Some become flooded by the minutiae, and get washed away in the tides of emotion, reality, imagination, fear.

That night with Nicholas, I was that flood. I was possibility incarnate.

We were part of each other and something bigger.

When I could breathe, I tasted him. When I floated away, I saw Lynch, creating. When my eyes fluttered open, vision came to me like the sun rising.

I had drunk the blood of a god and become one myself.

This. This was what it felt like to be beyond understanding.

When dawn broke and Nicholas was asleep on the low bed, Zen-like, I stood at the glass doors in his room and looked out at the woods the way I did as a human. Seeing just what was before me. I needed to slow down, and not let the power of who I was and what I was about to do become who I was. *Shinigami* love their myths and destinies and prophecies, and I was *Shinigami* in my heart.

Izanagi's *Shinigami.* Not the Master's.

Izanagi was as much man as he was god, and I wouldn't take for granted that he'd become one with me. He was there throughout my life, that wine and roses headiness that meant the consistency of funerals to me. He was the connection between what I was and what I became. I had learned through him that vampires are not perfect. They make their purpose, using the gifts given them through the blood.

The forest beyond the tree line was visible to me but I shut it out.

I would not let the grand vision of defining a new race of vampires blind me to everything in front of me. And it wasn't lost on me that Izanami could be in my head at any time, knowing what I knew, shaping what I did.

Like I'd watched Nicholas do so many times, I opened the doors to his little porch, its grass mat crunching under my feet. I used the breath I didn't need to take to ground me. *In through the nose. Out through the mouth.* I focused my every movement, forming blocks, strikes, kicks in slow motion, never leaving the immediate space. *Use what you have.* Learning martial arts in Japan leaves…an impression. A vitality all its own. I would channel it now to remind me that everything done well is done in steps.

I don't know how long I was out there, but a sheen of sweat touched every inch of me when Nicholas put a hand on my waist, bringing me to a halt.

"Eliza," he said dreamily, kissing my neck.

"You're awake." *Obviously.*

He spun me around, his skin glowing through its ashiness, like a pearl covered in dust. "You know you've been out here for hours."

"Oh." I looked around the woods, the signs everywhere. "You were asleep for longer."

"You win." He kissed me hard, making me giggle like I wasn't a vampire god. "So, you got a god in your head right now?"

"I don't know. Can't tell." I knew what he was thinking: Was that all me last night? "It was all me last night," I said.

"That's not what I asked."

"And you know what I'm going to say to that."

His laugh rumbled down through me, pooled in my belly, right back up and out in my own voice. I threw my arms around him, joy filling my aura for me to see. I wished he could see it too, hoped that he could in a way.

"Nicholas, we're really doing this. Aren't we?" I said it reverently, like we were a couple that decided to have a baby. This wasn't so different. The closest we could come.

I squinted against the image of the red-haired baby in my head, living in Yomi. What kind of a childhood was that? How was he…she…there?

And suddenly I felt such a kinship with this anonymous baby that was probably a tiny monster too, because we'd both been born to live among death.

As if called to the mere thought of it, Blue whipped by us in a midnight slash through the daylight, a haunt among the trees.

"Nicholas," I whispered. "What can we do for her?"

"An in-law cottage in the backyard hardly seems the answer, huh?"

We stared into the woods for a sign of her again. "Blue!" I called out. "Blue!"

But I don't think either of us really wanted her to come. I was terrified of what might happen when she did.

Little difference that made when Blue fell upon us from above, having found her way to the roof. Snarling and gnashing her teeth, she tore at my hair and clothes while Nicholas yelled her name, pulling her off with great effort. He threw her to the ground off the porch, eliciting a wild yelp from her. I wiped at the tears pouring from my face, leaving watery pink stains on my hands. Why, why did this have to happen to that sweet soul?

I had an answer for that. Because she could be used against me.

As Blue scuttled like a crab into the woods, whining and whimpering, I steeled myself against what I must do.

"I have to go to Yomi."

Nicholas more fell than sat on the porch, exhausted once again. *Dammit, Roman, feed him already!* My mind was reeling in so many directions, I had to remind myself of my original resolve: One step at a time. Focus.

"El, sending you into Purgatory now would be—and I can't stand myself for this not-quite pun—a death sentence." His voice was raspy, his breath short. "You—" he had to stop to take a breath, his chest heaving with the effort. "You can't be everywhere at once." He coughed, doubling over.

Once again, my priority shifted. From getting ready for Izanami, to stopping Lynch, to building a vampire coven, to going to Yomi itself, and now to Nicholas. Because if I did all those other things and couldn't manage to get Roman to heal the man he calls his brother in a way that only he could, then what was it for? What would my eternity be if I couldn't make that happen for the person closest in all the world to me?

I helped Nicholas back to bed. I don't know if I was seeing time move ultra-fast, or if it was a vision of the future coming to pass, but with every step Nicholas looked more and more frail. His health drained out of him with each breath that rattled through him. I shook from the waking vision, finally struggling not to sob as I laid him down—and he was little more than a corpse. *It's not real,* I told myself.

But it would be. I knew that.

He was skin and a skeleton in that bed. His T-shirt hung against his body, every rib visible, a death rattle in his breath. His upper arms were as thin as my forearm, his cheeks hollow and hugging his teeth. The only reminder of who he'd been were the fangs dimpling his cracked, colorless lips, and the slow swirling of his cocoa eyes before they went dark and still.

"Nicholas, no," I moaned, running my hands through his hair. I expected that hair to come off in my hands, but it felt healthy enough that I could convince myself I was seeing things. It wasn't real.

A trick to keep me here. A vision given to me by Izanami.

It wasn't real, but it would be. It was coming. Once again, I remembered first things first.

I was done waiting for Roman to come to terms with the secrets he held. No secret shame was worth Nicholas's life. Roman's time was up. He would feed Nicholas if it killed all three of us.

CHAPTER 116

I needed him when he was alone. I wouldn't use Nicholas as a tool to make Roman do what he needed to do. It hadn't worked so far.

We may not be any good at Stop-the-Abomination plans, but the Abomination was good for something.

Back at the mansion, I found Lynch in his usual spot on the couch, staring idly, this time with a glass of whiskey in his hand. Apparently he did have a taste for something again.

"Can I have one of those?" I said, making him jump from the thoughts he'd been lost in.

He turned his cold eyes on me. Unreadable. Intent but directionless. Dangerous. "You don't like whiskey," he said flatly.

Amusing. "You know that?"

"I never liked you. It doesn't mean I didn't notice you," he said, and got up, like a human, returning in a vampire second with a cold beer.

"You…keep beer here?"

"No. I have beer here. I don't know how old it is."

"It's not dusty, anyway. Let's go outside."

"Why?"

"You built me a treehouse. I can sit on the steps of it and have a beer with you, can't I?"

There was no twitch on his lips when he turned his eyes on me this time. Black eyes. "Like a doll's eyes," I remembered from Jaws, and smirked. *You don't scare me, Chris Lynch.*

The shocking thing even after all this time was that it was still jarring how quickly he changed from sadness to ambivalence to psychotic to depressed to charming.

"You want something," he said.

"Don't we all?"

He followed me—*he* followed *me*—to the spot I wanted. This was how it would have to be. I would establish dominance in little ways, but he'd know I was doing it. He was keen to tactics. I would have to let him know that we were playing this silent game together and that there could be only one winner.

I cracked the beer, sitting on the short steps to my little home.

There wasn't fear exactly in his aura—just hesitation. Fight or flight. But he sat beside me on the step, our legs touching in the narrow area, and that contact made him relax.

That was a shock I wasn't prepared for. I comforted him, even when he was unsure of me. Maybe *because* he was unsure of me. We were more alike than I thought.

"We have problems to solve, you and I," I said.

"What did you do, Eliza?" he asked me.

"What? Nothing, I'm not talking about anything *I've* done."

"You don't think we should talk about the things you're doing?"

"What?" I said again, aggravated that this conversation was being taken away from me. "No, it's about the things you're doing, so listen." But he was shaking his head, lifted his eyebrows in a *can you believe this* way, like I was crazy. It was impossible to go on without addressing it. "What, Lynch? What's bothering you?"

"You are!" he burst out. "You've been killing, like I do." And his face softened, took on a dark warmth. "Like me. Like you're sick with it."

"Sick?" I breathed out. "Lynch, I'm just not holding back now. That's all. I do not kill like you do," I growled. "You stalk, choose, get close to them, *you're* sick, I'm not…not addicted to it like you are." The disgust oozed from my voice like a sickness itself, and I remembered who I was talking to.

"And yet you're not trying to cure me, are you?" he said.

I shuddered as he penetrated me with that vicious gaze I remembered him having when we first met, and before Kat died. Like he was playing a one-sided game of chess and was just waiting to flip the board on me.

"No," I said. "I'm not. There's no curing you, we all know it. What I can do though is put you to use. You're the most conniving person I know."

"Gee, thanks."

"You're welcome. You want to redeem yourself in some way?"

"Never said that."

"I'm telling you that you do. Help me get Nicholas back on his feet."

"And how do you propose I do that? He despises me."

"What he needs is Roman's blood. Only Roman's blood will restore him because he drank…" I didn't need to say it; we both knew. "Here's the thing. Roman won't feed Nicholas because he's hiding something and he's afraid that his blood will betray him. Either to Nicholas through residue or to me if I drink from him… I don't know yet. But I do know that whatever I'm here to learn from your blood, it's a puzzle, and

Nicholas feeding is the first piece I have to place. Do you want to know why I was brought back here?"

"Not especially."

Something rose up between us like the tension in a funeral home. An understanding.

"Lynch… I won't just leave you alone here when I figure it all out, you know."

He glared at me the way a hurt child does when a parent apologizes. Reluctant and wary. "You want me to get Roman to feed Nicholas?" he said slowly.

"Inadvertently. Roman did that horrible… He killed Kat just to save Nicholas from having to do it. And now he's willing to let him wither away when he could so easily prevent it? Whatever he's hiding, it's powerful, and he can't be given a choice to tell us or not. You're the only person I know who can back him up against a wall. Corner him. I need you to do it now."

I was asking for an energy level from him that I wasn't sure he had anymore, and I didn't even know how he'd do it— which is why I had to ask him. He knew how to get under Roman's skin in a way I never could, and I didn't know what other options I could find.

Quietly, soothingly, I appealed to him. "Don't you think Kat would want you to know why we've been drawn togeth- er?" He snapped his head around at me in defiance. "She would want you to do this."

Rubbing a hand over his face, he sighed. "I'll find a way," he mumbled into his hands. "You might not like how I do it."

"Oh, I thought that was pretty much a guarantee. But I like the alternative even less. And Lynch, there's something else." I almost didn't tell him, but he knew how to use every bit of knowledge as a weapon, and he needed a lot of ammo. "Nicholas and I calmed Roman down about the vampires you've been creating. He almost murdered me for knowing and not telling him. But we've got a plan."

I told him that we were rounding up the vampires he'd left and creating our own coven, and the delight in his eyes was wildly malicious. He'd always loved to watch the world burn.

"I know what to do," he said.

T he three of us had agreed that I should be the one to tell Lynch about the new coven. He could hardly stand Nicholas, and Roman was too much of an angry father for him to listen. Lynch could find those girls through his connection to them, if he wanted to. He could just plain tell us where to go, for the ones he remembered. But not only did he want nothing to do with the vampires he'd abandoned, he was, as expected, using all the information he had to his advantage.

He would refuse to help Roman locate the women. Nicholas could scare him into doing whatever he wanted—but not in the weakened condition he was currently in. It had to be me who approached him. So we'd play them. It was the only way I could get everyone to work together.

My heart stank like rotten meat with the deception of it all. It churned in me, aching to be wiped clean. But secrets beget secrets, and vampires accumulated them in hordes. My own intentions changed with every passing minute, it seemed.

While the clock ticked, I pretended to be holed up with Lynch, convincing him to help me find the women. In actuality, we were simply *being*, and it felt pretty good. We played cards, I got him to drink tea, we listened to the rain fall on the roof of the treehouse. Two days passed while Nicholas wasted away and hungry vampires roamed without direction or help.

"You go, and you tell them I won't help you no matter what," he said when we thought enough time had passed.

"No way, you have to do it. They'll see me lying a mile away."

"You think I should go over there and tell them to leave me alone?"

"Yeah, sort of. Tell them you'll leave and never reveal the locations of these vampires if they don't get me off your back."

"Eliza, what if I told you I don't know where they are? That I don't feel them at all?"

"Well. I have a plan for that, too," I said quietly. The level of deviousness I'd reached was just staggering to me. *It's all for a good cause, Eliza. They're just lies. They can be forgiven. They're a means to an end.* I told myself that a lot.

"Let me guess," Lynch said with a sneer, "you're going to drink from me until you see them all."

It wasn't a stretch, after all. But I'd be doing it against his will—at least it would seem that way to Roman and Nicholas. And maybe it would be true. Lynch really didn't want anything to do with the new vampires. Whatever his purpose was, it wasn't being the leader of a fresh coven. Those kills had been a coping mechanism for him. Having them around would be a constant reminder of what he'd been trying to escape, or trying to bring back in a Frankenstein-like way: Kat.

I was apologetic, pitying, when I said, "There's no other choice for me than to get him well. You see that, right?"

He chuckled under his breath. "You have to win. That's what I see. You need this all to go exactly as you want."

"It's far from going the way I want." I laughed. We were about six degrees from the problem, but I refused to let Chris think he had the upper hand here. "Go, before I change my mind. Stick to the plan."

Daylight, and Lynch strode outside into the sunshine

without so much as a flinch. He'd been drinking from good people, with clean auras. And yet it did nothing to lighten him, left no residue to make him any happier.

I had not been feeding on the best quality folks. The light seemed to reach for me with hot fingers, scrambling for me when Lynch opened the door. Amusement was all over his face, but he left without a word. I would wait until the sun was low, and go to them. If all went well, hopefully Roman would see that the only way to make Lynch do what they wanted was for him to feel threatened by Nicholas. And then Nicholas would feed from Roman. Wildly convoluted plan, but then again, vampires aren't known for their simplicity of spirit.

But when darkness descended, I was trembling with the desire for blood.

Just a quick hunt.

I hadn't hunted since the men in Japan, my appetite all but gone. With the encroaching hunger came the lingering in the darkness. And then the desire for dark blood. It didn't matter that there wasn't time.

Lynch called it a sickness. I *wanted* to fall into it, for just a few minutes, let myself drift away in the lowliness of a kill and be gone, for just a little while. Then I could face all the lies, the responsibility, the haunting and the evil.

There was enough time for me to be a little evil myself.

Singing Pines Park was where I ended up, sitting on a bench. The place where I'd first seen Lynch lose control so much that he dropped the veil that hides us from mortals. I, just a girl then, saw him drink deeply from that young lady, her blood spotting the snow beautifully. Horrifying then— beautiful now. A romantically stunning scene of black, white, and red with the frozen pond and the trees singing in the cold wind, Christmas lights dotting the duskiness. Life meant something different to me then.

The ground was muddy—not the best place for a walk, but

that never stopped the starry-eyed nature lovers from dawdling.

Did I really want to kill one of them?

I did. I really did. But could I coach a bunch of newbies to do the same thing?

I dropped my head into my hands. "What in the holy hell have I committed to?"

No, the question was, what choice did I have? The vampires existed—I was only going to help them find their way, make good choices. I thought.

She walked by, alone, leggings and some fancy hoodie-thing but the kind that hugs every curve and shows off just how much time the yoga mat has seen. Her hair gleamed, up in an artful messy bun with strands straying flawlessly here and there. I could see darkness in her eyes. She was smiling ever-so-faintly, was certainly the head of the PTA, and a valued member of her community. Her aura floated airily about her as if to say "namaste." But other words were scrawled throughout. Vicious words that immortality made even more ghastly for how commonplace they were among so many. Words attached to skin color, to where someone grew up, to sex. The kinds of words that for so many became who they were, and to think that such an idea, a falseness, could follow a person for *eternity*… It certainly changed my idea of what a "good" person could look like, act like. If they were the type of person who should be made immortal. Or should it be the damaged ones, the recipients of that often silent abuse? Who *was* worthy of immortality?

Who deserved death at an immortal's hand? Or teeth.

Leggings Lady came upon me, and I made no attempt to cloak myself from her. Her aura was…forgiving…when she met my eyes. Apparently I was good-looking enough for her. And I was white, so I guess that worked, too.

If I killed her, she would be missed by many. The other

PTA moms, the clerks at the grocery store where she was always so kind. Her family. Both kids. But her thoughts smelled like sulfur and no wildly expensive facial cream could hide it on her skin. Not from me.

I guess the final question was, would the world be better without her?

"Hello," she said coldly but with a tight-lipped smile.

"Hi."

I was no longer hungry.

~

"Y ou're going to leave me alone."

Lynch had gotten to the cottage before me, as planned. I was still several yards away myself, approaching on foot, but of course heard everything.

"Ugh, why did you let him in?" Nicholas groaned. I laughed out loud, slowing once I reached the yard. Might as well enjoy the banter before it all went ugly.

"This idea is ridiculous, and I won't have any part of it," Lynch said.

Then Roman started. This was where it would begin.

"Chris," he said. Immediately, I pulled forth the red mist, creating a miniaturized version of the whole scene inside. The three men were clear to me. But I didn't need to see anything at all to know Lynch caught the one word, *Chris*, and knew he was being worked.

And poorly.

I thought of how he always called Nicholas "Nick," and how Nicholas fumed about it. And here Lynch was, not mentioning at all that Roman never called him "Chris."

Roman continued, "We have an opportunity, Chris, to do some good. You have a chance to do the right thing here." His words were loaded, the tone of his voice off, but I couldn't see beneath it.

"There have been plenty of opportunities for me to do 'good' before this. This time isn't different," Lynch said, some of that old shark sneaking into his words.

Roman's silhouette in the mist flickered and darkened, sharpened, narrowed and stretched like a thing finding its way into the world.

His aura was shifting.

The voice in my head—Izanami—burst into my mind. *"Focus harder, foolish girl. You've been given gifts."* And of course, she was right.

The *telling* was there. All I had to do was pull it along.

"Wouldn't you want to…to…create something," Roman choked up, "if you could?"

His words bled into his aura, blobs of pain and deterioration of his heart. *What is getting to you, Roman?*

"I did create something. Quite a few of them. Not much of a creator, it turns out. I feel nothing for them. Nothing you can do will make me be a part of your backwoods family, Roman. What will you do, bring them all here? Show them how to hunt, as if they have no idea what they want, like they're completely imbecilic and can't follow their own craving for blood? You going to show them how to hide themselves while they drink, as if that will do anything to protect them? You are no Master, and this isn't some mountain in Japan."

"No," Nicholas interjected, "it's a mountain in the U.S. and we can update what we've been taught, make it mean something. We can start the right way."

"The right way?" Lynch laughed. "You presume there's a right way to murder people. That's what you're saying."

"Goddammit, Lynch!" Nicholas exploded, shocking all of us. "We have to contend with who we are! I won't go through this for the millionth time. We are who we are and we do what we can do. But listen to me, you have to stop making new vampires until we get these ones under control." The argument was taking so much energy out of him, gray lines were forming around his eyes, miniscule to a human but like open veins to me. "No more vampires, Lynch."

In an instant, those condescending final words tipped Lynch over the edge into the voraciously cruel creature I'd first met. I had to stop myself from rushing into the cabin to protect Nicholas, stop Lynch. This was what we needed.

"And who's going to stop me?" Chris spelled out menacingly.

Only one of us could. A cascade of delight crashed over me —Nicholas back to himself, and knowing what Roman was hiding—I needed this like blood. Willing the mist to stay focused on the scene before me rather than give in to its own sentient excitement, I trained my eyes on the Lynch figure. Until the little silhouette glanced my way.

"Keep pushing them," I thought at him.

Lynch's image faltered as he tried to understand where my voice was coming from. I'd broken his concentration.

"Lynch," Roman choked out. The emotion there, the guilt and fear ate at me, itching for me to drag it out of my friend. "You don't have to help us guide them, but you have to stop creating vampires."

"Didn't you just tell me it would feel *good* to create something?"

"Something good! But more than that, to take responsibility for an existence you brought..." But Roman couldn't finish. His words hung in the air, traced like a shadowy finger through the scene in the mist, and I felt the stab in his heart— though I could never truly *feel* it.

Because I'd never had a child, and I'd never lost one.

I finally dropped the mist and entered the cabin, straight

past Nicholas and Lynch to wrap Roman in my arms, hoping that he could feel how sorry I was, while both trying to relay and hide my guilt at pushing him the way I had. Lynch may have said the words, but it was only because of me. Roman didn't embrace me back, though—a move entirely unlike this man made of compassion. Pulling back, I blinked hard, trying to see what I was missing in his aura, but nothing happened.

"Eliza…" he began.

That one word sounded like an apology.

I cocked my head, as if it could help un-confuse me. "What's going on, Roman?"

It was Nicholas who answered. "He's not going to let me drink," he said with a casual shrug.

Roman's eyes told a different story, though. He didn't plan to let Nicholas drink, no, but that wasn't what he was hiding. Why he needed to apologize to me.

Backing away, I shoved him off with a mere thought, and he stumbled backwards. "Whatever *betrayal*," I snarled, "you're smothering? It can't be worse than leaving your brother to wither away. You came back here, for what? Because you were too weak to say no to me?" Fury fueled my words, my hurt. "You just love this self-flagellation. The martyr. Right? You said you would bring Nicholas back."

"Did it ever occur to you that we aren't supposed to live forever, Eliza?" Roman muttered, and immediately dropped his head, remorseful.

But I'd already propelled myself across the space and slapped him hard. He hit the ground, me standing over him while Nicholas begged me to leave him alone. "No. It never occurred to me that Nicholas should die. And if you can look at him and think that, well then the wrong brother is dying."

"El," Nicholas whispered, defeated, hand on my shoulder. "No."

I stifled a scream that rumbled up from inside me, boiling

the mist in my body, exploding my soul. Because all I wanted to do at that moment was rip Roman limb from limb and gorge myself on his blood.

Then the voice of the demon goddess in my head cackled. She wanted this, this chaos.

She's doing this, I thought. And of course, she heard.

CHAPTER 117

"**S**top!" I yelled—but I was the only one doing anything to stop. They all turned to me, waiting for my next move, whatever latent crazy would show itself.

I had to wonder how far back Izanami had been messing with me. How much of this new vampire was actually *me*, not some extension of *her*?

And I shoved the crippling betrayal away from me at a thought that had no basis in reality: Did Izanagi somehow let her in?

"This fighting, the secrets, it's all orchestrated by her," I murmured.

"Her?" Lynch said.

"Izanami."

Lots of questions about that were to follow, but I could only shake my head, confusion rattling my brain as the voices came one after the other in an onslaught and I tried my hardest to work through the nagging thought that Izanagi had set me up. Could have been recently, could have been part of his escaping the mountain, could have been when I lost my parents and death hung around me. Waiting. Was this what fate really was? Betrayal by gods who befriended you, attached themselves to your soul and turned it inside out, made it unrecognizable? Ones you didn't know, manipulating you from a hellscape?

Goddammit, I only ever wanted peace and quiet.

"Eliza, what the hell are you talking about?" Nicholas barked, his chest heaving with the energy it stole. "Why is he here?" he said, raising a hand in Lynch's direction. "And what the hell does it have to do with Izanami or…" Flabbergasted, he fell into his favorite chair by the unlit fireplace.

Our plan to get Roman to feed Nicholas had fallen apart almost instantly.

I pulled myself out of the thoughts of Izanami for the moment, determined to stay on track, to get Lynch back into character. I snarled at him, angry that he'd failed to show his recklessness, what it *could* be, if he'd cared.

"I won't stop," Lynch said, unconvincingly. "I'll make as many vampires as I want to. It feels good to me now, better than killing. Like laying waste to a lovely hotel room." He grew more convincing by the second.

"We'll stop you," Roman said solidly.

"No," Lynch laughed, "you won't. When will you learn? After all these years, you still fight this ridiculous battle of controlling me, but you can't even control yourself. She was the kindest…" Lynch faltered. "You ground the sweetness right out of her. *Killed* her. She was your friend."

It was the healthiest way I'd seen him deal with Kat's death yet. *To think that I spurned him into it, forcing him to be a conniving jackass.*

What would Kat have said?

I stopped that right away. Kat would have said to do what was necessary to get what I wanted. She wasn't innocent. She was kind, yes, but she was sly, determined, seductive. All those things made me love her more—she was no angel, but she could act like one.

Lynch didn't need to act to get what he wanted right now, what *we* wanted. He was finally letting it all go.

"You killed her, the only person who mattered to me, and now you think I'll do what you want? Do the *right thing*? Tell me about what's right, Roman. Letting Nicholas die? That's right? You killed Eliza's dearest friend, you want to take him from her too? Who's the brutal one now? Hmm?" His teeth were bared. His eyes glinted with sorrow and the madness it brought along. "She was innocent," Lynch said at last.

I could see Roman's knees buckle ever-so-slightly when he heard "innocent," saw it hang around him like an aura in itself.

"If you only knew..." Roman said, trailing off.

"Knew what?" I butted in, grasping at the straw that might lead him to finally release his secret. If this was the way to get him to feed Nicholas, I'd take it. "Stop hiding, Roman," I growled. "What don't we know?"

But Roman was silent.

"Enough of this," Lynch spat. "I'll never help you. I'm not your brother and I never will be. We won't ever work together, Roman, do you hear me? If it's a coven of vampires you want, a coven you'll get. I'll make as many as I can, more than you can handle, more than you'll ever find. And rest assured, it's because of *you* that I'll tear their lives from them and make them eternal killers."

This was going too far. I'd seen Lynch start to deal with his feelings, and I liked it, wanted to see more of it. Instead I'd sent him spiraling into killing again. I'd only wanted it to be an act, and here I'd done...

My god, what had I done?

Lynch pounded out of the cabin like a man who needed to hear every footstep to remind him of what solid ground felt like. A man who had a god complex that could get away from him if he let it. And he most likely would.

This was the kind of chaos that Izanami wanted, and I'd handed it to her, just handed it right over like a goddamn moron.

Roman still stood there, dumbstruck, lost in thought, and Nicholas was trying to pretend nothing weird had happened. Though many terrible things had happened, actually. He sat in his favorite chair by the unlit fire, crossed his leg with a grunt, and put his head back to stare at the log ceiling.

"Don't walk out on this, Roman," I said quietly, hoping Nicholas wasn't paying attention. "You have to face it."

I couldn't care anymore about the defeat on his face that meant he was giving up on his brother. Roman had put a barrier between us that I had no energy to repair.

Speaking of no energy, I went to Nicholas's side, sitting on the arm of the chair, running my fingers through those thinner-than-usual curls that still framed his face like an angel's. "You'll be okay, no matter what," I said, more to myself than him.

But there wasn't a whisper or grunt of response. Not his usual lean-in to my hand in his hair.

There was no sign of life at all.

"Nicholas," I said, shaking him hard. Harder than a human would have been able to, rocking the chair on its legs—but Nicholas, eyes open, just stared straight ahead, a dead man, looking above for someone to bring him home.

"Roman," I choked out. Not even a vampire could have heard it. "Ro—Roman," I tried again, voice a strangled scream at the end as I shook the man we loved to no avail. His head lolled to the side, and I hastily lifted it back up, propped it, his eyes staring the same direction as nausea roiled in my gut. The salt of my tears stung my tongue as they slid into my mouth, dripped down my chin. Roman was a blurry ghost of movement on Nicholas's other side, but not moving fast enough for me, there was no glint of blood being poured into my lover's mouth, nothing to save him, nothing different than the bull-shit I was doing, shaking him like I could rattle the sense to survive into him.

"Feed him!" rumbled out of me in a violent, spittle-infused roar.

Everything stopped when Roman's eyes met mine and I was the one who drank.

Drank his terror, its faces as many as a rough-cut diamond. Grief for his brother washed over fear of his secrets revealed, flooded disgust over his selfishness, drowned out revulsion over his actions. Fear was the crest of them all and I imagined myself bathed in it until I lost myself in it. I felt my jaw unhinge, my chin brush my sternum as my mouth grew longer, wider, drinking in the multi-colors of fear that raced around Roman, crippling him.

NO. NO. STOP, I told myself. *Not now, this isn't you, this isn't you this isn't you not now...*

Roman fell, a marionette with his strings clipped but so much less alive.

Nicholas.

Now, with my every nerve on fire, having fed on fear and glowing with electric power, I could sense Nicholas—not dead, then.

Comatose.

I remembered those long hours before, me merely human, Nicholas the only god I knew, and how he snapped out of it, called to a victim that restored him completely. I remembered watching him emerge over the hillside, the snow a blank canvas with the white-trimmed dark forest framing him. My heartbeat when I'd see him...a feeling I would never forget and never feel again.

Could he come back this time? And here, the blood he needed should have been served up to him on a silver platter.

Roman was stirring, groaning. And it was totally me, not any god's intervention, that wanted to knock him out again, slit his wrist and pour his blood into Nicholas's waiting mouth.

And I wondered again, if Izanami played a part in all the events that had transpired, and Izanagi had been a presence in my life for decades…did he play a part in Nicholas's demise too? Would he betray me this way? He'd taken everything from me for so long, he would *not*—

That's when the birds came.

Like black lightning bolts, they tore through the front door, crashed through my favorite window by the fireplace, screaming and surrounding me, a black storm of motion in stark contrast to Nicholas's unmoving body. Hundreds of them, on the floor, perched on the chairs and the mantle, the exposed beams in the ceiling. They all looked to me—not just at me, but *to* me, waiting for a response.

This was Izanagi, reassuring me. The crows were always a part of him.

I kneeled down and looked closer. I noticed that their eyes… I'd never actually looked deeply into them before. I hadn't needed to. With a deep breath, I reached out my hand to one bird. He didn't move away or squawk in fear as I rested it upon his broad back.

Once again, I was overcome by yet another force—a vision.

I saw a green chair, occupied by a young man. A smiling little girl sat in his lap as he read her a book. The vision shifted, and the man was older, the little girl in his lap still, this time talking animatedly. Next, the man was old and the little girl was gone.

This was the green chair. That was the man Nicholas had

been called to, meaning that little girl was the one Lynch had turned into a vampire.

I bent further down, to truly see into his eyes, and they told me the story.

This bird and that man were the same.

Slow motion as I looked around at all the crows, all these souls that came for me.

Getting to my feet like a mortal, like clumsy Ellie who had to adjust her shirt and pants every time she moved, I tried to make sense of quivering Roman, motionless Nicholas, the horde of birds, of Lynch taking off, of Blue out there somewhere, waiting for a weak moment to attack.

"Roman," I breathed. "Stay with him. Do you understand me? Stay by his side and if Blue comes, you get her out of here any way you must. Any. Way. She's not herself. I'm going to get—"

What, answers? Help?

But Roman nodded solemnly without me having to finish. With one final promise to Nicholas to fix him, I let the crows lead the way.

CHAPTER 118

I raced through the woods, as I had so many times before, now with the murder of crows ahead of me in a midnight swarm. With giant leaps and bounds that cleared the trees, I furthered myself from Ossipee, but never from the problems there or my responsibility to them.

I was running right into a trouble I never could have imagined before.

Having gotten the mortal need to *do* out of the way, like I could outrun my own mind, the horror that my world had become, I pictured myself in the Yomi from my dream. Still running, leaping, I felt my body become less real. Less solid. But I didn't do anything except nearly fall from the air into the trees below. I tried to envision Yomi again, to no avail. But the surge of willpower made me jump higher, until I was brushing clouds.

Despite the circumstances, I was laughing hysterically, even as I came down to the ground to push off again. I knew that it was a matter of moments before I came to the ocean.

No way can I cross the damn ocean.

But what would hold me back?

I ran again through the trees, the black birds a shroud around me, a blur in front of me, and the ocean was close, the sea salt stinging my nose. Before I could think twice, talk myself out of it, I took the final leap over open water.

Exhilarating. The only word that could describe it.

Clouds tickling my head, waves lapping in tune with the flapping of bird wings, and just as black.

Until the plummet began. Panic overtook me and I flailed, screaming until I would have done anything at all for blood to soothe my throat. The crows screeched along with me, diving at the water in a massive streak. The time passed so slowly—maybe just regular time, but for me, it was an eternity—every vampire sense popping like fireworks in the darkness. My heart was paralyzed in my throat while my body couldn't stop moving.

And then I hit the water.

No crows to guide me under here.

In a heart-stopping millisecond, silence enveloped me. The darkness, velvety before, became impenetrable, thicker than gods' blood. Suddenly, time fast-forwarded and the still ocean I'd invaded sprang to life. Every speck of life within those waters swirled into a dance that my presence interrupted, an unnatural thing in an ancient environment. I hovered there, hair spread out around me, limbs weightless, my mind anything but. Tentacles whipped fathoms below me, scales gleamed, teeth glinted, and I was no longer the prime predator.

For the first time in a long time, *I* was the one afraid.

I swam hard for the surface but it wasn't anything like it was in mortal dreams, where you can't move no matter how desperately you flail. No, vampire strength still fueled me, and I torpedoed to the top, and I swear the beasts of the deep howled with rage.

"What a trophy you would be," the voice in my head said.

"Izanami?" I thought as I broke the surface, where I was met by the hovering gang of crows.

They grabbed me as I shot up, lifting me higher with claws and beaks clinging to every part of me, bringing me back up as close to the clouds as their strength would allow them.

And I clung to that feeling for as long as I could. Not the dreaminess of it, not the surrealness of realizing I wasn't the greatest power in my world—because that was how I had felt all the time since becoming *Shinigami*—but the feeling of not being in charge. For this time I was at the mercy of birds and sea creatures.

God, I was so tired.

The birds called out to me as they carried me, and I let myself reach out to them in my heart, even though I was just too drained of life and will to *interact* at all. I longed for Birch Tree Books, for the icy New England air and shaking snow off my boots, the *quiet* of being nobody but Ellie.

I curled my fingers around the claws of the crows holding my hands. I trained my eyes on them to see their auras. I felt so close to them, so invited *not* to speak.

Their auras didn't glow as one as I thought they might. No, these were human, complicated colors of a lifetime of memories, held behind a flourish of blue-gray that was the reinvigorated life of a creature with only nature to answer to.

No, not only nature.

I breathed in, encouraged by their simplicity and peace. The scent that greeted me wasn't the salt of the ocean below, but of wine. And roses.

I gasped, "Izanagi?" and whipped my head around. My hair pulled as it hung from the beaks of the—

"Tengu."

A sob broke free, and I rolled my eyes at myself for how goddamn exhausting it was, at how often I did that, how weak I felt. But Izanagi was here, somehow, and I'd needed him so much. I strained to find a way to see him, but he couldn't be seen—I knew that. So I let myself be carried still, and listened.

"Tengu. Spirits of the dead not pure enough for Heaven, and not terrible enough for Hell. They live between worlds, where neither matters."

Crows had followed me my entire life. And now they were bringing me to Yomi.

"Yomi is a place for others, *too, Eliza. The ones who don't belong. They may be called demons but there is no such thing as merely evil, there is only reason and belief. The demons of Yomi are the heroes of their own tale, as any hero is. Can you fault them for that?"*

"No…"

"Would you consider that to be abominable?"

"No…" What was he getting at?

"Do you not live between worlds yourself?"

My brain skidded to a stop at the thought, a clue, the *point* I'd always searched for. It was in those—

The *tengu* dove, eliciting a scream from me as we plunged toward the water. And even though I knew Izanagi had sent them and that he was on my side, terror of those monsters below strangled me and I struggled again. "Yomi is on a mountaintop, for chrissakes!" I yelped.

Seconds before we'd have smashed into the water fast enough to obliterate bones, they pulled back, and let me gently glide into the depths.

My own fear gripped me again.

That which consumes me makes me stronger.

Long ago words from Kieran that rang so true they almost drowned out the sub-aquatic screams of the marine predators that descended upon me.

I swear, they'd had time to gather their friends while the crows flew with me and Izanagi gave me riddles to unpack, but these ancient creatures had nothing but time. The further I sank, the thicker the swarm of tentacles, fins, teeth. I swung out an arm when a razor-sharp fin whipped my back, just in time for a blue streak of a shark to latch on and sink his massive teeth right in.

Pain, physical pain, is something I hadn't felt since being human and falling down the stairs in our crappy old apartment.

This far exceeded that.

Every nerve leaped to life as the shark snapped me back and forth, bones cracking so loudly in my own ears that I wanted to scream. But a flood of ocean water invaded my mouth, and I went limp for a second, just a second, because it would be really easy to give up.

The shark let go.

Taking my arm with it.

Agony came first in the form of nausea but my stomach was thankfully empty. Delirium hit me when my thought was, *Kat would laugh so hard if I was swimming in my own puke and limbs.*

The shark thrashed, sliced across my face with its tail. *That's what sharks do,* I thought, serene and without a hint of anger. *They're predators.*

Izanagi's words: *"Would you consider that to be abominable?"*

I laughed, swallowed more water. Did *everything* in my life have to mean something? Seriously, at some point it would be nice if I didn't live in a goddamn tapestry of Big Picture threads.

Of course, I wasn't going to live through it much longer.

This was it, then? This was how it all ended, torn limb from limb after *all that?* That...that...*ridiculous* life and the deaths and vampires and battling and winning and losing and now this was the end?

I watched the wide river of blood stretch between the shark and my shoulder. The pain came next, searing under the water, disconcerting. The trail of red never dissipated, just flowed thick and dark.

Because it wasn't my blood. Not all of it anyway.

My crimson mist extended from the gaping wound in my arm that had other sharks swimming closer and closer, faster and faster. But when they came too near, the mist lashed out, frightening them off in a rush of whitewater. Or was that my blurred vision? Fish darted this way and that, carefully avoiding the mist as it twisted in and around itself, thickening and strengthening.

The pain dwindled to a tingling.

The tentacles that had pulled at my ankles disappeared. And the sound of the deep overcame the noises of predators that only a vampire might hear. Never heard anything about those terrifying sounds on Nat Geo.

I was sounding more like myself in my brain.

The mist had reached the shark holding what was left of my arm and lunged at it. My mist exploded like fireworks, obliterating the shark in a flurry of actual blood, simultaneously stitching itself to my arm.

Slowly, magically, the mist slinked itself back to me in a cascade of winding tendrils. I dared not flinch when it approached the raw socket where my arm had been torn away, the bleeding stopped now. I didn't have my own blood to flow, not really. The mist-veins knit themselves together, braided and overlapped, stitched themselves around the two pieces of me, and with an odd sizzle underwater, re-attached my lost arm. A jagged red welt was all that remained of the nightmare.

"There is loneliness burrowed in the strength we have," Izanami said in my mind. *Christ,* did I hate having someone rattling around in my head, and here I had both Izanagi and Izanami sending me messages.

I'd been dragged so deep into the ocean I could scarcely see the surface. The sea still offered resistance to my body, vampire or not, as I swam upward to a place I never thought I'd reach.

"You aren't unmatched. That should frighten you, and give you peace."

What the hell was she talking about now?

The surface had only been a reflection of a shimmer of a wave before, a detection of another place, and now glimmered like stardust.

I would not be taken down.

I powered up harder, my injured arm now moving with greater and greater mobility.

My heart was not invincible, but my spirit would be. *Strength is more than constant bravery, constant vigilance*, I told myself. I'd told Nicholas the same thing, over and over against all our odds.

Nicholas.

The thought of him bristled Izanami, I could feel it like an aggressive tickle.

"Imagine the loneliness in my strength," she growled.

I rocketed higher until I exploded out of the water, met by the hundreds of crows again. Suspended in the sky by the red mist that had saved me over and over, I wondered for the briefest time if the mist was a gift from Izanami, too—but it didn't matter. It was mine. I had power in so many ways, and I would bring Nicholas back to life with it one way or another.

"Worth another try," I said to the birds, and they agreed in their silence, their knowing eyes all the encouragement I needed.

I closed my eyes, felt the soaked canvas of my Chucks. Somewhat invincible or not, Chucks were the only shoes for me. I felt my Overlook Hotel T-shirt clinging to me, and remembered always pulling it out from my waist, always sucking in my stomach. I didn't have to do that now, but I still did sometimes. Muscles pulsed in my back, ones I'd never had or used when I was human. They made my bra straps uncomfortable occasionally.

Because I was still Eliza and I'd survived so much. And dead, I was still surviving. Nicholas would, too.

The great purpose that constantly hovered over me could pound sand right now. I had to get to Yomi and save Nicholas first.

I said the word in my head, knew Izanami would hear it, knew it was the equivalent of wishing myself to Oz, but I pictured myself in Yomi anyway. Because if I didn't know the way, the mist certainly did.

At once, the crows screeched with human voices, making my stomach twist—or was that the way the air and sea seemed to create a vacuum with me in the center, sucking and pushing me apart at once? The demons of Yomi added their howls to the human crow screeches, and nothing made sense, nothing was real and everything was new but impossibly ancient. The smell morphed from briny to sulfurous and strangely sweet, the atmosphere nothing but a million auras melding into one. Screams and peace.

This was Yomi.

CHAPTER 120

"Well, I'm here," I said into the abyss as Yomi slowly came into view like human eyes going from Christmas lights to sunlight.

Izanami glided out of the tunnel of blackness, trailing red light behind her along with the bustle of an angelic white kimono trimmed in the colors of the sun. It was easy to see how Izanagi fell in love with her. Her seeming purity, her demure magnetism. She was a princess in this empty, over-flowing place where the dark was so monstrous it was impossible. Unidentifiable moans or animal noises emanated from the dark, more in shockwaves than sound. There was no ground below, no sky above, only dark.

Until she cast her eyes upon it.

One glance upwards with her pearly, glistening face, from her deep liquid eyes, the slightest smile on her dainty ruby lips, and the sky appeared, the deathly film wiped away. A blissful, baby-blanket shade of blue tried to peek out, but even this princess couldn't bring it forth entirely. Instead she revealed a dusky blue-gray riddled with slow-roaming thunderclouds, eerie and beautiful. A flash of lightning shocked the sky, creating a menagerie of gigantic creatures of the clouds, parading through the evening like carousel animals.

A second flash had them all turning their heads toward me. And they were not just animals at all. They were eyeless shadows in the shapes of all kinds of beasts that leered down at me—but in the next illumination they'd pulled back, their blurry holes of mouths downturned, their vacant eyes wide *O*s.

"They recognize the *tengu*," Izanami's sing-song voice said as she approached. "They are not so different from one another."

"Wha—what are they?" I asked, looking up to the monstrous clouds as they morphed from demons to common creatures.

Izanami smiled at me, her dark eyes meeting mine with only a hint of malice. "My souls," she said.

My throat sucked in on itself, frozen. *I have to get out of here.* "You know why I've come," I choked out.

She laughed, coming closer. "Yes! But do you?"

"I know exactly why I'm here."

"Liar!" she screamed, sending answering howls up from the darkness, the demons or souls or monsters hiding even from vampire eyes. "You think you're here to save him, the Golden Boy. But it was never about him."

More wailing from the shadows. "For me it is."

Her smile opened so wide I thought it would swallow me whole. *Like your own when you swallow fear, you freak.* But it was she who'd point out the monster that I was. "There!" She waggled a long, elegant finger at me. *"For me it is,"* she said, perfectly repeating my own words in my own voice. My stomach clenched. "Even though your friend Blue is drifting into madness, and Roman is being consumed by a secret, and Paolo—"

"Where is Paolo?" I demanded. But it was half-hearted.

Because I hadn't thought of him once since I got here, focused as I was on getting what I came for.

Her blood. Heal Nicholas. Bring him back.

Her power.

She'd drawn me here with her lovely "gifts" and I'd fallen for it.

"It's not about Nicholas, huh?" I said, cold reality sinking in. "You knew saving him would get me here. It's about me. Isn't it?" Fury quaked in my bones, my body shook with anger, at her, at myself for being lured in. "*This* is my great purpose?" I spat, sweeping my arms around me.

In a flash she was before me, her face inches from mine, and it was no longer the face of a princess or a god.

Decay poured from her like a fountain, stinking and rotten. Her skin slid from her cheeks, leaving gaping, meaty holes, bits clinging to the bare bone underneath. A tangle of black stringy hair hung over the yellow flares burning deep in her eye sockets. Teeth became daggers, lips became bloodless lines.

"DO YOU THINK IT WAS MINE?" she boomed, and all of Yomi shook with fear. It tasted like ancient blood and ashes and it all pooled around her. I licked my lips without thinking.

The dead thing that was Izanami calmed herself inhumanly fast, replaced her smooth smile, now on broken lips. It gave me a second to think, a second I needed because my mind didn't move the way it should here. Not in this place. But I thought: *She's right.*

When she gave birth to deities, when she and Izanagi were happy, was this the fate she was bound for? It wasn't fair. Fair may not matter, but still, it wasn't fair.

"You don't want to be alone anymore," I said quietly. Because she'd been alone for so long, with remnants of her former life clinging to her like the skin that fell from her skull.

Her smile was genuine, if not macabre. She turned away

from me in a gentle swoop of light, and when she turned back, she was beautiful again. "But I'm not alone anymore."

"Where is Paolo?" Everything was so jumbled here, confused, it was hard to keep track of even a sentence with the demon shadows looming overhead, coursing around me.

"I didn't mean Paolo," Izanami said.

She fed me images of the baby, dreamlike again. "She's real?" I said with a gasp.

"As real as anything can be in this place," Izanami said mournfully. Yomi groaned. "But hers is not the life I long for." When I gave her the pause she was obviously looking for, she continued. "Did you know my children were taken from me? We were *gods*. The goddess of creation is nothing more than a vessel, not to be worshipped but *used*. My children, stolen from me to create Japan itself, and I will never have them back. Except for the imperfect ones. They call this one 'leech child.' Can you imagine? *Fumeiyo*." Disgrace. She gestured down at a slug-like, bald toddler, with no arms or legs and slippery, wet skin that wiggled at her feet. I couldn't help it—I jumped back, grimacing. She leered at me. "Easy enough to see why they've been deemed the Devils of Yomi."

"I—I'm sorry," I choked out.

She came closer, slowly, each step terrifying me into paralysis.

"Of course you are," she sneered. "How dare you pity me? You. You who has my husband's blood running through her veins."

The slug baby wrapped itself around my feet like a boa constrictor and Izanami's eyes blazed.

"I—it's not my fault!" I cried out, hating myself for the weakness of it. I despised when people shirked blame, and if she blamed me for having Izanagi's affections, who was I to turn that around on her? When she was trapped here like a zoo animal in Hell? "But you have the baby now…"

Her voice boomed, sending up wails of agony from the devils of Yomi, every one of them feeling her pain as their own. "I created the islands of Japan! Born of my very womb!" she screamed, clutching her stomach as it morphed into one of a disgusting corpse again, maggots falling between her fingers to the ground. "One child is an insult, a consolation prize, a *travesty*! That child is nothing more than a sign that I am meant to mother once more."

Leech-child slithered around my feet.

"I don't understand what you want," I said, measuring every word so as not to spark her anger again.

"Your monster has begun a new race of vampires," she cooed to me, kimono stitching itself back together, recreating her pristine form. "One without a meddling old man to control them, thanks to you."

It began to come together.

"You want to be the master of the new vampires?" I asked, and was answered with a sinister smile.

"He creates them, satisfies his need, and I mother them. It satisfies my needs and theirs," she answered.

I dug through the words in my head, nothing coming together as smoothly as it should. Did she want to walk the earth again to be with Lynch's vampires?

"Izanami, you can't be released into the world, you must know that. You're not..." What could I say that wouldn't condemn me to death with her rage? "You aren't the woman you used to be."

Her eyes went dark, dead. "You are so much better than I? A murderer, consorting with a murderer, the pair of you digging your heels into the ground and poisoning it. Your Golden One would be fully restored to watch over me on Earth. Nicholas could be healed beyond your imagination with my gifts! This is where *you* belong, both you and the Abomination. With her."

The baby appeared in her arms, swathed in a pink silk blanket, a tuft of red hair peeking out the top.

It can't be.

I stumbled, my body turning against me in a way it hadn't since I'd been human, in those last throes of life. The ghouls and devils whirled around me in a sickening twister.

How foolish I'd been to not see it before. To have ignored what was too clear.

The baby.

She was Kat's.

"How is this possible?" The noxious, cavernous blackness spun.

"Ah, you've woven it together at last," Izanami said with a grin that was too wide, the thing of a demon, not of a goddess. "It is simple. Your friend was with child when she became *unmei nashi.*"

No, it couldn't be. Lynch was a vampire. How could he create life?

And yet, didn't he? With countless girls across the world, turning them into death gods.

"Gods do not play by human guidelines, musume," Izanami said into my whirling mind.

"I am not your daughter. Get out of my head."

"As you wish." But she was laughing at me. "You believe that all things were created for a purpose, do you not? And that the *Shinigami* had the greatest purpose of all—to keep that balance, and put a finite line where lives end. This Abomination has done truly godly things, in his own life, in his immortality. He has taken life and given it, created rules of creation himself. He has renewed the world of *Shinigami.* It is his reason. His purpose. His *mokuteki.* He has redesigned what forever can be."

My head buzzed with all that this meant, gurgled under the oceans of meaning. The Abomination that was Chris Lynch, the man was suffering personified. This race he'd made—was making—could be a new breed of predator forces that worked within the laws of the *Shinigami*. They could join the food chain, keep the balance as they always had with more choices and more independence, with more conscience than they'd have been allowed under the Master.

But they could become monsters like Lynch, who slayed people at random, without ever quenching their thirst. No balance. No humanity. They could become earth-bound devils of Yomi, themselves.

If I wasn't there to lead them, if Nicholas was in a coma, if Roman wasn't there to keep Lynch on the straight and narrow —as much as such a wraith could be—what would happen to those countless vampires?

But I could just make out Izanami's angle.

"If I take your place here," I said, unable to focus my eyes, my voice a tinny thing, "you'll save Nicholas. And if I don't…"

"Do you need to ask?" Izanami said. I didn't, really. I knew the answer. She would let Nicholas suffer forever, or until he couldn't handle it anymore.

The bigger question that I couldn't ask myself because she'd have seen the answer in my mind, was this:

Could I take the blood from her by force?

"Neverrrrr," she hissed, her face suddenly enormous, blocking all else from my eyes, her breath reeking of rotten meat. And just as suddenly she was back to the false beauty. Because there was nothing beautiful about her.

I had seen into her then; it had been impossible not to.

Not only would she refuse to give Nicholas the blood he needed if I didn't stay in Yomi, she'd turn him into a mad thing, like Paolo, like Blue. A creature whose greatest strengths attacked their minds, crippling them into subservient beasts. We'd said she was using them as weapons to get to us. But she was using them as examples.

"I don't need you," I croaked, not believing a word I said. "Roman will feed—"

Her laugh was startling, sending the crows that had been my companions into flight. "Roman? He allowed you to venture *here* instead of helping the Golden One! Watching as his *brother* withers into nothingness! At one time Roman was willing to betray you all in order to save Nicholas and what you had with him. Now the prospect of Nicholas's death is completely acceptable to him! Tell me, what do you think would change him so? What do you think he knows that would make his brother expendable in his mind?"

"I don't know what you're implying," I growled, "but Nicholas is the most honorable person I've ever known. He's done nothing to make Roman think less of him."

That laugh again. "What is it then? What changed, Eliza?"

"Nothing I can't change back." I felt blood drip down my wrists, I was digging my nails into my palms so powerfully. "Roman came back here to help Nicholas, I can still—"

"And even if you do have this persuasive power that you think you have, Roman's blood isn't enough now. *Kat's* blood isn't enough now."

She had me and she knew it. Because she'd caused this coma Nicholas fell under the spell of, and only she could restore him. Everything inside me deflated. My mist didn't even attempt to coil around me and comfort me, weakened by what we knew to be true.

"Did you poison Lynch's mind, too? Are you responsible for what he is?"

"You speak as if choice played no role in his life."

"But you did instill the seed of his...of the Abomination. Didn't you?"

That slash of a smile again, bright red lips against a chasm of teeth. "If only I could claim such extensive depravity."

Lynch acted on his own, then. He'd always been this.

"Imagine what I could do with the strength of the Golden One's mind," she said in my head and I couldn't help it, I sobbed, cried out. I'd never been backed into such a corner in my life or my death.

"I can't let it happen, Izanami. Even if you take Nicholas away, and restore Blue and Paolo. You and Lynch turning girls into vampires forever will be hell on earth. I can't ever trade the *world* for them. They would never let me, even if I could make myself do it."

"But it's not just about letting Nicholas die," she reminded me. "I would twist him into the most vengeful monster the world has ever known, with an army of the Abomination's creations to do his bidding. I would plunge him into a darkness of the mind with no escape, a golem of my own bidding, and if you dared to oppose him he would smite you down with the conviction only betrayed love can give him."

He'd always told me he'd love me no matter what I became. But would he love me no matter what *he* became?

All I had to do was stay.

Nicholas, Roman, Blue and Paolo, even Kieran would make sure Izanami was controlled.

Hell, maybe I *would have the power to control her, just like she's been messing with me.*

"Yes," she piped in, reading my thoughts. "My power would be what you have now, and you...you would have mine. We are the same, Eliza. We are both Izanami. You would rule Yomi, and I would be your anchor upon Earth. And when your Abomination discovers who I have here?"

Izanami inclined her head toward the baby, who became visible out of the darkness. That night-blooming jasmine whose petals had been stolen away.

Like my future had been, like all of the Shinigami *had been. But before she could ever begin to breathe a breath. Before she knew who she was, or how loved she would be. Trapped here, in this death place with devils and gods.*

"This child could turn his heart to light. The promise, and the memory, all in one. His beloved in all ways. His truest and greatest creation, the one that could undo all he has done."

The stipulation hung in the dank blackness like a cloud of devils.

"Or," I started for her.

"Or she could become more vicious than he's ever been, slighted before she ever knew what goodness or life was. A Master unlike any other vampire before her."

"She's a vampire?" I breathed out.

"Not yet," Izanami hissed.

The idea of Kat's baby—*Kat's* baby…

"But, the baby's not alive," I said, gulping back a sob.

"But could she be?" Izanami said, and then in my head, "*Gods create their own rules. Creation is ever-changing.*"

"Are you saying…are you trying to tell me that you could give her life again?" I said. "Wouldn't that be wrapped up with a shiny red bow, you could just *change* the rules, bring life and death together. Nope. If you had that power, you'd be out there yourself."

Izanami held the cooing baby out to me, her arms creaking like old doors with the gesture, her face alternating between ghastly and gorgeous each second, wielding the baby like a weapon, like she did with Blue and Paolo. And yet, I was drawn in. "Touch her," Izanami said, her voice hissing steam.

But terror gripped me as I relived touching the things all around Lynch's mansion, the connections to Kat that were everywhere. I backed away. The baby whimpered, but I couldn't, I couldn't. This was a trick. I was here to save Nicholas, not be lured into…into what? Taking care of a baby? Freeing a demon goddess? Trapping myself in a hellscape?

Could the soft pink beauty with sweet strawberry curls framing her delicate face answer all my questions?

Trap or not, I wouldn't be put down by my fears. *That which consumes me makes me stronger.*

Not humanly at all, I took the baby from Izanami in a flicker of vampiric swiftness and wrapped the little creature in red mist in my arms, careful not to contact her skin just yet. Her eyes—the softest doe brown with long, fluttering lashes. I blinked pink tears from my own, but one fell onto her peachy cheek, and she giggled. I brushed the drop away with the tip of my finger.

And that one drop became a flood the likes of which I could never survive.

CHAPTER 121

I thought I was screaming. Maybe I was laughing. I was no one.

I'd vowed to never let myself be swept into that ceaseless void of pasts, presents and indeterminable futures that the Master had subjected me to in Japan, stealing my consciousness, turning it into a tool, a monstrosity. But this time, I'd walked into it willingly and I wouldn't have had it any other way.

A culmination of the blood of the gods that flowed through me, of my love for my best friend reemerged into this tiny beloved soul. The prophecy that I would be the one to change the world of the *Shinigami* in ways no one else could, the desperation with which I would save everyone I loved, and the battle with fate that I forever fought.

This child. This was what purpose meant.

I let the mist fall away and pulled the baby as close as I could, terrified to feel any more. The idea that I could ever give up this feeling was reprehensible. I took a deep breath, closed my eyes to her perfection, and reached my mind out to force the images and feelings into order.

Because this was it. This was the moment it all came down to, and I needed to rise to a place I'd never been, where no one had ever been, to comprehend it.

The groaning shadow monsters hushed. Izanami's presence evaporated like everything else. Black light exploded from my body, death and stars and forever, and in the midst of it came Kat.

My red mist surrounding her face, brilliant smile bright, leaning in, conspiring happily with Roman over two cups of coffee. Black Bear Café, his brotherly love for her alight in his eyes. Then shock in his eyes. Then a smile. Then a hug.

She'd told him she was pregnant. She knew. She didn't tell me.

She told him.

And he killed her anyway.

Bile, human bile burst into my mouth. I struggled to hold the baby while the strange black light swirled around us. *Not from me,* I realized, *from* her. The black light bled into crimson mist. Everything bled into everything else: betrayal, *she'd told Roman and not me*; desperation to have changed it all; fury that he'd taken her life, *this* little life, *the baby is so cold, she's really not alive in my arms and yet she is.* And memories of Roman, the wound of losing his own child fresh, forever fresh in his heart leaked into sadness for him, for Kat, for us all. *And so this is what he'd kept from us. His much-deserved shame. The dirtiest secret any of us could ever have.*

Disgusting that he wouldn't risk Nicholas seeing it through the blood that would flow between them, would let Nicholas *die* instead. Even though it was for him that he'd committed the atrocity to begin with!

"All for nothing?!" I cried out, but it was silent in the chasm of energy the baby and I emitted.

The baby gurgled, brought me back to the thick of visions and understanding. Now of Roman, countless times arguing with Lynch, flickers of fear, anger, guilt as he tried to reconcile having created the Abomination, struggling to understand what purpose in it there could ever be.

Roman, vomiting bile like the burning in my own mouth and throat that kept coming and going. Him exploding into the woods behind the cabin, leaning defeated, sobbing against a tree, sliding down its trunk.

I didn't need a vision to tell me what horrendous turmoil my friend was suffering.

The baby screamed. I wanted to scream but I was paralyzed.

Poor Roman, I thought, despite my rage. Losing his own baby, losing the love of his life, his own life. The possibility of losing Nicholas, Kat, watching our happiness die as *Shinigami purpose* replaced us. Knowing he'd created Lynch, a serial killer, and then the girl we loved carried the Abomination's child…

If he could stop a new Abomination from entering the world, saving his brother's life in the process, would he?

Yes. He would. At the cost of his own sanity, his own soul.

"Did he know?" I cried out into the thick void of black and red that whirled like the cocoa and cream of Nicholas's eyes. "Did he know that—" I couldn't say the words out loud.

Did he know that the baby's soul would be trapped in Yomi?

Of course not. Had he even thought of it, he'd never have been able to take its life. He'd have spent another eternity trying to save the world from a father-child team of mass murderers rather than condemn a baby to this Hell.

For a split second, I wanted nothing more than to tell him what he'd done, but instantly sucked the idea into my subconscious. As hurt as I would forever be, I could never hurt Roman more than he was already. Never.

I was even a little relieved that he hadn't killed my best friend *only* for Nicholas, and for what we had.

Jesus Christ, is nothing simple or clean?

The baby shuddered, I cooed to her, as if we were the only two beings in this cyclone of power and horror. But I shuddered too as a cold chill inched up and down my body, slowly and all at once, and squeezed. Paolo had managed to find his way through the storm of crackling, screeching energy, and though madness was in his eyes, when he touched me I felt his intent. To tell me that there was more to know.

Trying to focus on him for just a moment, I covered his hand with mine, and memories of the days I spent immobilized in Japan by the Master, riddled with blood and visions, swept me away from the present.

"There was purpose then and there is purpose now."

That wasn't Izanami in my head—that was Paolo. Clear and cool like his eyes had once been, as if touched by the heavens. He was still in there.

I had to free him.

"Focus, Eliza," he said, his body buckling like a tortured animal's. *"There was purpose then, and there is purpose now,"* he repeated. And fell to the ground. I felt seconds tick by and knew it was too long, I had so many lives depending on me.

Purpose, purpose, purpose…

I pictured Nicholas—healthy Nicholas—his bare, muscular back to me through the French doors of his bedroom (*"They named these after me,"* he said), meditating on the moss mat on the little porch.

Purpose, purpose, purpose.

Breathe in…

The answer was in my arms.

I leaned down and kissed the baby's forehead, cold, but sweet-smelling. A mix of life and death. Balanced. She was the perfect balance.

Kat's bright sweetness and Lynch's cold monstrosity.

Living forever and killing forever.

Eternal life through death.

Monster and human.

Fate and choice.

Every one of us tipped the scales over and over, always questioning if our purpose was real, if we were more horrible than good, if there was hope for us. This little creature never had that conflict and yet she was the apex of it all.

Because when my lips touched her skin, it was all laid bare.

In a silent cacophony of images, my own purpose came to life—to reveal hers. Her alternate fates descended upon me as my murder of crows descended upon Yomi to protect me while I endured the throes of visions. *Show me.*

Kat holding this child, both their faces alight with smiles. Lynch coming to sit beside them, and he's human…he's *human.*

I shook my head as if flipping the channel, because had they even met while Lynch lived, Lynch wouldn't be the man he is now, this would never have happened. *Lynch was meant to be this way.*

Page two of the book of her fates showed me a flame-haired teenager, blood pouring from her mouth as she hunched over a nameless girl.

The next, the same except Lynch was behind her, ready to turn the ended girl into an eternal vampire. *Creation and death together.*

Then Kat, streaks of gray racing through her hair, laugh lines around her mouth and eyes, but she was not laughing now. For her daughter, only an infant, was draining the blood from her breast, a puddle of it surrounding them both as Kat cried, unable to stop herself from feeding her baby the only way she could imagine. I sobbed, bringing me back to Yomi, to the child in my arms. *That couldn't be her.*

The crows screeched, urging me onward.

A young woman, the picture of Kat. It came to me in a

tunnel, expanding outward like a camera lens. She sat upon a throne, for lack of a better word. *The Master's throne.* A black kimono wrapped around her lithe, strong body. Kieran standing at her side, guarding her. But this woman didn't need guarding. She was the new Master. And as the camera panned out, hordes of vampires grew into the frame, on their knees, heads bowed to her. And she sneered.

"No," I said aloud. The baby stirred, pulled a strand of my hair, but I couldn't see her, could see nothing except the image that replaced it.

The same young lady. Kat's life in her cheeks and eyes, Lynch's strength in her shoulders and jaw. The same kimono, pitch black but with white threading that sang of birch trees in the snow, and a smile played upon her cherry lips. She emanated life—but she was not alive. She was here, in Yomi still, which sent pangs of sadness through my body, even as I was unaware of myself. I would feel them later. Forever. But Yomi was…different. The monsters remained, but the horror did not. The shadow monsters surrounding us held no malice in their forms, and the crippled creatures, limping, crawling, mad, were no longer mad but at peace. Of sorts. As much as they could be, knowing what—who—they had. Having been part of Izanami's world. And now…

Now cared for by this beauty from both worlds.

Then a torrent of visions: a laughing group of vampires in the cabin kitchen, female and male, listening to…me. And Nicholas, healthy, telling some story that only he could tell filled with sarcasm and good intention; Roman—in Yomi— sharing a smile with a fully restored Paolo; Lynch holding his baby daughter, a shining look in his eyes that spoke of rebirth; me again, this time with Kieran, crouching in snow-topped mountains, such joy between us, blood on our lips and peace in our hearts; me, my arms around the child, now grown.

Holding each other as if meeting for coffee, but in Yomi. A gray and pink Yomi, with fewer shadows and more faces.

With a gasp, I came to, and Yomi returned in a rush, along with Izanami. I hadn't seen her in any of those visions. For as much as I knew this baby was my responsibility to care for, because she was more important than any of us, I refused to forget what I came there for.

"Bring Nicholas back to us, and I'll take the baby off your hands."

Izanami burst out laughing, a raucous thing that didn't fit her now-tiny body. "You're clever, and funny. I've not known humor for a very long time."

"Thanks, I pride myself on maintaining a sense of humor when faced with a manipulative demon goddess. Look, I came here for one thing, and you're trying to keep me here by preying on my loyalty to my dead best friend. A solidly unexpected twist—but not one I'm falling for. I'll take the baby—"

"You cannot!"

"—I'll take the baby, and if you want me to come back, then take Nicholas out of the coma. That's it. That's the deal."

"She cannot leave this place. She was born into it."

I held my chin high when I said, "We don't have to live what we were born into."

"I won't do it," she blurted. "Take her and I will take him."

Ice ran down my limbs, spread from my heart, made me think of Nicholas's cold, the way he could become it, release it. I couldn't take not having him in the world.

Take.

"I'll have to do some taking of my own."

CHAPTER 122

S he was in my head, even without me knowing, and so I had to act faster than I could think.

I dropped the baby.

I rode on the truth that my mist had caught me a million times in a million ways, and I let it carry me in a blink to Izanami.

She is only Shinigami.

As she shifted back to a six-story Amazon, I grabbed her, was carried up into the shadow clouds with my fangs buried in her neck. She cried out, and Yomi cried out with her. The ground shook beneath her feet, reminding me that no matter how much of a *nothing* place Yomi felt like, it was just a cave. Just a cave on a mountaintop.

Everything feels so small if you use the word "just." Especially me, clinging to this vampire goddess, and she would never allow me to leave here, not with her blood in my body. All these thoughts in a fraction of a second, because it was then that she plucked me off like a piece of lint and held me in front of her face.

She's going to swallow me whole.

I wrenched around and sank my teeth into her thumb, and she dropped me. Grabbing the sleeve of her kimono, I bit down onto her wrist and sucked up as much as I could in the second I had.

Black licorice and the briny smell of Cape Cod low tide. Evil, pure evil squeezed my veins as Izanami's blood ran through them. But not her evil—the evil of this place, and of the world that stole her children from her. Of a system that wasn't a system but a way of life, and the goodness born of it, and her stuck in the middle of it, forever giving and never receiving. And such hatred.

That part was all hers. I bit harder, to taste it deeper because I could absorb it and I could *handle* it. I didn't have any hate of my own.

Like the rush of blood, the realization that I only knew love reeled through me. Tears clouded my vision with red as Izanami's arm waved, me waving with it.

Only love. Any hate I had—for Lynch, for Death—had been transformed before long. I could never be as vengeful as Izanami was. I could never take her place. We were not the same. I had much, much more.

I'd drunk more than I thought, because she wavered. Flickering like an old TV, she faded in and out, and every time she stabilized she was smaller. Or I was bigger. At her weakest, finally her normal size, I curled around her like a crab, dragged her to the ground, punctured her skin with my short nails, bit as many places as I could in rapid succession. Moving so fast I generated heat, my teeth a high-powered stapler, drawing like a needle, my skin leaving burns on her where I touched. She wasn't crying out anymore. Yomi no longer howled. And I was FILLED. Full to bursting, like nothing I'd felt before. A sedentary power, without moral compass or fear or pain, just a sense of existing, waiting, but *dark*. And without promise.

But I did have promise. And so did the baby.

Heaving and exalted, I rose off of Izanami motionlessly, lifted by the mist. The same mist that cradled the baby, and held the shadow monsters and demons of Yomi at bay. They watched, stupefied, lost. Paolo stood at his full height, head held high as it normally was, a faint smile upon his pale, chapped lips. He had known me at my most lost, enslaved by the Master. He had felt it himself, now. I gave him a knowing nod.

"Give her to me," he said in that soft, lilting voice of his. I sobbed, relieved to hear him as he was meant to be. Taking the baby in my hands, I passed her to him, and it was heavenly to look upon. This man of God wrapped around this little enigma, made of promise and power and hope.

"I have to go," I blurted out, frantic with this blood roaring into my limbs and heart, my eyes and brain.

"I know," he said.

Yomi was just a place. A cave. A mystical one, yes, one human eyes could never behold, but for a *thing* like me, it was just a place now. And so I left it, without the aid of the crows, though they followed close by. All of their eyes, when they met mine as we passed through time and space like feathers on the wind, were cocoa and cream swirls.

Hurry. He needs you, they told me.

Teleporting didn't come to me, I just had to get there, had to feel myself get there.

The wind doused the fire of my skin, the steam in my blood, and I screamed wild as I flew without wings, desperate to go faster, faster, faster. My mind was an overflowing dam, a geyser that needed *more* even as it exploded. My senses were an army, both defending and attacking me. *Faster.*

I burst through the cabin wall like a bulldozer, ripping it wide open. Logs coursed through the air end over end but I didn't falter as I stalked to Nicholas, slumped in the chair by the still-standing fireplace. With my own teeth—sharper now, colder somehow, different with her blood fresh on them—I punctured my wrist. *Too hard.* Izanami's blood rang through me like a wild animal, weakened by endless captivity, making up for it with ferocious longing for vengeance. My hand hung by a few tendons, snapped bones, viscous not-blood flowing out of it, pungent and brighter, but darker than any blood I'd ever seen, fluffy like Roman's omelets. The ripe, flowery, hypnotic smell of it made Nicholas's nose twitch, even as his eyes, dead-still, never blinked, sunken into a body that was as still and as thin as a corpse.

I held my dangling hand over him, let the blood pour onto him in a life-giving shower. It had a vitality of its own, frothing out of me as a scarlet whipped cream, my mist infusing it.

Nicholas twitched under the rush, but his tongue didn't reach for it, his throat didn't bob.

"Come on, Nicholas," I pleaded, my voice hollow and tinny.

Gently, I pulled his chin down, massaged his throat like I was giving medicine to a puppy, but the blood just bubbled around him. I grabbed his arms, *so frail, so cold,* and sat him up straighter. But there was nothing.

And I was becoming nothing. The blood was looking more like my own blood now, normal. I was running dry. Powerful as it was, Izanami's un-life force hit hard and fast. But not hard enough.

I collapsed, the wind from the gaping hole of the wall slapping my hair into my face, and I willed the cradling mist away in order to feel the hard, splintered floor. Maybe knock myself out, maybe impale myself like vampires from stories and be *done* with this joke of an existence, this misery. Nicholas's foot was within reach—Roman had put his old plaid slippers on him. I held it, felt the bones beneath the fabric, the sedentary blood under his skin that wasn't strong enough to propel him, had nothing left.

Blinking, regrettably still conscious, I saw the rubble of the cabin in the yard shuffle. *Roman.* I couldn't face him, not knowing what he knew, not having let Nicholas die, not ever again. He emerged from the logs, shards of wood sticking through him all over, blood pouring from the punctures. A moan escaped me when I saw the one that went clean through his eye. I tried to push myself up, but one-handed now, I failed. Again. Roman toddled over, a monster Tom Savini would have been proud of, pulling the stick out of his eye—it had gone through the back of his head. Yanking more daggers out with every step, he waved me off as I tried to get up and go to him, desperate to help remove the debris I'd destroyed him with, *God, I destroyed another person I love.* He went straight to his brother's body.

I couldn't look. I turned to the disaster I'd created of our home, their home, knowing I should never have been there to begin with. I never should have met Nicholas, never should have gone to that party. Never should have gone to the bookstore over and over. Now, he was gone. I'd killed the one they all called the Golden One. This was my destiny after all. To be a harbinger of death, befriended by it and despising myself for it. Izanami had been right—I *was* meant to replace her in Yomi. Maybe I could make existence more livable for those beasts. I could raise Kat's baby—isn't that what I should be doing? Didn't I owe her that? Had I really thought I could escape Kat's memory, let time heal the wound? That wasn't the Eliza I was. No, I clung to memories, let them drown me. That kind of life was what thrived in Yomi.

Barely able to see through my pathetic, red-tinged tears, I wiped them away with my single hand, *forever losing a damn limb now,* sick to death of feeling sorry for myself, and turned back to Roman at his brother's side.

But he wasn't mourning. He was *doing.*

Roman's throat was pressed against Nicholas's lips, covering his face.

"Roman, it's—" I tried to say it was over, to stop torturing himself, but I couldn't get the words out. I couldn't say that Nicholas was…

I swore I saw Nicholas's leg move. My eyes, clouded as they were, could detect movement before it happened, but I couldn't let myself believe that we'd been saved from the fate I'd brought us. Roman shifted, and it happened again, this time a finger. I sobbed, wanted to retch, wanted to sing, wanted to punch and jump and drink and beg forgiveness, but couldn't believe it. Not yet.

CHAPTER 123

Roman stood, and I saw Nicholas, the foamy blood I'd given him spitting from the sides of his mouth and growing like suds when I'd overflowed the washing machine. It multiplied, pink and red and thick, and Nicholas attempted to roll over in the chair, to curl up, but the blood came from him in waves.

"Eliza, do something!" Roman cried out.

Do something? The blood I'd brought him had done nothing, and now erupted from him in a geyser.

There'd been too much. Roman's blood, what he should have had to begin with, was too much. Too much, too late. What could I—

In a black flash, Blue was cutting through the foam of Izanami's blood as she made her way to Nicholas. Terror-stricken, I rushed her, toppled her over into the pink and red clouds of gelatinous, yet bubbly blood, and it soaked into her.

"Blue, no!" I cried, but she was frenzied, jaws gnashing, eyes wild, staring past me at Nicholas. She bit me so hard I screamed, then kicked me off of her with the force I'd seen her fight with, this little woman who'd been such a powerful enigma. She descended upon Nicholas in that second, forced him down again in the chair, clung to him, and before I could move, with speed that wasn't hers, she buried her fangs into his neck. Nicholas didn't struggle.

Roman got to them first, tried to tear Blue off Nicholas, calling to me for help, and I rushed there, but she was done. Blue stood—straight up, not like she'd been, a humpbacked, feral thing. For a second, I was only grateful that she was back. But when she looked at me, she wasn't just Blue.

Izanami was there, too.

Blue's petite body, but held more regally. Blue's supple lips, but pursed thoughtfully. Blue's dancing eyes—thankfully, Blue's playful expression—but behind it, another presence, darker, stronger. She smiled at me.

Nicholas rolled over without as much effort as before, and I cried out his name. I could only see his back past her, but his spine wasn't prominent through his shirt.

"I'm sorry," Blue said, in Blue's voice.

"Is that you?" Roman said, coming up beside me. "Blue, you're okay?"

She reached out to him, took his hand. "I was never in as much pain as you were, darling," she said. With a wave of her hand, all the knives of tree bark tore out of his body. He gasped, doubled over. I didn't know what to do—didn't know if she'd done him a favor or put the final nail in his coffin.

"You couldn't kill me," Izanami said to me, a different voice from Blue's.

"I didn't want to," I said.

"I'm out now," she said.

"Not completely," Blue said. Their voices were distinguishable, like talking to two different people from the same face. But a *peace* emanated from them, a gentle melding together of two incredible souls. Souls beyond death.

Nicholas got to his feet behind them, and everything else

faded. He unfolded, it seemed, like a paper doll coming to life, and I lingered on every fold.

His arms were robust, the muscles straining against his shirt sleeves. His chest swelled up in a way I'd nearly forgotten, he'd been wasting away so long. The aging of his neck had reversed with pulsing, thick veins beneath. His jawline no longer sagged, but stood strong, his cheeks full, wrinkles returning to laugh lines, his lips pink, and his eyes...

His eyes danced, the cocoa and cream of my dreams, the warmth in them radiating toward me, long black lashes thick, and a new knowing behind them, a tinge of gold that hadn't been there before.

"God, I missed having good hair," he said, running his hands through the tousled locks that needed a good wash. "You count on having something your whole life, you know? Then *fwoosh*, first thing to go."

"Your *hair*." Roman had recovered, hands on his knees, and I thought I might pass out from all the goodness around me happening all at once.

"I know, it was probably nice to have the best hair for a while, but those days are over now. Sorry, brother."

As hard as it was to tear my eyes from Nicholas, his presence alone was enough for me to do what I needed to do, which was to observe Blue. Izanami. Whoever this new being was, observing us. What thoughts were going through their heads?

"Love what you've done with the place," Nicholas said. Roman and I looked at each other, both of us too shocked to know what to say, how to react, where to go from here. "So," he continued, stepping through some remaining globs of bloody stuff, and kicking aside debris. "Who might *you* be?"

Blue-Izanami raised their chin to him. "I think you know."

"Do I?" Nicholas said, stopping to wink at me. My knees

buckled. "Pretty sure you were one person when I saw you last. Sure doesn't seem like that now."

"I fed you Izanami's blood," I butted in. "It came back out." I waved a hand, gesturing at Blue, and realized it was my not-so-there hand. It just flopped against my forearm.

"Gross," Nicholas said. "We'll get that fixed up." He went closer to Blue. "A new god, goddess, somebody in there?" Silence answered him. Nicholas squinted, twisting his lip up in thought, and he crooned to her. "Tell me, are you a good witch, or a bad witch?"

"Good and bad are figments of the imagination," Blue replied. And it was definitely Blue that time.

He put a hand on her cheek. "Atta girl," he said.

Nicholas's willingness to just sorta let this new being *be*, at least for now, was enough for Roman and me. There was plenty more to do, to fix, to care for, to become.

"And how is our Abomination?" Nicholas said.

Roman winced. "Shit."

CHAPTER 124

I zanami's eyes lit up at the mention of Lynch, and the start of our encounter in Yomi rushed back in a flood of dread. What would she do when she met him? We couldn't find out.

But lo and behold, here was Lynch coming back to the scene of the crime. "Nice to not have any footwork, I guess," I muttered to Nicholas. He took my hand, for the first time in a million years, and the bird wing beating of my heart slowed. The ever-present fear that had become my way of life recently, diminished. I closed my eyes, breathed in the scent that was buried in him but *was* him to me: peppermint brownies on a cold day; pine trees and fresh snow; coffee and cookies.

When I opened my eyes, there Lynch was, covered in fresh blood. The way he strutted through the tree line and across the yard revealed how proud of himself he was. The thought of starting a new coven still thrilled me, and now that I'd seen who we'd be answering to…

Oh my God. I have to tell Lynch about his baby. Before Izanami does.

"Hi Nick, you're looking better than ever," Lynch said silkily. "Eliza," he said, turning to me. But his eyes stopped, his smooth smile became a happy grin, his self-involved bravado softened into a happy stance that radiated *enjoyment* of someone else. I don't think I'd seen him enjoy anyone, or anything, since Kat.

He was looking at Blue.

"Hi there," Blue said, no Izanami behind it.

"You're…different," he replied, eyelashes fluttering with an odd shyness. Odd for him. "I mean, I know we've…we haven't really gotten to talk much, but you've changed. Haven't you?"

Izanami's eyes appeared over Blue's, a double exposure where the shape and color and intensity of Izanami's eyes slipped over my friend's. "We are more," they both said in a symphony.

"Wow. You," Nicholas said, poking a finger into Blue's shoulder, "just took top billing on the freak scale. El, you're a silver medalist."

"Is it top billing like a concert, or silver medal like the Olympics? Can't have both," I said.

The whole time Lynch was mesmerized by Blue, and I just wanted to know what he was doing back here. And I was terrified of telling him about the baby. *Maybe time can just stop here, in this post-apocalyptic camp setting.*

"Whatcha doing, Lynch?" Nicholas asked. "Last we saw you, you were going to kill a bunch of girls, right?"

"The *Shinigami* has met its new leader," Blue/Izanami said breathlessly, eyes shining at Chris.

"Um, no it hasn't," I said.

"I second that," Roman said. "Lynch answers to us." He nodded at Nicholas and me.

"And we—" I couldn't breathe. "We answer to someone else. Someone *more*." I locked eyes with Nicholas, afraid to look at anyone else, excitement and anticipation swelling in my stomach like Izanami's blood across the cabin.

"Maybe we should, uh—" Nicholas looked toward the

kitchen, still standing, visible beyond the swinging-turned-dangling red door. "Have some tea."

~

Roman pushed the door aside, and it fell off. "Oh."

Nicholas strode past him. "Maybe we need French doors."

The kitchen was fairly untouched and I breathed a sigh of relief just to enter it. This was the time stop I was looking for. I plunked into an upright chair to examine my hand. While the others picked up the mismatched chairs and Nicholas put on the kettle, I created a little burst of red mist that wrapped itself around the wound like a bandage, holding it on. It didn't trouble me that it hadn't healed yet—I was exhausted, depleted, every part of me. And there was some comfort in not being 100 percent, if I was being my basest self. A predetermined excuse to not be the foreman solving all the problems.

Roman busied himself sweeping while Lynch and Blue/Izanami huddled together, murmuring at one side of the table. *Is she telling him the truth about his baby right now?* No, he'd have been wild, inconsolable and overjoyed at the same time. But boy, did they seem cozy. It warmed my heart. And it gave me a little hope.

The few minutes of quiet soon ended with the kettle whistling, and I steeled myself to give the news of the baby. The reactions were going to be...memorable. Nicholas poured tea, human speed, relishing the moment before the next storm. The ridiculous thing was, it didn't *feel* like a storm. Here we were. My friend Blue, possessed by a demon goddess who had manipulated us all for...who knows how long. Nicholas, who'd blown up into health like a bouncy house. Roman, who had no idea still about the baby or the fact that I knew *he* had known Kat was pregnant. A serial killer turned vampire serial killer.

And we were all putting a new coven together, *together*. Plus the house was falling apart because I had destroyed it.

Yet it was calm. As if maybe the storm had been there all along. The epitome of the fight or flight syndrome I'd been working through for most of my existence—always waiting for the next tragedy, seeking them out half the time.

"Okay, El," Nicholas said, leaning against the counter with his cup of tea. "We're listening."

"I don't know where to start."

"You came to me in Yomi," Izanami said in a layered voice that creeped me the hell out.

With a glance at Roman, I began. "Roman, you wouldn't help Nicholas, even after coming home, but when the coma happened I realized who would. It was her," I said, nodding at Izanami/Blue. "She's been in our heads," I spat, "working us. She's the one who immobilized you, Nicholas. And she was damn well going to fix it." I spoke through teeth gritted so hard I thought they might crack, nostrils flaring as I stared at the possessed Blue. "Then I went to her, which is exactly what she wanted me to do. Right?"

The woman smiled knowingly.

"And I...I saw why Roman wouldn't feed you, Nicholas. What he was afraid you would learn through the residue." I trained my eyes on Nicholas. The thought of seeing Roman's face when I revealed his secret, if he knew at all that the baby was alive, or in Yomi, or Lynch's reaction, too overwhelming. "In Yomi, there's a—" The words choked me. "I can only show you."

The mist, an extension of myself, recreated the scene for all to see in a haze the color of blood. When the baby came into view, for the first time ever, the mist cleared of hue and showed her to us like a clear picture, a still.

The room choked as I had. What could anyone say?

"Whose baby is that?" Nicholas said. Of course. "Where the hell did a baby come from? El?"

But Lynch was up silently, slowly, approaching the image of the wiggling child.

"No," Roman whispered.

"She's mine," Lynch said in a voice sure and strong. It made me smile.

Nicholas was watching Roman, whose hands were shaking so hard the cup of tea clattered against the table. Sharp as a tack, Nicholas got it. "Kat was pregnant," my love murmured.

"I never thought I could…" Lynch trailed off. "I need to see her," he said, whipping around to Izanami. "Bring her to me, please."

"She can't leave Yomi," I managed to say.

"That's my child," Lynch snapped. "And she will be with me."

"Chris," Izanami said, "she was never a child of this mortal plane. She cannot leave Yomi."

I think we all expected him to fly into a rage like only he could, barely sane yet in complete control, a calculated, venomous anger that he directed like the weapon he was. He was a monster, and I'd managed to forget it.

"Chris—" I started.

"Then I go to her," he said coolly.

"It's not a vacation spot," I said. "You can't just walk in and out of there." *Paolo*, I remembered, my heart sinking. "Izanami. Did you bring Paolo there or did he go on his own?" Kieran said he'd gone to Yomi, a pilgrimage of sorts as only a holy man could, looking for a renewal of faith. I think he got something else. "He went to you," I answered for myself. "You turned him into that thing he became to use against me—but he's not that now. Can he leave?"

Izanami's demure smile crossed Blue's lips. "It is not a vacation spot," she said in my own words.

"If I choose to go there, I can't leave," Lynch said. No one had to answer. And no one begged him to stay with us either. What argument could we give, even if we'd wanted to? He'd never felt at home with any of us. He was a monster among us, his brutality unforgiveable, and he'd despised us all at one time or another; a sting that never left him. Even now, his future was wildly uncertain. He created vampires out of spite, and to satisfy a need that had driven him for longer than we could know. But when I drank from him, I understood one thing—that he created these new vampires and left them, hoping they would hate him the way he hated himself.

It only became clear to me now that he had been hoping they would end him for it.

"No, that's not right," Nicholas said, shaking his head. "A baby, bound to Hell with a damn serial killer and *you*?" He pointed at Izanami.

"She can change that place," I said before I knew what I was doing. "I've seen that she can." All eyes turned to me. I stood up, like I was preaching or something, like I couldn't deliver such news sitting comfortably. Like I was a prophet, and I suppose that I was. "It's not Hell to her. It's not really Hell at all."

Izanami, nodded emphatically in agreement, her body tensing with excitement. "Yomi is a place *between*—and she is a child between. She's not out of place in Yomi. She isn't trapped. The child is beyond your created rules of good and evil, and can become so much more."

"She's right," I said, breathlessly as the vision of the baby shifted in the mist. "All of the *Shinigami*, every coven will emulate her. She will lead us without having to lead us. She is...everything." One would think all my years of reading would have taught me to say things powerfully, but there was no grasping the promise of that child. There was no way to say what I knew, and it was for me to understand alone.

Because I was her messenger.

"I want to go back with you," Lynch said, taking Izanami's hand in his. "I don't belong here," he said with a sad laugh. "I need to be where Eliza said, where good and evil aren't different. I knew it as soon as you and I met, Izanami, that you were here for *me*. An angel of death—to deliver me to a new life."

His words, so heartfelt, so *right*, and necessary, were true—he couldn't stay in our world forever, making vampires and pining away, resisting his murderous urges. He wasn't a good man, but he also wasn't always bad. He had a conscience, as much as he fought it. And the baby—his baby—could do so much for the man I'd briefly glimpsed, the one that Kat fell head over heels for. She could breathe new life into him. With Paolo there to soothe his tortured mind, the way only Paolo could, Lynch could finally have peace. Closure with himself.

"Izanami?" I ventured. Blue looked at me, the Blue-ness of her fading behind the goddess. "What about you, and what you've been doing, trying to break free of Yomi?"

She was soft, sweet when she answered. "I only ever wanted to feel free and feel love again."

"Oh, that doesn't seem true," Nicholas said.

She snapped her attention to him. "Yomi does not care for its inhabitants. It has worn upon me. Twisted me. *Honjitsu,*" she said, clenching a fist against her sternum, darkness welling in her eyes. "Changed forever. But you, Eliza, have changed me forever as well."

"Yeah, she makes a habit of that," Nicholas said.

Why me? was right there, wiggling behind my teeth to be said, but I held it back. I wanted to ask why me of all the vampires, of all the eons of undead. Why had she finally only tried to escape when I showed up? But the two-word question had weaseled its way into most of my existence. Why did death—or Izanagi—attach to me? Why me for Nicholas? Why me to lose Kat, why could I see alternate fates, why did I have the mist, why had I been victimized by the Master, why had Izanami chosen me? Why me, why now?

I'd spent much of my life feeling like I was meant for something *different*, but with nothing to back the feeling up. No special skills, no important lineage, nothing outstanding about me, and when the different things began to happen, I asked myself why plenty of times. But the real question was why *not* me? Why should I question what everyone else seemed to know? That I was a thing of prophecy waiting to fall into place? Maybe nothing had *made* me special, but that didn't mean I couldn't be special.

I was a creature of change, both reluctant and willing, and there was no reason it couldn't be me. There was no why. There didn't have to be.

Izanami watched me, and a moment of understanding came between us. She'd heard my thoughts, probably, I don't know. But between us was a presence of *more*, and I was done asking why.

"Uh, what exact weird thing is going on here?" Nicholas said, eyebrows raised, waving a hand between Izanami and me.

I snapped out of my mini-trance. "There's a baby in a cloud in the kitchen and you're questioning why I'm quiet for a minute?"

"Fair. Proceed."

"Thank you," I said to Izanami, surprising myself. "I don't even know exactly why, but thanks. I guess, thanks for saying I'm important enough to give you strength?"

"It was not you alone," she said with a smile. "Your friend, Blue, is extraordinary."

I felt Roman stiffen from across the room. I had to speak for Blue.

"What you did to Blue is unforgivable. Hijacking her mind like that, you made her an animal. You can't take Blue's body to move forever between worlds, she's in there. She's a person without you."

Her features shifted ever-so-slightly, and Blue's playful eyes dominated them. "Here I am," she said with a smile. "I'm not like, *possessed*, I'm right here." Her fangs poked out when she grinned. God, I loved to see her this bubbly. "And it's not like I haven't sequestered myself to a remote Japanese mountaintop before. I guess…" she said more seriously, "I guess this way we both get what we really want. I can hide away, and Izanami can leave, both of us together. I think we're both stronger now. This is what I want to do, go to Yomi, and you know what? If I hate it? You know I'll find a way to get out of there."

She would. She got her way all the time without hurting a soul to do it. Always managed to make everyone feel at home, loved.

Love.

"Blue, have you spoken with Kieran?" I asked.

"In the last hour, no. I'll tell him something, put his fears to rest. He's got his hands full with the *Shinigami,* and I wouldn't be insulted if he was happy to be done with me for a while. I'm kind of a lot, you know?"

Nicholas and Roman had been murmuring to each other for a while now, and I'd been blocking out their words. An irrational fear that Nicholas would want to go to Yomi too pecked at my brain. If any of us was a god, it was him. I didn't *really* think he could pocket himself into a cave forever—nobody there would appreciate him, his sense of humor, his tea, his strength and confidence, his determination. He was a man who needed people. A home that he created himself.

But Roman was another matter.

"Roman?" I interrupted. "Are you okay?"

He'd avoided speaking to me directly this entire time, and now it had to be done. "El, Lynch, I didn't know—"

"But you did," I cut him off. "You did know she was pregnant, I saw that she told you."

His eyes watered, his mouth drooped. "I did know. But it didn't change what Nicholas needed, and it was a choice I had to make."

"You did *not!*" Lynch boomed, heat generating from him. "You killed my child! You murdered the woman I loved, murdered our *baby* before I even knew she existed!" His entire body shook violently, like a human earthquake, but nothing around him moved. He was a contained disaster, but he would explode. I had to do something.

"I didn't know that the baby would make it! Kat didn't know you were a vampire, Lynch! What kind of creature might you have..." Roman couldn't finish, though. I'm sure we'd all thought it, as much as we hated to admit it. What kind of monster might the Abomination bring to life that way? Would Kat have even lived through it?

"Don't you dare pretend that what you did was for anyone but yourself. How you need the Golden Child. How you didn't want to see me happy. How you couldn't bear to see me with a child when yours is gone."

Ice raced across the floor, swallowed Lynch up in a tomb.

Nicholas, apparently more powerful than ever, was rooted to the floor in ice himself from sending it Lynch's way. Silvery icicles darted up his arms, under his shirt sleeves and up the sides of his neck, licking at his chin and ears. And his eyes had turned to a disarming shade of cold blue-white that chilled me as much as the frost coating the room.

"I've had enough of our friendly neighborhood Abomination," Nicholas said with a sarcastic downturn of his lips and a nod to Izanami. "How's about you pack him up and take him home now?" He joked but the fury under that layer of ice was as plain as day.

"No way," I scoffed, eyes darting between Izanami and Nicholas. "She's done all this to get out of Yomi. Not a chance."

"It feels…unlike me here," the goddess said, but I still didn't believe she'd go back to Yomi that easily. "Eliza, I see your doubt, but circumstances have changed. I have a reason to stay in Yomi now, don't I? And I can leave when I choose."

I supposed prison didn't feel so much like prison if you had a get out of jail free card.

"Well, you don't have to go home but you can't stay here," Nicholas said to her.

Blue straightened up with that flirty smile of hers, and turned her teacup upside down. "My tea was getting cold anyway," she said, as a solid block of ice fell out. She stood up, graceful as the Blue I always knew but with a regality that was all Izanami's. She held out her hands, examining the backs of them, turning them over, coming to terms with this new form of hers. She clenched her fists, closed her eyes, and took a deep breath.

Terror heated up my body, melting away the ice, and suddenly I was well aware that she was only beginning to realize what power she held now. What abilities she might have.

With a way in and out of Yomi, a baby to care for, a strange little family, a lifeline in Blue and Lynch, Izanami had what she wanted. She'd always had power; that didn't mean she had to flex it.

Except a new race of vampires all to herself.

Izanami was on our side for now. I couldn't think of what might happen if she weren't, but I was the one who needed to ensure our safety. I had to put the case closed stamp on this one if we were ever to just relax. Izanagi had kept her in his sights and in Yomi for so unimaginably long, he would be able to tell me. He had to.

With a gleeful smile, she swung her arms up high and clapped her hands together over her head. Living shadows slipped from the ceiling, down the walls like molasses, consuming the ice. I'd have known they were alive even without the lidless eyeball here and there showing itself, studying us as they covered Lynch in his cold cocoon.

"See you 'round," Blue said to me, then winked at Nicholas and was gone.

CHAPTER 125

And just like that, Nicholas and I were alone. For a moment, I could be still, forget that there was anything else to be done, anyone else to be responsible for.

"Where's Roman?" I always managed to ruin it for myself.

Nicholas didn't look surprised that Roman wasn't in the room.

"Nicholas," I said, "where is Roman?"

"He just needs a little time—"

"Oh, again? For a guy who'll live until the end of time, he never seems to have enough of it. Where did he go? He can't just go moping off whenever he doesn't want to face—"

"Could you face what he's done, if it were you?" he interrupted, head tilted, eyes pleading.

More gently, I said, "You know that I could."

He nodded, head dropping. If I was good for anything, it was owning up to my bad decisions. Nicholas was at my side in a flash, had gathered me into his arms. His strong arms, the Nicholas I first met at Lynch's stupid mansion, knowing and mysterious and yet so forward at the same time. Once again, we were where we belonged, no matter what ruin surrounded us.

But would it ever not surround us? When would *we* have time?

With effort, I released myself from him, kissed him until I couldn't think, and we tumbled to the kitchen floor, to take the time we deserved and desperately needed. My heart pounded, needing nothing but him. Not blood, not resolution, nothing but his body and mine. The standing walls shook with our bodies, the floor cracking beneath us. The preoccupying pain in my hand forgotten now.

"Stop destroying my house," he gasped into my ear. I answered him with harder kisses, squeezing closer, pulling him nearer and deeper, sweat smelling of ice and blood, black stars bursting in my eyes, his animal sounds reverberating through me like thunder.

"I think we've successfully melted all the frost you made in here," I said, spread on my back, my chest rising and falling as if I were human. It felt beyond good.

He rolled over onto me, kissed me gently. Not joking when he said, "Please don't leave me again. Not ever."

The thought of it was a car crash in my head. "I won't. I don't want to be away from you, from home... My purpose is mine. I've done what I needed to do, a million times over. Fate is coming to us now, everything we do next, we are the epicenter of it. And I don't care if it ever comes," I said, curling his hair in my fingers, relishing in the health of it. Of him. And of us.

His eyes drew me in again, as usual, mesmerizing, magnetic even as powerful as I was. It felt *good* to not be powerful in that stare. "You're *so you* right now," he said, kissing my lips with the taste of sugar and chill of winter. "Like you're here, and not obligated anywhere else. I've never known you this way, you realize."

"I've been searching and searching for so long, and running from what I really wanted for even longer… I've always been afraid. I'm sick of being afraid, nothing can hurt me now."

"But it's not about being strong."

"No, no, I mean everything has fallen—no, I've *put* everything in place. I've exhausted myself leaving behind the only thing I've ever wanted. A home. It's a terrible thing to long for something so much and still be so scared to get comfortable in it. Everything always goes away, is taken from me. But not you, and not this place, I'll always make it back here if I have to crawl. I deserve home. And it won't be taken from me."

He pulled me to him and whispered, "I love you," with such ferocity, I knew this home wouldn't leave me without a fight.

"I love you," I said back.

～

We didn't have to ignore our obligations for days after that. The things we wanted to do were ours to do. There was no axe held over my head, no prophecy that said I had to hurry, no ultimatums, no impending doom. We were fate's vampires, but fate didn't ride on us alone, not on me alone. Not anymore.

Once we'd finished with each other for a while, we did rebuild the cabin. The satisfaction of *building* something like that was one I'd never experienced. Simple creation, by my own hands. And it was fast. Nicholas may have built the cabin and most of its furniture the first time, but to do it together filled me with such pride and comfort, ownership. It was *mine*, this whole world we were making together, ours and mine. I carved our initials with my fingernail into our new coffee table—once I'd finally made it right. Putting things together came quickly, but doing it well sure didn't.

"Hey! Nice job," Nicholas said, knocking on the simple tabletop. "Could use some sanding."

"Yeah, that's your job."

"You carved our initials into it?" he said with a mischievous glint in his eye.

"Yeah, with this," I said, grinning, holding up my index finger.

"Pretty cool, El, pretty cool. Super strong fingernails."

"That's why I got into this whole vampire business. Kat could never make me get another manicure again."

"Can I say something…" Nicholas asked.

"Don't you always?" I said, sitting on the table.

"Since Yomi, after you came back, you don't seem as broken over her as you've been. You're Eliza, without the pain all the time."

I just nodded. It was true. I think when the events of my life, and my afterlife, fell into place, even if they didn't all click together smoothly, I could breathe with the thought of having lost her. And to have brought knowledge of the baby to all of us, to have put Lynch and her together in whatever way they were in Yomi—I didn't know—was as much as I could do. Quite honestly, the world was a safer place without Chris Lynch roaming around in it, and no matter what he was and the damage he'd done, I was happy to have given him some peace and someone to love.

I hope that's what's happening in Yomi, I thought, but dismissed it right away. That wasn't my problem to solve. Just like Roman wasn't, wherever he'd gone. He'd come back to us this time, and so would news from Yomi.

Nicholas did leave for a while; he'd gotten a calling. An *unmei nashi,* he said. It certainly looked like it always did when he had a calling, and now as a vampire I could sense more changes. His blood slowed down. His body went cold, as if the ice he could use had turned inward. Saliva flooded his mouth, the swirl of his eyes chugged to a stop.

When Nicholas went to feed, I went to feed as well. There was no blood calling, nothing special about this victim to me. The guy was in the wrong place at the wrong time. I'd gone to Singing Pines Park but it felt dirty there this time, like I was following in some of Lynch's worst footsteps—and some of my own. I hadn't realized how long, and how deeply entrenched in my head Izanami had been, the bloodlust she'd instilled there. She wasn't entirely to blame. Tired of being told who and what I was, of being thrust into an immortal society built on this puritanical righteousness, I loved making that choice for myself. I loved not guilting myself over my choice of prey. I didn't regret my more brutal kills now, but I didn't want that anymore. At least for the time being.

We both arrived home in the dead of night, sated and ready to be together, wrap ourselves in each other.

But we found we were not alone.

CHAPTER 126

"Um, hi?" I recognized her, this girl on our worse-for-wear sofa, but man did she take me by surprise. Nicholas peered at her warily.

The one we'd only ever called the Girl in the Green Chair.

"Hi," she snapped, uncrossing her skinny-jeaned legs and standing up proudly. She wore cat-eye liner and bright red lipstick, a shade darker than the red peach fuzz of her shaved head. "Mind telling me what the hell I'm doing here?"

"Delivery girl?" Nicholas asked. "Sorry, delivery woman? We didn't order anything. We already ate."

She shifted feet in her probably fifteen-inch black stilettos. "Look, some lady dug into my brain," she said through gritted teeth, jabbing a long black fingernail into her temple, "and wouldn't let go. She told me to come here," waving her arms around. *So animated,* I thought, ridiculously. "I wouldn't, so she *made* me." A hard swallow. This girl was not accustomed to being out of control. This one gave the orders, didn't take them.

"I know you," I said, voice cracking.

"Yeah, well, I don't know you."

"What's your name?" I asked, approaching her until she snarled at me.

"Sierra. Tell me why I'm here." She didn't ask our names. Didn't care.

Glancing at Nicholas, I began hesitantly, "You're a vampire."

"No kidding."

"We're the ones who will take you in and help you."

She laughed, so boisterously it sent chills down my spine. Emotionally tainted. Cold. "I was dragged here against my will so you could *help* me?" she said with narrowed green eyes. "I don't need your help."

"If I may," Nicholas butted in. "We are quite a bit older than you. Well, I am, anyway, and I know our history. Our world. Others like you. We can guide you, so you won't be alone."

"What makes you think I'm alone?"

Hadn't expected that.

Nicholas looked at me, shook his head with wide eyes. "I've got nothing."

"We know who your maker was, and that he left you without any reasoning, or telling you what to do—"

Wrong thing to say.

"I figured out what I am, I don't need a man to tell me. Instinct showed me plenty."

"You've been feeding then?" I asked.

She snickered, "Well, yeah."

I wanted to ask who, when, how often, but she didn't invite questions in any way.

Nicholas asked, splayed out on the couch, "Did you feel anything that made you pick those people to drink from?"

"Feel anything but hunger? No. And drink from? Not exactly."

"What do you mean by that?" he asked. But my blood had already run cold.

"Why only drink from them?"

"You...you ate..." I couldn't say the words.

She smiled. "You never have?"

Nicholas's eyebrows nearly crossed over each other they were so furrowed. Neither of us, for once, had anything to say. What on earth *could* we say?

"Suffice it to say, no, we haven't considered cannibalism," he finally said.

With a fingernail between her teeth, she smirked. "You're missing out."

"I just wanted to go to the grocery store. Get a cheesecake. Maybe like, half a dozen pizzas, watch a possession movie or six. I'm feeling possession movies today." I was rambling, leaving Sierra in the living room and storming my way into the kitchen with Nicholas on my heels.

"Eliza, why did your friend send a cannibal to my house?"

"Our house, and she's not my friend."

We plopped into the kitchen chairs, the bewilderment palpable between us. "Izanami sent this weird lady here for a reason," Nicholas said.

"Yeah, because she's twisted and likes playing games."

"Well, Izanami's got Lynch. And Lynch created Sierra, has a connection to her—"

"—even if he wants to deny it," I muttered.

"It's got to be strong enough that Izanami was able to use it. Use her. Jesus, do they ever stop *using* us? Why *her* and not the other newbies? Don't get me wrong, she's nice scenery, but she's a cannibal."

I rolled my eyes at him. "Maybe that's why Izanami sent

her here. Because she needs help even if she doesn't think she does."

The kitchen door—a swinging door again, now that we'd fixed it—slammed against the kitchen wall as Sierra busted through it. "I can hear you. I'd rather be part of the conversation than the subject of it. And no, I don't need your help. Maybe this lady sent me here to help *you*. Thought of that?"

Amusement danced in Nicholas's eyes. "If eating people isn't a cry for help, I don't know what is. And we definitely don't need your help."

"We have to talk to Izanami, there's no other way to get to the bottom of this," I said.

"Can you just walk in and out of Yomi, though? I feel like it won't go over well."

"I've bested Izanami. I can go back to Yomi if I want, and nobody will stop me from leaving. I need to make an agreement with her, and Blue, about what role they're going to play in the *Shinigami* coven now. What they're doing for the baby. I mean, it was the *baby* I saw that grows up and leads the *Shinigami*, not Izanami—but we have a while before the baby grows into that role. I don't want Izanami interfering with us down here in the meantime. She can't be puppet-mastering our recruits whenever the mood suits."

"*Recruits?*" Sierra said, arms crossed. "I'm not joining whatever thing you have here. And whatever this shinny-hey-hey is, I don't need it. I have my own people."

Sierra's porcelain cheeks lit up a happy pink as she described the Blue Hole in New Jersey to us—a mysterious but beautiful pool of frigid cerulean water that unnerves the locals. Unexplained currents pull swimmers under; quicksand grabs ahold of people on the ground around it; disappearances; the infamous Jersey Devil is known to frequently pop his head up from the seemingly bottomless depths. When we asked why she'd gone to the Blue Hole to begin with, she said she'd followed the smell of organs there. Closing her eyes drowsily, she took a deep whiff of the air. "The Blue Hole Devils reek of flesh and human parts. Stronger than anything I've ever smelled."

"I'm sorry," Nicholas said, and I anticipated his smartass comment, "but the Blue Hole Devils? Did you join a swimming hole biker gang?"

Sierra smiled wickedly. "There is no Jersey Devil," she said, eyes glinting. "Vampires live under the Blue Hole."

"Under a pond? They live under a pond? You live with pond people?" Nicholas prodded.

"It's *not* a pond," Sierra snapped. "It's an anomaly from the Ice Age, buried ice that burst like a bomb, creating the Blue Hole and leaving ice caverns below."

"Wow," I said in a whisper, fascinated. I wanted to know everything—what they looked like, living under the ice, like a cross between Nosferatu and Marvel's Ice Man. My mind conjured up images of them digging under the icy ground, sleeping beneath it. "Obviously the currents you say that pull swimmers under—"

"Right," she said. "And the quicksand. It's the Devils."

"Jesus Christ," Nicholas said, squeezing his eyes shut. "They must be absolute beasts, pulling people down, feeding off them—" He stopped himself.

"Nicholas?" I asked, fear leaking into my voice. "What's going on?"

"Picture it, Eliza," he said fervently. "The bastards suck people down and keep them there, eating them. Don't they?" He snapped at Sierra.

She shrugged, totally cool with it. "They can't live on the blood of one swimmer here and there alone, now can they? And the Devils learn from those swimmers! It's how they know about the world at all! Without those people the vampires would be trapped in a time cap—"

"Yeah, stop it, it's gross," I said. "And you could smell them all the way from here?"

"Sure. You can't smell that far?"

Clearly, she had some gifts of her own. And I was beginning to believe that she really didn't need our help at all.

"El, we'll find another way to contact Izanami. She'll find us first, actually, like she sent this one here," Nicholas said.

"Sierra, let me touch you," I said, suddenly able to think of nothing else.

She moaned, smiling at me.

"Not like that." I twined my fingers through hers.

I did see some of her past. I felt her heart break when she saw her father dead. I heard her anguish as Lynch made her. I saw the green chair. Forever with the green chair. But it wasn't enough, and she saw it.

I flipped our hands over, exposing our wrists. It only took a second for her to understand my hard swallow, the quickening of my breath and what it meant I wanted. She said, "Do it."

I pinned her hand to the table and bit.

First I saw the horrified faces of those people abducted from the narrow, scrub-brush trails around the Blue Hole. Saw nearly translucent vampires in the night, with bat-like webbed arms, dragging a screaming girl up into the trees. Through her blood I walked the glittering crystalline caves— and the stacks of stripped bones. And then I tasted past her skin to all the skin she'd eaten. Their lives before, how fast they ended, and how fragrant their flesh. Some bitter, others sweet and dense… An entirely different taste than blood. A different world of flavor.

But it was over in a heartbeat, and I watched an invisible force drag Sierra up through the Blue Hole, spit her onto the quicksand shore, then drag her through all manner of terrain and drop her here, in our cabin. Then Izanami's face filled my vision, her smile a thing between elation and mania. She shed her face in a wave, like removing a mask, to show me Blue.

"Blue, are you okay?" I thought. She smiled and simply nodded. I wasn't sure whether or not to believe her, but I'd learned not to underestimate Blue before.

"Can you hear me?" she asked.

"Yes," as I continued to drink.

"You're draining Sierra."

"She likes it."

"I'll be quick all the same. Sierra is different, independent and vicious. She doesn't want to be *Shinigami,* and she isn't meant to be. The Devils adore her. She's the only vampire they've accepted into their ranks in centuries because she came *looking* for them, these invisible monsters. Who knew that some of the most hidden vampires ever wanted to be found? Thousands of years, changed by this one woman. She's powerful, like you, but in a different way. What I'm saying is she's got her own coven now; she isn't your problem. You don't have to police who she kills, and you don't have to *do* anything for her. This isn't the *Shinigami* you know, and because of you, that's possible. Lynch…Chris…" She smiled when she said his name. "Wanted to show you that he's connected to her."

"Yeah, they're both psychotic."

She rolled her eyes. "That's not what he means. Like you and Nicholas, me and Kieran. Creator and created. He can watch her now, while you do what you must with the other new vampires."

Sierra moaned, and the wrist under my mouth twitched. I didn't have much time.

"I'll come down from this mountain again, Izanami and me. We will watch with Lynch, make sure no one goes too far astray. There's so much possibility now for me, Eliza, I can *breathe* it." Her eyes went wild for a moment, but I tried to tell myself, *not my problem.* "You're draining her," she said. "Time to go. But someone has something to show you."

With a great gulp of breath, drowning in the taste of knowledge, I let go of Sierra, a rush of savory skin taste going with her as she fell back. She waved Nicholas off when he tried to go to her. *Strong.* I was occupied watching a sheet of red mist taking over the wall behind her.

"What the hell is that, El?" Nicholas said. I could only shake my head.

Out of the mist emerged the maroon silhouette of Chris Lynch, then Izanami as herself, kimono, hair flowing freely like a veil down the middle of her back.

She handed Chris the baby.

The stillness in the kitchen was palpable, pained and expectant as Chris came nearer and nearer Sierra, who we didn't trust, who was so strange to us. It was stranger when I realized she'd taken the same sort of strides toward Lynch as he had toward her, sure and long, head held at a pompous angle. Stranger still when she held her arms out before her, cradling the empty air, just as Lynch cradled his child.

"Why is she mimicking him?' Nicholas choked out.

"She's not. Not exactly," I said. This was the connection between them coming to life, in a way we'd never seen, bridging two worlds. Sierra had become both part of the vision in the mist and the vampire in this world. Both ends essential, different and visceral.

Sierra's blood stopped pounding through me like a million hammers and settled into the lazy lapping of a river, an untapped peace. "She's perfect," Sierra let out in a sob, and I watched Lynch's shadowed lips say the same words.

Then the image of Lynch shifted. The presence of pure love, untainted by grief or murder became an actual golden glow from Sierra's body. The baby was suddenly in *her* arms, until milliseconds later the golden glow flashed again, revealing Sierra emptyhanded. But the not-quite-real silhouette of the baby had become a young lady, lithe and fresh, vibrant, hair bouncing around her with a life more than life.

"It's her," Nicholas whispered.

The child—no longer a child—grew larger as she came closer to the edge of the vision. But now, with every step, a black inkiness filtered into the mist, muddying it.

"This okay?" Nicholas murmured. But I couldn't answer, unable to reconcile that this darkness could exist in the same space as the sweet purity of that baby. But it was undeniably the same girl.

As the darkness overtook the red, she remained untouched, golden and pristine. Rather, she blossomed out of the darkness like night-blooming jasmine, growing faster with the love that poured from Lynch, through Sierra. Her heart, soul, flourished—a human, beautiful soul, just like our Kat's. Just like hers.

She lifted a wrist and sliced it open with a long fingernail.

"No!" I screamed. She could *not* hurt herself, she could never—

But rather than blood, blackness pinpricked with stars, like a universe in itself flowed from her veins in a perfect mix of darkness and light. A dark so deep I would lose myself in it if Nicholas hadn't pulled me back out.

I jumped when a grimace of cruelty slapped across her face as if assaulting her, unwelcome, unbelonging. *What's happening to her?* I wondered desperately.

Still so beautiful, but now with a greed that leaked into her heart, and that soul of Kat's didn't so much drift away as run. Behind her, an image of the New Hampshire woods, our woods. And littering the forest floor were limbs. Human limbs in a pile, others strewn recklessly, all with chunks the size of a human mouth taken from them.

"What in the holy hell is happening? Eliza?" Panic overtook

Nicholas and that scared me just as much as the monster in the mist. A human being, not a vampire, a *person* that looked a little like Kat and a little like Lynch, and a lot like something horrible. And without fangs, without immortal speed, without fate's calling and without a purpose but for her own lust, she had taken these lives.

Images of her with an array of knives, cross-legged and covered in blood on the forest floor, sawing slowly and steadily at human arms, tearing chunks from them and chewing as she went to her work.

A hand wrapped around my ankle, and for one horrific second I was sure it was *her*, come to take me, to tear me limb from limb with nothing but revolting, purely human determination. But a second was all it took for me to know it was Sierra—because through her I felt it, what Lynch, what the child, what Izanami and even the Master and Izanagi wanted me to feel. The reason why I'd been given the damned ability to see futures through blood.

When Sierra touched me, the victims' gory ends in the nightmarescape rewound, until I saw their lives. Straight through their deaths and into the future. All the promise that they'd held, the children left behind, the terrible choices those children would make because of all the *hurt* they had suffered. The missing parts of the world that would never repair. The thousands, *millions* of lives affected by the loss of one of these victims' ideas, until finally—

"The end of everything," Kat's child said in a gentle voice, beyond mortal and yet entirely human. It actually reminded me of Izanagi.

In my peripheral vision, Nicholas stumbled, his swirling, wide eyes glued to the girl, mouth agape. He reached for a chair but fell unceremoniously to the floor. The emotions cascaded from him in frost and reverence, demanding my attention, and I knew that look on him, I knew that humbleness. He'd been floating without an anchor since the Master had fallen, the core of his beliefs torn away by storm. Everything he'd come to see himself as, what the *Shinigami* meant, had been shaken and exposed, but her... Kat's child was undeniable proof that there was a bigger picture, no matter who had molded it to fit their own story.

Clean, clear tears rolled down Nicholas's face. While I saw the reason why Kat's child had never been born, he recognized the birth of a goddess.

CHAPTER 127

W ithout so much as a goodbye, Izanami had taken Lynch and the baby back through the mist and disappeared. Though Nicholas was too stunned to move, and Roman was…

Where was Roman?

I couldn't stop to think of the possibility that he'd gone to Yomi as well, but accepted that Roman was great at taking leave of emotional situations. He'd just flap right out of there like Dracula.

Sierra wasn't as tough as she seemed—okay, she was tougher, but she still let me help her up and get situated on the couch where she could rest. She'd need to feed, quickly.

Once Nicholas got his wits about him he joined me. "Don't suppose you'd eat pizza, huh?" Nicholas asked Sierra as he tucked a blanket under her feet. She was too dazed to answer. "What do you think we should do? Can you feed her? I mean, you *did* take all her blood."

"I didn't take all her blood," I huffed. I leaned over her, offering her my neck. She moaned but rolled her head away, wincing, which I tried not to take personally. Her residue clung to my insides, to the basest part of me, the memory of the taste of flesh. I took a long whiff of her, from her abdomen to the top of her head to *read* her, know what she wanted.

"You never stop getting creepier. When does it end, Eliza?" Nicholas joked, and I grinned, my heart pounding at how happy he was and how alive.

"She wants meat," I said through a smile. Overjoyed, no matter how confused I was by what we'd just witnessed.

"Ooookay, well, I'll make her a burger."

"No. She wants fresh meat."

"Gross."

I heard a feral hiss, and bristled—until I realized it was coming from me. "Sorry, got a little cannibal residue in there, I guess," I said. "She needs flesh, like we need blood. I'll take care of it."

"And we'll talk about what *that* just was later," he said, waving a hand at the kitchen like he was swatting a fly.

"Later." Kissing Nicholas goodbye, long and lingering until the transferred need for meat pulled me away, I left through the back door in the kitchen to head for the woods. For a second, I stood looking across the vast green field that was the backyard, ignoring the abandoned construction project, and remembered watching Nicholas come home in the snow-coated darkness, the trees great black golems behind him, the glow of his skin a halo. My heart leapt.

We'd be together now. I could watch him come home time after time, fresh senses awaiting his arrival, the hot chocolate ready. I could be at this back door to wrap him in my arms, smell the woods on him musky and mossy, and know that we had forever to be this way. For as much as had changed, for as much loss as we'd seen, in the trauma of *meeting* my best friend's undead daughter, seeing fate unfold and tell all in a flash, I was happy. We would be happy.

But for now, I had flesh to find.

I dashed for the woods, the scent of a thousand animals above ground and below sweeping through my senses, and I worked to ignore the scent of humanity in the town on the other side. It was one thing for a person or two to go missing in North Conway here and there, normal even—but to be dismembered wouldn't work out in our hometown. Sierra would have to save that for the Blue Hole. For now, I wanted to feed her and send her home. But I didn't want to kill an animal.

Funny how that works. I'll kill people, but taking down a fox is out of the question.

Growling with frustration, snarling at my predicament, I reached out with my mind for an answer where I wouldn't have to compromise. Red billowed around my feet as my gears turned, and black flocked overhead in the wings of a thousand crows. They circled above, the mist churning the opposite way below, until I was the center of the greater machine. Steady crow eyes looked down upon me as they swirled, humanoid and beastly, telling me something through the air. Then they took off toward the cabin. I followed as if on wings of my own.

The door opened with the rushing wind of their wings, much to Nicholas's annoyance. "Now what?" he grumbled.

A collection of the birds flew in, landing gently on the weakened Sierra. The first one trotted up her chest, nuzzling into her neck. When she didn't awaken from her semi-consciousness it pecked her, drawing blood. The scent of her own blood woke her, red-ringed eyes focusing on the crea-ture, and she turned her head to bite into it.

The bird didn't even struggle.

"No!" I cried out. The spirit guides had done enough, had always been with me. I wouldn't watch them do this.

"Eliza," Nicholas said softly, and took my hand. That was what sent me sobbing.

One by one the silky black birds went to her, peacefully, purposefully, and let the vampire drain them. These creatures, these souls, knew their reason for being and went to it willingly, took part in it.

"*As have you,*" I heard in my head.

"Izanagi?" I blubbered. I only needed to see beyond the cabin wall for my answer, to the trees beyond, to see a giant crow the height of moose antlers bending the branches where it perched. The sun blazed behind him, mist-red, filtering into my mind as wildly and completely as my dream had once of a moon sheathed in blood. The creature had the eyes of the god I loved—and three legs.

"*Heaven, Earth, and life itself, all components of creation. Feeding each other, branching and recreating, reforming.*"

"I've never seen you like this before."

"*You see me as* Yatagarasu *now as you have now witnessed those three elements and absorbed them within.*"

"Heaven, Earth, life…"

"*Heaven and Yomi are one in this cycle, my dear,*" he said, forging a path through my overwhelming clarity, the bursting of ideas and understanding. "*You have accepted them into yourself. As you have death.*"

He didn't need to explain that to me.

Death—wine and roses—drinking Izanagi's blood—becoming *Shinigami*—losing everyone, gaining immortality…

Death is who I am.

And life is what I give and take.

Izanagi said, "*And life is what you have given me again.*"

"Meaning?"

"*I am* Yatagarasu *now only. You have, in a sense, replaced me.*"

"No! I won't replace you! I need you!" I cried out, and Izanagi listened.

"*Eliza Morgan,*" he said, love pouring from every syllable, "*you have replaced me, allowed me to ascend to this form forever-*"

more. And with that you have relieved me of my duty to Yomi. Do you see?"

His plea for me to understand rang true in my heart. He was no longer beholden to Yomi, or to guarding his wife.

That was something I could do now in his place.

"I won't let you down," I said. I was answered by a warm breeze of wine and roses.

Nicholas tightened his grip as the ever-present residue of the creation god's blood blossomed into my mind. Izanagi had always been there, and he always would be, the closing of the back cover of my book. And the birds' peace became mine.

When I could see beyond the red glaze of my tears and the pulsing burn of the sun behind the great crow, Sierra was sitting up, pink flushing her cheeks, eyes glistening, the shadows gone. She cradled the remains of the *tengu*, murmuring to them. I did all I could to push the devastation away, knowing that they weren't really gone. They'd be back, they always were. *Kat would have laughed forever at me for buying into this circle of life crap,* I thought. But I realized I was wrong, because one second with her daughter would have told her that life and death were so much bigger than we were.

But the daughter she'd have known would have brought about the end of the world. Fate wasn't set in stone. We chose it, we created it like we did everything else. I knew what Izanagi was telling me. That the vampire race lived, too. It should thrive, as all life should. Izanami and I were one, after all—we were both creators of terrible, wonderful things.

And while one terrible, wonderful creation would rule us all, it couldn't be done without me.

CHAPTER 128

It was two weeks before I was able to be seen among people again. I might have handled the…everything… pretty well in the moment, aside from several instances where I absolutely did not, but when the dust settled, I broke. My insides felt totally clawed up, and I just wanted to be away from them. I told Nicholas we needed to go looking for Lynch's girls, and brilliant jerk that he was he saw right through it. He lit up with triumph when he figured out I was too weak mentally to just *find* the new vampires—until he realized that it meant I'd been depleted. Then it was all worry. And cringing from my now-overpowering voice.

Physically, I had cannibal blood running through my veins, mixed with the ever-present traces of Izanagi and short-circuiting memories of Izanami's. And with the vision of the three-legged crow, everything about me changed. I guess seeing a creature so beyond otherworldly, so magnificent and unimaginable was enough to alter even the vampire legend that I was. That I'd proven myself to be long before becoming a glowing, floating, buzzing, black-eyed mist monster with a voice like the tumbling of a thousand civilizations.

With full realization of my abilities as a…goddess, I guess…I'd been unable to control things like my voice and strength.

But what haunted me were the lives I'd watched unfurl and extinguished so brutally. By someone who didn't exist.

No matter how many times I told myself that none of it was real, it hit me like a thousand funerals.

And beyond that, I saw that Roman had done the right thing, and believed he didn't.

Once I finally was able to come out of the bedroom, Nicholas tried to make light of it. "Finally. Jesus, El, I was starting to think I'd have to make a church for you or something, with the halo and everything," he said, pointing at the reddish-gold glow emanating from my body. "It's weird keeping a god in your cabin."

"OUR CABIN," I said. Nicholas winced at the timbre and crushing boulders *weight* of my voice. "Sorry—our cabin."

"That's better," he said, shaking his head with his finger poking at one ear, working his mouth up and down. "If you sound like that around Birch Tree, the place will crumble."

"No, it will not," I said with a laugh—my own laugh. Not the laugh of a goddess who had changed the face of vampirism forever. I was still getting used to being *this*, so different from who I had been, and from everyone in existence, mortal or not. I was getting control back.

Nicholas took my hand, not tentative anymore. I'd felt his fear when I changed, but I didn't *take* it. I didn't need to consume it any longer the way I once had, to control it. It was never about control to begin with. It wasn't even about survival.

It was about living.

"You're sure you're ready?" Nicholas said. I couldn't stop looking at him, at how much like himself he was, the same as when we met. A civilized man of the woods with the aroma of baked goods and peppermint. "You haven't fed…"

"And I don't need to," I said, cupping his cheek in my hand.

After returning from my vision of the three-legged crow, seeing Sierra cradling the dozens of *tengu* that had given their souls for her to feast upon, I wasn't overcome with sadness. Not for long. What sadness I did suffer at their deaths was quickly eradicated when, driven by instinct and oneness with my companions, I dropped my jaw open in that straight-from-*The Grudge* manner that I hoped would go away soon, and I took a great gulp of air.

Every one of the crows was swept up in the cyclone of breath, and I took them all in, absorbing each of their stories, each of their souls, all of their lives, until they were part of me, and I was satiated. Until I felt at one with them. I hoped it wasn't a goddess thing that I'd have to do forever—but I thought it might be. A part of my life evolved into something incomprehensible to mortals. But not to me. The crows and I needed each other. We always had, when they were just black birds that followed me around all the time, and now when I was truly immortal. That which consumes me makes me stronger. And vice versa.

"I think it's time. I want to just go to the damn bookstore, Nicholas! It's been…how long has it been since I *read a book*, for crying out loud?"

"I know, I know," he said, nodding. "There's so much crap for you to read, all your favorite garbage."

"I don't read garbage."

"Prove it."

"Pr…prove it?"

"I know. You can't, can you?"

We drove to Birch Tree like regular people in the SUV that had been sorely neglected for a long time. It was kinda nice to anxiously wait for it to turn over, guess at what the grinding sound was when Nicholas shifted. Normal. Human. Zero fate of the world involved. We stopped for coffee at Black Bear, and I had to swallow back a lump at how much I'd missed it, how it took me by surprise that I needed the smell, the sound of our shoes on the floor, and autumn wind shutting the door behind us. The hiss and chugging of the pots and machines, and the friendly chatter, the smiles. Light and careless, if just for a moment, for everyone inside.

Leaves rustled in with us when we unlocked the door to the bookstore and flipped on the lights. The silence greeted me like opening a book itself, soft and warm with the feeling of promise and peace. Nicholas had given his few employees the day off, knowing how we'd need this place to ourselves today, and probably not a little concerned that I would do something totally weird to freak everyone out on my first day in public.

This was the start of our new life. This was the epicenter, and while the rest of our world surrounded it, here we controlled how much of it we'd contend with. Here, we were quiet.

Nicholas slipped his arms around my waist, planted his lips on my neck. Not a hint of teeth, only lips. No crows beat their wings outside. No visions infiltrated my mind. My mist was as subtly comforting as a pair of fuzzy socks inside my boots— negligible until the moment I wanted to feel it. I reached an arm up, my fingers in his hair, and pulled Nicholas closer. I breathed in today's concoction, created just for me, just for what my soul desired: cardamom and autumn leaves. Vampire senses allowed me to go beyond that—a hint of warm animal fur, a fox. The soil around damp moss. The memory of the scent of red velvet cake. But I chose to stick to the top notes because I didn't always have to dig deeper. No, I could be right here, right now.

This was a purpose, too.

"It's almost opening time," Nicholas murmured into my neck, barely words, but I understood.

"Almost."

I turned around in his arms, tangled my hands in his hair, tangled my heart in his, tangled his limbs in mine, tangled us forever, or at least until just before opening.

∼

We stumbled to our feet from behind the register where we'd ended up, Nicholas raking his hair back, me trying to make sense of clothes.

"I'll put the coffee on," he muttered, squinting hard as if he'd just woken from a dream. I felt like I had, too. More coffee would help.

The familiar clanking of the old coffee pot into the machine, the grounds being poured into the basket, the scent of it and Nicholas, and the spines of the books peeping out at me from the shelves—it was all I could ask for of eternity. Simple, constant, full of love and comfort.

That was not what eternity had in store for me, but here was quiet.

The coffee bubbled away while Nicholas and I put away a stack of books—or I put away a stack of books and Nicholas made a new stack of books by the window seat. Half the furniture in this place was stacks of books. The wood floor took on a new life now that I could take the time to glance it over—the depth of the knots was like looking into other universes. I smiled to myself thinking of little universes under our feet, like the Dr. Seuss story about Horton. Another story, simple and full of love and promise.

I opened the door, the string of jingle bells clanging against the glass. Brown, crinkly leaves breezed in. I didn't brush them out. I was wearing my favorite green sweater that I'd taken from Nicholas when I was still human, best thing to both absorb and cozy up against the fall chill. We settled together on the small window seat that could go unnoticed by unfamiliar faces, curled up with throw pillows on our laps and chipped coffee mugs, and watched the leaves blow by. We read —him, classics that were so pretentious I wanted to die, and me some new werewolf series that I kinda loved, but kinda didn't. Thing was, I could read the whole series in two days and have the rest of my life to read "better" books.

The day breezed by without a peep of vampiric activity. With Lynch in Yomi, and Blue...part of Izanami, and Roman running from all he couldn't actually outrun, everything was remarkably quiet. Turns out every day isn't full of crises. Sierra had been quick to leave. I didn't hear from Kat's daughter and she didn't appear to me—but I felt her. I felt her growing. First as a tremble in my belly, as if she were turning, a baby of my own somehow, nourishing each other through unseen blood and blackness.

With Lynch's love, she grew. They both did. And the world was safe from him.

It wasn't this day, but it was one not long after; another one that passed with the *shush* of pages turning and the steam of coffee, peppermint brownie kisses and crow calls. On this day, Nicholas's blood flow slowed and his pupils dilated, just enough that I would notice. He took his hands down from behind his head, dropped the front two legs of the chair behind the counter to the floor, and stood very slowly.

I'd noticed nothing, I was so entrenched in being normal. I'd forgotten that normal had once included Roman. But here he was. He wasn't alone.

She was red-haired; no surprise there. All of Lynch's girls were after Kat died.

Roman smiled when he saw me, and despite myself I

smiled back. The girl hung behind him, eyes darting wildly, as if some monster greater than herself would leap out from the bookshelves to attack her.

It was the same kind of homecoming that Roman always received after leaving us. We had a routine now, of hugs and murmured apologies, filled with love.

"This is Angelica," Roman said, putting a hand on her arm gently. She startled when we merely looked at her but his touch settled her. "It's okay to say hi," Roman whispered.

"H…hi," she stammered.

"Jesus, she's just a child," Nicholas said.

"No, not really," I said, neither of our eyes leaving hers as she half-hid behind Roman. "She just feels like one."

"I wanted to come alone, but she—"

"We understand," Nicholas said.

With a swallow of hesitation and a glint of excitement in his eyes, Roman said, "There are more. They're at the mansion."

It was a Tuesday, which meant not many customers, and so we were able to talk for a while after getting Angelica comfortable with a warm blanket and some coffee. She winced when she took a sip.

She wanted only blood.

"She hasn't fed, huh?" I asked Roman in a hush.

"She won't. But she can't eat anything else, it makes her sick." Angelica dozed on the window seat, weak from lack of food, obviously, and terrified of us to boot. Roman leaned in but we all knew she'd be able to hear us if she wanted to. He told us how Lynch seemed stronger, more peaceful and at ease. He could tell because their connection was more powerful than it had ever been, that they could speak to each other in their minds now.

"Between the power of Yomi—"

"By the Power of Yomi," Nicholas said like He-Man.

Roman laughed, and I laughed with him, even though Nicholas didn't do this stuff for laughs. This was just who he was. Nicholas caught me staring at him adoringly. I rolled my eyes to brush it off.

"Chris gleans energy from Yomi," Roman went on. "It's like he's finally found a home." His eyes shined. Mine had been shining since Roman called his offspring "Chris." It made sense—Chris hadn't ever fit in our world, or among humans. He couldn't abide by rules of good and evil because he was something else.

"Yes, he's home," I agreed. "And…Blue…Izanami…they're part of that for him. And the baby—"

"They call her *Chiisana Negami,*" Roman said, smiling wide. "Little Goddess."

After that there was only laughter and love between us. We were all so *overcome,* and everything felt finished. Not over, but finished. Ready for our next mountain to climb. This one wouldn't lead to Yomi, not for me.

As Angelica stirred, we got back to business. Roman told us how Lynch led him to the girls he'd turned, and how most —not all, but most—came with him back to Ossipee to be part of our coven.

Our coven.

"They aren't all well-adjusted to vampire life, that's for sure," Roman said with the huff of a parent talking about the teenager they don't understand. "Angelica is the most…traumatized," he said with a glance at her. "But I don't know if it's from being turned or before. Something from her own life. That's the problem—we don't know what their lives were like."

"They could be nothing but trouble," Nicholas interjected.

"Or they could be hurt beyond repair," I said, more to myself. Angelica gave off the aroma of a scared cat, one who couldn't truly see what they were afraid of.

"They belong to us, though," Roman said. "We'll take responsibility for them, no matter what. I will. That's my burd —my privilege."

Nicholas took his hand. "Finally," he said, and hung his head with relief.

For too many years, Roman had been a man of obligation. To Lynch, yes, but even before that to his wife, Emily's, family. Leading a good life without error. Helping these new vampires, this was something he wanted, and something not entirely *good* by the rules of the Lord probably. To see Roman accept the gray area made me grin.

"They're all at Lynch's house?" I asked, picturing who knew how many fresh vampire girls at that giant house. It was an MTV reality show waiting to happen.

"We sure as hell aren't offering up the couch," Nicholas said.

"Fair point. I suppose we'll...come meet them?" I said, looking to Nicholas.

But it was Roman who confirmed it with an eager smile. "I'll get them ready," he said.

CHAPTER 129

We lost some, sure. Like any new fanatical group of heathens, we lost some of Lynch's girls. The eeriness of looking around at two dozen other women who looked just like them, watching them go through various phases of accepting life a as a Vampire of Fate, well…it did plenty of mental damage. And a lot of them had some already.

Roman ran the Great White Mansion like a bed and breakfast, making eggs and pancakes every morning, place settings for all of them whether they could stomach human food or not. "Jane likes the eggs, reminds her of babies," Roman said with disgust. Changed my view of an omelet forever. When we dropped by early, Nicholas would steal hash browns off one or another's plate while I leaned against the kitchen counter with a cup of coffee. The whole place bustled with the clanking of dishes, muted bickering, laughing, life and life after death.

A couple of the girls came to help at Birch Tree, but nothing serious. It was only to get them out of the mansion, away from the others, including Roman. None of them were drawn there the way I'd been, none of them *needed* it the way I did.

Winter came, like an old friend. Some of our newbies had never seen snow. It was something to watch, the half dozen of them out there, hair like streaks of blood on the pristine white, making me lick my lips. The Christmas lights went up overnight all around town—on the lamp posts, in shop windows, and Jingle Bells played on loop. *Elf* was on every other day, and I only missed the invite to Kat's family's house with a brief pang. Stockings went up in our cabin, and the cat was home more often than not. Roman still showed up a couple of nights a week and walked right in. We still ate cookies and drank cocoa, like we had when I was human and crashing here. I woke in the same bed as Nicholas now, and once again, every morning was a wonder.

We settled into a rhythm of being together: Nicholas and I, Nicholas and Roman, Roman and the coven, the coven and me, Nicholas and the coven… It was random bouts, random but consistent bouts of togetherness. We could comfortably count on it every day.

I had had family before. I had missed them every day of my life. But this was family, too. Not a replacement family, not a next-best-thing, but a real family. Equal. Comfortable.

And when it became too comfortable, and nothing was changing except for hunting techniques and confidence, and nothing grew but love, things naturally changed. We could never get *too* comfortable. That wasn't the *Shinigami* way, or whatever our way was now. We hadn't exactly named our new clubhouse for orphaned vampires, we'd been so entrenched in enjoying it.

My own scent permeated Birch Tree Books on this, another simple day. Vanilla, sugar cookies, cardamom. Nicholas smiled at me, breathed me in deep. The swirl of his eyes sped up—a more intricate pattern now, at least to me.

The love in his eyes was thicker. Ever since I'd known what I would become, I'd feared I'd be too much of a monster for Nicholas to love. Of course, before that I was worried I wasn't interesting enough for him, too. Once I'd experienced blood-lust, though, once I'd become a mythical thing, it seemed impossible to me that we'd be able to have a happily ever after of our own. How could we go back? But it never became a question of knowing too much to go back—we'd experienced and changed enough to see what was important and choose it. I'd given Nicholas much more than just my love, when he'd had such conflict over taking lives, no matter what the circumstance. I'd given him the truth, and instead of just accepting who he was and what he had to do, I embraced it. *Became* it. Shown him by example how to own his nature and love himself more for it. After all, I'd torn through blood and ashes to achieve the eternal life I'd longed for.

With head held high, Nicholas was well-fed and enjoying the chill sun streaming through the windows. It was strange for him still to feed on just anyone he found appetizing, without the assurance that it would do the world good to finish them. That seed of an idea, that *unmei nashi* were born to die by his hand, had been planted and watered so much that it took over the garden. At first, I went with him—always together—and I'd feed, tell him what the future might hold for his choice of victim. But he came to terms with what I'd learned long before, that nobody has it all good or all bad, and everyone has worth to someone and hurts someone. Now Nicholas had developed his own palette, a fresh taste. Turned out, it was one for the elderly, who'd seen enough of life and wanted it to come to a close. He identified with that, the need to feel *done.* Most of the girls at the mansion thought it was gross. Not all, though. One thoughtful, under-the-breath-humored girl who barely spoke to anyone voiced that wisdom and fullness of life tasted like magic. Nicholas took her under his wing right away. It was this girl, Lafinn, who was dusting stacks of books-turned-end-tables when *it* happened.

"I thought that shelf would be full until the end of time," I muttered to Nicholas as the couple we'd just sold a tote bag full of bad biographies to held open the door on their way out.

He slipped in with a murmured thank you and a head nod, met the couple's eyes as if they'd given him a hundred bucks, and raised a hand holding a bagel smeared with jelly to them. *Toasting,* I thought, and nudged Nicholas, who I'd shared the joke with silently. Just as the door closed, the bells jingling, the man dripped jelly down his shirt.

"Bad shirt anyway," Nicholas said, leaning over, but his eyes never left the man. Neither of us could look away.

Past the terrible polo shirt of wide blue, purple, pink and red stripes, was the kindest, most unassuming gentleman. A young guy, twenty-five maybe. It was his lips that caught my attention first as he mumbled to himself, wiping jelly off his shirt, then looking at his hand in frustration. He talked to himself out loud, which I loved at that moment. A deep, rich voice, and beautiful teeth.

"Calm down," Nicholas said, and only then did I notice how hard I was breathing.

He approached the counter like it was an emergency, wide brown eyes pleading. "Do you have napkins? Or like a towel? Or...napkins?" He nodded toward the coffee pot.

"That's a coffee pot," Nicholas said.

"What?" he squeaked, wrinkling his forehead, squinting at Nicholas. "I know it's a coffee pot. Are there napkins near it, man?" He waved his jelly hand, gestured at his ruined, horrible shirt.

Lafinn shot across the shop. I panicked inwardly that it was too fast, another customer would see, but I underestimated her. She'd shielded herself quickly, almost by second nature. Her creator had never been quite so prolific with it, but Roman had been a good teacher. Lips pursed, eyes bulged, she slapped Nicholas's hand away from a coffee-stained tea towel. "I'll do it," she hissed. Nicholas put his hands up.

Towel in hand, she turned around slowly, purposefully, giving herself time.

Creating herself for him.

With every millisecond, she transformed, Nicholas and I watching her create a thrall.

"You always said you didn't control the thrall, and I always said—"

"Shhhh."

Well, my scent was all mine and every time it drew someone in, it was because I had done it. Willingly. Purposefully. Without apology.

Lafinn's began with her heart. It glowed under her blue sweater, then reached up like the naked birch tree branches made of light. They touched her jawline, bringing a golden shine to her features. It struck the tendrils of her fiery hair, even glistened around her glasses. She turned more, and the scent came next. It didn't come in a wave, but more of a tingle, like spice sneaking up on your tongue. She was cinnamon and pine, orange and cloves. The darkness of the wee hours of Christmas Eve after the party and after the wrapping, when it's so dark all you can feel is peace and cheer and anticipation. She handed our visitor the towel, which he took in a haze. Her light stretched out to him, inviting him to her.

"You don't belong here," she said with a warm smile.

Thank you so much for reading the **Vampires of Fate** series. I hope you enjoyed it!

I have so much more coming your way. Never miss a release by joining my free newsletter where I'll be sure to keep you updated on upcoming books!

To sign up, simply visit
https://juliehutchings.net/

Thank you for reading the VAMPIRES OF FATE! If you enjoyed the series, I would greatly appreciate it if you could consider adding a review on your online bookstore of choice.

Reviews make a huge difference to the success or failure of a book, especially for newer writers like myself. The more reviews a book has, the more people are likely to take a shot on picking it up. The review need only be a line or two, and it really would make the world of difference for me if you could spare the three minutes it takes to leave one.

With all my thanks,

Julie Hutchings

Charity Blake survived a nightmare. Now she is the monster others dream about.

By day, punk-rock runaway Charity Blake struggles through a stream of dead-end jobs and the haunting memories of her past. But at night she is the Harpy, sprouting wings with black feathers, and claws made for tearing the flesh of her prey.

Having survived a lifetime of abuse and torment from a sadistic man who broke her spirit, Charity's physical manifestation of her grief and anger allows her to hunt down those like her abuser. Only this time, Charity isn't a helpless little girl praying for things to end. Now she is the monster, and hell hath no fury like a harpy scorned.

Power always comes at a price though, and Charity's inner predator craves to take over. Torn between a life with no feeling other than the sweet satisfaction at ripping evil apart or suffering through her days to stay with the two people she cares for most, Charity must choose between her human existence or the wild and feral freedom of a flying avenger.

A perfect read for fans of Joe Hill, Anne Rice, and Chuck Palahniuk, THE HARPY is the first book in the chilling and deeply disturbing world of the Harpyverse where victims become vigilantes and power is a thing to be played with.

Get your copy of THE HARPY today and delve into the deliciously dark paranormal horror everyone is talking about.